About The Author

Stuart Goodwin was born in Sutton Coldfield in 1971 and lives in Lichfield. He is an educator, actor, tour guide and writer. This is his debut novel. Stuart has also co-written two musicals with Alan Rowe. Together they are Goodrow Productions. This novel was written to explore and explain the world created for their second musical The Legend Of Dinosaur George Muldoon.

About Goodrow Productions

www.goodrowproductions.co.uk

GoodRow Productions is a Film, Drama and Community-focused Production Company based in Lichfield. It was set up by Managing Director, web developer/actor/film maker Alan Rowe and Artistic Director, actor/entertainer/film maker Stuart Goodwin in 2014 as an inter-generational platform for kids, their parents and their grandparents to come together and act together.

The aim of the company is to tell interesting stories in a fascinating way. The process of bringing those stories to life involves physical theatre, new media, shaping and touring performances to fit specific spaces in multiple venues and sharing ideas. They use cutting edge tech with a DIY ethic.

GoodRow offers training, education, skills, knowledge and understanding in the fields of Drama, Film and Communication. Through improvisation and devised work it promotes problem solving, working together and the development of active imagination. We aim to facilitate and nurture people's talents to make them grow in whatever direction they choose.

This book was written to conceive of the world portrayed in their latest musical, The Legend of Dinosaur George Muldoon.

Denizens and Visitors of the Island

THE MULDOONS:
Dinosaur George Muldoon
Justice Wilberforce Muldoon
Patrick Muldoon **&** Great Uncle Muldoon

THE MAGICIANS:
Count Astapor (The Russian)
with Caleb and Lurch
Professor Augustus Crowhaven
with Smithers and Carruthers
Yabu with Meruvel
Mr Lapp Zhou
Mr Albert Hand

THE ALPHABET GANG (EAST SHORE):
Antelope, Beth, Crimson, Def, Edie, Frantic, Rudi and Semantic

THE ALPHABET GANG (WEST SHORE)
Zenith, Ox, Hen, Ultra, Tarantula

OTHERS:
Madame Fang and Herr Zoot the Man in the Yellow Suit
Lola
Madeleine
Hogarth Macready

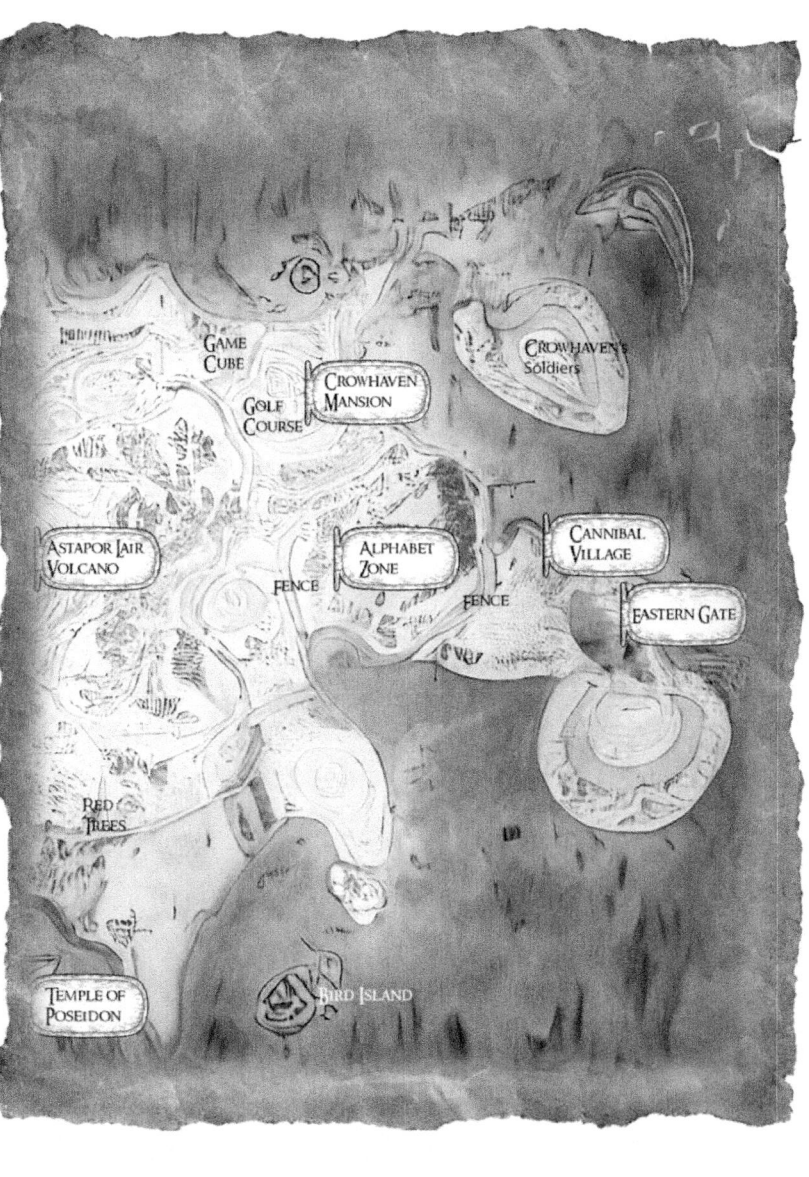

Prologue

It was over and all she could do was concede defeat.

She had tried and failed. That much was clear. What remained? She tried to force her thoughts to travel there but they would not. The future was a huge blank, an empty room, a towering wall of water that raced towards her and swept her away. She fought so hard to stop the panic from rising within and overwhelming what remained of her sanity but found she could not. Battered, bruised and bleeding as she was, this was not the pain that held her fast and dominated her thinking. It was the agony caused by the idea that her existence would be cut short, that her life would be taken from her and that she was powerless to stop it.

The midday sun beat down upon her. She felt its heat like the oppressive will of an angry God. Only it was not a God they were taking her to but a man. And why? Because she had been caught on his unholy mountain, two snatched treasures concealed upon her person whilst she made a beeline for the third. She knew that acts of mercy were not within his repertoire and that all she could expect from him were acts of torturous severity. The boy had confirmed her suspicions, whispering terrible stories in her ears, as they awaited the bearers. Eventually the bearers came, lifting the net wherein she was trussed and suspending it upon a long bamboo pole ready for carrying. At the boy's command they began the long march up the volcano, whilst overhead, the vultures circled.

She had run a good race. It was just that she had not run fast enough or been smart enough to outwit her adversaries. When eventually they arrived at the place from where he governed the island, he offered her a choice. She could live and be changed or she could remain as she was and die.

When finally she understood just exactly what the Russian was offering her, she chose death.

It seemed like the lesser of two evils.

1

The Real

The Boy waited at the top of the long drive for the bus to arrive. It was, as usual, late. And it was raining again. February. Deepest darkest February and it was raining. Why not snow, why not something to cover everything in a blanket of forgetting? What wouldn't he have given for a stint of Siberian weather? Snowed into his room by fifteen feet of icy snow. Snowed in without electricity and without parents. Fetching wood from the woodpile, the lakes frozen and fit for skating on, but best of all alone. Alone, abandoned, forgotten.

He couldn't think of anything better.

A sudden gust of wind, caused the lime and oak trees that lined the half-mile long drive that lead back to the Manor to creak and sway, sending down even more rain drops on his already damp form. He wore black jeans, a hoodie, also black, a waterproof jacket, likewise black and boots and gloves which were also a touch on the dusky side. What his father called his uniform.

"You look like a cat burglar or a ninja wannabe, Will. Why don't you try introducing some colour into your wardrobe? Who knows, smarten up your act and you could even snag a girlfriend."

Snag a girlfriend? Who spoke like that? Who even thought like that? Was it any wonder that they couldn't communicate? His father was no fool but he had a knack of saying exactly the wrong thing at precisely the right moment. He was a successful businessman who had no time for an adolescent son with problems or 'issues' as they were referred to by his former teachers. His father had always known what he'd wanted to do and thanks to the family business he'd had a smooth transition from a happy, high-achieving school life to a high-rolling and lucrative, working life. He hadn't had any issues, so why should his son. There was nothing wrong with him that a stint in the army wouldn't sort out.

As if that was the answer to anything.

Off in the distance, the Boy heard the sound of a bus rumbling down the A4091. It was hidden by a curve in the road but he guessed it was probably passing the Dog and Doublet, just under a mile or so away. He glanced at his watch, gave the driver ninety seconds and watched the seconds ticking down. The bus pulled up beside him on 85 seconds and, after an interval of five seconds the doors opened and the Boy jumped aboard.

The Driver didn't so much as look at him as the Boy slapped down his £2.20 and the ticket machine spat out its contemptuous response. The Boy snatched his return ticket and headed off down the aisle of the three-quarters empty bus. He sat on the back seat, in the middle, with his arms folded and a defiant expression on his face, staring straight ahead whilst the driver with small, sly hateful eyes, like a pig's eyes watched him balefully in the rear view mirror. There was no love lost between them.

The Driver, fat, bald and covered in tattoos and the Boy had had numerous run-ins and the antagonism between them had been exacerbated still further when the Boy had had the temerity to complain to the Bus Company about the driver's conduct. Normally the Bus Company would have dismissed his story as the lies of a snotty-nosed kid but the Boy had had the presence of mind to record his conversation with the driver on his mobile phone.

The Driver had received an official warning and had learned that the Boy was not to be trifled with, bullied or intimidated. No doubt he could have knocked the little weed out with a single punch but he had mouths to feed and few prospects besides driving. Best to shut up and hope someone else dropped a brick on the kid's head and plopped him into the Tame with his hands tied.

The Driver indicated and pulled out onto the carriageway. It was 9.47 on a wet February morning and the Boy was taking his weekly constitutional. Rain beaded on the windows as the bus picked up speed and traffic in the oncoming lane whizzed past in a blur. Down the road the bus rumbled, the Pig mindful of adhering to the speed limit and giving his problem passenger no cause for complaint. He hated that the Kid had the power to make his life a misery. He was so used to doing that himself he felt almost indignant.

Past the theme park with its coasters and flapping banners, past the empty Church and the tidy School and through the urban bottleneck that was Fazeley slowing, breaking, and begrudgingly stopping. Checked and blocked, gnawed by irritation, but inching forwards and then surging over the roundabout, forcing other traffic to screech to a halt. The endless road rage and the two-fingered salutes of those bested caused the hate-filled Bus Driver to smile to himself. That he could savour, that he could dine out on when times were hard and pickings lean.

The Boy looked left and saw the towering cranes of the wood yard. The place had always fascinated him, although he'd never been in there, never had reason to. Those large, faded, wooden gates, invariably closed, were always intriguing. His mind, always active, transfigured the interior from a wood yard into an elephant's graveyard, filled with tusks and sun-bleached skulls, positioned where the great, lumbering beasts had fallen.

The vision brought a smile to his lips and as the bus picked up speed, he began to chart a course through the town. He loved maps, was always poring over them in the library back home but here he didn't need the actual artefact. Didn't need an e-map either, a google layout. All he needed was the map of the town he had formed in his mind's eye and could survey from above, as though he were a bird gazing down from on high, circling, looking for prey. And that's exactly what he was doing, from a certain perspective. Looking for prey.

The bus skewed left and pulled onto Ventura Park Road. Past KFC with its deep-fat, artery-clogging wares and then right onto the Car Park outside of Costa. Before the bus had even ground to a halt he was up and running. The Driver, seeing him in motion, jammed his brakes on but the Boy had already anticipated the move and seizing an upright arrested his motion. Although the Boy never let on, he loved the game of cat and mouse, he and the Driver played.

The Driver edged forward, in a fitful pattern of acceleration and braking and the Boy surfed, micro adjusting his footing and handholds so he didn't fall. As always the Driver retained plausible deniability. If questioned he could always shrug and say he was just doing his job. It was the Boy's choice to stand or to sit. He was advised to sit but he took his chances and stood. Always he took his chances. He was not risk-averse as so many others were. If anything he was risk-seeking and thrill-addicted. Danger was attractive. The safe option, in his eyes, was a gateway to boredom. If that were your drug of choice; good luck, but the boy thought and lived another way.

Rounding the car park, the Driver pulled into a designated stop and flicked the switch. Before the doors were fully open the Boy had hopped out onto the tarmac and was out and running away at speed. The Pig cursed under his breath. Another round to the Boy but one day he'd have him, one day that kid would go down so fast and so hard he'd rue the day he'd been pushed out, between his mother's legs, into this world of blood and storm.

One day!

The Boy, mindful of Lot's example, cast no backward glance. He twisted his wrist, pulled back his sleeve and studied his watch. 10.07. The smile that ghosted over his face caused a passing woman with a pram to examine him with suspicion. But then he was gone and she was back to thinking about which of her four kids had most need of new shoes and what she'd be preparing for tonight's tea. Pizza and chips was the most likely option. Pizza was on offer at ASDA.

Along the walkway and out through a gap in the fence, the Boy headed northwards up the Fazeley Road, away from the Retail Park. Huddled like giants, the shop front facades of New Look,

Hobbycraft, River Island and JD Sports gazed down on the time-lapsed ants that hurried and scurried in and out of their product-lined domains. Not somewhere to linger, the Boy thought, no, rather somewhere to escape from. Shops gave shelter and warmth but their heating systems bred germs and disease. Everyone was always ill here, going down with bugs or one of the ever proliferating strains of flu virus and no one stopped to question why.

Was life this way because it had always been so or did modern life make you sick?

Not waiting for the traffic lights to change, the Boy crossed the road, weaving between lines of traffic. People in cars and on the recently-tarmacked pavement eyed him with disdain, united in condemnation. No one liked a rule breaker, especially here, here where you were ancient at thirty. The Boy ignored them. It was what you did if you wanted to get on. You learned to be invisible and indifferent to either praise or criticism.

To his right, the pavement dropped away down an eroded slope and trundled across unmown grass to the River Tame, often sluggish, but today due to the incessant rain, bullish and fast moving, swollen and angry. Wilber followed a muddy path, down towards the river and paused before continuing beneath the concrete bridge that carried Riverdrive eastwards to the SnowDome. Like the Dome of the Rock in Jerusalem, Tamworth's SnowDome was an iconic structure that hailed the arrival of a twenty-first century Midlands.

It had once been frequented, endorsed and promoted by Eddie the Eagle, celebrity ski-jumper and ironic emblem of England's lack of sporting prowess in the field of Winter Sports. To many, he had been an embarrassment in the 1988 Calgary Olympics, but through hard work and unflagging enthusiasm he had won the respect and affection of Snow Dome visitors and regulars alike. Not only that, he'd carved out a life for himself, helping in his own way, to put Tamworth, once the ancient capital of the Kingdom of Mercia, back on the map.

Tamworth was a town that remembered the past but was it a town that could escape it? Did it still deserve to be on the map? The Boy wasn't sure. The Romans had been here and left traces, the Angles too. The Danes had sacked it whilst King Alfred's daughter had rebuilt it. Plague visited and revisited the town during the sixteenth and seventeenth centuries, decimating the local population over and over but always it had rebuilt itself. Besieged during the Civil War by Cromwell's roundheads, its medieval castle had been condemned to destruction but for some unknown reason had escaped the passing of its sentence.

Always threatened, regularly destroyed but so often, phoenix-like, it arose from the ashes or from the flood to begin again. The town was a mirror to the Boy, in which he saw his own reflection. From shop windows and puddles, aviator shades and bird's eyes he was forced to confront the image he presented to the world. It was both shocking and scary, that image and it was always changing. The pallid face might be a Gothic mask one moment and a Manga cartoon the next, the haunted eyes, those of a medieval saint, or a sadistic torturer of insects.

Scarred, cast out and, more often than not, hunted, the image offered little in the way of hope for the future. What could he do with such thoughts, endlessly recurring and always circling but defying them. Sensing his sudden vulnerability, the Boy quickened his pace until he was jogging, quickly passing the explosions of graffiti that blossomed and bloomed in dayglo shades on the furrowed walls of the concrete bridge. Every step he took down the footpath, moved him ever close to danger. Less a footpath, more a warpath, he reflected. Why did he do this to himself?

Emerging from beneath the temporary cover of the bridge, the wind and the rain assaulted him again, with even greater vehemence. Stoically, the Boy absorbed the buffeting meted out to him by the psychotic wind and immune to the creeping fingers of icy water that climbed his spine, he surveyed the path that lay before him. In front of his steely gaze, the northern skyline rose up like an opposing army brandishing weapons. It was dominated by six High Rise tower blocks, slung up in the 1960s by careless planners in search of some kind of solution to the housing crisis. Dubbed by estate agents, with no sense of irony as 'apartments', they lumbered like AT-AT walkers over the horizon towards an enemy no one could see. Despite their reputation as being objectionable eyesores, the Boy loved the high rise towers almost as much as the inhabitants did.

The Council, rebranded and seeking fresh solutions for the Millennium had wanted to pull them down but the residents had all but rioted and the Six Towers, named like Medieval knights, as Harcourt, Peel, Stanhope, Strode, Townshend and Weymouth lived to fight another day. Like red brick layer cakes, they seemed to the boy, their rotting balconies edged in blue and white, forever glorious. His fantasy was to take to the roof of Harcourt and hit endless golf balls into the town below until he was arrested or gunned down by snipers in a blaze of glory. Perhaps later. After today's mission was accomplished.

Along the bankside path he trotted northwards until the path veered sharply to the left and, running aslant, collided with a second path spat out by the Fazeley Road. This path ran just North of West, straight as a medieval arrow towards an elegant footbridge that spanned the point where the Tame and Anchor rivers met and then passed one another. Here the whirling rivers were widest and the water at its most dangerous and turbulent. Swimmers were dragged beneath here or floaters rose or snagged on branches tumbling from either verge into the twinned rivers.

Rain, rain, a day of rain.

He paused at the entrance to the recently repaved bridge. At either end there were black bollards to prevent vehicular access. Both rivers ran deep and fast. He gazed into the waters seemingly entranced, as though in love with an idea he could not, dared not name. Glancing behind him he saw the Ventura Retail Park, Babylon and Mecca all rolled into one, always busy, always there. It represented the New town whilst over the bridge was the Old Town. Tamworth, a place where two rivers met, was a town divided against itself, not unlike himself.

He took a tentative step and then another step, then paused again, uncertain of what he was feeling. This was not who he was, this wasn't him. He had walked this way a thousand times so why was he reacting this way, today? He felt odd, poised on a threshold, that he felt both loath to cross and yet compelled to cross. Back to the New or into the Old. More uncertainty and another backward glance. In his head it was as though two great seas met here. Two great tides thundered together like opposing armies meeting on some vast and terrible battlefield.

It was as though he could hear the crish and feel the crash of those clashing waves. He was caught between those seas, powerless to resist. Yet he couldn't stand here. He wasn't Moses. There was no way he was going to part the waters. Between the tides the town stood. Like him it would be swept away by forces that mere bricks and mortar could never hope to withstand. It was a place that no one can save. Like him. Only he could save himself.

Almost of their own accord his feet began to move. Somewhere a church bell tolled eleven. He knew why he was here, knew what he'd come for. There was no backing out now. Crossing the bridge he began his search. He knew this place. Every street, every chipped cobble, the colour of every door, the haunt of every rat. He knew it.

Moving now with a purpose, up Holloway, rainwater rolling down the gutters. Ignoring the right turn into the Castle Grounds car park where bins overflowed and the ground was a patchwork of broken glass. Up the slight incline past a straining, sweating man in an ill fitting suit, a rolled newspaper under his right arm, cigarette protruding from the corner of his mouth.

As he passed he heard the man muttering, "jobless, hopeless, working class scum." It was almost a football chant. One for the terraces. In-ger-land!!! The boy ignored it, and was perversely heartened by it. He didn't belong here. Never had and never would, but he would never be broken, never made to bow his head, in shame or fear, by men like that.

2

The Label For The Dog

Past the disabled parking bays and up past the Castle Hotel to the corner of Market Street, he strides - agitated. Hands deep in his pockets, moving faster now, scanning from one side of the street to the other. The rain unrelenting, running like blood in the gutters. Heart beginning to pound. From an open doorway he heard the strains of Land of Hope and Glory being played, mingled with the sounds of laughter and someone shrieking abuse.

Walking the red brick street with its herringbone pattern. Compared with the New Town the Old Town was dead but it was still pretty lively. Far darker and more threatening, in his mind, like a tunnel narrowing. Faces in doorways watching. Suspicious, indifferent or just plain malicious. This was the Land of Elgar and nostalgia, of decency and fair play, or so his grandfather remembered it. Not so, him.

Once in a second hand book shop he'd heard one old woman ask another if she could recommend something to read. "Try this," she said, picking up a grizzled paperback and handing it to her compatriot.

"Looks violent. Is it?"

"Yes," said the connoisseur. "But then I loves a gory story."

The Boy had laughed to himself, hearing this and then he'd shivered and left the shop. That was what life was like here. It was a gory story, where all the doors were shut and there was no hope of escape. Other voices echoing in his head. Lines spoken by moving lips, words emerging from mouths he had known.

"Hell is a place without hope." And then. "Hope is the last thing to die." Not quite.

Past a shop with arching windows, with dozens of rolled carpets nestled in the eaves. Covered in polythene but still wet. Past a window filled with electric guitars and floors covered in glueless, laminate flooring. Round a parked van with ladders on the roof, towards the town hall. Dripping market stalls with plastic wraparounds, selling knocked off goods. Locks, dog leads, bird food, chicken wire, coats, T-shirts, bulbs, plugs, jeans, towels, cutlery and haberdashery. Everything you could ever need and much you never would.

And there he was, the object of the boy's search, leaning up against the statue of Sir Robert Peel, M.P for Tamworth, Home Secretary, Prime Minister of a more United Kingdom and father of the Modern Police Force. There he stood, tattoos on his neck, bleached peroxide hair, shaved at the sides, flapping tracky bottoms, Man U shirt and leather jacket, both battered and tattered. Eyes as black and turbulent as the water thundering under the bridge into which the boy had stared with such dread and fascination, just minutes before.

No beat, no second, no delay. Recognition was instant as was the rage that ignited in the eyes of the leaning youth. Straightening up his left hand dived into the pocket of his leather jacket and his fingers tightened around the handle of what the boy knew to be a knife.

"You're dead," he mouthed, as his eyes locked on the Boys who stood just metres from him, immobile, seeming fearless but with his heart pounding.

The Boy lowered his hoodie and glared back at the Youth, with flaming eyes. He had been well-named, the Youth, a legend in his own mind. Mad Dog they called him because he had teeth and once he started on you, he never stopped. Once there had been people close to him, people who would drag him off before GBH became murder. Not anymore. One by one his friends had dropped away, now it was just him, and the people he dealt for. The Big Boys, the Birmingham Crew who made their weekly deliveries with impunity. Despite the ever-proliferating number of surveillance cameras the right people looked away, the right people didn't want to know. Mad Dog ran Tamworth. Nobody messed with Mad Dog.

Only the boy didn't know the rules. But then he was as mad as Mad Dog. One day he'd ambushed Mad Dog and given him the kicking of his life. Then he'd taken the Drug Dealers stash and dropped it in the river. The Boy didn't know the rules, but worse than that, he came into town on a regular basis and taunted Mad Dog, in a way that could not be allowed. Today was one such day.

"Come on then. Catch me if you can," the Boy mouthed back.

As soon as Mad Dog began to move the Boy had turned and begun to amble off. Mad Dog followed at a discrete distance, never taking his eyes off his prey. Not running, never running. Undignified and it gave too much away. People who knew him looked the other way. People who didn't know him, did likewise. Now his hand moved to another pocket and he was removing a mobile phone and dialing a number.

A brief, whispered conversation of essential details and hurried instructions and then he smiled as he slouched down Market Street, placing the phone back in his pocket. The Boy he followed was retracing his steps, occasionally glancing over his shoulder to check Mad Dogs' position. Such a silly boy, he thought, as his hand tightened around the handle of his shank. A soon-to-be dead boy.

The Boy quickened his pace, and turned right, back into Holloway. The swinging sign of the Castle Hotel, the painted white columns, the drenched Union Jack, flapping on the castle ramparts, were just details his eye captured and discarded. Mad Dog, seemingly untroubled, picked up the pace too. The Boy, glancing backwards, was troubled. His pursuer was too calm; too controlled. Was there something he'd missed? Head turning, eyes darting, scanning the street ahead and then he saw it and his heart skipped a beat.

There was someone new, someone leaning against the archway that led into the castle grounds. Someone watching him with weird eyes. The game was afoot, the pieces in motion. No turning back now. A hundred metres, becoming seventy, becoming fifty becoming thirty. Someone detaching themselves from the wall, all teeth and dead eyes in a bleached face.

All he has to do is block, all he has to do is hold the kid. Mad Dog will do the rest and he will get a nice little kick back. He'll walk away as the kid bleeds out and no one will be the wiser.

Mad Dog, so calm and focused, changes gear and begins to jog. The watcher sensing his moment has come, darts forwards and snaps out a fat, scarred hand to seize his prey. His hand grazes the Boy's wrist, but the boy swerves and dodges, once more the full back of old.

Running now, all pretence abandoned, Mad Dog passes Cockeye in hot pursuit. The boy has taken to his heels and is running towards the bridge. Mad Dog is laughing and then the Boy sees why. Up head four more, someone's bearing down on him. Faces the Boy recognises, faces he doesn't like.

"Check mate," Mad Dog all but howls as they all converge on the site of the kill. Counting down, the Boy is sandwiched, caught in the jaws of the machine. Mad Dog hopes he will plead as he pulls the shank from his pocket. But the Boy has other ideas and swerves again. Climbing, climbing to stand on the wall of the antique bridge. Mad dog reaching but catching nothing but air as the Boy plunges into the racing, black, turbulent water.

*　　　*　　　*　　　*　　　*　　　*　　　*

The Boy had a name. He wasn't really a boy. In fact, he was fifteen years of age. It was what his father called him. It was what his father had always called him.

"Is the Boy in?" "What's the Boy up to?" "Don't tell the Boy, he'll only make a scene."

What had started as an affectionate nickname had become a boring taunt. There was nothing his father liked more than having a dig or rolling his eyes. And that laugh of his. It made the Boy's blood run cold.

Once upon a time, he had been a boy, both lively and opinionated, much loved and much commented upon. His given name was Justice Wilberforce Muldoon. That name, as you can probably appreciate, was quite a mouthful, so much so that most people shortened it. To his mother he was Justice, to his Grandfather he was Wilberforce and to nanny he was just Wilber.

To his friends he was just Will. Will he quite liked. He was wilful. That was why he went up to town, on the odd Saturday and jousted with Mad Dog. It was a game of shortening odds, as his most recent excursion had demonstrated. Mad Dog had gotten wise and made plans. He'd baited traps and then sprung them. It's just he'd never foreseen that Wilber would do what he did and jump.

The water had been shockingly cold and he'd hit and gone under. Up above he'd heard the sound of hoots and yelling voices. The pack were excited they'd had to do nothing other than spring the trap and that Wilber had jumped before he was pushed. Only Mad Dog had felt cheated. He'd wanted to plunge the blade in before they dumped the body in the water. But their cries had brought other people running and the pack sensing difficult questions and probable arrest had melted away.

Born along by the current, Wilber had surfaced some way down stream and with great difficulty had hoisted himself onto the bank. Breathing heavily and spitting out water, he'd clutched his knees and said a prayer of thanks to the God of Lost Causes. Then he was up and running again, away from the damage. Another round to him, he thought and he broke into a sudden grin. Not everybody's idea of entertainment but it worked for him.

He was soaked through and freezing yet he couldn't go home. Not yet. Then he remembered. There was a launderette in the old town where he could dry his clothes. The girl who ran the place was nice. She'd understand. If she was on. He had a few quid still, in his back pocket so that wasn't an issue. Just a question of whether she was working and whether Mad Dog and his crew had scarpered after his death plunge.

He was in luck, on both counts. Doubling back to the main road, he'd taken the long way round, onto Lichfield Street and then past the Fire Station. The launderette, which was down a side road, was all but empty when he arrived and the girl was there alone mopping up. As soon as he walked in, she brightened.

"What happened to you then Wilbs? Or are you trying out for the swimming team?"

In spite of himself Wilber laughed.

"Yeah the 100 metre sprint and crawl. New event. Think it's going to catch on."

"Seriously though Will, what happened? That's not rain-wet, that's proper wet, that is."

Wilber grinned from ear to ear.

"You're not wrong, Amy. That's river-wet. Couldn't afford the swimming pool at the SnowDome and came here so I figured a quick dip in the river would do."

Amy looked at him like he was mad but not entirely convinced he was lying. The Muldoon family were not short of a bob or two. In fact the Muldoons were a very large and very wealthy family. She'd read it somewhere in the local library after she'd first met Wilber. It was all there in black and white. Of course, he'd tried to tell her who he was when she'd first questioned him, but she hadn't believed a word he'd said. People like that just didn't come into her orbit. That had changed though after she'd been on her Fact-Finding Mission to the library. It was all confirmed then and the next time he had come in she'd looked at him with different eyes.

"I'm sorry I didn't believe you Will, about your family and all, but I went to the library and looked you up."

Wilber was pleasantly surprised.

"You did?"

"I did."

After that, they'd been confirmed friends. When she wasn't busy he'd come in and they'd chat, mostly about their mad families. Whilst the Muldoon families' fortune came largely from brewing beer and building luxury motor cars, Amy Shuttleworth's family had no fortune to speak of, just the money that Grandpa Jack had left them in his will. Her mum, brains of the family and the muscle end of the firm, had invested the money as soon as she'd received the cheque from her father's solicitor. Amy's father, a helpless drunk, had been told nothing, just sent to relatives until the business was over and Amy's grandfather was safely in the ground

"People are lazy," her Mother told her. "They'll always want their washing doing and their shirts ironing. It might not be glamorous but it's a living. Not only that, its bricks and mortar innit? It's a roof over our heads, it's security and at the end of the day, whether you like it or not our Amy, it's an investment. When I'm gone all this," and here she gestured about the launderette, with its six machines and seven driers, "will be all yours."

Amy too had looked about.

"Can't wait'" she'd said, under her breath and her mother had given her a look.

Wilber found Amy's Mother both irritating and amusing but her Mother, keen to see Amy's prospects advance, treated Wilber well. Much better than the glue-sniffing reprobates who sometimes hung around the launderette with an eye to the main chance. On more than one occasion she'd had to chase them away from the premises with a baseball bat. Wilber though was pukka, a real gent as far as she was concerned and Amy could do far worse than hook up with 'that'. So her mother insisted on telling her again and again and again.

Yet true love never bloomed for Amy and Wilber. They were friends and that was that. And on such a day as the one he was having, Wilber, was grateful for such a friend.

Amy, seeing it was best not to question the shivering youth too closely, took charge.

"Look Will, pop into the back of the shop. There's a boiler suit and one of me dad's old jumpers hanging up. Put that on and get a blanket round your shoulders. You'll find a kettle, milk, sugar and tea bags there n' all. Make yourself a cup and get warm. But before you do, drop your clothes and shoes in a basket and I'll sort out the rest."

Wilber did as he was instructed and by the time his clothes were washed and dry, Amy came back to find him curled up and fast asleep on the sofa. She hadn't the heart to wake him. He looked worn out. Instead she covered him with a duvet, which she retrieved from her bedroom and put the fan heater on.

When she'd finished she let him sleep and didn't wake him until shutting up time at five thirty. She awakened him with a second cup of tea and an Eccles cake. After he'd drunk up and eaten up, Wilber dressed, and having hugged and thanked Amy, headed for the door.

The world outside was getting dark. It was time to go home.

3

Tensions

Off the bus and into the still pounding rain. Endless. Relentless. Such a yawn. Still tired. The bus doors closing behind him, the driver, a different driver, indifferent. Raindrops beaded on the glass, soggy, mushy tickets in the stairwell. Pulling up his hoodie, mainly dry. Smiling at the thought of Amy. Picturing her face. Feeling the warmth of her duvet pulled up to his chin. Her smell. Her kindness. His smile turning wolfish.

Back down the drive, replaying the highlights of the day. A fast walk. The look on Mad Dog's face when he stood in front of him, the surge of adrenaline when he took to his heels, the thrill and fear as he sensed the net tightening, that leap from the bridge.

Hitting the water, and it all went cold. Immersed in darkness. A return to the swirling womb. Day glo colours. A different world. The shock enough to make his heart skip beats. Then the sound of a skipping rope hitting warm tarmac and then the rapid-fire flicker of imagery. Some familiar, some not. Odd that he should remember it now. Seeing the pictures reforming in his mind. The Tamworth towers warping, spat out into the air by unfamiliar trees, the sound of drums, screams of fear and warning. Surfacing, dragging life from the air as the oh-too-swift current dragged him down stream, then down under the water.

Pulling for the bank with all his strength. Heaving himself out. Kneeling, freezing, coughing up water and yet laughing, laughing, all the time laughing. And why? Because of the realisation that he was all alone in this world. And that it didn't matter. He truly didn't care and yet for the first time he really wanted to live. Knew that he was alive. But that there was no one he could rely on, but himself. Realisation after realisation, like dominoes falling.

A sudden flare of headlights coming towards him up the long drive, dragging him back into the present. Options. Thoughts. Feelings. Stepping off the road, running for the cover of a grove of oak trees. Shrinking into the shadows. Passed by the limousine with tinted windows. No way to see in. A limited vision from their side of the glass. Their side, looking out. They were a 'they', mum and dad. Vague shadows. Silhouettes. Always disappearing into the distance.

And him? How did he respond? By screaming, by making shapes, by drilling the air with hostile sound. Wanting to catch their attention. Enraged if they turned round to look at him, enraged when they didn't. Then the guillotine falling. Falling, falling... and a sudden change in his outlook. Seeing the scenes playing out like he was an onlooker. A watcher at his own funeral. Let it go. In laughter. In darkness. The car passing. Letting it pass. On up the drive. If they had seen him they hadn't let on, hadn't instructed the driver to stop. They'd just kept on going. No. It didn't matter any more. It was no longer even a question. The car pausing at the top of the drive, then turning left, heading for the city.

Lights, cameras, attention, glory.

Their world, not his. Alone and yet not lonely. A turning point. When he had seen the headlights, he could have stepped out into the road and flagged them down. But he hadn't, he didn't. Significance in all things. Significance in not hailing them. Mirrors disappearing into the darkness of forever. Gliding backwards like they were on runners. Reaching out with a child's hand. No. Louder No!!! Once enraged, now empty. No. It was pointless, trying to halt the inevitable. Attempting to stop the moon from turning, the sun from shining.

Now seeing with an adult's eyes. Those mirrors carrying images of a crumbling family into oblivion. And he was powerless to stop it. Something had died in him. And it wasn't coming back to life. He no longer believed in his family. But it didn't have to hurt. It felt like a liberation. Seeing with new eyes. Adult's eyes, wolves' eyes. The child, him, sinking into the current of the swollen river and never surfacing. Cursed, abandoned, pursed.

Then liberated.

No more car. No more headlights. Continuing down the drive. Away from the road. The lights of the Manor looming. Not welcoming, never welcoming. Past the lake, reed-lined. Level raised. Water roaring out through the sluice gate, feeding the streams, flowing away. Not bothering to side step the puddles on the drive. Splashing through them, oblivious. Round the bend in the road. The home fires burning.

Step after step, padding like a cat. Nearer. The front door getting closer and closer. It contains no mirror, just a wreath, a remnant of Christmas. Black and rain slashed. His first impulse is to skirt the 'issue,' the issue being Nanny, Nanny with her black eyes and permanent frown. Nanny with her jabbing finger and endless complaints. Nanny wheedling and sly with Ma and Pa, cunning and cruel with him.

Easier to go round her, to avoid the inevitable conflict but why should he? It's his house. The side door invites him. Bear to the left and follow the path past the stables to the side door. Use your key quietly. Put on no light. Ascend the back stair in the darkness. Press the door shut without a sound, sit quietly on the bed, undress, get into bed, fall asleep and dream of freedom. Or run from your nightmares. Run forever, just don't ever stop. Is that the way to do it?

No. And again no. That voice again. Cold, clear, assertive. Sure of itself. Not angry.

He stops to weigh his options. A fervent rain is falling full of twisted rainbows. How the drops fall. Like guillotined heads perhaps. He follows one drop down as it cascades through the ether, only to see it strike a window where blazes light. The mansion is gothic and isolated. He sees that now. A lair of lurking monsters. Rats and spiders, ants and bats. And nanny of course, the grizzliest monster of them all.

The lake lies just behind him and breaks the backs of its waves on manicured lawns. There are extensive lawns here. Patches of this and splotches of that. Groves of oak and beech, holly and birch. Ivy festoons the face of Muldoon Manor. The gardens are well maintained by Old George. He was working earlier when Wilber left for town. Getting his tools out of the van. Raking gravel or earth. Chopping wood, attending to the wood pile. He's always working, ever diligent. No need to mow in February with the trees black and bare. Leaves long tidied away.

Checking the drains and clearing the guttering of moss. Lichen on the roof is a good sign. A sign the air is clean. Or relatively so. Sweeping stairs. Laying traps. Keeping the Manor free of dust and grime, vermin and trespassers. A patient man in his mid to late fifties. Doing for others because paid. But aging and with no stake in the property. Nothing he does is for him. He exchanges his labour for money. Money for rent. He owns nothing. And when he can no longer work, who will look out for him? Will he be given a small room at the Manor in which to wheeze out a final breath. Or not? Probably not. Justice knows and understands his father.

Why is he seeing this now and who is he? His name is Justice Wilberforce Muldoon, knight errant and heir apparent. Rebel with Cause. Agent Provocateur. He has a head full of train wrecks and colliding suns. He knows he must face nanny, both Summoner and Pardoner, High Priestess and Punisher. But he will do so with a different head on his shoulders.

He climbs the steps and places his key in the front door. Turns and pushes, steps inside. The grand arch of the Great Stairway to his right sweeps up to the first floor, a balcony overlooking the hall below. The fire well tended, blazes and Nanny sits beside it knitting. Balls of multi-coloured wool in an old wicker basket. The current ball unravelling as she taps her foot to the harsh, pounding industrial strains of knit one, pearl one. The comfortable chair is not angled in towards the fire but faces out towards the door, so she can see all comings and goings without having to twist and turn.

Gargoyle and sentinel she is a fearful apparition. One foot in this world, one foot in the next. A familiar of spirits, crone and seer. When shall we three meet again, thrills the air around her. She stirs a cauldron, sees through the eyes of rook and crow, fox and badger. Gypsy blood, Egyptian soul born of an ancient line. Travelling people now settled. Caravans rusting on a back lot. A card reading, crystal ball gazing, lottery playing 24 carat nightmare. Or that's how the film of her life plays in Wilber's head.

She waits until he has descended the stairs and then she speaks.

"And what time do you call this?"

Her timing is spot on but then so is his. For the first time in a long time he has his eye in. When he speaks he is as cool as a cucumber.

"Bout eight."

She glances at the ormolu clock on the mantelpiece and sees he does not lie.

"Your parents have been and gone..."

"I passed them on the drive. They didn't stop."

"Oh," her troubled reply. There's something different about him. She inspects him with myopic gaze. As arrogant as usual but somehow stiller, more focused, less apt to jump. She considers her next attack whilst probing for an open wound.

"You should be ashamed of yourself..."

"But I'm not."

Deadpan. That guillotine falling. Like a body dropping through the air and hitting moving water. She reels backwards and he senses it. But she's not to be undone that easily. A swift recovery. Resetting, recalibrating her thoughts, she tastes the air like a snake. Smells no fear, only resolve. Tries another way. As soft as silk.

"Your dinner is under the grill Justice. I could reheat it for you if you like."

"I'll do it myself."

"Your parents are ever so worried about you, you know."

Wilber stiffened.

"Really?"

"They're afraid there's something not quite right upstairs." Here she tapped the side of her head with a crooked finger and a cruel smile swept over her face. Peel a layer off her face and you'd find only hate. That was the way she ruled the world, dominated her family and instilled fear into all she came into contact with. Cold, black-eyed, implacable hatred. The ability to sniff out and uncover any wound and the resourcefulness to exploit what she knew about other people's fears and secrets was what made her such a formidable opponent.

Wilber stung but not unmanned. Wilber still and smiling.

"Oh no, that's not it at all. I'm afraid the trouble is all downstairs. And it's only a matter of time before that particular problem gets fixed."

Nanny riled, black eyes flashing red, uncoiling the vast folds of her malice.

"There are ways and means of having you stopped, you know. You're not right in the head. Everybody says it."

"It's you who needs a check up from the neck up Nanny. And just remember I won't be fifteen forever. One day it'll be me who calls the shots here."

Nanny picking up her knitting, turning to one side.

"If you live that long."

Wilber still but not frozen. Neither burned, nor frozen. The snake was bested but not destroyed. Withdrawing slowly, never giving her his back. Moving back into the shadows and heading towards the kitchen, where meat and vege cool and congeal.

"Enjoy the fire Nanny, whilst you still can."

4

Home Invasion

Meal consumed, he heads for bed by way of the laundry. Still tired from his exertions he needs to rest. Clothes removed and placed in the drier. It's one of the witch's duties but he will do it himself. Never again will he be dependent on her. The worm has turned. He closes the dryer door, turns the dial and hits the switch. It will run for hours and irritate Nanny, he hopes. Gleefully he cackles.

Pressing the bedroom door shut he lies on his bed and is soon asleep. He'll sleep for hours or so he thinks. But that is not the case, not at all.

A short while later, he wakes in the witching hour in a darkness so cold he thinks he is back in the river. Waking with a start, he sits bolt upright, a zombie comes to life, freezing sweat slick on his skin. He has been dreaming of horrors, his head a serrated collage of swirling images, like a rotating buzzsaw. Usually when he wakes the images rapidly fade, but not tonight. No, tonight the images continue to scroll before his eyes. He is fascinated and not a little appalled, as if the last vestiges of sanity have finally left him.

He sees endless fantastical figures, many in silhouette and walks amongst them. Some are human but many are not. Most are rendered in stone but not all. There are statues of Goddesses and Monsters, Mermaids and Tritons, Centaurs, Gryphons and Minotaurs. It is a mythological feast. The level of detail he observes is unlike anything he has ever seen before and the colours.... Wow the colours, vibrant and alive, zinging with tang and vim, energise him. Through the statues he walks until the last one fades and he sees a cliff top up ahead. Silhouetted against the skyline is a woman with her back to him. He walks towards her, with a sense of wonder and excitement.

He knows her. Recognises her. She is important. She has answers. He speeds up, walking faster and faster and eventually breaks into a run. But the sky is changing and clouds are forming rapidly, oh so rapidly. Faster and faster until he is running. Excitement turns to desperation and soon he is screaming. She is close, oh so close he can almost reach out and touch her. But her back is still turned, he cannot see her face. And just as he reaches her, she topples forward and disappears plunging into the brine below.

He stands on the cliff edge looking over, scanning the water for signs of life, but there are none. His desperation shades into despair. And then he raises his head and it is as if he has left one movie and entered another. The screen has changed and the world has tilted, seemingly on its axis. The sea has turned red and a phrase enters his mind... the wine dark sea. Where has he heard that before? Then he hears a sound, as of a conch horn being blown. Then something in his head begins to rotate and the sky blinks and turns white. Through this snow white static black lightning lances the brine with deft, cruel fingers. The gathering storm has broken and now the rains come and a sound like that of a thousand exploding volcanoes almost shatters his mind. This is swiftly followed by a wave taller than the sky, that sweeps over the sea towards him. In horror he watches as away on the horizon a mushroom cloud rises to tower. The image transfixes him and the giant wave, the resultant tsunami sweeps towards him and over him, again and again. The flashback is caught in a loop. He is locked in shock, as he realises he is being gifted a vision of his own world albeit an ancient world. From out of the tsunami a vortex emerges that becomes a Galactic spiral, spinning his mind round and round like a deranged merry go round.

Eventually, in spite of his worst fears, the image fades and shivering he gets out of bed. He has on his pyjama bottoms, nothing else. An arresting tartan. The sound of his mother laughing and his father's mocking words fills his mind but he is strangely grateful. Overwhelmingly grateful that the image of the woman and the wave and the mushroom cloud have gone. Reaching for his dressing gown, he pauses. No. Better to go another way.

Putting on his bedside light he opens the cupboard door. It's full of his clothing. He dresses quickly in black. Back in uniform. Best to have multiple copies of the clothes you love. With sufficient cash and sufficient vision, you can be your best self every day. Almost forgetting, but not. Opening the drawer of his bedside table taking out a slim torch. Lamp off, torch on. Ready for action.

Opening his bedroom door quietly so as to escape detection he pauses, uncertainty clouding his judgement. Listening for, but hearing no sound of Nanny. No clicking needles, no air-sawing snore. Curious. The drier has stopped revolving and the air is freezing.

Out onto the balcony he peers over. Down into the darkness. The fire has gone out and the lonely rocker by the fire is empty. No sign of hated Nanny. Only there because of a legal requirement. But I don't need a nanny, I'm fifteen years of age. The echoing sounds of oft-repeated arguments sound and fade. Change and change in motion, the air shimmering. Something isn't right. The front door is wide open. He sees it and his heart leaps.

Glancing out of the rain-beaded window he sees a wind has blown up. Storm approaches, clouds speed like drivers on a six lane motorway. The trees rock and roll like patients on a mental ward. Black fingers clawing the air, ragged with tattered clouds. Craning forward, not just passively listening but active now, he scans the soundscape of Muldoon Manor with an ear bent for anomaly. Any way he plays it, something is wrong here. Drastic and potentially cataclysmic. All the doors are banging and a rabid wind prowls the stairs and corridors where family portraits are hanging. From paint to print. From sepia to colour. The chandeliers rattle like deadmen's fingers.

It's so spooky. Like a horror movie has oozed out of the silent screen into his waking world. Where's the turnkey? Where's the witch? Last thing he knew she was sitting in her rocking chair, knitting. Something is very wrong here. That much is clear. Everything is jagged and sinister. All the familiar things of hearth and home have been transformed, made strange by another mind. That much he knows, that much he can sense. Run down to the farm and raise the alarm. An inner voice teetering on the brink of panic, hisses.

Tiptoeing to the head of the stairs. All atremble, all aflame Wilber watches and reflects, even now obsessed by the inner-workings of his mind. The Manor is just another mirror. The mysterious history of his clan. That mad, bad line. Ceilings and drapery, stonework and masonry. House and garden both opulent and magnificent. Like the House of Usher, the House of Muldoon. Suddenly vulnerable. The heir exposed.

Go on. Oh I can't watch. I have to cover my eyes. His mind fills with the shrill cries of cartoon voices. Down the Grand Stairway, wide steps curving, clutching the wrought iron rail into danger and darkness, catlike Wilber creeps without a sound. Oh how he wishes he had security or a toothsome hound to offer him some protection. But no. He is alone. All alone. Pausing on the lowest step he glances at the fire, now just embers and ash. The wicker basket still full of wool, the log basket more than half emptied. His first impulse is to shut the front door, dart back up stairs and barricade himself in his room. Wait for mum and dad to come back, let them sort it. But no. He has lived today, become a greater self today. He will be damned before he will throw all that away.

It could be that the old witch is just trying to spook him. He wouldn't put it past her.

And then he has another thought. Even more fearful. Mad Dog. Could it be that he has found out where Wilber lives and has come to pay his respects? Wilber wouldn't put it past him. If you poked the beast enough it would bite and he had poked and poked. If Mad Dog didn't slap him down he would lose face and his City protectors would cast him aside in favour of someone who could keep order.

Wilber cursed his endless need to goad and provoke. Stepping over to the fireplace he picked up a poker and considered his options. Search? Hide? Hunt? Seek and destroy? What was it to be? He swung the poker around his head with a two-handed grip and felt marginally safer. Slashing downwards, then side wards he emulated the actions and postures of martial artists he watched and re-watched on his laptop. Endlessly. His was a looping, repeating culture. A labyrinth of images. His generation had been left with nowhere to go. Entombed in the apathy and boredom of societally approved rhythms and rituals or safe in the arms of a computer-generated game world.

All was well until reality intruded. With teeth and claws it came to rob or kill you. To bomb or imprison you. Was it any wonder he played Russian Roulette with Mad Dog, just to feel alive. Alive!

Moving through the Manor now with greater focus and purpose. The layout fixed firmly in his mind's eye. Blueprints of exacting detail. Out of the main hall, into the library. The shutters open and revealing that the drive side lights still burned. That the storm still blew clouds and rain across the rolling sky.

The library was his favourite room after his bedroom with its posters and wall paintings. Full of encyclopaedias and back issues of National Geographic, plays and novels, highbrow and lowbrow side by side, Airport fiction and leather bound classics, magazines from Vogue and Q, Horse and Hounds, Guns and Ammo... Guns and Ammo? Surely not his fathers? Grandfathers? No. Someone else's. He saw a face and pushed it back into the darkness. Too painful.

In one door and out of another. Keep moving! Into the dining room. Unbearably pretentious. Luxurious details and expensive cutlery. The candelabra, walnut table and Louis Quatorze chairs catch his eye, provoking sneers. A quick glance and out. Past the bar and the shining bottles, into one of the back lounges and then the drawing room.

Endless portraits. Patterned carpets. Gilt edged mirrors.

Everything lovingly restored and brought up to the standard of former glory. Money was the passport to it all, money the sanctuary, the gateway to taste and position, influence and significance. It helped you to walk taller, see what mattered, ignore what didn't, obliterate the voice of conscience and to put endless distance between those who wanted a piece of you and yet had nothing to offer you.

Looking into a darkened mirror Wilber saw his father's face staring back at him.

A sudden shift causes him to turn from the mirror. The wind moans, long and low, like it knows something. The windows rattling, shadows populating the rooms. The full moon lending light. Out of the drawing room, lured from comfort by a sudden thought. A flash, as of lightning. An image. A possible solution or at least a direction. Which? Both, neither? He's unsure.

Into the laundry room. The machines are still, the washing motionless. His socks and sundries dry and waiting. Remembering Amy's smile. Hitting cold water. Walking past the machines, the walls yellow, skirting boards white, in need of a lick of paint. To the far end of the room to the unpainted door he pads. Old and always shut that door. Shut and locked but not now. The key in the door, rusty-looking. Slammed in and turned, he sees scratches, the evidence of frenzied motion. Hand on the door resting. Uncertainty. Hamlet's dilemma. To be or not to be. Walk on or walk back? Wait for mommy and daddy to tuck him into bed, to tell him everything is going to be alright. Only it isn't. Walk on.

The black water is whirling and swirling below him. In his mind he walks a tightrope.

Through the door, past its creaking hinges, heart thumping in his chest, Wilber edges forwards. Door slowly swinging to, behind him of its own accord. Into the naked room. The wood room. For weeks now the fires in Muldoon manor have burnt long into the night and wood stocks have dwindled. The room, usually full, due to George's diligence has largely emptied, revealing...what is that?

Wilber freezes, stares, points his torch, lancing the mystery with a blade of light. It can't be and yet it is. A raised trapdoor, like an invitation to peril, grins back at him. That hole is the darkest he has ever seen. The steps leading downwards are the most enticing he has ever known. Why is that? Is it just him?

Such tension and yet something draws him on. Is it instinct or a voice that only he can hear? Perhaps, he'll never know. It's so cold inside it should be snowing. Wilber walks as though in a trance over to where the trapdoor casts its shadow, like a tombstone in the moonlight. He so desperately wants to stop himself but he can't. Pointing his torch down into the hole he steps over the threshold and with a sense of falling begins his descent.

Wanting to call out, "Nanny, Nanny?" but knowing he can't. She could have set this all up. Could be waiting there in the dark with an axe or a cruel smile. Like a spider ready to pounce. "Gotcha!!!" Wilber sinking like a holed battleship. Going down with all hands. If that were the case he wouldn't give her the satisfaction.

Step by step he creeps downwards until the stairs end and he finds himself in an unknown space. Casting his torch around he sees that it is both huge and dark. But what is it? Could be a basement, a wine cellar. Could be a crypt. It has the feel of a gothic tomb in a haunted house. It's so cold he can see his breath.

Flicking the beam of his torch from side to side he delves for answers. He feels like a detective in a minefield. The clues have led him here but have they led him to his doom?

Wide-eyed with fear Wilber scans around. Then he notices something. His roving torch spins and fixates on a far wall. What is that? He moves closer, and then even closer. Despite the cold his palms have begun to sweat. The fog in his mind lifting slowly. Gauges? No scratches. Three deep scratches. But what could have made such deep impressions? He goes over to them and examines them closely, then he hears a curious noise. A rhythm, steady and regular, pounding like drums. Thud and echo, thud and echo. Reverberations and something approaching at speed. Then it stops. The torch light flickers off. He taps it, it stays off. Taps again and a feeble light returns. He raises the beam and that's when he sees them.

That's when he sees the red eyes staring out of the darkness down at him.

5

The Vortex

The mind screams, not the mouth. The mouth has been paralysed and silenced by fear. By fear! Running, running as fast as his legs can carry him. His heart fit to burst, his adrenals pumping adrenaline into his blood like his life depended on it. And of course it did.

Up the stairs, two steps at a time, gasping for air. Hotly pursued. The roar of the beast behind him. The impossible beast, the beast that had been extinct for 65 million years. Cretaceous. Mass extinction. Meteor strike and lights out. Dust up. Ushering in the age of the mammals. Then the age of man. 100,000 years out of Africa. Every dog has its day. His mind reeling and creaking, overwhelmed by inessential facts, by things he didn't need to know right there and then.

There was only one thing he needed to know at that exact moment. He was being pursued by a T.Rex. A tyrannosaurus rex. Terrible Lizard. Lizard King. Twelve metres long, 3 and a half metres high, the adults. This one was half that size but still enough to swallow you whole. Feathered and toothsome. An apex predator. A small one for sure but they came into the world fully formed and ready for business. And right now he was business!!!

Bursting through the hatch like a Typhon Missile. Exploding into the room as the hatch detonated behind him. Splinters and bricks blown everywhere as the beast burst from its lair. Seeing it all now, playing it back in rapid motion as he scarpered towards the Wood Room Door, quite literally fighting for his life.

Every breath potentially his last.

Seeing it all now. Nanny's discarded handbag, the contents spilling outwards, like its guts had been ripped out. Then an item of clothing, a knitting needle and a boot. Running past it at speed, noting a remarkable fact. The boot wasn't empty. It was still full of foot. The shattered tibia and fibula a testament to that. The shredded muscles and severed sinews, all that remained of Nanny.

God rest her rotten soul.

Through the next door and slamming that. Not enough, not enough to keep the beast out and away from him. Stealing a glance as the laundry door exploded behind him. The slavering, bloodied beast clawing at the hole to make it larger.

Unbelievable size, unbelievable speed and aggression, only he had to believe. But more than that. He had to think. And do it quickly. Roaring past the washing machines and silent driers and through the open archway. Down the corridor and into the hall. Desperate for hope. Seeing everything, taking it all in, in a fraction of second. The recently vacated rocking chair would be rocked no longer. At least, not by Nanny. Suddenly aware he was still clutching his poker. No use. No good at all. Scanning the walls for new weapons, something more effective than the poker was needed.

Scanning and turning and Yes!!! There it was, up on the wall. Flinging a chair up against the wall and leaping onto it, reaching as the T Rex thundered into the room. Reaching, grasping, finding a wooden haft and yanking it down off the wall. Dropping to the tiled floor. Raising the medieval pike staff to the level of the Rex's throat. Heart thrashing in his chest. So close to death. So close he could smell it.

The Rex circling. Stopping to roar. Drool and bits of Nanny clearly evident on its curving, bloody teeth. Designed to puncture, shred and tear, those teeth, bigger than a Great White's, bigger than just about anything that had ever lived. The red eyes fixed on his. A battle of wills and skill. The Rex clearly believing it had the advantage. Lunging, snapping its jaws. Wilber countering with a thrust to the throat. The ancient blade finding flesh and puncturing it.

Blood pouring from the deep gash, the beast screaming in rage and pain. Wilber indifferent to its suffering. Yet marvelling at its strength and size. He would so have loved to have stopped his defensive manoeuvres, in order to study it, if it wasn't trying to tear him limb from limb.

The bloodied beast, easing back, using its large tail to steady it, to prevent it from toppling over, studied him with obvious intelligence. Wilber held the tiny torch between his teeth and shone it up at the terrible lizard. When the beam played over the large reptilian eye, he saw the pupil contract.

A stolen, sideways glance. Wilber angling. Looking for options. Opposite Nanny's knitting station, was a large, flat screen TV. Lifeless. Devoid of flickering images but interesting, nonetheless. The open front door, flicked too and fro by the wind's bored fingers. The slap and crack of wood on wood. Droplets of water drenching the stair carpet. Outside the sound of rain, then thunder filling the air. The storm was still building, many winds howling, opening their throats to give vent to their rage and fury. Let them. Let them howl. Let them come, Wilber thought. Sound, from whatever source could be a useful distraction.

Calculating, scheming, darting looks here and there, the Rex was also weighing its options. It wanted a quick kill, didn't wish or need to be wounded. Mostly its prey ran until felled and dispatched. This was a new experience for it. To be challenged and countered by a creature as small as this human was unusual, to say the least.

Away in the distance, a sudden flash of lightning illuminated the interior of the hall. The huge lizard, caught off guard, turned away momentarily, blinded by the harsh flare and glare of light. Wilber, seizing his opportunity, dropped back and grabbed the remote that poor, dead nanny had obligingly left on her chair, when she'd no doubt gone off to investigate mumblings and grumblings in the crypt. Jabbing at the on button, he activated the blank-screened device and jacked up the volume to its highest level.

The Rex in response, gave a low hiss, a growl and finally a

scream. It obviously didn't like TV. Wilber sympathised. He really did. It was mostly crap these days.

"Lean back, my dear, take a mouthful of popcorn and watch the show unfold. It's going to be quite a ride you know," he said. Pleased with his impromptu rhyme, he leaned back and hefted the medieval pike into the Rex's left thigh. The head or eye would have been the obvious target but Wilber didn't much care for being obvious. Eye too small. Head too far away he reasoned. Go for thigh. It'll hurt and whilst it might not be life threatening, it might at least slow the terrible lizard down.

The lizard screamed like a pensioner who'd just been told her heating allowance had been scrapped and rocked its head backwards in rage and pain. Tory scum! It seemed to cry. Wilber, now weaponless, made a break for it. The flapping, front door ignored, he hurtled for the library door, the screaming TV covering his tracks adroitly.

Slamming it shut he allowed himself a celebratory breath and then went looking for a mullioned window to open.

Outside the wounded Rex, in both a rage and a quandary took its frustrations out on the blaring TV set. It charged the screen and head butted it. Sparks and shards of glass showered down, then it took the screen between its jaws and crunched it. Not a great idea as the TV exploded and a few thousand volts of electricity coursed through its heaving Reptilian frame.

Inside the library, Wilber heard a terrible cry and a near-deafening crash and thud as the electrocuted Rex's body hit the floor and ceased moving.

*   *   *   *   *   *   *

Victory?

There was no way Wilber was going to hang around to find out. Having found a window that finally opened he clambered out and dropped down onto the wet earth. Landing just to the right of one of George's red and extremely thorny rose bushes, Wilber thanked his lucky stars and took to his heels.

In front of him stretched the open driveway. An 800 metre sprint and he would be at the road. He'd flag a car down and say the house had been burgled, get himself taken into custody. Either that or committed to a mental ward.

He was just completing his plans when the front door blew outwards and in a tumbling morass of brick and wood a disgruntled and wounded Rex burst forth into the rainy night with one thought on its tiny mind. Murder!

Out of the doorway, it raced, like a prize greyhound just out of the traps. Hotly pursued by the beast from another age, Wilber let out a Rebel Yell and roared forth. This was not good. You didn't need to be blessed with Einstein's intellect to know that the immediate future was so bleak, you would not have to wear shades. Out in the open, Wilber was doubly, trebly exposed and the Rex, in spite of its wounds in hot pursuit.

Racing, racing, the terrible lizard shaking the ground behind him Wilber found despair snapping at the edges of his mind. He would never make it to the end of the drive. Not now. The wood was closer, but he didn't fancy his chances there. Not if he chose to hide. T Rexes, like bloodhounds, he had read, had a terrific sense of smell. He could climb but could he get high enough? Up a tree he was cornered. The beast could shake him out or even climb up for him. He wasn't blessed with squirrel-like cunning and agility, and to the Rex, he would be like a lame duck to a seasoned hunter.

Only one thing for it. Instead of going right, he peeled off left. Into the botanical garden with the ornamental fountain. Crunching the gravel as he ran. Then through a hole in the yew hedge into a space he had never before been. Crouching, hiding, remaining immobile. Trying to silence his breathing. Terrified for the first time that night. Then a flash of lightning and a new shock. Five huge trilithons, arranged in a circle, leaning over him. Glowing faintly in the early morning air.

The huge hollow thuds of the Rex's feet. Close and closing. Sniffing the trail, hot on the scent. Reality striking like a falling tree. There was nowhere to hide. These beasts just didn't key off motion.

They were Jurassic Bloodhounds!

An explosion of foliage, sudden but not unexpected and the Rex was through. Stopping, it leaned backwards and roared. It had cornered its prey. Nothing to do but accept the inevitable. The T Rex was blocking the hole in the hedge, but still Wilber would not surrender. Leaping to his feet he rounded the circle not once, not twice, but three times with the Rex snapping at his heels. He was halfway around the fourth circuit when he felt a sudden and uncontrollable urge to move to the centre of the stone circle. A side step and a shimmy and the Rex thundered past him and planted its head in the hedge wall. Having attained his mark, the air around Wilber began to shimmer and blink, then it began to spin. Instantly nauseous. Falling to his knees, then flopping onto his back, Wilber looked up and saw a huge vortex above him, bearing down on him. Like a mouth opening. Presenting him a rabbit hole down which to fly.

A flash of lightning, the blink of an eye, sounds of tumbling and rumbling, the sensation of falling. Then blackout. The T. Rex having retrieved its head, stopped just short of the threshold, watched the boy disappear then retraced its footsteps back to the house.

6

Gateway to Paradise

Justice Wilberforce Muldoon awakened slowly to the sound of gentle lapping noises. At first he thought his face was being licked by a large cat. Possibly a Maine Coon, possibly a leopard. It was hard to tell. He tried to shoe the persistent feline away, but being persistent it persisted with its licking. Irritating. Very irritating, he thought but if he could just ignore it for long enough it would surely go away. That's the way cats were. No staying power. If he were a betting man he would have put money on it too. Face licking he could deal with. Verbal abuse from nanny he could deal with. Being excluded from school, no problem whatsoever. He was a man of iron will.

Time passed but still the licking went on and still he fought the urge to sit up and wake up fully. That was not an option, it was not the Muldoon way. Then he felt a second sensation, one that was harder to ignore. A wet warmth that was spreading outwards from the region of his groin.Gradually the horror dawned. Oh no! That wasn't possible. Had he really? He sat up and froze. Then he looked around him. What in the name of hell was going on? Had nanny spiked his tea with magic mushrooms? Where was he? He knew where he wasn't. He wasn't in his bedroom, he wasn't at school and he doubted he was even in England; it was February and the sun was out.

No, he was on a beach that was covered in whitish sand not feet-lacerating pebbles. Definitely nowhere in England. He stood up and looked down. Aah. That accounted for the wetness between his legs. He had been lying in the surf being lapped at by the waves, not a cat. The sea was a curious shade of green. Not exactly pea green but if an owl and a pussycat had floated past right then he wouldn't have batted an eyelid. This was beyond weird. The waves continued to roll over his feet but he felt no inclination to move. The water was warm, like being in a bath. He thought about stripping off and going for a swim, then he thought again. Great way to start the day but no he needed one or two answers first. Besides, the water might be shark-infested.

Turning around he encountered his next shock of the day. Towering above him was a trilithon. Not everybody would have known that word but archaeology was kind of in the family and the technical terms for things had been drilled into him when he was still very young or, as his grandpa had always said, knee high to a grasshopper

A trilithon was a stone structure made up of three stones. Two vertical or standing stones and a horizontal lintel across the top. The most famous trilithons were to be found in Stonehenge in Wiltshire. They had been quarried and hauled into place at least four and a half thousand years ago, if memory served. But whilst those stones were pitted and cracked, crumbling and eroding, the stones he was staring up at might have been cut, dressed and dropped into place just a few days earlier.

Another thing he noticed was that these stones were considerably larger than the ones at Stonehenge. He stared up at them nonplussed, and mused in silent wonder. Where was he? Initially shocked, then bemused, now he was perturbed and his mind began to fill with questions. A cursory glance was enough to reveal that he had landed in a tropical paradise. The white sand seemingly stretched on forever along two coastal beaches that beggared any resort he had ever seen in Spain. He stood on the tip of a point of land, shaped like an arrow, and the trilithons formed a point of entrance.

From where, to where though? Once more he wondered how he had come to arrive on such a magical island and whether it was deserted. He'd always had a Robinson Crusoe fantasy but in his head Man Friday was a hot chick who looked not unlike Lara Croft. Turning back to look out over the sparkling sea he watched the sun hauling itself up over the horizon, as if it too was just getting up out of bed. It was obviously daybreak, and if he was still on earth, he was standing on the eastern tip of the Island. Shading his eyes Wilber looked inland. The beach ran for about three hundred metres before it hit a jungle tree line. The jungle rose dark and brooding, the trees seemingly ancient and massive. No logging here. That forest was virgin.

Avoiding the temptation to walk through the trilithon, Wilber began to make his way up the beach. For all that it was early morning it was hot and it was probably only going to get hotter. Wilber was dressed in jeans and a T-shirt, an ironic Christmas jumper, boots and thick Winter jacket. Whilst practical for an English Winter it was not really going to work here. He stopped and removed his jumper and jacket and tied them quickly around his waist. Striding off he felt much better, but then he saw something that jolted him out of his new-found sense of complacency and pulled him up short.

There was a set of footprints in the sand.

So much for his Robinson Crusoe fantasy. Nice whilst it lasted, he supposed. Wilber examined the footprints and weighed his options. There was nowhere to run. I mean he could hang out on the beach and work on his tan but how long before he was bored and dehydrated? Island paradises could only be considered such if you had a swimming pool, a helipad and copter and a five-star hotel with a full complement of flunkies. Without all those conveniences it was work.

He needed to find somebody and quickly, so that they could give him the lowdown and point him to the nearest airport or boat. At this point he decided it would be best to follow the footprints. How bad could it be? The sand was fairly well compacted and easy to walk on and the footprints headed straight into the forest. Hopefully there'd be a nice path with a handrail there that would lead him up by gradual stages to a plush hotel. A rich heiress, sunbathing alone, but for a towel and book would invite him in for drinks and then a candlelit supper. He looked much older than his fifteen years, at least eighteen so everybody said and who knew where such an adventure might lead.

He was just beginning to get into the fantasy when something up ahead, sticking up out of the sand, caught his eye. It looked to be some sort of sign, so Wilber walked over to it, for a closer inspection. It was a signpost and painted on it, in Day-Glo colours, was the legend 'TROUBLE'. It pointed towards the jungle. When he read that Wilber laughed out loud. Somebody here had a sense of humour and he couldn't wait to meet them and exchange stories. The sign was old and battered and covered in smiley faces. It reminded him of nineties Rave Culture about which he'd watched countless U-tube videos. Bit retro but he loved the aesthetic and the attitude.

Suddenly Wilber heard a sound he thought he recognised. Yeah it was familiar. He craned his ears to listen and, having made the connection, clapped his hands together, with glee. It was the sound of beating drums. That was it, that was the Rave connection. It all made sense, he'd won a competition and they'd brought him to a Dance-Island somewhere off the coast of Spain. Like Ibiza but classier. Or maybe even in the Caribbean. Hence the green waters. It was clear now. Yeah. No doubt he'd flown in yesterday and gotten a little loaded and woken up this morning still a little worse for wear. The hotel was just on the other side of the trees. No doubt he had a luxury room and his passport was there. That was it. Obvious. It was just a bit troubling that he couldn't remember getting on the plane.

Oh what the hell. Wilber, having made an executive decision, made a beeline for the treeline but he was pulled up short when two shady figures, one tall and thin, the other short and fat, stepped out of the densely shadowed forest and began looking him up and down, as though he were a piece of meat for sale.

"Allo, allo," said Shorty.

"And what do we have 'ere then," said the Whip.

Now Wilber was not immune to political correctness. He didn't like the notion of labelling anyone anymore than the next girl in class did, but how else to think about this pair other than as a duet of outmoded clichés. Shorty was fat, round and balding. He wore Harry Potter spex and no doubt he'd read all the books and fantasised about being able to perform real Magic. His comb over was a hangover from the 70s as were his cut off jeans and sandals. His faded, tropical shirt was covered in toucans and tigers. Oh and it was covered in stains too and most of the buttons were missing.

Mr Whippy, likewise favoured the cut off jeans and sandals look. He wore a saucy postcard T-shirt with the 'Legend Slip Into Something Cool' emblazoned for and aft. The image was unspeakable but it made use of a slide and two polar bears.

Wilber so wanted to laugh out loud but not at the T-Shirt. His Grandpa would have described them as a pair of sketches, ice cream vendors perhaps or slaughterers of livestock. They were not wholesome individuals. They were, to use the common parlance 'dodgy' but they were there, standing in front of Wilber and they looked as though they were prepared to be questioned.

"So, have you come from the rave then?"

"The rave?" Mr Whippy repeated, adding a question mark by way of his intonation.

"Yeah, you know, the dance."

Shorty was quicker on the up-take than his confrere and stepped forward to take charge.

'Yeah, we've been here a fortnight already. Absolutely banging, mate every night. Best rave I've ever been to. Seven different DJs on permanent rotation, cheap drinks from dawn till dusk and the light show will blow your mind."

Wilber paled as he teetered on the brink of a flashback.

"Really?"

"Would I lie to you, mate?" Shorty said bursting into laughter. "Course I wouldn't," stepping in quickly to answer his own question lest Wilber contradict him.

"So how did you get here? Cheap Flight?"

Shorty glanced over at Mister Whippy who grinned, as though it were part of his job description. His teeth, whilst all present were far from correct. They were all of them coated in yellow slime and to be presented with them prior to any mealtime, however hungry, would have put you off your food. He looked a broken down racehorse who had been put out to pasture and boy was he ready for the knacker's yard.

"No, we came by train," Mister Whippy volunteered by way of an explanation.

"And then by boat," Shorty added. "Much cheaper. And the views, oh, stunning."

Wilber took a little while to digest this information.

"What, so you're from London?"

Both Shorty and Mister Whippy nodded and grinned.

"So where are you staying? At the hotel?"

Once again Shorty took the lead.

"Well that is one option and it's a good call but there is a second option, which we would advise. Shall I tell you what it is? Yeah I will. You want to know this. You really want to know this. They have a cut-price but luxury village here. It's called the Cannibal Grove. I kid you not. It's kind of informal. Sort of bring your own hammock sort of gig. You know. But don't worry, if you haven't got a hammock you can buy them here and they're very reasonably priced. There is a bar and there isn't a drink they haven't heard of. You can get a Thai massage, with all the extras, and up on the hill, there are heated plunge pools with loungers and umbrellas. Really luxurious and the staff are so laid back."

Listening to this description, Wilber felt increasingly buoyant, excited even, but at the back of his mind, a little voice was beginning to nag. Block it from his thoughts, deny it outright, but Wilber could not escape the fact that he hadn't flown in on Easy Jet. He'd come through some sort of portal and prior to that he'd been chased out of the house by a ten-foot-high dinosaur with teeth twenty times bigger than Mr Whippy's. Not only that, but Nanny, the Old Crone, love her, had been pawed, clawed and eaten alive by said Killa Dino. You didn't need to be a fan of Jurassic Park to know that your home had been invaded and ransacked by a Tyrannosaurus-Rex, Terrible Lizard King, archetypal theropod and Apex Predator.

As the reality of his situation began to dawn, Wilber stood stock still and stared into space. Long, red seconds passed and he said nothing. Something didn't quite add up here; he felt as though he had lost more than time but what? Agonise as he might, he couldn't quite put his finger on it.

7

The Welcoming Committee

Shorty looked questioningly at Mister Whippy, then back at the now pallid and vacant youth. This was out of the ordinary, even for them. The kid looked like he'd just wandered in from a war zone.

"You alright mate, you look as if you've just seen a ghost?" Shorty asked, doing as good an impression of concern as he could muster.

"Funny you should say that," Wilber replied in an almost whisper.

"Is it?" Mr Whippy added, sounding a little uncertain. "Why?"

"I'm not sure you'd believe me, even if I told you," Wilber confessed.

Shorty didn't like where this was going. All this kind of chat and staring into nothing was superfluous to requirements. It was time to get things back on track.

"What did you say your name was?"

"I didn't."

"Well, what is it?" Mr Whippy asked, beginning to lose patience.

"It's Justice Wilberforce Muldoon, if you must know."

Shorty laughed, as though Wilber had just told a joke. Wilber gave him a funny look and he stopped laughing. Suddenly nervous, he ran his stained, stubby fingers through thinning locks and cleared his throat. It was obvious he was about to make a speech.

"Well, Wilber, if I might be so bold as to call you that, I'd like to be the first to welcome you to our wonderful island. It is a paradise of sorts and I am sure you will come to love it as much as we do. If there is anything we can help you with, don't hesitate to contact us.

We'll give you your space but we'll also be on hand should there be any niggles or beefs that you want sorting. We don't shy away from danger Wilber, nor from confrontation and we will always do what is necessary. Whatever that is. Once more, welcome."

Mister Whippy applauded and his claps rang out over the white sands. A cool off shore breeze had begun to blow in their direction and Wilber felt a sudden chill. Away in the distance, and yet, not too far away, the Rave Drums picked up again and began pounding out a different rhythm to the one he'd first heard.

"If you'd like to step this way," Mister Whippy said in a rather solicitous manner, indicating with his oily right hand the path Wilber should take into the jungle. There was only one path so all in all it was a superfluous gesture.

"What is going on with those drums?" Wilber asked, suddenly suspicious. "That doesn't sound like a rave."

Shorty laughed out loud.

"African drumming workshop, mate. You can't dance for twenty-four hours a day, so why not drum? Gets the whole community in touch with one another and at the end of the day community is what its all about. We all love to participate, don't we Wilber? And there's some very talented people around here, as you'll find out."

They walked on and the drumming got louder and seemingly more frenzied. In spite of what he'd been told Wilber felt increasingly uncomfortable.

"Do they cater for vegetarians here?" he asked, somewhat disingenuously.

"They cater for all sorts," Shorty replied, with relish. "The food here is unlike anything you'll ever taste. You are in for a Culinary Odyssey of unbelievable discovery."

Mister Whippy was in total agreement.

"We eat things here Wilber that will astound you. Cordon bleu, gourmet, experimental, meticulously prepared, dazzlingly inventive are just some of the epithets that have been applied by the World's Greatest Food Writers to our cuisine."

Shorty nodded his head and laughed.

"And you're going to be part of that Wilber. In a big way. It's as if I can hear them now, dusting off the cutlery."

"Oh yeah," Whippy agreed, "no doubt, this very instant they are bringing up the very best napkins and table clothes from the scullery. I think it's time, my friend, for a taste explosion."

"For a taste explosion?" Wilber echoed. "What's that?"

"It's when the food tastes so good it quite literally blows your head off. You'll feel as if you haven't had a decent meal in years. You'll be drowning... in tears of joy."

At this, both Whippy and Shorty first howled and then hooted, then they danced around like they were at a Hoe-Down. They so obviously found Wilber hysterical and whilst he didn't want to rain on their parade, he found their attentions and responses to him most disconcerting.

The path led them onwards, towards a conclusion, and still the drums grew louder and louder. Wilber winced and screwed up his nose. The noise was, to coin a cliché, ear splitting. On either side, the forest pressed in on him, closer and closer, the trees dark, the foliage thick. It wasn't as he had imagined from the outside but denser and gloomier. The heat had built steadily since they had left the beach, and had grown tediously oppressive. He felt like he was being squeezed, in an ever tightening grip, funnelled into a future that might not be quite as bright as it had been billed.

Then a development; the path led towards two huge gates, at least ten feet high and made of bamboo. Lashed together with vines, they stood invitingly open. From thence the path snaked into a dark tunnel, likewise made of bamboo, that swallowed the meandering trail. It was like the entrance to a fairground ride but a little more sinister.

"In there?" Wilber asked, just checking.

"In there," Shorty and Mister Whippy chorused.

Taking a deep breath, Wilber plunged into the dark tunnel that lay beyond the gates. The roof of the tunnel was a little lower than he was, so he was compelled to stoop. In a state of discomfort, he cracked on, accelerating his pace, so that Shorty was compelled to run to keep up. The Comb Over King had no need to stoop though. His head fell well short of the tunnel's height. Being a dwarf was not without its disadvantages Wilber thought bitterly.

Up ahead he spied a light. Thank God. He was beginning to feel claustrophobic in this overripe tunnel, which had a smell somewhere between rotten fish and fruit gone bad. More and more light began to flood into the tunnel and Wilber felt a tangible sense of relief when he found himself reaching the end of the passageway. Stepping through the opening, ducking lower than he would have liked to, he entered a large, sandy clearing, situated in the midst of the forest. The floor of the clearing was dappled with a crisscross pattern of interlaced strands of light and shade. It took a while for his eyes to grow accustomed to the light and to understand exactly what was going on.

Opposite him, was the colossal sun-bleached skull of a giant reptile. Its mouth was open wide and gaping as if it had been exhorted to do so by a pushy dentist. Despite the lack of flesh, Wilber identified it immediately. It was a T Rex. Turning he looked back at the opening through which he had just stepped and instantly he understood he had emerged through a second set of jaws that both mirrored and echoed the one opposite. This wasn't the half of it.

Around the periphery of the grove, standing, clutching knives and forks were the shabbiest, motliest group of individuals he had ever seen. By comparison, Shorty and Whippy were Fashionistas who demanded respect. Clothing, where it existed at all, was rotten or frayed and each and every individual was caked with mud and something else that Wilber didn't want to have to think about. Few wore anything on their feet and none were groomed. Hair stuck out at odd angles and beards raged, hanging from upper and lower jaws like swarms of bees or clusters of grapes.

In the centre of the clearing stood the largest cooking pot he had ever seen. It was ash-black and clearly used on a regular basis. Water and root stock bubbled and boiled within its capacious bell as beneath it a fire blazed and raged. The cauldron rested on a giant brass tripod that had been scorched black with age and use.

Every eye was fixed upon him and there was, about the expansive grove, an atmosphere of expectation. Despite their down at heel appearance, the people seemed pleased to see him. In fact, Wilber might have said, without hyperbole, that the good people of Cannibal Grove were delighted to see him. There was not one amongst them who was not beaming from ear to ear. It was most heartening and he felt as though he had just won an important competition, and that he ought, perhaps, to make a speech.

The drums had fallen silent, possibly in anticipation of his saying a few words and he racked his brains for something to say. His father was good at this sort of thing. He had a relaxed formality about him that went down really well with large crowds of people. The basic message was that heh, we're in all this together and I know my job is to amuse you and not to bore you and if you'll give me your good will and your laughter I'll get off this stage quickly. His self-deprecating, ahh shucks, approach to life and business was one that Wilber was beginning to appreciate.

There were a couple of things that were beginning to bug him though. Looking around the grove, he could find no evidence of the much-vaunted sound system that Shorty and Mr Whippy had alluded to. It was obviously well hidden in the trees or under the ground and where for that matter was the light show? This was supposed to be a five-star gig and yet it looked more like a one-star parade. Perhaps it's fancy dress day and they'd all come as cannibals or something. The thought made him smile and he had to fight hard to suppress a giggle. Just then, a bare-footed woman in a red and white gingham dress, with an animal bone through her hair, took a step forward and stared at Wilber with a glazed look in her eyes.

"Hello," she said, "and who might you be?"

"Hi, my name's Justice Wilberforce Muldoon," Wilber replied, feeling ambassadorial. He was not without charm, when the occasion demanded it, and the fact that no one knew a thing about him worked in his favour. Life here was like life before the fall, innocent and jolly and he for one was loving it. The Gingham Lady chuckled and simpered in a slightly unnerving way, but Wilber, feeling expansive just grinned back.

"Is it? Ooh what a lovely name," Gingham offered in response, as though she were in the presence of minor royalty.

A second member of the welcoming party then stepped forward and the Gingham Lady stepped back. This one was dressed in patched and faded motorcycle leathers and a wife beater vest. He had tattoos of dragons and skeletons on his arms and his hair stood up on end in a way that made it look as though he had just been electrocuted. He had very peculiar eyes too. Blue eyes as his Granny used to say in that one blew one way and one blew the other. Whilst the left eye looked straight ahead, monitoring traffic, the right eye was at ten past two, checking out the weather. Most disquieting. They were odd colours too.

"Hello Wilber. I'm Maurice and this is Beef or, as we call her, Lady Macbeef, being of Scots descent and all. Scots Irish as the Americans say, whatever that means."

He tried to roll his eyes then but didn't quite manage it. Then he laughed and Wilber almost went into shock. Where the eyes were weird, the laugh was pathologically abnormal and not without danger either. To Wilber's ears it sounded like a hyena having an epileptic fit inside a washing machine. Nobody else seemed phased by the laugh so perhaps, in time, he too would get used to it.

"It is my pleasure and my privilege to welcome you to our humble island abode. I hope that Ian and Andrew are taking good care of you. They are part of our official welcoming committee, you know."

Wilber hadn't 'known' but he had guessed as much. Glancing behind him, Mr Whippy, who he figured was the being who answered to Ian, and Andy aka Shorty, stood with their hands clasped in front of them, watching him. They looked like Mormons or bodyguards or perhaps Mormon Bodyguards. Anyway they were both helpful and reassuring and Wilber was glad he had met them. Suddenly the image of the trilithon flashed into his head and he turned back to Maurice. For all that Maurice looked like a freak who should have been chained up and sedated, Wilber felt an odd sense of kinship with him.

"Maurice, you're not gonna believe how I got here, what happened to me this morning. First off I was chased by a dinosaur, then I I went through what I can only describe as…"

"A time gate?" Maurice asked innocently as though he were just checking.

Wilber was flabbergasted.

"You know about the time gate?"

Maurice rolled his eyes then glanced back at Beef and winked. Beef grinned inanely revealing teeth that looked as though they had been filed down to sharp points.

"How do you think we got here?" Maurice whispered in an OTT sotto voce stage whisper.

Curiouser and curiouser.

"So you didn't come by EasyJet either, huh? Look Maurice, I like you and feel like I can trust you. I'm still in shock I think. I mean one minute I'm in the family mansion, the next I'm here on a beautiful, tropical island…"

"Overrun by dinosaurs and all kinds of freaks that your family, were they here would probably advise you to cross the street to get away from. Unbelievable isn't it? But frankly Wilber, nobody here cares about where you've come from. They only care about where you're going."

The way Maurice said this pulled Wilber up short. The rest of the Ravers were all still staring at him, in a way that bordered on the rude. Surely they should be going about their business by now. He wasn't that interesting. Up above him, a cloud passed over the sun and the grove became gloomier and somewhat macabre. The fire leapt and spat and the people stood as still as states. Mr Whippy and Shorty wore odd expressions on their faces and a cold wind was beginning to blow. Wilber shivered and he felt his heart rate pick up.

"Is that so," he said in response to Maurice's previous statement. "And where am I going?"

The runaway laugh came out to play again, spinning end over end like a tumbleweed on the set of a spaghetti western, only this time everyone in the charmed circle joined in, like a Greek Chorus. Maurice went to answer and got so far as opening his mouth before Mr Whippy leaned forward and whispered in his ear.

"It's good of you to ask, my son. Actually we'd like to invite you to breakfast.

8

The Menu

The news was not unwelcome to Wilber as his mouth had begun to water.

"That's really kind of you. I haven't had a bite to eat in hours. I think, with everything that has gone on I'd slightly lost my appetite but now its back. So tell me chaps, if you'd be so kind, what's on the menu?"

All around the circle the good people of Cannibal Grove looked at each other and smiled wryly. From behind him Shorty and Mr Whippy, Andy and EeEe, draped their arms like beneficent spiders around his shoulders.

"Oh, Wilber," chortled Mr Whippy, "we'd love to tell you but it's kind of a surprise. You do like surprises don't you?"

Hearing this, the ragged ravers exploded into fits of laughter. It was as though the dam of propriety had finally burst and a flood of madness was sweeping through the grove. Taking to their heels they ran wildly, hither and thither, cheering and whooping as though a rodeo had just begun. Some ran about like headless chickens, clucking, flapping and pecking, others pretended to be whooping gibbons and swung their arms about and beat their chests with gay abandon, whilst others still, howled like hounds on a foxhunt. Everywhere he looked an orgy of unconventional, animalistic behaviour was taking place and it had come from nowhere. Or seemingly it had. The people were riotous and laughing so violently that many fell onto the sandy ground and convulsed as though they had been tasered.

On the one hand, it was insanely funny but on the other hand it was quite terrifying and Wilber was close to freaking out. Tamworth on a Saturday night was bonkers but never, in a month of Sundays was it like this. All he could do was stand and stare. This went on for a good few minutes and then it stopped abruptly, as though a secret signal had been given or a switch thrown. Then the action moved into a second phase, very different from the first, but just as freaky. The people began running around the Grove but not in a haphazard way. They had become purposeful and focused, clearly intent on getting things ready. They were still in a state of high excitement but for now it was as though they had lost all interest in Wilber. As the befuddled youth watched, the residents of Cannibal Grove began to prepare for an occasion they had obviously been looking forward to for a long time.

Trestle tables were brought out of the woods and laid down on either side of the bubbling, cooking pot. Under each side of the crude and roughly hewn tables, small three-legged stools, whittled from fallen or felled island trees were placed and the cutlery that each of the Ravers had been brandishing, since Wilber's arrival, was finally laid at designated places. Blue and white enamel cups, chipped and dented, were then produced from an old treasure chest that looked as though it had been retrieved from the submerged bowels of a Spanish galleon and set down ready for whatever beverage was to be poured and imbibed by the mob.

Some brought firewood and stoked the fire. Others hung buntings in the trees. Still others swept the sand with makeshift brooms or pounded the drums once more. Beef, in a chef's hat and frilly apron, was tasting the thickening broth with a large, wooden spoon that had had many notches sliced into the handle. Meanwhile, Maurice was sharpening a large and fairly intimidating carving knife that looked like it hadn't been washed in an age. In the midst of all this activity Andy and EeEe, Shorty and Whippy, chatted affably with Wilber about many island related matters as the others completed their allotted tasks in preparation for what was obviously going to be a slap up nosh. Oblivious to any sense of personal threat or danger Wilber chatted away, eager to compare and contrast life at Muldoon Manor with life here.

"Hungry Wilber?" Shorty asked as the preparations were clearly coming to a close.

"Truly famished," Wilber said, looking about him for any sign that the arrival of food was imminent.

"Well everybody's gotta eat," Mr Whippy suggested. This was eminently practical and Wilber couldn't help but agree.

"Can't live on love," Shorty added.

"Or wait for fleshy treats to rain down from above."

Mr Whippy considered something philosophical for a moment and then he turned to Wilber and spoke with as much sincerity as he could muster.

"You know Wilber, I really want to thank you for coming to the island and lighting up our lives. You don't know how much we appreciate what you've given us. As much as we love our place in the sun, it can be so lonely here."

Shorty was in complete agreement.

"It's true. You've given us so much already but whether you know it or not, you're gonna give us more. I feel it in my belly and in my bones, my old mate."

"Really?" said Wilber, a little nonplussed now. This was starting to sound suspiciously like overkill.

"Yep, in meeting you we struck oil." Whippy said, glancing over at the fire. He seemed satisfied that everything was in order, as good as it could be. Beth was grinning and nodding her head. Maurice had stopped sharpening his knife and now a whole line of people were moving forward with bowls and chopping boards.

Something was about to begin. You didn't have to be a rocket scientist to see that countdown had commenced.

"Yep we struck gold when we met you Justice Wilberforce Muldoon," Shorty said as the smile dropped off of his face and something else peeped out from behind his eyes.

"We are all on the threshold of one of the greatest feasts in living memory," the follically-challenged, pot bellied dwarf hissed with great relish.

This just wasn't right and why had the air begun to cool and chill?

"But its only breakfast," Wilber reasoned, "nothing special about breakfast."

"Oh but don't you know Wilber? Breakfast is the most important meal of the day," said Mr Whippy as he grabbed hold of Wilber by the neck and squeezed. "especially when you've been starving as long as we have."

Shocked and not a little amazed, Wilber tried to resist, but Shorty, as fast as a darting pike, lunged, seized and pinned the grimacing youth's arms behind his back.

"Nothing to worry about Wilber," he cackled, "It's all just a game. We don't want you in pain or worrying. Pain and worry poison a meat and we want to enjoy our food."

"Food? Wilber screeched. "What is the name of hell's bells, do you mean?"

Mr Whippy, tightening his grip on Wilber's neck leaned forward and whispered in his ear.

"You're the guest of honour at our Breakfast Feast, Muldoon."

Everyone laughed, everyone but Wilber.

"My Dear Boy," Whippy drawled, as he turned to Shorty, parodying, as far as he was able, the manners of a nineteenth century aristocrat. "How about a weeping little fig?"

The gathered crowd tittered as Shorty considered.

"Such a generous offer Old Boy, but me, well I'd prefer a mouthful of Long Pig." Then he let out a ripping squeal which reduced the crowd to hysterical laughter. All but Wilber that is.

Propelled forwards towards the bubbling, cooking pot, Wilber was forced to his knees as the drums went into overdrive and manic looks of glee broke out on every face. How could he have been so stupid? Why had he trusted these freaks? They were so obviously off their heads. Too late and to his great cost he had discovered that there was no sound system, nor was there a rave, nor were these people at a fancy dress party.

The inhabitants of Cannibal Grove were in fact Real Cannibals and the masks they wore were masks of irony and deception. The vision had revealed all this, just moments before he had met them. But deaf, blind and dumb he had ignored all of the signs. How could he have been so naive? And why hadn't he listened to the message of his vision? If he'd have had a free foot he'd have kicked himself, but a manic mop top with powerful fingers and a squint had both of his feet pinned firmly to the ground. Suddenly besides Maurice's sharp knife there were all manner of choppers, axes and saws being waved about under his nose.

He had always dreamed of dying heroically, of going out in a blaze of glory, in a hail of bullets to the strains of a lone guitar. He had never imagined he'd be hacked to death and boiled in a cauldron for the culinary delight of a bunch of sartorially distressed psychopaths with cannibalistic tendencies.

That was not part of his life plan, nor had it ever been. If he survived this little crisis, unlikely as that was now, he would need to rethink everything.

"I want his liver," somebody shouted out.

"I want his tongue," came the rejoinder.

Oh great that's just what he needed to hear. Before he'd even gone into the pot they were squabbling over who got what.

"I want his feet."

"Oh no you don't. I baggsied his feet."

"When?"

"Last night."

"But nobody knew he was coming last night."

"We had a meeting."

"To which I wasn't invited?"

"Well we looked for you but we couldn't find you."

"I was down at the beach washing my hair."

"Were you? If we'd have known, we'd have come looking for ya. But we didn't know, so we couldn't come."

"Oh that's convenient." The second voice shot up in pitch as the sense of indignation mounted.

Wilber had had enough. If they were to going murder him in

warm blood, he would much prefer it, if they did it quickly and efficiently. Give him a drop of grog, slit his throat and let him bleed out relatively painlessly before the carve up. That was the solution. If the Meat Feast became a free for all, the likelihood was that he would be hacked limb from limb in the most agonising fashion imaginable. He had read medieval accounts of people being hung, drawn and quartered. William Wallace, Braveheart himself, went that way. They had cut up his body and burned his bowels whilst he was still alive, then having hacked off his head, they'd dipped it in tar and shoved it on a spike. Like a toffee apple. And whilst that was bad, at least he'd been spared the indignity of being eaten alive."

"Look you pair," Wilber cut in, "shut it."

The voice of the indignant hair washer went up another octave. "Oh how rude!"

The Feet Baggsier likewise, was outraged.

"The Meat does not get to choose who gets what. That is the law here, so don't argue."

Wilber wanted to scream quite blue and violent insults at the two squabbling gulls, but he was a Muldoon and Muldoons didn't do that. Muldoons had dignity which meant that they carried themselves a certain way and, like Royalty, they never complained about anything or explained their reasons for doing anything. If he was due to meet death on this day, he would do so with his head held high.

"Listen, I have the perfect solution. One of you, get's the first foot. The other gets the second foot."

"But who will get the left foot and who will get the right foot?" The Hair Washer protested.

"Draw lots," Wilber said wearily. "I think that's the best solution, don't you?"

The Hair Washer and the Foot Baggsier looked at one another, nodded and shook hands. They, unlike Wilber, were not displeased with the outcome.

Having given up on the vain hope that the crowd of starving savages would be overcome by mercy and tenderness Wilber was resigned to his fate. All he wanted was a speedy dispatch.

"Most magnanimous," Shorty volunteered. "Well it's been lovely knowing you, Wilber. Hope you enjoyed the island- what little you saw of it and remember it's nothing personal..."

"It's only business," the drooling crowd shouted back.

"What sort of people are you?" asked Wilber, overcome by sudden exhaustion and despair.

"Can't you guess Wilber?" Mr Whippy quipped gleefully. "Well let me give you a clue. It sounds like Span-i-el and it rhymes with Hann-i-bal."

Laughter spread, like plague through a colony, and even Maurice joined the fray doing his manic hyena in a washing-machine impression. The atmosphere was festive, on the verge of clubbable one might say. Amazing what the thought of food could do to a starving multitude.

"Help! Help! Helllpppppppp!!!" Wilber cried, not expecting to be rescued, just wanting some well-meaning knife carrier to plunge a blade into his jugular, giving him a speedy deliverance.

Maurice, fond of Wilber, stepped forward and patted the kneeling meal.

"No point shouting Wilber. There's no one coming to save you. Surely that's obvious by now? But don't worry. We'll finish you off quickly and then ooh la la it's in the pot you go. It's time for you to bubble and squeak my old son."

Once again there were gales of laughter and then with a nod from Maurice the bowl carriers edged closer.

"Don't spill a drop, he urged. The blood will thicken the broth and put some colour in all our cheeks."

Suddenly Beef gave an eldritch screen so ear-splittingly awful that the Drummers suspended their tubthumping to see what had happened.

"What is it dear?" Maurice asked with concern.

"Don't do a thing, Mo until I've fetched me cook book. I was thinking Jamie Oliver but you're a little bit special Wilber. I'm going to go a little bit retro for you and get out me Fanny

Craddock."

"Help." Wilber screamed. Oh the horror, the horror. What was to become of him?

"Help. Please Hellllpppppppp!!!"

9

Dust Up

Wilber's screams drifted high above the jungle canopy and took to the air like birds. Flapping their wings, they travelled in every direction and despite the silence that appeared to greet their arrival, they were not ignored. Oh no, their presence was registered and tracked back to source. Thankfully for Wilber, he was not alone. Eyes watched, ears listened, minds processed, schemed, calculated vectors of approach and attack. Threat was assessed, risks weighed, benefits calculated, costs deferred.

And most importantly of all orders, were issued.

Down on the ground all looked bleak for the rope-bound arriviste but hope, for those that dare to hope, springs eternal. Whilst the cannibals salivated with extreme relish, sharpening their knives and stoking the fire beneath the cooking pot up in the trees adrenaline surged and pulses quickened. For if truth were known, neither Wilber nor the Cannibals were alone. And whilst the Cannibals laughed and smacked their lips, a net tightened. As they had surrounded Wilber so the hidden ones had surrounded them.

Beef, having found her blood-encrusted copy of Fanny Craddock's 1965 culinary classic, Home Cooking with Fanny, was champing at that bit.

"Don't worry Wilber, we won't waste a morsel. You'll love what we do with your remains. And I'm sure that Fanny would have approved."

"God rest her beloved soul," Maurice replied, lifting a sharp edged knife and pressing it against Wilber's carotid.

"Good night sweet Prince," Mr Whippy called, archly waving a snotty handkerchief in Wilber's direction.

Frothing words of rage bubbled on Wilber's lips but he never had time to deliver them, for suddenly, out of the trees sprang shadows, fully armed and intent on damage. Not only that either, for rocks, artfully thrown, found their mark. The first, and possibly most significant rock being the sharpened stone that struck Maurice on the occipital region of his skull rendering him bloody and immediately unconscious. Dropping to the floor, seemingly in slow motion, his eyes rolled over white, and his head hit the ground with a dull thud.

Wilber squealed like a cornered pig, having exhausted his repertoire of screams and watched the violence unfold with both joy and relief. The shadows were not shadows at all but a crew of what appeared to be adolescent girls sporting Dayglo clubs and staffs which they wielded with extreme precision and focused violence. Swinging into action, they set about the Cannibals with vicious relish. They clubbed and whacked, tripped and smashed anybody in the hallowed grove, who was not Wilber.

And they looked amazing. Lycra-clad in their morph suits of many colours, the gang had augmented their outfits with camouflage paint (artfully applied) muds of many colours, leaves and branches. Each had their own unique look, marrying circus with carnival and more than a dash of the MacQueens. One extraordinary individual had a headpiece comprised of Antelope horns and a bull's skull. They looked like something out of a Sci Fi Movie by way of the catwalk and the moment that Wilber saw them, he fell in love. With all of them simultaneously.

10

The Dinosaur Boys

As the two sides fought, the man watched from the sanctuary of the trees. He could have helped, could have joined the fight on either side and swung it one way or another but he didn't. Oh no, he watched and he waited, his brown eyes, dark and calculating taking everything in.

It was all a question of timing and when his moment came he took it, creeping forth with Ninja-like stealth and cutting Wilber's ropes with his Bowie Knife. Then he loosened the youth's gag and placed his longest finger against trembling lips. Wilber's heart was racing but he couldn't help but feel an instant and immediate gratitude for his would be saviour. The jungle hat and kerchief that the man wore, like the Lone Ranger, over nose and mouth served to conceal his identity but they did nothing to diminish his stature or to suggest that he was not a safe bet. The youth and the man looked deeply into each other's eyes and came to an immediate accommodation.

"If you want to survive you'd best come with me," the man whispered into his ear.

And all Wilber could do was nod.

As the man sped away from the Cannibal Village, Wilber followed him into the forest. Behind them the sounds of the fight raged on but that was not Wilber's concern. He glanced back, saw the cannibals and the gang smashing seven shades of stuffing out of each other, the highly-colourised sticks wielded by the girls, flashing in the morning light and he sighed. Wilber was not one to run away from a fight; he would have loved to have stayed and joined in but as of this moment he had other priorities.

Like his own survival.

Moving at speed, trying to keep up with the man in front of him, Wilber's head filled with racing thoughts. So much had happened in such a short space of time and he understood none of it. Or rather he did and could not accept it. One minute he'd been running round the grounds of his family home, the next he'd been transported through some kind of portal onto an island populated by cannibals and God alone knew what else. Either that or he'd had what Doctors called an episode.

Confusion was not always the enemy. Sometimes it was a friend and ally but right now he was having a hard time calling it. The confusion in the Cannibal village had enabled him to flee, aided and abetted by this mysterious figure but it was not helping him come to terms with his predicament or formulate a plan. Thrust from a life of meaningless boredom into a world of crisis, of ever present and immediate dangers, he realised he was in shock. Not able to take what was going on any more, Wilber stopped running and slowed to a halt. Then he folded his arms and called out to the figure up ahead.

"I can't go any further. I need a break and I need some answers."

The figure stopped moving immediately and, turning on a pinhead, ran back down the trail towards Wilber. His body language bore testament to the fact that he was not entirely happy.

"It's not safe here. We have to keep on moving."

"The hell, we do. I want some answers," Wilber shot back. Having perfected the role of moody teenager, he was going to play it for all it was worth. We'll see what happens, he thought when the unstoppable force meets the immovable object.

"We don't have time for this," the man hissed, "We are still in danger. Serious bloody danger."

Wilber tried a change of tact.

"Look, what's with the mask and hat? You look like you just stepped off a movie set. I mean who dresses like that, anymore? Who are you?"

"You mean you don't recognize me?" the man replied, hurt in his voice.

Wilber was incredulous.

"Should I?"

"Of course," the man replied, clearly exasperated. Removing his hat and lowering the jaw-covering kerchief he took a step back and spread wide his arms. It was not as big a reveal as he'd hoped for and the look of confusion that had been creasing Wilber's brow stayed firmly in place.

Was this the Royal Road to madness he was on, Wilber thought? The youth studied the man as an artist studies his model and in his mind's eye the man was transfigured into something larger than life. Mere man became Jungle Guy, a cartoon figment of Wilber's Manga-addicted mind and still he stood, arms spread wide awaiting acknowledgement. It was obvious that Jungle Guy thought that he had performed sufficient action to guarantee a positive ID but Wilber, Master of Sarcasm that he was, just shook his head from side to side, slowly, in a gesture designed to infuriate and smirked.

"No idea."

Jungle Guy sighed.

"You never used to be this thick."

Wilber's lower jaw dropped and he gaped.

"Excuse me?"

"Look. Its me. Don't you recognize me? I'm you, or rather I'm part of you. Genetically speaking that is. I'm your Uncle."

Wilber froze. Of all the shocks he had experienced this morning, this was the greatest. It felt as though he'd been wired into the National Grid and someone had just pulled the switch. 240,000 volts were coursing through his system and black smoke was about to start pouring out of his ears.

"That's impossible."

"Improbable, not impossible," said Jungle guy returning Wilber's smirk with some top spin, like a Hollywood Tennis Pro.

"Dinosaur George? You can't be."

"Oh but I am."

Wilber studied the man for some time and little by little he began to put the jigsaw back together. His conclusions were not altogether pleasing to him and fight as he might, eventually he had to accept that Jungle Guy and Dinosaur George Muldoon were one and the same. His disappointment was marked. George was older, greyer and paunchier than he remembered. Some of his teeth were missing and he was shabbily dressed. His boots had holes and his cords were torn.

And cords?

The George he remembered had been a Grail Knight. He had blue eyes and long, blond shining hair, that caught the light and blinded the unwary. He stood tall and true, well over six feet three and he was as muscled and toned as a Young Schwarzenegger. He was stylish or trendy as occasion demanded, always ready with a quip or gag. He could rock a tux, make a shell suit smoulder and would have given Usain Bolt a race over 100m. When he walked, the sound of the Old Spice Advert could be heard trailing in his wake. Women loved him and men half admired, half envied him. Kids wanted to be him when he grew up. He was a rock star and a movie star and Einstein all rolled into one. When he had left, Wilber had cried for a month and then mourned for a year.

Looking at this splintered, wreck of a man he would have preferred that George had stayed away, safely embalmed in his mind, as an icon and image of what was possible, of the man he might grow to be. But that was not to be. Time had coughed him up and spat him out and he had landed at Wilber's feet with a splat.

Neither wanted, needed nor expected.

George lowered his arms and looked at his nephew. Now it was his face that creased with a frown. The disillusionment he saw in Wilber's eyes caused him great pain. Okay he'd deserted the family, abandoned the boy but he'd had his reasons and they were very good reasons. Surely the kid would understand when he explained what had gone on and why he'd made the choices he had. He was older now, more mature and therefore more able to cope with disappointment and loss. Wasn't he?

"My life went to hell after you left," Wilber said slowly and with great deliberation. Suddenly the world became very still. "I was nine years of age. You were my hero and you left me hanging, without a word. Do you understand how that made me feel? About myself?"

The power in the boy's words unhinged George. All he could do was stand and stare.

"I can only imagine," he said after long weighty seconds had passed.

Wilber's face was a mask of rage.

"No you can't. You haven't a clue, not even the most basic conception of the pain you've caused. You are the most selfish man I have ever met and the most destructive. How do you live with yourself?"

That one was really a stumper and for once George found himself at a real loss for words. Wilber waited for the silence to be filled and when it wasn't he realised he would have to move the dialogue forwards himself.

"So Uncle, how did you come to be here? You've been missing for years."

This was turning into one of the worst days of George's life. He had always thought of himself as one of the good guys but his nephew clearly hated him and wanted him dead. And even worse now he wanted him to explain the choices he had made.

When he played it back George wasn't sure he could. Looked at in the cold light of day his story was totally and utterly insane.

Improbable, impossible and insane.

"Now therein hangs a tale," was all he could say.

"Something I'm hoping you can share, Uncle," Wilber returned, icy with sarcasm.

"I'll try."

Wilber sat down on a nearby fallen tree and prepared to be lied to. Why? Because it's what adults did.

"The world isn't what you think it is Justice. History is mainly lies told by men who have been bought. It's a bunch of stories that don't add up or lead anywhere. There's no pattern in it, no reason, no meaning."

Wilber stifled a yawn.

"But that's just one kind of history, the official kind. There are other kinds of history."

"Such as?"

"Unofficial history. Imagine the world is a car crash and around the crash, barriers have been erected. The people draw in close, to look at the crash, but the barriers prevent them from seeing. Then the Powers-That-Be erect barriers around the people. Now, not only can they not see in, they are barred from looking out. They are contained in holding tanks and they are not allowed to speak. Immobile they are silenced."

"That's really depressing," Wilber deadpanned.

"Yeah, but don't get caught up on that. Some people bust out. They sneak past the barriers or they tunnel."

"Or they make a stand with the Power's-That-Be," Wilber added, intrigued in spite of himself.

"Exactly!" George replied, delighted to affirm something positive for a change.

"Which is what you did."

"Partly," George agreed.

"You played their game your way, made them think you were on their side but all the time you had your own agenda which you were pursuing, covertly. With their Passcard you were able to look behind the barriers and that was when you discovered..."

Skillfully he built his voice up, increasing the speed and volume of his delivery gradually and on the point of climax he paused, like the born showman that he was and waited for George to fill in the gaps.

"And that's when I discovered that nothing was as it had been presented and that reality, so-called, was far nuttier than I had ever imagined. That there are things under the ground that beggar belief. That there are Government Projects, so evil, that if you knew about them they would convert you into an instant terrorist. That

Governments everywhere have technologies about which we are told nothing."

Wilber was sceptical.

"Bit X-files George."

"More than a bit X-files Wilber but that don't mean it ain't so. TV, Film, News it's all part of the Big Disinformation Machine. The lie is so big it has enveloped everything."

Wilber started to open his mouth with a view to slam dunking his now obviously lunatic uncle, but then he remembered the kaleidoscopic vortex of pulsating colour that had picked him up on one side of the ocean of time and dropped him off on an alien shore just hours earlier. The proof of the pudding was in the eating and the eating was in the island and that was where he had landed; smack bang in the middle of an enigma.

"Go on," he said wearily.

George beamed from ear to ear, then took a moment to prepare his thoughts. Not that that helped, he was still confused.

"It's time Wilber to stop the clocks"

"What clocks?"

"The clocks that whirl round night and day in your head. That trick your body and your mind into thinking that time is just one thing, that it moves in a certain way, in a certain direction. That just ain't so. The arrow of time can fly in any direction in any number of ways. I can see this is hard for you, that it 'blags' your head but stay with me, little man. Perhaps it's better to approach this a different way. Think of the Universe as a tape recorder if you will. You can wind it backwards or forwards as long as you have the hardware."

"And we do, have the hardware," Wilber asked quizzically.

"Depends on who you mean by we."

"Who do we mean by we?"

George looked uncomfortable with having to answer this particular question.

"Probably best that you don't know actually. Prepare for shocks and you'll be well prepared. Certain Governments, a few

Corporations, a bunch of Multinationals, one or two very wealthy individuals, a President here, a King or Queen there. It's quite diffuse."

"Sorry I asked," Wilber said, never straying too far from the sarcasm that served him so well on a daily basis. "So where did you go after you left us?

George had the good sense to look a little penitent.

"I went to a desert, to Guajira Desert. It's on a peninsula about seven hundred miles north of Bogota, right on the border between Columbia and Venezuela. We were on the Venezuelan side of the border on a dig."

"What, looking for fossils and bones?"

"Well yeah, on one level. That was what the grant money was for. We were looking for the remains of a new species of dinosaur called Laquintasaura Venezuelae. It's a Triassic bird-hipped dinosaur that's been extinct for about 200 million years. Not very big. About the size of a small dog. They'd found some specimens in a place called Quinta La Jorgera but they weren't in an especially good state of preservation. We had permission to dig to the north of this site, in the desert. We found other specimens, bigger and almost pristine.

"Why do I get the sense there's more to this story than you're telling me Uncle."

George shrugged.

"Because there is."

George, whilst loquacious when it suited him was notoriously tight-lipped when it didn't. Another Muldoon trait. Every minute Wilber spent in his company was crammed with more and more tension and irritation. The man was more slippery and evasive than anyone he'd ever encountered but by far the most damaging thing in Wilber's eyes was that he could recognise himself in George. The Dinosaur loving goon was a mirror wherein he saw his own reflection, darkly.

"So what happened out there Uncle? Did you find something besides this Venezuelan chicken or did something scare you?"

George puffed up like an agitated rooster as soon as the words were out of Wilber's mouth. The little git was deliberately winding him up. He had been far too accommodating he realised and Wilber had played the Blame and Shame Game brilliantly and to great effect. But hey it was time for a reality check. He'd rescued the little scrote and the kid hadn't had the good manners to even thank him. Perhaps it would be best if he took him back to the Cannibals. Then he'd see what side his bread was buttered on.

"Scared, me? Hell no, Bozo. I'm Dinosaur George Muldoon. I don't get scared. If someone crosses me I get even. I've got more attitude than a dog baboon. Ever seen an enraged baboon Wilber? They have teeth and they ain't afraid to bite."

"That a threat, Uncle?"

"It's a description," George hissed through his remaining teeth.

The forest had suddenly become very quiet. Justice leaned in, tired of the back and forth game they'd been playing. It was time to go for the jugular, to get the Dino man to commit to some kind of narrative truth, some species of openness that would move them forward and not round and round in circles.

"So George, help me put humpty back together again. Let's finish the jigsaw shall we because this is getting old. It wasn't just fossils you found in that stony South American ground was it?"

"Ain't you the smart one," George replied, all pretence at civility abandoned.

"So, go on Uncle, drop the bomb. Let me have it."

But George was like a dog with a bone and he was not letting go.

"Come on Big Man. Spill the beans. Break the habit of a lifetime and spill the beans. Tell me what happened or just go away!" Wilber urged.

By now the goading and the sarcasm had really gotten to George. He was ready to snap; to snap Wilber's neck and pull off his head. The kid was everything that he hated about the Muldoons. That had driven him to leave. The arrogance, the sarcasm, the sense that everyone not them was educationally sub-normal. That they were pathetic and lame and that they needed to be told what was what.

"What did you find George?"

"Alright I'll tell you. I found an underground temple just north of the desert on the coast. I grew friendly with the local Wayuu people and one of them, a pearl diver, took me to this cave. It was beyond belief, completely unknown to anybody outside the tribe. That's how much they trusted me.

"So was it big this underground temple? I mean was it huge. Like a cathedral?"

"It was ample, and that's all you need to know. We need to move, and now!"

George had had enough. Wilber as though possessed was hounding and harassing him like he wanted it all to kick off.

"What did you find in that temple? Did it make you crazy? Drive you outta your mind?

"What do you think I found?"

Wilber was on his feet and the Muldoons were nose to nose. Violence was imminent. There would be blood and probably broken bones. Things would be said that could never be retracted, punches would be thrown. There would be rivers of blood.

"You found?" Wilber said

"I found," echoed George.

"A map!!!"

This they said together, at exactly the same moment. Both of them had the presence of mind to look stunned. Telepathy was not an everyday occurrence in either Muldoon's world.

"And on that map I found the thing I was looking for."

"And what was the thing you were looking for? Gold, treasure, a Magic door? What?"

"It was..."

But George had no time to finish his sentence. Two juvenile, but still deadly Allosaurs raced into the frame, salivating like Pavlov's dogs, looking for a quick and easy meal.

"Hell Uncle this is so much fun but I think it's time to run. Run!!!"

No pounding drums but crashing feet zeroing in on a kill. A

walk in the woods and a trailside story were no longer appropriate so the Muldoons, coming to their senses, took to their heels and ran. When they came to a fork in the path, they split, Wilber going north and George heading south, the young Allosaurs in hot pursuit.

11

The Tower Complex

In the centre of the island, on its highest and only peak, one can see eight industrial looking towers, in two sets of four. They stand at well over 120 metres in height and unless cloud intervenes they, as features, dominate the skyline. Not only the jungle skyline but the island skyline for miles around. Rising, like oversized needles, they seem to pierce the underbelly of the sky, causing it some measure of pain, never relief.

They were originally constructed of white-grey metal, which, given the rapidly changing climate, and the schizophrenic state of the weather, did not last in its virgin state for too long. Bolts and rivets turned to orange mush and bled out. Surfaces blistered, then holes appeared. Soon after, structures began to sag and then to rapidly collapse. It was not a happy state of affairs and, whilst it might have given the Tower Complex a pleasingly Industrial come Gothic look, it rendered it no longer fit for purpose. Soon after this was discovered a makeover was ordered, planned and implemented. However, just a few months after completion a further makeover was required.

To this end, new treatments and coatings of paint, resistant to wind, acid rain and all manner of tropical storms were developed in the lab and then field tested. Sadly, they too, soon yielded to the elements, so necessitating further advances and developments. In response, a new lab was outfitted and a permanent staff put in place. They were given continual employment, both maintaining the facility and developing newer and more weather-resistant products. Their work was never-ending and they, for all that they were essential to the smooth running of the complex, were all but ignored by other departments within the facility. Regardless of directives from above, the Colony was not an egalitarian machine. Instead it was extremely hierarchical, not unlike the Hindu caste system, which the Buddha, in his wisdom, had seen fit to trounce and denounce.

The towers, like Thunderbirds, are numbered, one through eight. Each is different, each is unique and given over to a very different purpose. The four Northern Towers for instance are painted in hues of green, favouring curves and arabesques whilst the more rectilinear and angular, Southern Towers are painted purple. In some there are restaurants and spaces dedicated to entertainment. In others there are hospital wards and beds, labs and assembly lines. There are schematics of course, and new arrivals are advised to study them at length and in detail. However not all information about the structure and function of each and every tower, or indeed each and every floor, within each tower, is available. Some areas are highly classified and as such require a High Level of Security Clearance. One such area is Tower One.

Send over a drone, or a camera strapped to a trained bird of prey, and, zooming in, one would see more, much more. Amongst the eye-catching, if somewhat eccentric buildings, one might see anomalous features alongside of concealed things and hidden details. The top of the 'mountain,' for instance, whilst appearing flat is in fact not. It is rather part of a volcanic cone, around whose rim the towers, circle. The crater has a lid, a false top, covered in concrete which at the press of a button can be split in two and rolled back to reveal a bubbling lake of lava, into which, those who fail to please can be thrown.

Furthermore, around the entire complex there are fences crowned with razor wire. These fences appear at various places all over the island and must be navigated by the wary and the unwary alike. Wire cutters exist but one needs to know where they are hidden if one is to proceed unmolested and without multiple lacerations. One such fence can be found between the enclosures that house and separate the so-called Alphabet Gang from the Cannibal Horde.

Circle the top of the volcano and one would no doubt see and hear more.

For instance, at this very moment, someone is playing the organ, a la Captain Nemo, in Tower One. If you remember this tower is off limits to the majority of the citizens who staff the facility. The music floats down the slopes of the volcano and then out over the jungle eerily mingling and merging with other sounds. Tower One is the most ornate of the towers and is crowned with a Domed Observatory of Green Glass. Despite the fact it is the middle of the day, storm clouds are beginning to form overhead and everything is mist-swathed.

12

The Confederacy

The Lift doors slid open and Puharich, whom Caleb had dubbed Lurch, stepped out of the liftpod and into the dome. Once a Scientist of some promise he had been commandeered by Astapor to serve as an advisor cum valet. He typically wore a lab coat and a frown. Called upon to describe him Caleb, ever economical with words, as with praise, cleared his throat and made pronouncement.

"Sadistic Pseudoscientific Hunchback or a hunchbacked servant of sadistic tastes, if you prefer."

Astapor, not prone to expressions of joy or amusement, guffawed like a denizen of a London Comedy Club and Caleb's place was secured. For a little while longer anyway.

Today had started like any other at 3.00 a.m with sunrise. Astapor, self-styled Russian Count, Prime Magician and resident genius had watched the sun rise as he did everyday as he schemed and plotted the twist and turn of events that would unfold during the course of the day ahead.

Whilst he schemed and plotted the Russian loved to play his organ. Today he was hammering out Bach and Caleb, surrogate son, protégé and fixer was turning the pages of the sheet music trying not to look bored. Caleb clad head to foot in black with flashes of red, green and purple about his person was an Emo-Goth, white of skin and oily of hair. The hair was long, well over his collar and slicked back. There were one or two discrete piercings and a neck tattoo on display. He wore converse boots.

As Puharich moved round the back of the lift pod, Caleb plastered a wry smile on his face and began preparing insults. It was his favourite thing in the world and Lurch was his favourite target. Now that Puharich was present The Command Team, as Caleb had dubbed them, were all present, if not correct. Lurch, ever alive to the precariousness of his situation, waited for Astapor to finish playing before speaking.

"Master, there's been a development. We have a new visitor on the island and he is, or he was, being accompanied by an Old Friend."

Astapor, ever alert to the nuances of Lurch's voice, realised that something major was going down.

"Show me."

Astapor stood and moved round the lift pod to stand in front of the green glass dome. In seconds though the glass had been illuminated from within and became a screen. As the screens flickered on Astapor felt a stab of premonitory anxiety.

Then he saw him walking through the forest with a youth a little younger than Caleb. For the first time in many years he saw the man he both hated and feared most in the world. Dinosaur George Muldoon. His eyes blazed and then the smile came. There were so many possibilities in all this.

"Friends reunited?" the Russian asked.

"I believe its his nephew, Master. The boy came through the Eastern Gate at Sunrise where he was greeted and almost 'meated' by the Cannibals."

"What happened?" Astapor growled.

"He escaped with a little help from those....those girls." Lurch spoke with obvious distaste.

"Those girls," Astapor repeated after him, slowly, as if he were having a hard time processing the information.

"The escapees Count. They call themselves the Alphabet Gang," Caleb said helpfully.

"Thank you Caleb. I'm fully aware of who the Alphabet Gang are and I'm fully aware of what I'm going to do to them after I catch them."

Puharich and Caleb stood silent and still whilst Astapor

processed the information and began weighing options. Eventually he spoke.

"It' just after five now, right?"

"Yes Master," Lurch said, always happy to agree.

"And I'm guessing they were separated, the boy and his uncle. There are young Allosaurs on that part of the island. We hatched them about six months back."

"Right again, Master," Lurch affirmed. "Whilst the girls beat the Cannibals to a pulp, so George and his nephew, who's name is Justice Wilberforce Muldoon, beat a hasty retreat and ran straight into the Allosaurs. They then ran off in opposite directions. Muldoon was always a coward was he not, Master?"

Astapor swivelled his head and fixed his steely gaze on the Hunchback. His expression was unreadable.

"Dinosaur George Muldoon is a lot of things Lurch, but he is not now, nor has he ever been, a coward."

Lurch, taking the correction, bowed his head in shame.

"Apologies Master."

Caleb who had been watching the video feed with due care and attention was a little nonplussed. Astapor alluded to Dinosaur George Muldoon not infrequently, usually when he was angry, usually when he was going to do something that others, not of the island, would refer to as Great Evil. Muldoon, it seemed to Caleb, was justification for Astapor's every deed, particularly if someone was to be operated upon or transformed into something not quite human.

"It's unbelievable that he should be here, Count," Caleb offered.

Astapor exhaled slowly.

"I don't want to believe it either, Caleb but I have to. The evidence is there before my very eyes."

"Forgive me Sir but that's not what I meant. It just seems like its stretching the bounds of probability to suggest the boy and his uncle should arrive on the island within hours of one another, albeit quite independently."

Here he turned to Puharich and his tone changed.

"Do we have footage of Muldoon Senior's arrival on the island?"

Puharich shook his head.

"I'm afraid not."

Astapor up on the ball quickly chuckled to himself.

"It is as I supposed and neither of you would believe me. There are glitches in the system, gaps that need plugging. We've been too dominant, too much in control, for too long. We've gotten complacent."

Caleb, quick study that he was, had learned that it was best not to contradict Astapor. New information had to be introduced into conversation as if it was just an extension of Astapor's previous comments and ideas, a glossary, if you will. That way it would pass muster.

"I'm so sorry this has happened Count. What can we do to make things right?"

Astapor, as still as a heron, did not respond at first and then he spoke.

"Where are they on the Map?

Caleb reached in his pocket and pulled out a remote. A Map of the Island appeared, on the green glass screen overlaying the frozen video traces and illuminating their faces with green, yellow and orange splodges. Lurch moved forward and pointed with a bony finger to the Central Eastern Quarter. It was the best way they had of tracking the movements of their latest prey.

"When the Allosaurs got the Muldoon scent, they attacked them here Master. Young Muldoon came up off the Point and through the territory we know the Alphabet's frequent. Now, despite our best efforts, a lot of the cameras we placed down there are gone."

Caleb, keen to add to the narrative, for fear that Lurch would claim all the credit he thought rightfully his, jumped in then.

"I can confirm that Sir and bring you up to date. Of 28 feeds 23 are down. We sent in Tech guys but they didn't come back."

"And you didn't think to go in yourself," Lurch remarked with a sneer. Caleb didn't respond and the Hunchback regained the initiative.

"George Muldoon beat a trail southwards, back down towards the Blue Ruin whilst Justice Muldoon is heading North."

The Russian chuckled.

"Do you think Young Justice has brought his clubs with him Caleb?"

"Do you think I should lend him mine Count?" came the riposte.

"So my friends, he faces his first great test. Breakfast with our mutual friend and then a little light Opera. The little brat will have to sing for his supper though if he's to progress. Any other new arrivals?" Astapor asked, as though he didn't already know the answer.

"Yes, three children came in just after the Muldoon Youth. Crowhaven had people waiting by the Eastern Time Gate so once again the Cannibals went hungry."

Astapor glanced at the digital wall clock.

"5.15. Tick tock said the Atomic Clock. Good work Lurch. I'm impressed."

Outwardly Caleb smiled but inwardly he raged.

"Do you not think it is time to slow them down a little, Count?"

Astapor chuckled.

"You read my mind."

"I did?" Caleb asked.

"You did."

Astapor rose and moved over towards the map. Lurch, inclining his head, moved aside. Tracing a route northwards with his right index finger, Astapor skirted the edge of his forested mountain home and arrived at a point, a few hundred metres inwards from the North Eastern shore. There his finger came to rest.

"I want them met here after their breakfast with the Professor, if the boy succeeds that is. I want him flushed with a sense of confidence and self delight and then I want him crushed.

"How do you propose to crush him, Count?" Caleb asked, his

eyes sparkling with sadistic delight.

Astapor placed his fingers on a nearby keypad and then began moving them rapidly over the keys, inputting choices and instructions. The map, which had taken up the entire quadrant of green glass, moved to the left side of the screen, diminishing in size as it did so. The right side now displayed a schematic of an underground facility comprised of thirty-two levels. The facility, an inverted tower, had been inspired in Astapor's mind by the Taj Mahal.

Initially, legend held, the Taj had been planned as two magnificent structures, one black and one white. The black Taj was to have been built of black marble and situated on the opposite side of the Yamuna River to the White Taj. It would have been a perfect reflection of the white Taj but it remained only within the mind of its conceiver, Shah Jahan. Sadly the Shah had been deposed by his son Aurangzeb and his plans had come to naught. Happily Astapor had faced no such opposition and his dreams became reality on a not infrequent basis.

How he loved the game. It was mostly his invention, both the rewards and the punishments but it was the punishments more than anything else that excited him, that made him feel whole. And the fact that it was Young Justice Muldoon who was in his sights was justice indeed. He had dreamed of revenging himself upon Muldoon for so long it had become unreal. But now here he was back in the flesh, that all too fragile flesh. It mustn't be over too quickly. It mustn't be clumsy. The slow blade was needed, not the knife. Muldoon, before he faced total destruction, must witness the death of all that he loved and held dear. The edge of a plan began to surface in the ocean of Astapor's mind and his eyes glinted like plundered diamonds.

"It's time my friends to crank up the tension."

"Invite our guests to a Terror Convention?" Caleb suggested.

"Indeed, I like that Caleb. But the terrors I am about to release will be far from conventional."

Puharich leaned in.

"No problem, no fuss. Master, you're a genius. We'll dispatch the order at your convenience. If that is convenient."

"Indeed it is, Lurch."

The hunchback considered their options. Best not to over egg the pudding. Knowing Astapor he would want the boy taken out in a very specific way. One could hint but not direct. To overextend oneself would be to court disaster.

"Should we send in the Cannibal Army, Master? They are very hungry now, so they might be a little difficult to control, but it would be greatly entertaining to watch their predations."

Caleb scoffed and then spat like a Temple cat.

"Send the Cannibals in on a death safari? You're so unimaginative Lurch and that is so last season."

"So what do you suggest, Caleb," Astapor murmured, his voice rippling the fabric of the ethers and sending a chill down the Young Emo's spine.

"I think you know exactly what it is you want to do already. No doubt you've already weighed the Cannibal option in your mind, explored it in detail and rejected it. Am I right?"

The look that Astapor gave Caleb would have stopped a charging rhino, but then in the smile he gave, he returned everything he had taken away.

"You're so right Caleb. The Cannibal Army lacks the subtlety I require. Every death that I am responsible for here, must in my mind be a work of art. Or why bother? No, we'll leave the Cannibals for another time. Send in the creepers, they're far crueller and much cheaper.

*   *   *   *   *   *   *

Up above Russian fingers dance over the keyboard, dispatching the order, of which Lurch had spoken. A pulse travelling down wires, from above ground to below ground is the result. The tapping of keys is a magical act, an alchemical act converting will into action, thought into motion.

The eye reclines, the eye pans back, a camera in motion. We are all cameras recording. We see everything, store everything, as memory or fantasy. In the photon booths of our brains fantasy and memory couple producing what we laughingly call reality. But reality is a myth, a ghostly projection. Oh for the imagined order of symmetry with a white tower above and a dark tower below.

Travelling down the lift pod to the Ground Floor, to Ground Zero, we cover the span of human history. Through progress into civilization we are born, then we regress, going backwards in time and possibility. Civilised impulse is forgotten here as we transition from above to below. First conscious, now we are unconscious, fighting politeness and conditioning. Civilization has diminished us, robbed us of our personal power whilst promising dominion.

It is time for us all to continue that downward journey, away from the surface into the depths. Here we may recover our selves, our authentic selves. Here there is hope. The smooth running of the lift, purring through its gears is a distraction, but a necessary one as we prepare..

Multiple directives, multiple directions. Everything set in motion at once. The hum of machinery as gears are engaged and descend ever further into our most delicious nightmares. Terror is the only thing that nourishes us moderns. Intricate stonework, carved by artist masons has been left behind, abandoned to the tide of history. Personal intricacies have been swept aside. All that remains is the gaping maw of the digger, the earth eater with its merciless claws, the pile driver and crane.

Each level is a wedge of space, crammed between concrete crusts. Each level stands at two and a half metres high. There are thirty-two in total. Here everything is stored, awaiting activation. Everything hangs, lurks, dangles, suspended in darkness until the depressed keypad dispatches a pulse that conjures a sudden and shocking illumination. This is not an event but an act. The pulse dropping down from on high to Land in Level 5 or rather Level Minus 5. The slow illumination of the level through neon tubes. A sickly yellow light bleeding into the darkness. And oh the ripe smell of sickness and decaying flesh

The capacious lift door opening, onto the level, drinks in flesh and light. The crackle of electricity, a slight shake and they are awake. Eyes that were once human fill with malice. The flesh once healthy and pink has been bleached white as have the eyes that appear yolky with cataracts. Each is clad in a mockery of fashion, a three-piece linen suit with shoes that shine.

These are the Creepers, a stealth brigade. Re-engineered by Scientific process, they have been designed to stalk and to brawl, to chew and to claw. From out of the concrete silos they will emerge and howl, then silence will claim them as brothers. This will be just enough to let the hunted know they are hunted and inspire terror. Captured, modified and confined in the concrete vaults they are human attack dogs who will pursue their prey unto death. Today's targets are the Dinosaur boys. The Creepers drink in their images and their noise relayed through flickering feeds. Instantly they recognize them. They want their toys. They know them now and pouring into the lifts they ascend to the surface. Released from shadows into the light they dream of warm bodies, clutched, bitten and silenced.

Sniffing the air, they acquire the scent and set off at an amble.

13

Separation Anxiety

Wilber finally came to a halt and, bending over, gripped his knees, and tore hung lumps of breath from the air. He had never in his life run quite so far or quite so fast in such a short space of time, but then he had never been pursued by anything quite so scary before. Even when the Law had been hot on his tail he had never been faced with the threat of being eaten alive; locked up over night was about the worst they could threaten.

Little by little he came back to himself and soon he was breathing normally. Even in his darkest days he had never taken to cigarettes or alcohol and he thanked his lucky stars for it now. He craned his neck to listen. Nothing. He had given the Dino the slip. For now, anyway. He quickly reviewed the situation, playing it back in his mind as he'd learned to do.

"I can't believe it. George has gone. Again. Why does he always do this to me?"

Behind him Wilber heard the sound of a weapon being cocked. He immediately froze and then he turned around very, very slowly. What he saw make him gasp out loud.

She was tall, that was the first thing that struck him about her and she was beautiful. That was the second. Her pallid face seemed made of wax and her hair looked like it had been dyed in crude oil. Her clothes walked the thin line between fashion and hard-wearing practicality. This was a hostile environment after all. She was clad all in black although her eyes and lips were carefully painted with crimson make-up. There was nothing girly about her but then she wasn't butch either. She was definitely female as she had curves in all the right places.

Gothic Tank Girl. Manga Tearaway and Ne'er-do-well. Killer for hire. Survivalist and vivisectionist. That was a start. But where would it end? Her hands were wrapped in skin tight black leather and by the sawn off shotgun she was sporting Wilber could see she meant business. Her voice was, when she finally deigned to speak, full of razor blades and scorpions

"And who might you be?" she asked.

Wilber drawing as much on his sense of self-preservation as on his breeding held out his hand ever-so politely.

"Hello. My name is Justice Wilberforce Muldoon. How are you?"

The girl made no move to take the proffered hand; she just tightened her grip on the shotgun and eyed Wilber with distaste.

"Quite a mouthful isn't it? I'm very well thank you. Did you not read the sign?"

She bounded from question to question like a squirrel on caffeine. Wilber was non-plussed.

"What sign?" he asked trying to keep a tight hold on his rising indignation and not quite managing it.

"This sign," the girl replied, pointing to a large, yellow sign with black lettering in bold print. It read ALL TRESPASSERS WILL BE SHOT...DEAD!!! It was surmounted by a no-nonsense skull and crossbones that left no room for misreading or ambiguity. Wilber realized he had very little room to manoeuvre.

"Ah, no I didn't. I'm afraid. Sorry. Is that a problem?"

The girl was not impressed.

"For me, no. For you definitely."

The gun moved from her hip to her shoulder.

Wilber realized he would have to act now and with as much charm as he could muster.

"Look, I'm having the worst day ever. You can't even begin to imagine what I've been through. My nanny has been eaten alive, I appear to have slipped through some kind of inter-dimensional portal and I've just been chased by a Killa-Dinosaur. And Did I mention that it wanted to kill me. The Killa Dino?

The girl seemed vaguely amused.

"Well they tend to do that. They're hungry and everything's gotta eat, don't you know. To them you're just meat. Nothing personal."

Wilber was horrified by the girl's matter of fact manner but he was also quite impressed.

"Is everything and everybody on this island trying to do for everything and everybody else? This place is more hostile than Stoke. Look, I was just here with my Uncle."

The girl looked around in a somewhat ironic manner. Wilber's dander was well and truly up by now.

"So where did he go?"

This spoken with barely disguised sarcasm. It was enough to make a monk's blood boil. Wilber pointed back over his shoulder, just to the east of south.

"That way I think."

The girl didn't seem to think that was a good idea.

"I wouldn't go that way if I were you. Dangerous."

Wilber pointed to the West.

"I wouldn't go that way either."

"Why?"

"really angerous," the girl said. "Go that way." She pointed northwards.

Wilber considered.

"Is it safe?"

"No it's dangerous." Here she paused for effect. "But it's less dangerous than the other ways."

"Oh Hell," Wilber spat as he heard the distant sound of an Allosaur roaring.

"Don't stress. It's so unattractive." Another pause. "So uncool."

Wilber wanted to pull her hair when she said that, until she screamed. She was deliberately goading him in a time of great stress but he also wanted to laugh out loud at her. He wasn't sure her behavior was an act but she was entertaining. In a sly subversive kind of way. She also seemed capable of anything. There was no point trying to blag her, best just lay it all out before her and let her decide.

"Look, I need to find my uncle and I need to get off this Island. Preferably today. Now are you going to help me or shoot me?"

The girl considered her options for a moment and then lowered her weapon.

"Oh alright, but if you annoy me I'll blow your legs off. So…there's somebody I think you ought to meet. He can help you. He's been here forever and he knows the island like the back of his hand. Probably knows your Uncle too."

Odd.

"Don't you know the island?" he asked the girl, more than a little confused. She didn't look like a new arrival or one of the fallen for that matter. She was, for all the militaristic shabby-chic, too well groomed to be anything but a long-term resident with privileges.

"Only bits of it. They don't let me out that much."

Wilber felt the onset of a laughter explosion but had enough presence of mind to batten down the hatches.

"Really. I am surprised." He paused then a question popped into his head. "Say, there's a bunch of freakish girls running around dressed like some kind of guerilla army? Do you know them?"

The question seemed innocuous enough but the effect on the girl was anything but. In the blink of an eye she went from cruising in neutral to incandescent rage. It was like watching a volcano erupt or the dropping of an atom bomb.

"WHAT? The Alphabet Gang? Don't talk to me about the ruddy Alphabet gang. They're a bunch of saps. Sad, self righteous, pretentious wannabes. Stay away from them Justice. If you want to stay alive and if you want me to stay friendly. Now are you coming or what?"

Wilber stood rooted to the spot, still in shock. It took a few moments for him to recover his poise.

"We won't see any more dinosaurs will we?"

The girl shook her head emphatically. She had slid back into neutral and was once more her old, sardonic self.

"They're the least of your worries. Believe me, there are worse things on this island than dinosaurs."

Wilber gulped.

"That's good to hear. Look do you have a name?

"Yes. I'm Lola. But you can call me..... ."

And with that she turned on her heel and ran. Wilber followed her looking mildly terrified.

*　　　*　　　*　　　*　　　*　　　*　　　*

Moving at speed through the trees, the boy behind her, Lola was laced with doubt and foreboding. But other emotions were registered too. The sense of her own genius for starters. She had waited for just the right moment and stolen the boy right out from under their arrogant little noses. The Alphabet Gang. How she hated them. So precious, so elitist but not fit to wipe the mud from her boots. The boy, had he stayed with them, would have found out sooner rather than later they were not to be relied upon.

And the boy, well he wasn't really a boy...more a lad...well not even that, he was definitely well, male and well-made, teetering on the brink of manhood. He had curves in all the right places and for all that he was young he was tall and he looked like he was on the verge of shaving. The polar opposite to Caleb. But he was polite and that she found unattractive, worthy only of mockery. He had held out his hand for her to shake. I mean who did that, any more? It was as though he was a product of a bygone age, a throwback. Not ugly though. Not without merit. But too pure, too unsullied, too spotless to truly admire. She wanted to see him compromised, covered in filth, battered and bruised, screaming for help, bleeding out. She wanted to see the idealism kicked out of him.

Pulling the trigger on him would have given her no more qualms than offing a jungle rat. Bang. Bang. And he's gone. But they would have heard and come running. And for all that she hated them they were still a threat. She could so easily have become one of them but she had been too much of her own person. She wasn't taking orders from anyone, least of all Antelope. The silly little bitch. Who called themselves Antelope? I mean really. It made her want to gag. So stupid, so pathetic, so pretentious, the lot of them. They were a laughing stock, something to cross the road to avoid. Caleb thought they were stupid too but he never owned it.

No it was best that she had set them aside. To have become dependant upon them would have been to sign her own death warrant. Whilst it was true she was destructive, she wasn't self destructive. Nor was she stupid. If she was to sacrifice anything or anybody to save her own neck it would have been them. All on this island lived to serve her. She thought like that and she lived like that and that was why she was a winner. But in truth she would only be serving herself, her need for greater and greater knowledge and power and skill drove her. They saw this and they had seen it from the beginning, and that was why they had rejected her.

It didn't matter. Not now, not anymore. Sooner, rather than later, the Alphabet Gang would fall. They would end up below the ground again, caught in Astapor's net. If they allowed themselves to be taken alive that is. They must know what was in store for them, that the Russian had planned some hideous end for each and every one of them. God, but he was clever. He was a genius and he would stop at nothing. He was capable of anything. He would transform them utterly, cell by cell. He would eradicate their beauty, he would warp their bodies, he would torment them day and night.

But he wouldn't kill them straight away, he would keep them alive, even after they were broken. He would leave enough of their minds in tact that they would know and understand right up until the end, until they drew their final tortured breath. Some would die whimpering and some screaming and she would drink their agony down like wine. Oh if only she could be the one to deliver them to him, she would be happy. But he was so dangerous and could not be trusted to give her, her own freedom. But that was ok.

Everything, she knew, had its price.

THE LEGEND OF DINOSAUR GEORGE MULDOON

14

Family Reunited

George pounded through the jungle as though his life depended on it and of course it did. The Killa-Dino that was hot on his trail had been on an enforced fast for some time and it was ravenous. He could tell just by looking at it that it meant business. Poor pickings meant increasingly bold and more savage animals. The food supply was not what it had been. One look at the unhappy cannibals was enough to tell him that. It wouldn't be long before they turned on their own and began noshing away at each other, if they hadn't done so already.

The prognosis for the young and weak was increasingly bleak, he realised. Not that he cared particularly about what happened to them. Ruddy cannibals! They had made their bed, now let them lie in it. He had more pressing matters on his mind and a whole raft of complex issues to resolve, the main one being what to do about the family members he had left behind on the island. It was possible that they would not greet him with open arms. After all, he had kind of abandoned them to their fate, had he not? Guilt and shame were debilitating forces for anyone to have to cope with and that was a large part of the reason he had forced himself to come back. It wasn't the only reason, it was one amongst many, but it had played a part.

But everything was happening so fast. Seeing Young Wilber had been a shock and he hated that they had been separated so soon after hooking up, but in a curious way he was glad too. He wasn't sure he was ready to take on the burden of the family he had walked away from, not just yet, anyway. He needed to connect with himself first and to process what he could of the past. There were other things he needed to deal with too.

Whilst the island was anxiety-provoking, being away from it was more so. It was a paradox that George was only now able to address. For all of the terror that came with being chased by an eighteen-foot-high reptile that wanted to tear you apart and eat you whilst you were still alive, he had to admit it was also kind of exciting. Life on the other side of the veil was more comfortable certainly, but it was also bland in comparison. It was bills and lectures and responsibilities. It was laws and not being able to sock somebody in the mouth if you didn't like or agree with them. It was doing what others felt you ought to do, not what you wanted to do.

As fast as he'd run to get off the island, he'd run twice as fast to get back onto it. Meeting Wilber the way he had, had not been a positive experience though. And that was nothing to do with the situation being fraught with danger. Oh no. That wasn't it at all. The problems had started as soon as the dangers had stopped, and the cannibals lay safely behind them. As soon as they had stopped running and turned to face each other, straight away he'd felt compelled to explain everything. Who he was. What he did. Why he did it. How everything in the stories of their lives fitted together. And it was just so boring to have to do that and worst of all it was draining. It exhausted him and it irritated him to such an extent he just wanted to carry on running, even if it meant getting chased by things that wanted to eat you.

Why did everybody need so much detail anyway? He much preferred to keep it all simple. Locate the tower. Plant the explosives. Blow it up and let it burn. That was just the kind of Mission he enjoyed and the one he'd agreed to do. That was the kind of life he wanted and whilst hiding up a tree to escape the unwanted attentions of the Killa-Dino below he realised how much he'd missed life here. He carried on thinking and feeling it too until the sound of crashing feet died away and the All-Clear Siren sounded in his head.

Sighing, he descended to the forest floor and quickly looked around for signs of further trouble. None, unfortunately. He took off at a sprint then, zig-zagging from side to side to confound any would-be sniper until he was sure he was not being followed, then throttled back to a well-paced lope. No point wasting energy. Best to conserve it.

Heading just west of south, he sniffed the air and drank in his surroundings. He knew this place. Same trees, same plants, same animals but new smells, new energies and a totally different vibe than when he'd left. He couldn't quite put his finger on what had changed but it was there, picking away at him, vague and concealed. Best to watch and wait, let your unconscious do the work and when you were ready, it would pop it right into the frame of your new world view.

Away to his right, the ground began to slope upwards. Follow the gradient and it would lead, after a mile or so, to Astapor's lair, the magic castle on top of the hill. The Russian and his menagerie was a whole other show and one he would likewise need to prepare for. Until then he followed the path southwards, back towards the familiar. He paused then to check that he was not being followed. He wasn't. Thank God for that; he had lost the dino. Rather those killer teeth than his family though. They were hard work; yet they could not be avoided.

They would have to be faced and soon.

He arrived at the clearing he had once called home after a few minutes and, walking the periphery, scanned for signs that his Uncle and Younger Brother were in the vicinity. It didn't take him too long to pick up the scent and, bounding from tree shadow to tree shadow, he snuck up on them without them being in the least aware of his presence. Some things never changed.

His Uncle, obviously asleep, was flat on his back, leaning against a tree, with his hat pulled down over his eyes, snoring. His snores, as George remembered, were loud enough to wake the dead and they not infrequently did. How many legions had Astapor wasted on that old fossil, George wondered? Patrick, in stark contrast, was as nervy as he had always been, little more than a bag of nerves.

Forever looking around, checking for signs of danger but never seeing it, even when it was right under his nose. How had the pair of them lasted this long, without his constant vigilance and protection?

Away in the centre of the clearing was the old ruined temple, the marble remarkably well preserved, despite the passing of millennia. It made him ache with nostalgia and sadness, not just for his former life on the island but for the former age that had spawned the temple in which his brother and uncle often hid. The allure of Atlantis was so strong and it still exerted a tremendous pull on him. It lay both in the notion of its Futuristic Crystalline Technology, the stuff of future sciences, and its Magical knowledge and prowess. For all that he had seen and learned, it had never lost its mysterious otherness. It was an open invitation to every human living, to dream and to search, to scour the earth for artifacts and to consider the lessons such an advanced society could teach our own.

George watched his brother as he cleaned the mud from his boots with a large leaf and then, when he felt enough time had elapsed, he spoke.

"Still skulking in the ruins Brother?"

His brother, nearly jumping out of his skin, leapt to his feet and began sweating profusely. He raised his fists and wheeled around, fully expecting to feel flying metal raking his flesh. Instead all he saw was his Eldest Brother George, Dinosaur George Muldoon leaning up against a tree trunk, watching him with a wry smile.

Patrick Muldoon's lower jaw dropped and he gaped like an Atlantic cod. The shock had frozen him to the spot. How could it do anything else, George thought. How long had he been away from them? Time, like everything else, didn't function the same here as it did in that other world he had so recently left. That world of shadows. In time the shock lessened sufficiently for Patrick to verbalise his emotions.

"George, I'm going to kill you."

With that, he ran at his brother and swung at his chiseled jaw with all the rage he could muster. George, attuned to instinct, sidestepped and Patrick lost his balance and fell on his face. He hit the floor with a sickening crunch, enough that his brother winced. But it was not enough to stop him. Leaping to his feet Patrick spun round, like an enraged warthog, and attacked again swinging with the opposite arm this time. Left then right, left then right, then an uppercut and an attempted reverse sweep. None of these blows landed and the more he missed, the angrier he became. George, for his part, just ducked and dived, effortlessly, whilst Patrick swung again and again, each time just missing his brother, until he was spent and gasping for air.

Slumping to his knees, his face purple, he looked like he was drowning or maybe choking. George, folding his arms, eyed Patrick critically. He'd believed that life on the island would sharpen his brother up, make him leaner and more athletic. But it hadn't. Quite the reverse. He still moved with all the grace of a sclerotic elephant seal and it would appear he had lost a step in pace.

"I swear to God, George," he panted, "when I get hold of you, I'm going to destroy you."

"Not this side of Christmas," George shot back.

Patrick dragged himself to his feet and raised his dukes.

"Don't," George hissed, raising a warning finger, "you'll just embarrass yourself again."

But Patrick could not be placated. On he came, swinging again. By this time George had had enough. Softly, softly hadn't worked; it was time to retaliate. When Patrick was in range, George hit his brother smack bang in the solar plexus and he went down wheezing.

"Enough, already! I haven't got time for this."

He waited, hands on hips as his brother got himself right, and rose to his feet a second time, more than a little worse for wear. Patrick had obviously gotten the message and was going to take the scene a different way. Now he performed a comical double take and clapped his hands over his mouth in faux surprise.

"Oh my God! It can't be. And yet it is. Brother Mine. Where in the name of God have you been? Come here, embrace me."

With this he flung out his arms.

Frowning, George watched his brother with obvious distaste. Sarcasm was the obvious approach now that brute force had failed, he'd just hoped his brother would be a better man by now. Not so small-minded. Not so self-absorbed.

"Patrick, I know I left you here: I know you've suffered but we need to move past that. There are more important things to attend to. Bigger fish to fry."

"Bigger fish eh?"

Patrick stilled and the ironic mask dropped from his face. He was clearly thinking about his options and how he really felt. After a while his shoulders dropped and all the rage seemed to seep out of him. Without warning he moved over to his brother and embraced him warmly. After a while Patrick leaned back, and holding his brother at arm's length stared deep into his eyes.

"Yep, still here in the shadow of the ruins, brother mine. After all these years it's still the safest place to be."

George laughed when he heard this. Thank God for that. The Old Patrick was back. It was like he'd never been away. There was so much to say, so much to reminisce about, but where to start? He felt if he wasn't careful, he'd find himself in the same predicament as he had with Little Justice. So much to say but no inclination to say it. Patrick watching him closely must have intuited this and shook his head slowly from side to side.

"Look, Brother dearest, let me spare you any pain and unrest you might be feeling. Me and the Old Fart have absolutely no problem with what you did. You had to get off the island. Period. No explanations are necessary."

George couldn't believe his ears.

This was not what he had been expecting. More, accusations, flying fists, screaming fits, yes. But unconditional acceptance certainly not. It wasn't like his brother to capitulate so easily. Had he finally grown up? It took a while for this to sink in and for him to be able to speak again.

"You don't know how much that means Pat. It was the hardest

decision I've ever made in my life…"

Patrick nodding, reached out and clasped his arm.

"Let's just leave it at that, George. I don't want any more conflict, really I don't. I'm sorry I flew at you. I shouldn't have done that. Life's too short for bearing grudges and constantly looking backwards, wishing for what could have been. What you did, it wasn't even a mistake. Your leaving made me grow up and as far as I'm concerned your escape from the island gave everybody here who remained, hope. It also secured you the title of living legend. You know that. People when they talk about you talk about The Legend of Dinosaur George Muldoon."

George could hardly believe this.

"Really?"

Patrick nodded his head in confirmation.

"Shall we dig up the Fossil now and invite him to the family gathering or shall we leave him in the Land of Nod?"

By way of answer George knelt down beside his Uncle and gently shook him till he awakened. Snuffling like an old badger, he sat up and spat heavily to one side.

"How many times' have I told you Patrick never to disturb my noon time slumbers?"

Raising his hat above his eyes he prepared to launch into a diatribe, but seeing George smiling down at him, he stopped, cut off in mid flow.

"It can't be," the Old Man said, as stunned in his own way as Patrick had been.

"But it is," George replied softly.

"How long you been back?"

"Coupla hours. I came straight here."

The Old Man took a few moments to digest this information. Unlike Patrick he seemed troubled and anxious.

"Nothing's the same here George. You shouldn't have come back. Everything's changed and not in a good way." Here he paused as though trying to find his bearings.

"What happened to all the stars, George? I waited up last night to see the stars. I couldn't sleep. But there wasn't a single star in the sky and they're normally so lovely."

George didn't know what to say. The implications of how their Uncle was speaking were too painful to take on board. The situation here was not quite as rosy as he had surmised. George looked up at Patrick with questioning eyes but his brother, unable to meet his gaze, looked away. Eventually he felt compelled to speak.

"I don't know Uncle. Perhaps they just went away, far away. They do that sometimes."

There was a silence for a time and it was uncomfortable for all. Eventually Patrick moved to fill the silence.

"So what happened George? Why did you come back?"

"Lot of reasons but I can't go into all that just now. The main thing is that I am back but that I'm not alone."

"I don't like the sound of this," Patrick said, the nervousness back in his voice.

George took a deep breath.

"Brother, you're not going to like what I have to say but I have to say it. Our nephew is here. Justice came through the time gate."

Patrick looked stunned whilst Great Uncle Muldoon just looked confused. It took a while for the penny to drop.

"Justice? But how could that be? You told me the time gate back at Muldoon Manor had been closed, that you closed it yourself, when we came through."

George suddenly felt very tired. He'd been going over this in his mind too, over and over. How could he explain this to himself? Let alone anybody else.

"Look, I'm sorry, I know what I told you Pat. I thought I'd made it safe, thought I'd secured it but I was wrong. Somebody must have reopened the gate and driven the boy through it. That's the only explanation I can come up with. The Evil Curs."

Patrick, so calm and even just moments before, looked like he was going to explode. Great Uncle Muldoon seeing this, sat up and the vacancy left his eyes.

"Alright Pat. Calm down. We're in this together, remember?"

After a moment he turned to speak to his other nephew.

"Now George, we warned you about this. We told you, you should have rigged the stones to blow but you didn't, did you?"

"How could I? They are historical artifacts Uncle. Priceless."

Great Uncle Muldoon, looking both angry and pained, shook his head.

"Priceless and dangerous. You didn't really believe Astapor was going to let sleeping dogs lie. One way or another he was always going to pull you back onto the island and he has done. You took the bait."

Now George was angry.

"True as that may be, Uncle, Wilber is out there and he needs us. We have to find him."

"The likelihood of him having survived both the cannibals and the Dinos is slim," Patrick suggested.

"I'm not giving up on him Patrick. You coming or what?" was George's retort.

"Do I have any choice?"

"When did we ever?"

The brothers looked at each for long moments and then rose together. Great Uncle Muldoon, folding his arms, was having none of it.

"I'm staying to watch the Scorpion Soup. I ain't wasting good food on false hope."

"Suit yourself," the brothers chorused and then took to their heels.

Soon silence closed in around him, punctuated by the sounds of growling and prowling monsters. Being alone was overrated as was the taste of his scorpion soup.

"Stuff this. Boys, wait for me," yelled the old man as he thundered after them.

15

The Gentleman

The jungle cleared and much to Wilber's amazement they stepped out onto a huge, sprawling and recently mown lawn. They looked it up and down; first left, then right, then again, left and right, in rapid succession, as though they were watching a long distance Tennis game played by giants. There were large holes full of white sand scattered about and off in the distance a tattered crimson flag fluttered in the tropical breeze. After careful consideration, Wilber decided it wasn't a lawn but a golf course and hearing the word 'four,' yelled by a crisp English accent, and seeing a golf ball soaring over his head, confirmed his suspicions.

An English gentleman in a white linen suit and a light blue shirt and waistcoat was practising his chipping with a nine iron. Sporting a cravat and panama hat, he looked very much at his ease, not in any kind of rush, at all. Such a curious apparition, so out of place on this island in the middle of nowhere. Seeing Wilber and Lola his face lit up like a small child's on Christmas morning and he began gesturing for them to approach. He looked quite a benign figure but Wilber approached him with some caution, looking around for any sign of danger.

"Who is that?" he asked his companion, trying to mask his anxious curiosity. Lola's grin was wolfish in the extreme.

"Someone I think you should meet Wilber. He can help you. His name is Professor Crowhaven."

Wilber was impressed. "A professor, no less. From London?"

"No Lola," replied airily, "Nantwich."

Nantwich? How curious. Where in hell was that? Wilber picked up his pace to keep up with Lola. Such a bizarre name and such a bizarre setting, he thought. Seeing the Professor at his ease in all his colonial glory was profoundly disquieting. Wilber was baffled and perplexed in equal measure, as he had been since the moment he had first awoken by the time gate that morning, the waters lapping at his face like an overly affectionate hound. Whilst he was freaked Lola wasn't at all phased. She just strode out of the jungle, onto the well mown grass and over to the Professor who was watching, while a well-manicured servant gathered his balls together and stuffed them back in the pockets of a rather plush, cream-coloured, golf bag.

Lola stopped just short of the Professor and performed a half-ironic curtsey. The Professor appearing bemused, inclined his head in mock salute and grinned from ear to ear like the Cheshire cat in Wonderland. But the island wasn't wonderland; there were horrors here, horrors he had seen and others that were coming. He sensed that acutely. Furthermore, there was something about the Professor that Wilber found quite unnerving. What that was he couldn't quite put his finger on but it was there all the same. He would watch and he would wait for further disclosures before making up his mind, one way or the other.

"Professor, this is Justice Wilberforce Muldoon, Wilber to his friends. He's just arrived on the island."

The Professor looked at Wilber and smiled. His half moon glasses glinted in the morning sunlight.

"A newbee? Really. Delighted to make your acquaintance my dear boy," he chortled, thrusting his hand out for Wilber to shake. The boy took it and was surprised to find it possessed of great strength. He'd been expecting a wet fish. Retrieving his hand Wilber looked the Professor straight in the eye.

"So what do you know about Time Gates, Professor? My uncle began to tell me, but got a little sidetracked."

"Hmmm," the Professor said, nodding his head vigorously, apparently impressed that Wilber had cut straight to the chase. "Walk with me Wilber. I think its time for a little refreshment back at the 19th hole. Of course you're welcome to join us Lola. I'll bet you're both famished. I've asked cook to put two extra plates out for brekkie. A full English is the only way to start the day, as I always say. Come along Smithers."

He turned on his heel and took off like a rocket. Lola and Wilber found themselves running at a brisk canter to keep up with the Professor who was remarkably spry for his age. They walked back down the tree lined fairway trying not to pant too vigorously and listening intently to the Professor, as Smithers strutted behind them, hauling the golf bag he had placed in a little trolley with wide wheels and ne'er a squeak or rattle.

"The Time Gates are the only way you can get onto or off this island, Wilber. The Eastern gate, where you arrived with a bang this morning, is the way on; the Western gate is the way off. Sorry about the cannibals by the way. They're quite untamable and believe me I've tried. We treat them like a farmer with many cornfields treats crows, Wilber. We spend a lot of time scaring them off. With guns."

Hearing this Wilber felt his spirits lift. "So there is a way off the island, Professor? That's really good news." Rather unexpectedly he turned and grabbed Lola by the waist, picked her up and whirled her round, like they were at Ho-Down. "Yo Baby," he yelled joyously. "There is a way off."

Lola half shocked, half amused tutted and clucked. "Well I knew that."

"You did?" Wilber replied, arching an eyebrow.

Lola turned. "Best keep up." The Professor and Smithers were disappearing from sight rounding the bend of the fairway's dog's leg. It was a minute or so before they caught up with the Professor but he resumed his narrative as though they'd been there all along.

"From what I understand each Time Gate is a one-way option, a slice of Pi if you'll pardon the pun. The trouble is the island has some rather unusual properties."

"I've noticed," Wilber said, picturing the large cooking pot the cannibals had intended boiling him in just an hour or so previously. "And what would they be?"

The Professor considered the question, like a sergeant Major inspecting a rather large platoon of Soldiers who were about to go into battle.

"Each person who gets onto the island has only one day to get off it, to race from East to West, and this they must do so, within the hours of daylight. The sun rises at 03.00 hours, which is when you arrived, and sets at 21.00 hundred hours. That gives you 18 hours in which to complete your mission, should you choose to accept it."

Here he looked at Wilber with a wry smile but Wilber failed to pick up on the reference. Perceiving dim-wittedness the professor rolled his eyes and finished his thought.

"After that you're stranded; the Time Gate closes and you won't be able to leave the island. You'll be Muldooned here," here he paused to laugh hysterically, before resuming, "I mean marooned here forever, like the rest of us."

Up ahead a large white house had hovered into view, like a ship on a wide, vast ocean, an emblem of order, of hope and sanctuary. And hopefully of a decent bit of brekkie, Wilber thought. As the Professor had surmised, they were both famished.

"But where is the island?" he asked.

"Ah, well that's a little bit rickety. I mean a little bit tricky. Less a question of where, more a question of when. I know we're on earth somewhere. That much I can tell you. But when? That's any bodies guess."

Wilber looked puzzled again. Not the sharpest pencil in the pot, the Professor reflected.

"There's a lot to get used to Justice. In some respects, this island is the collective fantasy of all who inhabit it."

"Say what? I'm sure I don't understand a word you're saying."

Crowhaven sighed. This was going to be a long morning.

"But you understand the basic concepts I think. The island is only five miles long so theoretically it should be possible to traverse it in 18 hours. It's almost six o'clock now so by my calculation you have a little over 15 hours to complete your mission."

Lola nodded in agreement.

"And do what so many others have failed to do. Namely get off this island"

"And get back home," Wilber added.

"Yes, quite, the Professor," said. "Wherever and whenever home is."

They had arrived at the house. Through a little white gate, they went, as though into a secret garden, onto a well appointed lawn surrounded by flowers, shrubs and trees, to where a table awaited them. Another servant stood by the table, holding with perfect poise, a silver tea urn on a tray. They each of them sat down to find a full English breakfast standing steaming, ready to be devoured. Wilber looked at the bacon and pushed it to the edge of his plate. Having almost served as breakfast for the cannibals he was suddenly not quite so ready to gulp down gobbets of flesh. That meat came from something that had lived and breathed and suffered as he had. He'd rather acquire his energy some other way. All it took was a little discipline and self control. He looked up and saw Smithers disappearing into the house. Passing the other servant he had nodded an acknowledgement and right on cue the other had poured out the tea, adding milk and sugar, without needing to be told. It was if the man possessed a sixth sense about what was required and delivered it before a request was issued. Everything here ran so smoothly, like clockwork. It would be so easy to sink into complacency, to ignore one's mission, recline and bask in the morning sun. But there was more at stake here, more important matters to attend to. They ate in silence mindful of the birdsong and the occasional roar of something bigger, hungrier and more dangerous than the birds. It took a while for Wilber to pluck up the courage but eventually he did and asked the question.

"So, Professor, how did the dinosaurs get here?" Crowhaven stopped munching on the mouthful of sausage he had been enjoying so heartily and regarded Wilber with an air of the mildly miffed. He resumed chewing and swallowed the meat, then took a gulp of tea and regarding the arriviste with no small degree of self possession. After a minute or so he deigned to speak.

"Another question for another time I'm afraid. Tick tock said the clock. Now Justice...lovely name by the way, there's so much to get through and so little time. Pin back your ears, stitch your lips and listen"

Crowhaven reached into a bag that the second servant had left by his chair. It contained numerous objects; Wilber could see that, but the first thing the Professor drew from the bag was an ancient looking parchment which he promptly handed over to the boy.

"For me?" Wilber asked somewhat disingenuously.

Lola rolled her eyes and began buttering a fifth slice of toast with disdained amusement. She had wholly ignored the Full English.

"Yes," the Professor nodded in assent, "for you". It's a custom here, if you like. Everybody you meet will give you a gift, at least, whilst you're a Candidate.

"And that's me?" Wilber ventured looking somewhat unsure of himself.

"Just for today it is. You're not the first through today either Wilber. In fact you're the fourth. You'll meet the others shortly. They're waiting for you but more of that later."

Gesturing to the parchment, he indicated that Wilber should unfurl and study it. Eager to see what was written on the parchment Wilber complied and was amazed by the quality and detail of what he found there.

"This is a map, or rather the map," Crowhaven announced somewhat grandly. "This is the map of the House that Jack built."

"Jack? Who's Jack?" Wilber asked, more irritated than puzzled by the Professor's frequent diversions and allusions.

"Just a Game, a childish game. Forgive me, dear boy, my mind wanders. I've been here a long time, you know."

Wilber glanced at Lola who gave him an inscrutable look by way of reply. She was absolutely no help at all so why then did he feel drawn to her? It was, as Crowhaven might say, another question for another day.

"So this is a map of the island?" Wilber asked, returning his gaze to the parchment; "and we are here," he said, pointing to the area of the map swallowed up by the Professor's golf course, house and what would appear to be laboratories.

"Clever boy, indeed we are," said Crowhaven, clearly impressed by the boy for the first time since they had met. Perhaps there was more to him than met the eye. "Not very big is it? You've travelled almost a mile and a half, through your various trials to get here, but it's easy going on this side of the island and you, my dear friend, will have to penetrate to the interior if you're to succeed. That I'm afraid is a far less friendly place. You'll find the island has some very strange habits."

Funny way of putting it Wilber thought.

"Like what?"

Crowhaven's gaze became unfocussed for just a moment and his brow creased into a frown.

"Like an irritable old man, too long on his own, it snores, bites its nails and speaks when it should listen. Only joking Wilber."

Wilber laughed nervously and for the first time, since meeting the Professor wondered if he wasn't the slightest bit dotty. Reaching into his bag Crowhaven withdrew a second object and promptly handed it to Wilber. The boy took it with care and examined it with great curiosity. It was a beautiful old-fashioned watch that had roman numerals instead of numbers and a deep scratch on its gold face. Turning it over he found there was an inscription on the back.

"From Russia with Love."

That was the name of an old Bond film wasn't it? Why should it be inscribed upon the watch and who had given it to the Professor in the first place? Wilber wondered what it all meant and looked at Crowhaven quizzically, expecting some hints if not plain answers to his questions. But Crowhaven being Crowhaven sidestepped Wilber's glance and went his own way, pursuing another agenda entirely.

"Justice I'd love to chat but the clock, I'm afraid, is ticking. So let's get down to business shall we?"

Beginning to get a feel for the way The Professor thought Wilber readied a quip.

"Should I prepare for shocks Professor?"

Crowhaven laughed delightedly.

"Oh yes Wilber, that's good and you should." Here he paused, as if weighing what to tell Wilber, but Wilber knew by now that he knew exactly, and had known exactly all along what he was going to say and how.

Young Muldoon, although a slow beginner, was quicker on the uptake than most people gave him credit for. It was a habit, a defence mechanism he had evolved to put people off their guard so he could observe them and get their measure. This way he could draw them out without them really knowing what was going on, in a way that was advantageous to him.

"What would you think Wilber if I told you that the Island is a Game and it's playing you? To win the game you just have to run from East to West, collect five keys and spring the Five-Time gates on the Western Shore."

"I'd think you were pulling my leg Professor. Who ever heard of an island that was a Game? This isn't a theme park is it?"

"No." This time it was Lola who answered. She'd been silently following the conversation up until now.

"It certainly isn't a theme park. You should take him seriously, Wilber. Tick tock and all that."

"Okay then I will," Wilber conceded with a shrug of his shoulders.

"Five keys? What and where are they?"

Professor Crowhaven looked back towards the house and then returned his gaze to Wilber.

"One of the keys to success is learning to ask the right questions, Justice. Well done." Lola, ever impatient, sighed. "And?" She obviously wanted to speed all this up. Crowhaven, picking up on her cue leaned in towards Wilber and stared right into his eyes. Wilber held his gaze and felt the will, the power and the resolve that were so obviously at the core of the man.

"The keys are quartz crystals, each one in the form of a Platonic solid. Know what they are?"

Unsmiling, Wilber nodded.

"Yes: cube, tetrahedron, octahedron, icosahedron and dodecahedron. At least according to Plato. It's a good job I listened in Math's Professor. I guess my education didn't go entirely to waste. And who has these crystal keys?"

Now it was the Professor's turn to look slightly taken aback. This wasn't the response he'd anticipated. He'd obviously have to watch this one and closely. Against his better judgement Wilber impressed him.

"Alright then, I'll tell you. Five Scientists, or, Magicians if you will, hold these five crystal keys within their grasp. To acquire the crystals, you must play their games and solve their riddles, if you can. Five riddles, five chances to get it right. Five excruciating punishments if you get it wrong. As a Magus of Power and someone who attained his first PhD, in astrophysics, at the tender age of 21, I would have to confess that I have attained a mastery of all things physical. Know what that means. No? Well, I'll tell you. That means I can take a theory and make it work for me and not just on an intellectual level either. With the right resources, and appropriate levels of funding, I can turn my insights into machines that work. That do something. It also means I can make anything you imagine appear or disappear."

Wilber considered this for a moment.

"Does that include people?" he asked. This time Crowhaven didn't smile.

"Oh yes," he replied. "It most certainly does."

16

Japes

Breakfast was over and Crowhaven rose, like a stork from its feeding, and indicated they should follow him. Wilber put on the watch he had been given and carefully folded the map and placed it in his coat pocket, where he knew it would be safe. The pocket had a zip. Crowhaven watching him do all this, nodded distractedly and led them around the side of the house, via a well tended garden path, towards a side gate. They went through the gate and into another garden. This was quite a shock, as unlike the front garden, where they had eaten breakfast, this was wild and untended; to all intents and purposes a savage garden.

Wilber looked around carefully noting everything. He had an eye for detail and was good at remembering, albeit that he was sometimes slow to make connections. His eyes were drawn back towards the house and drifted upwards to a third floor window. The window was curtained and he was sure that someone was standing there, watching them. Despite the heat he shivered, then returned his gaze towards the garden where he soon picked out a path through the long grasses and coloured plants into another section of forest.

It was there they were headed. As soon as he had made the link Crowhaven had begun to move off, somewhat more stealthily than before, picking a cautious path through potentially lurking hazards. Entering a world of trees once more, Wilber felt his anxiety levels rise. Looking behind him with wide eyes he glanced at Lola who padded behind him, as silent as a hunting panther, a strange look in her eyes. Despite the fact he liked her he didn't entirely trust her. There were things she wouldn't or couldn't tell him, that much was obvious.

They walked on in silence for about fifteen minutes in what Wilber took to be a northwesterly direction. Birds chirped, insects buzzed and Wilber sweated. Suddenly a large building loomed up before them. It was well screened by the trees and Wilber surmised it was roughly where on the map, Crowhaven's laboratories were situated. Crowhaven strolled towards the building and over to the door. There was a device beside the door towards which, the Professor inclined his head. A red beam of light from an iris scanner flicked out over his eyes and the door swung open silently. The Professor went inside and Lola and Wilber followed behind him, somewhat apprehensively.

They walked through darkness initially, then down a tunnel illuminated by flaming violet uplighters. Wilber tingled all over and soon had a case of Goosebumps. He wasn't cold, it wasn't that, no, he was encountering something else he had felt on more than one occasion since his adventurous start to the day back at Muldoon Manor. He was encountering not just fear, not just a case of mild fright but cold, remorseless terror. Behind that, he sensed a silent mind of pure, unbreakable will watching, waiting in the darkness to shatter any who would be foolish enough to enter its domain.

Soon the corridor delivered them to a door, which Crowhaven opened, and they went inside, into a large cubed space with a ceiling as high as the room was wide and long. It took a while for Wilber's eyes to grow accustomed to the light and when they did, he saw that they were not alone. There were three other children in the room, each standing silent and motionless in an allotted corner. Entering the space Crowhaven clicked his fingers and the children came back to their senses and looked around them wildly, fear and confusion etched into their features.

"Wilber, I'd like to introduce you to Raoul, Matilda and Samuel. Like you they are new arrivals here and like you, they are on the path to future possibilities."

Wilber turned to speak to Lola only to find that she was nowhere to be seen and that he was alone. Crowhaven, seeing this, looked sympathetically at Wilber.

"I'm afraid Lola can't help you now, Wilber. She's one of the islanders you see, and as such, exempt from all of this. If you're to have any hope of getting out of this place and moving on, you have to play the Game yourself. Rely on your own resources at it were. Shall I elaborate?"

When Wilber said nothing Crowhaven smiled his funny little smile.

"I'll take that as a yes."

Removing a remote control from his pocket, Crowhaven pressed a series of buttons and from out of the floor, in the centre of the cubed room, a plinth arose. It hummed away merrily, as it rose and stopped at a height of just over a metre. Crowning the plinth was a crystal cube, which glowed with what Wilber could only describe as glory. It was magnificent! How he wanted to touch the crystal cube, to own and possess it. He was fascinated and mesmerised. In fact, truth be told, he was absolutely hooked. Wilber went to take a step towards the crystal but found he couldn't move. What on earth was happening?

Crowhaven stepped towards him, tapped him on the shoulder and led Wilber to the last uninhabited corner of the room. He was quite clearly setting the final piece on the board before starting the game. But what was the game and how was it played?

"All in good time Wilber," Crowhaven chuckled, as though he had heard Wilber's unarticulated questions. He promptly turned on his heel and glided over to stand beside the recently risen plinth. Wilber's eyes never left him. Nor, to be fair, did any of the other children's for that matter.

"So this is the game," he said, waving his arms to suggest the game was in fact the entire room, "and this is the prize," he said, staring down hard at the crystal cube in front of him, so nobody was in any doubt about that either.

"This room is unique in so many ways. Care to see how?"

Here he pressed another series of buttons on his remote control and the floor suddenly lit up with different colours. Casting his eyes downwards Wilber saw that the floor had been divided up into six squares of different colours, each embedded within the next, like Russian Dolls. The first and largest outer square, on which they stood, was red, the second orange, the third yellow, the fourth blue and the fifth, a rich imperial purple. The sixth and final square, which formed the base of the plinth, from which rose the column on which sat the crystal cube, was white. White as snow or oblivion.

Wilber found himself entranced.

"By virtue of your choices, since arriving on the island, you have already passed the first round and won yourself a step into the room, onto that first outer layer of red squares. The way to advance is simple. Answer the questions the room asks you and take a step inwards. Every question you answer honestly will take you one step closer to victory."

"So it's a general knowledge quiz?" the boy Crowhaven had identified as Samuel asked, rather snottily, as though all of this were beneath him.

Crowhaven smiled, somewhat, and then shook his head. Despite his joviality it was obvious he had little or no time for wrong-headedness

"I'm not interested in what you know, Samuel. I'm interested in what you're prepared to divulge and how far you will actually go before you break. This Game is a game of truth or dare. Tell the truth and shame the devil. Dare to lie and..."

"You disappear." Wilber completed his thought.

A genuine smile crossed the Professor's face.

"Indeed you do, for ever and ever my dear boy. Amen. Just like in the prayer. Now Wilber would you like to begin the game? Oh yes, I think you would."

*　　　*　　　*　　　*　　　*　　　*

Having positioned each child, or youth, in Wilber's case, in a corner of the room the Professor headed back towards the door, opened it and disappeared with not so much as a backward glance. It didn't take a genius to realise that the professor was a busy man, who loved golf more than children and science more than pleasantries. If this was part of his daily routine, it was only a cast iron discipline that kept him civil and performing a role a trained monkey could have done.

For a time, there was silence, total and absolute, and then there was a hum, like bees, but not. Like electricity but not. Wilber felt himself beginning to shiver. He did not like this one bit. If he had understood the Professor correctly there were no second chances here. Neither did one just lose. One was vaporised. Scanning the faces of the other children Wilber saw that they, like him, were more scared than they were prepared to admit.

A crackle of static thrilled the air of the cubed room and everyone jumped.

"Well Good Morning children," said a voice that sounded just like Crowhaven's. "You'll be glad to know that your wait is over and that the game is about to begin. I'd like to wish you all the very best of luck. And please should one of the others, as is perhaps inevitable, disappear, don't weep, don't wail, don't bawl or cry. Suck it up, because unless you deliver the goods, it'll be you next."

This was terrifying to hear and the wild, demented laughter, grossly amplified and horrifically distorted which seemed to spill from the walls after this pronouncement made them all freeze with terror. In time the laughter ceased and the voice dropped to a whisper.

"Unfortunately, there can be only one."

Silence. Nobody got the allusion, or if they did, they weren't exactly turning cartwheels. The Voice of the Machine was disappointed and irritation ironed the creases into its next words.

"Shall we proceed?"

Again silence.

"I'll take that as a yes. Answer the question and take a step forward. Take a step before you answer the question and you'll fizz and vanish. Take a step after you lie, same outcome. How does this happen? I could explain the physics but none of you would understand so it's best just to zip it and proceed. It's enough to know that all this is the product of pure genius and leave it at that."

"Is it painful?" a small voice piped up.

"Is what painful?"

"Getting vaporised," Samuel asked, who was trying desperately to stop his teeth from chattering. His snotty arrogance had dissolved and been replaced with something a lot more endearing. Childlike terror.

The Professor considered.

"What an excellent question. I don't think it's painful but you never know. Not really. It's a hypothetical postulate I've never really explored. All those who came before you, who didn't make it, disappeared forever and didn't come back. I couldn't ask the question so unfortunately there's no way of knowing. But that really is an excellent question. Well done."

The Professor's voice trailed away into nothingness. It was obvious he was really very impressed.

"Anyway. First steps. Easy peesy. Let's talk about human psychology for a few moments and leave experimental physics to one side. At least for now. Psychology, as you know, is the study of mind and behaviour. The most rudimentary study of human beings reveals that certain behaviours are common to all races in all historical eras and that one of these behaviours is lying. In other words everyone lies and there are evolutionary reasons for this. And why do they lie? Because it benefits them. It gives them a leg up in the daily scramble for continued existence. Costs, very little and the benefits, potentially are huge. Nevermind about morality. Nobody believes in eternal punishment or damnation anymore...unless they do... so everyone lies. It's kinda inevitable. It's just that some people do it much better than others. You see?"

"We see, we really do, but what does all this have to do with us?" Wilber asked.

"An excellent question Wilber. As I said to you back at

breakfast each of the Five Magicians, for want of a better word, has to come up with a game, a test that is set, for each Candidate to pass or fail. I could have come up with an obstacle course, a series of physical challenges but that seemed a little passe so I came up with this instead. In this game you have to both lie and spot the lie. Do that and you succeed. Fail to do that..."

"And you're vapourised," Samuel added.

The Professor chuckled.

"Indeed you are. Anyway, enough chat. Let's get on with the show. We'll call this Round Two, ok? I'm going to ask you something and you're going to either lie to me or tell me the truth. Let me decide which way you go and we'll take it from there. Matilda, you go first. Did you ever deliberately hurt an animal?"

The question, coming right out of the blue, was a shocker. No gentling in, no warming up. The Professor had gone straight in for the kill.

Matilda lowered her head and when she raised it again there were tears in her eyes.

"Yes...I did. I mean I have."

"Tears already and its only the second round my dear. What is it you hurt?"

"My dog."

"Why?"

"Because I wanted to see if I could get away with it.'

Crowhaven chuckled. He was clearly impressed.

"Well done Matilda. There is hope for you yet. What about you Sam? Ever deliberately hurt an animal?"

Samuel lifted his head, openly defiant.

"No, never"

Crowhaven tutted.

"Little early in the day to be lying Sammy. I do hope you'll be joining us for the next round, but I have my doubts. What about you Raoul?"

The Spanish-sounding youth shook his head.

"Never."

"Really. It would appear you are surrounded by saints, Matilda. And what about you Wilber, ever kill anything for sheer pleasure? An image flashed through Wilber's mind.

"Well?"

"Yes."

"What?"

"A bird. It had hit the window and fallen down onto the gravel path stunned. I rode over it with my bike. Its guts oozed out of its rear end. Horrible really."

There was a pause, whilst Crowhaven digested Wilber's story.

"Well done my son. Well done. Painful isn't it? But like the Bible says, the truth shall set you free. Now take a step forward, all of you, and we shall see what we shall see."

They all took a step and one of them, as promised, vanished into thin air.

17

The Cubed Route

It was horrible really. They had all of them taken a step, as they had taken many millions of steps throughout their lives, only this step was different. At least for Samuel, who seemed to pass through an invisible barrier into another realm. The others turned as the air around him began to fizz and churn. He screamed, but it was as if he had been imprisoned behind soundproof glass and his anguished cry made no impression, left no audible trace. His arms flailed, like he was doing a bad impression of a Catherine Wheel, and then he froze, like a paused video, and simply vanished. Faded out of existence, forever. For all they knew.

In the space where he had been there was a dull glow of mustard light and the unmistakable whiff of sulphur. Wilber scrunched up his nose in silent disgust. They had all of them moved one step closer to their goal, that white square in the centre. Beneath their feet the glassy floor tiles glowed with orange light. Behind them the outer tiles remained aglow with their blazing red light.

They all of them stood immobile. All in their own ways ashamed, heads lowered. The only sound that filled the room was that of Matilda's weeping. Eventually she stopped, wiped her eyes and looked around her to see where the others were at. Neither of the boys could meet her eye. In time the voice, Crowhavens or the machines, they couldn't tell which, spoke again.

"Well done children. You've survived. At least for now. Care to move forward into the third round? Of course you do. After all, there's no going back. You step when I tell you or you fizz and go out."

Here the voice paused, then let out a little chuckle.

"And so to Round Three. Here the game changes. I've caught you in a lie. Now you must catch each other in a lie. Simple really. Matilda you go first. Choose one of your friends here to be your partner. Turn to face them and tell them something about yourself, a simple statement if you will. It could be true or it could be false. You just have to sell it, that's all. The speaker speaks and the listener replies. Truth or Lie. That's all the Listener needs to say. The speaker is safe but the listener, if he or she gets it wrong, takes a step into oblivion."

Matilda's tears had dried and when Wilber examined her face he saw something else there, a quiet and terrifying change. It was as if the light of the child that she had been had gone out and all that remained was a ghost. Or maybe something else, something darker. Her eyes picked up the glowing light of the outer square and appeared glassy and quite, quite red. Yes, the effect was most unnerving She looked like something out of a fairytale now. Or possibly a nightmare.

Matilda looked first at Wilber and then at Raoul. It was obvious she was sizing them up. Who was the greater threat? Who had she the better chance of misleading? It didn't take her long to figure it out. She turned to Raoul and fixed him with her wide, staring, tear-reddened eyes.

"Hello Raoul, I'm sorry we have to meet like this. My name is Matilda. I am an orphan. My parents died when I was four years of age."

A single tear rolled down the girl's face and Raoul felt his heart open like a flower, in both love and pity.

"Truth."

Matilda smiled like a Medieval Saint and Crowhaven, or the Machine, applauded.

"You go next Raoul."

Raoul, following Matilda's lead, turned to Wilber and smiled.

"Hello Wilber. I am not an orphan but I do love mathematics. I am the best in my class and no one outscores me on a test."

The smile seemed genuine and he had told the truth about never hurting animals. Raoul was squeaky clean. His hair was parted, his teeth brushed, his clothes even here, were neat and creased in all the right places. It's just that it didn't feel right. The logical part of his mind said 'truth' but the creative, intuitive part said 'lie.' To which should he listen? This wasn't just a game anymore. This was life or death. In that instant lightning flashed through his mind and he had his answer.

"Lie!"

The word fell like a thunderbolt and the smile dropped like a thousand flakes of plaster from Raoul's face to be replaced by a scowl. His expression confirmed that Wilber had made the right choice.

"And now you Wilber," the Voice of the Machine prompted.

Wilber turned to Matilda who stared back with piercing eyes.

"My family is very rich and I live in a mansion."

Matilda studied him for a while before answering.

"Truth."

Then they all took a step, and Raoul, like Samuel before him, fizzed and disappeared. This time Matilda did not cry and the third yellow square that illuminated their features revealed that both were in it to win it. No quarter could or would be offered here. No laugh this time greeted the elimination of a competitor.

"And then there were two. Like an Agatha Christie Dinner isn't it?"

When both Wilber and Matilda looked blankly at each other the Voice sighed.

"Never mind. On with the show. The great thing about Round Four is that no one needs to lose. It's a bit of a throwaway really. It's called Fact or Opinion. I will offer a statement and you will simply judge it to be a fact or an opinion. It could be something like the moon is blue, the earth is round, God exists. Get the idea?"

Both nodded.

"First question to you Matilda. Ready?"

Another nod.

"Your opponent is far more intelligent than you are."

Matilda froze and her face paled. It was a cruel thing to do but then the game was cruel. How to answer. What was intelligence? Could it be measured? Weren't there different types of intelligence? Did age matter? Wilber was much older than she was. That was true but was he more intelligent? Perhaps intelligence depended on the type of question or problem under investigation. But she couldn't answer 'depends'... She could only answer 'fact' or 'opinion'. And what if it was a false fact...

She glanced at Wilber then and she knew with a sense of sinking what the answer was. It hurt her to think it. It would hurt her even more to say it but say it she must. Wilber was looking at her blankly. Outwardly he was an open book. There were no signs of deception or even the ability to deceive about him and yet behind the expression she sensed a mind in motion, a mind that was rarely on the leash, faster and more unexpected than hers. A mind that worked on many levels, submerged, hidden, yet active nonetheless. Knowing this she could only answer one way.

"Fact," she said, a slight quaver in her voice.

"Ouch," Crowhaven's voice responded, entirely without empathy. "That had to hurt."

Matilda did not comment and Crowhaven, or his simulacrum sighed.

"Back to you Wilber. Your Uncle George has betrayed you. Fact or opinion?"

Without so much as a pause Wilber replied.

"Fact!"

"So sure? Not too late to change your mind."

"Fact."

"How can you possibly know?"

"Fact."

"Oh dear."

The pause was an eternity, the silence a snare. But there was no way Wilber was changing his mind and eventually Crowhaven was forced to concede.

"Advance."

Both took a step and neither disappeared.

"Interesting," was Crowhaven's only comment. "You learn something new every day."

That was true and Wilber's mind was spinning like the reels on a fruit machine. Not only that, his heart was pounding. How did Crowhaven know about George? What did he know about their shared past? Had he been watching him and if so for how long? The Professor had a habit of generating complete panic and mental chaos, for all that he was an absolute gentleman with impeccable manners.

"So kids, Round Five. So far you've done very well and I'm more than a little impressed. Two rounds to go and it's back over to you. Three statements. One lie, two truths. Pick out the truth. Wilber you go first."

No time to think. When the fighter plane hit a snag; an inbound rocket or an exploding engine, the call was eject, eject go. No time for analysis, no time to question why. You just had to do it. Like now. Three statements. One lie, two truths.

"I've never had a girlfriend. I'd never knowingly lie. I want us both to get out of here."

"Excellent. Now you Matilda. No pauses dear one, or you'll fizz and fade."

But Matilda didn't need the threat. She already had her statements.

"I am an American. I am a murderer. I love you."

The Voice of the Machine gasped. It was enjoying the action greatly. Oh that it had to end.

"You guess first Matilda. What is the lie? Ten seconds on the clock."

The clock ticked down to zero point before Matilda gave her answer.

"You're a good boy Wilber, perhaps a little too good for this world and certainly for this island. I guess you'd prefer it if we both got out of here...so that's true. I think you'd never knowingly lie, so that's true too but I can't believe you've never had a girlfriend. Far too good looking. So I'm going to go with that. That's the lie."

Wilber lowered his head and stared at the lighted blue panels beneath his feet. She had him. Okay his turn.

"That accent sounds English but you feel American. The English are more well...self effacing, less assured, and you'll do anything to get ahead. That's obvious and obviously true. Murder or love? When I look in your eyes I don't see love for anybody other than yourself. So you are a murderer and it's the final statement that is the lie. You don't love me."

"Take a step"

Wilber closed his eyes and took a step forward.

18

HMS Victory

When he opened them again he was alone. He turned round and saw all five of the grand coloured squares lit and glowing. He then counted the squares within the squares from the inner layers outwards; 8 purple, 16 blue, 24 yellow, 32 orange, 40 red and 1 white. He turned then from within his purple square and reached out for the glowing cube.

"Slowly slowly catchy monkey."

The youth froze, his hand suspended in mid air.

"But I won," Wilber said, his voice a mere whisper.

"Not quite."

"But there's no one left."

"Oh yes, there is. There's me," Crowhaven responded. "You have to beat me. Two lies, one truth. Then you get the crystal."

It was as pointless to argue as it was to resist.

"Shoot."

"I am three hundred years old. I can predict the future. I I will be the death of you."

Wilber's blood iced over and he thought of Dante's ninth level of hell in which Judas was frozen, like straw in glass, looking up, for all eternity, at him who he had betrayed. Christ. His mind was full of rolling columns; the marble columns of an Ancient Temple, glowing not white but flickering with countless images. Both in time and out of time, Wilber walked around the Temple structure seeing images of Crowhaven from many angles, at many different times. Thrice he circumnavigated the temple and he was half way around a fourth time when he stopped and the lie dropped into his lap, like an apple falling from a laden tree. Gravity was a wonderful thing, but levity was better.

Wilber blinked slowly and began to laugh.

"You're not what you appear to be, Professor."

"Who is?" the Voice replied.

"Another question for another time I think," Wilber commented philosophically.

"So what's your answer?"

"You're older than you appear. You have seen certain futures but not the future. And you will not be the death of me."

The Voice was quiet for a time.

"How do you know that?"

"I just do," and with that Wilber reached out and took the crystal. The whole room lit up with white light but he didn't stop to enjoy it. He was at the door and turning the handle before the Voice had time to reply. Stepping through the door he sensed a presence and span. Crowhaven reached out and handed him a brown leather satchel.

"Why?"

"Because you'll need it."

And Wilber understood. Down the corridor he ran, and as he ran, he placed the first crystal, the glowing cube, into a hollow space inside the bag. The cube fit perfectly into the hollow space and he knew the two were meant for each other. He couldn't believe that he had emerged victorious, couldn't quite believe that he had survived to fight another hour, the crystal cube swinging at his hip, in the less than fashionable satchel. But it was the truth. The other children Raoul, Matilda and Samuel had all disappeared into thin air as Crowhaven had said they would. That too was the truth, albeit it far less palatable.

Hours earlier, that would have been unbelievable but now it was almost commonplace. This Universe ran according to different laws and rules to the one he was familiar with. Back at Muldoon Manor he had slept the sleep of the just, but now he had been thrust out into the world of the island, a place that was a moral maze. Here there were no certainties, only pain and torment. On the island you played the game or the game played you.

Removing the compass from his pocket he checked his direction. He was heading due west and Crowhaven's labs lay behind him. He stabbed the map with his index finger. He felt guilt, enormous guilt but he also felt some measure of exaltation. For the first time, in a long time, he knew where he was and what he had to do.

Examining the map closely, he picked out his second destination. It was in the far northwest corner of the island and to get there he must traverse the northern shore. Soon the trees would thin and he would be exposed to the elements and whatever else was stalking about. There was savannah to negotiate, deep grass which could conceal God alone knew what. But it might also conceal him. A double-edged sword if ever there were. He glanced at his watch. It was almost nine o clock. He had used six hours of his allotted span and acquired just one crystal. But he had acquired it. How many people came to the island and fell at the first hurdle. Hundreds? Thousands? It didn't bear thinking about.

He took a bearing and, reassured that he was travelling in the right direction, with the right strategy, looked about him. Lola was nowhere to be seen. What had he expected? She was part of the world of the island and no doubt performed a function here. She was nobody's friend, just another person looking to survive. And who was he to blame her?

Through the trees he walked, his face grim, his will fixed, mind focused. Crowhaven had disappeared back into the darkness, from where he had come, as he had intimated Wilber would, if he failed at the game. The idea of obliteration and oblivion didn't trouble Wilber, it was the idea of being disembodied in a sea of nothingness forever that played on Wilber's mind. There were all kinds and shades of suffering here. The world of the island was not a world of the comfortable coma; it was a hell realm. Stripped of all nicety and certainty. And suddenly a voice from in front of him, stirring him from his revelry, crying out in warning.

"Wilber behind you." Wilber's heart leapt with joy. Lola was back. But then he felt icy talons clutching his ankles and pulling him down to the ground.

The sky was no longer bright; the sun no longer shone as it had in the early morning as Crowhaven had swung his nine-iron, calling out four, the very epitome of the English gentleman. But whilst English, he was by no stretch of the imagination, a gentleman. It was just a mask he wore, a mask that Wilber longed to drag from his smug, pasty face and shatter. The blue Technicolor sky above had gone, replaced by a canopy of gunmetal grey, a sky filling with clouds that were in their turn, filled with red veins. They scudded by, ready to burst and rain down, who knew what, blood-smeared acid horrors.

Dragged to the floor, held down, he looked up and saw a face out of a nightmare. A once-human face staring down at him. A body denuded of flesh clad in a long black coat and a trilby hat. A parody of 1950s fashion. Hands with elongated fingers, more talons than fingers, fingers surmounted with sharp claws reached out towards him.

But the faces, the faces were worse than anything. More skull than face. Yellow, jaundiced eyes staring out of deeply recessed sockets. Teeth crooked and oversized, the incisors; fangs, curved like those of an ice age sabre-tooth. Moving towards him. Moving inexorably towards him. Faces edging closer, saliva dripping from those too prominent jaws. They didn't walk, they didn't run, skitter or skulk, these creatures crept. They were creepers and they wanted to feast, to consume his flesh to assuage the hunger that gnawed at them.

Wilber screamed and screamed, his soul filling the air around him with a shiver and a shimmer of terror. The island watched and did nothing. It drank in his terror as the desiccated face and the dripping fangs moved closer, closer...oh so close, close enough to bite and to tear. He could already feel the flesh being ripped from him, the gaping hole it would leave, the hot blood that would flow, the cold shock that would both numb and anaesthetize him.

But he had to think...no he had to act. Now! More than anything he needed to move his limbs. To fight back, but how could he; he was frozen. It was all so hugely comic, so hilarious. So iconic, so laughable now that the cold stinking, maggoty breath was being exhaled onto his skin, spewed onto his shocked features.

Bang! The body of the reaching Creeper flew to one side with a screech that almost deafened him. He was wrenched free and suddenly the air was full of flame and the black coated figures were running amongst the trees. Only they were in flames now. Burning flesh, screaming bodies. Running, lolloping away, running anywhere so long as they could escape the flames. But it was too late for them and Wilber felt no pity. The smell of their burned flesh rode the whimpering wings and he felt no pity. Soon they were gone and no trace remained. Trembling, he brushed himself down and looked around him. Once more he was surrounded only this time by sweet, sweet girls not monsters from out of the pit of hell.

"Thank you," was all he could say. Wilber realised that he was in a state of shock. The girls around him stirred, they recognised the signs, having been through the process themselves but they also knew that he had to pull himself together and now. There was no time for rest and recuperation. You simply had to get on with it, to suck it up. It, being the pain and shock and agony of life here. Why should this be so? No reason. It was just the way it was. The biggest girl stepped forward and put her hand on his shoulder.

"I'm sorry but we have to go. He'll know you're here. He'll send more."

Wilber was shocked all over again.

"More of them? Why... and who are you talking about?

"Astapor, another girl replied. The first girl, the leader, was getting impatient. "Look, we'll talk but only on the move. Do you have it?"

Intuitively, Wilber knew that she was alluding to the first crystal but he decided to play his own game, to use the ropes in order to play possum.

"Have what?" he replied.

"The crystal you mule, the hexagram" said a rather plump girl, covered in tattoos and piercings and porting some kind of oversized mallet around on her shoulder.

'Yeah I have it," he admitted. The girls exchanged knowing glances.

"Well let's go then," said the leader. "We'll take you to the next place. You can acquire the second crystal there."

"What? You're gonna help me?" Wilber was dumbstruck.

The Leader nodded an affirmation.

"Yes and you better be grateful. We don't do this for everyone you know."

"But what about Lola?" Wilber stammered.

"Gone," said the Hammer Girl.

"And good riddance to bad rubbish," another added.

"We can't leave her behind. She's my friend," Wilber said, his voice raised in protest. Despite his mostly composed demeanour he had a temper every bit as fiery as the Hammer Girl. The Hammer Girl seeing this lost what little patience she had.

"She ain't nobody's friend, brother and if you'd spent any more time with her you'd have learned that in a very painful way."

Wilber just couldn't accept that.

"Well I'm not going anyway until you tell me who you are."

"We're the Alphabet Gang Wilber. I'm Antelope, this is Beth, my Second in Command, Crimson, that's Def..." this she said pointing to the Hammer Girl, "Edie, Frantic, Rudi and that's Semantic, our language expert and code breaker. She's also a whizz with electronics."

And with that they were moving. Wilber had his own praetorian guard. It should have reassured him but whenever he closed his eyes all he could see was that fleshless face and those dripping fangs moving into him, wanting only to have and to hold, to clutch and to bite.

19

Don't Walk and Talk

Whilst they walked no one talked. They moved quickly and before long Wilber found himself slipping away into a sort of reverie. Since childhood he'd had a weird ability to see things in his mind's eye in incredible detail. It wasn't just the result of an overactive imagination either. Sometimes he saw events or the shadows of events before they happened. Car crashes, natural disasters, the break up of relationships, the coming of storms.

He had a good eye and a sound ear for the macabre, did Wilber. He especially loved horror movies with a supernatural edge. Anything dystopian was nectar to him. Life lived on the edge of extinction was what mattered. Pain and fear brought people into the moment. So many lived in a sort of comfortable coma, hypnotised by notions of their own success and the praise of others who aspired to have what they had. People had such an overweening pride in their own possessions. But things were just things. They were either useful or they were not. A house was just a big box, a car a smaller box. A body was a suit of earth, air, fire and water. It was the human mind that mattered. Experience and the Spirit of Adventure that made life worth living.

George understood that. More than anybody he had ever known George understood that. The Muldoon family were obscenely rich and had been for generations. George, being the eldest, had been groomed to succeed as Patriarch but he had refused the title and handed it on to Wilber's own father. His father, unable to believe his own luck had taken the reins of the family business and grown it still further. Now the Muldoons were a global brand.

But to what end? It meant nothing to him. It had done though, up until the age of 10. After that he had changed, almost overnight, in a way so profound and shocking, he and everyone around him was still reeling. What had caused him to change though? There must have been a moment. It was a mystery and the answer was always on the tip of his tongue. Always dancing in flame. He just couldn't articulate it. Couldn't reach it. All he could do was replay the memories endlessly, the before and after shots. Like those images on the net of Crystal Meth addicts. Before and after the addiction began.

Nine years of age. The before time. Together. Happy and with friends. Always popular, always invited to things. Kicking a ball around in the park. Going down a slide, sitting on a swing. Riding a rollercoaster at Alton Towers. Dancing at a disco. Taking part in a school play. Winning a prize. Helping to wash the family cars. Taking a bag of carrots out to feed the horses. Writing a thank you letter to his Grandma. Taking pride in his appearance. Wearing colourful clothes. Offering praise and being helpful. Dressing smartly. Tidying his bedroom. Doing as he was told.

Ten years of age. The after time. Alone. Everybody walking away from him, everybody critical. Damaging and breaking things. Hurting people. Getting into fights. Kicking down a wall. Desecrating a grave. Vandalising a car. Slashing tyres. Burning down someone's garden shed. Visits by the Police. Meetings with social workers. Being read the riot act by his father. Sitting cross-armed outside the headmaster's office. People shouting at him. People whispering about him. People leaving him well alone. Dressing in black. Never washing. Wearing hoodies and shades. Not wanting to be seen. Not wanting to go anywhere. Just wanting to sit in his room on his own. Just wanting to read and to forget about the world.

Such a bad time, such a dark time, the after time but it was also a magic time. It was as though someone had wired him into the cosmic grid and pulled the switch. He'd been blasted, electrocuted but he'd woken up from the sleep of childhood. His mind had lit up and the world had come painfully into focus. What he had gone through, he could see now, was the agony of an awakening. During that time he had been forced to confront his own reflection, to own his fears and limitations and to face down his shadow, the dark and destructive part of himself that he would have preferred not to exist.

But it did exist and it had a purpose. Sometimes those dark impulses, the ability to fight and if necessary kill were what kept you alive. Most people wanted to be liked and most parents wanted to see a smiling face. But what if the child did not want to smile and laugh and play along, what then? He knew, had learned the hard way. They turned from you, abandoned you and they cast you out. But whilst in the short run that might be terrible, a scarring, a maiming, it did not destroy you. It made you stand up on your own two feet. It forced you to grow up and take responsibility for your own life and your own baggage.

Looking at the Alphabet Gang he saw something different, something that in some vague way echoed his own experience of life. These kids had not been born into poverty. Most likely they had been born into privilege like him. They had never suffered a day in their lives, never gone without. No doubt they'd been driven round in big cars, big American cars, chauffeured from venue to venue, from school to after-school club. Life was an ever revolving series of delights. Of endless parties and sleepovers, of texts and calls, makeup and shopping. Protected, cosseted, entitled. Sold the idea that they were everything and that they could have anything and why, because they were worth it.

This, they called empowerment.

Yet like him, just as in his life, it had all changed for them too, in just one day. For some unknowable and most likely unbelievable reason the middle finger of fate had pointed at them and then the hand of fate had hauled them out of their comfortable first world lives and hurled them back through time into the dark ages. No soap, no washing machines, no makeup, no Golden Arches, no phones, no change of clothes, no teachers, no parents, no help, no nothing, just unrelenting hostility.

What daily terrors had these girls had to face since coming to the island? Hunger. Rain. Extremes of heat and cold. No shelter. And that was just for starters. They would have had to learn to hunt and camouflage themselves. To kill animals and harvest fruit. To be ever vigilant. To fight and to train. To be disciplined. To follow rules. To cope with loss and grief. To run and run fast. To hide. To avoid detection. To accept that they would always be hunted and if caught, killed, or worse. That things from their worst nightmares could be launched upon them at any moment. That they could be experimented upon, eaten, blinded, mutilated, made to rue the day they were born. All this and more.

God but they had come a long way. For as long as they had lived on the island, Wilber perceived that they had lived in a state of conflict. All around them in the jungle, dry laughter floated on the wind. Leaves drifted down from the canopy, to the jungle floor and evil circled and grew in strength and cunning. The odds for a lengthy survival here were not good ones. Would they all be destroyed by forces they could neither understand or even define? Did it even matter? The energies in this place were like vines, twisted together. Out in the jungle where they slept, unnameable terrors crawled amongst their dreams, twining and twisting.

Words come out of the light, dancing through the mist, piercing all with blades. Was that a face? Mist was not a terminal condition. It could be burned off, turned off, travelled through. Mr Hand and the white woman are crook-backed and broken with age. How can this be so? Why should this be so? They howl, plaintive. The same thoughts circling like wolves or echoes of a man screaming in a cave, with a dead child in his hands, a dead woman, lying bloodied on the ground, surrounded by old women with bowed, covered heads.

Exhaustion and questioning Why? Why me? Why this? Why now? The answers were there in the energy forming, there, but just out of reach. They have overstretched themselves and are on the brink of breaking. The others who heard the voices, who had had the intention to come, never did, they found reasons to stay home, to lose themselves in flesh and death. Those that did come were soon lost or killed. They all in some way lacked the vigour, the juice, the drive, the restraint coupled with the killer will.

Yet this pair...this pair did not. They crossed desert and river, braved drought and flood and the predations of other humans and animals. They lived by strength and cunning and they survived and in time they arrived in the valley where the watchers awaited them.

But would it be enough to sustain them, what they had learned on this journey? Once again, the howl, the agony of a human mind, small, trapped, bound in a nutshell, exposed to a force that cracks and opens it.

Wilber ran back in his mind, his time on the island. He'd been here just a few short hours and yet he had experienced so much already. Waking on the beach. Being snatched by the cannibals and prepared as meat. The pounding of the drums, the gleeful laughter of children who believed they were about to end their enforced fast. Busted free by the Alphabet Gang. The savage beating of the cannibals by the alphabet gang, Meeting Lola. Taken to Crowhaven, treated to breakfast. Given the map and a Mission. The story of the five crystals. Did he even believe that? The game inside the cube. His guilty victory. The faces of the disappearing children. Sam, Raoul, Matilda. Their cries and agonised screams. And just now their battle with the Creepers. Once more the resolve and fearlessness of the Alphabet Gang astonished him. It was all so unbelievable yet he believed and for the first time in a very long time he felt vital and alive.

Questions shot through Wilber's mind like a shoal of ever proliferating minnows chased by a very large and hungry pike. A voice echoed in the chamber of his head. Why me? Why am I here and why do I want to get off this island? Its paradise compared with where I come from. I could make a life for myself here. I would never have to go back home and re-enter a world full of people I loathe, whose values aren't mine, who's goals aren't mine. I was lost there and for all of the insanity here, I at least feel alive

And why are these girls helping me? They've no need to. I'm an encumbrance to them. A risk and probably an embarrassment. What makes me so special? And what of the island. How did it come to be here? Where and when was it? Does it even exist or have

I gone insane? And if it was a time gate I came through, is everybody from the same place and time? What happens to the aging process when you come to the island? Is it suspended and does that mean that everybody remains the same age they were when they first came to the island? Does that mean, should I fail in the Quest, as everybody else here obviously has, that I will stay forever young? Does that mean, should I survive, I will become immortal?

And what of the Magicians and who was Astapor and why had he set up such a vicious, monstrous and yet ultimately exciting game? What kind of mind did that?

And why?

20

The Next Step

There were four kinds of vulture on the island, but the Black Vulture was the most populous. Over the years that the Russian had been in business their numbers had grown steadily. They particularly haunted the northern slopes of the Great Mountain, as food was most plentiful there. If they came into the compound and roosted on one of the eight towers, they would be shot. As much as Astapor loved them he would not suffer that, and the birds, alive to the absolute realities of life and death on the island, dwelt for the most part beyond the perimeter fences.

Today, they crouched in expectation on the fringes of the forest, looking with black eyes up at the looming towers. Their stillness was unnerving. They did not seek the air to wheel high above the land, searching for the flesh of the dead as their kind did in other parts of the world. No, they simply watched and waited, wings either outstretched or folded. They were neither tame nor blunted but highly alert. It's just that food would be brought to them. They knew that. It was just a case of waiting patiently. Today, of all days there would be meat in great abundance.

Back up in the Green Dome, on top of Tower One, the air was alive with tension. Indeed, the space, which doubled as Astapor's Control Centre, had never been busier. There were monitors and screens everywhere which allowed The Big One and the Little Two to track the movements of each candidate as they moved around the island. And today there were many movements which needed tracking.

There were limitations however. It was a stated rule of the Company of Magicians that no cameras could be placed inside any other Magician's domain. It was fair game to place them just outside a domain but never inside. To do so would be to contravene the spirit of the game. Moreover, this, it was felt, would lend too much advantage to the Magicians. You had to give the candidates at least the appearance of a fighting chance.

For all that it was still early and the game young, Astapor was anything but happy.

"It would appear the Creepers have failed me, Lurch. As have you. You did not factor the Alphabet Gang into your calculations. Such a basic error, and you, a scientist."

Lurch had the forethought to look apologetic.

"We need to develop a new batch of serum Master, even more potent than the last one. The Creepers, whilst disappointing, are still a wonderful agent of delivery. They just need tweaking, that's all."

Caleb, ever impatient, failed to see the logic in Lurch's statement.

"Forget about the Creepers Lurch. They're too slow and ineffectual."

"What makes you say that?" the scientist retorted, stung by the brat's impudence.

"Observation and analysis supported by more than a modicum of intelligence. They are neither smart enough nor vicious enough to do the job they are required to do. Like someone I know."

Here he stared pointedly at Lurch, who stared back balefully at him. It was all in the game they played, the game of vying for Astapor's favour. The Russian followed the sawing motion of insults between the two with mild amusement, whilst revealing nothing.

"We have options Caleb, so many options," he opined.

"Would you care to elaborate Count?"

Astapor pulled up a menu on a nearby screen and began to scroll through them. Each Level of the Storage facility was filled with human variants. It was an ever changing smorgasbord of delights. New procedures were coming to light every day. More and more flesh and mind-warping chemicals were being manufactured by the hour and all had to be trialled. The only limiting factor was the amount of human flesh he could lay his hands on, but soon that would cease to be a problem. He had begun to map out in his own mind a breeding programme and for that he would need the Alphabet gang.

Astapor began to read from the list.

"Well, let's see. We have boss-eyed wombats, skilled in combat, pouncers, mekons, melt-ons and crunchers, scourers, peelers, squealers and feelers, slappers, pokers, jokers and skewerers, yappers, trappers, knobblers and cobblers, gaugers, impalers, mucky-fingered leerers, Robo Dog-headed bananas (sans pyjamas) and Psycho side-kicking lamas."

Caleb picked up where Astapor had left off.

"Stalkers, stranglers, biters and leapers, drainers, guzzlers, puzzlers, and nubblers.

Lamb-whackers, Jaw-crackers, Scratchers and Dampeners, Danglers, Janglers, nonces and ponces, slashers, flashers, desiccated worm lickers, Flesh rippers, nail strippers, mollycoddled kipper-whippers, Wreaking, rabid baby eaters. Hairless Happy slabbers, Hawkers, squawkers, talkers, prodders, Cat-slappers, smilers, whiners and mewlers, hairless goons in oversized trousers, blowers of crumpled trumpets, humpits, crunchits, black meats and collywobbles

zombies, creepers, sleepers and weepers..."

Astapor screwed up his face with obvious distaste.

"Who names all of these things Caleb? Desiccated worm lickers? Really?"

Caleb shot Lurch a quick glance.

"We both do Count."

"We may have to review that."

The silence was more than just a little uncomfortable and it needed filling. Desperately.

"Hold on, hold on!" yelled Caleb suddenly. The light of electricity crackled in his eyes. "We've got it," he shouted, exuberant and charged with life for once.

"What have we got?" Lurch sneered

A thought had just occurred to Caleb. Always a dangerous thing.

"I'm not entirely sure but we need to make a decision. Or maybe a revision..." he added as an afterthought.

Lurch made a face. Any suggestion that came from Caleb was to be treated with as much contempt as he could muster. He stroked his moustache and began to assemble and polish his own proposals and counter proposals.

"We need to move towards a decision, Master. The pack is on the move and time is of the essence. I have a tentative proposal to make, if I may. The boss-eyed wombats could do with an outing. Now I know that they are only Level 1 creatures but why not send them out with the desiccated worm lickers. Why slap when you can both slap and stab?"

Astapor's face was an inscrutable mask that would have been the envy of any poker player of note. Caleb watched him like a hawk.

"You have an unhealthy obsession with those wombats, Lurch. You treat them more like pets than Attack Beasts. And as for those worm lickers, well they can dish it but can they take it? I fear not."

Lurch bowed his head and tried to smile but sweat filmed his brow and he had begun to shake. Raising a remote he clicked a switch and a Camera feed crackled into life.

"What is this?"

"Level 5. A new batch of Creepers."

Astapor hissed like a snake, and Caleb darted in, raising his remote and changing the channel. A steaming, fetid den filled with huddled shapes hove into view and Caleb instantly began to curate.

"Check this out, Count. Level 10. We call them Liberty Smashers. All flash and stab or smash and grab merchants this lot, of the highest order. A terrible beauty is born, eh? They mug and they maim. They sling acid and wield a blade like the Count of Monte Christo. Not really finishers, this lot, but they make a real mess. After they have been to the party no one gets out without major wounds..."

"Caleb..."

"Yes Count."

"Shut up."

Caleb shut up whilst the Russian considered his options.

"What level are the Zombies on?" he asked, as though he didn't know, but of course he did. He knew everything about the island and he took especial pride in his human menagerie. A smile licked the edges of Caleb's lips.

"Level 20 I believe, Count."

Lurch screeched in disbelief.

"20?" There was a note of agonised hatred in Puharich's voice that Astapor was not slow to pick up on. The enmity between the scientist and the boy was quite something to behold. It was a fire he would have to feed. It was something he could warm his hands on.

"We never normally need to go much beyond Level 10 do we?" Lurch asked in that wheedling voice he had all but perfected.

"That is true, Astapor conceded but then you've never had to deal with a Muldoon before."

"But he's only a child. What is he, 13?" Lurch asked, unable to suppress a snigger.

"He's 15," Caleb said. "And a Muldoon. He already has one crystal. We don't want him getting another, now do we? It will give us all a bad name. The other Magicians will begin to think the Count is losing his touch. They may feel inclined to challenge him for the centre."

The Russian considered this for a moment before responding.

"Thank you Caleb. A sound analysis but I don't think we need fear a coup just yet. There are other forces in motion and other plans too. Of which you know nothing."

Caleb bowed his head in deference to the Count but then he turned and winked at Lurch who began immediately to add to his list of Caleb Death Fantasies.

Astapor cleared his throat and then continued.

"Yes, dear boy, I think my suggestion is best. We'll proceed to Level 20 and release the zombies...."

Here he raised his remote and clicked.

Caleb winced, then raised his remote and counter clicked. Outside the world appeared to freeze. It was a terrifying moment for all of them. The boy had only wanted to show the Russian his latest work on Level 21, on the Leaping Biters, but it was a serious miscalculation and they all knew it. Without further ado Caleb clicked back onto Level 20 and without a second glance the Russian resumed his narrative. The Camera revealed an eerie host of yellow skinned giants frozen in various poses beneath muted half lights.

"We've made one or two modifications to the latest cohort. They are faster, more sensitive and much more vicious than before. Oh and they are yellow. They'll tear Young Muldoon and his protectors to pieces and then they will feast on their flesh. "

"How long?" Caleb asked, grinning manically.

"After release? Thirty minutes, give or take, before they catch up with them. By that time they should be well and truly lost in the swamp. I think a celebratory dinner is in order, don't you, Caleb? Something fresh and recently killed. Perhaps it's time to send for the chef. See to it, Lurch."

21

Down at the Farm

The sun had risen higher and shone down on the island where it could, in an ever-shifting patchwork of light and shade. Such a strange colour, the sky. Not clear but sickly looking with no hint of blue in it. If anything it was more of a bronze colour, shading into oyster at times. Cloud afforded some cover but the temperature had climbed steeply since Wilber's arrival. Glancing at the watch Crowhaven had gifted him, he saw it was nine o'clock. He had been on the island for six hours but it felt much longer. Strange, how in such a short space of time he had lost all sense of the world from which he had come. He wondered what it must be like for the others.

The Alphabet Gang moved fast and no one spoke. Senses were dedicated to ascertaining whether any threat was imminent and if so what to do about it. The usual responses were run, hide or kill; simple responses that had kept all of the girls alive. They moved along the Northern Shore of the island, in not one line but two parallel lines. One walking on the edge of a great stretch of sandy beach, the other through tall grasses. The grass patrol had a harder and more tiring slog but the grasses afforded them some cover. This was the line in which Wilber had been placed. Best not to put all of your eggs in one basket, Antelope reasoned.

When they stopped for a brief water break Wilber turned, and shading his eyes, gazed at the tree-clad mountain that dominated the centre of the island. He studied the eight towers that cast the longest shadows with due care and attention. They made his blood run cold and not for the first time he found himself wondering what went on in there. Semantic had mentioned it was best not to think about it too much. It was enough to acknowledge that a clear and present danger existed and to be mindful in every moment.

"Astapor can and does launch attacks from his Tower Complex at any time of the day or night", she had said. "We've seen some pretty horrific things in our time but we've survived them all. So far…"

Half way down the beach Antelope stopped and signalled for the second group to come over to where she was standing. They cantered over at pace, looking around like Meerkats and then the group, as one, dropped to their knees and started feeling for something in the sand. Wilber stood looking down at them, somewhat dumbfounded.

"Lift!," Antelope commanded.

They lifted, and hauled what looked like a screen made of branches and leaves from the sand and placed it to one side. It had been exceptionally well camouflaged. A six-foot pit was revealed into which Frantic leapt without prompting. Immediately she landed she began handing up some rather formidable longbows, which each member of the gang rapidly slung over their shoulders. After the bows came quivers full of arrows. Wilber picked one up and inspected the arrowhead. They looked pretty bloody lethal and he was just about to test how sharp the point was with his index finger when Edie growled at him.

"I wouldn't do that if I was you, Wilber. Poison." She added by way of explanation.

Wilber dropped the arrow in shock and shaking her head Edie stooped down to recover it. Leaping out of the hole Frantic landed beside Young Muldoon and handed him his own quiver and bow.

"For me?" Wilber asked with a note of trepidation in his voice.

"For you,' Frantic confirmed.

"Know how to use it?" Edie asked.

"Yeah I had my own archery range at Muldoon Manor. Mummy and I used to shoot on a daily basis. She is an excellent shot. Can't say we ever used poisoned arrows though."

Def, overhearing this, scowled.

"Well perhaps Mummy and you never had the need." She didn't bother trying to disguise the sarcasm in her voice. Justice regarded her with some measure of coolness.

"Can't say as we ever did."

Antelope flashed Def a warning look and Def arched an eyebrow in silent response. Frantic leapt back down into the pit, without warning and each of the girls handed her a staff. Amazing to think such a simple weapon could cause so much damage. As one the girls knelt and hauled the screen back into place. When next they arose they looked like a different outfit.

"So what's with the bows and arrows?" Wilber asked.

"We're going to need them where we're going," Crimson deadpanned. Without further word the group divided once more and continued their journey. A cold wind blew in from the north and Wilber shivered. Not so tropical now he thought. The grass swayed to some inaudible music and mesmerised, he stopped to watch. A sharp tap on the shoulder by the ever glowering Def launched him on his way again.

As before, they made good progress. They had come a long way from Crowhaven's estate, although the trees that fringed his golf course were still just about visible. The long grass dropped from shoulder to waist height and then down to a point just level with the ankles. They crossed a rocky plane strewn with boulders, which made Wilber feel very exposed, and then each group came to a halt on the edge of a somewhat sinister looking jungle. The trees were taller here albeit closer together, the canopy thicker and less light penetrated. Not somewhere you'd choose to go, not somewhere you'd dare venture unless you absolutely had to.

"So," Wilber said in a stage whisper, "remind me why we're here again."

Rudi leant forward and placed her mouth next to Wilber's ear.

"We're here to protect and guide you, Vilbur and you are here to collect ze second crystal. Ze crystal of air. It is called an octahedron and it has eight faces."

Something didn't compute.

"Air? Why air?"

Wilber twisted his neck to look behind him. Rudi gave him an apologetic smile, whilst Def, who stood behind her grinned from ear to ear. It was a curious thing. The more he suffered, the more she seemed to enjoy it. With friends like Def who needed enemies, he reflected.

"You vill see," she said and patted his shoulder as though he were a loyal and affectionate dog. It was a less reassuring gesture than it might have been. No doubt it was well meant but Wilber felt anxiety laced with irritation clouding his mind.

'Who's in there?" he asked, forgetting the rule of silence to which the group adhered so assiduously.

Antelope, at the head of the first group, swivelled her head sharply and with blazing eyes placed her right index finger on her lips. The sign of silence, a Universal sign beloved of teachers, was not what he wanted or needed right now. As far as he was concerned this wasn't Sunday School. His blood got even hotter and his inner Irritonomer edged up a few more notches. Once more Rudi saved the day. This time her round lips were pressed against Wilber's right ear.

"The Magician who resides here is called Yabu. He, the second of five Magicians you will encounter, is of African origin."

"What's he like?" Wilber said, pressing his mouth to Rudi's ear.

"I don't know. Ve normally have nothing to do wiz him. He is considered very dangerous and not altogether honest."

Great. Without warning Antelope was off again. The girl was a law unto herself. Beth, leading the second group, to which he belonged, followed soon after. Once again they moved in parallel files. This forest was darker than he had imagined and had a markedly eerie atmosphere. The air was cold and yet it seemed to crackle with some invisible force. It was not an entirely pleasant sensation. Electrical yes. Enjoyable no.

More curiously, the forest floor was moister than he'd anticipated and soon they were slogging through viscous mud. Up above the wind was building and the trees jerked from side to side in rapid and unpredictable staccato motions. Appropriate, he guessed, in that he was, if Lady Luck was with him, on his way to harvest the Air Crystal.

The further into the forest they went, the thicker the mud became and soon water began to seep into Wilber's boots. This was no forest; it was a swamp, something his protectors had neglected to mention. Just when you thought the island couldn't get any more unbearable, it did. Suddenly up ahead Antelope paused and raised her right arm. The Alphabet Gang, like the well-drilled militia that they were, slammed to a halt and drew their bows from their backs, then each notched an arrow. Wilber followed suit. In spite of the cold he found he was sweating.

Being here suffused him with dread, a feeling that was soon confirmed by the shrill wail of a siren splitting the air. Antelope cocked her head to one side and then moved off in the direction from which the siren was coming. As soon as she did, the sound immediately cut out. Wading through the ever-deepening water was tiring but this was not to be a problem for too long. Before he had time to roll up his trousers both lines were clambering up out of the swamp onto a slatted walkway covered in mesh to reduce the general slipperiness.

"Thank God for that," Wilber muttered to himself.

Moving with Ninja-like stealth, two lines became one on the wooden walkway. With bows drawn and arrows pointing down into the water, the Gang made their way forward slowly and cautiously. The sense of threat had grown more acute and now everyone was absolutely on edge. God help anything that dared thrust its nose up out of the swamp to cock a snook at the Alphabets. It would find itself pocked with arrows at the very least. Step by step they advanced into the gloom and then suddenly, without warning, up ahead, light. Or rather flame, blowing from side to side in four crackling torches that had been positioned in the corners of a wide platform, into which the walkway fed.

Upon that platform, wonder of wonders, was a white throne

and on that throne there sat a very dark-skinned man with an aura of elegant malevolence. The gang edged down the walkway and fanned out around the throne. They lowered their bows and arrows if not their heads in deference to their host but no more. They were armed and ready for action, should action present itself for their entertainment and delight. The man upon the throne surveyed them all, with a bemused air and flashed his dazzling teeth at them.

"Good afternoon rabies and gerbil men. It's a real pleasure to finally make your acquaintance. My name, as you may have surmised, is Yabu. And you, you must be Wilber."

This he addressed to Young Muldoon.

"News travels fast," Crimson commented wryly.

"Even in a swamp," Def added, never the optimist.

Yabu looked pained. He was not as Wilber had foreseen. When Rudi had mentioned that the Magician was of African origin Wilber imagined some kind of wild and leaping witch doctor in a grass skirt with ostrich plumes, jangling beads and dangling bones strung out on ornate necklaces. A pointer of sticks, a rattler of skulls, a stirrer of pots was what he had expected to face. Voodoo and wide, with friends on the other side. Instead he was presented with an image of contemporary elegance, an urban sybarite, Gucci clad, scented and perfumed. With his Jimmy Choos and his Raybans he looked like he had just flown in from New York by LearJet.

Wilber made a mental note, for future reference, to beware of stereotypes and clichés. As the Alphabets studied him, so he studied them. It was Beth who broke the silence.

"You live in a very out of the way place, Yabu," she ventured.

The Magician shrugged. "Each to his corner, eh Beth? This just happens to be mine. I find it odd that we haven't been formally introduced, friend."

"No doubt it would have happened a lot sooner, friend, if you hadn't been on quite as intimate terms with the Russian, as you so obviously are," Beth replied with an edge in her voice that nobody present missed.

"Thick as thieves I'd say," Def, the Resident Agent of Provocation added.

Yabu's lips curled into an ironic smile.

"Whilst we may be as 'thick' as cream we are certainly not thieves. We take merely what is offered, be it service, hostility or friendship. We have no need to steal."

Antelope's face creased into a frown.

"That is not our experience of Astapor. Many of our friends are dead because of him. He is our sworn enemy and if you persist with this BS so will you be."

A deep and brooding silence ensued in which they regarded each other. Yabu could see that he had underestimated his opponent.

"Let's just agree to disagree eh? If you are to remain here, you have to do business with the Russian, as you call him. He is the Prime Magician after all and as such occupies the centre. Whilst he reigns, it's his game and we all have to play it."

"And if he's toppled?" Antelope asked with a voice colder than liquid nitrogen.

"Then we play a different game," the Magician replied.

His face was an inscrutable mask, that Antelope for all her guile could not crack. The spaces between them were filling with possibilities though, which would need to be explored more fully in any future they might choose to share.

"Quite a change for you I should imagine; having company?" Antelope suggested heading out on a different tack."

"Oh I always have company," the Magician replied somewhat enigmatically.

"And what does that mean?" Wilber shot, throwing his hat in the ring for the first time.

Yabu turned to face him.

"So Wilber, do you know why you're here?"

"I'm today's Candidate. My name is Justice Wilberforce Muldoon. Most people call me Wilber but..."

"That's not what I asked, but it will do for a start. Shall we get going"

Wilber opened his mouth to say something cutting but then thought better of it. Yabu glanced at a very expensive Omega wristwatch and Wilber, in unconscious imitation of the Magician, did the same.

"It's 9:43. Nae man can tether time nor tide and here we are gossiping on like a pair of old fishwives as though we have all the time in the world. But whilst we do Wilber, you don't, so let's just crack on shall we? Please follow me, friend. You're very welcome to join us ladies but only on condition that you don't shoot me in the back. The poison on those arrows looks especially toxic. My, oh my but you have come a long way."

And with that he was up and moving. Turning on his heel he strode off down the walkway that emerged from the rear of the platform and Wilber scurried after him. The Alphabets were a little more circumspect but followed at well spaced intervals, their bows aimed into the swamp as they scanned the muddy waters for signs of hostile life. None presented itself for inspection but it was there, nonetheless.

All felt it.

22

New Balls

Yabu didn't so much walk as glide. He was a very centred and grounded individual and he walked with his head held completely immobile. He did not, as the Alphabet's did, scrutinise the swamp for signs of life. He felt no sense of threat from anything, it seemed. Master of himself and all he surveyed he was a very attractive figure to Wilber, with a sense of self and style that the youth felt compelled to emulate, should he survive this current ordeal. Nothing was ever wasted in Wilber's head, just filed away for later use.

They barreled down the mesh-covered walkway towards a tree-obscured future. The gloom persisted but then so did Wilber's sense of anxiety, vague and nausea inducing. The game had taken a very odd turn here, like pop music in the 60s when it had gone psychedelic. Most disquieting. Without warning the slatted walkway split into three pathways and lifted up out of the swamp and into the trees. Now they were aerial walkways, torch lit and hand-lined. Beneath each walkway a now-bubbling swamp and an odd amalgam of scents and odours he couldn't quite place, rose to assail his nostrils.

"What's that smell Yabu?"

He couldn't put his finger on it, but soon his attention was directed elsewhere. Now looming up out of the swamp were houses on stilts, He counted at least nine, of varying shapes and sizes and in various states of dilapidation. Each set of houses was served by its own walkway and towards the largest Yabu was headed. The Alphabets were still behind him when he checked but they were lagging, caught in the spell of Otherness that the swamp effortlessly conjured.

Quickening his step, Wilber caught up with Yabu as he entered the Big House. Turning to face Wilber the Magician beaming from ear to ear, flashed his ivory teeth in fair imitation of a Great White Shark. Wilber slammed on the anchors and swayed backwards, almost toppling over but catching himself in the last instant.

"Welcome to my home, Wilber, to my beautiful home. So simple and yet I have everything here that I could ever want."

Wilber glanced around him. The Big House whilst capacious was as austere as a monk's cell. Made of a combination of mahogany and bamboo, it struck one as being a fine example of Jungle Gothic, if such a thing had ever existed. When the wind gusted, the house, like the trees, swayed from side to side. Earlier, out walking through the tall grass he had felt the wind blowing in from the north. Now it was as though the winds were blowing in from all directions at once.

Thanks to Crowhaven's generosity he had a map of the island, but not only that, he had been able to orientate himself. This had always been very important to Wilber and in his darkest hour this sense of knowing where he was, if not who he was or what he was there to do, had guided him away from the abyss. Since he had turned ten, that abyss had been a stark reality, far more real than friends or school or home. Why, he didn't know. It was as though someone had flicked a switch and the Universe had spun itself into a hitherto unimaginable configuration.

In the darkness he had wandered, the bane of everybody's life. His parents had tried, then teachers, then the doctors had prodded and probed. He'd been written up and then written off, prescribed medication and plenty of fresh air. He fell further behind in his classes and his schoolwork. Nothing more was expected of him. Finally he was excluded and he spent most of his days in the family mansion reading existentialist literature and listening to loud, angry music. His parents' wealth both protected and alienated him. Out on a limb he drifted and waited, Nanny, like Madame DeFarges, knitting at the foot of his guillotine until the blade fell and the island reached out for him.

And here he was with a man who, in all seriousness, called himself a Magician. It was all so odd and yet it was more real than the world of shadows he had left behind.

"Do you live here alone?" he asked, piqued by more than curiosity.

Yabu beamed that same smile again.

"Like I said Wilber. I'm never alone. I've so many friends, friends without end, you might say."

Out on the walkway the sound of the Alphabets approaching caught his ear. Yabu caught it too and he cupped his right hand in his left and rested both on his flat stomach. His black suit was of the sharpest cut Wilber had ever seen. It accentuated his lines and curves in just the right measure. The yellow T-shirt was an oddity, the black shoes just right. The shaven head, the glow of health were alluring, envy-provoking. It was all so perfect and yet it was all just window dressing, a visual distraction. It told you nothing about the man. About who he was and what he did.

"This is the middle section of your journey. Where we are going next, your Protectors cannot follow, Wilber. You will have to rely on your agency, much as you did back with Crowhaven."

Wilber nodded.

"News travels fast here. I'm guessing you Magicians are in touch. All, if not most of the time."

Yabu's smile did not falter.

"Most of the time. Do you have it safe?"

Wilber knew, to what the Magician alluded, without prompting. He twisted his shoulder round so that Yabu might see the satchel he had been gifted.

"Might I see it?"

"Do you have something for me? A gift," Wilber urged.

Yabu nodded but made no further move. Wilber set down his bow and arrow and undid the strap, reached in a hand and withdrew the first crystal. The cube, or hexahedron, as Def had called it glittered in the ailing half light and changed the energy and atmosphere of the room. The room seemed both brighter and lighter and Wilber felt less in thrall to this strange man with his beautiful suit and expensive accoutrements than he had done.

He knew now that he was in the presence of a very dangerous animal. A man, if indeed he still was a man, who was capable of anything. Deception, cruelty, murder. And that was just for starters. All that glistened was not gold and not every smile proceeded from a true heart.

Since he had removed the cube from his pocket, Yabu had not taken his eyes off of it. He seemed enchanted.

"Might I hold it," he asked.

"No!" Antelope's voice sliced an icy course through the room and fixed Yabu in an unblinking stare. The rest of the Alphabets spilled into the room, bows drawn and arrows notched, and every arrow pointed at Yabu's heart. You didn't annoy the Alphabets unless you had a death wish.

Yabu reached into his pocket and drew out a spherical object of about 15 cm diameter. Like him it was completely black and absolutely mesmerising. As he did so Wilber placed the Hexahedron back in its compartment within the satchel and re-fastened the strap. Yabu held the object up to the light, which spilled in through the open doorway directly behind him.

"What is that? Wilber asked, as ever overcome by his sense of curiosity.

"One of his balls," Antelope quipped.

"Excuse me?" said Wilber as he turned to look at her, half amused and half surprised.

"It's made of crystal." Beth added, ever helpful.

As if that explained anything. Wilber sighed.

"Isn't everything here? What does it do?"

Now it was Yabu's turn to look amused.

"Well, it won't get you a girlfriend but it might just save your life. This is a crystal ball, much better than a surveillance camera if you know how to use it. It's kind of like having your very own eye in the sky, Wilber." Looking deep into the crystal ball he nodded and smiled knowingly. "Ah I see you were followed. Somebody is coming and they bring violence. There isn't much time, Wilber. We have to go on alone and without them." Here he nodded to the clustered bow-touting gang of Alphabets. "I have something to show you. Something I think you'd like to acquire. You will be tested on every level here. Crowhaven's test is more cerebral than mine. Mine is more physical if equally as psychological. Are you ready to take the test, friend?"

Wilber glanced at his watch; bang on 10.00, then at Antelope. She nodded in silent affirmation and Yabu without further word, shot out of the back of the hut, with Wilber in hot pursuit. Down the aerial walkway they thundered and across a rickety bridge, then following the walkway down for a couple of hundred metres they descended to a landing platform against which two large powerboats had been moored.

Yabu leapt aboard the first and started a large motor at the rear of the craft. Meanwhile Wilber unslung the mooring ropes and off they sped, Yabu skillfully tracing a course through the swamp. The trees gave way to twisted mangroves rather rapidly and once again that sense of threat, he had first detected the moment they had entered the forest, reared its ugly head. It was palpable and it was close but he couldn't see it yet. Wilber stared down into the water. The muddy brine with its subtle currents masked the thing that watched, the unnamed and unknown malice that waited with infinite patience.

"Where are we going Yabu?" Wilber shouted over his shoulder to the standing man who held the tiller behind his back in his left hand.

"You tell me. After all you are a Muldoon and we've had your sort here before. Adventurous types as I recall and brutal in all kinds of ways, you don't want to know about. Met your uncle once. Once was enough. I was lucky to escape with my life that time."

Wilber nodded, his eyes full of darkness, his face a mask of scarcely controlled rage.

"That's what happens when you cross a Muldoon."

"Where is it?" Wilber shouted back over the controlled roar of the engine.

"Just up ahead. We're close now."

Yabu, grinning, throttled back and whilst the boat still shot forward it did so almost silently.

The boat burst through the last tendrils of mangrove out into the open air. Up ahead he saw sand and beyond it sea and rising from the seabed four pinnacles of rock; twisted, crumbling stacks either placed there, or the product of millions of years of weathering and erosion. He didn't know which. Nothing and no one was what they seemed here. The swamp gave way to an estuary. Dipping his fingers in the water he tasted it and found it was part salt water, part fresh.

A short ride northwards, down the estuary and they beached the boat on a sandbank and jumped out. From the sandbank they gazed up at the pinnacles of rock. Wilber estimated they were about sixty metres in height. Another boardwalk led out towards the pinnacles of rock, then split and ran horizontally along the base of each one. Yabu stared up at each of these pinnacles like he was examining a priceless art treasure.

"Not many even make it this far, Wilber."

"Not everybody's a Muldoon. How many?"

"Ten percent. Give or take."

Give or take. Definitely take. He had in younger, keener days done a fair amount of climbing. His uncle, far seeing in most things, had taken him on long weekends in Wales and then in Scotland. George didn't believe in gentling anybody into anything. It started difficult and rapidly became severe. It exhausted him and boy was it dangerous but he said nothing to his father or mother about it. As far as they were concerned, George and he did a little walking and maybe a bit of bouldering. No photographs of their activities ever changed hands. They were confined to the obligatory gurning competitions snapped in hotel lobbies or in car parks. It was all such a laugh or had been. After George went missing everything headed south but even through the dark years he'd kept working his upper body. That kind of strength was important to maintain. And now hopefully he would reap the benefits.

"Up there," he pointed.

"Indeed," Yabu affirmed.

"Which one?"

"Take your pick."

Oh great. He had to choose.

Wilber's gaze moved from stack to stack. The rock did not look as if it was in the best condition. It was either too smooth or too crumbly. Not a particularly enticing combination. And on top of that he had to guess which stack housed the crystal. It was like trying to guess which cup the ball was hidden under. Not a game you wanted to bet your life on. Misdirection was the magician's stock in trade so he had to be careful and he had to resist the temptation to believe that Yabu was there to help him. It was one of the most challenging situations he had ever been in and he would have to deploy a level of guile he had only observed in others.

"I'll take my chances," Wilber said, trying hard to match Yabu's dazzling smile. Better to believe the glass was half full than half empty. Better not to imagine yourself maimed or drowned. Better to imagine you'd always be able to evade Astapor and whatever he sent after you. The horrors of an overactive imagination were best driven back down into the unconscious, not given room to roam.

My, but the mind loved to play its tricks.

"Best of luck," Yabu returned breezily.

Wilber was just about to head off when a sudden thought occurred to him. Well, not so much a thought as a question. It had been frying his noodle for some time, but now he just had to voice it.

"So what do you do here Yabu, when you're not, you know, being a Magician?"

The smile returned with a vengeance. It was like watching a lighthouse being turned on and off.

"I'm a farmer."

"A farmer? And what exactly do you farm Yabu?"

"Why those," the Magician said, looking out over the sea and then pointing with his chin. Wilber followed his gaze and then froze. As shocks went this was a whopper. Out on the boardwalk, which had just moments before been clear and free, lay four enormous crocodiles, sunning themselves, their huge jaws open and ready for business.

Maths had never been his strong point and he had loathed measuring things but Wilber would have put their lengths, tale to snout at well over three metres. As if the prospect of the climb hadn't been daunting enough now he had the reptile threat to contend with. If he fell he wouldn't just be hitting warm water, he would be hitting crocodile-infested water and whatever else was swimming around out there.

"Like I said Wilber, I'm never alone."

Wilber shook his head slowly from side to side, as he looked down the boardwalk at the seemingly insouciant reptiles. What the hell, there was no going back now. He was in it to win it and lest he forget he was a Muldoon. Filling up with pride at the thought of his lofty heritage, and what that had come to mean, in light of his arrival on the island, Wilber removed his jacket and began to stretch as he would have before an important sporting event. Yabu watched him with evident bemusement.

"Anything else I should know?" Wilber asked through gritted teeth,

Yabu considered.

"Wilber, I like you. More than most. Not everybody can deal with the island. Most people who come here are incapacitated. They bitch, whine and moan about what it is they perceive they have lost. Or what they were never given. You're not like that. It seems to me that you have been asleep for quite some time and that the island has awakened you."

Wilber was surprised by these words. They were insightful and honest.

"Thank you. That means more than you know."

"As Magicians, we can't have favourites as we have important functions to perform here. Without us the island doesn't work. We Magicians must always be five. That part of the plan was not Astapor's; it was preordained. Learn as much about the history of the island as you can, my friend. It might just save you."

"I will and once again thank you. Here goes nothing," he said as he set off at a sprint.

Behind him the air filled with the sounds of Yabu's laughter as the winds began to howl.

23

Croc and Zombie Apocolypse

Despite his advanced age, it wasn't long before Great Uncle Muldoon had caught up with his younger, fitter nephews. As the Aged Relic staggered to a halt, Dinosaur George stood with his hands on his hips surveying the surrounding jungle, like he was in a TV advert for deodorant. His regulation-length designer stubble and tanned complexion lent him an air of film-star allure. This was checked somewhat by the sweat stains that drenched his under-arm regions. More Bear Grills than Indiana Jones he was a man who inspired both respect and incomprehension in equal measure.

"Where are you hoping to intercept him George, at Crowhaven's?" Patrick had asked as the Old Man staggered into view, mirroring his brother's stance in the hope that George's cool would someday rub off on him. George, deep in concentration, shook his head and rotated his wrist to look at the timepiece strapped there.

"No, we wouldn't get there in time. No point backtracking. It's almost 10 now. If he's anywhere he'll be heading towards Yabu's. If he survived the Dino chase, if he survived the cube and if he collected the first crystal."

"Lot of 'if's' there," Great Uncle Muldoon wheezed out, still catching his breath. He was bent double clutching his knees like he was about to give birth. Not a pretty sight.

"Don't I know it," George shot back, not bothering to mask his irritation.

He had weighed his options carefully. He'd thought about heading south of the Eight Tower Complex, through the Red

Trees and then venturing northwards, past the Crash Site to the Northern Shore. That was one possible interception route and it would be unexpected. The second option was to take the direct route across the mountain in a north of west direction. A third option was to head north west and skirt the mountain. It was a slightly longer route but it did not have the gradient of the more direct option. After careful consideration he made his pitch.

"What do you think Pat?"

Patrick dabbed his brow with a soiled cloth, that like him, had seen better days.

"Moving at speed like this, in broad daylight, makes us all vulnerable. As we all know the Russian has eyes everywhere."

"Not everywhere," George retorted.

Patrick eyed his brother suspiciously and George turned to look at him. This was so typical of George. You had to push him to loosen his tongue. Just like their father, an excellent poker player, he conveyed as little as he could, without actually lying.

"Know something I don't George?"

His brother shrugged.

"Just heard one or two reports is all. The Russian isn't having everything his own way. That's obvious. The island, it would appear, is fighting back."

"Not something I've seen much evidence of George. Care to elaborate?"

"There's a pack of feral girls on the loose. Some kind of gang. Mostly American teenagers with survivalist genes I think."

"First I've heard of them."

"Well, they're definitely out there. Whatever you've heard. I think it's best we head straight over the mountain. It'll be tough but it's the most direct route. You up for it?"

"Do we have a choice?" Pat whined, but his brother was already gone.

*   *   *   *   *   *   *

Wilber on the white sand sprinting. Yabu's laugh fading behind him, more deranged than the Joker's. Pumping his arms like pistons. Breathing through his nose in short, sharp staccato breaths, as he had been taught to, by his games coach. Thinking about his time on the cross trainer. So much rage, so much resentment. Setting the machine to the highest level of difficulty and then pounding his arms and legs until they ached. The pain felt so good. The agony fanning the fires of rage in his blood. After everything he'd been through it was all there to burn off.

Come on the machine! A voice shouted from the sidelines of a rugby match.

An image of himself, dispatched from the void. Pale yet toned. An ice Prince. Pale blue eyes. Blond hair. Looking at himself admiringly in the mirror. Sculpting his body so there was not an ounce of fat on him. His life may have been going to hell in a handbasket but that was no need to neglect the physical.

Thankful now, for his rage and hard work, he launches himself from the sand onto the boardwalk. Feet on wood, sawn planks that have been sanded then swathed in some sort of wire mesh to aid the grip. Was that chicken wire? Picking up the pace, feeling the rhythm of his breathing change, the world wheeling. Running, running, for all the world running. The crocodiles still, nothing but hurdles to vault. At twenty metres.

Approaching the first, counting down the metres. Fifteen, twelve, ten metres...feet skimming the deck. Then the vast head, turning and that seeming smile, snaggle-toothed, offering greeting. Remembering the power in the jaws. How many pounds of pressure per square inch could they leverage? Someone had told him, but he couldn't remember now. Best that way. No point in imagining the damage they could inflict. Not on his flesh.

Close enough now to see the green eyes, packed with age and cunning, calculating like roadside crows dragging meat as cars approach. Slow, slow, so slow as to be invisible. The armour-plated back, darkening to black in places, the clawed nails on the dainty feet and that huge, pendulous belly. Not starving these saltwater monsters, remnants of another age. Giants dwarfed by dinosaurs but terrifying nonetheless.

Not starving. But what did they eat? Chicken? Did Yabu feed them pieces of chicken like they were amusing household pets? He could see the slow beast lumbering over the sand towards him. Ready to arch the neck, rear and lunge. Slow, slow so very slow until they were not. The fencers lunge, faster than a sprinter over 30 metres.

Five metres, four... now or never.

The jaws opening.

Three, two, one and leap. Airbourne. Sailing over the recumbent form. The snap of turning jaws as images interlace. Road accidents, plane crashes, burnt flesh, charred remains. Dripping blood and splintered bone. Bodies seized and dragged apart as the high pitched whine of agony shifts in pitch. Torn, bloodied fabric. High enough to shatter glass.

The comical waddle of the croc as it hurtles down the gangplank after Wilber. A second reptile turning to charge. Peril fore and aft. Wilber shimmies like a full back and jumps again. Two down. Two to go. Nothing to it. Just like doing the hundred metre hurdles on sports day. Feet pounding the high decks, lungs burning, he jumps again and feels the jaws snapping just inches from a trailing hand. The hot just of rancid breath exhaled. Too close for comfort.

The last croc waiting, heart aflame, fit to burst. No time to count. Total focus as he leaves the gangplank...as seconds pass...as he lands only to sprint again and dive.

*　　　*　　　*　　　*　　　*　　　*　　　*

The Muldoon clan had made good time, first up, then down, like the Grand Old Duke of York. Not only that, they had made it to the edge of Yabu's swamp and George, as keen as an African Hunting Dog, had picked up the scent.

Away to the east, a moaning wind ruffled the yellow grasses as it descended to the shore. Behind them, to the south east, the thinning palms and banana trees, from which they had emerged, swayed from side to side like tired revellers slow-dancing the last few songs of an epic disco. A mile-long descent leading from the volcanic dome and tower complex lay behind them, like a sundial and permanent reminder of the Russian's presence.

"It would appear they are just up ahead," George said pointing down at a row of footprints that pocked the mud and led directly into the mangrove swamp. Clumsy and careless. Not the done thing, not here. One did not leave traces.

"Keep up Uncle," Patrick yelled over his shoulder, whilst simultaneously gasping for breath.

And off they ran once more, away from the jungle and into the swamp, down the path the Alphabets had trodden shortly before. George, Patrick then the Old Man sticking to the trail like glue, following the many footsteps from dry earth to wet mud. The Old Man sinking into the quagmire up to his knees, George hauling him out, shaking his head. Then taking off again. Perpetually in motion, always in flight.

The swamp smiling like it had a secret.

*   *   *   *   *   *   *

The air swarms with threat. The buzz of fear and darker possibilities whirl and draw nearer. Eight sets of eyes watching. Eight hearts keeping time as the adrenaline courses through their blood. Too many variables, too many unseens, Antelope thinks. One can only deal with the moment here. With probabilities.

Nothing is ever certain, despite their prayers. The Alphabets wait and pace, irritated and anxious, boxed within the hut of grass and straw or spread out on the dangling walkways. Waiting for change, for some sign of progress or danger. Bored and yet alert. Beth drumming her fingers on a handrail, Crimson biting her nails. Def listening for sound-laced threat as dark trees lean over them like dirty uncles offering sweets. Soiled bags and stained fingers.

Always shifting, never still; Frantic the least able to settle with genes pitched halfway between a Meerkat and a monkey. Too disciplined to talk though. Too many accidents. Too many sisters lost. Pain, the first and best teacher. And there it is. The detail alerting them their worlds are about to change. Hearing the sound of crashing feet and curses resounding through the jungle. Through mud and then on wood. Not subtle, quite definite. A smile licking Antelope's lips like fire.

"Prey!" Def mouths the word like an act of worship.

Bows are raised and steadied. The gang are ready to pore back down the walkway from whence they came. Wilber, forgotten for now. Only Rudi lingers by the rear door, looking fearfully backwards. Where is he, that man, where is Yabu? She doesn't trust him one jot. Wilber is in peril as are they all. Rudi hangs back, not out of cowardice but because she cares.

The Alphabets move so smoothly, so soundlessly whilst the Muldoons trample and stampede like a herd of cape buffalo. Closer the two forces draw together. One within the house, one outside, on the path. Almost there Def thinks, as her hands grip the blood-stained mallet. The Alphabets pause. Six bows and a hammer. Let them come to us, Antelope thinks. Why sacrifice a strong position? Let them come to us

Twin fates approach. When at last they meet they will surely clash.

24

The Tightening Net

Down the winding trail the Muldoons hare, crumpled and gasping, since the moment they first entered the swamp. Earth first moist, becomes sodden, and then bog. The air is close, swarming with insects and fear. The humidity is off the charts and each of the men is slick with sweat. The Old Man looks like he has just emerged from the sea. Patrick looks like he has been drowned and declared dead. No one is ready for what is set to happen next.

Squelching through the stinking mud, George finds the first one and then a second set of footprints. He points and yelps like a bee-stung dog. Why? Because it's what he does, he looks for answers in the earth and more often than not he finds them. Dinosaurs tiptoe not infrequently through time's tulips in his dreams.

Taking to his heels, once more, he yells for the rest of the family to follow him. His Uncle and Brother have lurched to a halt, but with curses ringing in their ears they attack the trail again.

Patrick and Uncle have always complained, always moaned and whined, only now they have just cause. This time it's about the pace that George has set but they understand his hand has been forced. This isn't just about George getting his own way. It's about saving Wilber. Its about rendering aid. Not that that is easy now. The air is so corrupt here, its scarcely breathable. It is the colour of rotten flesh and just as rank.

The Muldoons previous sufferings are as nothing compared with what they are currently enduring. It is as though time is hammering nails into their extremities, forcing them to reassess their lives and every choice they have ever made. All their instincts can do as they kick in is advise terror.

The 'why' is no longer as important as the 'what'.

There is something up ahead of them that threatens with teeth and foams with hungry purpose. Ragged lumps of breath saw the air neatly in two, like a circus trick, as they run, faster than they have ever run. Above them black branches wave and point. It is as though they have been caged and pinned and only await their torturer and executioner.

The net around them is tightening. You don't have to be a genius to smell death on the wind. Scrambling out of the ankle deep sludge they hop onto a conveniently placed duckboard, sighing with relief. Only George registers anxiety at the transition, understanding that now they follow the trail to where they are directed. No diversions, no shortcuts, just the straight road that may lead straight into the open mouth with its dripping fangs.

Slipping and sliding in worn shoes and battered boots, in spite of the hexagonal wire, chicken or otherwise tacked onto the wooden slats, they feel hope dissolving. Eel-slick the planks of the walkway feel jellied. Nailed together but rotten or rotting at best. Rotten as a pear. The stuff of nightmares. Yet through it all they run, hot on George's smoking heels.

Above them concealed in the black branches and hunchbacked trunks, multiple cameras record their progress. According to the intel they are broken or malfunctioning or recently sabotaged. But this is patently false. Nothing is broken, nothing smashed. The machine continues to watch and to record and those watching eyes are as creepy as spider's eyes and just as black. Shining, revolving, staying in focus, relaying the feed. And always the question. Who watches the watchers?

But to that question there is no answer. No words of explanation, no directing sounds just the hollow groan of the winds up above their bobbing heads. The sky once comically blue rusts like ancient iron. Pink rot mingles with vermillion blood. They are like drowning men hanging suspended in the amniotic waters of time or maskless soldiers running through yellowing fields of gas.

Let me tell you, those who doubt, silent cameras do not whirr, insect-like for the eagle-eyed and the keen of hearing to register. They do what it says on the tin and remain silent. Not one, no solitary machine succumbs to either time or entropy here, not in this forest. Oh no this lot were maintained, are maintained, by Astapor's armies of little techies, tech bots, lovers of technology, computer boffins, programmers, phone-jugglers, jargon swallowers, electrical experts, engineers, designers, bloggers, Visualists.

In spite of what the Other says. He is not to be trusted for all his charm.

All of them know what's at stake, all three. Watching the foliage change and birds taking to the air as they run, they understand their lives have always been headed for this moment. Nothing makes sense here though. Nature riots. The trees are both ancient and futuristic.

Gone these millions of years past or yet to exist. Time is not singular here but multiple. It wavers in fronds and filaments that collide, showering sparks and groans, that fall just beyond the range of most human's sense.

The Elder Brother leads the way as, that which was hidden to Wilber, below the dark waters, begins to rise, like moons or rent. Hanging suspended, the reptiles watch, smiling like the recently diagnosed. Jaws open wide, they yawn death at those they perceive as prey. Open wide to receive me, open wide, whispers the smiling priest and Yabu the dentist leaning over the rotting stumps, clucks and tuts, amused and appalled.

George, suddenly aware, screeches to a halt. He registers change in his environment, looks around and his heart thumps him like the playground bully was wont to, over and over. Uncle and Patrick, skidding to a halt behind him, see what he sees, and their lungs scream like speared birds.

Up ahead, out of the swamp, all glistening scales, seeming bejewelled, the first crocodile hauls itself through mud and froths up onto the walkway. George's mind flashes back, scrolling through geological ages to a time when the fish first emerged from the oceans.

If only it was all academic. But it isn't. No one here gets a free ride and the gator doesn't lumber. No it is a lithe as a rabbit, faster than any would dare expect, deadlier than any coiled snake, as unwound, it counts the beats between human breathes.

No time to weigh or balance probabilities. George sets off at a sprint. The gator, twenty paces ahead grins like the Cheshire cat. If it had lips, it would lick them. Fearless George running at full tilt is only the next meal. It will seize him by the thigh and plop back into the muddy water where it will roll and roll, until he squirms no more. It's in the bag; the reptile only needs to wait.

Then out of the rickety house, trembling on its bamboo stilts come the girls, spilling out into the open air like enraged ants. They have heard the yells and the crashing footsteps of the Muldoon Clan. Taking in the scene, in the blink of an eye, they hurtle towards George who rushes full tilt towards them. Antelope leading, drops her bow and hoists a scimitar aloft. One of Yabu's playthings, the razor sickle, is her toy of choice. The hundred-metre champion beats George to the drop and with a thousand years worth of hate, she swings the blade in a downward arc.

No guillotine fell faster or with deadlier intent. Gators are supposed to wear their armour as well as medieval knights, but this living fossil takes its last gulp of air in shock as the blade slices through skin, flesh and bone and the severed head, all bloody spray, tumbles back into the churning, muddy waters.

George, yelling out his grateful thanks, vaults the tumbling body and continues on his upward trajectory, the wooden slats bowing under each pounding foot. The Alphabets, young, yet wise, step aside as he hurtles past. These men represent no threat; they do not belong to Astapor.

Hope sparkles in Crimson's eyes. Perhaps they are in with a shot. Long odds but worth a punt, worth risking some spilt blood for. But George doesn't have the time.

"Where's Wilber?" the Running Man cries.

"Down on the Dock," Frantic returns, "With Yabu."

Not what he wanted to hear but at least he has a direction. Beth calls out words of warning but George is already gone, intuiting the need, anticipating the play. And all over the swamp, everywhere, gators are rising, their tales sining from side to side as they move, as one, towards the walkway, multiple points of entry open to them.

It is obvious, but terrifying nonetheless. The reptiles swim at a leisurely pace. And why not? They have all the time in the world. Muldoons and Alphabets are conjoined and ready to meet the threat. Tactics and strategy are required, not mindless rage. If rage is to be weaponized, it must be focused.

As one they retreat, withdrawing on tiptoes once more into the rickety house that is Yabu's Palace of grass and straw. Yet the gators are the least of their worries. Another net has been cast, a mobile net that morphs and mutates, a net that is not easily recognizable or even comprehendible, but which closes as the seconds thunder by.

Rudi, with her bat's ears that miss nothing, hears a sound that chills her blood. Her eyes widen and her palms sweat. Fear renders her mute. She cannot quite articulate the words, but soon the others will her, the splashes of mud-caked feet, swollen with pus and lymph are splashing through the swamp.

Everyone not running, freezes to listen.

The air conveys their worst fears to them in the form of growls, hisses and yells. From every direction the splashing feet approach. Uncle peering out of the doorway of the rickety hut, stares back down the trail, down the wooden walkway, into the face of a newly minted horror.

"Patrick, I think we have a problem."

"Those Gators may be mean, but they're no match for me Uncle," Patrick shoots back, over confident but lacking knowledge.

Great Uncle Muldoon shakes his head slowly.

"I wasn't referring to the Gators, Patrick. Look!"

As one, the Muldoons turn and listen to the sound of splashing feet. Patrick, like Rudi, feels his blood cool with terror. The

Muldoons have finally joined the party. Now they know what all the Alphabets have known for some time, but Patrick must confirm what he fears.

"Oh no, that isn't what I think it is, is it?"

"Depends what you think it is," The Old Fossil quips.

"Zombies," he yells, his voice mashed, his eyes wide with terror.

Frantic pokes her head round the door and pans left and then right. Zombies it is, yellow headed, white eyed, steroid-infused walking nightmares. Converging on the swaying rickety house that Yabu built.

"Oh crap."

Patrick racing to the door joins her. Flickering eyes, lit up with the red lightning of burst veins, perform a quick headcount. Twenty at least and fast, very fast. A present from Astapor. Dispatched at a moment when danger is closest and the risks greatest. This is an escalation and young and old alike grit their teeth and prepare for battle.

They are on their own. George is long gone and Wilber may not be coming back. It's all too much for Patrick and he slumps to his knees.

Antelope, though, is young and fearless and she clutches her bloodied sickle and stands her ground as the yellow peril approaches. If she has to go out, she'll go out defending her girls, the only family she ever really cared about. There would be no retreat and no surrender. They would make their last stand here and they would not be going out with a whimper.

It is what it has always been, in her mind, war.

25

Something Sparkles in an Unknown Eye

Back on the sandbank, Wilber's progress is watched by Yabu who is taking his ease, enjoying the moment. He has brought a wicker hamper and a red and white striped deck chair, in which he sits. Next to the chair is a wrought iron table on which stands ice and glasses. He pours himself a Pina Colada and nibbles at pieces of barbequed chicken. At least it looks like chicken, even tastes like it but Yabu being Yabu, suspicions are aroused.

Taking a set of binoculars from his hamper, the Magician scans the open water. The time for ifs, maybes and supposes are over. Action is called for and the Kid from Tamworth has answered the call, launched himself into the fray. Does he have a shot?

Yabu undoes the top button of his shirt and sighs. In his mind's eye he replays the sight of Wilber running shirtless down the boardwalk, vaulting the idling crocs and then diving and hitting the breaking wave before it rolled over, exploding into foam. Slicing through the surf, his dive propels him first five then ten metres. He is forty metres away from the rocky stack when the crocs plop, one, two, three, four, into the water and begin their pursuit. Stroke after powerful stroke, crashes into the brine but will the crocs be faster?

All that Wilber is certain of is that they have seen him and they are moving towards him at speed, aided by millions of years of evolution. He pulls until he is fit to burst, as though his life depended on the outcome, which it does. It is obvious to Yabu that the youth prefers breast stroke but here that will not suffice and he is forced to crawl, churning the waters with his windmilling arms and thrashing feet.

The green water is clear and warm, reminding Wilber that under other circumstances the island would be a paradise. But it is not. Because of the Game. Because of Astapor and the Magicians. Because of the way that life is here. The rage of his personal circumstances begins to colour his vision and he is forced to let it go. The twisted revenge fantasies, the self pity, the messianic self regard. None of it will work. The only thing he has to do is get to the sea stacks before the crocs get to him.

Yabu counts the metres down, watching with his binoculars. This is the life, more exciting than any horse race, more exhilarating than roulette, more dangerous than telling a woman what you really think, about the way she is dressed. Yabu is psyched and sweating and why? Because of the stakes, because of what could happen should the youth succeed. Can he make it? Can he? Yabu's heart begins to race, his palms to grease with sweat. Thirty metres away and there is still everything to play for. The crocs are relentless. Yabu can almost taste their excitement. They are close and closing in on their prey. Four of the beasts converging on his racing form. Closer, closer until it is almost certain the boy will succumb and be dragged under, torn apart limb by limb and then jammed in various holes to rot and tenderise.

Twenty metres, fifteen metres, twelve, nine.

Yabu, holding the binoculars with one hand, begins to make circling motions with his free arm. It is unbelievable but he finds himself routing for Wilber, not the crocs. This is a first.

"Go on boy, go on."

The excitement in his voice would be contagious if there were anyone there to hear him, but he is alone. Go on. Go on. Wilber is there. He has reached the rock but so too, are the crocs. With a sinking heart, Yabu acknowledges that it is all over. The reptiles have won like they almost do.

But no! Wait.

With an extraordinary surge of skill and power, Wilber has gathered his strength and at the last moment heaved himself free of the water. With his right arm he reaches, stretches and grasps the rock of the second pillar on the left hand side of the centre. Bat-like he clutches and dangles, his fingers remembering old strength. He pants, he gasps but adrenaline fuels him and he climbs. Below him are only swirls and ripples. Yabu senses the rage in the blood of the thwarted crocs as hand over hand, the boy climbs to safety. Well, relative safety.

Yabu finds himself standing and punching the air, whooping like a carnival barker, spinning like a top in celebration. But the show isn't over, not by a country mile. Yabu reminds himself of this terribly exciting fact as once more he raises the binoculars to his eyes.

Wilber is climbing with some measure of skill as below him the crocs swim in circles around the brine swamped base of the pinnacles. He is ahead for now, but for how long? Yabu knows what is coming, and his anxiety begins to rise and spike.

Nothing matters to Wilber now but survival and the need to achieve. Fear anchors him in the moment and he focuses, focuses with deadly intent.

God but he's quick, Yabu thinks, as Wilber zips up the second stack. 'Where did he learn to do that?', the Magician thinks. Having cheated the crocs of their meal, at least for now, he moves closer and closer to that special prize.

But where is it? Where the second crystal is, Wilber thinks and he nears the top of Crumbling Stack. He wrestles with his doubts but soon he will need to wrestle with quite another kind of terror, Yabu reflects. Will he acquire the crystal? Suddenly it matters to Yabu that he will. He must.

Just then a chilling sound carried over the waves, assails the ears of both youth and man. Reaching the top of the stack, Wilber hauls himself to his feet, steadies himself and looks back towards the sand where the Magician is watching. He chuckles when he sees the deck chair, the ice and glasses. Why not? Then, the hideous noise again, dragging him away from his sense of achievement.

Uneasily he turns, then shades his eyes as the sun momentarily dazzles him. Squinting he looks, squinting he peers. What is that?

Two specks approaching at speed, heading straight for him through the tumbling air. Could they be birds, eagles? He watches and waits, a sense of acute anxiety growing within him. More screams, more terrible cries forcing him to press his hands to his ears. In the distance another sound, almost imperceptible, like the buzzing of flies.

*　　　*　　　*　　　*　　　*　　　*　　　*

The bamboo village receded at a rate of knots, like a train of rattling, swaying carriages, diminishing in size and importance as it raced towards its vanishing point. The point where it was no longer visible was the point at which it could be forgotten and ceased to be a current concern.

As much as it pained him, George forced himself to forget what lay behind him. Patrick, Great Uncle Muldoon and the Alphabets were no doubt in peril, it was just he couldn't help them right now. Wilber was the priority and they must help themselves. Down the walkway, heart pounding, but not exhausted, he bounded, like a wolf hunting. Adrenaline, anxiety and a certain kind of hunger combined in a heady mixture to give him a dangerous edge.

He was not unaware of the screams and roars behind him but he had shut them out of his mind. Where was he? Where was the boy? He moved his head from side to side, scanning the mangrove swamp for a sign or a possibility. Something registered suddenly on George's radar. A boat, Yabu's boat. 'Note to self; steal boat. Retrieve Wilber. Easy!'

*　　　*　　　*　　　*　　　*　　　*　　　*

The howls and shrieks got louder, as did the splashing. Bodies approached and with them came a new level of threat and the possibility of doom. Frantic notched an arrow and let it fly. It struck the neck of a lumbering zombie and lodged in the voice box. The zombie let out a muted howl and plucked the arrow from its flesh. Then gripping the arrow with hands of unbelievable strength it began to gnaw on the shaft, as though the arrow were a corn on the cob, until the wood splintered and the arrow broke. Disregarding the pieces, it clambered onto the walkway and sniffed the air. Even from a distance, it stank so bad that no self-respecting fly would go anywhere near it.

The white eyes bulged and the yellow flesh, covered in suppurating pustules, seemed to ripple in the changing light. Each member of the Alphabet Gang froze and watched it with a curious mixture of both fascination and horror. Turning with agonising slowness the flesh-eating zombie looked up towards the Big House and seemed to smile. In the doorway Frantic shrunk and Rudi let out a fearful yodel. Even Beth gulped and faltered.

Behind them, on the Walkway, that just moments before George had thundered down en route to the dock, two more zombies appeared and began to move with an unnatural calm and deliberation up towards the house where the girls and the Muldoons had taken temporary shelter. In a matter of minutes the Bamboo Village had been overwhelmed and the Big House surrounded. Great Uncle Muldoon, ever the pragmatist, weighed up their options in the blink of an eye.

"Patrick, girls, quick into the trees."

"Wouldn't it be better to barricade ourselves in and fight from the sanctuary of the House?" Semantic reasoned.

"Screw that!" Antelope spat through clenched teeth, pushing the door-hugging girls aside and heading for the grinning zombie. It didn't matter that the beast towered above her, Antelope had both reach and audacity, not to mention a razor sickle. The zombie went the same way the gator had, crashing back into the swamp minus a head. As one, the girls cheered and punched the air as though their shooter had just scored a basket from the halfway line.

Antelope curled her lip into a sneer and blew a troublesome hunk of snot out of her left nostril.

"Right girls, do what the Old Man said. Up into the trees! Now!"

And up they shot faster than speeding monkeys into the uppermost branches of the swaying trees. Thankfully the village was surrounded by trees. Either Yabu was lazy and hadn't bothered to clear them or they had been left as a matter of policy, for camouflage and cover. Not that the kids were interested in the history of the village. They just wanted to escape the gnashing jaws.

As did the Muldoons but neither of them were climbers, one on account of his advanced age the other on account of his level of alcohol consumption. Def, swinging the axe and knocking over the attacking zombies, like they were coconuts at a church fete, was forced to give each man a hand up, before taking to the trees herself.

Finally, everyone but the Gators and Zombies were safely clinging to high branches up in the forest canopy. From the sanctuary of their swaying nests the Gang watched as the dog-faced, jaundiced-looking zombies swarmed up the bamboo stilts and into the compound. Bursting through the doors and roof they tore up the place before realising the prey they sought was safely ensconced in the trees above them. Then they too began to climb.

*   *   *   *   *   *   *

The smell on top of the pillar was bad but the sense of paranoia was worst. Everywhere, there were branches, and it took a while for Wilber to put it together. A nest, he'd landed in a bloody, great nest. And then he saw them, incredibly well camouflaged but unmistakable. Eggs. And they were huge. Bigger than ostrich eggs, bigger than dino eggs, about the size of a human head.

The thought caused him to shiver for all that the day was baking hot.

Anxiety gnawed and clawed at him and he glanced at his watch. 10.27. Time wasn't that much of an issue. Not yet anyway. But staying alive was. Peering over the edge of the sea stack, Wilber took in the forty metre drop and the circling crocs with a dry-mouthed gulp. Then the sound of screeching caught his attention.

Like a top, the youth spun and looked out to sea. The dots were getting closer. Only they weren't just dots anymore. Now they had wings. Wilber cursed and looked frantically about him. Where was the crystal? Dropping to his knees he began frantically scrabbling amongst the heaped branches. Wrinkling his nose and fighting hard to keep his breakfast down, Wilber found both his rage and his fear spiralling ever higher, twin threads in a nightmare strand of real-time DNA playing out like a sped-up nightmare.

It didn't take too much searching for the penny to drop. That smell was meat, rotten flesh and from the look of the splintered bones and cracked skulls it looked like the nests were where momma and daddy ate breakfast, raw and alive.

Oh dear. What to do? Another glance. God but the birds were fast. What were they? Eagles? Condors? No...no... That would be too easy, too predictable. This was the island. A place where everything was warped and mutated. Here, even the butterflies were killers. What to do? The voice in his head was screaming. Wilber felt like he was in a burning car in a multiple car pile-up, strapped into the front seat, with multiple lacerations, bleeding out, leaking blood and plasma, as the roaring flames raced towards the tank.

Whatever else happened he didn't want to burn to death. Not here. Not anywhere. He dropped to his knees again and resumed searching. Damn it! This was one pillar, there were four. 11-11. What was this? Some kind of gateway. No, more likely it was some kind of graveyard. His thoughts were racing and his skin was drenched in sweat. There just wasn't enough time. He had to eliminate the eggs from his enquiry. It was just possible that the second crystal was inside one of the eggs.

And if it was; lucky him. Easter had come early. There was just the question of the birds racing towards him and that was no question at all. By virtue of being up on the stack he was already the enemy and no doubt late breakfast.

Hoisting the first egg aloft Wilber hurled the speckled form down onto the rock at his feet. Instantly it cracked open and bloody yolk spattered his trousers, lower belly and face. His sense of disgust almost unmanned him. Then he clamped his left hand to his jaw. Something limp and leathery had flopped out of the egg and lay unmoving on his left foot.

Wilber felt his stomach turning over but he forced himself to look into the shattered pieces of egg. Damn. The egg wasn't empty but sadly no crystal. No, its treasure was more of a carbon-based confection. A sudden burst of agony burst through his foot and Wilber hopped backwards, almost losing his balance, tumbling back down the stack into the waiting mouths of the crocs. It took a few moments for him to work out that the 'thing' had bitten him.

Enraged he flipped the chick over with his foot. It was undoubtedly a bird but when he saw the head Wilber let out a scream that would have shattered glass.

*   *   *   *   *   *   *

Yabu took a sip of his Pina Colada and let out a low chuckle. Ice and a slice, just how he liked it. The birds were inbound and Wilber had just discovered the alarming truth about what he was about to face. What a show! The early morning clarity of blue skies and sparkling waters had been replaced by a dirty, pink sky filling with polluting clouds, and darkening waters. This constituted a far more Gothic palette and much more to Yabu's taste.

The Magician lowered his binoculars and wiped the sweat from his brow, then raised them again. The birds were closer and Wilber was standing on the edge of the ledge nerving himself up ready for the jump. His first search had yielded nothing but the horror of what was growing in the eggs, all of which the youth would have to crack open if he was to find the object of his quest.

Such a beautiful vision. Those four pillars out in the bay, crumbling, yet perfect. And the Game, his creation. A physical and a psychosocial trial and just when you thought it was all over you realised it hadn't even begun.

"And there he goes!"

Yabu was guffawing. The kid was unbelievable! He had flung

himself off the ledge into the gap. Yabu was sure he would plummet to his death but no, he'd made it and was clinging to the edge of the second ledge. Now he was hauling himself up. Another top, another nest to explore and the birds close and getting closer.

Engrossed as he was, Yabu didn't hear the footsteps until it was too late and the knife had been pressed against the side of his neck, tight against the carotid. The blade was sharp; he could feel that. A little pressure, a gentle slash and he would squirt and spray the sand with his life's blood. Thirty seconds and it would be over. The Observer had been observed and would soon be dispatched. It was the way of things. Nevermind.

"Enjoying the show?"

"Heh, George, long time no see. How you been?"

Yabu lowered his binocs but didn't turn his head. Even he wasn't that dumb.

"You know I don't need you, don't you?" George was whispering in Yabu's ear, trying hard not to carve the hated Magician's face up like it was a kebab on a spit.

Yabu chuckled. Oh he was loving this. George was so dumb.

"You might not need me Old Sport, but the island does and you know how nature abhors a vacuum. Kill me and you have to become me. Feed the crocs, run this stage and you can never leave. How about it, wanna trade up?"

George thought about this for a matter of seconds, then brought the weighted handle of his machete down on the back of Yabu's neck. Instantly the Magician and his consciousness parted company. Quickly, George flipped him over on his belly and tied his hands together, picked up the binocs, then running over the sands, returned to where he'd ditched the speedboat and powered it up.

Yabu could wait, Wilber couldn't.

As the Magician had before him, George scanned the stacks with the binocs. Wilber was up there smashing eggs and the birds were almost upon him. Only they weren't really birds, they were something far worse, as he knew from experience.

George looked down into the back of the speedboat and his gaze alighted on the thing he had found there. A gift from providence or just luck? George believed in neither but who cared. Spinning the wheel, George opened up the throttle and the boat roared over the waves and round the second pillar.

Up above Wilber was preoccupied. George only hoped he wasn't too late.

26

Climb, Climb, Climb!

The Girls and the Muldoons, like Wilber, had their own problems. They watched with fear-haunted eyes as beneath them the yellow-skinned zombies climbed ever higher up the swaying trees, pausing every now and again to grunt or bellow, craning their necks to ensure their prey was still trapped, with nothing but sky above them. Antelope stared down at the rising menace. She was damned if she was going to succumb to fear but they had never been in a tighter spot than they were now. And all because of Wilber, because they'd wanted to help. No! Best not to be bitter. Best not to blame anybody for their predicament. There would be time for that later when they were being pulled apart by the lumbering squad of yellow meat sacks.

It was hopeless. Each zombie was possessed of such strength, it was hard not to envy them their enhancements. They were no longer merely human. The human had been driven from them chemically. They had been transformed entirely into a different species whose one and only thought and drive was the acquisition of human flesh. Looking down between her legs Beth gulped. She still had a machete handy but the odds were firmly stacked against them. Beth, realist that she was, doubted her slices and terrified hacking would detain her pursuers for very long. Would she die with courage or go out screaming? Little by little it mattered less and less, as hand over hand, the zombie army closed in upon them all.

Their bellows and howls were more joyful now but no less frenzied. Def wondered whether it wouldn't be better to drop from her tree and take her chances in the muddy, bloody water below but a still, small voice of reason within implored her to stay put. The last few feet were being climbed by the dauntless monsters and the moment the Alphabets all dreaded was approaching. They all of them saw this, understood it, pinned and virtually powerless as they were. It was only a matter of seconds now, before powerful hands gripped them and dragged them back down from their lofty perches, or hurled them screaming, into the teeming water.

Rudi observed the unfolding scene with calculating eyes. Her mind was detached, almost calm in spite of the impeding calamity. Memory nuzzled at her like a friendly dog and without knowing why, she began tearing a length of wound fabric from her camouflaged arm and wrapping it around an arrow head, removed from her back-slung quiver. Then steady, if dirty fingers, reached for the buttoned pocket on her left leg and slipped inside.

Slowly, she withdrew the small bottle and held it aloft for the others to see, the clear liquid seeming to glow in the ailing half light. Turned heads arrived at the same conclusion instantaneously. Time and silence had moulded them together as a thinking unit. No words needed to be spoken as each Alphabet, acting on her initiative, drew out their own clear bottle of liquid, dousing rags and torn pieces of fabric, with the scented infusion, which were then wound around a firmly held arrow head and its upper shaft. With muscle-knotted legs, each girl clutched her tree trunk, ensuring that hands and arms were free to unsling bows and to notch arrows ready for the final assault. Precious seconds passed and then the simultaneous click of plundered lighters could be heard, setting the tightly wound rags alight. The zombies, as one, paused and the horror of flame danced in every filmed eye. The realisation was sudden and fierce and they all of them surged as the first wave of arrows just a few feet above them sped down into their climbing bodies.

The effects were immediate and devastating. Each yellow body ignited and was engulfed by avenging flame. Roars of rage and agony filled the mangrove swamp and silence consumed the clambering killers as, one by one, they plopped into the muddy swamp and the waiting mouths of the grinning gators. Even the raucous birds that haunted the forest canopy were quiet, marking the moment as a kind of victory, for the island was rid of one more horror, one more terrible menace. Nothing and no one would mourn the passing of these terrible killers for all had suffered at their hands. But that was as nothing now. Wave after wave of arrows sped down bringing their reign of terror to an end. Others might follow, more noxious and more cunning than this latest crop but not for a while. Perhaps never. The Russian was not one who rewarded failure, for so their extinction would be perceived.

The girls were calculated and unhurried for there was nothing the zombies could do to arrest their downward trajectories. There was nowhere for them to go but into the swirling waters and the snapping jaws.

Fight as they might with their terrible strength they were no match for the hungry gators, who clamped them in their jaws and dragged them down into the cold, churning waters. For all that they felt no fear, they sensed, with rising desperation, the extinguishing of their lives as the amassed force of gators tore them bodily, limb from limb, turning the waters vermillion red in the process.

Semantic counted off the bodies as they were reduced from humanoid forms to bloody hunks of flesh and splintered bone. It was quite a sight, and the girls, like the birds, watched in satisfied silence. They felt no pity, not one iota of remorse, for had they not acted, they would have been torn apart and feasted upon by their pursuers. It was the law of the jungle that operated out here. Kill or be killed. What could be simpler? The gators certainly weren't complaining, for they had never in their long lives, harvested such a crop of deliciously rotten meat. In their delirium they rolled end over and over in joyous frenzy, as the deathly waters closed over the last of the flaming zombies, as it edged from hateful life to harmless death.

The girls waited until the waters had stilled before descending cautiously and silently from the upper reaches of the forest trees, down onto the walkways that threaded their wired planks through the swamp. They stared into the slack flows of water that had, just minutes before been threshed into a bloody foam. Such horrors constituted their staple diet of images on the island and they were no longer appalled by what they saw. Blunted, they had been, but still they remained sharp. No one spoke, not even the Muldoons, who had had to be helped down from the treetops they had been guided into, when the splashing feet of the zombies had first been heard. Each absorbed the lessons of this encounter without comment. What didn't destroy you here just made you less inhibited and more resilient. Life was cheap and passed in the batting of an eyelid. Antelope was the first to move and the others filed into place behind her, without comment, padding along the duckboards back into Yabu's now wrecked hut to await the results of Wilber's trial.

The doors had been yanked from their hinges and the walls shredded and smashed. Bizarrely though, the Magician's throne was still intact, leading Edie to wonder whether the Magician hadn't deployed his considerable powers to safeguard a symbol of his own ascendancy and the rule of law. As they awaited developments Rudi, along with the others, pondered the far-sightedness of Mr Lapp, their friend and ally, who had distributed the small bottles with the clear liquid within them, to each member of the gang with the instruction that they were only to be used in the event of dire emergency. No-one doubted that their encounter in the swamp constituted just such an emergency.

27

The Reckoning

George, dumping Yabu unceremoniously onto some oil-soaked rags, in the bow of the boat, roared off the sandbank and out towards the centre-right pillar where Wilber was wilfully smashing eggs with a pointed rock.

As the boat shot forward at full throttle the magician groaned and sat up. He had an egg shaped lump on the back of his head where his long-time adversary had struck him with the handle of his machete and he touched it gingerly. There was no blood but the lump was sizable and throbbing. Yabu shot George a contemptuous look but the fossil grubbing thug was having none of it. He growled low in his throat, like a guard dog who had a prisoner cornered, and Yabu raised his hands placatingly.

Some people you just didn't get in the way of.

George, seeing that Yabu was no threat throttled back, fearful he would either capsize the boat or strike one of the sea stacks. At a near crawl he circled the rocky pillar, neck cranked backwards so that he could watch his nephew. But Wilber wasn't watching him. He was too busy focusing on the task at hand, smashing the last of the four eggs nestled amongst the stones and bones on top of the crumbling sea stack.

As George gazed upwards it was obvious that Wilber had not found the object of his search and that whilst aware of the impending arrival of the parent 'birds', he was not in full possession of the facts and, as such, extremely vulnerable. Like the rest of the Magicians on this Gothic Shagpile of an Island Yabu had stacked the decks in his favour. Despite his smile, the man was not a friend.

Wilber would want to jump and he mustn't. He would believe himself invincible and he wasn't. This Game was set up that way; to make you believe you could do anything and then to demonstrate you couldn't, that your belief was erroneous and that you were deluded, abandoned and without hope.

Oh yes, that was the way it was played. Take this problem as an example and you would find an apt illustration. The central two pillars were doable but the outer pillars were not. Jump and you would fall short and even if you got a hand hold, the rock would crumble. Cruel, so cruel.... the island and the minds that inhabited and ruled it were capable of nothing but cruelty. Refined nonetheless, but cruelty all the same.

Just as well Wilber had George in his corner. The birds were fast approaching and George felt his pulse beginning to race. He told himself to breathe and to calm himself. If it had just been him he wouldn't have given a stuff but it wasn't just him anymore. It was his family and guiltily his thoughts returned to Great Uncle Muldoon and Patrick.

Cutting the engine, he let the boat drift into the central stack. Then he took a line and made fast the boat, using a protuberant rock as a mooring point. Shooting Yabu a threatening glance he reached down and picked up the bolt action rifle he had placed in the bottom of the boat and checked the weapon was loaded. It was, so he stooped once more and picked up a long, stout piece of bamboo that was at least nine feet in length and prepared to climb.

Yabu scrutinised his every move, a sly expression on his face. He understood exactly what George was up too and saw no reason to lunge at him in an attempt to stop the Adventurer or to be foolish in any way. Events would go the way they were going to go. It was not his job to intervene, merely to observe. Intervention was God's prerogative, wasn't it? Thinking this, made him chuckle aloud, and George, gun slung over one shoulder, bamboo pole over the other, spun round with suspicion etched into his features. His left arm was outstretched and touching the volcanic rock, both feet were up on the side of the boat. It didn't take a genius to see that his position was precarious. The man had poise and an ability to find a point of balance in most situations, but not all.

The sudden bang beneath his feet could not have been anticipated and before he could stop himself, George was tumbling over backwards and the boat was dipping and tipping towards the landwards side. The gunwale on which he stood reared up, like a striking cobra. His mind raced, desperate to understand, which it did almost immediately, as fear clutched his heart in its talons. The crocs had awaited their moment and at the point of greatest vulnerability they had struck.

Falling through the air there was nothing he could do to arrest his momentum. All he could do was try to land correctly, to right himself and avoid the terrible punishment that awaited him if he fell into the churning green sea.

The fall seemed to last forever and when he finally struck the deck George found the gun and the pole strapped to his back lent sufficient weight to unbalance him further. With a dread he found difficult to control he sensed himself toppling over backwards. The port side of the boat was raised above him, the water into which he was headed, now down below him. Full of teeth and things keen to rend his flesh to shreds, the ocean sloshed and slopped.

His mouth was a comic 'O' whilst up, on the sea stack above, Wilber, hearing the commotion in the boat, peered down over the edge, shock and fright registering in his eyes, as he beheld the scene. Behind him the whoosh of wings and the outstretched legs with their hooked talons implied his own doom was near, but Wilber was oblivious.

It was over and George was closing his eyes. He'd outrun the odds for so long but they'd finally caught up with him. The ocean would claim him, the lustful, laughing ocean along with those salt-water loving crocs. Not long now, not long.

Time was slowing down further and further as a hand reached faster than a snapping turtle to seize George's broad and seamy leather belt. Strong, black, nimble fingers closing and then heaving, arresting his fall and pulling him back into the safety of the boat.

Two bodies falling backwards, one landing safely on top of the other, as the body beneath reached round the neck of the saved man with a crooked blade, pressing it against his throat, savouring the irony.

As the water bubbled and thrashed and the boat righted itself Yabu held George fast in his embrace. Croc, cobra, boa all in one person. Saved for the noose. George's blood turned to ice and the curse in his throat rattled his teeth. To come so far only to lose it this way was hard to bear. And Yabu, with terrible strength, was pulling him closer to whisper something in his ear. Not long became no time, then less than a second.

The stroke of the knife would be like the drawing of a bow across the violin string of his throat. Would the blade be so sharp he couldn't feel it?

Nothing. Nothing? And without warning and in a state of shock George found himself launched into mid air, catapulted back towards the rock face. Scrambling hand over hand he raced up the crumbling rock as Wilber suddenly, cognizant of the terror approaching him on beating wings, turned to face his own Waterloo.

The shock was great but less now that he had observed the developing young in the mottled eggs. Shattered, scattered shell and stinking yolk was everywhere but he didn't care, because it didn't matter. The bird with the human head was hovering above him, poised to seize and kill. To drive its poisoned talons through his back into his heart. To eat him on the wing.

The second bird was wheeling above him, giving the first, room to manoeuvre, only they weren't birds, but neither were they humans. Wilber knew what they were but he hesitated to name them. They had emerged from Graeco-Roman Myth, a story recounted to him by his Grandfather in the nursery. His Grandfather knew his Homer and had taught Wilber well which was why he remembered now.

The cries of the birds were terrible, which was why Odysseus had had himself bound to the mast of his ship. Others hearing those cries had gone mad or leapt overboard, drawn by feelings of lust and notions of love to those that called from the nearby island. But arriving on that rocky shore they had found only death, torn to pieces by the merciless and voracious sirens.

Yes, sirens, for that was what these creatures were. Sirens. That was what he was looking at now. The half-woman, half-bird, hovered above him weighing him up. Myth made flesh, nightmare brought to life by the horror-obsessed Russian. Literature supplied the inspiration, Astapor the genes and the surgery.

Wilber stood up as the Siren swooped and lunged. He stood up and he stood stock still, master of his fear. His arm reached backwards and his fingers closed around the single arrow head in Alphabet-gifted quiver.

The teeth were neatly vampiric and the hot breath upon his face sweet and tinged with cinnamon. But all he did was smile and thrust the arrow head through the feathers, into the pounding heart. The beautiful head crowned with its copper locks arched backwards and the body tumbled down into the seething sea, compensation for the meat-deprived crocs.

When she hit the ooze, her mate's scream split the sky but not for long. George, cresting the summit, quickly shouldered his rifle and sent the second beast arcing downwards into the hellish brine. The roar of the blast from the rifle was strangely satisfying, even soothing, as though something human were being asserted. The crocs made swift work of the feathered monsters and before the waters smoothed once more, Wilber had vaulted across the divide onto the outer right stack. Nine eggs lay there toasting, and eight had been shattered before the ninth yielded the prize of the yolk-smeared crystal.

Kicking the young into the sea, Wilber felt no remorse, only a renewed sense of resolve. Holding the octahedral crystal up to the sun he felt its power entering his mind, like a series of speeding light rays. The light sped up his mind, a structure itself composed of light, but largely hidden, mostly remote and unknown. But not for now. The evil sun might glower but the crystal, buried within the protective egg, still glinted. Its sparkle leant Wilber a spirit of malicious defiance. That he would not borrow. That he would keep.

Placing the second crystal in Crowhaven's dripping satchel, Wilber vaulted back onto the second stack where George watched and waited, a smile curling at the edges of his lips. Wilber, in landing, ditched the bamboo pole and stared deep into his Uncle's eyes. Nothing was said but much was communicated, then both man and youth climbed back down the crag and into the bobbing boat.

Yabu sat cross-legged in the prow of the boat playing a game of patience with himself. As George took the wheel and started the engine, Wilber untied the mooring line and they cast off. There was no need to race now. George at the wheel took his time, looking every inch the unshaven hero. As the sea stacks receded into the distance the Older Muldoon mulled over his options. Momentous things had just happened, things he did not understand. He did not look at Yabu and Yabu did not look at him but both were aware of what had happened. Both had had the chance to kill the other but neither had. Now why was that?

Down past the jetty where the now sated crocs sunned themselves, past the sandbank and back into the swamp. Throttling back even further George almost let the boat drift its way back home. The river arced and the river bent and hidden eyes watched them from the sanctuary of the trees or the water. It was not too long before the jungle jetty loomed and a new set of problems presented themselves. As the boat bumped into the pier, George took a length of rope and yanking the Magician to his feet, bound his wrists. Then taking a second, longer length made a noose which he placed over the Magician's head and around his neck. He wasn't exactly gentle about it either and anybody watching would have questioned the necessity of such an action. Yabu winced once or twice but did not complain. Wilber secured the boat both fore and aft and then leapt nimbly onto the jetty and strode purposefully up the boardwalk back towards Yabu's Bamboo and Ebony Palace.

His eyes shone bright with the light of success whilst simultaneously burning with the fires of rage. His satchel swung behind him, a little heavier, since the successful completion of his second mission and the retrieval of the Great Crystal of Air. George trailed in his wake, dragging Yabu on the end of the knotted rope. The Magician's hands were tied behind his back, whilst the cruelly knotted rope circled his neck. With every yank and pull, the bound man gasped and wheezed for air but George was indifferent to his suffering. Through the forest they trudged until finally buildings began to appear. They were back.

Upon entering the village, they saw about them the signs of a great and violent struggle. Many of the bamboo structures appeared to have been hit by a tropical storm but Wilber knew that this was only partly true. The storm was human or it had been once, before it had been 'adjusted'. As Uncle and Nephew approached Yabu's hut, the hinged rear door creaked open and a blood and mud stained Def and Edie stepped out with questioning looks.

Wilber tapped his satchel and smiled and Semantic, reading the signs, did a little victory dance until Def skewered her with a Death stare. Seeing that Wilber had returned triumphant, the Alphabets gathered round to slap his back and offer their congratulations, but for all their chattering pleasantries, Wilber was not amused. He moved them aside and pushed his way through the battered door. Entering Yabu's pad, the Muldoon Youth walked over to the vacant throne, which he kicked over, whilst George dragged the prisoner over the floor to where the throne had been situated. When he was happy that they were safe and no dangers lurked, George loosened the noose without removing it. Yabu cleared his throat and looking around his formerly luxurious residence, flashed Wilber his most charming smile. Even in adversity he was a joy to watch.

"Ahh Wilber. Welcome back... to my once beautiful home," he purred, as silken as ever, but Wilber was having none of it.

"I ought to kill you Yabu, you treacherous dog."

"You're not the murdering type Wilber and like I said, we

Magician's don't have favourites. If you make it here you can make it anywhere."

Antelope, seeing Wilber's reaction, stepped forward and, raising her bow, aimed it straight at the Magician' heart. As before, Yabu seemed unphased, but Wilber shook his head. Everyone understood and the Alphabets, followed by Patrick and Great Uncle Muldoon, filed out of the room and began their return journey to the edge of the swamp. Last to leave was Def, who unsheathed and then handed Wilber her Bowie Knife and then she too was gone. George, ignoring Yabu, watched Wilber, whilst Wilber, ignoring George, only had eyes for the Magician.

"Why would anybody want to live in the middle of a swamp populated by Crocodiles?" he asked, his voice ringing with incredulity.

"Gators in the swamp, crocs at sea. Pay attention, Wilber." Yabu said in gentle reprimand.

For a time there was silence and then the Magician spoke.

"The island chose me, Wilber. I just made myself available. It's not for everyone, this life."

Wilber was unmoved.

"Of all the things you could have been. All the things you could have done? Why this?"

Yabu seemed disappointed.

"Why not? This is me, Wilber. It's what I am."

Wilber nodded.

"Would you give us a moment Uncle?"

George said nothing and he wouldn't look at Wilber. He just walked out of the door and without a backward glance followed the others back through the swamp. A short while later, Wilber emerged from the shredded hut with a grim expression on his face, wiping the blade of the knife. It was time to move on.

28

The Clash

It didn't take Wilber too long to catch up with the others for all that they were moving at quite a lick with George in front and Great Uncle Muldoon at the back of the queue line. Immediately Frantic dropped back to walk beside him?

"So, did you finish him?" she asked.

"As if. I cut him loose. I'm not a murderer."

"Not yet," Antelope muttered under her breath.

Wilber hearing this, sped up to walk beside her. He needed to have a word.

"I'm having a hard time with this," he said.

"Welcome to our world Wilber," Def interjected, as sour as a crab apple.

Beth was more sympathetic.

"Think of it as a lovely afternoon stroll Wilber," she said consolingly, putting her arms round Wilber's shoulders.

"Ja, zat is just the way you should think about it. It's much more fun if you do zat. And also you von't end up suffering from Post Traumatic Stress Disorder," Rudi declaimed joyously. In her world every cloud had a silver lining whilst for Wilber every silver lining had a cloud.

"But people are dying," he whined.

Semantic was unimpressed.

"What, you mean those zombies? They were already dead, Wilber."

"No," Wilber shouted, suddenly furious. "Not just the zombies and even they were human once. Anybody who finds their way into this swamp is croc bait and you know it. Question is, what are you going to do about it?"

Semantic, ever-literal shrugged with indifference.

"Everything's gotta eat! You, me, them, everybody!"

She stated this simply, as though it were just a matter of fact, not open to debate or discussion. She stated it as though she were talking to a child who lacked even the most basic grasp of reality.

"Even the crocodiles?"

Edie nodded.

"Especially the crocodiles. Like us they are part of the food chain. What gives you the right to judge another animal's lifestyle, to say that the crocs don't have a right to live the way they choose to live, that they should eat this and not eat that. Evolution is evolution buddy, life lives on life. Humans have had things their own way for so long they have become isolated from reality. They kill millions of animals every day and nobody questions it but if just one of them gets eaten by another animal they go into shock or they go on the rampage."

Edie, normally so level, had gotten aerated and that was enough to make most people back down but not Justice Wilberforce Muldoon. He was not one for rolling over.

"This isn't about evolution Edie. This isn't the natural order. This is a game set up by some sicko for his own amusement. He's sat up on the top of that hill, in a tower, playing a god-damned computer game, only this ain't no virtual thrill, it's real."

Great Uncle Muldoon was not impressed.

"Don't say 'ain't', Justice, say 'isn't'. That is not the way you were brought up."

George rolled his eyes.

"I'm not entirely sure that matters Uncle."

Great Uncle Muldoon folded his arms.

"It matters to me."

Wilber tensed, then took a breath.

"What all of you have to realise is that you've all been converted. You've joined the cult of Rasputin and you're playing his Game, his way, like it's the only game that's real, or possible. There are other things you could do here besides collecting these crystals."

He slapped his satchel and the girls gasped.

"I mean what would happen if I just tossed these crystals into the swamp. What would you do about that?"

There was silence as the girls just stared at Wilber and considered his question. In the end it was Def who answered, her voice quiet and low.

"We'd slit your throat," she replied

Wilber froze, shocked at her response. So much for friendship!

"But why? Why Def?"

"It's like this. You just got here. We've been here a while. And for every one of us that's here alive and kicking, there's a hundred that didn't make it. That got cut in half, or drowned or eaten. Whether you like it or not the Game is the prevailing reality here and we play it until somebody wins it. If that somebody is you, great. If not we'll support the next Candidate and the next and the next until somewhere down that very long line, someone wins it and we all get to go home."

Wilber stared into her eyes and saw a killer staring back at him. She hadn't been made this way, the island, or rather the Game had turned her into this. Did he want to face her down? No, not at all. It was clear she would kill him without a second thought. Not only that, if he managed to best her, to disarm her or knock her out, he would lose the support of the Alphabet Gang and they, he knew without being told, were the only thing keeping him alive.

Justice looked at his watch. 11.11. It was decision time and everybody was watching him. Make up or break up, that was the question. The atmosphere had changed markedly in the last few minutes. It was a different kind of dangerous now and the next few minutes would be crucial to his survival.

It was Antelope who asked the question.

"So Wilber, are you still with us? Are you going to carry on playing?"

"Yes. Yes I am Two down. Three to go and over nine hours to

get the job done. Let's do it. Let's play his game our way and let's win it."

Smiles broke out all over and if champagne had been to hand, it would have been popped and passed round. Instead they had to settle for High Fives and a Group Hug. After the hugs and high fives had finished they got into a tight circle and began to discuss their options.

"So what's left to do?" Wilber asked, suddenly all business.

"More a question of who. Three Magicians remain. There's Mr Hands, Mr Lapp and the Russian," Antelope responded. "Just a question of which order you do them in."

"Who do you suggest going after first?"

Antelope weighed her response carefully.

"Look, the Magicians are a law unto themselves. We have nothing to do with Astapor and Yabu obviously. Crowhaven creeps us out and Mr Hands ignores us but Lapp is friendly. He helped us in the early days. He didn't exactly do things for us but he gave us tips and hints, warned us about stuff, showed us the ropes. Never in a way that would leave him open to censure by the other Magicians but always in a way that helped us to help ourselves."

"Why?" Wilber interjected.

"The rules are the rules," Def shot back. "The magicians aren't here to be anybody's friend. No enemies and no allies. It's as Yabu said. You need to listen more carefully, Wilber."

Wilber took a breath to stop himself screaming out in rage and Antelope cut back in.

"A while back Lapp said you were coming and that you were important and I believed him. Besides, Something's happening on the island."

"Yeah," Patrick chipped in. Speaking for the first time in front of the group, he was nervous. "The vibe has definitely changed hasn't it Uncle."

"Sure has," wheezed Great Uncle Muldoon gasping like a fish out of water. Then he nodded and spat, unable to gather enough breath or energy to extend his thought. They had arrived at the edge of the swamp and he for one needed a rest.

"Look you lot, I'm knackered. I need to sit down before I fall down. That okay?"

Antelope peering out through the trees at the edge of the forest turned her head and stamped her left foot in a fury.

"We haven't time for this."

Wilber, suddenly tired of Antelope's relentlessly bullying tone, folded his arms in defiance.

"Well I say we have. What is it you were saying, Great Uncle?"

"There's been all kinds of comings and goings. No starlight, no decent weather, animals spooked. Hours of cloud and darkness even in the middle of the day. Worse still, the things that are coming out of Astapor's bunkers are more dangerous than ever. People who have been here a long time are falling prey to the Hunting Parties. Time was, you'd settle down, keep out of trouble and you'd live an okay sort of life. Primitive? Yes. Rustic? Yes. But relatively safe? Now? No. Not anymore."

"So what changed?" George asked. Everybody regarded him with surprise. He'd been acting like a Trappist Monk for so long that everyone assumed he was incapable of speech.

"Good question," Patrick replied, keen as always to support his elder brother.

"Something is coming", Great Uncle Muldoon asserted. "A shift. Some kind of revolution but Astapor and the others are trying to contain it, to prevent it from happening. And let me tell you, spaceships are involved."

Patrick rolled his eyes and groaned.

"Please Uncle, spare us your conspiracy theories. Nobody wants to hear them now. We just don't have the time."

"I do," Wilber cut in. "What do you mean Great Uncle Muldoon?"

"The island's been here a long time, thousands of years, right?" said the Old Man, "but is that five thousand years, ten thousand years or a hundred thousand years? No one knows, but spend any real time here and your dreams fill up with all kinds of weirdness."

"Go on," Wilber urged.

"You end up leaving your body and travelling. Know what I mean. Lights surround you and then they lead you into the Crash Zone."

"Where's that?" Wilber asked as his blood ran cold. "Is it on the map?"

"Oh yeah," George replied. "Less than a mile to the south of here. But nobody goes in there unless they absolutely have to. It's the twilight zone."

"You been in there Mr Muldoon?" Antelope asked.

"Please, call me Dinosaur."

"I'd rather not."

"Alright then, George. I've been in there once and that was enough. When I came out I couldn't remember who I was or where I'd been. It took a week of Great Uncle Muldoon's scorpion soup to restore me to health and sanity."

"I'm not sure you were ever fully restored", Great Uncle Muldoon muttered under his breath.

"All I remember was the place was filled with crashed spaceships, of all shapes and sizes. There were flying saucers, cubes, cones and even cigar shaped objects just hovering in the air. It was the freakiest place I've ever been, worse than Stoke, and that's saying something. Just walking around was enough to fry your brains. I felt like I'd been pumped full of drugs and then subjected to Electric Shock Therapy."

"But did you learn anything Uncle?"

"Yeah, I did. I learned not to go back. There is enough craziness on this island without going looking for more."

Wilber was intrigued.

"And what about you, Great Uncle? What did you learn."

Great Uncle Muldoon put his head in his hands and then shook his head from side to side as though he were both trying to remember and to forget.

"Like George said there's all kinds of ships there. Some you can enter, some you can't. The things they show you leave you addicted, always wanting more. Everything else here pales into insignificance when you've been on board one of those ships. Such beauty and such complexity but.... Oh, it's too much for the human mind to comprehend. You end up just whiting out and hanging suspended in a daze for days. Fit for nothing."

"Go on. There's more isn't there?" Wilber pressed.

Great Uncle Muldoon looked pained.

"I'm sorry Wilber, I don't know that I can."

"Please, for me Uncle."

"Alright. Alright. The Game is the Game and you're playing it. It's important, but I don't believe it can ever be won without the Runner on Point going into the Crash Zone. It's not just that there are space ships there, its that there are answers there. To everything. The origins of the island, the civilization that grew up here, what happened to it. What's coming? It's all there but how to access it safely and to bring those answers back for people to profit from. I don't know that anybody can."

"Look, Mr Muldoon Sir, I'm not saying you're wrong, it's just we don't have time for this right now. We have to get moving and we have to decide where we're going next."

It was Antelope who spoke, demonstrating real leadership as ever. But Wilber was hooked and wanted to know more

"I think he should be allowed to speak, Antelope. This is important right?"

Beth stepped forward.

"It is important Wilber but its also a question of priorities right now."

"And that isn't a priority," Def weighed in.

"Damn straight," Frantic added. "We've been here a long time, Wilber and what we've done to survive would shock you. Like I said, don't get drawn into the dramas. Do the job, get in, get what you need and get out. Fast. The spaceships were here yesterday and unless by some miracle of fate, you've won the game and everything and everybody has gone back through the time gate, they'll be here tomorrow. You can play then, on your own time."

Wilber was flabbergasted.

"But this matters. What he's saying is the key to everything. You can't just drop him from a great height as if what he's telling you doesn't mean anything."

Antelope had had enough.

"That's exactly what you do, if you want to survive and if you want to win the Game. Everything else is speculation, as far as I am concerned. You get one shot at this and one shot only. And tomorrow it'll be somebody else. So decision time Wilber. Do you want to get off this rock?"

"And are you going to get with the program, or do we dump you in the swamp?" Def added, looking grim and murderous as ever. It was after all her default setting.

It was George who answered.

"He'll get back on the program girls and he'll roll up the hill. No more sneaking around. A full frontal assault is what's called for. It's time we took the fight to Astapor."

Even Def looked gone out when she heard this.

"But Astapor has an army and an army is armed. They are not going to stand by whilst we walk into Tower 1, go up to reception and ask to have dinner with Astapor and the gang. It just ain't gonna happen Mr Muldoon. I think you need a reality check."

"And I think you need to man up," George hissed.

"Inappropriate George," Great Uncle Muldoon roared.

"Sorry, ladies but it's time to go for it. He is the one and only chance you're going to get, to do this. He already has two crystals and I know where the third one is, the fire crystal."

Everybody was shocked by this.

"Where?" Antelope asked with great urgency.

"Way down under the ground in the midst of a lake of fire. That mountain didn't just happen. It's a volcano and it's far from dormant. Those tremors you've been feeling aren't due to Astapor's mining operations, despite what you may have been led to believe. That volcano is powering up and it's going to go off any day now. Which is why we have to act. And act now."

"What he's saying is true. It's time to act."

The voice of the stranger rang out behind them and the group turned as one. As always it was Justice who called it.

"Lola, you're back. I knew you wouldn't let me down."

The group fanned out with lightning speed and bows and arrows were hoisted into firing positions.

"Make your peace with whatever you believe in Lola. It's time to die!"

29

Traitor In Our Midst

Despite the vehemence of the threat, Lola seemed unimpressed. She just folded her arms and exuded attitude. It was what she did best, after all.

"Well if you're gonna do it, just do it already!"

The girls held firm, arrows drawn, strings and bows creaking. Great Uncle Muldoon was aghast, Patrick was agog and George seemed largely indifferent. Only Wilber appeared interested in steering the outcome into a place where nobody died.

"Err, Antelope, would you be so kind as to get your girls to lower their bows. And Lola, if you would be so good as not to antagonise anybody, that would really help the situation."

Lola chewed her gum and stared away into the middle distance.

"Wilber, I will not kowtow to these cows. Either they accept my help, or they don't. I'm sick of them and their so-called attitude."

Wilber stepped forward, placing himself between the Alphabets and Lola. George watched him, saying nothing. His attitude was hard to fathom at times.

"Lower your bows girls. I won't ask you again."

Slowly the girls complied and Lola gave a slow and ironic handclap.

"About time too."

Wilber shot her a glance that would have stopped a charging rhino. She was such a difficult person to get on with but then why did he like her so much? The Alphabets loathed her and perhaps with good reason. She was surly, rude and uncooperative. She was not a team player and she was the least trustworthy person he had ever met.

But there was always a but, where Lola was concerned. And the 'but' clinched it.

"So why are you here?" Def said, "Come to infiltrate so you can betray us again."

Lola faux-grinned.

"You're not worth the effort. They used to be a full alphabet Justice but take a look at them now. Just eight of them left. Just eight crumbling letters. A rag bag of psychotic scraps with no hope and no direction."

"Take that back," Def hissed, "or I'll kill you!"

Tension-filled, the air crackled.

"Why should she, she's right."

The gang gasped as one. It would have been understandable if the words had been Lola's but they weren't, they were Beth's. Ever faithful, ever positive, ever true. Antelope's loyal second in command sounding as though she were ready to throw the towel in.

"Beth, how could you?" Edie said, her voice aflame with shock.

"I can because it's true Edie, and we have to face facts. Astapor has the upper hand and he's held it for a very long time. He's wearing us down, little by little. Whilst he sits up in that tower, feasting on gourmet food, getting a good night's sleep every night, planning his every move carefully and meticulously, we are stuck out here, squatting, boiling by day and freezing by night. Always on the move, always hunted. Getting more and more tired. This doesn't end well for us. Oh it's been lovely playing the Game and we've done well to get this far but we have to do so much more than just get by and it's time we all admitted that. I'm sorry Antelope."

Antelope shook her head.

"No need to apologise, I agree with you Beth. Astapor has had us on the back foot for a very long time. I've led as best as I can. Where possible I've consulted you, but when I've needed to, I've taken the decision squarely on my own two shoulders. I know you don't always agree with me, especially you Def, but you've followed me and for that I thank you."

There was silence for a while, as the girls digested what was being said and what it meant. It was Frantic who spoke first. Whenever there was uncertainty it was always Frantic who spoke first.

"So what are you saying?"

Beth and Antelope looked at one another and something unspoken passed between them. It was Beth who turned to address the group.

"It means we have to step it up, do stuff that we've avoided in the past. We've always given people the benefit of the doubt. To live like soldiers means more than wearing a uniform and following orders. It's about cutting yourself off from your own humanity, from the idea that you are a good person. It's no longer about trying to see the best in others, in the hope that if you show folk some decency, they will be decent back. That kind of thinking doesn't work, not here. We have to become like Astapor, like machines. We have to treat others as assets to be used or threats to be eliminated."

Here she fixed Lola with a steely gaze.

"I'm addressing you now Lola. These words are just for you and you better take on board that things are different now. You've played us for fools again and again, you know you have. You betrayed our friends to torture and death. You lay with the enemy. And we knew all this and we tolerated you. We allowed you to live. So what happened to us was not your fault, it was ours. But from this moment on you help us or you die. The first whiff of sarcasm or betrayal, you die. The first time you place us in jeopardy, you die. If you've come here today with nothing new to offer to us; you die."

30

Bait

After Beth's speech, there was silence, as the others began to assimilate the new order that had begun in the moments following her final words. Before, they had all of them, lived in a grey zone, between childhood and adolescence. This latest directive took them forward into a new chapter, into a blank space others referred to as adulthood, but more than that, it signalled the end of a certain kind of relationship. Each of the Muldoons felt this in their turn. It wasn't just Lola that Beth was addressing, but them too.

Lola slowly removed her glasses and turned to Beth. The ironic smile had vanished from her lips. It seems she had gotten the message.

"If you'd have let me in when I first asked to join, I'd have been loyal. But you didn't and you paid the price."

Here she paused and Beth said nothing. A frown creased Lola's brow as she realised that if she failed to impress in the next few minutes she'd be going the same way as the zombies. Straight down a crocodile's throat!

"Alright. What's past is prologue. We all need to move on..."

Def had circled around behind Lola and was watching her closely. As though waiting for something. Lola, sensing this, wheeled suddenly and staring straight at Beth, was confronted by a frightening smile. Lola gulped. Def's expression and the way her grip had tightened on the handle of her hammer, spoke volumes. Wilber glanced at his watch.

12.03. Just past the halfway point. Time lost could not be recovered. Lola continued to stare at the hammer. Decision time. It was obvious to everybody that her mind was racing. There would be no more discussions after this one. She needed to make an offer that the Alphabet's found attractive or, as the Police in England were fond of saying, she would be eliminated from their enquiries.

"Okay. Okay I get it. Time to shape up, time to deal. Time to lay my cards on the table…"

Def grunted. She was angry and she was bored and looking for somewhere to put it. If Antelope raised so much as an eyebrow she was going to swing that hammer and usher in the new era with a dash and a splash.

"Astapor is losing his grip on reality."

"Astapor had a grip on reality?" Great Uncle Muldoon asked incredulously.

George considered.

"Once."

"It's like Jungle Jim said, the island is changing. It's as though its waking up after a long sleep and it isn't happy. Everywhere you look, the signs are there. The animals are running wild, the skies are schizophrenic and as for the plants…don't get me started on the plants. Want a metaphor for how things are? Just look at that rumbling volcano. The volcano is as unstable as Astapor has become. More so. It's not a question of if it will erupt, it's a question of when. No one can live by the old rules anymore. If we do, we will all die."

Here she looked around the circle of impassive faces. Wilber could tell she was anxious and with good reason. Death hung at her shoulder in the form of Def, lugging a hammer bigger than Thors. If she didn't speak persuasively and to some definite end, it was all going to go a bit Pete Tong for her.

The Alphabets and the Muldoons continued to listen but patience was wearing thin. Sensing this, Lola began filling the air with more words. But could mere words save her?

"I'm not going to lie. It's as you said. I lay with the enemy. I did Astapor's bidding. I wanted a comfortable life and why not? I've lived here just about my whole life and if I've learned anything in that time, it's that you have to take care of number one. Whatever the cost. I ain't helping you because I like you...frankly I hate you all...I'm helping you because you and him (here she pointed at Justice) are the future and Astapor is not. If he remains in power he will kill us all!"

Justice interjected without warning or invitation, causing Def to scowl.

"But do you really believe that Lola?"

It was Dinosaur George who answered.

"You can't believe a word she says Wilber. She's a pathological liar. A narcissistic psychopath with sociopathic elements in her make-up. It's how she's lasted as long as she has."

Patrick, mirroring his brother, folded his arms and nodded.

"Couldn't have put it better myself."

Great Uncle Muldoon put his arm around Wilber's shoulder.

"She's a bad apple Justice. Just one in the barrel and we all rot."

"I can't accept that Great Uncle. Everyone deserves a second chance. Even her. She is what the island has made her. Well her and Astapor."

Edie, following the conversation with some care, shook her head.

"She is what she chose. Like Sartre said, men and women are the sum of their deeds."

"Ain't that an existential kick in the ass" Lola muttered under her breath. "So at least give me a moment to explain my plan before you send me to the guillotine."

Antelope glanced at Wilber's watch. 12.07.

"OK. You have three minutes Lola. Consider this as your elevator pitch."

"As always Ant, your generosity is overwhelming," Lola beamed, her mastery of condescension once more on display.

"On with the show then," Def said through gritted teeth.

"Like I said, Astapor is on the slide. He's obsessed with Jungle Jim and that's why he brought Half Pint to the island. It was no accident you got chased through the time gate Wilber. It was part of his plan. Isn't that right Jungle Jim?"

George had a face like thunder.

"Watch your mouth Lola."

"As a family you really need to share more, you know that George. That way Wilber wouldn't come over as confused at best, retarded at worst."

"I said watch your mouth Lola. You're running out of rope and it's a very long drop," George roared, puffing himself up like a cane toad and using the index finger of his right hand like it was an offensive weapon.

Lola rolled her eyes.

"What does she mean George? What's she saying?"

"Oh keep up Wilber," Semantic shot, clearly exasperated. "Isn't it obvious? Astapor has links to the outside world. He's not confined to the island. He sends people topside to hunt. That's how we came to be here. Your uncle thought he could run but Astapor's reach is long. As an escapee, George was and is a legend, who can bring hope to people on this island. Astapor doesn't want that. He wants everyone in fear and without hope. Isn't that what hell is, a place without hope? So you were brought here as bait."

Wilber was outraged.

"Bait?"

"B-A-I-T." Frantic said helpfully. "Bait."

"So you went through the time gate, Uncle?"

"Yes and no," said George, looking and sounding uncomfortable. "I went through a time gate, not the time gate. Not the Western gate anyways. And not with any of the crystals."

"Well this is news," said Wilber, adopting Lola's tone and look. "And you were going to tell me this when?"

"Oh shut up! Shut up you self-pitying ass! There isn't time. There's never enough time." Lola yelled. "The Western gate, if activated, can get everybody through and off this island. Not just a few individuals. The others can't. As much as it grieves me to say this, you are our best hope. Now Jungle Jim. Tell me about the Fire Crystal."

George looked indignant.

"I'm not going to be interrogated by you."

"George!" Great Uncle Muldoon cautioned.

"Oh alright. The fire crystal is below the Tower Complex. There's a lift that takes you all the way down. It's in an underground chamber, beside a lake of lava. Like I said. And of course it's guarded."

Patrick was looking confused.

"You never told me this. How did you find this out?"

George looked immediately sheepish.

"Madeline told me."

Wilber's ears pricked up immediately.

"Madeline? Who's Madeline?"

"It's a long story, for another time. Suffice it to say, I have a map. Or at least I memorised a map. I can take you there Wilber. I can help you find the third crystal. We just need to get into Tower Complex and then ride the elevator down."

Lola, already grinning, now burst out into a laugh.

"Which is where I come in. I can get you into the complex and into that lift pod. But we can do so much more than just acquire the third crystal. We can destroy it all. Astapor included."

*   *   *   *   *   *   *

Antelope and the other Alphabets were clearly intrigued and Lola had a captive, if still murderous, audience hanging off her every word. It was like a dream come true. Or at the very least a nightmare deferred. Her elevator pitch had obviously worked and this was as it should be. She had spent considerable effort and energy formulating a whole series of plans. They were as plates on vertical rods that must be kept spinning, spinning, spinning lest they fall. Every winning strategy entailed an element of risk, only in her case it was an elephant of risk. A big, lumbering male elephant in musk, with flapping ears and upraised trunk and tusks. It thundered towards her, trumpeting. Murderous, charged and dangerous. In her mind's eye she saw it clearly. The Alphabets had swooped down in a balloon and hauled her away to safety.

For now!

Safety and security were temporary measures. She had played and won for the moment only. Her three minutes were up but she had been granted a stay of execution and more importantly additional time to outline her intentions.

Would they buy what she had to sell them? They might...they just might.

"So Lola, what's next? What do you have in mind," Antelope asked, grim of expression and maxed out on tolerance.

Lola's grin of response was both cruel and cunning.

"After your last incursion I saw that you were going through the change. You were growing bolder and more daring in your methods and modes of attack. Unfortunately your execution was flawed which led to two of your girls..."

"Ultra and Zin,"

"Thank you Edie, Ultra and Zin getting blown into cubes of dog meat. After that, Astapor relocated the High Explosive. At first it was deep underground but recently he's moved it back up into the Observatory, in Tower One. Why? I don't exactly know. Perhaps he feels paranoid and he wants it close to hand. Anyway, he moves around a lot. Or he used to. Now he spends most of his time in the Observatory."

"What, that green dome?" Wilber asked.

"Exactly that. He has protection of course. The Surveillance cameras cover every angle of the complex and he has ways of piping poisoned gas into the observatory, should anyone ever get up there."

Beth looked gloomy.

"This isn't a happy picture you're painting."

"But everything has a solution," Lola countered. "Astapor created an antidote for the gas which I just happen to have about my person. Like polio, a sugar lump is all you need, and you're safe."

"And the surveillance cameras?" Crimson prodded.

"I had Caleb create a gadget for me, so we could come and go from the towers without Astapor knowing. Live feeds can become recorded feeds at the press of a button. The latest explosives have timers. Plant them, set them and run away laughing. Within three minutes the towers are gone."

"But what about Astapor and what about his guards?"

Lola looked at George, who had asked the question and then at Antelope. The grin dropped off of her face like a mask that had melted.

"This isn't a bloodless coup, unfortunately. You girls have bows and arrows and the guards have machine guns. They aren't idiots either. They are well trained and not apt to flee at the first sign of difficulty. Astapor has eight personal bodyguards and an army of about a hundred. In the compound anyway. More are scattered about the island, most of them looking for you."

"Anything else?" Beth asked.

"Lots of things. Things that were human secreted away in holding tanks beneath the tower complex. You've sampled some of his work but by no means all of it. God alone knows what he has held back."

"More frightening than the creepers? More violent than zombies?" Wilber asked, barely able to keep the tremor from his voice.

Lola looked Wilber square in the eye.

"They were just hors d'oeuvres Wilber. After the starter comes the main course. If you're still hungry and alive that is."

Having delivered her pitch, Lola folded her arms and prepared to wait. Had she done enough? Would they go for it? She would find out and soon. If she'd failed to pitch her plan successfully she hoped they'd kill her quickly. She didn't much care for pain. Least of all her own. Other people's pain did not bother her at all!

*   *   *   *   *   *   *

The girls withdrew into a huddle and George was left holding the hammer. If Lola had thought him a softer touch than Def, one look at his expression convinced her otherwise. Like the Alphabets George had been hunted and like them it had changed him. If nothing else, Astapor was an element of transformation within the psyches of all he met.

After a few minutes the huddle broke and the girls returned to the communal space where Lola and the Muldoons watched and awaited developments. Antelope without preamble, addressed Lola.

"Alright Lola. You can breathe easy. For now at least. We're gonna go for it. We're gonna follow your plan."

"Whoopee," Lola trilled, never far from an ironic utterance.

"But if we walk into a trap, your shadow here," and here she pointed to Def who had once more taken up the hammer, "will pound you into oblivion. Comprendez?"

"Oui," Lola intoned, happily back in the game. "Je suis content avec ça. Tout est en ordre."

Antelope continued. "George, we'll get you to the lift. After that you have one hour. Patrick and the Old Man will stay with us. We're gonna need all the help we can get."

George digested this information in a heartbeat.

"If everything goes according to plan, where should we meet?"

Antelope considered.

"Do you know the temple about a mile to the south east of the Tower complex?"

"Of course I do. Me and the other members of the family used to hang out there."

"Some of us still do", Patrick added, grinning inanely.

'We'll meet there. Oh and George if you're not out in an hour we're gonna blow the complex anyway. So make it snappy. Comprendez?"

31

On The Lamb

And off they went, at a fast-paced walk at first, until they had warmed up and then at a jog. No more time for planning. No more need for discussion. Lola up front, Def hovering behind her, hammer in hand, ready to strike. Slow or fast, Lola's shadow. Unshakeable. Two lines not three, moving at speed, with deadly intent and purpose. Bows and blades, sickle and hammers. The primitive returned, ready and poised to strike. Feet skimming the ground like skaters hurtling over water. Soft and subtle and fast.

Over rough terrain, the shadows of birds gliding overhead. The exotic and the mundane in endless procession, the known and the unknown shadowed and exposed. Here a lizard, there a spider, a skipped beat and a peering deer behind layers of leaves. The only constant here was change, wherever you were, in whatever direction you looked. The ever shifting palette of the sky. Now dark, now light. Through mournful blues, to bleeding reds to bruised purples, every shift in colour bringing a corresponding change of mood. Anger, sadness, despair, exhilaration, warlike rage, suspicion and joy would be registered in the course of a mere minute.

Then away beyond the canopy, the growl of thunder and the ever-swinging winds.

Running, slowing, accelerating, looking about, ever vigilant, fear heightening the senses to near levels of toxicity. Anomalies sought. Anomalies explained and discarded. Threat and the assessment of risk built into every glance. Fight and flight activated but the aesthetic sensibilities still engaged. On the edge of a precipitous ledge poised to fall at any moment, delivered into the mouth of death but still aware of beauty. Still feeling the micro changes of temperature. Dripping with sweat one moment, shivering the next. A twinge of calf or a sudden scratch, drawing blood from beneath the skin to taste the air. Branches and thorns reaching out with cunning fingers. Obstacles to duck or swerve at every turn, to address with every footfall.

The gaze shifting, like the rotating barrel of a kaleidoscope; eyes focusing through sudden bursts of blinding sunlight. The zing of a yellow flower or a flash of blue petals. Red leaves rustling and empurpled earth, moss-covered and occasionally slippery. Watch your footing, the oft-repeated note to self. The endless trees from countless ages dazzling the mind, regardless. Every moment filled with mysteries and puzzles. An open air museum of enigmas. Greenery, lush-hued and multi-faceted, fascinating with every breath. And everyone is in motion. Running in one direction but thinking in many. Multiple planes of mind engaged, a veritable Jacob's ladder and an always-complex series of interactions evolving through every hour, minute and nanosecond.

Reading the lay of the land. With varying abilities. The sophisticated and the coarse, side by side. Alternating layers. Merging seamlessly with the contours of the slope. A volcanic slope, now steep, now gentle. Basaltic rock pounded and covered. Here black sand, here white. The volcanic and the sedimentary brought together. White sand hauled up from the sea's depths, swept inland by the tides and deposited like coin in a bank vault.

No paths and yet all lines, over earth, available. Everything possible and left to choice. A mile to cover and infinite options. Led by the tall girl towards the towering eight, the rectangle of white towers with their criss-crossing walkways. Wire and cameras and the conjoined sound of chirrup and whirr.

Drawing nearer and nearer to the high fence of barbed wire. Razor wire. No other purpose but to tear flesh. The Russian's barbed wire smile into which Lola has carved her mark. Made her hole. All is ready and waiting. The complex has been infiltrated if she is to be believed. Can she be believed? Can anyone? Their hopefulness has made them weak, yet given them strength. Wheels within wheels turning. In every mind. Multiple plans of attack. Multiple contingencies vying, competing for space, in the rotting rooves of possibility. Where nests were strewn. Antelope thinking, playing and replaying the angles. Is she even the leader anymore or has something else taken over?

Beth changed. The darkening of her shining eyes. Matt black like the walls of a night club. Ink black like octopus venom. Or so Antelope thinks. Images roar through her inner space like dragsters at a race track. Beth different. Challenging and yet compliant. Deferring and yet reaching out, into spaces beyond the known. What was between them has changed. The old has dissolved, along with sets of responses, behaviours, reactions. New adjustments are being made and inclinations long-suppressed are given form and expression.

Five hundred metres closing to four hundred. Like a trap being sprung. Like iron jaws closing. Going on a bear hunt. Are you coming with me? Are you? Antelope wonders. Is Beth still with her? Did she always want to lead? Not that that matters now. All talk is done, just eyes watching now, bows half-drawn, ready to fire, even on the move. God but they've all come such a long way. All of them. Words echoing. George's words to the gang.

"If we get separated we'll meet at the Old Temple on the South Eastern side of the Tower Complex. You know where that is? They all confirmed that they did. Even the Old Man. The Uncle's Uncle.

The Old Man's words to George.

"Please take care of Justice." And a knowing squeeze of the arm.

So little, communicating so much. Each aware of the other. The Muldoons, the Alphabets and Lola. Lola the odd one out, the Judas bird with shaded eyes and black lipstick. The multiple piercings and tattoos. The black hair and black coat. Long. The body meatless, barely there, scarcely feminine. The polished boots. Polished? Here? No. None of it adds up. It's all just camouflage. Isn't it? Misdirection. That is not who she is.

The voice in Antelope's head screaming like an alarmed bird.

Who and what is Lola? Lola is a line of crude crosses. Sticks bound together by vine and planted in the black, volcanic earth. Crosses. Like anyone is Christian anymore. Like anyone ever was. Crosses over empty graves. All those girls. All their friends gone. The ones who didn't make it. No time to bury them. Bodies left for Astapor's vultures.

"We can make use of this meat," said the voice and then the laughter of jackals, the hilarity of hyenas following. Hot winds from the fires of experience have dried all of Antelope's tears. People are bodies. Just meat for the factory. The dead are safe, she tells herself. It's the living they left behind that she fears, that trouble her nightmares. What have they become? What has he turned them into? They have all suffered a sea change? But into what? Something rich and strange no doubt.

Walking, then jogging, then walking, then still. Her face angled to meet the world but her mind always on Lola, attending to business. The enigma of she. Aware of the world on the other side of the veil, but she has never been there. Antelope thinks and then remembers. And her eyes tear. No! She drives it from her. In the final moments of her life she will allow it in. Allow her father's face to form and her mother's and sister's. Only then will she allow that other world to return, when she is broken and there is no possibility of continuation.

The Russian triumphant. His rich golden laugh polluting the air. The razor between her teeth as he bends over her to taunt her and exalt in his own brilliance. One final word and it will be over. Slashing and then showered in blood as her eyesight fades and the blackness covers her for ever and ever.

If only she could keep them all safe. If only she could do that, what wouldn't she sacrifice? It's an easy question to ask. Not so easy to answer. Her darkest fantasies are only and ever cartoons. Despite the act, she is still a child, and she knows it. Until she confronts him. The Dark Father, who lures them all with baited hooks, will always be in charge.

Bait. B-A-I-T. bait. Frantic's explanation brings a smile to her lips.

And then she looks at Lola and the smile dies. Bait. Let her think she has won. Let her think they are weak and easily fooled. But Antelope knows...how she knows she knows, she doesn't know...other forces are in play. But she knows. Other elements will create an opening here. The island is the invisible hand that raises the wave, makes the connection or severs it.

No, she thinks. Let her believe she has won. It will be easier for everyone that way.

32

Forming

Lola had stopped and was pointing through the trees at something none of them could see.

"It's through there, the Tower complex. That's where you'll find him. It's close, so very close. I hope you're ready. You'll get one shot at him. That's it. After that, he wins."

But she wasn't herself, not any more. Not as she had been. Wilber, trudging behind Def moved forward, placed his hand on her shoulders as The Old Man had placed his hand on Wilber's shoulders. To soothe and to calm. A human gesture in a place where to be human was not encouraged. Actively discouraged in fact. The island was a place where nothing could be taken for granted.

"What is it Lola? What do you see?"

Lola quivering and still. Lola terrified, her mind enveloped by a cloud of associations. Transported back to a childhood no one could ever imagine. Here amongst the trees, walking, watching, knowing even as a child that he did terrible things. That it wasn't natural but that she must pretend that it was.

Something hanging
Simply dangling
Forms unwinding in the air
Like mist suspended, time upended
Flickering shadows on the stair
Don't you see them floating there?

Everyone still and somewhere different, although occupying the same physical space. Transported into different parts of themselves. Shifted sideways; becoming aware in different ways. Frantic agitated and in on herself, birds trying to peck her eyes out. Edie watching, remembering her own childhood and its many fears. Antelope half there half not. Wondering about Beth. Fearing her. Afraid of the loss of control, though putting a brave face on it. Beth changing, aware of forces moving into her consciousness from deep within. Welcoming change but unsure of what she would become. How much she would darken. Crimson fascinated by Lola's change. Hating her but pitying too. Def wanting to finish her. Wanting to hoist the hammer aloft and finish this wand of a girl. This black and twisted stick insect with her mocking laugh and shaded eyes. Semantic reframing the language patterns that had formed around Lola. Rudi sensing a different kind of future, beginning to unwind.

And then the Muldoons. The Old man tired, wanting to just let go and be at rest. But knowing a job had yet to be done. Knowing it wasn't all over until the family was safe. Drawing on hidden reserves of energy. Getting in touch with his younger self for strength and direction.

The brother Patrick unsure about everything. Uncertain of what to say and do. Looking to others for his cues. Feeling hideously exposed and yet grinning inanely.

That word again. Inanely.

And George. A mass of secrets. A seething nest of contradictions. Strength like a lion, though weak as a lamb. His mind is full of snakes. Trapped in his guilt. Fighting always. Irritated by attachment, the need to help and protect others binding him, depriving him of breath. Loving and hating his young nephew. Ashamed of his feelings. So wanting to be alone yet needing to be here. Little or no sympathy. A whirling mass of unresolved questions.

And Justice. The boy. The fool. The genius. The unknown quantity. He whom the others rally round. He whom they feel compelled to help. But why? He is nothing special and yet some deep signal within him pulses outwards and draws them inwards. Draws water from the well, draws the wandering lost to the fire. They all sense it but none can explain it. Each and everyone has to fight not to smash him, to seek to crush him. He has that effect on everyone he meets. It made the boy feel unclean and pathetic. Like he should be put out of his misery. And yet the seeds of greatness are contained within.

His voice moving out towards her, replete with gentle strength, prompting without pushing.

"What is it Lola, what can you see?"

Silence and then a word.

"Them."

The shiver running through him, like a ripple through water. The panic in her voice

"Don't you see them?"

Wilber looking, staring into the trees. Looking through things, not at them. It takes a moment but then all of a sudden there they are. Suddenly he sees a quite different world. A world he might dare to imagine but never to describe. At least not to others. He has been laughed at and mocked too cruelly in the past to want to do that.

But with her, with Lola in this shared now, with the other's scattered he can do it.

"Yes, I see them. They confuse me but they draw me in too. Like a sweet you can't quite get enough of. What are they?"

Silence intrudes but it is a knowing silence. Knowing passes between them in an endless two-way stream. Words are an encumbrance, not needed, yet the impulse to speak them is still heeded.

Lola muses.

"He calls them wisps. But what they actually are is far more disturbing. They were people but they aren't any more. They're people who've been turned into ghosts. Flesh and blood and bone has been...well translated... into what you see there, white wisps of presence.

Wilber stared at a nearby wisp but after a while he had to look away. He felt his energy levels beginning to dip.

"They're serene and yet terrifying. What is it they do to you Lola?"

For a while Lola said nothing. It was as if she was only half there. Wilber much preferred the old Lola. The sardonic tank girl with killer style and verve. The kind of kid that nobody liked but everybody wanted to be. Rather that brat than this blunted child.

"Just another act in the circus, Wilber. Think of them as Astapor's latest trick and then write them off. Write them out of existence because no good ever came of fixating on a wisp. I found that out the hard way. What are they? They are an addiction if you let them in. They take on the faces of those you love and desperately want to be with. They mimic their voices and whisper things in your ears at night that you desperately want to hear. What are they? Do you really want to know Wilber? Do you really want to know? To me they are magnetic hypnotists, by far the deadliest weapon in Astapor's arsenal."

Wilber shook his head slowly, from side to side. He felt drunk and spaced out. Both woozy and queasy. Like he was walking through quicksand in lead boots or on a planet with twice the gravitational pull of the earth.

"First the Creepers, then the Zombies and now the Wisps. Doesn't he ever give up?"

"He has too much to lose," Antelope replied. "If he let go of the reins of power everybody on this island who has suffered because of him would tear him limb from limb."

Wilber nodded, only half listening. Try as he might he couldn't take his mind off the wisps. With zombies and creepers, it was easy. They were out to kill you. You either ran from them, blew them to smithereens or fed them to something with teeth. But these wisps, they made it far more difficult, because they played on your need for love and acceptance.

As he watched, he saw one turn to look at him. It was a featureless mass of glowing white light. The archetypal ghost. It seemed to be watching him, yet how could it, it had no eyes? Wilber felt a sudden pressure on his arm and turned to see what it was. Crimson stood beside him clutching his muscle.

"Be careful Wilber. They're more dangerous than you know."

Unable to stop himself, he looked back to where the wisp hung suspended. Something about it had changed and a shiver of electricity ran through the air and then up and down his spine. It felt as if he were being caressed by ice-cold fingers. Half painful, half exquisite, he didn't know how to feel about what amounted to a guilty pleasure. Did he want it to stop? Yes! But no. Not really.

Absolutely not. The roar of inner force.

The air around the wisp had darkened and the creature, if that is what it was, had begun to shimmer. Wilber was mesmerised and found himself taking a step towards it.

Crimson, growing more agitated with every second called after him.

"Wilber, you are making really bad choices here. You need to stop looking at that thing and walk away. They are not a trick. They're real, albeit they aren't physical but they can really mess with your head."

Listening to Crimson's tirade, Wilber grew angry.

Who was she to tell him such things. She knew nothing. These things weren't harmful. They were friendly. Why shouldn't he be friendly back? If people were more friendly towards one another the world wouldn't be such a messed up place.

The wisp pulsed and the blank face flickered, then assumed the contours of a familiar profile. Before he knew what had happened Amy was standing before him, holding out her hand for him to take. Amy from Tamworth? What was she doing here, away from the launderette? Why, she was on holiday of course, just like he was. She'd followed him to the island to tell him how she felt about him. That was it. Of course it was.

With this thought filling his mind he took a step forward only to find himself being grasped by the shoulder, yanked back and turned around.

Def! But of course. Who else? Always there to air an opinion nobody wanted to hear. Always there to spoil the fun. Wilber was about to tell her exactly what he thought of her when she clamped a pudgy hand over his mouth.

"Don't! Just don't! Ok? We asked you nicely and now we're telling you. Don't look at the pretty lights. They'll mess with your head and turn you into a raving addict. If you feel unable to comply with our commands, in this situation, we'll have to blindfold you. Nod if you understand."

Wilber nodded and Def leaned in to give him the eye of warning.

"Remember Wilber if I catch you sneaking so much as a guilty peak it's a slap and a blindfold for you. We need to destroy them, not encourage them."

Wilber was perplexed.

"But how do you destroy something that isn't physical?"

"I'm not sure you can," Edie opined. "They're etheric, nothing but white vapours with the merest hint of a human form. I'm not even sure they can be said to be living things anymore. They don't fit into any classificatory system I've ever seen. They'd probably bamboozle Carl Linnaeus!"

33

Jumbling The Alphabet

Trust Edie.

"George, do you think they are conscious? Have you encountered them before?" Wilber asked his Uncle.

"Only in my nightmares Wilber. There was this one time I was walking though the jungle. It was night. I turned around and I saw what you've just been looking at. At first there was just one of them, only one, and then with a blink of an eye there were nine and in the time it took to light and smoke a cigarette there were a thousand. They watched me, watched me intently. Then they tried to break into my mind."

This pulled everyone up short. George had a way of making everyone pay attention whenever he spoke. He was more absent than present, lost in some twilight zone that only he had access to. But when you needed him, he was there 200%, armed and dangerous and ready for action.

"That's impossible!" Edie countered. "You're talking out of your...hat George." As a Gradgrindian Science buff she was a lover of facts. Demonstrable, replicable, verifiable facts. Life on the island had stretched her definition of what constituted reality but it had done nothing to scotch her belief in scientific method. Much of the time, like George she was silent, but when she felt there were principles at stake she became fierce in her defence of reason or truth or some other privileged abstraction.

George hocked up a greenie and spat.

"Improbable not impossible Edith. Keep up."

Edie bristled like a porcupine. Her big sister had constantly referred to her as Edith and it had become one of her triggers. Edie had had to train herself not to react. Had he known or was he just probing for a weak spot? Difficult to call. Dinosaur George Muldoon had an uncanny knack of giving offence, and Edie suspected he had issues with strong women, issues that needed addressing.

"I would dispute that George. It's probable you were in an altered state, possibly the hypnagogic state. That is the liminal state between sleeping and waking where hallucinations are not unheard of. Either that or you were engaging in a little projection. It's not unheard of, particularly amongst those who have suffered trauma. As you obviously have."

The last part of her commentary she muttered under her breath, but George had the ears of a bat.

"You're probably right Edith. It was only a dream. And I am prone to hallucinations. Trouble is when I woke up they were still there watching me. And no matter what I did and where I went they followed. I wasn't the only one who could see them either. "

In spite of the sound of the ticking clock in his head Wilber was intrigued.

"What did you do?"

George beamed from ear to ear.

"I went to see a friend."

"A friend? Do you mean a friend or do you mean a 'friend'?" The insult was all in the emphasis. Now Edie was digging for dirt, proving that she was not averse to a little light innuendo, not afraid to strike back at a would-be tormenter.

George eyed her with disdain.

"I mean a friend Edith, a real friend, someone who doesn't run when it's safer not to hang around. Someone prepared to take a stand and put it all on the line. Know anybody like that?"

Edie stared right into George's eyes.

"Yes, I know seven really good people like that George and they're not a million miles from here."

"I'll guess we'll find out in about ten minutes whether that's true or not."

Wilber, feeling the tension ratchet up, thought it was time to intercede.

"And what did he do, this friend of yours, George."

George looked away and thought about it. He had never talked about this before. One, because there was no one who had ever asked and two, because it had been just too painful. To spend any significant time on the island was to put yourself in the way of harm. To open yourself to the potential for damage. Not just physical damage either. Astapor thought that crude. He much preferred to inflict lasting psychological damage. Whilst Topside, George had tried to put the tragedy of what had unfolded on the island behind him. He'd immersed himself in work, travelled the world and the seven seas but wherever he went, he cast a long shadow. And that shadow invariably invited interest. The down side of celebrity, or rather his celebrity was that he needed to keep one eye on where he was going and one eye looking over his shoulder.

Now everyone in the group was listening in, even Lola. By taking pot shots at Edie he'd laid himself open. Truth or dare. What was it to be? He knew the answer before he'd even asked the question. Whether he wanted to or not he had to share.

"He went into my mind. And once there he was able to get rid of them."

Wilber's eyes widened. It was unlike George to be so confessional.

"How did he do that?"

George glanced at Lola but her eyes were hidden, as oft times before, behind her shades. No help there. No show of solidarity or support. He was on his own.

"From my mind, he travelled into their minds. He was skilled at that sort of thing, this man. It's not something you can learn from a book Edie, it's something you have to experience first hand and pray you have a good guide to get you in and bring you out. You leave one reality and enter another and if you don't have a strong will and a good map you are destined to shatter. This man was a master and he worked alone. He didn't much care for people but for some reason he took a shine to me. Thankfully when things went bad he was able to help me, but only because we'd established a friendship built on trust. I had to open my mind to him fully, when those things invaded. There was no other way.

He got to see all the dark and twisted corners of my soul. There was nothing he didn't know about me by the time he'd finished his clean-up operation. But he didn't just charge around like a bull in a china shop. He was gentle and he didn't pry. Unless he absolutely had to, that is.

You see he was a man who understood people very differently from the way most people view others. You can be biological or sociological or psychological in the way you approach humans. Or even anthropological, for that matter. And those disciplines and ways of seeing are useful but they have their limitations. They explain from the outside. They don't always place you inside. That's where his skill lay. That's where he was different.

To him, the human, and by extension the human mind, was a safe with a combination that only an expert could crack. Get the combination right and you could open all sorts of doors into all sorts of minds. Doors of iron, doors of fire, doors of numbers, many leading onto corridors of light.

He knew that to get rid of these parasites he had to travel to the place that they had come from, a place where the lost congregate, and that he had to show them something they would never forget. An image that would haunt them and follow them wherever they went. Whichever way they turned."

Now even the jungle was silent, listening in on George's story. Despite her earlier sniping, even Edie was hooked.

"What did he show them George?" she asked, her lips atremble.

"He showed them their own reflections," George replied in a near whisper. "It was the one thing they couldn't bear to look upon.

Frantic, who had been expecting a gorier conclusion to

Muldoon's story, assumed a scornful expression.

"And that was enough?"

George turned his head and looked at her with dark eyes.

"For some it was enough; they just vanished, like smoke into rain. But others were darker, more stubborn, more intense. They were quite prepared to look on the horror of their own reflections. So my friend took them to a place none of them were prepared for. A place of screaming forces and terrifying voices, of whirling threads of time. An inescapable vastness. And in that vastness he placed two objects in their minds."

"And what were they?" Wilber asked, every bit as hooked as Edie.

"The first was the smallest possible thing in creation and the second was the biggest possible thing in creation. Its one thing to encounter the idea, quite another thing to experience the reality."

"And that was enough?' Edie asked quizzically.

"Hell yes!" George almost roared. "Know what happens when the unstoppable force meets the immovable object? It's the same deal. He stretched their minds to breaking point. Ever had your mind stretched to breaking point, Edie? I have. First, the corners of your mind begin to whine and creak, then to fray and unravel. After that invisible bullets begin to shred the fabric of your mind and finally you fall in an unblinking scream into the abyss. The further you fall, the further you travel from yourself, and your mind becomes like a glass balloon, with the thinnest walls imaginable, walls that could shatter at any moment for ever and ever."

Edie allowed George's images to fill her mind and after a while wished that she hadn't. It took time, effort and will for her to locate her equilibrium once more, longer still before she could speak.

"That would probably be enough," she eventually conceded.

Dinosaur George Muldoon smiled the smile of the recently vindicated.

"I'm glad you think so Edie and that we finally agree on something."

"What was your friend's name George?"

The quiet voice belonged to Lola and all eyes swivelled to fix upon her. Eyes of raging contempt. The smile that played about her lips was proof enough that the damaged child with the wisp-like demeanour had been driven back into the wasteland of her own mind and that the knife-wielding tank girl was back and ready to play.

George rolled out a chuckle without mirth.

"It's so nice to have you back Lola, sweet Lola. Ever cynical, ever true. Always ready with the right question."

"So who was he?" Lola pressed, unperturbed.

"In the Old Tongue he was known as Yalla Mallai." George stated grandly.

"And in the new?" Edie asked, all pickles and gherkins.

"The same."

Wilber stifled a laugh.

"So," he asked, "Does it mean anything?"

"It means everything to me."

"Don't be so pedantic George. Just translate the words," Semantic instructed.

"The words mean Song of Madness."

"Yes but who was he?" Lola hissed.

George grimaced. "He was a Magician and Astapor's predecessor. As to where he is. Let's just say he's at one with the island and leave it at that."

34

Storming

The kneeling huddle rose as one and then broke. All around them the wisps hovered, faceless with malevolence, until George approached them and fixed them with a stare. Then they popped, like squeezed zits and disappeared. Pop, pop, pop, they declaimed in parting, like party balloons falling to the trickster's pin. Yet another one of Astapor's weapons disarmed, Antelope noted, a satisfied smile creeping onto her face. George was the magic key here. She wondered if he would open all the doors that stood in their way.

But there was no time for conjecture, they were in motion again, the Muldoons and the Alphabets breaking into two lines, streaming forwards and upwards, moving with both focus and intent. Every heart was pounding, every adrenal gland working overtime to keep them on task and on time, primed to fight or flee.

The shadows of the swaying trees around them striped their pale faces with deadly purpose. Even the Old Man had lost his air of comedic buffoonery and looked deadly serious, like a warrior of old. An ancient knight maybe, riding off to the crusades. Through the trees they ran, Antelope glancing at her compass to verify that they were still heading in a south-easterly direction, Edie cataloguing the trees that they passed. Ticking off the Palms and Redwoods, Ebonies and Oaks, Rubber trees and pines, Banana Trees and the Heavenly Lotus she felt happy, albeit anxious. There were still some trees she could not name. The frustration vexed her, making her wish she still had access to a library or computers. There was still so much she wanted to learn. It was doubtful though that life here would ever fulfil her needs in that particular direction.

From time to time Wilber found himself watching Edie. He felt protective towards her. Of all the girls she was the one who most felt like a sister to him. He told himself that it was important not to get too attached to anyone here, but he was finding it difficult. There was just something about her, stranger than she was, that touched his heart. Different currents and forces seemed to meet in her. She was both ancient and futuristic in a way that was difficult to define. Perhaps in a way that had yet to be identified, let alone studied and understood. Even in the midst of danger she was always questioning, searching, making connections. He loved that about her.

Rudi and Antelope, in stark contrast to Edie, were always looking for traps. As they ran, they both scanned for cameras and searched for weapons. On occasion Antelope raised her right arm in a signal for the group to stop. At such moments they ceased moving as one, silent and deadly, dropping to one knee to listen. Quickly the Muldoons caught on and followed them. After moments of listening Antelope would raise her left arm, to signal the all clear and they'd resume moving once more. Def and Patrick kept a sharp eye on Lola who moved in the middle at the Alphabet's line, as though she was now, and had always been one of the gang. Nobody needed to be told just how precarious their situation was, and everyone understood how easily everything could unravel if Lola had lied. If the Judas bird had sung her song in Astapor's ear, they would all swing. Or worse.

Swivelling his head, Wilber caught sight of Def, who was positioned fifth in the Alphabet's line, just behind Lola, who was fourth. She, like him, was sweating like a pig en route to a barbeque. Lola, ever nimble, ever quick, ran without effort and at great speed, forcing Def to work hard to keep up with her long-coated charge. She was a big girl was Def, well in excess of 200 lbs, but for all that she was as light on her feet as a dancer. Do what she would, Lola couldn't shake her shadow and Wilber found himself grinning at this.

Without warning the terrain began to change. The ground seemed to grow steeper and the trees began to thin out. Lola, breaking into a sprint, passed Crimson and then Edie to take the lead from Antelope who fell into step behind her. Sensing Lola was pulling a fast one Def sprinted past the other girls, resuming her role as Lola's shadow. Ordinarily this would have irritated Lola but she was too focused on the task at hand to care. Swinging suddenly right, she led the group towards the looming towers, their silver-grey cladding visible through the thinning trees, and then raising her right arm as she had seen Antelope do, forced every member of the group to a stop.

Everyone dived behind a tree to hide and to drag air into their oxygen-starved bodies. The last hundred or so metres Lola had really forced the pace and they were all feeling it. Wilber felt both excited and anxious and only when he turned, did he see how high up they had climbed. Away to the north-west lay Yabu's mangrove swamp and whatever remained of the zombie horde. Out at sea the crumbling stacks of rocks caught his eye and he shuddered when he recalled his clash with the sirens. God, but that had been too close for comfort and without his Uncle George's intervention it was unlikely he would have made it. God bless Saint George, he thought as he grimaced.

Beyond the treeline, where they were hidden, Wilber caught sight of the twelve-foot-high perimeter fence they had discussed earlier. Impossible to climb, as it was covered in razor wire, but not to cut. And that was the plan. Snip, snip, snip to breach the perimeter wire, and to get onto the top of the volcano where Astapor lurked in one of the towers, both fenced in and fenced off.

Would he play the game and give Wilber a fair bite of the cherry as the other magicians had? That seemed unlikely but they'd cross that bridge when they came to it. They were about 150 metres from the front door, the front door being Tower One, the Tower in the North West corner of the complex. Surmounted by a green dome of sparkling green glass it seemed the tower most likely to be Astapor's Control Room. Yes, the Russian was close enough to touch and not only him either, but those explosives too, if Lola hasn't lied. Suddenly the plan seemed very precarious and shot full of holes.

Lola had stated that all the towers were linked together by tunnels and that numerous lifts ran day and night, from each level, of every tower down, all the way down, into the bowels of the volcano. Down into the lake of fire via the sulphurous pit, he suddenly thought. His grandmother, when she had lived, had been a big churchgoer and fond of delivering fire and brimstone sermons to anybody stupid enough to listen to her. Hypocritical old cow that she'd been, she'd instilled within Wilber a love of the apocalyptic. He dined out on all that imagery, especially in the Book of Revelations, with its dragons and pale horses, its crystal rivers and that woman clothed with the sun, with the moon under her feet.

He could almost imagine the sounding of those angel-blown trumpets, and the opening of the seven seals. He could almost see the beast unchained, crawling up out of the abyss to wage war against them, and that beast destroying them and leaving their bodies scattered about the island in pieces. Only his imagination, fertile breeding ground that it was, transposed the face of a beast into that of a black eyed Russian, whose soul blazed with hateful fire. It was almost too much and yet not quite. He was made of sterner stuff, was Wilber. He wasn't going to have an attack of the vapours and faint for all that the Island felt like the ideal setting for Armageddon.

Lola, kneeling down behind a large pine tree, was looking at him with a frown on her face. Everyone else was watching her and paying attention so why wasn't he? He mouthed the word sorry when he caught her eye but Lola just sneered and, retrieving a trowel from one of the inner pockets of her great coat, began digging in the dark earth. The others moved to help but she waved them away and in just a few minutes she had unearthed a carved wooden chest adorned with sequins and golden glitter. Heaving it from the earth, she sprang the lock, lifted the lid and began pulling out the goodies hidden inside.

Def, always suspicious, watched Lola's every move, ready, at the first sign of trouble to spring in and hammer the Emo Chick into the earth. But Lola, well used to hostility, just got on with the job of emptying the chest. One of the first things she removed and handed round was a bag of sugar cubes which she claimed contained the antidote to Astapor's poisoned gas. Everyone took one without argument, Beth and Antelope looking each other in the eye as they popped the cubes and swallowed. Lola, observing their anxious faces, smiled cruelly at the paranoia whirling around the circle of faces. Only the old man crunched down the cube with any degree of pleasure, transported as he was into far off days of untroubled youth.

There were other surprises in the box too. Snapping on her purple medical gloves, Lola handed round a collection of blowpipes and darts. When she got to George, he just shook his head and feeling in his backpack removed a holstered pistol that looked like it had been pilfered from the set of a Western. He then proceeded to check that each chamber of the old fashioned pistol was loaded with a Dum Dum bullet onto which had been etched Astapor's name. Whatever had happened between them in the past was not over, not in George's mind.

After handing out the blowpipes Lola returned to the chest and took out a weird smelling black paste that she kept in a sealed jar. The others, understanding what it was, stared at her open mouthed. Lola, cold-eyed, looked at Antelope who without a second thought nodded her head to grant permission. That simple gesture signalled an escalation in the conflict between the Magicians and the residents. But it was war, and it had always been war. In her nightmares, Antelope still heard the screams of those dragged away and pulled beneath the black volcanic earth into the spaces filled with Astapor's jagged plans. Once human, now they were not. It was easy for her to make the decision when she remembered how her many friends had died. Lola in her purple medical gloves, did not need to be told twice and began smearing the black paste on all the darts and arrows she had handed.

"What is that?" Justice asked.

"It's curare," Lola purred. "Something to relax the guards into a state of paralysis, to freeze them whilst we go about our business. With aid they might all survive; without it they'll probably perish. But looking around this circle I guess no one cares either way."

Hearing this, Wilber fell silent. Now the smearing was done everyone was armed, ready and dangerous. Reaching into the chest again Lola took out a gleaming black, remote control. Raising it to shoulder-level she depressed a series of buttons, just as Caleb has shown her, then dropped it straight back into the chest.

"That takes care of the cameras," she whispered, "at least for the next hour. The live feeds are gone. The screens in the tower will show only recorded feeds from hours earlier. To prying eyes we will be invisible."

Ingenious. She had thought of everything. So now it was time. Back into the box she went, one last time, pulling out two pairs of industrial looking wire cutters, one of which she handed to Beth, the other to Antelope.

"You know what to do, right?"

Both nodded. The plan was well known. Signed and sealed. Now all that was needed was for it to be delivered. Whilst they gathered into their two Operations Groups, the first headed by Antelope, the second by Beth, Lola reburied the box, speedily and efficiently. When she had finished there was no sign that the earth had ever been disturbed. And then they were up and running again, spreading out, speeding silently from tree to tree, anxious to avoid the armed guards patrolling within the perimeter fences. The Alphabets were both sharp and tight, the Muldoons less so.

Beth led her group out first. They had further to go and more to do to cover the distance from the north west corner of the Northern Fence to the south east corner of the Southern fence. It took them three minutes to get into position, Wilber watching the seconds ticking over on Crowhaven's watch, with some trepidation. Once they were in position a flashed signal propelled

Antelope and her team into motion. Antelope, with Lola and the Muldoon's moved straight to the outer perimeter fence, in the corner, whilst Beth did the same with her crew. Both encountered guards but speed, efficiency and camouflage won the day. Lola, as might have been expected, was deadly with a blowpipe and the bored, yawning guards fell in quick succession. At the southern fence it was Rudi who spat like a viper, dropping her targets like a trained pro.

35

A Quick Snip

Patrick, taking the wire cutters from Antelope quickly snipped a large hole in the chain linked fence and soon the group were through and taking weapons from the drugged guards. At the Southern Fence, Beth and her team had done likewise. Now it was time to move inwards. Whilst two members of each team waited inside the fence by the outer wire, to serve as lookouts, the remaining members headed towards the inner fence. It was a fast and slick operation, with both teams, so well drilled, that they seemingly mirrored each other's moves.

More snipping and the inner wires of both Northern and Southern perimeters were breached. And suddenly they were through and running towards towers one and eight respectively, momentarily hidden from one another. Now that they were so close, the looming towers seemed more and more threatening, as did the vile smell that hung upon the wind, half sulphur, half rotten meat.

Where before everything had been safely notional, now everything was terrifying real.

Rounding the base of Tower One, Antelope and the Muldoons suddenly stopped dead. There was something wrong, terribly wrong. What was it? No one could say. It was as if the stillness contained all the answers, but that no one could quite interpret it. Beth and her little troop of warriors had emerged from behind Tower Eight and, like Antelope's band, suddenly froze and stood stock still, staring at their opposite numbers on the other side of the compound. Half a football pitch separated them but they may as well have been oceans apart.

And then it began to happen and all of them just froze. The air above the courtyard that separated the two sets of towers, started to crackle and fizz as though it were the abode of demons. And then little lightnings began to traverse the space, whizzing here and there, whirling madly and then linking up and making of the air something like a TV screen, only three dimensional, a volume, not flat. The air took on the appearance of static and all the watchers below were agog as though they were watching a mid air disaster, a collision between aeroplanes or the explosion of a space shuttle.

The air changed state again and something began to appear, slowly at first, but then with increasing speed and clarity. In time the vague and nebulous became defined and observable and all of them beheld it; a man forming in the air over the courtyard, but not an ordinary man, a giant, over twenty metres tall, made of light, not flesh and blood. A hologram with a Russian face. A giant with a gleaming bald head, black suit and mandarin collar. A giant with black eyes and a facial scar. Part Peter the Great, Part Ivan the terrible, wholly Rasputin. Monster and monk, scientist and artist.

Astapor!

"Welcome Wilber to life on top of the volcano. This is my beautiful home. I've been watching your progress with some interest and a little amusement. You will, I hope, forgive me for not meeting you in the flesh as it were, but I fear your Uncle's rage is at such a pitch he would not allow me to leave any such meeting alive. We have a shared past, he and I, but that is perhaps best left for another time, a less-pressured time.

You've done very well, so far, harvesting the crystals of earth and air from my Brother Magicians, and with over eight hours on the clock you are in a very strong position. Of course you've had a little help along the way but I don't begrudge you that. You have had, after all, one or two obstacles thrown in your path. But you are a Muldoon and as such, much can be expected of you.

Anyway, enough chat and onto Game Three. It is a Game of Fire and requires a descent into hell. Let me show you what hell looks like."

As soon as the words were uttered, new sounds filled the air around them, but issuing from the ground beneath their feet, sending distressing vibrations into their bodies. There were many sounds of grinding, clanking pieces of machinery, which were swiftly followed, and somewhat bizarrely, by buzzing sounds of swarming angry insects. This was succeeded by the sound of churning cogs and juddering chains on one level but also the simultaneous hum of hydraulics on quite another level. What did it all mean?

This soon became apparent when the concrete courtyard split into two halves which began to move in opposite directions. The split was no smooth line but formed a jagged, irregular set of jaws filled with teeth that fit perfectly together. All too quickly the concrete courtyard disappeared, folding back into the volcano to reveal a flame-filled void, into which both the Alphabets and the Muldoons could not help but peer. Far below was a bubbling lake of lava, the sulphurous pit that Wilber had but minutes before pictured in his mind's eye. In the shimmering air, now filled with sulphurous fumes and the stench of the volcano, the hologram of the Russian hovered, an enigmatic smile on his lips. Clearly he had more to impart.

"This afternoon's hell is a hell of fire and into that maelstrom you must descend. It's a simple game really, of Hide and Seek. Nothing like the other games you've played and won Wilber. No lies to detect here, no crocodiles to outswim, no, none of that. Just a search with a series of elemental choices to make. What could be easier? All you have to do is pick a door and take a lift up or down. Choose carefully my friend. My house has many mansions and all are full of things that should be approached with a degree of caution. Those creepers, zombies and wisps were nothing but hors d'oeuvres. This is the main course. Here he paused and gave a little chuckle, and as he did so each of the eight doors leading into each of the eight towers slid open in invitation.

"Such an easy game to play, Wilber. Shouldn't detain a man of your talents for more than an hour. The only thing I will say is the crystal, whilst in plain sight, may be buried deeper than you imagine. Also, unlike the other crystals in your possession, it may not be static. Best of luck anyway. George, why don't you join me for a drink. We have so much to discuss."

And with that the hologram faded, disappearing from sight, if not mind. Instantly George's eyes darkened as, rage-fuelled, he broke into a run, heading straight towards the open doors of Tower One. Patrick, seeing what had happened, followed, in hot pursuit, with Great Uncle Muldoon trailing a little way behind him. In fact, the only Muldoon not running pall mall towards the tower was Justice Wilberforce Muldoon. Unlike the others he just stood and stared, but not at the towers, no, away to the south and out over the sea. It wasn't fire that was running through his mind but the water of a green ocean and what lay beneath it. Lola, immobile beside Wilber smiled wryly as though she recognised the signs, whilst the Alphabets on both sides of the smoking divide, just stood and stared, like rabbits caught in a spotlight.

George, at the open doors of Tower One, suddenly became aware that things were not proceeding as planned. Wheeling he froze, and then let out an enraged cry. Wilber, up to now, so decisive was rooted to the spot, staring out over the sea. There was no time for this, not now. Just as Patrick arrived in the doorway the youth began sprinting back the way he had come, passing the Old Man who was wheezing like a punctured bellows as he did so. Screeching to a halt, he took hold of his nephew and began shaking him like a rag doll

"What's the matter with you? Get a move on. The clock is ticking!" His voice rose in pitch to a scream and his eyes were blood-shot but Wilber was both deaf and blind. In fact, Justice was out of it, staring through the world at nothing, having some kind of fit maybe. Lola with all the time, in the world, a feline of no fixed abode, just shook her head slowly."

'I've seen this before Muldoon. So many times. The terror gets them all in the end and they're good for nothing. You have to let it go."

George, not believing what he was hearing, stared at the girl hatefully. It was clear that he wanted to strangle the life out of her but Lola, for her part, was indifferent. The gaze she returned was ablaze with defiance and George, suddenly murderous, was only checked by Patrick's restraining arm. Lola, absorbing every detail, kept her gaze locked onto George's as Wilber broke away and into a run. Everyone watched in horror as Wilber hurtled past the doors of Tower One, through the hole in the inner fence, past the immobilised guards, towards the outer fence. Without breaking stride he leapt through the second hole and taking a sharp left ran down the line of the outer fencing towards the southern slope.

Antelope, stunned by the sudden turn of events, span round and signalled to Beth to sound the retreat. Beth likewise stunned, rallied quickly and broke away leading her troop out of the compound via the south east exit they had used to get in. It was all about getting everyone out now. Tactical retreat be damned, this was just about survival now.

The Old Man who had paused at the door, on the threshold of Tower One, understood this too and like Antelope he was thinking furiously and juggling his options. Wilber, for whatever reason was out of there, and was even now sprinting down the Outer Perimeter fencing. For good or bad he was safe. No, the real problem now was that his rage had unbalanced him to such an extent, he was capable of anything. With heart sinking and mind filling with terror, the Old Man ran over to his nephew and seized him by the arm in an attempt to drag his nephew away. But Dinosaur George, like Wilber before him, was having none of it. All he could do was stare back into the haunted nightmare that was his past.

"Please, George, come now," the Old man pleaded in a near whisper.

Seeing this had no effect, Antelope took over with tones far less sympathetic.

"George, you have to go now!" she ordered.

"No," he roared, and again "No!"

As Antelope was desperate, so Lola was silent. She was still and saying nothing. Not my circus, not my monkeys was her attitude and as infuriating as it was, it was a powerful position. The Old Man had worked the angles, and realising that George was lost, slipped away. Following in Wilber's footsteps he moved with more of a comical waddle than a run, pumping the air for breath. For all that Wilber had freaked and run, he still needed protecting and should the day end in failure for him, as it must surely do now, he would need sanctuary and the occasional bowl of scorpion soup. Clambering through the clipped fence the Old Man cast a winsome glance backwards towards his nephews, locked together in a heated argument. Ah well, it was down to them now, he thought. They were old and ugly enough to decide their fate for themselves.

Back in the compound, George caught sight of his Uncle disappearing through the hole in the inner perimeter and the red mist descended. He was so close, the Russian, that George could almost smell the borscht and samovar. Why had he been born into a family of cowards and traitors? What had he done to deserve that? It wasn't fair. Patrick stood where his Uncle had stood before him, pumping his arm and trying to get George to see sense.

"We have to go, George. We have to go! Regroup and return to fight another day. In another way."

"Screw that, Patrick. It's now or never

Beth was signalling frantically from the other side of the compound for Muldoons to get the hell out of there.

"Do it! Just do it!" she screamed. But George was deaf to advise.

The mix of blinding light, of stinking air and tower-cast shadows obscured and confused everything. The stunning view from the very top of the mountain was something that only Edie saw. Def, realising all was lost, had broken into a sprint. Like race horses running for the finishing line, the Alphabets ran. Everyone was desperate for some kind of resolution but the plan had gone to hell. And what about George? What about George!

Antelope, unable to wait any longer, took to her heels, leaving

Patrick, George and Lola alone in the compound. Patrick, panting for breath, clutched his brother's arm, like a vulture, then grabbed hold of his brother's shirt. George, standing ready to kill, cocked his pistol and stared at the tower.

"George, you need to go. Now! Take the boy, my son. The tower will wait for another day as will the Russian!"

George just shook his head.

"I have to finish this, Patrick. You don't know what he did to her!"

"We need to get out of here. Head for the rendezvous point! Now Before it's too late!"

"It's already too late," George screamed. "We need High Explosive to finish the job".

"What?" Patrick asked nonplussed.

"I need to finish him and now!"

"But what will that achieve ultimately? The machine will remain intact," Patrick fired back. "You need to take on board the bigger picture George. Destroy the machine. Not just the man who built it."

But George was immune to reason and the lure of that open door was too much. A sudden sprint and he was at the door and then over the threshold. All Patrick could do was follow with a sense of falling and of the arrival of impending doom. Now inside the building the brothers headed straight for the lift with Lola padding behind them.

Just as George was about to hit the lift button Lola called out from behind him.

"Take the stairs, Muldoon. More options and a better chance of success."

George, surprised to see the girl was still there nodded slowly.

"Alright. Will do. You coming too?' George asks, "to point the way."

Lola shook her head slowly.

"I'm out of here George. No way I'm staying for this party. You're on your own mate! Give my regards to the Russian"

And with that she was away and running, the last of the rats to leave the sinking ship. Def, ever vigilant, awaited her by the outer perimeter fence, a scowl on her face. Lola, in arriving, smiled and quipped; "Ah Def you shouldn't have. People will say we're in love."

36

Norming

Up in the observatory Astapor, Lurch and Caleb were watching the scenes below them playing out with exceptional glee. It had gone down far better than anyone could ever have imagined, with one exception, no resistance was being offered. The Alphabets were fleeing en masse back down the hill and into the forest and there was no one to stop or follow them. Caleb for one had been anticipating a big fight scene, with shots fired and bodies dropped. He found the Alphabets almost as tasteless as Lola and deserving of punishment if nothing else. They had set the trap but then they had failed to spring it. Surely Astapor hadn't grown a conscience in the last thirty minutes. Why was this happening?

Glaring at the screen Caleb gestured wildly at what he was seeing.

"Those yapping mutts are escaping Count, with the Old Man. As for the Boy, well he's long gone. Surely we need to send the mop up crew after them. They're sitting ducks."

It was true. The Team needed to act now if they were to capitalise on their success. The Old Man was through pleading with his nephew and had broken into a trot in an attempt to keep up with the girls who were disappearing through the hole they had cut on the western side of the Northern perimeter fencing at a rate of knots.

Lurch, standing behind the seated Russian, was delighted at Caleb's loss of composure. This would not go down well with the Count who was a stickler for the observation of etiquette. Still Caleb's loss, as ever was his gain. He cleared his throat and addressed the Russian respectfully, in sharp contrast to his rival.

"Should we pursue them Master? We have men stationed in all of the towers, armed, ready and waiting. And we have others in the forest. What would you like them to do?"

Astapor appeared to consider but his decision was already made.

"Let them go, Lurch. Stand the men down. We have bigger fish to fry."

Spinning in his chair he turned to face the top stair of the spiralling staircase. Each turn of the screw had a barrier door, which had been opened to allow George to thunder upwards without obstruction towards his fate.

Astapor, as keen of ear as George, heard the brother's footsteps on the carpeted stairway before he saw them. He readied himself for his latest guests and both Lurch and Caleb took up their agreed places, behind him, the screens flickering off and the observatory shifting into semi darkness.

George burst into sight and rounded the final turn of the staircase with a look of wild joy on his face. Seeing Astapor seated and apparently waiting for him, brought him up short and he walked the last few steps with a cautious look on his face. Crossing the threshold from the stairway into the room he raised his revolver and grinned.

"Such a pleasure to find you at home Astapor. How come you never came outside to meet and greet me personally?"

The Russian shaped a face of mock horror.

"It's dangerous out there George, as well you know. Here I'm safe, safe to watch and safe to work. And you know how seriously I take my work."

"Yes I know all about you and work."

"So how have you been, Old Friend?" the Russian asked with apparent interest.

"Well I was fine. Happy to move on with my life, to put the past behind me. I didn't mind the fact that you sent people to kill me from time to time. In fact, I expected it but when you went after Justice, well you crossed a line and I realised I would have to put an end to you and your little games once and for all.

As he spoke George edged into the room, his eyes fixed on Astapor, his revolver raised and pointing at his Adversary's heart. The Russian was flanked by his aides, who had taken a discreet step away from the Russian's chair. It wasn't long before a red-faced Patrick came panting up the stairs behind him.

"Perhaps we should introduce him to Granny, Count," offered Caleb.

"Perhaps, but let it not be said I'm not sporting."

"Oh perish the thought," George added, his voice laced with sarcasm.

"One wrong move Georgie and you're toast," Lurch said. "Now, look behind you."

From out of the darkness stepped a number of well-armed men with joyless faces. The largest, a brute of huge proportions stepped in front of Astapor and looked enquiringly at Dinosaur George Muldoon. George looked back up at him and froze. Best to know when to act and when not to. There was no such thing in his mind as a dead hero.

Astapor observing all of this felt his energies soar. Born aloft on eagle's wings he floated and gloated. Some things were well worth waiting for.

"Perhaps it would be best George if you dropped your weapon. Then perhaps we could talk."

37

All The Way Down

Astapor's Guards trained their weapons on Dinosaur George who complied with Astapor's request to drop his antiquated revolver.

"Close but no cigar." Astapor's laughter rang out as he rose from his chair and stepped out to meet his guest.

"I've waited for this moment for such a long time; you've no idea."

Two more guards stepped out of the shadows and seized George, pinning his arms behind his back. Their size and their strength would brook no refusal.

Walking over to Muldoon, Astapor swung his fist into George's lower belly. George took the shock without flinching until Astapor removed a Taser from behind his back and zapped the wild-eyed fossil hunter below the belt. Stunned, George fell to the floor writhing in agony.

Lurch stepped forward and cuffed the recumbent man, then put some kind of hi-tech collar round his neck and fastened it. After a while George got unsteadily to his feet.

"If I ever get loose from these bonds I'll kill you."

Astapor laughed and took a remote from his pocket. He pressed a button, laughing with manic delight. The collar around George's neck tightened and began choking him. Once again he fell to his knees.

"One more word out of you Georgie and I'll make you wish you'd never been born."

Immediately George stopped struggling. The Russian

scrutinised the Dinosaur Man's every expression as though he were preparing to paint him. In Astapor's mind he was both an artist and a scientist. Sometimes the two warred for expression within the battleground of his skull. It wasn't enough to win, to beat your man to the canvas, to have your arm raised by the referee and to be proclaimed victor. No, that was not Astapor's idea of victory. Victory was only to be found in the absolute despair of the vanquished. This could play out over weeks, months or even years.

"Right, into the lift."

George stood and walked over to the lift. Once inside the lift he bided his time, watching Patrick out of the corner of his eye. Astapor fondled the remote and looked exceptionally pleased with himself. Suddenly George sprang forward and kicked the remote from his long white fingers.

"Patrick, the remote," yelled George.

Patrick unbound lunged for the remote, seized it, stood up and looked George full in the eye. Then he levelled the machine and discharged a near fatal dose of electricity into his brother's body. George lay prone for a minute or so and then slowly revived. Sitting up against the liftpod door he stared at Patrick with disbelief.

"Patrick, how could you?"

"Too many cold wet nights out in the forest Muldoon," Caleb crowed. "You should never have left him. He's weak and he lacks your resolve."

Patrick bowed his head in shame.

"So where are we going?" George asked.

Astapor reached out and pressed a button; the elevator stopped immediately.

"Take a look."

Through the clear glass frontage of the lift door George could see out.

What he saw made him gasp. There were dozens of people in cages, most in hideous states of disarray. Starved or bloated, smooth or torn, all were in pain and distress. White coated scientists were moving around with syringes, obviously happy to be working.

Burly guards manhandled the starving people, holding them so the scientists could inject them or force-feed them certain foodstuffs. Then they were loaded back into their cages, there to await developments. The people were obviously being experimented on.

"This is where we do all the work."

Lurch hit the lift button and once more they began to descend. Past a certain level, daylight was lost and they were obviously moving deeper and deeper underground.

"And here is where we store the products of our work. Layer after layer of human variants; transformed by me into things that would turn your stomach. More than human or less than human? You decide. Take a look out through the glass. Go on, enjoy yourself while you still can.

George looked out, mesmerised in spite of himself.

"So these are the holding tanks where all the fun happens. Way down under the ground where no one can see. I wonder what your Brother Magicians would say if they saw what you get up to in here. I'm guessing that isn't in your charter"

Astapor shrugged.

"Who's to say that they know and they just don't care. Who's to say they know and approve of my work. It's amazing really, what we've achieved. With just one or two neural tweaks the tweediest flower presser can become a lethal killer. Once they have your scent, they never relent; they'll track you till you're theirs and once your theirs...well lets just say they leave no trace. Not so much as a blood stained rag."

Down and down they went and the deeper they went the more twisted and manic the caged humans became. On the upper levels they were warped but rather sedate, in the mid levels they were hollering and growling, rattling the bars and being sick for sport, on the lower levels they were jabbering in psychotic states of rage, frequently turning on one another and tearing their cell mates to pieces. It looked like the inside of an abattoir or the results of a suicide bombing.

Astapor nodded to Lurch, who once more, pressed the button

that made the lift stop. This time much to George's horror, the lift doors opened, revealing a dingy dungeon with three dishevelled looking women, holding oversized beasts in their arms. Closer inspection revealed them to be cats but they were at least the size of Doberman Pinschers.

"Something I cooked up for you personally George. Meet the Cat Slappers."

At this a siren sounded and a poor boy of about twelve was dropped into the room through a hole in the roof. He landed with a dull thud and then slowly got to his feet at which point the women attacked. Their modus operandi was horrific. Initially they swung their cats by the tails like clubs. As they swung the cats bit and scratched and the boy screamed out in agony. After a while he dropped to the floor and both the women and the cats fell upon him, like ghouls, to feed.

Patrick couldn't look but George forced himself to and eventually the doors closed and the lift began to descend once more.

"How many levels?" George asked through gritted teeth.

"32. From the uppermost to lowermost."

Astapor glanced through the glass doors and grinned.

"This is almost as low as I go but not quite."

"I find that hard to believe."

Suddenly the lift came to a smooth and definitive halt.

"Ahh. Here we are. The basement, as you can see is full of medieval devices of torture. Caleb calls it the nursery, somewhere to play and have fun."

George looked around him and shrugged.

End of the line huh?

"Not quite, unfortunately"

Lurch thrust his hands into George's back, propelling him forward. In this way they moved away from the lift shaft towards the first of a series of deep vents

"Welcome Muldoon to the Pits of Pain."

"I always said you were the pits, Astapor, and now I have proof."

Another truly dreadful pun hit the dirt. Astapor looked at his nemesis with scarcely disguised loathing.

"These are entrance points to the labyrinth, George, and each one contains some form of terror. The labyrinth honeycombs the island and it's full of things too dangerous to be released onto the surface of the island."

"The uncontrollable, the unstoppable, the unbelievable. The things that most people only meet in their nightmares," Caleb crooned.

"Thank you Caleb," the Russian said in a voice colder than Siberia.

Patrick, looking down the first hole into the darkness, felt suddenly queasy.

"I'm not sure I need to be here. I did what you asked. I delivered him. Now its time to keep your side of the bargain. I've had enough of living out there, amongst the monsters. I want a little comfort and a lot of safety and the best food you have in your larder."

Astapor's grin did nothing to put Patrick's mind at rest. Then he cleared his throat.

"All in good time Master Patrick. I can assure you, you will know nothing but comfort. There are seven pits of pain here my Dinosaur loving friend, each with its own form of mythological horror. You get to choose which one we throw you down.

"Would you be so good as to tell me what terror lurks in each pit?"

"Unfortunately that's against the rules."

Astapor nodded to his guards. Two grabbed George and the others, to Patrick's horror, grabbed him. Patrick was cuffed and attached to a winch as was George, and back to back the brothers were hoisted high to dangle above one of the dreadful pits. When George caught one of the guards under the jaw with a vicious kick they hit him so hard he blacked out, then they bound his legs.

38

Slappers

Somebody was slapping his face. Over and over. Big hand, heavy and powerful. Callused and trained. Not somebody to cross. It hurt.

"Wake him up! Wake him now!"

The voice belonged to the Russian and George heard a note of anxiety within the cacophony. Astapor did not care about him per se, but he was concerned, lest he be robbed of his prey. George's pupils dilated as a beam of torch light was shone into his eyes. A sharp slap caught him off guard. Then another slap. He winced as his consciousness returned fully and he opened his eyes to find the Russian staring at him fiendishly.

"You had me worried for a moment then George. Thought you were slipping away into the Big Nothing before your time. Before I had given you permission anyways."

George snorted.

"Like I need your permission."

"That's my boy. So what's next? Shall I tell you? Do you really want to know? Course you do. Possibilities George. Always possibilities. I'm nothing if not fair. Another descent. Free-falling in the dark...that's you and him.... then the crack of bones and agonised screams until you're both silenced. Not exactly a chip off the old block is he, your brother? Your lovely brother. So easy to crack. Not really a man, not even a mouse. Far more pathetic."

"If you want pathetic, just look in a mirror."

At this the Russian guffawed.

"Flabby George. You've gone to seed, lost a step or two. You used to have such a smart mouth."

"Let me out of these chains and we'll see who's lost a step."

More laughter, increasingly manic.

"That's not the way we play George. You should know that by now."

George tutted.

"You're such a disappointment Astapor. Can't win without loaded dice. eh?"

"Well I have to level the playing field somehow. You don't begrudge me that, do you George? We have to keep it interesting. Boredom, after all, is the one and only curse."

"No. You are the one and only curse my friend."

"How can I disagree," the Russian replied, his mind clearly in motion, heading for the next stage of his revenge.

"So George, down to business. As much as I'd love to stand here trading insults, we have to move on. Everything is ready, after years of careful planning and now I am ready to make my presentation."

George faked a yawn and Astapor clucked. Seconds passed before George relented and asked the necessary question.

"So what's on the menu, my little Russian friend?"

"You're going to love this George. It's a genetic smorgasbord of delights. The best of the worst or the worst of the best. You decide."

"Please, just get on with it," Patrick pleaded. "Whatever you've got planned, just unleash it!"

Astapor was not amused.

"Open your mouth again Patrick, without my permission, and I will relieve you of your tongue. Not that you're going to need it for much longer."

The Russian was right on the edge and gleefully prancing. Patrick needed to be careful. If he pushed him too much the deranged Slav would snap his jaws shut on some much-needed part of Patricks anatomy.

"Been busy have you?" George asked, keen to distract.

"Idle hands are the devil's playthings, as well you know George."

"So what has mummy been cooking up in the kitchen?"

The smile dropped off the Russians face and reappeared on George's. There was nothing quite like bating Astapor. It was like poking a crocodile in the eye with a pointed stick. Quite exhilarating until it wasn't.

"George, there are all sorts of monsters in this world, most are broken but some are whole. If scarred. It's one thing to make them, quite another thing to train them to do your bidding. Suffice it to say I have done both. Cue applause."

Lurch and Caleb dutifully clapped.

"I've taken my inspiration from all over the world, from all ages. I have drawn my materials from every mythology and legend that had something nightmarish to add to the mix. There are bestiaries and demonologies, books of magic and of the imagination that I have plundered for ideas and inspiration. As well you know I have a well-stocked book shelf. And I have dug deep into the darkest places, places even de Sade wouldn't dare venture. Against the greatest minds I have measured myself and I have emerged triumphant."

"Pray, do tell," George prompted, seasoning his voice with as much ennui as he could muster.

Astapor could scarcely contain himself. His laughter was virtually epileptic. The guards were laughing too and in spite of his terror, so was Patrick.

"I don't want to let the cat out of the bag just yet George. Not until you have been lowered into the crypt and the cat has had a chance to claw its own way out of the bag. Suffice it to say you will encounter monsters, magnificent monsters. Genetic kinks and throwbacks at every turn. All equally maleficent and eminently venomous. And rest assured all of them have been bred to respond to your scent."

"Fancy," George trilled.

"Fancy indeed. You're going down that hole tonight George to face the crooked teeth. Nothing you ever dug up out of the earth is quite as terrifying as what I've cooked up for you. So, it's time to blow away the cobwebs and to prepare for one last dance."

Now Caleb was edging closer, a grinning vision of psychosis.

"It's not all bad down there boys. Don't think that. You won't be entirely alone and without friends. Why, Granny lurks in the labyrinth. Surely you remember Granny? She's so alone down there. Hasn't been petted in years. She knows you're coming though. It's to be admitted that she's put on a little weight. In fact, you may not recognise her at first. Not until she gets up real close and clanks her mandibles in your face."

"Thank you Caleb, that's quite enough."

Astapor's hiss was enough to silence even the most demented. Now the speeches were finally over, it was time to pay the ferryman. Astapor looked almost sorry that the moment he had dreamt about so frequently and recurrently had finally arrived.

It was one thing to plan, quite another to see one's plans realised. He had learned early on that one's reach should always exceed one's grasp, or one was prone to fall into a depressive stupor. The only antidote to the terror of boredom, was to create ever more outlandish and preposterous plans. In his inverted world Heaven and Hell had exchanged places. But, for all that, moments of significance must still be marked, with a gesture or with a silence and when all that had been done, a final requiem.

"Such a pity you've got to go now. I can't remember a time I enjoyed myself quite as much George. Goodbye, old friend. I'd like to be able to say that your death is going to be pain-free, but I can't. I'd like to be able to say that your life has had significance and meaning, but I won't and I'd like to be able to tell you that I'm going to let your young nephew finish the Game unmolested, but I haven't got it in me to lie. I'm going to hunt him down along with all his little friends and I'm going to transform them into something truly warped. They won't die immediately. Oh no, that would be too easy. But they will die screaming."

George shook his head sadly.

"Everything we know and love must always have an end. Madeline knew that and she told me as much."

Astapor's face darkened.

"How dare you mention her name."

George laughed bitterly.

"Why shouldn't I? You've got nothing more to threaten me with. You're going to kill me anyway so what the hell."

Caleb looked at Astapor uneasily, whilst Lurch looked away. One way or another someone would end up paying for this.

"She loved you enough to believe that you were worth saving. That day on the cliff, she had come to tell me it was all over, that she was going back to you. In her head, she was the only person who could save you."

"Save me from what?" the Russian asked suspiciously.

"From yourself."

Astapor reeled, then he began to convulse with rage. Normally so calm and controlled he had become something else now, someone different and it was frightening to behold. Even Astapor's minions looked away. Only Caleb dared watch, wide-eyed with shock and fear.

"She was mine, she was my wife and you took her from me."

George shook his head.

"No, she was going back to you. As much as she loved me, she loved you more. She believed in you, believed that you were the only person on this island who had the will and the vision to govern it, to safeguard the people and create a fair and equitable society. And what have you done with your will and your vision, you've created hell on earth. You've betrayed yourself and you shame her memory."

With a yell Astapor wrenched the control from Caleb's grip and the mechanism released. Both George and Patrick, still attached to the chains that held their arms aloft, fell into the darkness.

Below them something roared.

39

Down In The Labyrinth

Hanging, swinging from side to side, the once-loving brothers, bound and dangling, awaited their fate. The initial fall had all but unmanned Patrick. His screams had filled the darkness and when they had lurched to a halt, he had vomited. George, alternating between fits of violent rage and tender love, felt that of all the moments in his life, this was the most challenging. He had every reason to hate Patrick, and if the moment came when they were released from the chains he would have the opportunity to kill him. He knew of Astapor's tastes and could half feel, half sense the arc of this particular narrative.

It was just a Game for the Mad Russian's amusement. It would please him to watch as they were both torn apart by whatever horrors awaited in the pit, but it would delight him more, if George was so enraged that he killed his own brother. He must resist this temptation at all costs and in that moment of realisation they dropped again and Patrick resumed his screaming. When next they stopped, they shuddered and spun, the chains winding them together. Then lights flickered on and off in the labyrinth, creating new uncertainties. Now, bound face to face, in this moment of intimacy there was an opportunity for revelation.

"Patrick!"

No answer. Patrick just stared wildly into his brother's eyes and the lights went out. A few seconds later they flickered on again and George saw that his brother's eyes were closed. Could they still be considered as brothers? What, after all, was a brother? Humans who had emerged from the same womb, grown up together, laughed together, learned together. Who loved and protected one another, were loyal to one another. Or was it all just a lie, a fabrication. A biological co-incidence.

"Patrick." That word again, spoken with savage and heartfelt desperation. Almost a whisper. The eyes remained closed, for all George's pleading. Patrick. The word echoed in his brother's skull and Patrick opened his mouth and screamed. He was already in hell or on the cusp of it. Hell was a mouth full of broken bloodied teeth. He hung above it, hanging on to a few shreds of sanity. Soon he would fall in an unblinking scream forever. The thought almost broke him, but from deep inside, Patrick felt something stirring, saw a faint glimmer of light and hope. And somehow he found the strength he needed and he opened his eyes. His brother's eyes were open too, staring deep into him. For a few seconds they remained in that state, gazing deeply into one another.

It was Patrick who broke the silence.

"I'm sorry George," he said simply and tears ran down his face dropping into the darkness below.

"I know," George replied and a faint smile played on his lips. "And I forgive you."

'You do?"

"Yeah. I abandoned you, left you here in this God awful place. So I guess we're even."

Patrick pursed his lips, considered his brother's words and then he spoke again.

"And I forgive you."

"Don't push it," George responded, after a brief pause, speaking through gritted teeth.

Another pause and then they both burst out laughing. The hysteria of the moment gripped them and they laughed and laughed until the terror that had loosened their bowels slunk away, back into the shadows from whence it had come.

"So what's down there Pat?"

"It's not good, George. "

Typical Patrick. High on emotion. Low on content.

"So bio-engineered horrors."

"Pretty much," Patrick said breezily.

"Greco-Roman?"

Uh Huh."

"Cyclops, Minotaurs, Satyrs?"

"Yeah. He also has a Gorgon, you know the gorgons, those crazy women with snakes for hair and a gaze that turns you to stone."

George had heard of them and what he had heard was more than disquieting.

"What else?"

"Ogres, goblins, a werewolf or two, a few Tory MPs, giant snakes and spiders..."

Here he was interrupted as the lights went out and they dropped again. More jerks and twists and this time blasts of hot air and explosions ripping through the air around them. For some reason though it had ceased to be frightening. A few breathes and they were able to resume their conversation.

"So how are we going to play this George? What's the Game plan?" Patrick asked, suddenly serious.

"Haven't got one. We just have to go for it Pat. Whatever's down there is going to come at us at a hundred miles an hour with a view to turning us into foaming strips of meat."

"Yeah I agree. So we just go Rhino and charge in."

George tried to nod but the chains that bound them impeded his movements.

"There's no other way to do it."

Patrick, aware that time was ticking down to zero point, tried to think of one last vital piece of information that might make the difference between life and death for them. Suddenly a flash of remembrance lit up his eyes like lightning going to ground, splitting a tree in two in the process.

"It's not hopeless George. There is a way out of the labyrinth. That much I know. Something about mirrors. Don't look in any mirrors. They will only deceive you."

"That's good Patrick. Very good. We just have to keep on

running and as we run we look for weapons. There has to be something down there we can use."

"Let's hope so," Patrick said, not altogether certain. "Astapor has a habit of stacking the deck in his favour, you know. He's not going to leave loaded machine guns lying around."

"Yeah but he's gonna want a show," George countered. "He doesn't want this over in a few minutes. He wants us to suffer"

"Let's hope so," Patrick replied, trying to smile but failing miserably.

At this point the lights went out and they dropped into the darkness, one last time.

*　　　*　　　*　　　*　　　*　　　*　　　*

In creating the labyrinth and its contents Astapor had been tireless, his energy boundless. He had known way back in the beginning that it would come to this. Dinosaur George Muldoon could run but he couldn't hide. It had been so naïve of him to believe that he, Astapor was capable of forgiveness, of forgetting.

Spider-like he worked tirelessly in the dark spinning his many webs to catch a single fly. It was more than a point of honour with him. It was his nature.

The liftpod doors opened and he strode out onto the chequered floor of the green dome, exhilarated and impatient, quickly followed by Lurch and Caleb, who both had remote controls in their hands and were jabbing frantically at buttons to ensure that events transpired in their allotted order. The show, if their Master was to enjoy it, must be flawless.

As soon as Astapor was through the doors, the lights were lowering and the screens were flickering on. There were multiple feeds from multiple cameras, positioned within the labyrinth and the domed screen scanned from any number of possible angles. The cameras were everywhere; above and below the action, gliding on runners along the walls to track the running, screaming prey. They could flip sideways, zig-zag, even loop-the-loop. All shapes and sizes of lenses had been included too. There were wide angle lenses, fish eye lenses, close ups, mid shots, long shots. All manner of permutations had been explored. Infra red, low light and spotlight options had all been catered for too.

Caleb had put the initial plan together, which Astapor had approved and augmented with his own suggestions. Then Caleb had set the rig up himself, at great personal risk. Astapor trusted no one else on the island to do this as no one else, in his eyes, had Caleb's vision or technical competence. It was quite hard to find this blend of traits in a single person, but in Caleb he believed he had his man.

Before the 'set' had been ready for today's action they had tested it many times. The island was generous, ensuring an endless flow of screaming meat for the denizens of the pit to feast upon. After each entertainment, Caleb had adjusted the rig, repositioning cameras and replacing lenses where necessary.

The action could be watched live but then after the main event, he could edit the many feeds into a post show Match of the Day, which included the best angles to view the chase and kill with, and, best of all, all the boring bits cut out.

Periodically Caleb would edit together the highlights of numerous matches, compiling a Season of Horror for his errant Master to gorge on whilst he ate his nightly meal, usually alone. If Astapor was in a particularly foul mood this was the only way to soothe and placate him. His skill in the editing suite, and his general usefulness, was what kept Caleb alive, or so the youth thought.

"Is everything in order, Caleb?" Astapor asked in that effortlessly menacing way he had perfected so long ago.

"Indeed, it is Count."

Caleb pressed a flashing button on his remote and a camera positioned at the bottom of the pit, its lens angled upwards, crackled into life. It showed the Muldoon brothers dangling just metres above the ground, wound together by their wraparound chains.

"One more drop and out they flop. What would you like me to release first, Count?"

"Send everything Caleb, empty every pit. I want to be entertained so go on. Entertain me!!!"

40

The Labyrinth Revealed

As Caleb's index finger jabbed the last button in a sequence of six, the dangling men dropped the last twenty metres of their staggered fall and hit the ground. As soon as they hit, the chains that had bound them unravelled, as though by magic, spilling both brothers out onto the floor unencumbered. Springing quickly to their feet both Patrick and George rapidly patted themselves up and down to ensure they were still in one piece. Good. Nothing broken and no serious cuts. Patrick had a slight limp but then he'd always been a bit limp, so no change there.

"What now George?" Patrick whispered.

"Quiet!" George hissed back.

They had been dropped into a chamber, of some kind, lit with low-grade green light. Some kind of foul smelling mist, or vapour hung in the air, twisting and turning in the diffuse light as though full of snakes. Patrick covered his mouth with his left hand to stop himself from gagging.

"What the hell is that smell?"

"I can't be entirely sure but I'd say it was a cocktail of skunk, sulphur and elephant dung. Now will you please be quiet."

George, having delivered his initial diagnosis, turned around slowly, listening intently at every turn and pausing occasionally. Up above, there had been screams and cries, roars and bleatings, but now it was silent. Deadly silent. Whatever lived down here was used to hunting in the dark, or at the very least, in very low light levels. It was slightly unhinging. They had both expected to be attacked as soon as they touched the ground but no, that was not the plan. And yet, and yet... they were not alone down here. Something was approaching, something with deadly intent.

George, ever hopeful of escape, focused on the walls and the doors, whilst Patrick scanned the floor of the chamber for whatever weapons he could find. After a while, the silence got the better of the younger brother and despite misgivings, he was compelled to speak.

"So what do you make of it George," Patrick whispered.

"Interesting, most interesting" George responded as though he were faced with nothing more baffling than the Sunday Times Crossword. "It would appear we are in a hexagonal labyrinth. Three full walls, three broken walls. Three open doors in the broken walls inviting us to run, treating us as if we were idiots. But we are not idiots, are we Patrick?"

"No, indeed we are not... but if we're not idiots, what are we then George?"

"We're Muldoons Pat, and don't you forget it. Find anything?"

Patrick considered his next response carefully.

"Yes. Now do you want the good news or the bad news?"

George rolled his eyes.

"This isn't panto Pat. Just give it to me straight.

"Alright, alright, don't go on."

This was so typically Patrick. They were in the gravest danger, possibly the worst situation of their lives and yet he couldn't deliver simple information in a clear and concise way.

"Please", George pleaded. "There isn't time."

"Well," Patrick said, somewhat ponderously, "there aren't any conventional weapons down here but there are these."

And at this he hoisted what looked to be two smooth sticks with swellings at either end into view.

"Great," George ejaculated, reaching out for, and then snatching, one of the sticks in a sudden flurry of excitement. "Not quite up to the standard of baseball bats but probably the next best thing. What are they, do you think?"

"Well I'm not entirely sure, brother dearest, but I think they might be bones."

George was nonplussed.

"Why do you say that?"

"Look down there," said Pat pointing with his free hand. George followed the pointing finger to what appeared to have been, prior to Patrick's predations, a perfectly preserved skeleton. It was in pristine condition, without a shred of clothing or a morsel of meat attached, but otherwise human in every aspect. Each and every bone gleamed white in the ailing half light, as though sanded and polished, and ten fingers and ten toes could be counted on the immaculately-maintained hands and feet. In fact, the only thing that was noticeably lacking was a head.

When George saw this, he gulped. Patrick, observing his brother's reaction, merely shrugged.

"Well everything's gotta eat George."

George was about to take issue with this not unreasonable point of view, when a sudden hiss alerted him to the fact that they were not alone. Standing in the doorway, facing them, was a tall woman with black eyes and a writhing nest of snakes for hair. There was a hint of the badger about her in that she wore a long grey robe and had a black stripe of paint across her eyes. Her face was geisha-white but she was nowhere near as beautiful as a Japanese lovely.

Her teeth were positively Vampiric.

"The Gorgons!!!" Patrick yelled, and right on cue, the two remaining doorways filled with similarly adorned snake-haired monsters. In Greek mythology, it had been said that they could turn men to stone. Perseus had slain them with the aid of a Magic Shield, whose reflective surface allowed him to behead the women without having to look upon their loathsome, hate-filled faces. Unfortunately, the Muldoon brothers were not quite so-well armed as Young Perseus. All they had was a pair of femur bones yanked from the skeleton of a recently-devoured human. Nevermind, they would improvise.

George, thinking on his feet, indicated that Patrick should get behind him and within two whisks of a lamb's tail, the brothers stood back-to-back, ready for action. George, sensing something amiss, sniffed the air.

"My God, and I thought the chamber reeked; they smell just awful!"

"I'm afraid, that isn't them George, it's me," Patrick admitted dolefully.

"Oh no, you haven't."

"I'm afraid I have," Patrick whimpered.

Slowly, the Gorgons began to advance on the brothers, their black eyes mesmerising, their writhing hair terrifying. Each head must have contained thirty red-eyed snakes, each chock full of deadly venom for which doubtless, no antidote existed. George thought it was a look that would have suited Jordan, but then berated himself. This wasn't a time for inconsequentialities. It was a time for ingenuity backed up by swift and savage action. But what to do? The situation looked bleak for the bone wielding brothers. Had they run the last leg of their race and backed themselves into a corner? Was the curtain about to descend?

Patrick, realising how hopeless the situation was, broke formation and reached into his pocket. Out of this, he yanked a half-empty bottle of scotch, unscrewed the cap and took a long and desperate swig. George, sensing the movement, spun round and gaped.

"Where in the name of hell did you get that?" he thundered accusingly.

"It was on the floor," came the plaintive reply.

"Well, give it here," yelled the elder, seizing the bottle as though it were contraband, a deft and cunning plan forming almost instantly in his devious mind.

Reaching behind his lapel, George, with the fingers of his right hand, retrieved a hidden match. Fortunately Astapor's guards had failed to find it, secreted away, as it was, on his person. With a little luck, it might just provide them with the much desired opening. Hefting the bottle of whiskey to his lips, George took a generous swig. Without swallowing, he quickly lit the match on his unshaven chin and held the flaming timber just before his eyes.

It was all just a question of timing now. The unsuspecting Gorgons came on and by some hidden, and yet prearranged signal, dashed forward as one, for the kill. Big mistake! George, apprentice circus freak, trainee juggler and fire eater, spat what Patrick had swallowed, onto each screeching body, which combusted on cue, in quite spectacular fashion.

Screeches of hunger-filled lust turned to screams of rage, then fear and finally agony. Swatting the flames aside with well-manicured fingers and bony white hands did nothing to help them, and soon the air was filled with smoke and the smell of burnt flesh.

Both Patrick and George found themselves salivating, but that was only to be expected. Neither had eaten anything in quite a while. In time, the Gorgon's frenzied motions ceased and they collapsed, as one, to the sand-covered floor. There they continued to bubble and smoulder. Patrick gave a little cough and then, remembering his manners, clapped his hands in enthusiastic applause. George, almost against his will, gave a little bow.

"That was impressive," the younger brother conceded.

"Unfortunately it's not over. I think it's just the first course in a very long banquet of horrors. What's that? Can You hear it?"

"I can hear something."

"Listen! On second thought, don't bother. Run!"

There were more shrieks and howls and the sound of running feet coming towards them at speed. With deadly intent. George was right about that and Patrick wasn't wrong. All their nightmares had come out to play, or so it seemed, and none could be placated with kind words and the application of reason. Only brute force would liberate them from their plight. Down the passages of the labyrinth they hared, dodging this way and that, sometimes side by side, sometimes separate. Now ducking, now swinging, now attacking, now retreating. Always pursued. Always on the edge of going under.

A swarm of killer bees, an army of deadly ants and a rabid mongoose came in the first wave of the attack. George drank and spat more flaming whiskey, Patrick stamped and stomped with his Grindstone Boots, and both pounded mercilessly, with their bloodied femurs.

In the second wave, things became more serious. A phalanx of shamed Tory politicians, defrocked priests and the violently mad assaulted them without mercy. Some pinched, most kicked, all bit and scratched. Thankfully the Muldoons were a tough breed and their frequent recreational bouts of cage fighting served them well.

Patrick was a master with the well-placed knee, whereas George favoured the head butt or the nut as he called it. Before long their foes were neatly piled in a bleeding heap of dangling limbs and protruding bones.

It was unlikely that many would see consciousness again but that wasn't the Muldoon's problem. Only survival was. They resumed their flight, Patrick a headless chicken, George a mobile planner and master tactician.

Before too long a third wave of horrors came out of the walls with a view to scaring the brothers to death. But after the politicians and the priests, little moved them. They had supped full with horrors, as the cliché ran. The headless ghosts were rapidly exorcised and sent screaming back to their numerous hells, whilst the demonic goblins were laughed out of court.

After a while, there was silence and the brothers stopped running and paused to rest and reflect, leaning on their bloodied femurs as though they were Old Men's walking sticks. Patrick was panting as though he'd just run up and down a mountain, but George was in good nick, and his breathing returned to normal, before too much time had elapsed. Their boney weapons', despite being well-used, had not splintered, shattered or split. For this the brothers were grateful.

George, hoisting his weapon aloft, examined it with care and wondered whose the bone had come from. Some unfortunate soul, most likely, condemned to roam the labyrinth until felled, killed and eaten. Or perhaps eaten alive. It didn't bear thinking about. And all for Astapor's pleasure. The swine!

"Do you think he's still watching?"

At this, George leapt, swung and smashed another camera. The green lights above them flickered, then rallied. They did not go out and the brothers were, both of them, licked green by the rancid spots and shins. Their illumination was not for their benefit though; both understood this.

"Who? Astapor?" he asked needlessly.

Patrick nodded.

"Undoubtedly."

Things didn't get much better for the Russian. He had his prey and at last his revenge could unfold. Such a highlight for the crazed Slav. George could well imagine how he'd spent the years of his absence breeding and corrupting life. Taking the beautiful and making it bestial, converting impulses to love, into the need and the drive to kill and maim. It was the Russian's aesthetic. Beauty destroyed and became ugly but it was still potent and alluring. And to Astapor, the ugly was beautiful.

His was a world of tortured inversions.

George, meditating upon his and Patrick's fate, came to understand something important. That the labyrinth was a model of the Russian's mind. It was perfectly ordered, but there was no way out. It had been filled with the Count's wrath and as such contained things that scratched and clawed, stung and bit. It was a cave of plagues and endless torments. Of memory and regret. Death was the blessed release, survival the unendurable horror. So many terrors here and a single error or a moment of mercy would ensure one's doom. As hopeless as it all was, it was also an education on how to survive the island.

No mercy, only severity. No pause, only action. No end, only more and more terrifying beginnings. Never relax. Never lower your guard. Never give up. Fight always and that was when George saw it. The next instalment of the latest wave. White, not black as it should have been. A snowflake of malevolent intent bearing down upon him, rearing up and striking out again and again with its hairy limbs. Pounding them downwards, raining down blow after blow.

In his auditory imagination, he heard the sound of crunching bones. His. The eyes, unlike the body, were black and there were eight of them, clustered together like rancid grapes. In every eye, he saw not his own reflection, but Astapor's.

A trick of the light, or a distortion of his mind. He didn't know anymore and for the first time since hitting the island, George felt weariness engulf him. Above his head, a light flickered on and Patrick yelled out in warning.

He had seen what his brother had not. The end was nigh.

41

Bullseye!

The spider gathered itself for a final assault. Its prey was tiring, it could see that. Anyone watching could see that. It was to be expected. The odds were stacked against anything that dropped into the labyrinth, however skilled. Too many horrors were stored there for even the strongest of humans to contend with. Chains would rattle and lights would flash alerting the waiting monsters that something was about to drop into their lair. Something that would scream and run and put up a modicum of a fight but not for long. The odds were too long, and the hunters were starving. Ruthless and ready to run. Poised to strike and tear, shatter and shred.

Gates would slide open, upwards or sideways and out they would rush into the pale green air. Everything that skulked and scuttled, crept or loped was a source of terror. And there was no end in sight. If the first monster didn't get you then the second would, or the third or the fourth. An endless chain of horrors, all with needs, would be focusing on just one thing; your death.

All this ran through George's mind as he gazed into the eight black, lens-like eyes of the edging spider. One last lunge and it would be over. He counted the seconds as his heart pounded in his chest and his life flashed before his eyes in bite-sized chunks. Image piled on image.

The moment arrived and the hirsute arachnid wavered, then surged forward, its legs pumping like pistons, its clanking mandibles oozing stinking venom. George tensed, convinced the game was finally over. The stench of its breath turned his stomach and felt the bile rising. Just at the moment when the spider's jaws were set to close around his throat a black shadow detached itself from the labyrinth wall and hurtled towards the spider's head.

An arm was hoisted aloft and descended rapidly, the sickle it carried slicing down through the spider's head, severing it from its body. It fell with a thud and a splat of black blood like a bucket of paint dropped from a high ladder. The creature convulsed and collapsed but behind it a second beast leaped and landed on the shadow; the shadow that was Patrick.

The scream emitted from his brother's lips was enough to galvanise George into action. Adrenaline coursed through his bloodstream and he dragged himself to his feet. His first impulse was to run but he willed himself to a halt. His brother lay on his belly, his left leg clamped in the spider's mouth, a shattered bone protruding through the flesh. Reaching out he clasped Patrick's hands but it was all too late. The second spider was already dragging his brother away into the darkness. George wrestled the sickle from his brother's grip but he was gone. The last image he had of his brother was the blank staring eyes.

It could not be doubted that the spider's venom had already stopped Patrick's heart.

It took George a moment to process what had happened. Patrick had hurled himself in harm's way and offered his life for George's. There was no doubt in Muldoon's mind that his brother was being eaten in his stead. The sounds from the darkness confirmed as truth what he had surmised. Oh, let him be dead. Let him be oblivious, George prayed.

No greater love existed than he who would lay down his life for a brother.

Tears came to his eyes but George quickly wiped them away. This was no time for grief. That would have to come later. He must ensure that Patrick had not died in vain. A quick glance upwards, to where the wall of the labyrinth met the ceiling. Black eyes staring down, the cctv lens revolving silently, focusing. Astapor. George flicked his middle and index finger into the Agincourt 'V' and then hurled the sickle.

The bloodied blade clattered into the camera and it exploded into a shower of sparks. Bullseye. Up in the control tower Astapor screamed with rage and pounded his console. George ran down the corridor, rounded a corner only to find a mirror staring at him.

He raced towards it as the lights went out.

42

Jabbing Buttons

Silence.

Up in the tower everyone froze and all eyes turned from the blank screen to the staring Russian. Astapor, seated on his elegant throne of white leather, was at first incredulous and then furious. For what seemed like minutes he just stared at the screen, unable to process what had happened, whilst Caleb's blood turned to ice. His bodyguards fingered their triggers and awaited orders, all eyes fixed on Caleb, until now the Golden Boy. Lurch hung suspended beneath his smile.

The Russian was in that moment a more terrifying apparition than anything down in the labyrinth.

"Where is he?" he hissed, scarcely able to contain himself.

Caleb hoisted his remote and began jabbing buttons. One by one the camera eyes flickered on, filling the screen with multiple viewpoints. They revealed a shattered world, diced by Cubist brushstrokes. A fragmentagram that echoed the shape of the hexagonal labyrinth. All were filled with action but none showed the scene that Astapor had waited for. Planned for. Meticulously, year after year. Namely George's death.

"Get the beasts back into their pits."

Caleb, his brow beaded with sweat, jabbed another sequence of buttons and the green lights began to pulse and the air below, to fill with a deadly stream of high-pitched tones and whines. It was agony to the beasts and so they slunk back into their lairs and gates slammed or slid shut behind them.

A perfect construction, yet another product of the Russian's genius, Caleb thought, as he stared at an image that would haunt him forever. The last bloodied remains of Patrick Muldoon's life on earth. That could be him and soon.

Caleb stood as still as a statue and waited for his fate to unfold. He was aware of the position of every bodyguard in the room, how focused they were. Once they had been his to command but not now. Not anymore.

How soon the Old Order faded.

A glance at the screen revealed there was no movement in the labyrinth.

"Where is he?" The Russian asked.

"He's gone," Caleb said simply.

"I can see that,"

"Yes, but where?"

And that in a nutshell was the ten million dollar question. Think, Caleb told himself; think. He closed his eyes momentarily and breathed deeply. Then he opened them again and began scanning the fragmentagram. At least sixty feeds into that space and one lucky shot by George had turned the outcome of the game in its dying moments. Like a last minute penalty in a world cup final. One half of the crowd screaming with fierce exhilaration, the other half with agonised disbelief. It didn't look good. In fact it looked as though George may have been helped and that did not bode well for anyone, least of all Caleb.

Think.

He clicked rapidly through each of the feeds. The tension in the room began to mount and he became suddenly aware that in one of those machine guns was a bullet with his name on it.

Think. Don't panic.

The feeds span end over end, last glass falling in the darkness.

Glass falling in the darkness?

A surge of energy coursed through his system as he jabbed at the remote, freezing the action.

"There."

He pointed.

"There."

"What are we looking at," Lurch asked, his voice a spider-like whisper.

"The glass," the Russian replied.

Sure enough there were glass fragments on the floor of the labyrinth.

"Only two doors in," Caleb said, stating the obvious, "only two doors out."

"Yes. Mirrored doors which I insisted upon. Got to give the prey a fighting chance, eh Caleb?"

Caleb said nothing. Astapor's words were baited traps.

Astapor was on his feet staring at the frozen image on the screen. The camera was zooming in and panning upwards. The mirror had been designed as a final moment of torture, as the running man, or woman, ran hopelessly towards their own reflections.

The last image of their sorry lives was to watch themselves being chased down and then eaten alive. But the mirror was no longer intact. It was a black hole into which George had vanished. No cameras down there. No light. But there were answers. At least for Muldoon there were.

Astapor got to his feet and moved over to the screen. Without turning he addressed the youth.

"This is all your fault Caleb. I favoured a simple electrocution in the chair but oh no you had to be flash. It had to be the labyrinth in your eyes. Eaten alive. You are even more twisted than Lurch."

A pause. So dangerous, the desire to fill that silence. But let it hang suspended, like a guillotine poised to fall. Let it hang. Caleb counted the moments and felt the danger build again. There were no hard and fast rules here. He would have to speak.

"What do you want me to do?"

Astapor turned slowly and looked straight into Caleb's left eye. His gaze was enough to stop a charging rhino. It contained all the terror of the world's worst nightmares.

"I want you to get after them and quick. If they are not back under lock and key by lights out it'll be you down in that labyrinth and I'm guessing you'd be no match for the Minotaur."

"Of course."

"You've failed me once Caleb. Don't do it again. If you had followed my instructions none of this would have happened."

It was all a lie, total nonsense but no one could contradict the Russian. Those that did, met a fate worse than death. That was not a fate he wanted for himself but still he must know what was required of him.

He formulated his next question with care. It would tell him much about the Russian's state of mind.

"What about Lola?"

He held his voice steady, terrified lest it would crack and reveal his feelings. Exposing his vulnerability.

The Russian stared fixedly at his eye. He dared not break that gaze.

"Lola is with them now Caleb. She's a betrayer so she goes the same way as the dinosaurs. Understand?"

More lies. Punishment and a test. The test that was never ending for the Russian. The test of loyalty.

"I understand Count. I'll go now."

"You know what you have to do."

"Yes."

"Be relentless and remorseless."

"Yes.'

Now his voice was a whisper, a lullaby.

"Oh and Caleb, don't you ever betray me. You're the son I never had, my son and heir. You know that don't you? Just remember your priorities son and we'll get through this. Together."

He waited as long as he could bear it and then he turned and walked away. All eyes in the room were fixed upon him. His first thought was the lift but that would never do. Too presumptuous. Too much of a risk. He peeled off to the right and took the spiral staircase down.

Down, always down. Bouncing softly as he followed the curling spiral downwards, away from the fierce gaze of the Russian. It pulled at you, that gaze, like the earth pulled at you, all the time making you gravity's slave. Strong and weak forces pulled at you relentlessly from within and without. Doubts and fears. Ticking time bombs and lights that burned.

The tower was no sanctuary, not anymore. Best to leave it to Lurch. Let him dance with the Russian. Let him cook in the heat and the pressure of Astapor's wrath.

Up in the green domed control room, atop of Tower 1, they waited until Caleb's footsteps had faded and then they spoke.

It was Astapor who broke the silence because it was he who owned it.

"I don't trust that boy anymore, Lurch. I want him followed."

"What about the cameras?" Lurch asked in response.

"I don't trust them either."

Lurch took a moment to digest this information. He knew in crisis, there was opportunity, but that he had to be careful not to lower his own neck onto the block, as Caleb had done.

"What options do we have?" he asked his Master.

Lurch was edging, only and ever protecting himself in what he advanced.

But the Russian wasn't playing. Now was the time to step up or be thrust to the wall.

"What do you suggest?"

Lurch had his answer ready.

"I would suggest the Stalkers Master. They are, as you know, on Level 17. I feel they are somewhat under-used."

"They are unpredictable," Astapor countered.

"But hideously efficient."

"Alright then. On your head be it. Yes and at the first sign of anything that whispers of betrayal I want that boy offed. I want him bled. Think you can handle that? Course you can. You've been waiting for me to give that order for years. You're so transparent, Lurch."

Lurch bowed. "And the girly gurls?"

"Now that they've joined forces with Young Muldoon we know

279

exactly where they'll be. Down with Mr Hands. Time to revive that time honoured classic: Cowboys and Indians. I think the flesh rippers and the lamb whackers deserve a go. Don't you?

"What about the Rabid Baby Eaters?"

"Yes. Why not? Turn them all loose. And send the Cyclops out with them."

Lurch arched an eyebrow.

There was going to be a bloodbath.

43

Flight

Wilber ran down the fence line as though the devil himself were hot on his tail. At the corner of the compound he paused briefly and turned back around to look up at the tower topped with the Green Dome. Tower One. Astapor's lair. How he gaped and then gagged, vomiting up Crowhaven's breakfast, retching and retching until there was nothing left to come up. Gripping his knees with what strength remained in him he took three great ragged breaths. It wasn't enough, but it was a start. He had strength enough to raise his head then, to stare at the sliding doorway into which George and Patrick had disappeared. His first impulse was to retrace his steps, to make good what he had done wrong, but something deep within him held him back. It was as though hands had seized him and were propelling him away from temptation.

Behind him Wilber saw a ragged line of figures shrouded in smoke running towards him and surmised that it was Antelope and her crew. A swift turn of the head to his left and he saw a second line likewise making their way towards him. Vultures converging on the sight of a kill, he thought. What would they think of him? More to the point, what would they do to him now that he had thwarted their plans and in the process betrayed them. He wanted to run away and hide as he had as a child but he knew that would do him no good.. They would hunt him and kill, speedily and without remorse.

Nothing to do but wait. Wait and watch as both sets of feet pounded towards him. From his corner of the compound he ran his eyes back to the pit from which sulphurous fumes now drifted, obscuring his view of the towers and the running girls. Occasional gaps in the smoke allowed him to study the differences in each tower. To his eyes the four towers on the Northern side of the complex were more elegant than the Southern towers. They seemed sculpted and highly individualised whereas the Southern Towers could have come from IKEA. He detected the influence of Art Nouveau in their design with the flavour of Gaudi. Curlicue forms of silver metal, rusting down and that mesmerising green glass. Now light. Now dark. Changing with the lighting states of the island. Responsive to cloud and sunburst. At least 120 metres high, nevermind what was beneath the ground.

But it was all just a distraction, a way of taking his mind off what was coming next. Antelope, as expected, was the first to arrive and the first thing she did was whip out a six inch Bowie knife and hold it to Wilber's throat. In spite of the fact that his heart was pounding, Wilber knew that to have any chance of survival he had to look her straight in the eye. He turned and did so and it was like looking into the eye of a ravening tigress, as she prepared to pounce and kill.

Wilber counted long red seconds as his brow beaded with sweat. Soon the others had arrived and like Antelope they stared at him with barely contained rage. Even Edie. Wilber's eyes flicked around the circle quickly and he was glad to see all nine girls had escaped along with his wheezing Great Uncle. Lola stood with her back to him, her arms folded, her face an unreadable mask. If he had expected to find an ally in that quarter it would appear he was sadly mistaken. She looked as likely to kill him as any of the others. It was Antelope, who predictably, spoke first.

"Give me one good reason why I shouldn't slash your throat, Wilber."

Instantly Wilber thought of a joke, but then just as quickly suppressed it. Humour was all about timing and now was exactly the wrong time for jokes. What to tell them...how best to explain it. He wasn't sure he could. Already images from his past life were flashing before his eyes, as though his mind were getting ready to rewind the tapes and call it a day. How to explain it. The words tumbled out of his mouth before he could stop them, before he could edit, censor and shape his message.

"It didn't feel right."

"What?" the Alphabet's all gasped together

The look of fury on their paint and mud smeared faces convinced Wilber that he had best get a ruddy move on and elaborate. In the air, the buzzing air, a sense of terrible danger was present.

"I can't explain it. It just didn't feel right. There was some instinct, deep within me, that told me to leave."

"Yeah, they call that cowardice Wilber," Lola quipped. "In war they shoot you for that."

Wilber could have stabbed her. She was not the most sympathetic of characters, even at the best of times, and in moments of danger it didn't take a genius to see she could easily turn into a rabid nightmare, making trouble for all, especially him. He had to steady the boat and quickly.

"It wasn't cowardice Lola. It was something else. Call it a sixth sense, if you like. We were walking into a trap that we wouldn't have walked out of. Astapor doesn't play nicely..."

"We know that," Beth hissed, "and we were ready for the fight. Ready to die if need be."

"I don't want anybody to die on my account Def. There is a better way."

Semantic sighed.

"You do know Wilber that to win the Game you have to collect all the crystals."

"Yes but I understood that you could do it in any order."

Frantic shook her head, as though she were having some kind of fit and then stopped abruptly.

"He is right, you know. And I think if we were to kill anyone it should be somebody other than him. There are a thousand people more deserving of death on this island than he is. Don't you agree Antelope?"

The murderous look in Antelope's eye did not soften one iota and still she kept the blade pressed to Wilber's jugular. It would be so easy for her to do it. With all the rage in her. With the many disappointments she had suffered. Best to trust no one and hope for nothing. Best to just live moment to moment. A sudden hand on her shoulder caused her to shudder.

"Lower the knife girl, everything'll be fine. You just have to trust him."

The voice was that of Great Uncle Muldoon and for some reason Antelope complied. Beth watched in amazement. Like the Old Man, for some reason she couldn't explain, she believed in Wilber.

"The Old Man's right Ant. We have to trust him!" Beth said.

"And why?" Def shot back. "He bottled it!"

"No he didn't, "Edie hissed. "He didn't bottle it. He changed his mind. It was a trap all along and I for one didn't sign up for a suicide mission. Wilber's choice was the right one and whether you can acknowledge it or not he showed true leadership back there. He made the right decision. The Russian doesn't make mistakes and like Wilber said he doesn't play nicely. If you want somebody to punish, then take it out on the one who led us up there; Lola. And if you want somebody to cut her throat I'll gladly do it."

Everyone was shocked by Edie's words, shocked and impressed, not the least Def. Antelope calmly handed her the Bowie knife and Edie turned to Lola, with the sudden and immediate air of a butcher.

"Charmed, I'm sure," Lola deadpanned.

"Thanks for your support Edie," Wilber chipped in, "but I think it's best that no throats are slit. Not just yet anyway. As far as I'm concerned Lola was acting in good faith and we must honour that."

Lola gave a wry smile.

"Your support is touching Wilber. You are a purveyor of justice after all. Now should we go back for your Uncles, or...."

"No way," Wilber said, cutting her off before she could finish.

"It's too dangerous. I'm afraid we have to accept that they are both gone. At least for now."

But whilst he said it, and convincingly, he didn't believe it. Not for a moment. Whatever Wilber did or didn't have to accept, forgetting about his Uncles was not part of any contract he would willingly sign. As infuriating as George was, as vacillating as Patrick was, they were blood, and blood, as his grandfather was so fond of saying, was thicker than water. He had to go back, even if it meant his death but not now. He had to bide his time and trust that the two men could stay alive.

Lola watching Wilber closely nodded her head and cast an eye aloft to the now darkening sky.

"Wilber's right. We have to get behind him and stay behind him. No unravelling now girls. His Uncle, lost the plot, went radio rental, started foaming at the mouth like a rabid dog, then he started swinging his fists and pushing us about. We had a plan, a plan he didn't or couldn't follow because of unresolved issues with Astapor. It was he who betrayed us, not Wilber. I, for one, am with the kid. Let's go for the fourth crystal, then the fifth and then loop back round for the third. We have to be adaptable so this is us adapting."

The hateful rage in Wilber's eyes was painful to behold. He knew why Lola had said what she'd said but it still burned. Beth watching this, stepped in yet again with soothing words, ever the diplomat.

"Lola's right, we have to refocus and keep on going. Down the side of the volcano, past the Old Temple to Mr Hand. Keep the prize in sight and we'll have our shot at an exit. Antelope said nothing, just nodded.

"George is far too smart to go anywhere without a plan," Wilber said suddenly.

"As much as it pains me we have to make like he's gone and keep on moving Wilber," Edie said consolingly

"But he's not dead, right. Never say that. He's just temporarily unavailable."

The placement of a wizened hand on Wilber's shoulders brought him back to his senses, somewhat sharpish. It was Great Uncle Muldoon. Touching the right shoulders again.

"I believe that too Wilber. He's a Muldoon, he'll survive, they both will and they'll catch us up later. But for now we have to run."

There was something in his tone. Something persuasive to which Wilber responded in spite of himself.

"Ok. Ok," he said, whipping out his map with a view to locating the next base. But the other girls were already up and running. Led by Antelope they skirted the Southern Perimeter fence now heading west to east.

Lola and Wilber were the last to join them and both of them heard the whine and whirr of machinery as the great lake of fire was one more covered over. Within a short while it was as though it had never been there.

44

Searching

Caleb emerged blinking into the sunlight. It was the first time in many days that he had been outside. It was not an unwelcome break. Being around Astapor had kept him on his toes but it had also drained him. Even the Duracell bunny could not drum forever and things were not great up on the hill.

George's escape had enraged the Russian to an extent that Caleb had not believed possible and everyone on Team Astapor had caught it. A number of the guards in attendance had been executed or were being tortured, Lurch had been put on a cleaning detail and he had been exiled, albeit temporarily from the Garden and sent forth to atone. Despite the fact that his mission was a punitive one, he welcomed the break.

It wasn't difficult to find the pathway the Alphabets had taken. They travelled lightly but even they left traces that the trained eye could identify. The flattened grasses and broken twigs bore testament to hurried flight. To anxiety and shock. They had carved a passage for themselves, cutting holes in the fences through which they had gone and run, following the chain-linked fence all the way to the eastern edge of the compound, then south, down through the forest, towards the Old Ruins.

He knew intuitively where they had gone and why. Tracking them was not a problem but what he should do when he found them was. Oh yes. That was another question entirely. Looking around the Tower Complex he saw what he believed to be his home. Everywhere else he'd ever been was just a space through which he had passed. But here he belonged. Here he made a difference. Of course he had earned his place. Unlike Lola who was a resident and to the manor born he had had to work for position and advancement. And worked he had converting Astapor's plans and ideas into flesh and blood reality and at no small cost to himself. He had gone from being a child to being an adult in a very short space of time. There was nothing naive or ignorant in his make-up. He wasn't fearful or squeamish and he had learned long ago how to disconnect from his emotions so that he might function. Oh there had been doubts and there always would be.

Over the years he had spent here he had often asked himself why this, why me? Why had the hand of fate plucked him from obscurity and brought him here? What special quality did he possess that had spared him from that lift ride down into the darkness. The darkness. It was all about him now. It surrounded the island and it suffocated every soul here. All those who stumbled into the spider's web and flailed away until the final sting or crunching bite dragged them away into the oblivion. It hadn't always been that way though. When he had first arrived; a boy of nine the island been a place of light and hope. Of cloud free skies and days on the beach.

But ever since Astapor had flipped and become what he now was no one had known a moment's peace.

Caleb climbed through the fence and began running along the fence line, following in the Alphabet's footsteps with no doubt he was being watched. He found himself pondering George's escape and wondering what he would do next. Now that he was free in the heart of the mountain Astapor had no control over him. There were no maps for the tunnels that wormed the mountain's guts. Least of all none that he had seen. But he knew there were chambers down there filled with more than just magma, more than liquid rivers of molten rock and steam.

About all this Caleb was conflicted. Muldoon's escape meant peril for them all but it had also demonstrated that the Russian could be rocked, that his feet at least were made of clay. If he could be rocked he could be toppled. Caleb contracted in fear as soon as he thought this and stopped running. He was out the outer limit of the eastern fence and turning a corner he began to head southwards. The further he ran the more the towers diminished in size and soon the canopy of the forest hid them from view.

Astapor had warned him he was being tested, that his loyalty was all that mattered, that he was being groomed to succeed. But first he must prove himself. The Russian could not be fooled. He had seen that, as the Russian had seen what he had tried so desperately hard to conceal: his feelings for Lola. His love for Lola. Just thinking the word chilled his blood to liquid ice. It made him vulnerable because if you cared about just one thing that thing could be weaponized and used against you. If Astapor had taught him anything, it was that.

Caleb had never felt so alone as he did now. He had been sent out into the wilderness with a mission he could accept or reject. If he was to reject it, Astapor would kill him, unless he killed Astapor first. There was no running away from the island and from what he would be compelled to do to survive. As of this moment all he could do was keep on moving, like time did, inexorably towards its conclusions. Oh time took its toll but at least it gave one room in which to manoeuvre. Terrifying, yet liberating was the prospect of the Russian's death. An ecstasy of sorts and after that, the very real possibility of holding Lola in his arms. Of kissing her, of loving her and being soothed by her.

He closed his eyes in order to better savour the fantasy and out of the dark cave of his mind, he saw Astapor watching him, more frightening than any dinosaur. The dark glint in the monster's eye contained a chink though through which light spilled. Was that a portal, something he, Caleb, could travel through in his search for a future, where he ruled the island and the Russian was dead and buried. How could he make his dream a reality?

45

The Hand Speaks

Away down the slope they moved, in three lines, the full complement of the Alphabet Gang, plus Wilber and Lola. But minus George and Patrick. Behind them Astapor and the Eight Towers of looming death cast their very long shadows. It was 13.37 and the clock was ticking. The clock was always ticking. Less than six and a half hours remaining and the mood of the island was ominous. Lola and the Alphabets still weren't talking and Wilber still only had two crystals. As far as he was concerned Astapor was winning and nobody was going to convince him otherwise. In spite of her usual rule of not talking whilst marching, Antelope made a beeline for Wilber and initiated a conversation.

"How you doing champ?"

"I'm alright," Wilber said, but clearly, he was suffering. In the few hours they had been together he had gone through a series of terrible ordeals, losing not one but two of his uncles and most of his remaining illusions about life. He had had far less time to adapt than they had and yet he was uncomplaining. Antelope found no trace of the spoilt brat they had first encountered. Instead there was a decent human being, walking beside her, one she respected greatly.

"How much further?" Wilber asked.

"Just under a mile. Fairly easy going," Antelope added smiling, "most of it downhill."

"It's going to get worse isn't it?"

Antelope was silent for a moment. It was a rule amongst the Alphabets that no matter how bad things got, they always told each other the truth.

"Yeah, he's been toying with you up till now but with your Uncle..." here she paused, searching for the best way of relaying what she considered essential ..."with your Uncle gone he can give you his full attention. You've survived cannibals, creepers, zombies, crocodile attacks and wisps. That is a pretty impressive role call but he has a much fuller arsenal at his disposal and he's going to start deploying it against you. Knowing him, I'd say he's going to start dispatching multiple opponents against you and there's nothing to say he won't arm them."

"What about his militia?"

"He likes to keep them close, as a personal body guard. Also they keep an eye on the Complex. We've tried to burn it down a few times and once we got real close. Unfortunately, we lost too many girls on those raids to keep up the pressure. Astapor knows that without his little lair he's vulnerable. We've gotten too smart and too well drilled for him just to blow us away. If he sends people out after us, we send them back broken."

"Yeah, I saw what you did to the cannibals," Wilber replied, smiling.

"That was just a gentle mauling."

Wilber took a moment to digest that information and to phrase his next question with infinite care.

"How did you get like this Antelope?"

"I used to play a lot of computer games. You know the kind of games? Where you have to blow stuff up and form alliances? I was good at it and when I wasn't doing that I was captain of the girl's basketball team. I was never a girly girl. I lived with my pop in California. My mum died in a car crash and me and dad argued a lot. We were too alike to get on. Always competition, never cooperation. Then I came here."

She was on the verge of saying more but they had come to the edge of a clearing. Antelope raised her right hand and immediately the girls broke rank and took cover behind the trees. Bows were unslung and arrows notched in readiness. A second signal brought them all together again and after a quick huddle they divided into two groups. Lola being Lola did her own thing and followed sulkily at a distance. Wilber watched her, partly affectionately, largely irritated. She was such an unknown quantity was Lola. Not a team player exactly but always surprising and often ready with the one strategy that no one else had thought of.

Silently they split and stealthily they crept round the edge of the clearing, alert to every rustle and birdcall. In the centre of the tree-lined space was a partially shaded but very beautiful ruin with columns and walls of marble. It was somewhat overgrown but Wilber found it very alluring; somewhat Grecian in Spirit, but more ancient and more mysterious. He wanted to stop and explore but knew that was not the play that Antelope had called. Instead he dropped back, to the rear of his line, and surreptitiously studied the colonnade and portico. There were faded paintings on the portico. Some kind of dramatic scene was depicted of a figure with a trident and a huge wave rearing up like an agitated cobra behind him.

Wilber felt a sharp pang of excitement and in spite of himself stopped walking. The sun, which had, until that moment been largely hidden behind thickening cloud, suddenly broke through and dazzled him. In that instant he received a sudden shock, that all but unmanned him. Standing between the central columns was a figure looking straight at him. The figure was clad in a hooded cowl and the face was largely hidden but he was sure it was fixed upon him. Feeling a sudden painful pulse in the space just above his eyes, he raised his hand to his brow and groaned.

In front of him, Antelope turned and frowned. Why had he stopped, she wondered? She tried to get his attention but no cigar, he was oblivious. When Wilber finally lowered his hand and returned his gaze to the space between the columns, his blood turned cold. The figure was no longer there. A trick of the light perhaps? Time was snapping at his ankles and back in the world he sought direction. Up ahead, Antelope was looking daggers at him and the last thing he wanted to do was annoy her. Wilber raised his hand in acknowledgement and picked up his pace to catch the rest of the group up. Immediately the frown vanished and safely out of the clearing and back into the cover of the forest, she called for a second huddle.

"Okay Wilber?" she asked, her voice free from any trace of irritation, but laced with curiosity.

"I'm good. Sorry I stopped. I got dazzled by the sun back there. Thought I saw something."

"Yeah what?" Beth cut in, clearly intrigued.

"It was a figure standing between the columns. It was wearing some kind of hooded cowl and it was looking straight at me. Weird though. The cowl wasn't black, it was magenta. Now why would I see something like that? Never seen anything like it before.

Beth and Antelope exchanged looks.

"Just your mind playing tricks, that's all," Def chipped in, cheerily dismissive.

"Or maybe it vas an echo of the future. Or von of its shadows…"

Whilst Rudi had other ideas, Def was not impressed.

"Alright Space Girl, tone it down."

Wilber was intrigued though. Further clarification was required before he was ready to walk the line to the next Magician.

"What do you mean by that Rudi?"

"The future sometimes casts its shadows in ze same vay as the past does. If you're sensitive zat vay, you shouldn't ignore it Vilber. It's a gift and not von to be taken lightly."

True that, he thought, remembering his weird waking vision, prior to his encounter with the Cannibals.

Antelope waited until Rudi had fallen silent and then she spoke.

"Okay Wilber, Mr Hand lives about two to three hundred metres beyond the tree line. There's knee length grass there, like up in the North west of the island but there's very little cover besides. Whatever Astapor sends against us we need to be ready for. We will form a perimeter which will give you whatever time you need to complete the next task. If we are separated we'll catch you up at Crescent Bay. Do you still have your map? Because if you don't, we might have a real problem!"

A look of horror crossed momentarily over Wilber's face.

46

Where's Lola

Wilber reached in his Satchell, retrieved and unfolded the map, which he then laid carefully upon the ground, ready for inspection. Antelope walked over to him and knelt beside him and they both began studying the map. She pointed to a crescent of white sand that was almost directly to the south of The Tower Complex. It was perhaps a little over a mile, perhaps a mile and a half from Astapor's lair and a definite point of danger.

"Bit exposed isn't it?" Wilber asked, clearly unhappy.

"We've burial pits all along the East shore of Temple Bay. In some of the pits there are weapons, in others, boats," Edie said.

"Weapons? What kind of weapons?" Wilber asked, excited and intrigued.

"Some spear guns and a bunch of harpoons," Frantic replied beaming. "One of the boats has an outboard motor. We stole it from Astapor's thugs on a wet Tuesday afternoon, then we tarred and feathered them and buried them up to their necks…"

"Alright Frantic, wind your neck in," Def growled, albeit with a manic gleam in her eye and a twisted smile on her lips.

"So remind me, what's he like, this Albert Hands. What's his thing?" Wilber asked.

Semantic cleared her throat and adjusted her spectacles.

"Something of a loner and where we are concerned, something of an elective mute. I'm not sure that he approves of the philosophy of our little band; in his eyes we are nothing more than white savages who engage in terrorist activities. He's a Native American or First Nation personage if you prefer and we, as representatives of the white race, are not to be trusted. He has a point. There is not a treaty, made by an American Government, be it Republican or Democrat, that the White man hasn't welshed on. According to Mr Hand, his people have been betrayed, enslaved and sold down the river, over and over again and the less time he spends interacting with us, the happier he is."

This did not bode well.

"Anything else?

He belongs or belonged to the Navajo Nation and has a highly unusual skill set. We have seen evidence to suggest that he is an excellent tracker, linguist and hunter. He writes and sings aloud and engages in sand painting and weaving, which I believe is a cultural trait. There are ritual elements to his make up and he has a particular fondness for collecting skulls."

"Skulls?" Wilber repeated tentatively.

"Skulls," Semantic affirmed, "which from time to time he can be seen holding aloft and chanting with."

"Animal skulls?"

"All kinds of skulls," Crimson said with some relish.

Wilber gulped.

"So, what do you think he's up to?" he asked.

Semantic sighed.

"What his 'project' is, none of us can be sure of. He's one of the Big Five and that's all we can say with any degree of certainty. Around here they are referred to as Magicians, as you know, but what they actually do, how they influence life on the island, that's all open to debate."

"And debate is something we don't have time for," Def concluded. "This ain't High School Dubya. It's war and the first casualty of war is truth. If you want my advice, go in there with all guns blazing. Do what you gotta do, to get that third crystal and don't take any of his BS. Albert Hand, like the other Magicians, has a job to do and if they stop playing by the rules, stuff breaks down and they get ousted. He's down there, when you're ready."

The rest of the Alphabets rose as one, happy with Def's no

nonsense summary. Fight now, talk later, win. Otherwise they'd be back the next day ready to do it all again.

"Hold on," Wilber called out, suddenly panicked. "Where's Lola?"

Everyone looked around searchingly, except Frantic who had information to impart.

"She dropped out of sight at the clearing when Wilber had his vision of the ghost in the Temple."

"Good riddance to bad rubbish," Def pronounced, wiping her hands clean.

"Sorry Wilber, we have to go," Antelope said, "her eye always fixed on the business at hand.

Glancing backwards, Wilber looked pained. He wanted to go hunting for Lola, but more than that, he wanted to poke around in the ruins and see what was inside that Temple. An image flashed through his mind; of a Red Indian in buckskin trousers and moccasins and a full eagle-feather headdress, which ran from his head to the top of his thighs. The chief or shaman or whatever he was, was holding aloft the skull of a bison and chanting, chanting, chanting up a storm. Behind him, a great wall of water rose and Wilber froze. The same image as on the mural.

What did it all mean? He didn't know and he probably wouldn't find out as there just wasn't time.

Through the few remaining trees they plowed, back once more in their three-line formation. The sun, by this time, had passed the zenith and Wilber moved in the centre-spot of the middle group, placed just behind Antelope, with Def behind him. Beth led the Left Hand Group, with Rudi and Semantic, whilst Crimson took the Right hand group with Edie and Frantic. Frantic had a dual role in that she also played sweep and watched for signs that they were being followed.

Out of the trees and into the tall grasses they padded, immediately on edge, exposed like rabbits with raptors circling. A soft wind blew in from the south and the yellow grasses swayed and rustled. Then a sharp wind blew in from the north and Wilber shivered, chilled to the bone. Siberian weather, his mother had always used to say, when the wind grew icy teeth and gnawed at your extremities. With every step he fought to keep such memories at bay. They didn't help, they simply plagued him and filled his mind with distractions.

The sky, he noticed, was again shifting state. Now it was poised somewhere between gunmetal grey and cobalt blue. Down they dropped once more, heading in a southeasterly direction. Fleeing Astapor's lair, the slope had fallen away sharply. It felt like a mountain descent. Tough on your knees but good to build up a head of speed, which they had done. Then instead of going downwards, they'd gone sideways, zig-zagging and backtracking to keep the rabid dogs from the scent. A secondary slope had kicked in then and once more they'd run, until the ground had levelled off, leading them into the temple clearing.

This was a gentle slope like an alpine meadow where yellow grass gave way to bands of sand. Wilber was amazed to see the colours shifting through unpredictable hues. Where the grass ended the sand was blue and then within fifty metres it had turned white. Another fifty metres and it was red. Was this a natural phenomenon or something else? The slope reached its nadir and then began to climb. The stretch of red sand lasted a few hundred metres before another swath of blue and then white sand and beyond the white sand a simple dwelling arose. Antelope gave a signal and the girls broke formation and formed a long line, with intervals of roughly twenty metres between them and then they began converging on the shack.

It was a perilous business, this creeping game and he felt greater anxiety in this moment than at any other time on the island. Why this should be so, he didn't know; he just felt it. Step-by-step they edged cautiously forwards and before too long, they saw that Mr Hand was home, seated on some weird kind of high-backed chair, in a seeming trance. It was the kind of chair you'd expect to see in a care home for the elderly, not a savage island overrun by zombies, cannibals and mad Russians. About forty metres downwind of the immobile Magus was a large, circular target made of coarse straw bound with wire. The target had been peppered with arrows.

Closer and closer they crept, until Wilber, just behind Antelope, inched up to her and whispered in her right ear, "what's that on his lap?" Before she could answer, the mute statue had raised a longbow, fledged, drawn and released an arrow which flew straight and true, finding the dead centre of the target.

"Bull's eye," shouted Frantic, unable to keep a lid on her admiration. Mr Hand, as though activated by the wild cry, rose smoothly to his feet and marched with some pomp and a little ceremony straight over to where Wilber was standing. The Alphabet's as one, raised their bows in an act of both threat and protection. For his part Mr Hand was oblivious. He just stared right into Wilber's eyes and then he began to recite.

Up beyond the clouds
The winged steed rears,
Peddles the air and flies away.
I fly beside him or perhaps I am him,
Seeing through his eyes
Accelerating through the air
The atom beleaguered air.
He's my ride,
Now he's me.
Cloud and speed
What does he see?

Then he was silent and stood, mute and still once more, staring directly into Wilber's eyes, as though awaiting a response. But what was expected? What to say. Wilber wondered. Hovering at his elbow was the ever-dependable Antelope and it was to her that he turned now, in his moment of need.

"What do you think he's on? Mescaline?"

Antelope pulled a face that signalled uncertainty.

"Could be or then again he could be having a vision."

Def in the meantime had sidled up.

"If you ask me it's his antipsychotic medication talking. He's balmy, off his rocker, crazy as a shit-house rat. Let's torture him into telling us where the crystal is. No point in asking nicely he's too far gone!"

Antelope, normally so reasonable and fair, gave Def's suggestion serious consideration. After a few seconds of that Mr Hand started up again.

> Up beyond the clouds
> The winged steed rears,
> Peddles the air and flies away...

Def, past reason and past caring, was having none of it. "Yes thank you, we've had quite enough of that."

Mr Hand fell silent and they all went back to waiting. Wilber glanced at his watch, then up at the darkening sky. Ten minutes to two. Not good, not good at all. Without warning Hand sparked up once more, like a rocket which looked as though the blue touch paper had not actually been ignited but which had been smouldering all the time.

"With the visual element removed, we are compelled to remove our eyes, hurl them into the void and just...." Here he paused.

"And just what?"

Mr Hand, obviously pained, reached for the void and groped for the answer.

"Just feel," he replied. Then turning on his heel he marched back to his shack. "Well come on Wilber, I haven't got all day. Hurry up."

Wilber's jaw hit the floor and his eyeballs inflated. Frantic took a step.

"Not you," yelled Hand, without so much as a backward glance.

Wilber took to his heels and began to run and the Alphabet's converged on Antelope to get the skinny. Antelope for once, was lost for words.

"Well he is a Magician," Crimson offered.

Def was less impressed.

"Magician? He's a nutter. Certifiable. Where I come from he'd be in a padded cell in a straight jacket."

Rudi, normally so sensitive, was having none of it either.

"Ja. he definitely needs a check up from the neck up".

47

Snack Chat

By this time, Mr Hand had disappeared into his shack. Reaching the door flap, Wilber turned around. The girls were watching him like abandoned orphans. He imagined kohl-lined eyes filling with tears and trembling lower lips, the result of his perceived betrayal. But it wasn't a betrayal. He had a job to do. There was really nothing else he could do, was there? No! He had to grasp the nettle. Seizing the dangling flap he parted it and shot inside. Mr Hand was waiting for him with his arms folded. Close up he looked less like Geronimo and more like an extra from Dances with Wolves.

"Nice shack," Wilber said looking about him. "Minimalist like."

"It's not a shack. It's an octagonal structure called a Hogan and before you ask, it isn't here."

Wilber glanced at the floor and pointed.

"What's that?"

"A sand painting."

"What's it for?"

"To pass the time of day. I hear you have two crystals and that you're in with a shout."

Wilber was more interested in the sand painting.

"I thought the paintings were for healing purposes only and that they contain images of the Holy ones. I read about it in National Geographic. Who are you trying to heal?"

The sand painting was intricate and colourful and upon closer examination could be seen to be constituted of a series of inward pointing arrows, 32 in total, aimed at some great black cloud, full of animal faces. The animals were many and varied. Wilber picked out a bear, a wolf, a rabid dog, a crocodile and a tiger. There were others but the one thing they had in common was that they were all demented. Suddenly the penny dropped.

"Of course. It's Astapor! You're trying to heal the Russian or engineer his downfall. Which?"

"Aren't we the clever one," Mr Hand said, flopping down into a broken down armchair in one corner of the Hogan. For all that it was dilapidated and worn, the chair looked modern and not uncomfortable.

In the opposite corner of the oddly symmetrical structure was a second chair, the mirror image of the first. Mr Hand gestured impatiently for the youth to sit down and Wilber, keen to cut to the chase, obliged. Flopping down, he breathed a contented sigh and the two, man and youth, glanced at their wrists at precisely the same time in exactly the same way. It was not so much a co-incidence as a synchronicity.

"So did you build this Hogan yourself?"

"Enough of the small talk," The Magician snarled, peeling off his headdress and arranging it on a dented, polystyrene head, fixed to what looked like an altar. "Down to busy-ness. Do you have the crystals?"

Wilber nodded then tapped his satchel.

"Yep. From Crowhaven and Yabu. Why do you want to know?"

"Because I have a vested interest in the game. You've got that Russian freaking out. That's obvious. And that's never happened before. Of course the island's freaking out too. The weather's gone to hell in a handbag and the animals are going crazy. Signs and symbols everywhere, lightning storms every night and portals opening up in places they simply shouldn't be."

Wilber, both cute and astute, heard alarm bells and backtracked to a line of Mr Hand's that had him perplexed.

"What do you mean the island's freaking out."

Hand regarded him silently, as though counting flies caught on sticky brown paper.

"You're just what we feared you would be, only more so."

"And what's that supposed to mean?" Wilber shot back, his voice rising in anger. He hated being taken for a fool and given the runaround. Hated being patronised and ignored. And he was beginning to hate this flake.

"Calm down, I'm here to help. It is 14.05. Less than seven hours before the bell tolls and its Game Over."

Wilber, previously enraged and puffed up like a cane toad, rapidly deflated and put his head in his hands.

"It's already over. I failed back at the Towers."

His voice cracked and his eyes filled up with tears as the weight of his failure hit him.

"Astapor captured my Uncles, then he launched them into the labyrinth. They're dead."

"One of them is, one of them isn't?" the Magician said half mysteriously, half dismissively. Wilber wiped his eyes and sat bolt upright.

"What do you mean and how do you know?"

"Never mind, never mind. It's not important. Focus on what is important."

"Which one?" Wilber screamed, his face contorted, a demonic mask.

Mr Hand sat stock still. Wilber stared arrows of hate at him but it was no use. After a while he just collapsed back into himself and sat back in his chair.

"You back, you in control? Ready to hear what I have to tell you."

Wilber nodded, tears streaming down his face.

"Good. Now here it is Wilber and you need to hear this. You're special. Always have been, always will be. And as much as it pains me to say it, I have to. Because you need to hear it. Are you hearing this?"

Again Wilber nodded.

"When you were nine years of age, something happened, something terrible and at the same time something wonderful. And it scarred you and your life was never the same. Just nod if I'm right."

Wilber nodded, his heart pounding in his chest.

"Don't have a heart attack Wilber. Just listen." He paused, then he resumed his tale. "After that event everything went to hell. The world darkened and all your friends and all your family turned from you and suddenly you were alone. In hell and alone. But there was always a light in the darkness."

"My uncle."

"Your uncle. And he left you, but not really."

"Really?"

"No."

"I hated him."

"Because you loved him and you missed him."

"Yes," Wilber whispered, halfway to crying a river.

"But like you, he came here because the island called out to him as it called out to you. It had need of your services and it still does. You see the island isn't just a hunk of rock and sand, rivers and trees, its conscious and it's alive. It was part of a once great continent that your people know of as Atlantis. Many believe it's just a myth, a faded legend but those in power know that it's real. They hide this from you and they bury the artefacts from this culture, that not infrequently come to light. They lie and their lies go unpunished. It's time to take all that back.

Astapor is part of the Great Lie. The lie that Caesar told, the lie that Stalin told and Hitler told. The lie that every King and President and Dictator has always told. And that lie is like a statue that has long been crumbling and is ready to fall any day now. Shall I tell you what that lie is? It's just this. The lie is that you, the people, are powerless. You, the people, are worthless. You, the people, are slaves, born to do our bidding, to never question, to live as we decree and to die as we decree. You, the people, can never be free. You, the people, are to be denied the truth. You, the people, have fallen. Do you want to live as part of that lie Wilber, I know I don't?"

"Help me then," Wilber said simply, his eyes pleading.

"We Magicians must remain impartial, bound to our functions by forces you can't even begin to conceive of. Not yet anyway. All I am asking you to do, is to trust me and to trust that that Fire Crystal which Astapor has hidden so deep in the volcano, on which he sits like a roosting vulture, will be drawn up out of the earth, out of the lake of fire and into the light of day. The Russian made a fatal mistake dropping your Uncle into that labyrinth. You think the horrors of the Underworld could really do for the legend that is Dinosaur George Muldoon?"

"Hell no," Wilber cried, the tears still streaming from his now blazing eyes. "Never." As the story was told, he felt his heart opening and his spirits, so long bound, lifting and opening their wings. Angel's wings they were too.

"Hell no indeed. The Legend is on the case, but he is hidden. Let Astapor remain ignorant of this. Let him think the crystal is safe and that he, himself is safe. Let him think the game he is playing is one where he has loaded all the dice. But we have taken those dice and reloaded them. Trust your Uncle Wilber, trust that he will join you prior to End Game, that he will bring you that final crystal and you will succeed where all others have failed. Now get on with the job at hand."

It took a moment for Wilber to compose himself and to wipe his eyes and when he had done and his shaking hands had steadied, he saw that Mr Hands had replaced the feathered headdress and resumed his antic disposition.

"Where now?"

"Outside. I must talk to those crazed friends of yours and then to the cliff face for the final piece of the puzzle that I must pass to you. Are you ready?"

"Yes."

Mr Hand gestured with his hand and Wilber stepped outside.

48

Spreading Out

The Alphabets had spread out, each watching a different direction, each surveying a possible vector of approach. Of attack. Not one of them was what you might call happy.

"This is not good," Antelope muttered under her breath. "It's taking too long."

Def, less happy than Antelope, stalked up to the group's leader, a look like thunder on her face.

"We are too exposed here, Ant. They could hit us from any number of directions."

"Think I don't know that? He needs time, so we give him time."

Def, her face red, struggling with untold rage, looked like she was capable of anything in that moment. It took her a few seconds to turn her feelings into articulated words of threat.

"If any one of this group is hurt, injured or killed, I am going to hold Prince Charming personally responsible. If any..."

"And you'll do what?" Antelope spat. "If you touch him, I'll end you Def. As of this moment he is more important than anybody in this group. Understand?"

Def, normally so unflappable, appeared shocked.

"Yeah, I understand."

"Now get back to your post. I don't want to hear another word out of you. Clear?"

Def stalked off muttering obscenities and if the other members of the group had heard the exchange, they weren't letting on. Wilber emerged from the Hogan first, followed soon after, by Mr Hand.

"Ooh", he said, surveying the scene "tension!"

A look of exasperation flickered over Antelope's face. To think that all their futures hinged on the help of such a man as this, was not to her pleasing.

"So what have you got for us?"

Mr Hand draped his arms around Antelope's broad and muscled shoulders and the rest of the troop broke formation to join them.

"Beware my friends, for you cannot stay, take the ancient passageway. Under the watery arch, into the sunken temple, buried treasure in a fishy hollow you'll find the thing you need to borrow. Or some such thing. Anyway, enough! Evil approaches, with sharpened teeth and a solitary eye."

Beth placed her head in her hands. It was all getting a bit much. Mr Hand was oblivious. One minute lucid, the next spouting gibberish, like a Politician.

"They're coming," he said simply.

"Aren't they always?" Antelope quipped. "Who is?"

"Someone you'd rather not know. How will they attack? Hmm. Clear out, go backwards or you'll suffer setbacks. Let that be your strategy. Don't you get it? Can't you see it? There has been a new influx of energy here. Battle looms and with it the possibility of a paradigm shift."

Frantic, like Def and Antelope, was not impressed.

"What's he gibbering on about?"

"Actually he's speaking in riddles but he is making sense. Kind of."

What kind of sense Semantic didn't know. It was Mr Hand's turn to roll his eyes.

"Wilber you have been brought to this island for a specific purpose. Here nothing is as it appears. You must work together to defeat Astapor. Work this space. Win the race. The island is a riddle wrapped in an enigma. Crack the pattern before it's too late. Five wizards dominate!"

"And he's one." Crimson added, keen to state the obvious if

only for Wilber's benefit.

"But what kind of Magic does he use?" Frantic pressed.

Mr Hand seemed to think that was a good question.

"A curious blend of black and white my friends. We're beyond good and evil, here, in case you didn't know. Everybody has their own agenda. Everybody functions according to their own set of rules."

"Even you?" Edie asked.

Hand nodded.

"Especially me. Make a note of that. Here, anybody who's anybody, has an army. Just cus they're hidden doesn't mean they ain't there. Here, every frame is an equation that requires a solution. Time is important. Make a note of that. Because all time has its own signature, its own prompts and its pauses. It tells us when to sleep and when to wait."

"When to act and when to do nothing?" Frantic added, trying desperately to follow Mr Hand's illogic.

"My point precisely," Hand said. Wanting to agree, but looking confused. Then he pointed and a look of glee creased his face.

"Oh look. Trouble"

At this precise moment Lola came ambling out of the forest and into frame. She loped like a wolf but always at speed. Not straight, but zig-zaggy. Nobody, except Wilber and Mr Hand looked entirely happy to see her. Def could cheerfully have strangled her there and them.

"And where have you been?" Semantic, an even blend of huffy and hissy shot back. She was normally so academic, but Lola got her goat on a regular basis.

Lola, happy to offend, flashed her teeth in a gesture, calculated to offend.

"None of your business, Pedantic."

Hands on hips, in a full strop, Semantic, cobra-like, looked ready to strike.

"You take a perverse delight in winding us up, Lola. Don't think I haven't noticed. You spread chaos where there should be harmony. You could never have been a part of our group. Never!"

Lola, looking like she was sucking a wasp, considered her options. She appeared to be right on the brink of starting an all out war with Semantic when some higher force of will redirected her focus and purpose.

She spoke in a gratifyingly candid way.

"Wilber, we're under attack."

"No we're not," Semantic almost shouted, rolling up her palms.

"Oh yes you are!"

The voice boomed out of the trees. Then it emerged. A being nine feet tall, clad in garlands of skulls, a loin cloth and a well-worn pair of doctor martin boots. Carrying axes. Slinking out of the trees, it paused and a long line of tooled up miscreants and variants fell into place beside it. Growling and making gobbling noises like turkeys. The line was long. About fifty. A militia of some depravity and some distinction, or so it appeared, was forming up against them. The Leader was not unknown to the Alphabets as one or two of their number had fallen to his predations. He was simply called the Cyclops on account of the solitary eye in the middle of her forehead. A thing out of the pages of Greek Myth made real.

Def, still smarting from Antelope's threat, hoisted her mallet onto her shoulder and eyed up the Cyclops with a mixture of glee and psychotic rage.

"He's mine!" she growled.

"Be my guest," Antelope offered, keen to make amends.

Without further ado, the lines of adversaries raced at one another and the Alphabet Gang, with some precision began to demonstrate why they, and not others, had survived so long on the island. As the action unfolded and more and more bodies fell into the sand, headless or dead, Mr Hand performed a 180 and began walking off towards the cliffs that he had referred to earlier. Wilber had visions of Hand disappearing over the edge and plunging to his death but it seemed Mr Hand was back in control of himself.

"Do you still have the Map the Professor gave you?"

"How do you know about the map?" Wilber asked, suddenly

suspicious.

"Never mind that now. Do you still have it?"

"Yes I have it here."

Wilber reached in his bag and pulled it out. Mr Hand took it from him with some trepidation and examined the map's features as he walked. When next he spoke, he did so with some urgency.

"Wilber the map is not the territory. Remember that. It might just save your life." Here, he leaned in. "You are surrounded by deception my friend. Trust nothing or no one, not me, and certainly not this map."

"But how will I find my way?" Wilber returned, suddenly confused.

"First, seek new allies, then avoid the jungle. It's dangerous. Head out to sea... which is dangerous too, but essential. You'll need a ride, but you'll also need a boat and someone to row it."

"A boat, but why would I want to go out to sea? Where's the crystal? Isn't it here?"

Hand smiled.

"Listen to your heart, Wilber. It's the truest compass of all. It will point the way."

Wilber grimaced, understanding that Def and he were not complete opposites.

"It will? That's nice to know." He didn't bother keeping the sarcasm out of his voice.

"I have a gift for you. It's not a thing exactly. More a story. A vision perhaps. Down there is where you came onto this island. Can you see it?"

At this, Mr Hand pointed, and Wilber looked out across the bay, over the edge of the tumbling cliff to the distant shore where he had landed. Beyond the green water was sand and then jungle. He followed the shoreline with his eye, from west to east, and saw the land narrowing to the point where the time gate stood. Through the trilithon he had first emerged onto the island. Remembering his moment of awakening in the warm bath-like waters, he nodded, and shivered, mindful that time was ticking down. Away in the distance the trilithon remained, exactly as when he'd first awoken. The only difference was that the sun had shifted and the shadows along with it. The sky had changed colour too and was filled with cloud.

"You really need to look more carefully, Wilber."

Something in Mr Hand's voice alerted Wilber to the fact that he did actually need to pay attention from time to time.

"Yeah I see it. So what."

"The Professor gave you the map and the watch. Yabu gave you the orb. Astapor gave you grief. I'm going to give you a memory. Take a mental picture of the moment you first stepped onto the island."

Wilber closed his eyes and snap, an image flashed through his mind. Chased around the stone circle, not once, twice but three times. Arrested on the half. Moving to the centre of the maze. Click. The T Rex watching him as the air span. Click. The Cannibal Grove. Click. Claiming the crystal in the heart of the Cube.

"This is all great, man, but what's the point?"

"What is the point?" Mr Hand echoed. "What indeed?"

There was a sudden intensification of light and then a flicker. Wilber raised his arm to shade his eyes. He was first dazzled and then transported back home. He was nine years of age. Yellow lorries were thundering down the drive of Muldoon manor, covered in tarpaulins. Wilber counted five big lorries, watched the workmen spreading out through the grounds. Working in secrecy. Sent away on holiday. To Greece. Athens and then the islands. On a private yacht with outboard engines. He remembered the beaches and the amphitheatres, swimming in the pellucid waters. The white marble. Olives and fish, possibly sardines. So vivid. But prior to leaving he'd asked his mum about the lorries.

"It's just workmen. They'll be in the grounds for a few weeks. There'll be dust and upheaval. That's why we're going away."

The night before they went away, there was a big storm. Thunder and lightning. Lightning going to ground quite near the

Manor. An ancient oak struck, split in half. Seeing fire descending from the heavens. From the sanctuary of his room. Driving out the next day, seeing George cutting up the fallen branch with a chainsaw. For firewood his father mouthed. As they headed for the airport. But drawn back, back into his room where he had spent a feverish night. Tossing and turning. On the brink of a fever.

And then Wilber found himself spinning through space and the air around him shimmering. He was cold in spite of the heat and then he was hot in spite of the cold. Whatever he thought or did, he couldn't get comfortable. He was troubled and his mind was unravelling like a ball of wool. He found himself dragged along an ancient shore, protesting.

Looking out across the bay once more, he shaded his eyes to look at what? Temples. Complete and whole, not ruins. Columns and painted walls. Hundreds of buildings, thousands of people. A city laid out in concentric rings. Now land, now sea. Now city, now harbour. Ships and boats, celebrations. Health and vitality. The sound of laughter. The feeling of joy. An ancient culture but one with meaning, purpose and direction. Then huge objects hanging in the air. Immobile. That seemed to be watching. They reminded him of the mobiles at school, made of wire and coloured paper, hanging from the ceiling of the classroom. Dangling. Spinning. Unwinding like lines of time within a mind. A flash and he was back, Mr Hand watching him closely. Wilber woozy, confused.

"What was that? What did I see?"

"Part of the picture. The mystery that unhinged you, the story you've carried all along. It has to be told. You have to tell it, but first you have to remember."

A sudden cry of great urgency. Lola, running towards them.

"Come on Wilber. They're breaking through. We have to go."

Wilber, angry. "No. I need to stay. I need to work out what happened."

Mr Hand, soothing and real. "No you must go. Please Wilber, you must not be taken. It will unfold now. All of it. You should know that even the most evil people have good in them and that the best people have hidden evil. Don't get complacent. Change is essential."

Lola, grabbing him and hauling him away. Running away from the forest and the pitched battle. Running to elude capture. Running and processing. Running and then remembering.

"What about the crystal? Where is it?"

Mr Hand pointing in the direction Wilber was running. Over his shoulder.

"In the bay. Flow with the tides, my friend, they'll deliver you. Good luck."

He waved and smiled as Wilber ran, with Lola just ahead, leading the way. The headdress of eagle feathers was suddenly lifted by the winds as Mr Hand began walking backwards towards the Hogan, ignoring everything but Wilber, light behind the eyes. The Alphabets fighting, men falling and blood spilling. The cries of battle. And a final image. The creature watching them from the sanctuary of the shadows. A veritable giant with a single, burning red eye in the middle of his forehead.

The Cyclops!

49

The Mind of Yabu

Mr Hands's consciousness soared upwards, like an eye, out of the top of his head and into the sky, fast, so very fast, yet it didn't blur the world beneath it; rather it took everything in. It saw what was significant, understood the points of tension and possibility. The Alphabets, fighting below, hacking and bashing and generally making mincemeat of the opposition. Def swinging her hammer. Antelope giving a rebel yell, plunging a blade into something raw, dripping with foam and hungry purpose. Rudi picking off the stragglers with poisoned arrows. Everyone, playing their part.

Yes, a bloody incursion, an intensification of the conflict was underway, that much was plain, to the meanest gaze. That was what the eye saw as it moved away, as it flew higher and higher, so Lola and Wilber ran, away from Mr Hand, through the wavering grasses westwards. Away from the Alphabets too engrossed in their all-out war to notice and away from the watching eyes that hugged the tree line.

Lola in front, thin as a whip and just as cruel, running like nothing mattered through blue grass, a sly smile on her twisted lips. So insouciant. It might have been a holiday outing for her. Then five paces behind her, Young Wilber. Fit, but not as fit as he thought he was, despite those endless pounding hours in the gym counting steps, panting, sweat dripping from his brow, watching the colours of the grasses change. The eye took it all in as it sped away, the wavering grasses swaying against a purple sky, flicked back and forth by the wind's bored fingers. Still the eye flew, as Lola broke first through the blue and then into the yellow grass before heading for the tree line. And the foliage there, changing from Lincoln green to ferrous red as though the trees bled and wept their tears through eye-shaped leaves.

Back in his Hogan Albert Hand was seated, cross-legged, his eyes closed but seeing through the Flying Eye. Hearing the rush of the wind as beneath him the Tower Complex was revealed. Away down the tree-covered slope, north westwards flying, as true as an arrow through the mangrove swamp, scudding the rippled surface of the crocodile haunted swamp towards the bamboo hut. Slowing to hover and pulse, to seek and then to find a way into that intimate space. Finding his target, finding Yabu, his mind silent and unmoving as he watched the Dark One peering into his glowing white orb. Watching as he watched, seeing what he saw. Now was the dangerous time. Now was the point when the game hung in the balance. It could go any way. All were poised for change and that was why they watched, with a more than passing interest. Yabu too. Especially him.

Yabu scanned the orb with some irritation. It was not a single thing, the light the orb emitted. Not one plane. Not a lake or a mirror. Not an easy screen to read. Rather it was comprised of endless layers of vision, many of which ran together. Merging, shredding, overlapping. Here time collapsed. Here light was a collage, here the eye was a kaleidoscope of ever shifting patterns. It was enough to make a weak man mad. He watched the Alphabets fighting, saw Astapor's beasts falling, one by one, their screams rippling the fabric of the ethers. The girls fought with an undeniable fury. But with skill also. Yabu saw the watching man beneath the concealing trees and grimaced. The Watcher was assessing the strengths and weaknesses of the girls. He would let this small force fall and return with a much greater force, knowing how to exploit every recorded weakness.

Astapor was ever the cat that way. Fighting by proxy, analysing, tweaking, refining his techniques. But he would have to be careful. Forces long hidden were emerging and were aligning themselves with the boy. Doors that had been long hidden were suddenly reappearing, rearing up out of the sands of the past, and where before they had always been locked, now they were springing open. And things, best chained, were pouring forth.

Yabu's brow was beaded with sweat as he held the white orb outstretched in his left hand. His elegant black suit was soaked with perspiration. Something was changing. Was it him or the island? He was losing touch with the beasts over which he had held sway for so long. The Old Order was fading. It didn't take a genius to see that. The only question was which way to turn, with whom should he side? Traditionally he had sided with Astapor. The Russian favoured him, because he was vicious and sly but recent events would seem to suggest that Astapor was slipping. Everything was up for grabs. If the boy drew the Russian from his lair, then would be the time to strike. The Central throne would become vacant and perhaps he would be the man to fill it. He would redefine the Game and the crocs would feast on Slavic Flesh. Was that the reason for the disconnect? Was he being prepared for even greater glories?

Yabu twisted the glowing orb and let out a frustrated sigh as Lola and Wilber faded from sight. Normally he could control the flow of images but it was becoming ever more and more difficult. Perhaps it was time he undertook a journey, got out of the swamp. A flicker of images and he blinked. His ears filled with tribal beats of unhinged sound. It reminded him of his ancestral past, but to him, Africa was not even a memory, just a photograph on someone else's mantelpiece.

Another flicker and three new faces filled the glass. He gasped when he saw the Russian, younger but still noticeably the same. And then Muldoon and the Woman. Madeline. Or the mad one as he had called her.

Why should he see them now? The images scrolled and he watched the drama unfolding in a way he had not anticipated. The Russian was talking in an affable manner with Muldoon. It would appear that they had been friends. Muldoon shared his thoughts with the Russian and the work of reconstructing the island had moved on apace. They were not enemies as Astapor had always maintained. It would appear from these images that they were allies, friends even. Then she had arrived and it had all changed.

Astapor had loved her from the outset and she had obviously felt a great affinity with the Russian. Their first encounter was a meeting of minds and only later a merging of flesh. Their connection was a profound one, and profoundly shocking to Yabu's gaze. The Russian had melted, shown he was capable of love, of being held, of weeping and expressing his deepest hopes and hurts. Why should this be so hard to accept? And yet it was. Simple and yet so powerful. The healing power of love, the journey towards self-acceptance, the total trust of another. And then the change as Madeline's gaze shifted from the Russian to the Englishman. Subtle at first but building to a gradual crescendo. Surreptitious glances stolen at shared meal times, then the lingering gaze. Muldoon denying his feelings. Madeline attempting to conceal hers. The Russian's laughter and Madeline's doting eyes, straying from the Russians face when she thought he wasn't looking, but always the work progressed.

And always the project came first. The towers reclaimed from strangling jungle. Metal drawn from the earth and worked. The towers reclad, laboratories equipped. Everyone with a purpose and freedom to enjoy the space and peace of a cloudless sky and the benign and healing waters of the green deep. New people arrived every day and were put to work in areas of interest or skill. The Magicians in balance and each pursuing their own agenda. Astopor working to heal the sick, biochemically and psychologically. Exploring what the human might evolve into in the coming Age. All this, in spite of the horrors of his past. Or perhaps because of it.

Yet the hold was a fragile one. So profoundly damaged was he. And Madeline was the only thing that kept him together, kept him healthy and productive. Because of her love. Muldoon saw and accepted the Russian's genius and he believed in the project. The World they had all left behind was a place of great evil. He held that world in his hands sometimes and looked at it with horror.

Here on the island they had a place to begin again. To create the kind of society they wanted to live in, free from corrupt and corrupting governments and the relentless push for more and more power. The Old World was soiled and damaged, a fallen world where irreplaceable riches were dragged from the torn guts of the earth, forests felled and oceans polluted. Where populations in every country spiralled with less and less space for more and more people. Where there were ever greater divisions between rich and poor. Bigger and better bombs. Less and less caring societies. With no empathy, no compassion and no time for anything other than their own acquisition of wealth. For lies and delusion. On a collision course with disaster. The warnings of Hiroshima and Auschwitz discarded. The hopes for a better kind of world, forgotten. But not here. Not with Astapor at the helm. Not with the chance to engineer a perfect society.

Yabu saw all this and was agog. This was before his time. It was not the history he had been sold. Looking deeper into the orb. Seeing the arc of the story like the arc of a cannonball reaching its zenith and then beginning its descent. The earth, reaching up with skeletal fingers ready for the impact, ready for the explosion.

And then the boom... The lovers meeting and embracing for the first time. Lips tasting lips. Clothes discarded. Bodies conjoined. Fighting it at first, but weak, unable to prevent the expression of their passion for one another. The blades in Astapor's mind, the endless guillotine, suspended, finally falling and heads rolling and endless rivers of blood pouring into the green seas in which the island bathed.

The Russian, mad. His mind shattered. His rage, boundless. The sound of his screams, from his tower-top lair silencing the island. George, hearing and holding his hands to his ears. His eyes filled with tears, Madeline's with dread. George, running from his lover down the hill towards the bay. Madeline, repairing to the cliff top, looking back down the island towards the eastern time gate, shrouded in a deep green gown. Astapor finding her at dusk. The love in his heart extinguished, fires raging in his eyes, the hiss of an Auschwitz wind escaping from his lips in accusation. Holding her in his arms, squeezing her until she screamed and then dragging her away to the tower where her screams pierced the air and filled the sky with storm.

And thus the Golden Age passed and Hell poured out of Astapor's mind onto the island.

Yabu saw it all and saw it clearly. Saw the walls and fences erected. The shift in policy, from health to sickness. Endless punishment, not just for Madeline and George but for all the human race. Astapor's mind was full of hooks that sought only and ever to pierce the flesh, and chain the human to a world of pain. Because of his betrayal all would suffer and all had. The white light from the orb began to dim but in it Yabu saw one final image.

Astapor on his knees weeping, cradling the lost woman with the vacant mind. He has broken her mind and left her body intact. He hugs her to him and she hangs limp in his arms. Soon she will rot, soon she will collapse. He could freeze her in the ice; He has done it before but a voice says no, no. He must burn her, having the gift of fire, he must burn her and move on to all the others who will surely come. Those who fall into the net and those who are lured into it. And the eye sees too and for the first time since arrival, Mr Hand understands what before was hidden.

50

Friends Forever... or Never

In spite of his rule to only look forward and never back, Justice kept glancing over his shoulder for a sign that they were being followed by the Alphabet Gang, but there was nothing and no one. He and Lola were alone.

Once again they had entered a different vegetation zone. Here most of the trees, although tropically familiar, were red and not a subtle red at that but a screaming red like they had been painted by fauves or madmen. "Expect the unexpected, expect the unexpected" Wilber's inner voice chanted over and over. Sweat rolled down his brow and he was breathing heavily. He wanted to eat and he desperately needed to drink. Lola, aware he was flagging, slowed to a halt and spun round to face him, hands on her hips. She had a face like thunder and by the looks of it, an itchy trigger finger.

"You need to keep up Muldoon, or you're gonna get us both killed."

Something in her tone enraged Wilber and immediately he saw red, which, given the pigmentation of leaves in this part of the forest, was not entirely surprising.

"Why didn't you wait for the girls?"

"Girls, smurls, we had to get away from them, Wilber. They were holding us back! They are desperate, useless and helpless. It won't be long before they are facing an extinction level event."

"Just exactly who are you Lola?"

Lola, always sly, sidestepped the question.

"I've never claimed to be anything other than who I am. A razor girl with a booby-trapped mind and a bad attitude!"

"You sound like an ad-jingle, not a person. Could we try that again without the attitude?"

Lola's response was to flash him her trout pout. Wilber flung out his arms in comic exasperation and then flopped to the floor in real desperation. He crossed his legs, took deep cleansing breaths and cast his mind back over recent events. Up on top of the volcano it had all gone wonky. George had wigged out and he, Justice had floated away, carried off by the fairies. Why should this happen at such a crucial moment and was Lola implicated? She had been remarkably calm up at the Tower Complex like she was reading from an autocue no one else could see. And yet there'd been no guards, no interception, no gunfire. The whole thing stank to high heaven. Could he believe her? Could he trust her?

"Why are you helping me Lola?"

"Because I've this deep and abiding love of lost causes," came the reply.

Suddenly there was a rustle in the bushes and in a shot, Justice was on his feet, eyes wide and breathing hard. He looked around for a stick, a rock, a bucket, anything he could use as a weapon but there was nothing, just his fists. He raised them and wondered what being eaten alive felt like. A pasty faced youth with black, spiky hair and a starvation camp look, stepped out from behind a tree and raised his shades.

"Afternoon each."

"And you are?" Wilber asked suspiciously.

"Amazed that you are still alive," the youth said as he turned away from Wilber diverting his attention towards the obviously far more desirable Lola.

"Back in black Lolals and out on the range. You just can't help yourself can you baby? Always playing with the meat."

"Who is this?" Wilber asked moving to stand beside Lola. "He seems to know you."

Lola had never looked more bored of anything in her life but a sense of etiquette compelled her to make the introductions.

"Wilber, meet Caleb. He's a sick little puppy who likes machines and torture. Ignore him and he'll go away. In no circumstances should you give him food or show him any kindness."

"If only that were true. Lola, why are you helping this walking corpse?

"I'll tell you what I told him. It's because I love hopeless causes." She paused and smirked. "Well, not all hopeless causes. Some just make me sick."

Caleb scrunched up his face as though he could smell something really bad. He appeared to think of an insult, prepared to deliver it and then changed his mind.

"I came to warn you, you're in danger."

"You think?" Lola quipped. If sarcasm could kill, everyone within a hundred-mile radius would already be dead.

Justice had been studying Caleb's face with due care and attention for at least a minute before he made the connection. Immediately his dander was up.

"Wait a minute, he's with Astapor! What have you done with my Uncle?"

Caleb's smirk spoke volumes

"We had a little chat and then we let him go."

"Liar!!! You lying..."

But he never got to finish his insult as he was already flying through the air. Hitting Caleb like a freight train, he knocked the breath out of the spindly youth and bore him to the ground. Landing on top of his hated adversary, Justice tried to grab his throat for the stranglehold that would end the little worm, but Caleb was quicker and batted Wilber's hands aside. Then the wrestling began in earnest. Quickly, Caleb reversed their positions, spinning Wilber beneath him and pinning his arms with his knees. Then he began to pummel Wilber's face, slowly, methodically and with terrible effect. Lola, rolling her eyes, walked over to Caleb and round-kicked him in the head. Slumping forward Caleb hit the ground with his chin. Out cold.

"Boys, boys, get a room."

Picking Wilber up with one hand Lola carried him ten feet away and dropped him unceremoniously into a heap. Then she returned to Caleb and quickly revived him with a sharp kick to the ribs. Caleb, by way of a response, sat up and grunted.

"Chill out the pair of you or I'll hammer you into next week!" Lola commanded.

That seemed to do the trick. Reaching in a pocket, Lola retrieved a hanky and handed it to Wilber. His nose was bleeding and he had a black eye. Caleb was stronger than he looked and about as vicious as a leopard, Wilber thought, pinching his nose and trying to staunch the flow of blood.

"Thanks for the First Aid, Lolals, always appreciated."

"Who is he Lola and what is he to you?"

Caleb's ears pricked up when he heard this. It was a good question and he wanted to know the answer.

"Yes Lola, what am I to you?"

Lola looked at the seated, sprawling youth and considered her options. They had a long history of apparently mutual loathing, did she and Caleb, that much was apparent. To look at them you might say they were distant cousins or evil emo twins. They seemed cut from the same cloth, or perhaps it was truer to say that they had just had to adapt to the same conditions. Everyone on this island orbited Astapor, that was obvious but that didn't mean they couldn't be useful. Perhaps it would be safer to trust no one, but to use everyone.

"So?" Wilber prompted.

"Caleb's mad and Caleb's bad and Caleb's far too dangerous to know. Least of all, trust," Lola replied, hammering the final nail into the nasty, little emo's coffin.

Wilber beamed from ear to ear. He felt like he had just won the lottery.

"My thoughts exactly. Caleb, I really don't want to hurt your feelings but I think its time for you to leave the Big Brother house and head back to Siberia." Caleb, clearly enraged, banged his clenched fists into the soft earth and yelled.

"I'm not here for you Muldoon. I don't give a damn about you frankly but the times they are a changin'. Everything's falling apart up on the hill and the ship is sinking. Astapor is no longer in charge. He's evil, which is fine but he's nuts too, which isn't. We need a change of leadership, but first we all need to get away from him."

"But isn't he like your daddy substitute. Don't you idolise him and want to be him?

"Watch your mouth, Lola, or you'll end up on a meat hook!"

"Charmed I'm sure," Lola said, laughing maniacally and obviously enjoying herself. "Wilber, whatever you do, never wind up alone with this creature. He's the most twisted vine in the forest."

Caleb flik-flakked to his feet and stalked up to his tormentor.

"Look Lola, I didn't come here to trade insults. I came to help. By all accounts the Boy has two crystals and the count is freaking out. The other Magicians feel his vulnerability and are already circling, looking for a way onto the Volcano. They all want to be the Prime and Astapor knows that. He's ripe for toppling and the further the kid gets, the more he's weakened. I don't want to break the island or smash the system, far from it. I just want to move up the rankings... "

"Fancy yourself as a Magician, do you Cay?"

"Why not?"

"Aren't we the ambitious one?"

"Look, Astapor is rocking and he's going to fall any day now, but I'm not foolish enough to try to stick the dagger in myself. Oh no. Others tried before me and ended up being fed to the zoo. Oh no, I won't play that game. He could retain his position or he could fall... I want to back both horses. I have a good cover story. I've told him I'm going to bring you back home, back into the fold so to speak. But my time chasing after you is limited. It has a cut off point, after which time he's going to think I've turned."

Wilber, listening in, whistled and shook his head.

"God Caleb but that's a dangerous game."

"I just want him off the island Lolals. Gone. He could be the one who brings the Russian down. In which case everything is up for grabs. Or he could be just another 'also ran', in which case it's just been another day in paradise. With a little weather."

At this point he cast his eyes aloft, like a Renaissance Cherub, and surveyed the gathering storm. Taking a breath, and a peak at Wilber's reaction to what he was saying, he wrapped up his oration.

"I'll help get him to the time gate, but not for any altruistic reason. I want him gone so I can advance. Then, if and when the Count is toppled, things can get back to how they were before he came."

"Exactly the same?" she asked flirtatiously.

"Well perhaps not exactly the same. I didn't always treat you as well as I might have."

"Always the Romantic."

Caleb cast another irritated look in Wilber's direction. It was clear he had rehearsed his speeches in order to carefully elaborate his rationale for becoming a turncoat. He was uncomfortable, he was squirming and Lola was loving it. Come to think of it, so was Wilber. Within minutes of meeting, they had formed quite the little love triangle. Or was that a hate triangle? With teenage hormones it was so difficult to tell.

"Look, we can work out the details later. Lots of moving parts, lots of what ifs. Know what I mean? Anyway, we have to get moving and quick. Astapor is letting all sorts of things go and no no one is safe."

"What do you mean?" Wilber asked.

"There isn't time for this," Caleb snarled, his inner leopard out of the cage again.

"Tell him," Lola commanded.

"Alright! For some reason Muldoon you've really narked the Russian and he's thrown caution to the winds. He's usually so calculating, elegant in his solutions really, but that's all gone. Like I've said, he's cracking up. You have to understand, the island is an experiment with controls, but remove the controls and no one is safe."

Lola was impressed.

"Succinctly put amici."

"Anyway, as a kind of peace offering, I've brought you some gifts," Caleb said, disgusted with the notion of charity but compelled to win trust and build a positive relationship with the other two.

"Gifts?" Wilber shot back, like the very notion was obscene.

"Tools really. Oh just follow me."

Caleb stalked off behind a large banana tree and Lola and Wilber followed him, Wilber guarded and uptight, Lola loose but ready for action. Caleb came to a halt beside what looked like a deep hole. At first Wilber imagined the worst. Caleb had dug his grave and was going to bury him alive. Then he peered over the rough-hewn edge, down into the hole. There was a wooden crate in there, painted letter-box red. It was open and full of what Caleb referred to as tools. Lola let out a gasp of delight.

"Is that what I think it is?"

Caleb squirmed with repressed delight as Lola reached down into the crate and picked out her tool of choice: a portable chain saw! Instantly she pulled the chain and fired up the mechanical beast and began swinging it around her head as though it was as light as a swishy stick with a ribbon on the end. As well as being incredibly light it was virtually silent, like the buzzing of a wasp. Wilber stroked his chin, reached down into the hole and drew out a baseball bat. Caleb was not impressed.

"Woos! You need something with a blade. Something like this."

Caleb stooped and his fingers closed around the handle of something that made his eyes gleam. It was a Samurai Sword and it looked as if it were both ancient and priceless. Caleb drew it to him like others would a lost kitten. He removed and discarded the scabbard and admired the blade. Yet another case of love at first sight.

"I once read a poem in which one of these beauties was referred to as a Japanese Decapitator. I loved that. That made the world right for me at that moment. Know what I mean Wilber?"

Wilber didn't and the more time he spent with Caleb, the more the emo freak bothered him.

"Oh goodie, right on time," Caleb announced gaily.

Wilber wheeled and saw something vaguely human, standing in the bushes, looking at him. It was well over six feet and hideously muscled. Sartorially challenged, it wore a tropical shirt, or at least the remains of one, and shredded shorts, revealing more of itself than Wilber cared to see. Its hair was as spiked as Caleb's and dried blood caked the edges of its mouth. Wilber was reminded of a three-year-old who had eaten too much chocolate cake at a sibling's birthday party. The eyes were wildly-staring blood-filled boils, without feature and the hands, when it raised them, were coarsened pads, as though they had been adapted for scrubbing kitchen floors or dirty bricks in an industrial landscape. The beast smiled at him and emitted a low growl. Wilber's blood iced over, as he saw more forms lumbering towards him, from out of the forest. They had come down the hill, looking for a light snack or maybe a three course meal and it would appear that they had already finished their starters.

51

Anyone For Cricket?

"I count eleven," Lola declaimed gamely. "What are they Caleb?"

Caleb, clearly and alarmingly, was at last, in his element.

"Glad you asked Lolals. That is a Scourer. A Level 30 Variant with Unique Gifts. The modified hands are a cross between barbed wire and steel wool. And they do what it says on the tin. They scour! Skin, flesh, bone, everything and anything! Not only are they strong, they are remorseless in pursuit and they have very healthy appetites. One of these things can consume a six-year-old child at a single sitting. Disgusting. Horrific. Yet truly amazing. Better than TV!"

There then followed the sound of rustling leaves and a new emergence. Caleb, like a deranged Wildlife Presenter spoke in exaggerated whispers to Wilber who was quivering with fright. Or adrenaline.

Possibly both,

"Oh and look, coming up just behind it, on the right, is a Peeler. Where the scourer scours the peeler peels. They are usually housed together, albeit they are separated by mesh, for obvious reasons. Hooked thumbs and clawed fingers, these guys are our tribute to Freddy Krueger of Nightmare On Elm Street Fame, from whom we drew inspiration. These guys are skilled but a little bit retro, and whilst they like your meat they love your skin. They'll take it off with a single cut. You have to see it to believe it, it simply beggars belief. It's art I tell you, Art! Whoa! And here come the shock troops, the slappers..."

Out of the underbrush three wild-haired women came charging. Like rhinos. Wilber screamed like a prepubescent girl, but Caleb and Lola whooped like they were shooting rapids in a canoe. Swish, swish, rrrrrrr and they dropped like flies. The sandy floor became as red as the trees and Wilber watched open-mouthed as his partners in crime high-fived like they were playing in the semi-finals of a volleyball competition.

"Slappers slap, Wilber" Caleb called over the buzzing of the chainsaw. "Their job is to stun you so that the peelers and scratchers can get in close and finish you. It's a weirdly symbiotic relationship they all have, like sharks and remoras. Scourers and Peelers cherish their Slappers and will often let them feed first after they make a kill. They love a sweetmeat and are expert at extracting them with just their fingers.

Wilber felt as though he was going to be sick. Caleb catching sight of his green gills and pasty face grinned like a malevolent goblin.

"Look lively Doon, behind you!"

Sprinting towards him at a rate of knots were two more slappers. If anything this pair looked even more charged than the first assault team. Wilber swallowed hard and gripped the handle of his baseball bat and assumed a strike position. Crazed thoughts ran through his mind. Was he really going to try and kill these things or was he just going to knock them out. He had to defend himself but did he really have to use lethal force? In spite of the things that had been done to them they were still strictly speaking humans. If he killed them then he would be a murderer!

His deliberations ended quickly as the first slapper launched herself through the air at him as he had with Caleb, just minutes earlier. Wilber swung his bat but not hard enough as the bat just glanced off the wild-eyed slapper's shoulder and she bore him to the ground. He hit the blood-stained earth with a thud, the air knocked out of him and the slapper began raining blows on him from every angle. The second slapper was on him soon after and clamped her teeth to his upper thigh.

Again Wilber screamed but this time with as much rage as pain and brought his bat down on the head of the biting slapper. There was a sickening crunch and the body went slack, and then without warning Slapper number one stopped hitting him and fell sidewards, minus a head. Caleb towered above him laughing insanely, blood dripping from his Japanese blade.

"Isn't this fun Wilber?"

"Fun?" Wilber screamed, incredulous.

"Isn't this just the best game you've ever played?"

"Rugby it ain't! Nor is it badminton for that matter!"

Now he was babbling, quite clearly teetering on the brink of shock-induced insanity. Caleb thrust out an arm and helped Wilber to his feet. The remaining peelers and scourers still lurked in the bushes, awaiting a sign.

"Here they come," Lola yelled, revving her chainsaw, "and they're off!"

It was like some mad human variation of a horse race and the combination of shock and adrenaline starting Wilber laughing maniacally.

The first peeler fell to Caleb's whirling blade, the second to Lola's saw, the third again to Caleb, but the fourth, the fourth was Wilber's. He gritted his teeth and swung like he wanted to hit a home run and something flew off the body and arced up into the uppermost branches of a nearby palm. The once dry earth had become a thick, slick, glossy pool of blood. The fifth was Lola's and she carved it up like a Thanksgiving Turkey but the sixth and last was Wilber's.

This time he went low and a knee crunched and shattered. This slowed the irate scourer down to a crawl. But still its rage and malice were undiminished. The orbed eyes shrieked scarlet and revealed the intention behind them was always to kill, kill, kill. There was nothing left to reason with here. No human remained. Nothing he recognised as human anyway. Wilber had always considered himself to be vaguely Christian. Not that he went to church and sang hymns on a Sunday, that wasn't him. But occasionally he would go into a church alone, sit in a pew and talk in his head to something he imagined might be there and listening.

It never solved anything but it helped him to believe in those moments. To believe that better times were coming. To believe that there was meaning and purpose in the world beyond just making money and screwing other people over. To believe that the world's leaders weren't insane enough to blow everybody to kingdom come on the strength of a whim or the desire to show how strong and powerful they were. To believe and to hope that he could forge a future life where he wasn't ashamed, afraid or alone.

The scourer let out a bloodcurdling shriek as it continued to advance towards him. It was just a few metres away now. He couldn't let it get any closer. Whilst it had breath in its body it would keep on coming, keep on coming. But how to deal with it. How to cope with what he had been compelled to do. An image of Christ on the cross flashed through his mind and the words,

"Forgive them for they know not what they do."

Wilber winced. Nice sentiment but that didn't really work here. Another snatch, this time of the Salvation Army. "Fight the good fight with all thy might, Christ is thy strength and Christ thy might..." Men and Women in black and red uniforms banging drums and shaking collection tins. Definitely better but again, it didn't quite cut the mustard. And then an image of the Archangel Michael with his sword raised aloft. God's Right Hand Man and his Executioner. Even God needed a Hit man.

If these beings had souls then giving them a quick death was a mercy. If they didn't he was just despatching them to oblivion and it didn't matter. From nothing they had come and to nothing they would return.

He swung the bat, felt the impact and heard the thud of the body dropping to the floor.

Then he dropped the bat and let out a terrible cry that seemed to split the very air in two. Damn Astapor! Damn this place! Damn everything! Tears streamed down his face and he sobbed and wept uncontrollably, all the pent up griefs of his life spilling from his body, dripping into the terrible earth. There they swirled, dregs merely, that mingled with the many bloods already spilt, and seeped away, soon to be forgotten.

Caleb and Lola watched Wilber without offering any support or comfort. It was something he had to go through alone. No one could help him. And if he couldn't deal with it then he would just have to give up. Hurl himself off a rock or ask one of them to dispatch him quickly. But that didn't happen. In time, the tears stopped flowing and the sound of crying faded away and Wilber stood in the forest clearing with a new resolve, amongst the hacked and broken bodies of the fallen foe.

After a while Wilber asked a simple question.

"Which way now? Back up the hill and round the towers, or through the forest to the West?"

"No" Caleb said, "it's not safe there anymore. New eggs have hatched. Believe me you don't want to go that way. You'll get eaten or worst."

Wilber reflected on the past and weighed his options for the immediate present. It was not looking especially good. He didn't mind admitting that, not even out loud. But he had to find a way through all of this. If he lost, it wasn't like they would leave him alone to play in the sand pit. No, there would be repercussions and then there would be punishment. And he didn't mean a clip around the ear, or a week of detentions. He would end up trussed up in one of Astapor's labs with needles in his arms and head and electrodes attached to his extremities and sooner, rather than later, he'd go green or yellow and develop an insatiable hunger for human flesh. Tough choices were required and once made he would have to stick to them.

"Can't go forwards, can't go backwards. So which way do we go?"

Caleb and Lola gave each other an inscrutable look.

"Across the bay. There's a boat. I'll take you. But we have to go now," Caleb said.

"How do we know we can trust you?" Lola asked.

Caleb smirked.

"You don't. But if you stay here you're gonna get eaten or worse. Trust me."

"Alright we'll trust you for now. But one false move and you're gone," and she revved her chainsaw and laughed the laugh of an innocent child.

"Always the Romantic, Lolals."

And Wilber had thought romance was dead. How wrong could a kid be?

52

The Mind of The Monster

Spiderlike, Astapor sat up in his tower, in the green-domed control room musing on his fate and on the fates of those around him. The Game had entered another phase and for once it felt different. That was both good and bad, interesting and perturbing and presented an entirely new set of problems. Suddenly original patterns had begun to emerge in the world around him and not all of them yielded predictable outcomes.

Should that concern him? No. It was an opportunity. He was a Chess Grandmaster, not a man condemned to death. Not yet, anyway. The boy was not a threat, not really. Nor was his Uncle. Muldoon was...

What was he? Dead? Probably Possibly.

No. He very much doubted that. Muldoon was not a man to go quietly into the night. He had learned that from bitter experience. He lived that others might suffer, he being one of those others. Astapor in spite of himself cursed. It wasn't fair. That man spoiled everything and he had so been looking forward to watching and then rewatching his death, playing it over and over again. With stilton and port and endless hours of laughter. But not now, he had been thwarted. But worse than that, for the first time in an age, he was anxious.

After he had sent Caleb off into the forest, he had instantly regretted it. It was not the boy's fault. He was a ruthless and dedicated servant, schooled by he, Astapor since he was a small child. Such a mind. Such tolerance and cruel enthusiasm. He wasn't blood but he may as well have been. Two bodies, one mind, that was the way he thought of Caleb and himself. The son he had always wanted and would no doubt have acquired if Madeline had stayed true, if Muldoon hadn't come between them.

Furious, he rose from his chair and gestured for Lurch to leave him. The hunchbacked vulture bowed and left and upon his disappearance, Astapor's bodyguards melted into the shadows once more. Irritated and suddenly claustrophobic, the Russian reached for the remote in his pocket and stabbed at a button. A door in the green dome arched upwards and he stepped out, through it and onto a walkway that rounded the green chamber. The door, after a few seconds, slid back down into its original closed position.

"Alone at last," he murmured to himself.

The air outside felt cool. It felt good and he inhaled deeply looking out over the forest, past Tower 5 and down towards the Bay of Sharks. The cloud had come rolling in, some hours earlier and was obscuring everything. He felt like he was losing his grip. His once inviolable plans were being thwarted again and again. Get a grip he told himself. It's just Muldoon. After he is captured then things will return to normal.

Or rather abnormal, as they had been before.

The cloud cleared and he saw a boat with a red sail on the green sea at anchor just beyond the Bay of Sharks. He frowned, irritated. Could that be MacCready? The man was a menace but for now he was just beyond reach. Out in the Bay there were secrets he had never uncovered, but given time he would. With Muldoon gone he would go down to the harbour and indulge himself. He would dive again into the Great Ocean. He would search for pearls and sunken cities and buried treasure. He would indulge himself, take a holiday from the horror. Let Lurch or Caleb run the facility, if only for a time.

He would ensure that the Muldoon boy suffered agonies before he changed him into something less than human. Let Caleb keep him for a pet after that, drag him round on an iron chain and jab him from time to time with a cattle prod. A prod with multiple settings and endless possibilities. It would be an early Christmas present for the boy, a just reward for his loyalty and aid in securing Young Muldoon's capture.

It couldn't be far away now. Victory. The boy had done well. He had to admit that. But he would never complete the Game. Not without help. And Muldoon was... No he wasn't. He was very much alive and down in the fiery darkness where the third crystal was hidden. Terror gripped him. His face whitened and his heart pounded.

My God, Muldoon was in the place where he could do the most harm. Beneath the mountain where he had hidden the fire crystal, the tetrahedron. The odds against him discovering it were astronomical but there was always that thin slither of a possibility that he would. And why wouldn't he? He was the most doggedly, persistent imbecile that Astapor had ever met. Nothing could be left to chance where that man was concerned. He had to be stopped. And soon. But then again...

No. No. He couldn't intervene. Rules were rules. Rules he and the other Magicians had agreed upon when he had first come to power. If he broke his own rules he would leave himself open to being ousted, to being thrust from his throne in the centre of the island. Hurled down from its highest crag. Even he had to know and accept that there were limits to how far he could rig the game in his favour.

Shaken and even a little stirred he set out to walk what they referred to as the Upper Circuit; the unbroken chain of walkways a hundred metres high that connected all of the towers within the complex. It was a relatively simple route; eastwards from One to Two to Three to Four and then southwards to eight and back westwards through seven to six to five, then the final leg back to One. The design was as elegant as it was simple, each path breaking both left and right as it encountered a tower, allowing one to walk round each turret in a complete circle or resume the straight way of the circuit.

It was a long time since he'd been outside to take in the air and view with human eyes, not machine eyes, the lands of which, he was the unquestionable Lord and Master. He hadn't felt the need but today was different. Today it seemed all ordinary laws of policy and procedure were being suspended.

As he walked, Astapor recalled his own past. It was a place he tried to visit as little as possible. When Astapor had first come to the island, Astapor had brought with him a skill set that was very different to that of anybody else on the island. That was why he had risen to prominence so rapidly. Of course the games had been in play, but in a very diluted and watered-down form. Of course there were always five crystals, five platonic solids to collect. It's just that all the other paraphernalia wasn't in place. He had shaped it. He had shaped it all.

And all he had had to do was activate each monolith.

Better the others never knew about his past. Best they focused on the work and not the reasons behind it. Oh there had been speculation down the years and speculators, but anyone who grew too curious ended up being asked to leave the program and escorted into a cell with gently pulsing lights of many colours. Black through red and purple to yellow and back again to black.

In time all questioning of his motives ceased and the work proceeded without hindrance. The work... it was endless and yet forever progressing. His ideas changed, but the ideal remained the same. The application of his will to create endless suffering for the human species, of which he was only nominally a part. A species he despised and wished to convert into extensions of his hellish and tortured imagination. That was what kept him focused, the fact that his mind was perpetually in motion, endlessly searching for new ways to reshape human anatomy, corrupting and perverting it in ever more breath-taking turns.

Astapor spent a lot of time thinking about volcanoes, largely because his house was built upon one. He loved lava, loved that it was molten rock and that it could incinerate people. Drop people in lava and within moments they just weren't there. Vaporised, obliterated. It was a great game to play, something a child would enjoy. Much better than pooh sticks. Over time though, lava hardened creating a new black kind of rock. Basalt. He thought of himself like that. Hardened rock, eroded by wind and experience, into smooth and elegant stone.

He'd spent too much time outside. Fresh air didn't agree with him. It was time to get back into his bubble and return to work. Jabbing the button of the Remote, the curved glass door rose once more and he stepped inside.

"Lurch," he yelled, at the top of his lungs, "where are you when I need you?"

In a flash the scientist was at his Master's side and the door slid shut, sealing as it were, the entrance to the tomb.

"Nothing's working Lurch. The Stalkers and the Lamb whackers... and the... the..."

"The Rabid Baby Eaters?"

"Yes, them too, they have been a tremendous disappointment. I blame you of course. We'll see about your punishment later, but for now I have more pressing matters to attend to."

Lurch cowered. Things were getting out of hand. The tower had been attacked and he had been personally exposed to violence. That was never supposed to happen. Bomb from on high, from far away. Kill everyone and anyone but never expose yourself to danger. Rule number one. True they'd caught Muldoon, but the Bone Collector had evaded the horrors of the labyrinth, as Lurch had feared he would and escaped into the lower levels of the volcano where nobody went. For which no maps existed. It made him question everything. Was Astapor slipping? Could he be toppled? Or was it all part of some great Master plan, masterminded by the mad Russian to test them all. As time went by, the Count became more and more unpredictable. He made Rasputin look like a teddy bear.

"It's true the trail has gone cold, for now, but it will warm up again. Just like the volcano."

Astapor flashed him a look that would have frozen an explosion and made Lurch like an ice sculpture.

"We mustn't give in, Master. Now is a time for unity, not

division. Once more unto the breach dear friends. Once More."

Hearing Shakespeare quoted at him by the sweating scientist did little to sweeten Astapor's mood, but he had to appear amenable. Lurch was right. Unity, not division, was what they required. Muldoon would exploit division. Putting his right arm around Lurch's shoulder he squeezed his charge affectionately.

"My sentiments exactly Lurch. The Amazing Adventures of Dinosaur George Muldoon have only just begun. I fear however, there'll be no happy ending on this leg of the voyage."

"Not if I have anything to say about it Master".

"It's time we had a little more malice in Wonderland."

Lurch smiled, yet he looked perplexed.

"What a wonderful turn of phrase Master. Whatever can you mean?"

Astapor fired up a nearby screen and began scrolling through images. What he was looking at wasn't exactly prime time and wasn't fit for Disney. It was a little more r-rated. The mug shots he was scrutinising comprised a who's who and a what was what of terror on the island. There were things in the menagerie that even Lurch wasn't aware existed.

"It's time to explore our options. The Resistance is proving a little stiffer than we'd anticipated. Either it's improving or you're losing your grip Lurch. And as for the Cyclops, despite your protestations to the contrary, it has been an absolute failure and the cause of much disappointment."

"But he's still in the Game. Still following, still watching, awaiting his moment to strike."

Lurch darted forward, thrusting out an arm like a fencer and accidentally knocked over a vase containing one of the Russian's prize orchids, as white and and as pure as a narwhal's hide. The vase rolled over the carpet, scattering soil and petals. Eventually it came to a halt, trailing silence in its wake. It was not a comfortable silence.

"Not one of your better days."

Lurch considered.

"Not really Master but let's focus on the positive."

Without looking up from his screen, Astapor shook his head. "I'd prefer it if we focused on what has to go."

Lurch winced but accepted what was a necessary correction,

"Well obviously the Creepers, the Zombies and the Wisps are out. The Lambwackers, Stalkers and Baby eaters too but there's still the Vampires on Level 19. They haven't had a flap about for a while now and I have it on good authority they're feeling toothsome. The werewolves are hank marvin' n'all and the ghouls are keen to right past wrongs. Killer bees are looking a bit tasty this season. Worth a punt? Maybe."

Lurch was suddenly unsure. What else had he come up with...oh yes.

"Piranha in the paddling pools was one thought. Now I know you're not too keen on the chainsaw-wielding nuns but they have been on HRT and steak diets for the past year and they are hot to trot. I know they're unpredictable but nobody can carve like they can. Just saying. I recently weaponized the komodo dragons too. Difficult to control but once they get the scent they are unstoppable. Anyway it's an option.

The Russian yawned, like a Siberian tiger, and revealed his fang-like incisors as he did so. It was not a terribly reassuring sight but the Scientist could do nothing. He couldn't bolt, he couldn't rage and he couldn't reason. He simply had to wait for the Tiger to make its move.

So he waited.

And after what seemed like minutes waiting, but was in actuality only a few seconds, the Russian spoke. And what he said brought little or no comfort.

"Alright, send them out Lurch. Despatch them all.

A pause in which the Russian just stared at him, through him, into the depths of Lurch's withered soul.

"Empty all the cages if you must, but you know as well as I do that none of it will do. None of it. Those girls are on fire. It's like they've been trained by someone who's making all the right noises but making none of the right moves, if you catch my drift. It's time to really stop the clocks, to up the ante and to proceed to Def Con One. I've made up my mind. I want you to bring in The Hunters. Summon Zoot. Summon Fang. Let it all come down!"

The look of dread on Lurch's face was a picture, and Astapor, who wasn't exactly a bundle of fun, found himself laughing out loud when his gaze alighted on the quivering wreck that was his assistant.

"No Master. Not them. Not Zoot. Not Fang. His methods turn even my stomach and to say she's a loose cannon is a mild understatement.

Astapor stood up and looked Lurch in the eye. He didn't need to try and intimidate anyone. He just did it as a matter of course.

"Are you disagreeing with me Lurch?"

"No, Master, no, no. I'd never do that but I have learned to be a critical friend, to ask those difficult questions that nobody else will."

Astapor chuckled.

"Beautiful recovery Lurch but let me remind you of something. Herr Zoot, the Man in the Yellow Suit and Madame Fang have never let me down. They will succeed where all the others have failed. They will bring the Muldoons down and trim the weeds in this savage garden. The Alphabets won't stand a chance." Lurch gulped. This was an unwanted turn of events. Like using a sledgehammer to crack a nut or a nuke to clear out the rats in your cellar.

"I'll summon them Master."

Astapor smiled eerily.

"No need Lurch, they are already on their way."

53

Out of The Rabbit Hole

George burst out of the crumbling tunnel into the sunlight scarcely able to believe his luck. For a while he just stood there, breathing clean air, unable to process what he'd been through. Then he dusted himself down and wiped away the cobwebs that clung to his clothes, giving him an appearance of the walking dead. Looking around for clues, he quickly orientated himself. Up above him was the Tower Complex, whilst away to the North, was Crowhaven's Golf Course and Manor house.

The sun had already slid past the zenith and was headed towards the Western Lands. It served as both a pointer and a timepiece if only you knew how to read it. And he knew. He'd come out on the eastern slopes of the volcano. Incredible really, for all the time he'd spent on the island he had never known that there were caves and tunnels beneath the labyrinth. A backwards glance towards the tunnel opening had him shaking his head in disbelief. You wouldn't know it was there. So well was it disguised, covered in creepers and low-slung vegetation. Was that deliberate or had it just happened that way.

"It's quite deliberate."

George froze and then he turned round to find himself facing Professor Crowhaven, immaculately clad as ever in his cream suit and trilby, his cuffs starched and his shoes polished. Behind him stood his bodyguards, their automatic weapons pointed, somewhat inevitably at George. Bill and Ben the Flowerpot Men was how George thought of them. That wasn't entirely helpful. Brought, no doubt, through the portal from the Old Country to loyally serve and never question their orders, however ludicrous.

"What is?"

"The placement of that tunnel. We had a hell of a job excavating it without his nibs finding out what we were up to."

"Quite an act of Magic, I shouldn't wonder," George suggested archly. "But then if you want to be top dog, I guess you have to put the work in, do what the other fellow won't."

Crowhaven nodded an acknowledgement.

"I know the drill. That's all George. It's a preposterous title, that of Magician. Today's Magic..."

"Is tomorrow's science." George cut in. After all he had been through on this bloody island, there was no way he was going to be lectured by this effete and arrogant snob. For all that he was English he hated most of his fellow country men. Wherever he was in the world, when he came across them, he tried to avoid them. The Aussies referred to them as whinging pommes and God was that the truth. They were either moaning or complaining or both and they comported themselves with such airs and graces. It was as if they still had an Empire on which the sun never set, but it had, and they needed to grow up and stop dreaming. Stop fantasising about deeds of derring do in the Battle of Britain, lapping up Churchill's bile like it was mother's milk. Loving their queen, hating everything and everybody who had verve, drive, vision and ambition. And above it all thinking they were still superior to everybody else. It was all so tiring, so disgusting.

Whilst George thought all of this, he smiled amicably at Crowhaven. In spite of himself, very much an Englishman. Such a paradox. What was it the Queen said? Never explain and never complain.

"Sorry, you were saying..."

Crowhaven cleared his throat.

"Magic is the art of being where you need to be, at the right time, with the right people, in the right way, isn't it George?"

There was a pause.

"Sorry Professor, I was expecting an oration. Something in the line of John of Gaunt's speech in Richard the Second... You know this earth, this realm, this England."

"Oh George please, be civil. I don't give a damn about any of that rot. I'm concerned with now. Or rather I'm concerned with the future and my place within it."

George scoffed.

"Don't think I don't know what you get up to down in that little Manor house of yours Professor. You're always so correct, so perfectly attired but your experiments are every bit as horrific as the Russians'. And probably more damaging to humanity's efforts to acquire a future, than his are."

Crowhaven chuckled.

"How many humans currently reside on earth, George? Eight billion. In your time, or at least in time as you know it. And how many of those humans are actually useful? How many actually contribute anything new to human culture? Advance it? Most of them are just mindless cows, endlessly consuming. Happy for their governments to perform endless atrocities in the name of National Security. Just so long as they get to live the quiet life, the smug life, the life of comfort surrounded by family and cars and houses and swimming pools and tennis courts and cheap flights...but that world is coming to an end George. As well you know."

"Sorry professor, what were you saying? I must have nodded off."

The sound of the guard's machine guns being cocked wiped the smirk from George's face and Crowhaven stepped towards him, his smile gone, his eye blazing.

"Astapor's vision is the right vision, Muldoon, it's just him who is finished. Every thinking being on this island knows it too, and not just my Brother Magicians. He is the past and I, I am the future. I am the one who will deliver the vision not him. I will put the flesh on the bone, I will make it all concrete. For that I need your help. Your nephew is a threat to everything I've worked for here for the last thirty years. Problem is he has some powerful friends who will not allow us to just wipe him off the board. He must be allowed to succeed but he must not be allowed to complete the game. Otherwise everything here will crumble. And if everything crumbles here, then everything on earth will crumble too. The systems are linked, as well you know."

"Why are you so threatened by this boy?"

"It's not the boy, Muldoon, it's the mind behind the boy. You've been blinded by your devotion to that ridiculous family of yours. You need to see beyond the surface, beyond the fading photographs on the piano and you need to understand that the vaults of time are being opened. Hell, time itself is changing its nature because of what we have done, what I have done with the technology the Atlanteans left behind. You could be part of it George. A space has been cleared for you at the big table. Just change your shoes and dress appropriately. I am prepared to do business with you but are you ready to do business with me?"

George looked first at the guns then back at Crowhaven.

"Yes. I am Professor. I truly am."

"Are you sure?"

George turned and pointed back towards the entrance of the concealed tunnel.

"Do you know what goes on down there Professor? I mean really, beneath the volcano. I caught a glimpse of it myself just now and what I saw terrified me. I always sensed there was something different about this island but now I know."

"And I know that you know George. And I know too."

"Beneath the labyrinth there's a tunnel that leads down, way down to a series of chambers. Some of them are vast. I mean the size of aircraft hangers. Bigger. I did what I had to do for the boy and then instead of coming straight back to the surface I went deeper. Only I wish I hadn't. There's this great flat circular dais, about thirty metres across and it has a moat around it, only the moat isn't filled with water, its filled with fire, or rather lava. And then I see them standing around the edge of that circle, all in their different coloured robes, all hooded. And I just look at them, gone out, then one of them turns and looks straight at me and slowly lowers his hood. And I just freeze. I've never been more terrified in my life. I'm looking at a human face, that isn't human. It's an ancient face and its eyes are crystal. It looks at me and it looks straight through me and it knows me in an instant. And it just turns away, raises its hood and they stand there in silence. And in the middle of the circle there's this flame, an amethyst flame and above appears to be floating this huge crystal in the shape of an eye..."

"George, George," Crowhaven said softly, laying his hand on the Dinosaur Man's shoulder, "forget all of this, it can't help you and it won't help the boy."

"But the Ancients didn't die, they're still here."

Crowhaven nodded sympathetically.

"I know George. I know. I've seen it too, but the others haven't."

A look of bewilderment crossed George's face.

"But they need to see it, they really do. I should bring them back here."

At this Crowhaven shook his head.

"You can't and really, it doesn't matter George. None of it matters. Not really. Let it all go, focus on what's important. Remember what's important. The Game is what's important"

And with this Crowhaven touched George softly between the eyes and tapped three times.

"You will forget that we ever spoke. You will forget everything you saw within the volcano except when you took the crystal from the Guardians. That you can remember. You still have the crystal don't you George?"

George tapped his pocket.

"Oh yes."

"Good, you've done well. Remember, George, magic is about memory and forgetting. I want you to remember what you've been through, all the pain and the horror and I want you to focus on the good you've done too. Forget the rest. Forget the Ancients and their ceremonies and those chambers. It's fading now. Let it all fade. Go now George. Go to your Uncle. He's waiting for you down below. Be a family again George, but remember, the boy can never be allowed to succeed."

George nodded and began to move, downhill on his directed pathway.

"Remember George," Crowhaven called out behind him, "I'll be watching. Always."

And George began to run again and as he ran he remembered. He remembered leaving the labyrinth and the famished horrors of the pit; he remembered leaving the beasts to feast on his brother's flesh. He remembered finding his way into the lava chambers and he remembered fighting the creature with the crystals embedded in its head. He pulled the third crystal, the tetrahedron from its head and then he ran and beyond that he remembered nothing.

And now he was running, running through the trees. Listening for sounds of danger with every pounding footfall. Listening for sounds of pursuit. He knows the island so well, even now, even after all this time. What is it? Five years, eight, ten? What does it matter, what is time here? He can only run so far before he has to stop and gasp for air. Fit but not as fit as he was. Overhead the sun breaks through and shines ecstatically. The whole forest lights up and George smiles at the lush greenery of the leaves, but then the clouds engulf the sun, swallowing it like a wolf swallowing a lamb.

He would never return. Once the Game was over they would be a family again. He knew where to go, he knew exactly where to go. Down the sloping forest bank towards the rendezvous point, wondering about the cameras, wondering if he was being followed even now. He'd know soon enough. Down through the trees and then breaking through the trees to where his uncle was waiting. He knew he'd be there. Somehow he'd just known. Then he was sprinting, sprinting those last few hundred metres as though his life depended upon it. His uncle, upon seeing him, stood up and as his eyes grew wide, a smile erupted all over his face. Joyous, even though shocked, the Old Man flung his arms skywards and soon they were dancing around in circles, jubilant, triumphant, together again.

"George, you're alive. I knew you'd make it." Then the speech faltering, the dance halting. "What happened to Patrick?"

"I left him at dinner." Quick as a flash.

"Really. Up at the castle?"

George turned his body, looking back the way he had come, back towards the Tower complex, focusing his gaze on Tower One, the tower with the domed observatory of green glass. Astapor's lair. His Uncle called it the Castle. Perhaps that way it seemed less forbidding.

"Yes."

Easier to lie than to tell the truth. Even to his own flesh and blood. George winced and tears came into his eyes. What would Patrick be now? Just flesh and blood? Would there be any flesh and blood left? He heard his brother's screams then saw him reaching out with his hand. Save me, save me George, the terrified eyes implored. He drove the images out of his mind, as though they were a pack of wolves, hunting him. No profit there, no gain, there were other things that required his attention.

His Uncle was staring off into the middle distance.

"I haven't had a decent nosh in years George. Oh just thinking about it... I'm salivating like Pavlov's dog. What was the main course?"

"He was." The words were out of his mouth before he could stop himself. The shock unhinged him.

"Sorry, didn't quite catch that." His uncle looked confused.

"Sea Bass." Beautiful recovery.

"Ooh, I love a bit of fish. Especially Captain Birdseye's Fishy Fingers. You remember Captain Birdseye don't you George."

"Never knew the man," George replied, distractedly.

Great Uncle Muldoon rolled his eyes

"Oh Georgie you are hopeless," he chuckled.

"Sorry Uncle. Look, I wish we could stay here. I know you're tired but we have to keep on the move. Astapor's relentless. He'll just keep sending new horrors after us. We have to help Wilber get off the island. Everything else is secondary now. You understand."

His Uncle stood up and nodded his head. Overhead the skies

were darkening.

"I understand George. I'm glad you're here. Just wish Patrick would hurry up."

They both glanced back towards the Green Domed Tower. George said nothing, but began preparing mentally for what lay ahead.

"So what are we running away from today George? Stegosaurs or tyrannosaurs, sharks or crocodiles, ghosts or ghouls, zombies or vampires? Or is it the wild dogs with their wolven fangs? Go on, give us a clue."

George smiled grimly.

From whatever they send after us Uncle. We need to catch up with Wilber and his friends. That means we'll have to run through the Red Forest? Catch him on his way to Mr Lapp. You up to it?

"Do I have any choice?" Great Uncle Muldoon asked plaintively.

But George was already running towards the forest, its leaves red, as though coated with blood.

54

Row, Row, Row, Row Your Boat...

Lola and Caleb looked at each other with scarcely disguised hatred. The sun had clouded over and rain had returned, cold, stabbing and vaguely acidic. What should have been a tropical paradise was more like a miserable autumn day in the Black Country. Away down the beach, Wilber could see what looked like dogs and hogs dueling in the surf, in front of what on the map was referred to as Wrecker's huts. The sandy beach curved like a white tusk around the bay, ready to impale the unwary. Wilber looked at the boat and then at the two dueling Emos. It didn't seem like a particularly good plan to him.

"Why do we have to take the boat? Surely the beach is safer?"

Lola rolled her eyes.

"Wilber we've been here longer than you have, much longer and if we've learned anything it's that things that look safe, never are safe. You dig?"

Wilber looked across the bay then down at the map. The name had been scratched out.

"What's it called again?" he asked, a note of uncertainty quavering in his voice.

"Used to be called Dolphin Bay..." Caleb said cheerfully, "then the sharks ate all the Dolphins so now it's Shark Bay or some such thing."

The look of incredulity on Wilber's face said it all.

"You've gotta be kidding."

Caleb exchanged glances with Lola who smirked in spite of herself.

"Course I'm joking. It's hmm, it's called Mermaid bay"

The uncomfortable silence that followed was enough to propel Caleb around to the front of the boat and to begin hauling it into the surf. Somewhat unwillingly, the others followed suit and before long they were dragging the boat out into deeper waters. Lola jumped in first and took the tiller and the boys followed quickly, each taking an oar.

"Well put your backs into it, we're running out of time."

Wilber opened his mouth to say something uncharitable then thought it was better to say nothing. Although tired, he found the energy to heave his oar over and over again. Caleb did likewise. Despite his skinny frame he was tougher than he looked, stronger and fitter too.

They rowed for ten minutes, moving at quite a pace. The rain slackened momentarily then intensified. Soon they were soaking wet and not a little cold. In Wilber's mind's eye he saw the clock ticking. Glancing back towards the shore he saw the dogs and the pigs had stopped fighting and were watching them with sly psychotic eyes. Nothing was normal here. Everything wanted to kill you and feast on your flesh. Beyond the white sand the spreading forest reared, ripening with doom like a diseased womb. Caleb began to sing.

"Row, row row your boat
Across the sharky bay
Merily, merrily, merrily, merrily
Throw your life away…"

"Will you shut up!" Lola hissed, "I've just about had enough of you."

Wilber concurred. Caleb was a royal pain in the posterior. Perhaps he was being a trifle unfair but the kid had made an art out of being irritating. He was helping, but at what cost? Sheets of cloud moved out over the forest, bringing more rain. The towers in the middle of the island were, for the most part completely obscured, but every now and again one hove into view. Wilber shuddered. Tired, stressed and oppressed he let out an exasperated sigh.

"I feel like I've landed in the midst of some kind of war,"

Caleb grunted and Lola shook her head looking grim.

Back on the shore the dogs and pigs had begun fighting again. The whines and howls, grunts and tortured squeals were enough to put anybody off their breakfast. There was no respite to be had anywhere. The atmosphere was relentlessly grim wherever you went.

"What is it with those things on the beach? Why can't they just shut up and leave each other alone."

"Just dogs being dogs, pigs being pigs," Lola said with a shrug, making an adjustment to the tiller.

"Are they dangerous?" Wilber asked.

"Everything's dangerous here. Even the sheep," Caleb quipped.

"Really?"

Again that note of anxiety in the voice. Wilber was so easy to tease and so gullible. Lola couldn't believe he'd made it this far without collapse. They really should be nicer, she and Caleb, but she just couldn't stop herself. It was too much fun.

"Yeah, savage," she said

They rowed on in silence for some time before Wilber spoke again.

"So how did you get here?"

Lola tutted and shook her head suddenly serious.

"That's the one question you never ask. Anybody"

"Why?"

"Because the answer is invariably the same, Wilber," Caleb spat. "Everybody comes from some future city you'd never comprehend or a long vanished world you'd never survive. We don't do backstories here," he said, feigning a yawn. "Safer for everybody in the long run."

"But history is so fascinating and so are stories. And what are people if they are not stories?"

"Teeth and attitude," quipped Lola.

"You could learn so much," said Wilber, the disappointment in his voice obvious.

"Or die of boredom," shot Caleb. "I've been close once or twice on this trip I can tell ya." Switching tack, he turned suddenly to the Girl at the tiller. "Lola, why don't you ever talk to me?

His voice was full of longing.

"Because there's weird, which I can just about deal with, and then there's where you're at, which is some place I never want to go to. Ever. So back to you Wilber. To answer your question. Wherever or whenever you come from, there's little hope of getting back. You need to accept that."

"You're so negative," Wilber shot back, "but you're also kinda cute." This last thought he muttered under his breath but Caleb obviously heard as he began to scowl.

"It's a survival mechanism, Wilber," she explained with maternal patience. "Believe me, it's the reason we've lasted as long as we have."

Wilber nodded, accepting this.

"Ok, ok. I have one last question. Can I ask it?"

"If you must," Caleb said begrudgingly.

Wilber scrunched up his brow, unsure of how to express himself without giving offence. It was a tough call. In the end he just opted for being honest.

"How did you end up working for Astapor?"

Caleb and Lola looked at each other without speaking. Caleb carried on rowing and Wilber had to work hard to keep up with him. After a while Caleb spoke.

"Look it's real simple; you either work for Astapor or you end up getting worked on by Astapor and getting a zombie makeover. Ya dig? I chose the former. Got a problem with that. We'll discuss it later. If and when you fail to get off this island."

Caleb's words hit Wilber like a falling tree and he felt rage rising in him like never before. He gripped the oar tightly and stopped rowing. His voice when he spoke was as taut as steel cable.

"No way I'm getting marooned here Caleb. I'm getting off. Wild horses won't stop me."

This seemed to amuse the dark-eyed boy.

"But Astapor will. You don't know him like we do. He's remorseless and relentless. He won't stop until he has you in his clutches. You've annoyed him and frustrated him and he can never forget that. You'll end up as one of his experiments Wilber and he'll leave enough of you conscious to know what he's done."

"Never!"

Caleb smiled at this.

"He's close Wilber, so close and he has eyes everywhere. The cameras see everything and it's only a matter of time before he closes in and snap; off go your legs. Or worse."

Wilber bristled but he bore down hard. He knew he was being got at.

"Astapor can send what he likes against me. I'm rad and I'm well 'ard. He'll never defeat me, not with an army behind him. I'm A Muldoon. We're a tough breed. We don't crack."

Caleb shipped his oar and Wilber did the same; they drifted and the rain continued to fall. Caleb turned to face Wilber.

"You've never been here at night have you? Not yet. The moon rises and it's a terrible sight. Not a pleasant moon, not a romantic moon oh no, it's a monstrous moon, dark and red and filled with blood. And it drips as it rises higher, ever higher, seeking its zenith. The drip, drip, drip of pus. When it's pulsing and bloated that's when the carnage really starts. That's when the true terrors arise.

Here Lola continued

"Everything you've seen till now has been tame in comparison with what comes at night."

"You'll be glad of the sanctuary of Astapor's Observatory," Caleb whispered.

"Or indeed any one of the five magicians," Lola added.

"They'll shelter you, keep you safe from harm but they all demand a price."

Lola nodded.

"That's if they even want you, if you're useful to them."

"Some people just end up as bait," Caleb said.

"Other's end up as experiments."

Here they both laughed, working well together, like dogs herding sheep or orca herding dolphins. Ready to pen or to kill.

"Yes, Astapor doesn't have friends, he just has experiments," Caleb said, the line obviously rehearsed, his coup de grace."

Their laughter when it came, washed over him. Wilber looked from one to the other. They weren't nice, either of them. Cruelty shone darkly in their eyes. Bruised and bored, they were more than happy to turn on the runt of the litter, the weaker vessel as they perceived it. Had they started off this way or had the island seeped into their pores? Could people as damaged as them be healed, saved, changed? He had to believe it was possible. Had to believe that love was the answer, like the songs said, but he was having considerable doubts.

"Not everybody here is like Astapor. That's a real positive. I've had help from some of the Magicians, the Alphabets and you. I have two of the five crystals and I'm going to get the others. No one is going to stop me. I intend to get off this island."

Here he lifted the map from his paper bag and waved it in Caleb's face.

The youth was unimpressed.

"But today Wilber you're a Running Man and it amuses them to give you hope. They like to give you a sporting chance, to extend you every courtesy but when you're no longer a prospect..."

"Or sport," Lola added.

"You're just a potential recruit," Caleb concluded, looking more than a little smug.

"And remember hope is the last thing to die," Lola added for good measure.

Suddenly there was a bang and the boat stopped abruptly. Had they hit a reef? Caleb and Wilber looked at one another searchingly. Then agreeing to temporarily suspend their war of words, they dipped their oars into the water and pulled hard. They went nowhere and then a shock. Both oars were suddenly wrenched from their grip and pulled, down, down beneath the water. In a state of incredulity Wilber stood up and peered down into the oceans' rain-stippled depths. What was happening? Suddenly the water around them began to bubble. Oh God. Oh no. The realisation arrived with all of them at the same moment.

Something was rising!

*　　　*　　　*　　　*　　　*　　　*　　　*

The marble temple loomed above them, once brilliant white, now yellowed, covered in seaweed. The columns looked Grecian and yet somehow more elaborate. It was like the Parthenon in Athens, only bigger, more majestic. How was that possible? No acropolis. No city on a hill. No, this was a temple that dwelt beneath the waves, that's what it was. Their boat nudged up against the rocky mound on which the temple rested.

Without oars there was little they could do.

"What is this place?" Wilber asked in a hushed whisper.

"I don't know," Caleb replied genuinely in awe.

"It reminds me..."

"Of what"" Lola prompted.

"Of the Temple of Poseidon."

"But isn't that...?

"Yes," Wilber said in a near whisper.

Lola and Caleb exchanged knowing looks. It took a while for the penny to drop and when it did Wilber saw it, the edge of the plan, the edge of a colossal idea. It shook him, disturbed him and yet, he had to consider it, to allow it to play out. It was one of his Uncle's favourite topics after all, the Legend of Atlantis. For all that he was a fossil hunter, a lover of those terrible lizards, Atlantis was his greatest passion. He believed in it as passionately as others of his age and generation believed in football or technology or the diplomatic genius of Donald Trump. He had searched for and maybe even found part of that lost civilization, or so he had hinted when last they met.

Just hours before. What was George doing here? The question returned in a surge of near panic. Nothing added up. Why was that? If only they hadn't been separated. Before he knew it Wilber was up and out of the boat, scrambling up and over the rocks towards the temple. The others behind him were calling but he ignored them. Between the dripping columns into the dark temple. To the greatest shock of all. A figure in a tattered purple robe, clutching a trident, looking straight at him. Wilber stopped and froze, but he'd come too far to lose it to fear. He approached the figure who, like the columns, was dripping wet.

54

It's Just Down There, Beneath The Waves

Approaching, getting nearer, Wilber felt the hairs standing up on the back of his neck. The hooded figure didn't so much as move a muscle. The rain fell harder and blacker than ever, stinging the skin like iced needles. Nothing was as it had been, the joke that was his laugh had receded into a vanishing point. The green sea he had thought familiar, likewise had darkened and heaved with anguish. His hair was plastered to his scalp and his clothes were soaked but questions and the need to succeed prodded him forwards.

Land was nowhere in sight, it had vanished into cloud and driving rain. All that remained was the seated figure, motionless amongst the crumbling white columns, unaffected by all that surrounded it but aware of his approach. Justice felt anxiety shading into fear, then edging into terror. Something was loose and rattling around in his mind and he couldn't see what. He must control himself, that he knew. The rumble of thunder, and the accompanying flash of lightning did nothing to steady his nerves, yet still he must advance, step by step, toe by toe. Nearer, so much nearer now. To what? Why answers of course. He had beaten around the proverbial bush for too long. He needed answers and finally he was ready for them.

Another flash of lightning, closer and somehow more personal, stung his eyes. He blinked. There had been no lightning. So why the flash? He suddenly felt woozy and a sharp, rank stench hit the back of his throat prompting him to gag. Holding his hand to his mouth, Wilber wretched. The smell was unbelievably vile, like rotten eggs but far worse. A word rang out in his mind. Sulphur.

Was that what it was? Holding his hand to his mouth he crept forward. The seated figure was almost within reach, the drenched violet robes hanging down in lank tresses, like seaweed, the fabric sun-bleached and discoloured. Another flash and Wilber closed his eyes, temporarily blinded. He tottered, then staggered, fearing he might fall and hit his head. His senses reeled and he felt close to vomiting. Only a supreme act of will kept him upright.

"Who are you?" he hissed through clenched teeth.

The figure, as though in mockery, remained immobile and silent. Wilber wanted to swing at him, to smash his jaw and break it. He had never known such uncontrollable surges of rage. What in the name of hell was happening to him? Then the thing he had never expected occurred. The figure spoke.

"Poseidon. That is what they named me. Poseidon."

*   *   *   *   *   *   *

Wilber shook his drenched head from side to side and laughter oozed out of him. No such figure existed. He was a myth at best, at worst a deluded fantasy. What he was not, was a God. Chuckling he felt his rage shading into cruel mockery, a mockery he wanted the other to feel as a lance through the heart.

Poseidon, draped like a marble statue, rose from his throne and pointed with his trident at the boy who had dared approach him. Then he tossed back his head, like a petulant stag and his hood fell backward revealing the hidden face. His glistening beard, his great crowned head, his muscular, powerful torso were as nothing when compared with his eyes and the flames that seemed to burn within them. Like raging suns they were, scouring, and devouring, all that they surveyed, yet refracted through crystals. Now sapphire, now amethyst, now emerald. Ever shifting fires, that reflected every change of mood and every dawning thought within. Such vision within that vast head, that saw the greatest and the smallest things side by side, that understood the nature of causation and was able within the blink of an eye to identify the most significant events transpiring within the Universe from moment to moment and age to age. All time was contained within those eyes. All time coloured by pain and rage and love and indifference.

Truly it was the gaze of a God.

The boy stared in exhilarated wonder at the God Man, caught up in the majesty of creation and his place within it. Poseidon stared into him and his very gaze seemed to turn the boy's blood to fire. The boy began to fill with something he had never felt before, and exalted by the dawning of a new consciousness, of the rising of things within his oceanic depths he peered through the obscuring night into a future place where whole cities of light rose from the sea to pulse and shine. Poseidon was the beacon, the transmitter of the vision but was he worthy? The boy paused then, aware that he stood upon a threshold. Behind him lay darkness, in front of him trial and pain. Poseidon regarded him as though he were a painting and then he spoke.

"Why have you come here?"

In spite of himself Wilber smirked, then tapped his dripping satchel. Poseidon nodded.

"You came for the crystal. It is close. It awaits you but you cannot retrieve it. Not yet. There are things in the way, boulders on the path. Traps and snares. Things that block you."

"Like what?" Instantly he knew the answer. His mind and the questions it generated endlessly. Poseidon saw that he understood yet he did not mock or comment. He questioned.

"What does it mean to be a Legend? To be beloved of the people? To ignite their hopes and dreams, their passions and their devotions? To give them pride and a purpose? To be a hero, with a tale worthy of the telling for an eternity or more. To be cast in statues of marble and bronze by the greatest artists of every age. To be celebrated, dissected, discussed, mourned, grieved by world upon world."

"Yes. All that and more," came the boy's excited response.

"So to be a Legend is an honour? The Greatest Honour? Really?

Is it not rather a curse, a trap wherein one lies bound, eternally a prisoner. To have no life of one's own, no thought of one's own, no hope of one's own. To be a slave to a story one didn't write. To continue revolving in an endless hell of repetition for all time."

Wilber clenched his fists and shrieked at Poseidon, his flaming lungs full of rage.

"No! No! Do not say these things. Do not overturn hope. Do not kill our heroes. Do not destroy our legends for what would we be without them?"

"What indeed?

Poseidon lowered his arms so that the palms faced downwards towards the rocky outcrop that formed the smooth base of the temple floor then he raised and as he did two great urns rose up on top of the floor.

"These great urns you see, that might have carried water, bear only ash and bone. But think not of the bodies burned, think of the one who made the pots. Such artistry, such mastery. They are not water jars."

Wilber looked and saw, but he did not understand.

"Why are you showing me this?"

Poseidon gestured again and in front of him, the surface of the rock bubbled and cracked, then it opened into a circular space. The revealed hole became stairs spiralling downwards into the depths.

"See beyond the surface. Let the object become a meditation. Let it tell its own story. Then dare to listen. Don't object. Don't contradict. However terrifying, however implausible. Let it all unfold."

Then he moved forward and stepped down, taking the spiral stairway he had presented to Wilber. Soon he had disappeared and all Wilber could do was follow.

Down, down, all the way down they descended. Spiralling round the spiralling tower, following the Sea God wherever he might lead, Wilber for some reason thought of the Pied Piper. The tower sank beneath the temple to hang suspended beneath the ocean. At the bottom of the stairway the tower widened to form a cylindrical chamber, lighted and filled with a single curving glass window. Two other figures there, hooded and waiting. Standing beside what looks like a suit of medieval armour.

Wilber descending then stopping to stand in front of the suit as though it were his reflection. And in a way it is. It is not armour but an antique diving suit but unlike any he has ever seen before. Almost a model for an astronaut's space suit. Slowly the knowledge dawns and a black sun of horror rises on the parched white horizon of realisation. The crystal awaits but he must descend into the crushing depths to retrieve it.

No. Any way but this. He glances at Poseidon who returns his gaze with neither smugness nor condescension. A gauntlet has been passed to him. He has only to reach out and take it or let it drop to the floor. With a feeling of crushing weight bearing down on his shoulders he takes the gauntlet and sets the gears in motion. The attendants gesture and he steps into the brass legs. The upper body and arms, now suspended, are lowered onto him from above and finally the head is added, a head like none he has ever seen. No single face glass but many, many. Like a mirror ball.

Then the winch lifting him and lowering him into the water. Hello image he thinks. His entire culture, his British values seem both ridiculous and necessary. A stiff upper lip is required and ear plugs to block out the shrill, whining voice of the terrified child.

Drown it. Drown it, a voice chants. Drown the child. Lowered into the long and watery night by a silent mechanism. Descending once more. Wondering at the mind who had devised this sick game. Will it ever be finished? All around him the crushing weight of the sea. The creaking suit. The unbearable sense of pressure. And the endless descent in darkness. No green sea here. Only rushing noise. Bubbling, rising, unseen, but felt. Counting moments until he runs out of numbers, until order dissolves and the steady stream becomes a random jumble of shapes and then a language even he can't understand.

Totally befuddled, bewildered, lost. No awareness of up or down. It is as if he is falling in all directions.

The pounding heart will burst out of its shell and he will fade into nothing, either that or the suit will groan, buckle and fold inwards. Like a Japanese blade folded in upon itself over and over, again and again, pounded by that terrible hammer, Wielded by the Smithy God Hephaestus. And then a flicker and a glimpse of Pegasus, winged steed of cloud and breath of wind. From blackness into whiteness, from the heaving, freezing oceanic depths to the deft and nimble whizz of air.

Then losing all fear and finding the stillness that had for so long eluded him. And in that instant, within the helmet, a light flicking on, beaming out of his head in multiple directions, illuminating the one shape he had never hoped to encounter in these ocean depths. The form he had dreamed of since he was a child, in deep green swimming pools of icy water, pellucid like the prose of a literary master.

Black and white, white and black. The yang to his yin, the yin to his yang. Hanging suspended, the first and final terror and the word forming in his mind as the eye of the staring creature finds him and holds him in its intelligent gaze.

Still, suspended, unmoving, like Poseidon on his throne. All knowing and all powerful. And the word forming in his mind, the name of the nameless terror that has always been with him, travelling down the years, pursuing him over endless, boundless oceans.

And the name, finally escaping from his lips to rise as a bubble, towards a surface it will never reach.

Orca.

Hanging suspended, facing his greatest fear, Wilber felt for the first time, a mastery of fear. The Orca like him just hung and watched. It could crush him, destroy him, pierce the suit or chew him in half. It could tow him down into the blackness as the bubbles hissed from his severed hose. His one and only life line.

But it wouldn't. Of that Wilber felt certain.

The eye that watched was not the eye of Moby Dick. Not a hateful eye, but a curious eye, a knowing eye. Gazing into the depths of that eye Wilber felt no malice, only reassurance. Hitting the descender, he held the button and sank even further into the blackness, the Stygian gloom. And as he descended, the orca swam with him, spiralling round and round his descending form, in benediction and blessing.

The thing he had never believed in has finally happened. He is safely across the river, the river of boyhood, of adolescence. The kingdom he has entered is not that of the blind, but of adulthood. Dare he say it? Of manhood.

And as this new word echoes in his mind his feet touch the bottom of the ocean floor. Not sand but stone, polished stone. The light from his illuminated helmet shines in all directions and he gasps in wonder. He has landed in what appears to be a replica of the Temple he has just vacated. Only this temple is no ruin. There are no broken columns here, no broken tiles, no crumbling stairs, just a pristine form, as perfect as the day it was finished.

And in the midst of the temple, in its inner sanctum and still pulsing heart, a statue of marble, like the columns, china-white, unmarked and unblemished. The face he recognises, the robes and trident too. He gasps in wonder. It might as well be Christmas. The figure is seated and a wry smile licks at the lips. Immobile for ages and yet the illusion of animation. Is it really an illusion?

And then the final touch, the essential detail, the thing for which he'd preyed, held in the outstretched hand of a statue thousands of years old. The third crystal, the glittering octahedron and his prize. But not won, not yet. Not until he has walked the seven sacred paces, struggling against the pressure and the weight, against the exhaustion and the pain, until finally his metal clad fingers reach and clasp the confirmation of his victory.

56

The Temple

Pausing, with some difficulty, he stared away into the swirling mist. Off in the distance the yellow light seemed to puff and bud and a hovering white floret appeared, soon growing into a snowy, tear-shaped droplet, which touched the ground and filled with an ethereal figure. It was the first of many petal-like processes, appearing out of the thinning air all around him, birthing, or perhaps rebirthing many others. They seemed to move around in this fog, each and every one seeking, searching for answers that had so long eluded them.

Old men and older women, aged and bent, groped around in the nothingness. Young boys and toddling girls, arms outstretched like sleepwalkers or hunting zombies, staggered about, drawn by some unknowable pull into a fool's parade. Wilber hated the indignity of it all. He wanted to cry out and rage, to rain down blows upon the hooded figure. But the more he felt like this, the more drained he became and the harder it was to remain standing. Damn the creature, whatever it was.

Flickers and ripples in the fabric of time, spreading outwards in puddles of sound. The air around him seemed to fill with a strange and tragic music and he glimpsed a vision. A flash of guillotine light, travelling downwards and outwards through thousands of rainbow orbs, hanging suspended, bubbles of time, hope, possibility, warping and buckling, folding in on themselves, their glistening arcs contorting, darkening into rainbows of chaos, spiralling inwards, in ever diminishing scales, into that fabled nothingness. Unreachable sub atomic realms where dwelt cacophonies of fallen waveforms, the music of hell and the defective electron rose and fell as did the ocean, electric in its blue, deepening, darkening into cold indigo, then freezing in the swallowing dark, black, forever and ever.

The column-lined temple sinking, along with its memories and its relics, its sacred artefacts and polished crystals into the containing deep. Such white marble, such lovely stone. How could that be lost? How? The question rang out as a heart-rending cry in the oceanic soul of Atlantis. Why? And only the cruel, green birds gliding in the time-burnt skies seemed to know or to care. They searched the waves for the broken bodied, clinging to wreckage, holding on, vainly hoping for the salvation of the reaching hand and the gently drawing sail, bearing them away. But the birds swooping and plunging their stabbing beaks into the soft, white, exposed flesh of the screaming men and women, lived only to thwart their plans, to punish and to feast.

And in the heaving waters, objects raining down; stones and wheels, fountains and ships, animals and children, the broken in body, mind and spirit falling into the darkness of memory lost. A city sunk, a continent sundered, a race forgotten, and with them all of their culture, all of their learning and all of their attainments. For days and days their screams and then nothing, the silence of eternity, swallowed by the gaping, tooth-rimmed mouth of time. But why? Why? Why?

George believed that relics had been found but that they had been hidden by men of power and cunning who wished their brethren to know nothing of what had gone before, lest they learn anew the lessons of history and alter the deadly course on which humanity was now set. All lived within the configuration of the lie, fed false images, nurtured on dead, meaningless tales, which led them further and further away from the truth of what they had been and what they might again become.

If only the people could be shown, what had been, then they would rise up in their millions and pull down the altars to Mammon at the Stock Exchange and in the High Street, they would burn the gorgeous palaces and drag down the High Towers, fling the rockets of death and pestilence out into space and create a system that fed and nurtured all.

The Atlanteans' had gone astray and the world had punished them, drowned them. But it had left the memory of what they had been, what they had achieved to serve as a warning for future generations of men, who would advance once more at breakneck pace towards an horizon dominated by technologies of death. The human had been reduced and was being replaced by robots; the human was lost and enslaved in its own creation, governed by dark forces it had been conditioned to worship and fear. No more. No more.

Wilber felt a power rising within him unlike any he had ever known before. It drove away the billowing clouds of nausea and despair and filled the space around him with a crackling energy, of electricity, of lightning, of activation.

"Poseidon, Sea God, roar. Roar."

The words poured forth from Wilber's taut, stretched lips. Where they had come from he knew not, but it was enough that they had come. Off in some hidden corner of a long, vanished century, a royal lion roared, Wilber felt its strength and drank it in, became the lion, and feeling himself once more watched the yellow mist dissipate. When the miasma had disappeared and the air was once more clear and fresh, he felt the cooling wind caress his cheeks. The sky above him was still dark, still growled like an angry, cornered dog but it no longer frightened him, He had a new sense of resolve and purpose and that was all that mattered.

Wilber looked around him, curious and enthralled, knowing and shocked. The robed figure had vanished, as had the throne upon which he had been seated. In its place there was a dark square, where a large slab had been moved aside, revealing a marble stairway leading downward. It was an invitation to follow. That he knew. That went without saying. Gritting his teeth, Wilber walked over to the lip of the stairway and stared down. A glow of amethyst light faintly flickered illuminating the suggested depths. Without a second thought or glance he set off, disappearing from view, walking the ancient passageway towards his destiny.

*   *   *   *   *   *   *

Down the ancient passageway he walked, old and vastly matured, so much more than his fifteen years. His brain was aflame, teaming with new sensations, capturing images, dispatched from distant realms, into his now. Multiple image streams converged on his present. Many the senders, many the messages, many the agendas; he knew that now. So long waiting in the darkness of Muldoon Manor for this moment to arrive. His whole life had been one long wait. He'd resented it for so long, had hated himself, and what he'd become. Such a fun loving and outward child of ten, but at 15, what had he become? A withdrawn and nervous wreck, haunting the shadows and haunted by them. A stranger to family and friends. Unreachable, unknowable, unlovable. Doctors could find nothing wrong with him. Psychiatrists poked and prodded and tried to medicate him, but he refused. He had will enough to do that. Just a phase they suggested. He would grow out of it. But he hadn't and now he knew why.

All along he had been destined for the island. The island had called to him, the island had awaited him. Nothing was certain but he would rather be here than any other place in the world. The further down he went the warmer it became for a reason he could not fathom. Arriving at a junction he found two flaming amethyst torches. He took one and examined his options. Only he could choose his pathway.

The amethyst glow of his torch in the darkness revealed the white marble, rubbed smooth by the passage of many feet in time.

57

Up From The Depths

They had been waiting some hours when Wilber strode purposefully out from between the central pillars of the temple portico, his bag a little heavier than when he had gone in. Both Lola and Caleb, who had been sitting on opposite sides of the oar-less boat, making out neither was interested in the other, shot to their feet and simultaneously tumbled over, Caleb landing in a heap on top of Lola. Of course Lola screamed, bucked him off, gave him a slap for good measure, then clambering out of the boat ran towards Wilber and hugged him.

It would have been difficult to gauge who was the more surprised, Wilber or Lola. Realising that she had perhaps revealed more than was prudent she disengaged herself from the newly returned hero and smoothed her dress down. Looking back over her left shoulder in Caleb's direction she found it impossible to suppress a smirk. Caleb scowled and folded his arms, looking like he would be happier pulling the wings off of sea birds, rather than spending his precious time in the company of peeps who just didn't do cool.

"Wilber, you're back," she beamed, unable to suppress her joy.

Behind her Caleb snorted. "Thank you Lola. We're so lucky to have you here, so you can state the bleeding obvious."

Lola's smile vanished faster than a speeding bullet.

"Oh shut up Caleb. Make yourself useful and go boil your head."

Wilber rolled his eyes. He had been away from the Twins of Goth for a few hours only, faced peril upon peril, charted a course through perilous waters and retrieved the third crystal and what was his reward? To return to this kitchen sink drama and the prospect of a day filled with unrelenting bitchiness.

"Will you two just go easy," he pleaded. "This place is enough of a nightmare without you making it worse." Lola arched an eyebrow. "I'll try Wilber but he doesn't make it easy. Surely you can see that." Caleb threw first one stick leg and then the other over the side of the boat and stalked over to where the two were standing. His dark eyes narrowed and he licked his thin lips

"So did you get it then?" he asked, trying vainly to mask his interest.

Wilber eyed him up and down, wondering at the sudden shift of mood. "Yeah," he answered a little reluctantly. He'd rather Caleb kept his distance and sulked. More predictable that way.

Soused with impatience Caleb almost spat.

"Well let's see it then."

Reaching into his bag, Wilber retrieved the icosahedron, and withdrew it, so that all might behold his prize. Begrudgingly. Then he held it up to the light. It shone and sparkled majestically, lightening everybody's mood and drawing a startled 'wow' from Lola.

"Isn't it amazing?" Wilber said, staring deeply into the flawless crystal as he rotated it slowly between his thumb and forefinger. The faceted quartz spat out rainbows and even Caleb drank them in, feeling ecstatic.

"So what's next Big Boy?" Lola asked coyly.

Wilber pursed his lips, unsure of how to answer. Lola was so light and shade, so all or nothing, innocence and experience combined, ridiculously optimistic and hopelessly cynical, all at the same time.

"Well obviously I'm going for the fourth crystal," he said, almost tripping over his words as they tumbled out of his mouth.

Caleb scrunched up his nose.

"Don't you mean the fifth crystal? You just collected the fourth, remember? You had the first and second already but unfortunately you failed to acquire the third. Astapor has it still. I hate to have to remind you but you can't get off the island unless you have all the crystal keys. The gate won't open. Everybody knows that. So what are you going to do?"

Lola draped her arm protectively around Wilber's neck and gave Caleb her measured disdain.

"You're so negative Caleb. Wilber is doing fine and he still has six hours on the clock."

Wilber felt instantly better. Curious was the effect that Lola had on his moods.

"It's time to get going," he stated simply, looking back towards the distant shore.

"Easier said than done, old sport, we're still oarless," said Caleb in a botched, English, upper-class accent. Ignoring him, Wilber put the icosahedron back in his paper sack. Whilst Lola and a slightly chastened Caleb climbed back into the boat. Wilber then pushed them off the grinning rocks, before jumping in himself.

"So what do we do now?" asked Caleb, " do we just drift, is that it?"

"Bang on," replied Wilber.

So they drifted unspeaking, boredom and fear passing between them with every passing cloud. It began to rain again and Wilber turned up the collar of his coat. He glanced at his watch and huffed a little. Instead of drifting back in towards the land they were drifting further out to sea. Now why was that? Bang and a rock of shock splashed in the waters beside them. The waters around the island had begun to bubble again and as the triangle of frenemies watched, the Temple sank back down into the depths from where it had risen.

"So that's that then," Caleb muttered, a smile of flames licking at his cracked lips. Quietly satisfied he leaned back to enjoy the splash of raindrops. Wilber began to catastrophize. What if the wind continued to blow, what if they sank, what if the sea was filled with sea monsters? What if...

"What's that?" Lola said, pointing out to sea, where a speck of something on the horizon moved towards them at speed. Wilber and Caleb turned to look but neither would venture an opinion. Seconds passed, then minutes. The shape grew and a ship emerged from the speck. It bore down upon them and was soon pulling up beside them. An old man, as gnarled as a barnacle, appeared on the port side of the boat and raised a hand in greeting. Lola arched an eye in obvious disdain. Caleb reverted to his default setting and smirked. After a while of just staring at each other, as rude as you like, Lola broke the silence.

"Who are you then?" she asked, ever impertinent.

The relic of a bygone age didn't seem unduly perturbed. He flashed his teeth, which looked like crumbling tombstones and batted his eyelids.

"I'm just an old sea dog looking for love, " he admitted.. This answer didn't seem to faze Lola

"That's nice to know.

"Are you looking for love?" he ventured, less than tentative. Sailing the seas had obviously worn away any inhibition he might have had. Lola didn't drop a stitch.

"Not today shipmate but thanks for asking." Here she paused and inspected the lowering skies. "Actually we're looking to get back to the island." She mentioned this as if it were a thing of little importance. The Old Sea Dog scrunched up his face as though he were chewing a wasp.

"Hmm," was all he could offer. Then, "winds picking up, pushing you out to sea, you know." A pause. "Nothing out there but sea."

"Could we swim for it? Ditch the boat, like?" Wilber asked.

The Old Man shook his head, mildly pained.

"You could but you'd be swept to your deaths. Perilous undertow and if that don't get you there's about a thousand things swimming around that will."

Not a good prognosis. Wilber felt his spirits sinking.

"Any chance you could take us back to the island?" Caleb asked, inspecting his nails.

"Sorry, no. It's forbidden. Only allowed to take fares between the hours of nine and three. Strictly a night time service we are. I'd get into trouble."

Nobody seemed remotely like they wanted to hear this. The Sea dog was apologetic.

"Look, rules is rules."

"Jobsworth," Caleb spat.

"Sorry?"

The Gang of Three looked at each other, then back at the Old Sea Dog who almost got caught in triangulation. They weighed their options, some of which were violent and involved storming the floating ark and tossing the dog to the sharks that circled below. Wilber, usually so polite, sighed deeply and fixed the Old dog with his steeliest gaze, one his father had long since perfected.

"Look. I need to get off this island, I have one chance to do it, one day. After that I'll be here forever."

The Old Man seemed suddenly fascinated.

"So you're today's Candidate? That explains the desperation. I'm Hogarth Macready. Lovely to meet you and all. Sorry it couldn't be under happier circumstances."

Wilber felt his irritation rise and crest.

"It would be happier, for us, if you'd let us get in your boat."

Once more the Old Fossil looked pained but was he actually enjoying this? Perhaps piracy was the answer. The hands were raised placatingly.

"Look, it's nothing personal. It's all about the rules. The rules you don't know and never will. The rules you follow and the rules you don't. The rules you change and the rules you break. The rules you cannot challenge and the rules you can. The fact that everything begins and ends with rules, with language, with the decisions you make and the decisions you don't is what makes this island what it is."

Silence. Wilber clenched his fists. Caleb prepared an insult, only Lola was unfazed.

"I'm guessing you eat on the boat. That you cook your own

food. That you have a galley kitchen, and that that kitchen, not to put too fine a point upon it, is minging. Just nod if I'm right."

He nodded.

"Right, let us on board and we'll scrub every inch of this tub, we'll wash every plate and we'll darn every sock you ever put a hole in."

The Old Man slung them a coiled rope.

"Welcome aboard shipmates," he said. "Galley's that way."

58

Bellies in, Fangs Out

As all of the lifts were broken, they took the stairs down out of the towers and emerged blinking into the smoke-filled air. Even that took time. As the electronic doors had stopped working they had to be forced open. Such a humiliation. It had been a long time, in fact none of them could remember a time when the Russian had last stood out in the open air feeling the caress of light on his ghost-sick complexion. It just didn't happen.

All of them watched him, yet all did so surreptitiously.

Astapor was running out of options and he knew it. The towers he had spent so long fortifying, were crumbling. Three had been set alight and burned. The remaining five had cracks in them and whole panes of glass were missing. More and more cameras were going down every hour and the electronics were shot. The underground had been emptied, all 32 levels despatched and the labyrinth overrun. All in the course of one day.

And worse than that, they had drawn him out of the tower. The complex was now a smashed system without a power source. It was to all effects and purposes, useless. He had made mistakes and he could see that now. Too much reliance had been placed on Caleb and not enough caution taken with the Alphabets. He'd played with them for his own amusement, let them run but instead of running, they'd stopped, turned and brought the fight to him.

It wasn't just about Young Muldoon anymore. It was about regaining order and asserting control. His past, which he had believed buried, had surfaced and assumed a terrifying face. And do what he might, he couldn't escape it. The face of Madeline came out of the shadows wherever he looked. Hers was a skull face, with eyeless sockets and she pointed with bony fingers to the one place he didn't want to look.

So many storms. So much lightning at night. Red, white and blue sizzling on his retinas. Exciting and exhilarating and oh so alluring. Pulling the ships in with a synchronised pulse. Deliberately crashing them in their multiple and multi-coloured forms; the eye shaped, egg shaped, cigar-shaped, the spinning discs, cubes, torus's, orbs, octahedrons, tetrahedrons and those deliciously mind-boggling Calibau-Yau manifolds. Those he loved to look at. Those he loved to study.

Then, containing them. So much of their collective technology had gone into the construction of his Mountain top lair. He had much to thank them for. Each and every species. But he hadn't thanked them. There'd been promises, treaties made between him and the Visitors. Tech for Transit, so he had phrased it. Advancing through technology. They had traded in goodwill and he had reneged. He could have opened any number of portals, let them slip out, but he hadn't. He clutched the keys to his chest, broke them off in the locks or buried them. The only treasure worth having, or so he believed. And the visitors remained here. Trapped. But always there, watching, waiting, requiring containment. Upping the ante, increasing the pressure.

As if he didn't have enough on his plate. He looked around him and counted his men. Seven. Eight with him. Lurch didn't count. Good. All strong, all armed. The guards who had remained were the best and the most loyal. They had come through on the first day with him. Back in 45. And none of them had aged a day. Because time on the island wasn't the same as time spent in the world. It was enough to make you laugh. At least it had been. But on this day of days there wasn't that much left for Astapor to laugh about. The net was tightening about his neck and he was beginning to feel the wire bite.

Turning his body, looking down the mountain towards the Crash Zone, he felt the volcano stirring beneath him. The flash of images in his mind. The sudden arrival of new awareness. Pressure building, lava churning, the explosive rumble. Clenching, releasing. Shuddering, easing, building, subsiding. The micro tremors, the signs and portents that betokened doom.

Or at the very least cataclysmic change. Enough! "Drull, come here."

The largest guard, without a second prompt, came straight over to where Astapor was standing. His face was a network of scars, his hair cropped. How many had he killed? Both he and Astapor had lost count. It didn't matter. The only thing that mattered was who he would kill next. One of those pesky Alphabet's he hoped.

No, he wanted them for himself. Especially the eldest one, Alphabet. His hand went straight to his side, to where his lump hammer hung. On the opposite side was a razor sickle. In the final analysis no one could say he was not a patriot. Mother Russia had spawned him. Her cities and wars had forged him. Made him what he was. Gave him an unstoppable belief in himself. And she had taught him the most invaluable lesson in life.

Do what no one else dares to do and you will always be victorious.

"It's time Drull. We must summon her."

Drull just stared at the Count, uncomprehendingly.

'Her? Madame Fang?"

A smile lit up Astapor's face. He had played most of his cards but he had kept her in his top pocket. She was the Queen of Death, an Ace in the Hole, his Trump card. Winning was all that mattered. It was all that had ever mattered. From here on in he would be operating a scorched earth policy, like they had back in 42, with the German army closing in on Stalingrad. Burn it all. I may not be able to use it but then neither will my enemy

"Yes Madame Fang," Astapor confirmed.

"I have never understood her, nor trusted her Count but I defer to your greater wisdom in this matter."

"As you have always done my friend. And with good cause. She is without mercy and like her aide-de-camp, Herr Zoot, she is a free

378

agent who can be hired to do any Magician's bidding. She is impartial, the head of a race of hybrids, half human and half…"

Drull's eyes widened.

"Half what?"

"Nevermind. Send up the flare."

Drull saluted and reached into his backpack. He took out a flare, placed it in the ground and lit the fuse. Within seconds the rocket was airborne and speeding into the troubled and ever darkening sky. It exploded in a blaze of magenta light and the sky growled with thunder. Hairs rose on the back of Astapor's neck and the air seemed to chill. The guards scanned the trees for signs of threat or motion but detected neither. The forest had grown completely still. The winds had dropped away to nothing. Not so much as a leaf stirred.

Astapor glanced at his watch. 16.04. Just under five hours on the clock. Time droned by, and Astapor found his mind drifting back into the past. Twenty minutes went by before Drull tapped him on the arm. The guards had all seen the same thing at the same time and had raised their machine guns in one swift and well-trained motion.

"Lower them," a female voice commanded from under the cover of the tree line.

The guards as one obeyed without Astapor's intercession and Old Ma Fang crept out of the shadows. Behind her lurking in the bushes was Herr Zoot, the Man in the Yellow Suit. He moved like a jaguar, and stung like a sidewinder missile. Not a man to annoy but all Astapor's attention was focussed on the Queen Bitch, spawn of hell and the abyss, so Zoot became wallpaper.

"It seems I'm running out of cards to play," the Russian confessed.

"You should have come to me earlier, Astapor. Everyone else has failed you. Your creations too. Not deadly enough, not dangerous enough.

"Yes and that makes me very upset."

"You don't seem upset," Fang countered, not averse to a little schadenfreude.

Astapor, would for now, have to eat a little humble pie. His arrogance and over-weening confidence had landed him in this predicament and instead of raging himself into an early grave, he would have to go cold, colder than liquid nitrogen.

"Looks can be deceptive Ma. You of all people should understand that. Caleb has betrayed me."

Like a pecking hen, Lurch was instantly at his elbow, clucking away.

"I told you he could not be trusted, Master."

Without emotion and without turning his head, Astapor spoke in an elegant hiss.

"Shut up you little worm or you will taste the lash and more besides."

Madame Fang seemed to enjoy this. She had both height and poise, the skin burnished copper, the eyes green, bordering on yellow, the pupils a vertical slash. Dreadlocked hair was bound in a faded headscarf and a long black, faded coat, still elegant, stretched from the high, neck-concealing collar down to the ground to trail in earth, or surf or leaves. She was both spear and lash clutched in a remorseless hand.

"You wanted an heir Astapor and you created a mediocre monster with both airs and graces. Every son wants to kill his father, as well you know. Better that every father kill his sons if only by proxy. I will catch him and he will die in a very creative way. Unless that is, you want him back to pet and forgive?"

The Russian shook his head slowly. Things had gone far enough.

"No, there are no second chances on my island."

A smile lit up the woman's face.

"Very well. He will go and soon but this will cost you dear, Astapor in all kinds of ways."

"I'm willing to pay any price," the Russian conceded, emptying his face of expression.

"Of course you are and it's most gratifying. So where are they now?"

At this, Lurch stepped forward and laid a map of the island out on a table he had brought up from one of the lower levels. Everyone gathered round the rickety piece of furniture and looked down at the map. It was a little course, a bit 18th century but it would have to do. Realities on the island were shifting and the electricity was down. Lurch tapped the map with his finger.

"They have crossed the Bay of Sharks and entered the Temple. They are en route to Mr Lapp."

Astapor turned and spat with savage impatience. "That's not good enough. Where are they exactly Lurch? If you can't tell me I'll find someone who can!"

Fighting hard to control his fear, Lurch held the Russians' gaze for as long as he dared, then he looked down at the map again and scratched his chin.

"It's so hard to tell Master. Unfortunately, many of the cameras have been destroyed by the Alphabet gang. All we know is that they are crossing the Yellow Sands, that they have, in all likelihood, taken Mr Hand's crystal and it's probable they are on their way to Lapp. If he helps them and they are successful they will have all the pieces of the puzzle and they'll be ready to play for End Game."

Ma Fang let rip with a cruel laugh. "All of the pieces bar one. They did not acquire the fire crystal or am I mistaken?" Once again Astapor felt ice cold beads of sweat stippling his temple and running down his back. How did she know what he feared? Of course she was no fool, in possession of formidable gifts. In spite of it all, he must not let her rattle him. She had to be armed and used and that way she could be useful.

"You are quite right. The fire crystal is still safe, hidden where none will ever find it. Young Muldoon has impressed me though. Of all the runners, we've ever seen he is the one who has come closest to succeeding."

Lurch sidled closer to his master

"Too close for comfort, Master. He must be punished. Not just barred from passing through the gates but thoroughly destroyed.

We must make an example of him in front of the others. He has given them hope. We must remind them they are in hell and that hell is a place without hope."

Old Ma Fang watched Astapor closely. Something wasn't right. Every instinct in her body told her so. The Russian hadn't lied, but he hadn't told the whole truth either. If she was able to extract that truth she would be able to turn it to her own advantage. But she couldn't interrogate him here, not in front of his men. She must be careful not to inflict too great a loss of face upon him. To do so would be to risk her own head.

"There is something I would share with thee Astapor but not in front of these others. Step with me into the forest awhile and I will speak."

Lurch screwed up his face like a used paper bag and Drull, stepping forward, raised his weapon into a subtle, if definite attitude of threat. He looked at his Master with a quizzical air but Astapor just waved him away.

"Prepare to move out in ten Drull. Make sure your men have as much ammo as they can carry. They're going to need it. Oh and Lurch give them anti venom and administer the injections we talked about. I don't want anybody changing if they are bitten, as well they might be. Don't think, just do, little man! Everything is prepared. Father Francis has what you need up in lab 604. He wont be joining us."

An expression of slight confusion creased the scientist's face but he knew better than to argue. Of course the Russian kept things from him. He, Lurch was only part of the Masterplan as was everyone else in the group. But it didn't matter. Astapor was already in motion following the tall, cruel woman and her yellow shadow down the hill and into the forest. Out of the complex and into danger. Shaking his head, and clucking like a bantam, Lurch took to his heels and headed over to Tower Six. Out of sight, if not out of mind, Old Ma Fang stopped walking and turned on the Russian suddenly, as if to pounce.

"What is it? What do you know?" the Old Woman almost spat.

"Come on Astapor", she coaxed, "out with it."

"Name your price," Astapor returned, still and cold and full of power. The Old Woman recoiled. Most people she could roll over but not him. He needed her at the moment but as soon as her purpose was fulfilled he would end her or worse.

"Tell me what I need to know."

"Muldoon is loose beneath the mountain. He broke out of the labyrinth and escaped into the lava pits. We have seen no sign of him since."

"Dead?"

"Wishful thinking I'm afraid. No Ma, he lives."

"But you buried it deep and safe, didn't you?"

Astapor shook his head slowly.

"Not deep enough. Not safe enough to keep him away. The Guardians are formidable but they are not invulnerable. I suspect Muldoon and his clan are receiving help. I have to believe nothing is safe, that he has a chance, that he has more than a chance. He must be stopped; we must use whatever weapons we have to hand."

"Indeed we must, but first I want my own tower and I want to be one of the Masters of this Island. One of the five. You'll have to let Mr Hands and Lapp go. Herr Zoot and I will relieve them of their duties."

Astapor threw back his head and laughed.

"That is rather more than I was looking to pay but needs must when the Devil drives." Here he paused to consider. "Very well my dear. You drive a hard bargain, but then you are the best at what you do. Give me what I want and I'll give you what you want. But it needs to be done and soon. The Muldoons, the Alphabets and Caleb must all go the way of the Dodo. After that we'll work on Lapp and Mr Hands together. By close of play today Justice Wilberforce Muldoon will no longer be anyone's problem."

Evil laughter filled the air. They had finally reached an agreement.

59

Shore Leave

Hogarth Macready, the Old Sea Dog, had stayed true to his word. Behind them lay the sunken temple, divested of its treasure, in front of them, the forbidding shore with all its dangers. Yes, he had been true, had the Captain, reaffirming Wilber's faith in humanity, but then they had kept their side of the bargain too. Lola had taken care of the kitchen, cleaning it deftly and efficiently, leaving no trace of the former ravages of time and tide. The boys had been set to swab the decks and syphon the bilges, which they did with a little grumbling and much slopping of buckets and mops. Peering over the ship's wheel, steering with one hand, Hogarth seemed mightily contented with the way events had turned out and when Lola appeared with a full cooked breakfast, of kippers, dino eggs and chutney he grinned from ear to ear.

"Nice having a woman's touch about the place again."

Lola's smile was all ice and frosted roses.

"Don't get too used to it Captain," she cautioned, handing the Old Dog his plate.

Macready sighed and, handing control of the wheel to his diminutive assistant, took the plate and raised it to his nose to sniff. Letting out a contented sigh he set about attacking the steaming breakfast, wolfing it down with great gusto, if little panache. Like giving an elephant a strawberry Lola thought. First Wilber then Caleb came to stand beside the Captain as he looked wistfully towards the shore, chewing on the last of his kippers.

"So boy, how goes it?"

"Pretty well," Caleb answered.

"I wasn't talking to you," Macready growled, "I know who you are. Worse still I know what you are." He gave a disgusted belch. "You best watch out for this one Wilber. Snake, scorpion and rat all rolled into one."

Caleb hocked and spat.

"Always a pleasure captain, remaking your acquaintance. Word of advice though. Never run aground."

Macready gave him the evil eye and after returning the Captain's stare with interest Caleb went below decks muttering to himself. After a while Lola followed him down.

"Yeah, scurry along and while you're down there clean the karzi, it stinks worse than you do."

So you've met Caleb before, have you Captain?" Wilber asked, unable to stop himself chuckling.

Macready snorted.

"One of the few who has and lived to tell the tale. He's pure poison. What are you doing with him boy?"

Wilber shrugged.

"I'm sure I don't know. He rocked up an hour or two ago mewling and whining about the Russian, saying Astapor was finished and how he wanted to help me. Actually he doesn't really want to help me, he just wants me dead or gone so he can carry on sniffing round Lola without interference.

"What's that you say about the Russian?" Macready asked, clearly intrigued.

"The other Magicians think Astapor has lost the plot and they are circling him, waiting for him to weaken so they can dash in and seize the crown. And the better I do, the worse it looks for him. So suddenly I have allies."

The Captain snorted.

"They're using you boy and as soon as they have what they want, they'll snap and break you."

"I'm under no illusions, Captain about anything or anyone here."

Wilber looked behind him to check that Caleb and Lola were

still below decks and when he saw that they were he turned back to face Macready.

"So what can you tell me about Mr Lapp Captain?"

"Nothing that's going to help you, Wilber. They're a law unto themselves those Magicians. Impossible to know how they're going to act in any given situation. They both giveth and they taketh away. Just cus they treat you well one day don't mean they won't feed you to their beasts the next. I'm not in the habit of giving advice to anyone but trust no-one, especially not those boyos. They're not really men anymore. Perhaps they never were."

"So what are they?" Wilber pressed, fascinated by Macready and where his head was at.

Macready turned and looked to the horizon, as if there he would find an answer.

"Just a bunch of plans you'll never see or fathom. They are the sum of their agendas and they shift every day along with their alliances."

"So, how many crystals do you have?"

"Three."

Macready whistled through his teeth.

"Four and a half hours on the clock and you are definitely a prospect. Ain't nobody got that close in years. About a decade ago there was a kid of about 18. Mad on knives and guns he was. A survival nut. You know the type; climber, runner, shooter. He could do it all. With two hours on the clock he had four crystals jangling about in Crowhaven's satchel. Looked like he might make it too. He was doubling back for the fire crystal when they got him. Least of all that's what I heard. That third crystal is always the one that trips them."

For a while Wilber said nothing, but eventually curiosity got the better of him. He had to know.

"So what happened?"

"You don't want to know."

There was a long pause before Hogarth Macready spoke.

"He was bitten in half."

"By Yabu's crocs?"

"No, by Astapor's people. By Variants. Boy could that kid run."

"Just not fast enough, eh?" Wilber quipped.

Macready looked at him and they both burst out laughing. Gallows humour was the only humour that made sense on the island. The Captain reached in his pocket and pulled out a hip flask. He unstoppered it, took a swig, and then handed the flask to Wilber.

"Go on. Have a nip. Put hair on your chest that will."

Wilber took a swig, swallowed and felt the warmth spreading through him.

"Island wasn't always like this, you know. It's been raining for weeks. Sky, all kinds of strange colours. Weird cloud formations too. And the sea, the sea has been so difficult to read. Sometimes stormy, sometimes, dead calm. But always this feeling that something is coming. Something invisible and deadly. But something the island needs... It's not about the Magicians Wilber; I mean they're part of it, yes, but it's not really their show. It's the island that matters. Make a friend of the island and maybe you'll win where everybody else has lost."

He was silent for a moment and in the silence Wilber tried to digest this new information. In the end it was too big for him and he had to let it go.

"Better go and call those friends of yours. It's time to haul ass."

Wilber did as he was bid and soon Caleb and Lola had rejoined them back on the deck. Lola had her chainsaw slung over her back and Caleb had his sword. Without a word he handed Wilber his baseball bat. Very kindly he had hammered in some nails he had found in Macready's hold. Seeing this Wilber smiled approvingly.

"Time to go huh." Lola said.

The others looked at each other and nodded. It was time. The rain may have eased but the sky was leaning forward, frowning down at them. Quickly, oh so quickly they shot across the bay, the sails doing the work, now the engines were silent. As they neared their destination the little troop said nothing, just mentally prepared themselves as best they could for what lay ahead. Finally, it was time to disembark. Hogarth headed the boat up into the wind and let the sails luff. They were about two hundred metres from the beach. The captain had no intention of running aground. He was far too experienced a sailor.

"This is far as I go", he said, folding his arms.

Lola thanked Macready, then she swung her body over the boat rail and splashed into the ocean before the Captain had time to lard her with thanks and compliments. Sighing he raised his eyes to the heavens.

"One day," he said with great feeling.

Rolling his eyes, Caleb followed Lola into the sea and only Wilber took the time to shake the Captain's hand. Macready took his hand distractedly and looked over Wilber's shoulder.

"Best get going son. And remember to make a friend of the island. It may just save your life."

By the time Wilber had lowered himself into the water the other two were already halfway ashore. The waves came up to his chest but the ocean was warmer than anticipated. Battling through the waves he made for the beach, ever alert to the unwanted arrival of a black dorsal fin, carving a passage through the racing green waters.

"Any time," Macready called after him. Wilber heard but did not turn to watch the sails of the boat being drawn in until taut and then swelling with wind. He sensed rather than saw the ship's wheel turning and the Captain and his Boy heading back out to sea. Soon the water level dropped away and he felt more secure. First to his waist, then to the top of his thighs and finally down to his knees. Striding purposefully through the surf he soon stood beside his dripping compatriots.

"Onwards and upwards, eh," Caleb declaimed.

Neither Lola, nor Wilber spoke but walked quickly over the sands. Away on their right, up above the treeline of the Great Jungle lay Astapor's Laboratory and the sky-piercing towers of eight. Despite the dangers, Wilber would have preferred to be there than out in the open. Yet he must risk more now and hope his luck held. Over the burning sands, they moved like shadows, heading just South of West and moving towards a high wall of what appeared to be very strange trees. It was here Mr Lapp lived. The trees, even from a distance, appeared to be festooned with jangling charms, but there were no animals to be seen or heard. Of all the places he had been on the island, here he felt safest. This made him nervous. He wasn't supposed to feel safe. Any time he had felt close to relaxation, Wilber had been closest to being delivered into the jaws of death.

60

The Great Mother

Mr Lapp was the fifth and final Magician that Wilber would meet on the island. From what Antelope had told him, between snatched breaths and flying arrows, he was an Old Chinese man with a long white beard and a fascination with combat. Mr Lapp helped the girls from time to time and he was highly skilled both martially and strategically but he was also highly unpredictable bound neither by pity nor loyalty, he was a law unto himself and as such beyond good and evil. Mentally perusing what he thought he knew, Wilber ran like the wind, with the dual scents of terror and excitement clogging his nostrils. Beyond good and evil? What would such a man be like and what would make him like that? Glancing over his right shoulder, Wilber could see plumes of smoke rising from the tower complex. Three, whirling, twirling threads of possibility had woven their way into his consciousness. Who had done this? Who was responsible and what did it mean? It was all so exciting.

Behind Wilber, Caleb and Lola jogged along looking fantastic and chewing gum. If cool was a beach, they owned it. From time to time one would cast the other a look of disgust or sneer in a highly antagonistic way and the other would harrumph and then snort with extreme derision. It was a nasty, childish game but one they played with great relish, immune to what was going on around them. It didn't matter that the island was, quite literally, going to hell in a handbasket before their very eyes, they were only interested in getting one over on each other. It was so pointless and so draining, just listening to them. It was like trying to make sense of the chatter of apes. In the end Wilber just tuned out. As far as he was concerned they could just go and boil their heads. He had a game to win and the game was on.

Since Hogarth had dropped them off on the far side of the Bay of Sharks, they had raced over darkening sands towards the most south westerly point of the island from which two peninsulas sprang, sharpening down to needle points that cruelly lanced the brine. Off of the volcanically-darkened silicon they ran onto a red band of magnetic sand that would make a compass spin like a Catherine wheel and ionise the blood. It made you high and it made your heart pound in such an intense way you felt as if you'd just stepped off the world's fastest, highest, deadliest rollercoaster onto a rapidly melting iceberg. Wilber thought that at one point his old ticker might burst out of his chest and fly away. But it hadn't, thank God. He felt simultaneously spaced and drugged as he ran over the sand and straight into an eighteen-foot-high wall of bamboo. Immediately he slammed on the anchors, pirouetted to a halt then staggered back.

"Greetings my friends" said a disembodied voice, which came floating through the bamboo thicket with a certain insouciance. Caleb and Lola pulled up behind Wilber scarcely out of breath, whilst Wilber gasped and sucked the air like an out of work dustman who had just crossed the finishing line of the London Marathon. A door opened in the bamboo wall and Mr Lapp stepped out, giving Wilber the once over.

"Thank you, but no milk today," he said deadpan and when Wilber's jaw dropped, Lapp let out a high-pitched guffaw and clapped his hands in delight. "I had you then. I got ya. Didn't I? Go on, admit it, you believed me, didn't you Wilbs?"

Wilber was having a hard time believing that this gurning monkey was the final piece of the puzzle but that's the way the island was. A riddle rapping in an enigma ticking away like a time bomb. A cross between a Theme Park and a Concentration camp. All you could do was flow with the tides and accept whatever popped into your lap, even if it had a long white beard and was dressed like it was about to go on stage for the final number of a psychedelic Panto, with no plot and and no budget.

"Yeah you got me," said Wilber wearily, "now where's the crystal?"

Mr Lapp cocked his head to one side like a once endearing parrot and cawed.

"You've come a long way!"

"About five and a half miles, all told, now where is it and no messing about or..."

"Or we'll shoot you," said Lola, drawing a Luger from a concealed pocket in her long coat, cocking the hammer and pointing it at Mr Lapp's head."

Wilber swung his fist into Lola's belly and when she doubled over he kicked the gun out of her hand and over the high bamboo wall. It was a feat worthy of a stuntman or a circus performer, yet Wilber did it like he was opening a can of coke. Mr Lapp's eyes bulged, almost out of their sockets.

"Now that was impressive, but you know Wilber you should never hit a girl."

Lola straightened up and shot Wilber a hateful glance whilst Mr Lapp marched back into his compound, moving with a strange chugging motion. The inner sanctum was festooned with Chinese lanterns and wind chimes but there were also untold Christmas trees full of lights and a whole slew of sculptures scattered about, all obviously works in progress.

"Home from home," Lapp said, flinging the words over his shoulders as he headed for two banana trees, between which, a hammock was slung.

"Nice place," Wilber muttered. Mr Lapp, clearly indifferent to Wilber's sense of urgency, leapt into his hammock and immediately he was enveloped by a halo of blue light around which occasional lightning could be seen flashing. Infuriated, Wilber aimed a savage kick at the hammock, but Lapp, anticipating the blow relaxed, rode it and then catapulted himself out of the sling, ricocheted off the taller of the two banana trees and landed in front of Wilber, standing on one leg, with his arms folded and the grin on his face cheesier than a cheese Wotsit. In spite of himself the Young Muldoon laughed.

"What's with the lightning man?"

"It's a clue."

"About where I'm going next?"

"Wilber, I'll be honest, there's a lot of things about you I don't like, but I have to admit that you're smart, not algebra smart, not mathematically endowed, but you are fast on the draw and you understand how to play a hunch. When you were first proposed I thought 'no.' I thought if that is the best the world has to offer this island's doomed. Yet in spite of every obstacle placed in your way, here you stand with three gems in that satchel of Crowhaven's, looking for the fourth!"

Mr Lapp nodded and then rose in the air as though borne aloft on a magic carpet; he seemed to float without a care in the world. From standing on one leg, Lapp crossed both legs and assumed the lotus. Now, the blue ball of light that had enveloped the hammock spread out and engulfed Wilber too. The world around him seemed to fade and he found himself in a state of tingling excitement in the bluest blue he had ever seen. It was deep and it was dark, like a liquid ball of polished wax but as he watched it, it lightened, like a dawn and became steadily more electric. The world of the bamboo grove had gone. There were no banana trees now, just as there was no hammock, nor were Lola or Caleb there. There was just him and Mr Lapp, to whom something was happening. As Wilber watched he saw the Old Man's body dissolve and become a sizzling white space; the mere outline of a human form.

"Go on Wilber, go through," Mr Lapp laughed.

"Who are you?"

"Who do you think I am"

"I think you're an instructor for a new reality," Wilber offered.

"Really? Well then that's what I am."

Mr Lapp was every bit as odd as Antelope had said he was but Wilber could refuse him nothing, so he stood and walked towards

Mr Lapp. Then he walked right through him. Immediately, time splintered and cracked like a calving iceberg. He was going back into the sea. Into the Mer. Into Mare. The Great Mother. Mother as Ocean. Cradling him in her arms, she was. And at last he understood, the ocean was a place of origin for all humankind, just as it was a place of return. Into the deep one went, from whence one had come and once there, one would just dissolve and experience the one again. Deep dark blue, becoming electric and lightning issuing forth again and striking him in the forehead between the eyes. And as it struck, that sense of falling into forever, in an unblinking scream.

And as he fell, time split and coloured trains of time roared through his inner space as though he were Clapham junction. Hundreds, if not thousands of trains all travelling in different directions but never colliding. And not just back and forth. And there he was stood at a station, at a million stations, in infinite regress, watching the trains go by. In sequence. He blinked and more trains appeared. He blinked again and there, yet more, so finally, he stepped off the station into one of the trains. Once on board, he found himself seated. He tried looking out of the windows but they were yellow and begrimed. The world outside if it existed at all was just a blur. A smudge and a streak of something unpleasant.

Suddenly he rose and began walking through the train, to what he perceived to be the end, passing from one carriage to the next. The lights blinked on and off as he walked and he found himself transitioning through numerous emotional states. First he felt buoyant and electric and then he felt heavy and buried, almost unable to move. Then he was consumed by a fiery rage and he wanted to destroy everything. Then fear and tears came and with them an overwhelming sense of hopelessness.

He began to move faster and faster, down the train, passing from one carriage to the next in joyless monotony and eventually he began to run. A voice in his head was panicked and wailing. Let me not be trapped here, let me not be stuck. Had Mr Lapp led him into a trap? Antelope had intimated that like all of the other magicians he was not to be trusted. They were none of them right in the head. Each marched to the beat of his own drum. As he thought this, Wilber heard a paradiddle rapped out on a marching drum and then the sound of laughter, a snake's laughter.

Through the swaying carriages he ran, faster and still faster, passing from one to the next, over and over until he lost count, until he began to scream and curse. Then the lights began to blink and before long complete blackness had enveloped him. It was then he stopped moving and just waited. If this was it, if this was how he would spend eternity, then so be it, but he wouldn't scream and he wouldn't run. Not anymore, he had run enough. He would just be calm and still, like a forest where no wind blew. He would be dignified and accept his fate with grace. There were worse things than darkness in the Universe; some of them he'd seen on the island. And with this resolution he took a step and the last door slid open and he found himself on the last step of the last carriage looking down the line to a vanishing point of light, disappearing into forever. And there he hung suspended, a spider on the end of an unravelling thread which was about to snap and drop him. Wilber, sinking into forever, the one place from which there was no escape. Free of panic and the driving rhythms of other people's drums, he was able to formulate the one question that really mattered in that moment.

"Just what are you a Master of Mr Lapp?"

"The only thing that matters," the voice beside him whispered. "Space."

As soon as the word was uttered, everything froze and hung suspended in a timeless moment. And Wilber, with the greatest courage he had ever known stepped off the back of the last carriage of the last train in existence into forever.

"And just what are you a Master of, Justice Wilberforce Muldoon?"

Wilber spoke without considering. "Why fear of course." And he was loose in his own mind and it was a giant playground full of big boxes of colour that only he could fill. This one was orange and this one was grey. And this one was full of children and this one was a fairground. And this one was... Wilber turned round slowly. Just what was this one? He brought all of the colours together, snapped them together at a hinging point and walked between them. They were zones of memory and learning, of course.

He walked with his arms behind his back, as though he were Napoleon and as he moved from one coloured space to the next he watched each of the Magicians materialise and move about their business in turn. Years passed in seconds and days were reduced to a single image. Such beautiful things, like a museum filled with all the best objects in creation. His mind, if that is what it was, was able to distil essences and ideas into icons, into symbols that would stand for all time as concentrated centres of force to be contemplated again and again.

Each space contained a record of all the Magicians had ever been and done. Space begat space and he moved freely between them observing and inspecting. No more trains, no more monotonous carriages swaying in the night. Each unit of space here was productive. There was so much to see. Each life was so rich. A mixture of darkness and light, but he knew intuitively not to get lost in the details. The experiences he was observing needed to be ordered and placed within a structure that he could navigate. He thought of a circle and divided it into five equal pieces and allotted each, colours. Astapor was the orange of fire, Crowhaven: dark grey, Yabu: blood red, Mr Hands was white and Mr Lapp black.

First he walked from zone to zone, but then he stood in the centre and rotated his wheel so that he might see what interested him at any given moment. In this way he could rapidly cut between zones. Zone 1 contained Crowhaven. Zone 2 revealed the wonderful doings of Yabu, elegant beast that he was. Zone 3 reared up a lift shaft and then dived down beneath the ground to reveal Astapor's blood-winged chimerical fancies. Zone 4 took to the skies with Albert Hands and Zone 5 was in the here and now with Mr Lapp. At any moment Wilber could rewind the reels and see what each of the Magicians had gotten up to at any point in their lives. Of all the gifts he had been given, this was the most powerful and the most wonderful.

And yet, and yet all was not right here. Exasperated, Wilber froze, everything in motion about him and all the Magicians stopped moving, stopped thinking and stopped doing. As if on cue Mr Lapp appeared beside him like the proverbial genie of the lamp.

"What's the matter Wilber, bored with your new toy so soon?"

"Something isn't right here."

Lapp, fully embodied once more, smirked and clapped his hands.

"What's missing from this picture? Go on spell it out."

Wilber considered.

"There's so much detail here but everything's past. The machine just goes on forever replaying what has been. But I don't know that everything it's showing me really happened. I don't know if it isn't cutting in lies with the truth, showing me what I want to see as opposed to what happened. How can I trust this?"

Mr Lapp nodded.

"Scepticism is good. So, is there no way you can test the veracity of these images?"

"Why should I? That could take a lifetime to resolve and I'd still be no closer to my objective."

"Which is?"

"Gathering the fifth and final crystal."

Mr Lapp smiled.

"Aah and there we have it!"

Wilber turned to Mr Lapp and smiled back at him.

"Your spaces, as wonderful as they are Mr Lapp, are just distractions. I could fill them and watch them for an eternity but would I be complete? No, I wouldn't, I'd just be an addict confusing information with power. These spaces are as much prisons as Astapor's laboratories ever were. I think I'd like to close them down now Mr Lapp. Forever"

61

Lines of Force

From the centre point stretching out in all directions, were the endless coloured lines of space-time, replete with the images that constituted the lives and deeds of each of the so-called Magicians. Each was lit like a room in a house. As soon as Wilber said the word 'forever' the lights in each and every room began to go out, like fireflies extinguishing their flames. From the furthest to the nearest, the lights went out in every room taking with them the faces and actions they contained. One could never know enough. It was the unquenchable thirst and the great hunger. Knowing, always wanting more as Astapor always wanted more. More power, more knowledge, more pain and more death. He could never be assuaged. Oh he had been a lesson for Wilber, but that lesson was over.

He had always been taught that the light was good, that illumination was the desired thing, but here darkness was perfection. It revealed a true lack of desire for anything other than what one was and what one needed to do in any given moment. And with that thought, the last light in the last frame went out and Wilber stood alone in the darkness. Only it was not completely dark. In his hand he held something that gave light. He lifted it up and peered into its depths. It was the fifth crystal! The dodecahedron with its twelve pentagonal faces. Light danced in his eyes where now tears formed, like blossoms in a cherry tree, ready to fall.

"It's perfectly useless isn't it?" he murmured.

"But isn't it beautiful?" replied Mr Lapp.

"It's a power you can never use, like a nuclear bomb."

"Aaah you have such wisdom Wilber. Yes. Like a nuclear bomb. As such it is a thing men will always kill for, this vision that seems to confer ultimate power upon them."

It was a terrifying thought.

"Am I the first to come here?" Wilber asked, his voice as soft as silk.

Mr Lapp's face was suddenly inscrutable.

"Not everyone chose as wisely as you did Wilber," was all he said.

Wilber nodded. He had been tested and he had found the path but it was not the end and the questions that began to fill his mind suddenly seemed sinister. More chatter and more distractions he realised.

"It never ends does it? The human mind just isn't wired that way. I think it's time to go back."

"Bravo," said Mr Lapp and he clicked his fingers.

And with the blink of an eye they were back. The banana trees remained but the hammock was gone. In its place was an old stove on which was perched a kettle with the campest spout Wilber had ever seen. It was tarnished and battered, was the kettle, but Wilber guessed the tea it made was of the best.

"Care for a cuppa?"

Behind him Caleb piped up.

"We don't have time you stupid old goat. We've come for the fifth crystal."

Wilber, with a flourish, held his prize aloft and his two companions gasped and ran to join him.

"How on earth did you get that? Did he just give it to you?" Caleb asked incredulously.

"Not exactly," Wilber replied, taking one last look at the fifth and final crystal, the dodecahedron, the Crystal of Cosmos, before placing it, along with the other three crystals, into Crowhaven's battered satchel. They all sat down around the old stove waiting for the kettle to boil. Wilber glanced at his watch. It was 19:08.

"So how did you get it?" Lola asked, always suspicious, forever looking for the angle.

"A door opened and then it was shut," Wilber replied cryptically. Mr Lapp's influence was finding expression in his speech now. He liked that but he wasn't sure the others did. Lola spat like an Arab camel.

"I saw no door."

"Doesn't mean a door doesn't exist. Doesn't mean I didn't go through it. Lola, why are you here?"

Lola was taken aback. In the space of a few minutes it seemed Wilber had been utterly transformed from a mewling, self pitying idiot into something far more substantial. Each trial strengthened him in ways that made him difficult to understand and worse still to control. She stood up, flustered, turned around and folded her arms. Wilber stood up too and Caleb followed him. They looked at Lola's back and waited for her to turn and face them. Only Mr Lapp remained seated. The smoke up on top of the volcano continued to drift into the darkening air.

. "So Lola you came here to betray me!" Wilber said, a grim smile on his newly minted face.

"How dare you!" Lola exclaimed, clearly stunned.

"I dare, Lola. I dare. I don't want to get to the finish line only to have you plunge a dagger between my shoulder blades. You're working for Astapor aren't you?"

"You can't survive on the island without making a deal with the Russian. You know that."

"You had a choice, same as the Alphabets. You sold them out and that's why they hate you."

Lola stared into Wilber's blazing eyes and something inside her broke.

"Alright, alright Wilber I can see you've put it together. There's no point pretending anymore but before you cast me out into the wilderness, you need to hear what I have to tell you. I've been on this island all of my life. He could have processed me at any time but he preferred to keep me close. People came and people went all the time here, that's all I knew. Sometimes there would be a new little friend for me to play with, with pigtails and a gingham dress. All teeth and smiles and so desperate to please. You know the kind of kid I'm talking about. And we'd play so happily for days with dollies and we'd build sand castles and dress up and it would be idyllic. How the little girls loved it, at least at first.

"My job, as he explained it to me, was to tell them that their mummies and daddies had sent them away for a lovely holiday and it was down to me to look after them in the compound on the edge of the jungle. They could have anything they wanted, any toy, any food, quite literally anything. Nothing was out of bounds. We even had servants assigned to us, in livery, to fetch and carry, to serve us tea and entertain us when we flagged. And up in his eerie the Russian would look down on us and he'd smile and we'd look up and wave, so grateful, so happy.

"The little girls would ask me about him and all I could say was that he was our mysterious benefactor, a kindly uncle without wife or children of his own who lived only to make others happy. So we'd go on and hours would become days and days would become weeks. And there was only one rule, just one rule they had to obey. No tears. They could do anything they wanted but they couldn't cry. Not for a skimmed knee or a scratched hand or for mummy and daddy. As soon as they cried, and they all did, eventually, a man in a white coat and horn-rimmed spectacles would appear and take them away. He'd say it was time for them to go, that the car was waiting to take them to the airport.

" 'Back to mummy and daddy?' they'd ask all hopeful smiles and pleas.

" 'Oh yes,' the man would say and he'd look at me as he took their hands in his and he wouldn't smile. And I knew as long as I did not want to share their fate I couldn't blub. He was watching you see. As much as I loved them and I loved them all, in varying degrees, I couldn't show it. That if I showed it, that man with the white coat would come for me and he would lead me away too. But I knew that I had no mummy or daddy to go back to. So where would they send me? The island was home and if I wanted to stay home I had to do as I was told. I had to.

"And there were other things I had to do as well. The first thing I had to learn was to freeze my emotions. Other people just have them and express them but I couldn't. His game with me was to deprive me of any joy and peace of mind. That merciless presence, always on high, always gazing down, like God seeing everything, had to be placated, appeased every moment of every day. Like God, he was and is a relentless agent of punishment and torment. There's no love there but he has power, total power. The power to do anything and everything without limit.

" 'Your life is so easy Lola,' he'd say. 'All you have to do is obey me.'

"And I did. And after I'd learned to freeze my emotions I learned to act, to simulate emotion. So when the man in the white coat came and took them away I'd laugh and smile and tell them they could come back again, another time and that I'd been here waiting. We'd play again and their job, whilst they were back home with mummy and daddy, was to come up with new games and new things for us to do. And that way they'd always go away smiling. Keen to leave but excited to return.

"As much as he watched me, and he was always watching me, I never let my guard down, I never broke. I learned early on to make places in my mind where only I could go and be me. But I wasn't a girl with pigtails and a gingham dress there. Not really. I was something that others used to hunt with, something that herded the flock with smiles and hugs towards the spinning blades. In my imagination I was the Queen of my own island. But there were no trees on my island, just jagged rocks and a tall house on top of a very high step. All the rooms were cold as ice and there was never any wood to make fire with. Come to think of it, they were more like caves than rooms and I would squat in the biggest room, a mermaid newly hatched from the sea. I'd sit and look out of the window, every hour of every day on a throne of red coral.

"Life on my island wasn't exactly a rave but I would sing to myself and in my misery I would know a kind of peace. But it wouldn't last, couldn't last because even in the deep places of my mind I knew hunger. And torment. Pain is the past. It's a memory even if that memory is only a rumour loose in your head. For me it was the memory of my mummy and daddy, how they were anxiously searching for me and every day, without me was an even greater misery for them.

"Every day it was as if more weight was piled on their shoulders, the weight of grief. I'd see them young and joyous holding me in their arms as a newborn baby and then I'd see myself placed in a boat and set to drift on the sea. In time the boat would rot upon the waves and I would sink down into the deepest ocean. But I wouldn't die, as much as I wanted to, I couldn't cease to exist. Mine was a light that could not be extinguished. I could sleep but I couldn't die. And down in the deep, an egg formed around me and I grew in an aqueous ooze of pure evil. It seeped into every pore and that little bundle of joy was totally transformed into something else.

"When I hatched I found I could swim; as half woman, half fish I could breathe the water. With my long black hair and my sumptuous figure I was a beauty that would ravish men's souls. Women's too. All would love me, all would trust me but my eyes for all their seeming softness were just black caverns of nothing. I simply learned to hide it, that's all. And up from the depths I swam from the darkest deep to the faintest light, until I broke the surface and gasped, then suckled on the air, once more a greedy newborn, a neonate albeit I was fully grown. And I sought out my island and I hauled myself ashore and when my flesh had dried the tail would wither away and in that place would be these legs, long and beautiful, and oh so deadly.

"Don't look at me like that Wilber, don't judge me. You see, everything has to live, everything has to hunt and kill. There were no plants on the island for me to feed on and I had no taste for fish but human flesh, although cold, well, that served me just fine. And that was my life, my inner life anyway. The only choice available to me was which hell to live in. I couldn't decide, so I chose both, because I wanted to live. We're none of us born evil, but as you can see my life is a malignant tumour that needs a treatment which does not exist."

Everything was still, even the winds that swayed the trees and battered the rocks of the island had stopped to listen to Lola's story. The kettle had boiled and Mr Lapp had set out four cups with red dragons on them. Winged dragons with fiery breaths that flew through white porcelain. And now he was pouring the tea.

"Any questions Wilber? Any clever or pithy observations you want to make. Well, can I suggest you erase them? I don't need your approval and I could do without your judgement. Life here is all about survival. At least it was, until you came and made us believe there was a possibility of a different kind of life here. Without towers, without torture and most of all without fear. You don't know what I've risked to be here and if you fail, I'll have nothing left to go back to. Just the guillotine of his wrath suspended above me by a thread and poised to fall at a moment's notice. Only they'll be no mercy, not for me. He'll stretch it out indefinitely. For as long as he has life, I'll have life, he'll see to that. But what kind? One of infinite pain and distress."

They stood as though in the eye of a storm and listened to the sound of a clanging bell that was being carried over the waves, from the sea and into Lapp's compound. Macready was still out there in his little boat, recently cleaned by the three of them, so that he might continue to keep the resistance alive and well. Astapor for all his genius couldn't reach the Old Man, for sea and tide were his allies. And for all his genius, Astapor would never risk the wrath of the sea.

In time, Wilber nodded his head and sat down. Lapp handed him a cup and the others joined him. For once there was no bickering, no more snide comments or cutting remarks. There was just peace and the low growl of thunder from beyond the horizon. In the wake of Lola's story they were as close as they had ever been. They had a shared purpose at last, and better still, they had four of the five crystals.

It was Mr Lapp who broke the silence.

"So Wilber have you given any serious thought to how you're going to acquire that elusive crystal of Astapor's?"

Caleb lowered his cup, slowly.

"He knows?"

"Of course, he knows, he knows everything," Lola said, arch as ever. So much for the truce and the wonder of unity, Wilber thought.

"I've just had this weird feeling throughout, Mr Lapp, like things would just sort themselves out where that crystal concerned. It's all about the sequence. That's what I've come to understand, at least since I went beneath the ocean waves and met...." He allowed the sentence to trail away, unfinished.

"Astapor's was always the last crystal," he added.

"What did happen down there?" Caleb asked, as inquisitive as a cat on a midnight spree.

"I'll tell you later," Wilber shot back, trying not to sound exasperated but failing dismally. "It's not important now."

Mr Lapp sipped his tea and Wilber weighed his next words carefully.

"Mr Lapp, when we were at the Tower Complex with the Alphabets and Lola something happened. I don't know how to say this but George just wigged out. He went crazy, like he wasn't himself. The plan that we had spent so long formulating just went out of the window and we all just ended up running away. George and I were supposed to go down in the lift, into the labyrinth together and the others were supposed to storm the towers and acquire the high explosives that Lola had told us were hidden there."

"And yet none of this happened?" Mr Lapp prompted.

"No."

"Yet things appear to have worked out, Wilber."

Wilber paused. This was all so very subtle. How far should he pursue this in front of Lola and Cale? He trusted them, but not completely. It wasn't that they were bad people, that didn't matter anymore. The only thing that mattered was what they would do, how they would behave in any given situation. If they were to be believed, they followed him because he was the only real chance they had to break Astapor's hold over the island and its inhabitants. But would they revert to type if and when the Russian were to appear in their midst? This was tricky because this was End Game. Wilber was seeing more and more things clearly, but would it be enough to secure victory?

There were great and mysterious forces at work here, moving behind the metaphorical curtain. Hidden hands dispatching waves of intention that altered real-life events. Was this the essence of magic? Did magic really exist or was it just a future science in magical garb? Questions, always questions accompanied by flashes of image and lightning. The way was strewn with rocks and boulders. It was gnarled and twisted. You had to untwist it, clear the path of refuse, fill in the ruts and then drive a truck straight through it. Think he told himself! Think!

George was strong but George had melted in front of that tower, becoming a crazed beast. Had that just happened or was it engineered? Was it by intelligent design? Yes, of course it was. He'd been fixed. Hypnotised. Reprogrammed. That was brutally apparent now. Wilber broke out in a cold sweat. Yabu had told him that the Magicians were bound by rules they couldn't break. To do so would be to surrender their power, but given certain signs and conditions, could those rules be suspended? Was that happening now on the island?

Mr Lapp sipped his tea and observed Wilber as his mind travelled from memory to idea, from idea to plan, collecting, sifting and then processing data, making connections and forming a new picture of the rules and realities that underpinned the island. It was always a joy watching a mind activate, watching the eyes that suddenly understood, seeing the horror and the wonder commingled.

Crowhaven's watch told him it was 19:21. He couldn't rush this. There was no point running off. He had to figure out the rules by which the Magicians were bound and work around them. Lapp wouldn't just tell him what he needed to know. He couldn't do that, but he could answer questions. It was all breaking down, the system that contained them. The centre which had been so strong was beginning to crumble, but it wasn't broken yet. All that had happened was that Astapor had been driven from his lair out into the island. And now he had been flushed, he was more dangerous than ever. He still held most of the cards, for all that he appeared weakened.

"Mr Lapp, is there something different about Astapor's crystal? It's the only one I haven't felt compelled to go after."

"Astapor doesn't leave anything to chance. You know that." replied Mr Lapp. "Something else you want to ask Wilber?"

Wilber tried to speak, to express what was coursing through his mind but all he could do was stutter and sputter to a halt. Words wouldn't come and his ideas had stopped connecting and begun to fade. If he couldn't complete the arc, then the circuit wouldn't fire and if it didn't fire, he wouldn't have what he needed. And what was that? In his mind's eye he saw a sudden flash of lighting against an electric blue backdrop. His eyes lit up at the sudden illumination. Yes, that was what he needed. Lightning. But where would he find it. Hogarth Macready's words came back to him in an instant.

"Make a friend of the island and maybe you'll win where everybody else lost."

It was something he'd never really considered because it wasn't part of his culture. Could a place be conscious, influencing humans on a subconscious level to achieve select ends. Island as friend, not just rocks and sand and trees and sea. What would a friend do? Put you right and keep safe. It would help keep danger at bay. He'd never known what it was to prey, yet he could talk to it, the island, in his head. Maybe it would talk back, maybe it would flash pictures at him. Show him an escape route or a necessary exit. Mr Lapp watching and appearing not to look away to the North

"So Wilber, do you have what you need?"

"I believe so, Mr Lapp," Wilber replied, following his gaze northwards.

Lapp smiled and as Wilber rose to his feet, Caleb rose beside him, looking perplexed.

"Is that it? Are we done? What just happened? Where do we stand?"

"Good question Caleb. Let me give you my thoughts. I think we stand alone, regardless of what others tell us. Everybody arrives at this place with a history and a story. Mine is..."

"Shrouded in mystery," Lola suggested.

"How did you guess?" You must be psychic!" And laughter filled the air.

62

Decisions, Decisions

The fire up at the complex had intensified and was moving from tower to tower. Not everyone had got out, not because they couldn't have, but because Astapor wanted it that way and his well-trained staff had seen to it that his orders were obeyed. The Russian stood amongst the trees looking up at the smoke-filled sky smoking a black Sobranie cigarette. It was a sight he'd never thought he'd see, an eruption of kinds. Yet there was a kind of poetry in it too. Black smoke against a red sky and white ash raining down. Quite the backdrop, so movingly filmic. If only the trees were on fire too.

Towers 2, 3 and 7 had gone up in flames as the fire had jumped rapidly from floor to floor, consuming everything in its path as it reached for the sky. Or so the reports said, coming in as they did every few minutes, carried by whey-faced messengers, terrified that what they had to tell would land them in boiling water. Astapor however was unconcerned, unnaturally calm, and waved them away with a wan smile.

Suddenly there was the low boom of an explosion and a shock wave pushed outwards, in all directions, flattening everything in a 100 metre radius of the volcano's summit. But Astapor was well clear of that. He was off the hill and moving down the volcano in a south-westerly direction, towards a new set of goals. Above him the prognosis was bleak, now that there was even more smoke, thicker and blacker, spiralling out of the raging flames that issued from the rapidly disintegrating tower complex. His life's work. A record of all he had striven for. Yet he was indifferent.

Drull, Astapor's most-intimidating guard approached and

stood some metres away, clutching his weapon, his eyes glued to the earth.

"Yes, what is it Drull?"

"Tower 5 just blew."

"Is that so? Nevermind. I never really liked it. We'll rebuild it when this is all over."

"Yes Sir."

"Something else?"

Drull glanced over his shoulders to a bedraggled gaggle of red-gowned surgeons and white-coated scientists who stood together like a flock of turkeys awaiting Christmas execution. Despite the size of their intellects they looked terrified and with good reason; the jungle was full of cannibalistic monsters, many of them experiments that they had helped to engineer, on search and destroy missions for fresh meat. The irony amused Astapor and he found himself guffawing heartily as the sound of a spine chilling scream indicated yet another had succumbed to the beasts that were legion. On and on the screaming went, until it suddenly cut out, like the end of a record.

"How many left?" Astapor asked.

"About ninety or so. What do you want us to do with them?"

"Take them to the bunker on the Northern shore. Send as many guards as we can spare."

"But the northern forests are crawling. It's a massacre up there. Hell on earth..."

"Perfect. They'll draw the heat from our little party and allow us to attend to more pressing matters."

"Master, look out!" One of the soldiers screamed, as a young Allosaur hove into view and charged straight at Astapor. The Russian turned to face it. Everyone else froze, caught in a moment of unimaginable horror. There were some sporadic gun shots as Astapor, cool as a cucumber reached into his pocket, possibly for a last cigarette. The Allosaur, pounding the earth it was born to rule, opened its mouth and grinned from ear to ear, like the Cheshire cat. It stank of rotten meat and body odour. Off in the distance a bell tolled. Twenty metres, fifteen, ten... Drull stepped in, gallant Drull raising his weapon and squeezing off a clutch of rounds. Ask not for whom the bell tolls. Was that the sound of the dinner gong?

Bang, bang. But all for nought. Drull recoiled as Astapor raised his hands and clicked. Another bang, a different kind of bang and the Allosaur's head exploded from the inside, its brains showering down on the Russian's loyal stooge. The lifeless, reptilian body crashed to a halt and slid along the earth landing two metres away from where the Russian stood, poised like a Young Nijinsky, ready to leap.

"Always best to have an insurance policy," Astapor said, handing Drull his handkerchief. The guard wiped the blood and brains from his face and looked at his boss, with a look that was part shock, part wonder. No matter how long you spent with the Russian he never became predictable. And that was not the end of it, not by a long chalk. It was all kicking off.

A sudden cry and then shouts; listen carefully and you could tell that orders were being barked. Shots dispatched into the air and the sound of running feet. Astapor stood with his hands behind his back, tapping his left foot, his eyes fixed on the cooling Allosaur. Dinosaur's weren't really his thing; they were just a sideline. He preferred death to come from a human hand. No, he'd leave the dinosaurs to Muldoon. For now.

A deafening roar and yet another bang! Everyone ducked, but Astapor, as even more smoke whirled into the darkening sky and debris rained down. Already a messenger was running down the side of the volcano to give Astapor the bad news. The Russian waved the wide-eyed man away before he was able to tell him that another tower had fallen to enemy action. Not that it wasn't interesting news, it was just that Astapor was more focused on a little knot of soldiers advancing towards him with a struggling bundle.

Navigating around the fallen theropod, they stopped just metres away and dumped the bundle on the ground. Although the bundle's hands were trussed, it rose swiftly to its feet and spun wildly around, this way and that, kicking out at its tormentors. The soldiers laughed until Astapor fixed them with his steeliest gaze. Then they had sense enough to fall silent. The bundle wore a bag on its head and Astapor reached out with his long, pianist's fingers to snatch it away. When he saw what was concealed beneath it, he let out a coo of delight.

"Finally, results."

"Get away from me!" the bundle yelled, clearly infuriated, its eyes closed to avoid the sudden influx of light.

"Calm yourself Semantic, we're all friends here."

The captured Alphabet froze and stared, astounded.

"You know my name?"

"Of course I do, I know all your names but then I have been watching you for months. Collectively, you are my favourite experiment even though you will insist on blowing things up Semantic. Actually I think Semtex might be a better name for you."

"Well daddy was Special Forces and keen for me to learn the tricks of his trade."

Astapor gave a thin smile.

"Don't romanticise your father, Semantic. He was an alcoholic who beat your mother senseless on countless occasions before he drank himself into an early grave. Great soldier but a lousy human being. Without people telling him what to do all the time, he was nothing."

"My father was a hero," Semantic hissed, as her eyes teared. "He gave everything for his country..."

"And absolutely nothing to his family."

"He gave me enough to do that to your tower complex, Mr Astapor," she replied, looking back over her shoulders to the smoking wreckage on top of the volcano.

The Russian nodded in acknowledgement. That he'd give her. So smart, so damaged, so fascinating. Such a pity her time here was at an end.

"So how many of my towers are undamaged Mr Drull?

"Three Sir."

"Just three. Quite the destructive force aren't we Semantic? Did you wire the lift pods yourself? Yes, I expect you did. Best way to wreak the most havoc and to get the fires to spread. You know there are lifts into each and every one of my 8 towers, going up, up, up, all the way up to a place amongst the clouds that is full of laboratories. And then down, down, all the way down. But they aren't the only access points. If only you'd done your homework you might have done some lasting damage."

Semantic scoffed.

"You're losing the war, Mr Astapor. In spite of all, you know you are losing. And whilst you stand here talking to me, Wilber gets closer and closer to his final objective."

Astapor rolled his eyes like a severely unimpressed teenager.

"You've inconvenienced me, that's all, Semantic. By the close of play today I will be more firmly in control than I've ever been for reasons you won't comprehend. I could explain it but I'm not going to."

"Why do you hate us so much?"

"I don't hate you. It's just that you don't appreciate my work."

"Your work?" For the second time since meeting Astapor, Semantic was astounded.

"Yes, I know it may be a stretch for you to understand but I am reworking humankind so that it may once again be useful. I have entered into an artist/canvas relationship with their DNA and through them I'm reaching for the skies, back to our point of origin. With what I know I have become a God and the Human Mark 2 is my greatest achievement. Civilization softened them, led them away from their true selves. I've led them back, like Moses, across the Red sea of their blood, into the future. They will emerge truer and more authentic. They will be lethal and effective but best of all they will be expendable."

"You're insane, you know that? You think you're in charge but you're not. The island is waking up and it's coming for you. I may not have your mind but I know enough of the history of this island to know it will not stand for your debasement and corruption of the human spirit. The Ancients learned that to their cost. Abuse the privilege of knowledge, abuse power, abandon your humility and you lose control. And in losing that, you will lose everything. Those who do not learn the lessons of history are doomed to repeat them!"

"What a wonderful speech, Semantic. I've enjoyed it as much as I've enjoyed you. But now it's time for both you and your words to go."

63

A Philosophical Discussion

Caleb, running through the jungle, realised that the hour of decision had arrived. He could no longer put off the inevitable and play the double game. He must decide who he was and what he stood for. More importantly he must decide who he stood with.

His Dark Father or the Love of his Life?

Glancing behind him, he saw that his partners in crime had slowed to a virtual halt. Quickening his step, he slipped away, leaving Lola and Justice locked into discussion as they finalised their plans for End Game. The sun was well past its zenith and was beginning its descent. Soon the horizon would swallow the flaming orb and in that moment Wilber's only chance of freedom would vanish.

Caleb ran without sound until he was far enough away from his companions that he might be in peace, then he sat down crossed-legged and placed his head in his hands. After a short while he began to rock backwards and forwards. And this was where Dinosaur George found him. Great Uncle Muldoon, he had left some way behind, but the Old Man was a skilled tracker and would follow the trail that George had left. George, man of heightened senses that he was, detected that Wilber was nearby with the girl, but curiously, he felt no compunction to go to him at that moment.

Suddenly it seemed more important to focus on Caleb. Hiding behind a large palm tree, George watched as the boy contemplated his future, head in hands. After a while he got up and returned to where Wilber and Lola were waiting, some distance away. George, hearing the crack of a twig behind him, span round to find himself staring down the barrels of seven guns.

He tensed, ready to spring, then out of the shadows came the sound of cruel laughter. This was followed by the sound of padding feet and a figure emerging to stand before him, half in shadow, half in the light. George gasped when he saw who it was. Astapor.

"Pathetic isn't he?"

George looked over his shoulder to where, just moments before, the boy had been seated, singing, working out, no doubt which way he was going to play the situation he found himself in. To help or to hinder. To hold true or to betray. Those were the options he was presented with.

"Poor kid. He is whatever you made him," George said through gritted teeth. "What is it you tell everyone you meet? I don't have friends, only experiments. I'm guessing that's still true."

Astapor chuckled again

"I'm afraid it is." Here the Russian paused and regarded his adversary with, what to an outsider, might have looked like affectionate curiosity. But nothing could have been further from the truth.

"So Muldoon, you survived the pit and the volcano. I'm guessing the same cannot be said of your brother. I suppose he's in pieces now, fermenting in the gut of one of our lovelies."

George felt himself tense. His mind filled up with raging fire, but as soon as the flames rose up he doused them. That was not the way. Many years ago he had come to that decision. Like Caleb he had been at a crossroads. Pledge himself to revenge and murder or try to understand and to forgive. Try and build a life that had meaning and hope and significance even without the one he loved. The one Astapor had taken from him.

"Yes, I survived the pit. I wonder if you would have, in my place."

"Still taunting I see."

"Still hiding I see. Ever the spider in the centre of the web."

Astapor smiled, his lips sharper than razors. The cut and thrust of debate was what he loved. It had been some time since he'd been pitted against an adversary that could match him blow for blow, strike for strike. Muldoon was that adversary. He was relentlessly challenging but he could be broken, he would be broken and soon.

A flicker deep in the endless recesses of his web, an image glittering among the gossamer strands of his mind froze him momentarily. The outer world vanished and his inner world loomed and reared up at him, flashing teeth and foaming hungry purpose. Just like Old Grandmother Spider, he thought. But no. The horrors of the pit were as nothing when compared with the hell he had crawled from.

The glittering fragment he pictured, hanging by many threads of memory, sought to derail and betray him. It was no crystal, no diamond he saw glittering but a mirror, one of any number that he had tried to root out of his mind and destroy. Unfortunately, they were resistant to most forms of assault, those mirrors. They had an uncanny knack of showing him his reflection, images and memories he would rather not see. Like Judas, in Dante's Inferno, he felt himself, frozen in the lowest level of hell, looking up at the face of he who had betrayed. Not Christ, no. Not him. But her.

The agony was as much as he could bear and he had to will himself back into a state of quiescence. Self control was what defined him. He would never allow his conscience the upper hand. He could withstand whatever battery his chaotic mind might hurl at him from the past but only so long as he had the island and could control everything on it. That was the truth no other could know. All this in a fraction of a second as Muldoon peered at him through a shifting patchwork of shadows. Best to lead the hound from the scent, to fill the air with distracting sounds.

"You never learned to see the world through my eyes did you? Other people's suffering can be so beautiful, George."

"Not to me, it isn't."

"I'm surprised you haven't tried to kill me yet. If I've learned anything about you, it's that you have total faith in your own ability. Reality tells you that you are finished, but something inside of you refuses to die. I wonder, will the light finally go out of you when I crush your boy and the light leaves his eyes, never to return?"

Hearing Astapor's goading words, George gritted his teeth.

"You'll never crush him. He's too strong for you. He's a chip off the old block."

"It's true, he has surprised me. Gone further than any other."

"That's obvious."

"But what isn't obvious is the gap between what appears and what actually is. You always assume that I'm working on one level, when in actuality I'm working on nine. At least."

"Oh spare me the BS. Admit it. You're beat. Something has changed on this island and your power is on the slide my friend. It's just a matter of time now."

A sudden noise up ahead, caused them both to turn and listen intently. The sound of running feet crashing through the undergrowth. Lola and Justice were on the move and it sounded like they were being pursued. George made as if to follow them and was stopped by the sound of many weapons being cocked.

"You've been out of the loop too long George. Your world has made you soft."

"That's as maybe but this island you call home has blinded you. You think you're invulnerable and invincible Astapor and maybe you are here but not back there, in that other world you left behind."

Astapor held onto his poker face but he was intrigued.

"Those with a weak hand are compelled to bluff George. It is I who hold all the aces."

"But I, who have the Royal Flush, my little Russian friend. You see in spite of your best efforts to bury your past, I did a little digging when I got back home. It's what I do, dig up the bones of dinosaurs. And who is a bigger dinosaur than you?"

"Keep it civil Muldoon or we'll cut you in half."

"With those lovely German Machine Guns. MP 38s unless I'm very much mistaken. Now what would you be doing with guns manufactured in the Second World War in Germany?"

"Go on then, astound me."

"Those guns you're pointing at me now, you had last time and they were the clue that led me back to your secret past and to your lost name. You're not a Count, although some would say you are...and you're not an Astapor. Where did you dig that up from? You're an Ashinsky. Leonid Ashinsky. A Russian Jew born in 1917, in Arcangel and shipped west to Auschwitz where you collaborated with the Germans finding ever more efficient ways to dispatch your people in return for your own life. You survived the war and then it was you who helped certain high ranking Nazi's escape to South America. In time they returned the favour and got you out of Russia and funded your secret research. Your ideals and theirs were very much in line. Nazis and Jews working hand in hand. Enough to make you think that anything's possible."

"You don't know. You don't know what I went through."

"You're no victim Ashinsky. You went willingly to work."

"It is as you say. I went willingly, Muldoon. Those men and I shared a vision of the New World. Total domination of the human artefact through Scientific Procedures. Vorsprung Durch Technik. Advancing through technology. Technology was never meant to liberate the masses, only to enslave them. The humans of your world are past saving. They are well on the way to destroying themselves as well you know. All I want to do is try out my theories on captive flesh, away from the prying eyes of the governments of your world. The things I have created, the things I have done with humans are simply my love letters to a God I have never believed in."

George took a step backwards and as he did, he watched the machine guns being raised. His fingers went to his pocket. Still there, but all was failure. The soldier's faces were a blur. The only thing in focus was those fingers squeezing those triggers.

"Fire," Astapor hissed.

And there were seven clicks. Dead men's clicks. And George was running away from the cold metal of the machine guns, following Wilber into the Burning Grounds, the zone of crashed spaceships

419

where he would have to activate the final crystal, Astapor's Crystal which lay hidden in his pocket, dormant but by no means extinct.

64

If Only

Wilber stopped at the sound of the gunshots and Lola pulled up beside him. He felt a pain in his heart that did not bode well for someone. But who? His mind raced with images in a way he could not control. It was like he was being turned on, that faculties that had long remained dormant were rapidly being activated. But by who and to what end? Wilber felt a sudden stab of vertigo and his world began to whirl. The paths available to him were getting narrower and narrower. He understood that without being told. It came as a deep inner knowing, something he could never explain, even if he had wanted to. His consciousness was heading in directions that words found hard to follow.

"What is it, Wilber? You look weird."

Wilber snapped to.

"Nothing; we have to keep on moving."

Lola didn't seem convinced. The look on her Giaconda face told the story, yet the story of her face was no longer convincing to him either. Wilber's patience was wearing thin and he snapped again, this time out loud.

"Get out of my head Lola, its rude to trespass."

Behind her dark glasses Lola's head was buzzing like a swarm of angry wasps. A friend of Wilber's mothers had once squatted on a nest of hornets en route to relieve herself in a forest. A most painful lesson. Not that that mattered now. Why should he think of it? Of course, hornets came heavily armed as did Lola and they always carried a sting in their tail. Was she getting ready to sting him?

"How did you guess?" Lola asked.

"What, that you're telepathic?"

"We don't call it that here. It's just something the island does to certain people. Not everyone of course and not all the time. Just when you're useful to it."

"You talk as if the island were alive."

"Well it is."

She said it so matter of factly, like she was announcing the sea was blue or that fish swam in the sea. The old order was breaking down so rapidly. Of course it had been filthy and corrupt but that didn't stop him from being assailed by pangs of nostalgia for what was passing. As much as he hated what had been, he feared what was coming more.

"Look Lola, if you're going to stick me in the back do it now. I'll even turn around so you don't have to look in my eyes when you do it."

Lola, absolutely still, considered him in silence.

"Why would I want to do that, Wilber? Don't you trust me?"

The game was so old it was cold and yet still she played it. Maybe it would be better to finish her now. His game was too important to throw away. Too many people on the island were dependent on him for their salvation. Could he do it? Could he kill her in cold blood?

He had learned in the last few hours he could do anything. When faced with the age old dilemma of kill or be killed, he had killed. With qualms at first, and then rapidly without any kind of consideration, he had taken life after life. As the endlessly altered people ran through the foliage to get at him, he had ended them. It wasn't murder, it was more like weeding. But this, this was different.

"Lola, please. Torture me, disembowel me, gauge out my eyes with rusty spoons only please, please level with me. I don't think I can handle another minute of doubt as to who you are and what your real intentions are."

Lola nodded, exquisitely reasonable.

"As you wish."

"Since I got here, all anybody has been telling me is that I'm an idiot who doesn't understand, a fool being led round the farm by the ring through his nose, a pawn. If I'd listened to those people, those voices, I'd have given up. But I just kept on going. I have four crystals and I get the sense that George may have the fifth or at least know where it is. So unless you've got anything of substance to add to my story I'm just going to carry on, running for the finish line. The clock, as you know, is ticking. The clock is always ticking."

With this he turned and began to move off. Her next words brought him to an abrupt halt.

"I did it, you know."

"Did what?"

"I completed the Game."

"You did what?" Wilber spat, his voice ringing with disbelief.

"I know you don't want to believe me. Hell in your shoes, I know I wouldn't. You've too much invested in what you've been told to be able to take on board a counter narrative. Cognitive dissonance is a powerful force and like the python's coils, you are firmly in its grip."

"What in the name of all that's sane are you babbling on about?"

"The reason I'm alive, Wilber, is because I completed the Game. The only problem was that when I placed the final crystal in the final slot nothing happened. The sky didn't open, no bridge across forever materialised, Jesus and the Angels did not descend to earth in a thousand crystal space ships ready to take me and all the other islanders into another dimension. All that happened was that Astapor and the Other Magicians gathered round me and applauded and then they told me from then on I was safe. Not one of them, just free to come and go. My reward for completing the game was that I would be left alone. And then it began to rain."

Silence.

"I don't believe you."

Lola laughed.

"You don't want to believe me Wilber."

Outraged silence.

"You're lying."

"Of course I am. I have to be lying because you need to believe there is a way off this island. Only there isn't. I mean I believed too. Believed absolutely. And if anyone had told me now what I'm telling you, I'd probably have killed them. After everything I'd been through, everything I'd done, I wouldn't have been able to handle it either."

Wilber took out the base ball bat from his pack and looked at the dark red blood stains on the business end of the stick. He had suddenly turned very pale and his breathing was laboured.

"So you want to know why I'm here, do you, what my intentions really are? Are you sure you want to know Wilbs? I mean, really sure?"

Wilber shook his head, unable to speak.

"Because of a bet with Astapor. Hard to believe isn't it?"

Wilber gripped the baseball bat like he meant business and took a step towards Lola.

Lola laughed. It was all such a hoot.

"Yeah I know it's hard to take. Like being told you're not that good in bed. But it's true. You see Astapor had you down as a stone killer from the start. That's his favourite thing you see, working out what really makes people tick. He starts out from the position that everyone is evil and that all you have to do is to create the right conditions for that evil to manifest.

So before you know it you're letting kids fizz away into oblivion, or you're leaving your friends to get massacred or you're clubbing the brains out of zombies or even out of the girl you secretly love. All for the love of the game. All for the love of winning. You see, that's the real game. The crystals and all that jazz is just wallpaper, window dressing to sell the big lie. The real deal is what Astapor and I have going on the side. The bet. You see he bet that at this point in the game you'd be willing to do anything to 'win,' even if it meant killing me. Whereas I bet you wouldn't."

Slowly she took out her sword and dropped it to the ground,

then Lola walked over to where Wilber was standing, knelt down in front of him and took off her shades. Her eyes had never looked as beautiful as they did now.

"And if I win, I get to keep you, to own you, to make you mine. You'll be my slave and my every whim will be your least command. And if he wins well... I guess you're going to have to get a little more blood on those beautiful hands of yours. So what's it to be Wilber, him or me? Me or him?"

Red curtains fell in front of Wilber's eyes. It was all a lie. The show was over. He was done, his turkey cooked. They'd played him and flayed him, they'd turned him into a fool and a killer. The island was a hell from which there was no escaping. It was a game that no one could win. To win was to be so morally compromised that one could hardly bear to live with one's self and one's past actions. The only ones who won were the dead, those who chose not to play the game, those who chose not to compete and allowed the savage engine of the island to consume them.

Wheels turned within wheels in his mind and Wilber fell through them, in an unblinking scream, into the hell that had been prepared for him. The soft doe-like eyes that stared up at him were the eyes of the woman he loved but they were also the eyes of a Machiavellian torturer, murderer and manipulator. They were the eyes of the demon that had become his master.

Without a second thought he hoisted the bat above his head and brought it down with a crashing thud.

65

Hard Loving

Moving noiselessly, as he had been trained, breathing in and out of his nose, Caleb saw what was in front of him, screeched to a halt and froze. He shook, only partly free of the turmoil that had gripped him just moments before. Yet he had come to a resolution of sorts. Wilber stood with his back to him, head bowed looking down at the ground. In his hands he was clutching something. Caleb edged forward slowly, without sound, his heart pounding, to see what it was. He had thought as much. Wilber was holding the much-used baseball bat they had given him. In the slanting beams of light, that lanced the spaces without leaves, it seemed to glisten. Caleb shook his head in disbelief and tip toed forward to get a better look. When he saw what was on the ground he took a deep and convulsive gulp and then he began to laugh.

"My Wilber, you have come a long way."

Wilber spun round and hoisted the bat over his shoulder, ready to take another swing and, mindful of his own safety, Caleb took a step backwards. With his left hand he reached over his right shoulder and removed the decapitator that he kept in its scabbard there.

Many bloods encrusted the blade and he would have to clean it, but not yet, not today. For now, those exotic strains of blood would have to taste the air, shaming the blade, by making it filthy. Acutely aware of this, Caleb brought the sword down and to the left, in a position that would facilitate either attack or defence and waited for Wilber to respond. But when Wilber didn't, he felt compelled to fill the void.

"She's a hard woman to love Wilber, I know that and believe me I've tried but when you love her..."

"You love her forever."

Curious. Wilber had spoken and yet his lips hadn't moved. A figure arose and stood beside him. It was Lola, risen from the dead and she was smiling coyly, like a Geisha might. An origami smile with the fragrance of orange blossoms washed over her visage. So pure, so seeming innocent. Yet Geishas were not innocents, although they strove to appear that way; they were trained professionals with keen eyes and minds, trained on business and self advantage. As was Lola.

Wilber looked lost, his eyes unfocused. Looking through and not at things now. The tourist who became a traveller had in the last few moments become a pilgrim and things of this world, of the island, no longer seemed to hold his gaze. It was a familiar look to Caleb and Lola but one they never tired of seeing. Especially when it was as new as this. The death of faith, of belief in anything was what they prized most highly. In this they were Astapor's children, products of the culture that had spawned them. Now Wilber believed in nothing, he could finally be useful.

"So what's next champ?" Caleb asked Wilber, whilst looking at Lola.

Wilber, looking sullen, responded to Caleb's half question, half taunt with a deadened voice, a voice drained of emotion.

"What happened to you Caleb? Where did you go? You seem different."

Caleb seemed momentarily nonplussed.

"What do you mean? I just took a comfort break. You know, a call of nature. I may be thin Wilbs but I have an active metabolism. I eat and drink, capiche? Anyway I'm here and it's now, so what's next? Tick tock and all that"

The silence was painful and Caleb became increasingly edgy.

"What is it, what's with you guys? I just took a break, is all."

Lola, in shades and a long coat, gave a smirk.

"You can drop the act Caleb, he knows."

"Knows what?" Caleb responded, his eyes flicking from Wilber to Lola, in the backwards and forwards motion of a tennis match.

"He knows that the Game is phoney. That it's all a set-up, just play, invented by Astapor to pass the time of day here. He knows all this is just a side project for the Russian, a theme park full of distractions to amuse him. The main event in his world, the key reason he is here, is hidden. You can't beat him, appearances to the contrary, you can only join him, as have we."

Caleb beamed from ear to ear and immediately seemed to relax.

"Well I'm glad we've got that out of the way. It's such a weight, having to keep up the pretence. You and Astapor have a little side bet going on I'll bet, eh Lola?"

Lola's laugh of affirmation was rich and ripe.

"You bet. Wilber took it really well though. I mean he's still in shock but at least he didn't try to club my brains out."

Caleb cracked up at this.

"Lucky you Lolals. That would have really sucked. So you live to play another day eh? You called it and won another round. Wonder what you'll win. When you get into it, Wilbs, it's just so addictive, this game. You'll wonder how you ever lived without it. Such a great game and you get to be somebody new every day. But tread carefully, it's a game played with loaded dice..." he quipped.

"And live ammo", she rejoined.

Laughter filled the air and not a wisp of breeze stirred.

"When you came back Caleb you were sweating and shaking."

It was an odd observation for Wilber to make.

Caleb raised his blade and rested it on his shoulder. Lola was on the move, repositioning herself. All casual like. Slinky and not really committed. Not enough to raise any suspicions. Wilber was aware of it but he was focused on Caleb. So still, so very still. The island had changed the kid and made him difficult to read. What a difference a few hours made.

"Well it's hot and I've been running."

"But you run all day Caleb and you never sweat. You see I've been paying attention."

"Really", Caleb sounded bored. The roll of the eyes signalled boredom.

Wilber tilted his head to one side.

"Like Lola said, no one here is who they appear to be."

Wilber said the line like he'd coined it himself. Lola and Caleb have glanced at each other. Lola was saying nothing and Caleb shrugged.

"Actually it's kind of a line, Wilber. Scripted really, by Astapor. To sow the seeds of doubt. Doubt is what we work with here, on the island. It's our bricks and mortar, our road and sea lane. Most humans don't function well with uncertainty. Build that into your spiel and little by little the cracks appear. By the end of the day they are turning to you for instructions. That's the game we play here..."

Wilber shook his head.

"That's a game but it's not the game. Not the one you're playing anyway. You left us for a reason, albeit for a few minutes. You spoke to no one in that time. You did relieve yourself but only of your own uncertainty."

Caleb looked Wilber steadily in the eye.

"Ok Wilbs, ok. I can see you've got a bee in your bonnet so let's all think carefully about our next moves shall we? Me and her are just fine. The Russian will take us back..."

Wilber smiled and shook his head...

"Like that." And Caleb clicked his fingers.

"You're still sweating Caleb and it's not even hot. It's almost 20:00 and you're used to heat a lot more intense than this. In the forest you took a moment didn't you? And something burst through. A new resolve. To kill the monster and to rescue the stranded princess."

"What are you talking about?" Caleb's voice was suddenly all steel and razors.

"I'm talking about you Caleb," Wilber said. "the boy who believes in nothing and yet, and yet, he so wants to believe in the fairy tale ending. Even though he knows she doesn't love him and she never will...because she only loves..."

Caleb's scream seemed to fill the jungle. The blade in his hand flicked upwards.

"Lies...all lies..."

And with the blade grasped tightly in his two-handed grip he surged forward and brought the cutting edge down on the top of Wilber's head.

Or rather the place Wilber's head had been. He'd had the sense to move it. And taking his cue from common sense, and not a misguided sense of heroism, he took to his heels and ran...

66

Relativity

Through the trees they sprinted and into the treeless glade, where trees had burned and even rock had melted. Into the arms of one of the deadliest adversaries the island had to offer. Old Ma Fang. She was waiting with words and strategies too final to contemplate.

"One last indignity to endure I'm afraid, Wilber. I felt it was time I made my presence known."

Wilber pulled up short, baseball bat in hand, with Caleb close behind him. Of the two, Caleb was the more put out.

"Oh no, not you, anybody but you. I felt something circling, something crawling towards us."

Ma chuckled.

"Nephew!"

"Aunt."

Wilber felt his Zen-like cool deserting him for a few moments.

"You're related?"

At the thought of this Caleb blanched.

"Distantly."

Ma with her twisted stick, held behind her impossibly straight back, grinned encouragingly. There was a smouldering cigar clamped between her teeth and aromatic smoke drifted through the air towards Wilber and his pursuers.

"Oh no Caleb, we're much closer, in blood, than you could possibly imagine. I would elaborate but well..."

She smiled wanly and consulted her watch, a chunky gold affair that could have been a Christmas gift from Yabu.

"I see it's time."

Lola, long-coated and bespectacled, the last to enter the glade, had lost her usual sangfroid and broken out into a frown. It was the most animated she got until she began to kill things.

"Time for what?"

But Old Ma Fang said nothing. Just went on puffing her cigar, exhaling the smoke into the rapidly cooling air, her fingers twirling the cane behind her back, backwards and forwards. Over and over. Away to the west, the sun was beginning to sink. The seventeenth hour of Wilber's Quest had just passed and the final hour had begun ticking down. With the setting of the reddening sun it would all be over. Wilber studied Fang closely. The dark black eyes, kohl-lined, the dreadlocked hair, the elegant, if battered, long coat, worn like Lola's down to the ground, the cruelly pointed boots. She was a very real figure, was Old Ma, virtually fleshless but substantial in her sense of presence and in her unforced theatricality. So if the Game wasn't real, why dispatch her?

Turning round, Wilber saw it all, and once more the heavens flashed with lightning and the illuminated sky snarled. Lola was still frowning, staring daggers at Old Ma Fang who gazed back at her impassively. After the endless hours of frenetic movement this stillness was unnerving. Caleb held his decapitator in an attack stance, blade vertical, hands by his left side. He too frowned, but he looked less certain than he ever had. And then the sound of footsteps and after a brief interval, a tall form emerging from the darkness behind Fang. Lola gasped when she saw who it was. It was Herr Zoot, the man in the Yellow Suit. Yet he no longer wore his jacket, just the yellow pants, and a checked shirt and waistcoat. His tie and hat were gone too. The boots, unlike Ma's, were impeccably clean and so well polished you could see your own terrified face in them.

He was holding something that looked heavy. Something egg-shaped. Yet it was too large to be an egg. Wasn't it? Wilber gripped his baseball bat tightly and despite all he had been through, all of the ordeals he had faced, began to shiver. Old Ma Fang's eyes switched from Lola's to Wilber's and she puffed a voluminous cloud of smoke into the cooling air. Rolling the cigar from the centre of her mouth to the left side, she spoke.

"Time for something to hatch. You were so close Wilber, the best we've ever seen, by far. I hope that can be a consolation to you, in the end, when your heart slows and the black blood pours out of your eyes."

Wilber winced. Time for a little gallows humour perhaps. Just to keep the show moving along.

"Really Ma, you are not somebody I'd ever consider taking home to mother."

Madame Fang's eyes glowed when she heard this, the same colour as the end of her cigar. Unlike the other loons and hags he had so far encountered on the island, she could not be intimidated.

But just how far would she go and what were they up to? All any of them could do was watch.

Zoot, intent on his own task, was setting the large, egg-shaped object down carefully on the ground. Following his actions closely, Wilber could see a large indentation had been dug or hollowed out of the earth and that the egg, if that was what it was, had been placed to stand upright within its own crater. The light here was odd and fading and something seemed to thrill the air with buzzing and whirring sounds and oddly coloured shapes.

Wilber blinked twice in rapid succession. He was having trouble focusing his eyes on what was happening. It was as though he was only seeing part of what was present. The earth all around him was scorched and yet to his mind somehow alive. Blue veins of some unknown mineral ran through the ground and the rocks rose up like termite mounds, curiously alien and unsettling. Like the forest glade that lay just fifty metres behind them, this was an open space, yet beyond the perimeter there were trees and darkness.

All but the red sun had been swallowed by the black sky. He had never experienced anything like it in his life and the effect upon him was most unnerving. Within him, he felt things rushing and zooming. It was as if his body had become less physical and that it was no longer full of blood and bones, tissues and organs but something else beside. Just space maybe! He sought to understand it, tried to scramble through the mist and fog clouding his mind, but he couldn't. Wilber sensed he would just have to watch and wait. There was no point trying to run before you could walk, but it was just so infuriating.

Another flash of white lightning illuminated the glade and Wilber was shocked at what it revealed. There wasn't just one egg-shaped object, but many, set out in a semi circle. Wilber wasn't sure, but he thought he had counted at least eight, possibly nine. They were all about a metre high, some bigger and some smaller. A sense of immanence ran through him like a shiver. Yes, something was about to happen.

Could they be eggs?

It seemed unlikely, but this was the island, and anything was possible. Wilber focused on the eggs through the gathering gloom and began to assemble his conclusions. They weren't covered in shells, like a bird's eggs or leathery like a turtles. No, if anything they seemed as though they were made of rocks, rocks that had the look of a dark, coarse fabric. They weren't smooth either, but lumpy.

Could they be dinosaur eggs?

Having deposited what appeared to be the last of the eggs, Zoot had turned around and passing behind Old Ma Fang, had disappeared back into the darkness from whence he had come. His bright yellow trousers were the last thing to disappear and for some reason Wilber couldn't quite fathom, he thought of the paintings of Caravaggio and began to laugh. Beautiful horrors, agonised humanity often on the point of death but always looking their best. That was what he remembered and what came to mind now. He had always loved art but furtively. It wasn't something he could share with anyone, but it shaped the way he experienced his world. It had also helped prepare him for what the island was in the process of serving up, by way of experience.

Alone, in the semi-darkness, Old Ma Fang walked forward

slowly, her twisted staff still held behind her back, twirled back and forth, back and forth by her long, gnarled fingers. Swaying from side to side, as she walked, like some Great Old Bird, she moved into the centre of the space and came to a halt.

Time hung still just for her, like a viand on a meat hook.

Lola and Caleb edged forward too, until they stood on either side of Wilber. For all that they were close enough to strike at him, young Muldoon did not consider them a threat. They were just as mesmerised as he was. Ma had a curious light around her, a light that seemed to come off of her in waves, and for some reason, as the air around them grew darker, she appeared to glow more brightly.

The expression on her face was not in any way threatening. Far from it. It was, if anything rapt; part bemused, part amazed. It was an expression that none of them had ever seen before. She was as fascinated by them as they were by her. It was confusing though, like words had to be spoken and yet nobody was quite sure who should be doing the speaking. As the seconds passed though, it became obvious whose tongue would loosen first. Ma's! Yes, she had come to deliver them all a bedtime story, a sweet good night. Each member of the group; Wilber, Caleb and Lola, was so excited as to be scarcely able to breathe. Ma had poise, Ma had style and Ma would tell them a story that would electrify them. It would dazzle and thrill, shock and captivate and best of all it would be just for them. The performance of a lifetime, a memory to treasure forever. Unmoving, staring wide-eyed and child-like, the trio waited for the show to begin, all thoughts of purpose and enmity forgotten. Their only thought, the thrill of the ride they were about to take. And then she spoke.

"Welcome my children, welcome to this, the very last story of the current age. You stand on the edge, on the very crack of doom, wavering like a spider's legs, on the very precipice. This point in time will never come again. Your life will never be quite so electric.

"Can't you feel the spirit of the new age waiting to be born. It prowls the winds like a hungry dragon, testing each and every moment to see whether time is ready for it, whether space can bear the load of its coming. Surely you can feel that?"

They each of them nodded and Ma laughed with unconcealed delight.

"You can't rush a good story and this is the best. Shall we proceed?"

All affirmed she should and Ma beckoned them forward by raising her chin and flashing her eyes. Each took three paces closer to the centre where the old woman stood. She watched and waited and she seemed satisfied, but also impatient, as if the story she had to tell was one she just had to get off her chest.

67

Hatching

"You are part of this story, in fact you are pivotal to its success. Don't be afraid, as the story proceeds, all of your doubts and fears will be allayed and all of your questions about the island and your purpose in being here, will be revealed. You see how special this story is. It's really something."

With that, she brought the staff that she had held behind her back, round where they could see it and hoisted it high into the air. A shock of red lightning descended from the vaults of the heavens and struck the staff. All three of the watchers gasped aloud, each set of youthful eyes reflecting the red lightning. Each expected the Old Woman to be flung lifeless, backwards; to hit the deck with a heavy thud and to move no more. But no such thing happened. The Old Woman remained erect and the lightning whirled and swirled up and down the length of the twisted staff. The trio gawped in amazement.

Then Old Madame Fang wheeled slowly round and pointed the staff at the egg furthest from her, on the outermost reaches of the circle. A bolt of red lightning hissed down the length of the staff and shot across the circle into the egg. Old Ma Fang paused for a moment and then turned and pointed her staff at the next egg in the semi circle. The same thing happened again and as the lightning struck the egg, it glowed red, but not from the outside, from the inside. Here Ma paused and glanced back at her audience. They were very much captivated by her performance, fixated on her every word and gesture. She had no need to worry or hurry.

The trio felt the electricity crackling within them. It burnt away the cobwebs that festooned their minds and allowed them to see clearly, as Ma had intimated they would. Not only did they see with a newly pristine vision but they could also hear every leaf fall and every scurrying insect, crunch, grasp and slither on its solitary course through the jungle. It was quite the gift. But the show wasn't over. It was nowhere near. A third and then a fourth flash issued from the staff, and after each electrical discharge, Ma turned her hips, repositioning her staff so that each of the eggs was lit up in turn, until all nine had tasted the red fire. When she had finished her round, Ma once more swung the staff behind her back, held it in her fingers, parallel to the ground, and twirled it back and forth. As the long, red seconds ground down, there was no cue or clue as to what had just happened or what would happen next.

The tension built, and each of the trio watched the eggs in silent terror. An eerie light crawled upwards, from out of the ground, illuminating Old Ma Fang's face to ghastly effect and as the kids watched in mute terror and fascination it began to change, to become somehow less human. Ma seemed to swell in size, enveloped by her own shadow which ballooned and filled the grove, and her face took on a hellish aspect, swirling yellow, red and black. Off in the distance, they heard the sound of tribal drums, as if the cannibals had kicked up again but then the sound shifted and seemed to come from nowhere in particular. All sense of direction faded and sounds whizzed by on impossible tangents like an army of ghost trains.

The effect was singular and most disconcerting. One had the sensation of stepping off a rollercoaster, feeling the ground move, watching the world around one wheel. But the island wasn't a fair ground and this was no circus. The blood on their weapons testified to that. It had all been a game up to now, but the story was turning bad. The clowns had turned into zombies, the big top was a canopy of pox-ridden clouds pressing down on them, filled to the brim with the contagion of madness. Then bad became worse and fascination began to creep towards panic!

The atmosphere was changing; the hot, heavy air was turning

chill, needling them with icicles and the shivers. Ma Fang watched them and her black eyes turned red and blazed with the rage of an empire on fire. In the air around her, wheels of fire and eyes began to spin. Wheel upon crooked wheel in wonky rings showering the grove in sparks. For all that they had braved the horrors of the island, not Wilber, not Caleb, not even Lola was ready for this. This took them out further than they had ever gone. Yet for all that terror gripped them, they could not act! And Ma knew, knew that she had paralysed and mesmerised them and that there was no way out for the hapless trio. She began to speak again but now her voice had changed. It had lost its sweet, sing-song cadences and become demonic. It was enough to make one's hide crawl with the cold lick of primal fear. Now she was half singing, half chanting phrases that had the ring of demented nursery rhymes.

"Don't look back, kids. Know why? Eh? Eh? Go on, try! Try to guess. Awww bless! Cus you can't go back, kids. Turn around if you dare kids. Pull out all your hair, kids. Peer through the dark. Watch you don't burn your eyes on them sparks kids. See who's behind you. This is ju ju. My gift to you hoo is this old voodoo. Look behind you. It's Mr Zoo Zoo."

Her laughter crackled like an out of control fire and she spun each of the trio round like Catherine wheels as she showered them in sparks. Music split the night in half; drums warred with fiddles, flutes duelled with banjos and hell itself split the ground asunder and poured legions of demons into the bubbling air. Now raging flame, now freezing ice cap, there was no rhyme or reason to any of it. This was a state of pure and utter madness!!! But for all that, Old Ma Fang was enjoying herself immensely. It had been a while since she had partied this hard and she'd decided to rip a leaf out of the cannibal's cookbook and get jiggy with the meat, when the business of killing was over. Still it was just too much for one person to enjoy so out of the darkness, from directly behind them popped Herr Zoot. He sprang forward like a turbo charged tiger, hands clawed and his face a mask of feline rage. The frenzy had him by the tail and when Caleb looked in his eyes, his legs gave way and he screamed like a girl. Now Zoot was weighing in with the banter. Advancing on the terrified gaggle, who had wheeled and now stood back to back, weapons drawn, he howled like a banshee, then whirled like a dervish.

"Weirdos in speedos, eating nachos and eyeballs, ain't got nothing on me. I am out of my tree. Old Zoo Zoo, you see he gone Bu Bu. I am the man, yes I am the man with the plaguey breath and the plan, I am death, death in a yellow suit. Boo!!!"

With that last exclamation he leapt forward and Caleb swung the decapitator, just not fast enough. Laughing with insane glee, Zoot leaped backwards, out of the way of the slicing blade and did a mad taunting jig. He shook and convulsed like a man possessed, shaking all over, like he had just been spiked or was having an epileptic fit and all the time he laughed more and more loudly and in an ever ascending pitch. Wilber's eyes were out on stalks and he shook with terror. Oh let death come quickly let it fall with the speed of a guillotine. He just wanted out and he wanted it now.

Old Ma Fang advanced towards him with malevolent glee. The look in her burning eyes seemed to suggest she could read his thoughts. Wilber had tried to block her out, to stop her from entering his mind but unlike other mind invaders he had encountered, she just did not play ball. Like the mad music that was frying their brains, she came from no particular direction but all directions at once. Staring Wilber down hard, Old Ma Fang raised the crooked staff above her head and spat.

"No! No, no you can't look back. Your minds will crack. You gotta look forwards, seawards, landwards but never backwards. Wanna tip? Shoot from the hip! Grind away, now sway. Now focus behind me, you three. What can you see?"

The trio spun their heads round to face Ma and then felt their eyes drawn outwards to the fanned array of eggs. Ma cooed with delight.

"The eggs! Can't you see them kids. They got legs they 'av! You'll beg for death. What's inside you won't abide and they are all beginning to crack. Oh Lola, you're so solar. Coulda, shoulda been lunar. Easter came early for you little girly. And you're going to love. You're going to love what's inside. Yum, yum. Care to take a ride?"

On the opposite side of the circle, blocking their escape, Zoot's eyes shone with glee.

"Longer than a garden rake, our loving, laughing killer snakes. They could be real or they could be fake. You decide. The tide has turned. Now burn!"

Caleb, for all his fear of what was unfolding, was having none of it. Zoot and Ma Fang's rhymes were execrable. Worse than anything, they offended his sensibilities.

"Oh please. Get a life!"

Ma looked momentarily confused. "But we have life. In fact we have three. Three blind mice in for a surprise. Such a surprise to confront venomous eyes. Quite the shock. Ever looked down a well of bottomless eyes Caleb. Ever looked into the eyes of something trying to kill you? Eh, eh?"

"Every day!" was Caleb's snort, by way of a retort.

Ma's face blazed with sudden wrath and then was still again.

"One little nip and they'll permanently still you. In the end you'll beg for death. Me? I'll just suck down your final breath! Goodnight children. Good night."

And with this the ground ceased to glow and darkness enveloped them. All any of them could see was Ma's red eyes and Zoot's yellow eyes, twin poles of a whirling, spinning circle, a round in which they were imprisoned. Above them the thunder roared and the winds began to pick up, now groaning, now howling. Caleb gripped his sword, glancing rapidly, first right then left, then right again, from a world of red pain to a world of yellow fear and back again.

The red sun, going down, had almost been entirely swallowed by the black cloud. No light, nothing to see by, just the reality of darkness. Hope? No. Anything but. Red light burst out of each of the eggs, sending up twisting, fluted columns. The tops had popped! For too long the eggs had been fit to burst and now they had, their innards had convulsed and things were beginning to emerge, forced out into the fevered air. From the leaden, lumpen masses, forms were rising and the eggs were glowing, as if with excitement. The course, dark ovoid forms had lightened up and begun to glow, streaking the burned grove with iridescent light.

"What's happening?" Wilber yelled above the noise of the impending storm.

"Don't quote me," Lola deadpanned, "but I think we're about to be eaten alive. Hope you washed under your armpits this morning Wilber. Don't want to leave a bad taste in anybody's mouth."

68

Flow With Death

And just when it looked bleakest, just when the rainbow eggs were propelling their sinister cargoes out into the world, hope arrived in the form of pounding feet and flaming torches. The Alphabets were back! Wilber's heart leapt in his chest and he would have danced a fandango, were it not for the still-encroaching danger facing them. Now there was light to see by, he could see into the rage-twisted eyes and contorted face of Old Ma Fang. To say she was not a happy bunny was something of an understatement.

She was hopping mad and ready to kill each and every one of them.

Whipping around Wilber, studied the form of each of the Alphabet's, as though they were champion greyhounds he was preparing for a race. But wait! There was something wrong. He only counted seven in total. Who was missing? He scanned again and his blood iced over.

"Antelope, Antelope, where are Semantic and Edie? You didn't leave them behind did you?"

Five of the seven had formed a line to face down the creatures rising up out of the eggs, whilst the final two, Def and Beth stood with Lola to address the menace that was Zoot.

"No time for explanations Wilber. You have to go and now!"

"I'm not going anywhere."

"But there isn't time, Wilber."

Antelope's eyes were spilling tears and Wilber's heart melted. He understood without being told what had happened. She was right, was Antelope, there wasn't time for anything other than the essential, not now anyways, they could grieve when it all was over. Lest he forget this was war.

"We'll see this lot off, and then I'll go," he called back, steel in his voice, hate in his heart.

Old Ma Fang let out a cry like nails being dragged down a chalkboard.

"You ain't going nowhere but straight to hell, lil worm."

"I think not," Crimson spat and charged headlong into the fray.

The forms that had gestated within the eggs had now all uncoiled and stood majestic, but they weren't in motion, they were waiting for orders, expecting a round of applause or perhaps rosettes from the lady running this whole gymkhana. But, whilst they were terrifyingly snake-like with their gleaming skins and crested heads of red and gold, they weren't the brightest bulbs on the circuit board.

Caleb, running alongside of Crimson, let out a rebel yell and swung his sword horizontally, with all the power he could muster, and as a reward for his courage and due diligence, a slime-covered head 'geysered' blood and then arced through the air and landed at Old Ma Fang's feet. Her mouth, when she saw Caleb's gift formed a perfect 'O.'

Wilber was next out of the traps, swinging his bat like Joe DiMaggio and hitting a home run on his first ball. Indeed, all around the semi circle the rage-fuelled Alphabet's were cutting and slashing with perfect precision. It was as easy as docking swedes or nipping the heads off of daisies. Ma's children dropped one after another; and eldritch screams followed by sudden silence was the order of the day. Wilber was delighted and amazed to see that the girls had retooled and were now porting double-headed axes, which were already slick with black ooze.

But not everything would go their way that night.

Caleb delighted to have drawn first blood, foolishly turned his back on the action, seeking out Wilber in the fray, to boast of his prowess. It was just a game after all, wasn't it? Something to share and celebrate with one's fellow players.

Wrong move!

Seeing her chance, Old Ma Fang leapt in like a prop forward racing for the try line and sunk her long, yellow fangs into the skinny emo's neck. Then, viper that she was, she hung on, pumping all of the venom that she possessed into Caleb's bloodstream.

Wilber spun, when he heard the scream, and watched as Caleb sank to his knees, a thin line of blood oozing out of the left side of his mouth, the whites of his eyes already turning black, as though full of octopus ink.

"No!" he screamed but whilst he raced to meet his fallen, sometime-comrade, he knew it was already too late. Mid sprint he heard a muffled thump and a splat and turning yet again saw an even greater tale of woe.

Beth, sprawled belly down in the dust, her neck at an impossible angle, stared with unseeing eyes up into the cloud filled darkness. It was just too much to take in and rage mingled with grief took the Alphabets to a new level of frenzy.

Antelope and Frantic began hacking at the back of Old Ma Fang's thigh muscles with their axes as though trying to fell a brace of stubborn pines. Whilst the Old Viper was tough she wasn't so Teflon-coated that she couldn't be dropped. Releasing Caleb, in an absolute agony, she too slumped to her knees and Crimson quite literally disarmed her, with hands up to the elbows falling to earth with a phut-phut-ahhhh.

As for Zoot, his overconfidence and delight in destroying Beth led him to over balance and Lola and Def took either leg off at the knee. Like Fang he went down hard and stayed down, his chin buried in sandy soil.

So much for the best of Astapor's Agents.

This pair were minced beef, but it was small consolation for Lola. Leaving Zoot, half the man she had found him, she raced to join Wilber at Caleb's side. Wilber leaned back to give her space and in a jiffy she was cradling Caleb in her muscled arms. Shots could be heard off in the distance but nobody reacted. Everybody just stood and stared, some at Caleb, some at Beth. Not a tear fell amongst them.

In the last hour, all of the gang had undergone a quantum leap. In the unfolding battle that was to come, no quarter would be given, no prisoners taken.

It would simply be death or victory.

The wind continued to whine and howl, whipping everybody's hair up on end and making the trees dance like demented puppets. Now hot, now cold, it defied all reason. It was as if a hundred different winds from all points of the globe had converged on the island and were chasing each other's tails like yapping spaniels.

"It's the end of an era Lola," Caleb said quietly.

"It is that. Can you still see me sweet?" Lola asked tenderly.

"I'm afraid my old headlamps have gone out, thanks to that evil witch over there. Tell me she's suffering, Lolals."

Lola threw a quick glance at Fang, bleeding out in agony all over the burned earth. Fang stared back at her in utter hatred but they both knew she was finished.

"Don't worry angel-cake she is.

"Are you still there, L?"

A pause.

"Yes."

"It's just that I can't see you."

A longer pause.

"Really?"

Lola sounded a little bored.

"But in my mind's eye I can still see you. It was always you Lola, in spite of everything you did to hurt me, it was always you I loved."

Wilber, on the opposite side of the body to Lola, wanted to feel sadder than he actually was, and felt a little guilty when he stole a glance at his wrist watch."

20:20. It read.

OMG he thought and looked with pleading eyes at Lola who nodded at his unspoken request.

Caleb was drifting so Lola pinched him and he gave a little yip.

"I'm cold Lola, so cold, but I can see the waterfall. It is filled with rainbows. They sparkle and enthral. They make the cold bearable. It's just up ahead. Keep moving, you're so close. I'll wait for you there."

Lola, holding the body, was counting the seconds now.

"Oh Caleb don't die. It'll be so boring here without you."

She didn't sound entirely sincere and Wilber, caught between a rock and a hard place, winced.

"I can't feel my legs," Caleb announced suddenly.

"You always did have bad circulation. Oh Caleb I, I, I..."

Lola had run out of time and words.

"You what?" Caleb rasped. "You l...you lo.. Tell me you love me Lola."

Lola tried to form the words but they didn't come to easily.

"I, I..." she said.

But it was too late. Caleb's death rattle shook the wind and he was gone.

*　　　*　　　*　　　*　　　*　　　*　　　*

Counting down from five, Lola pushed the body away from her, like a used plate, and stood up. Wilber rose with her, like a stork from its feeding. Neither wanted to speak but the hour was late, very late, and it was Wilber who eventually broke the silence.

"So is it real? Is the game real?"

Lola went to say something, then looking in Wilber's hard, cold eyes she thought better of it and shook her head in a resounding affirmation.

"It's real. I lied. We need to go."

"We?" Wilber asked fighting hard not to slap her.

"If you'll have me".

Antelope standing beside them, arms folded was watching Old Ma Fang with what looked like more than a hint of enjoyment. With three of her girls dead in the last hour she had every justification and yet Wilber was saddened when he caught her eye. It was frightening how quickly people changed.

447

Was Astapor watching this and if so was he happy?

"I don't want to rush you or anything," Antelope said through clenched teeth, "but time is ticking. I'd hate to think we'd been through all of this for nothing. So if you could just get moving..."

Crimson stepped forward.

"We're not going anywhere. We have to bury Be..."

Antelope's slap was ridiculously hard. It caught Crimson on her left cheek and almost spun her round.

The remaining Alphabet's gasped as one. Even Def.

Only Wilber watched unmoved.

"There isn't time," Antelope said, her strangled voice sounding like a Dalek's.

No one said anything but out in the forest, to the east and to the south could be heard the sounds of distant screams and shrieks. They were getting nearer. No doubt Astapor's legions had caught a whiff of the scent of blood and were coming for a slap up gnosh-up. That didn't bode well for somebody.

Any guesses who?

Walking up to Wilber, Antelope reached behind her and drew a gun from the back of her pants and handed it to him without ceremony.

"Know how to use it?"

"Yeah."

"if you need to, use it. You have six bullets. Don't waste any."

They both of them, looked at Lola and Wilber nodded.

"What will you do?"

Antelope considered.

"We, none of us can follow you into the burning grounds. You're on your own. I hope for your sake that she can help you Wilber and that she will help you. She knows more about this mad island than anyone on it, even Astapor." A pause. "If anyone can do this, Wilber, you can."

Wilber checked his watch again.

"I'm sorry, Ant, I have to go."

"I know."

"Will you take care of Zoot and Fang."

Without speaking Antelope shook her head.

"It's more than they deserve but we'll do it. Now go. We'll be waiting for you on Black Sands by the Western Time Gate. Everybody will be there."

"Everybody?" Wilber replied in surprise.

Crimson, her face well... crimson stepped forward

"You've triggered End Game Wilber."

"What does that mean exactly?"

"All out war," Def chipped in.

Antelope grinned maniacally.

"Everybody has to choose a side and fight. They will either oppose you or assist you. It's as simple as that. Astapor and the other Magicians are no doubt, by now, on their way to the sands with the five armies. It's all kicking off. Please, you have to go now if you're to have any chance of succeeding. Don't let Beth and the others have died in vain.

Antelope handed Wilber her torch and almost against his will Wilber and Lola took off, running towards a place where compasses span without stopping and nobody else dared follow.

Left alone, the Alphabets stood silently, eyes fixed on their leader. The sounds of yelping and screeching were growing deafening. Soon Astapor's beasts would arrive.

"Well," said Def suddenly, "I'll do Zoot if you do Fang. Deal?"

Antelope eyed her coldly.

"No. Leave them."

And before anyone could protest she was off and running towards the Western Gate. The others were soon after her. Only Def tarried, curious to see what Fang would do. Holding her torch up to the witches face she saw that Fang clearly understood and that for the first time in her life the witch was actually afraid. Def gave a laugh and followed her friends.

Behind her in the darkness she heard the sound of anguished sobs.

69

Reunion

Something was definitely kicking off. You didn't have to be a genius to work that out.

More and more gunshots continued to sound all over the island, and not just on the Western side either, all over. With them could be heard the screams of the recently deceased, the dead and the dying. Howls and barks, shrieks and wails tore the jungle apart. Everything that Astapor had buried beneath the ground, all his nightmares made flesh, had been released. They poured out into the world full of rage and the need to destroy whatever and whoever they met, and because of this, none were safe. The once human, when they encountered one another tore each other to pieces and feasted on shredded flesh. Danger was close and getting closer. It was no longer behind bars or safely contained within a screen. Now it was out and about, bearing down on those who remained. It was a gust of hot breath upon your shoulder.

A vast equation of being was being reformulated and every superfluous term was being crossed out or cancelled. Young Muldoon saw it as he ran northwards with Lola into the burning grounds, the plan of an old world, of a Universal model, coming to the end of its life. Millennia to build and unfold, then a few hours to destroy. But it would not go quietly, that Old World. It would fight tooth and nail for its survival and who could blame it. The New World would have to be built along more powerful lines than the Old, if it was to survive its infancy.

Wilber ran away from Burnt Grove, happy to abandon the mess and grief he had left there. He ran, as he had run, since the first moment he had stepped on the accursed island and he did not look back. Now, as they entered End Game, there could only be more and more casualties in the War for the Island's Soul. Caleb, for instance, lay cooling with unseeing eyes and a body drained of blood alongside Old Ma Fang. She had succumbed, in terror, to a party of flesh rippers and squealers who had torn her and her young to foaming strips of meat. She had screamed, at the last, in a crazed sort of ecstasy, as her head had come away from her torso, in an explosive fountain of blood and gore that was quickly followed by the frenzied detachment of her arms and partially severed legs.

For all that she was totally foul, the squealers had seemed to enjoy devouring her. They cracked her skull and gulped her brains down with enviable relish and squealed with full bellies and the taste of blood still on their lips as they took to the jungle once more.

As for Herr Zoot, a squad of Pouncers, Mekons and Crunchers had done for him. When they had finished, his suit no longer looked like one of Jim Carey's castoffs. It was a crimson mess and he was fingerless, noseless and clueless thanks to the Crunchers whose oversized teeth made short work of his spindly, if powerful, fingers. The Pouncers leapt and leapt again till sheer weight of numbers bore him down to the ground. Then the lumbering Mekons had dragged him by his stumps into the underbrush as he bellowed like a gored bull. His end was slow and painful as the band of brothers, who had so often tasted Astapor's lash, tasted the flesh of one of his most loyal retainers. They ate slowly and with relish. They ate Herr Zoot alive and none lived that felt one iota of remorse.

There was so much rage in the forest but then what else was to be expected? People who had been so cruelly used and abused, once released were not going to forgive and forget. Their minds may have been smashed but they were still capable of action. They could run and hunt and they could kill and eat and by Jove they did.

*   *   *   *   *   *   *

The Russian watched as his island came apart at the seams but he did not seem unduly phased. Not by any of it. His expression was blank, almost autistically so. More and more of his loyal retainers fell, in the process of keeping him safe, but that was to be expected. It was what they were trained to do, after all. So why should he show surprise? End Game was unfolding and only the ruthless and the lucky could or would survive.

Back up the hill, on top of the volcano the last of the eight towers was exploding, sending up wave after wave of sparks and then raging, devouring flame. Black smoke spilled into the air and drifted up into the black cloud, which absorbed it without comment. Semantic had done a thorough job in laying the explosions. Her father had taught her well, Astapor would concede that. If she hadn't been so damaged, she could perhaps have been turned and made useful, but her pathological hatred of him rendered her unsafe. So he had given the order and one of his bodyguards, he forgot which, had blown a tunnel through the back of her head and despatched her to infinity. And beyond! It was all so pleasingly apocalyptic, yet to observing eyes, it did not appear that he cared. Drull approached, watching his master carefully, looking for signs that danger might envelop him.

"We've picked up the scent!"

"Man or Boy?" Astapor asked without a moment's pause.

"Both."

Astapor nodded.

"No mean feat in this melee. I commend you Drull. We'll follow the boy and deal with Muldoon Senior later."

Drull set off at a run after the man with the straining tracker dogs and Astapor joined him, closely followed by his surviving bodyguard and a trembling Lurch. It did not take them long to reach the Burnt Grove, where they quickly identified what little remained of Beth, Fang and Zoot, along with Fang's children. For some reason though Caleb's body was untouched.

"Seems like the Crunchers, Pouncers and Mekons had a field day," Lurch said, examining a partially gnawed foot. "Nice to know something still works around here."

Astapor kneeling beside the boy addressed one of his soldiers tersely.

"Take the boy to Mr Lapp."

The soldier complied and Astapor rose.

Drull and his tracker were again examining tracks that led from the Burnt Grove in any number of directions. It took a while, but they soon had it figured out, and Drull, aware of the limitations of time, was immediately moving over to where Astapor stood awaiting his report. Without further ado, he began to speak.

"The boy and the girl both survived. They have headed off into the Burning Grounds. The remaining Alphabets look as though they are headed West to Black Sands. My guess would be that they are arranging their defences against us."

Showing no sign that he had heard, Astapor moved to the Northern side of the Burnt Grove where Lola and Wilber had exited on their way to the Burning Grounds and stood looking off into the gathering gloom. Perplexed for a moment, he suddenly saw the reason why and nodded grimly, applauding the boy's foresight.

So End Game was really on.

As much as he was drawn by the pull of the Burning Grounds, the Russian knew he could not enter them and live. Turning on his heel, he moved to the Western Side of the grove and without a word of explanation headed off into the darkness. Drull and the rest of the party followed, knowing better than to question their Leader. From here on in anything could and would happen.

*　　　*　　　*　　　*　　　*　　　*　　　*

As soon as they left the Burnt Grove, Lola took Wilber's hand in hers. Turning, Wilber looked her in the eye, surprised and just a little afraid, because in spite of what his instincts told him, he felt his heart give a little flutter.

"What are you doing?"

"What does it look like?"

Wilber gulped.

"What it is."

Lola removed her shades and put them in her coat pocket.

"Yeah okay, let's go," she said impatiently.

Wilber wheeled and lifted his torch high into the air. Then they took off. Through the few remaining trees that surrounded Burnt Grove they ran, hand in hand, until a deep crack in the earth brought them to a halt. It was not yet entirely dark and thank god for that, or they wouldn't have seen the cleft ground. Patches of red sunlight still burst through the cloud here and there, illuminating the barren landscape with splotches of colour. Not much, but just enough to see by.

"What do you suppose did that?" Wilber asked.

Lola shrugged.

"Well it wasn't a cannon ball, I'm sure of that."

In spite of himself, Wilber laughed.

"What a leftfield thing to say."

"If you want a commonplace commentary you have the wrong girl."

And seizing Wilber's hand again she dragged him into motion and on they jogged, one eye on the ground and one on what was coming at them, from out of the semi-darkness. In a matter of minutes, smoke or mist of some sort had begun to drift towards them. At first, Wilber assumed it was a cloud but when he examined it he saw that it was yellowish-green. His first thought ran to sulphur, what with them being on the slopes of a still active volcano, but the vapour did not carry the tell-tale odour of raw eggs.

"What do you suppose it is Lola?"

Lola, still running, harrumphed.

"It's the Burning Grounds. That's what that is."

And as if to support her assertion, something loomed up before them out of the fog. Something huge and wholly unexpected. Wilber gave a gasp and almost pulled up short but again Lola dragged him on. The shock almost unhinged him but quickly he got a grip. Moments passed before he was able to articulate a clear thought though.

"Was that what I think it was?"

"Depends what you think it was," Lola deadpanned.

"Well I'm no expert but I'd say it was an eighteenth century galleon of some sort."

"Napoleonic," Lola added, keen to inform, yet equally keen to save her breath.

Wilber's silence was not entirely healthy, and sighing, with a fair degree of exasperation, Lola felt duty-bound to elaborate. But not wholly.

"Well, they are the burning grounds. What do you expect?"

Wilber couldn't believe his ears.

"You've got to be kidding! Come on Lola, play the game. Give me a heads up. Tell me in words of one or more syllables what in the name of all that's holy are the burning grounds?"

"They're just up ahead," she shot back.

Wilber let out a low groan as if he'd just been hit by a flying cannonball. Lola, aware that she had run out of ground back-peddled.

"I'm sorry Wilber, to be so vague and all but I was kinda hoping we could go around them. It's not healthy in here. The Burning Grounds are a sort of No Go Zone where we islanders are concerned, what with all the crashed spaceships and the radioactivity and all."

This just about finished Wilber off and he shrieked, like he'd been cut and burned at the same time.

"That is not what I wanted to hear Lola!"

Fighting hard to control herself, Lola let out an explosive sigh that ended in a curse.

"Well I'm sorry Wilber, I really don't know what to tell you. The burning grounds are the burning grounds, and that's that. I see them as being like the elephant's graveyard in an old Tarzan movie. They are where things that are old and outmoded go to die. Only the things in here were dragged in against their will. They were caught up in storms or in the doldrums from all over the place. And I don't just mean on Earth."

This shut Wilber up for a while. But only for a while.

"You mean there's like, stuff in here from other worlds?"

"I do."

The fog or mist was getting thicker and the ground was becoming more and more uneven, yet unlike before, they seemed to know exactly where they had to go. Why this should be the case neither could say but it was though they were being pulled along on invisible cables.

"You mean like spaceships?"

"That's right."

"But how do you know that?"

Without sign or warning Lola stopped running and Wilber was forced to stop too. She turned to face him with a look that was half anger, half desperation.

"Because I've seen them up close. I mean like really close Wilber. Like I've been on them, sometimes for days at a time. Only thing is when I wander back up the hill I've lost all memory of what I've seen or done. I just know that I've been away. Oh I've been interrogated like, dozens of times but always my questioners draw a blank and let me go. So now you know. Satisfied?"

Wilber let this sink in for a moment before speaking.

"Look Lola, I'm only here because I don't have all the crystals. You know that right?"

Lola shook her head in affirmation. Suddenly she looked incredibly tired.

"You're being used, Wilber, don't you understand that yet?"

"All I know is that I need to find that crystal and in the next ten or fifteen minutes. Have you any idea of how I can do that Lola?"

Looking utterly defeated Lola let out a cry and then collapsed in a heap on the ground. She seemed exhausted and totally broken. So lacking in energy that she couldn't even lift her head.

"I can't go on. You'll have to do it on your own Wilber. Look for clues amongst your memories, follow the images that flash like lighted signposts in your head. Things that nobody else but you can see. This isn't an easy game to win, Wilber. It's a game played with loaded dice. On this island nobody is who you think they are."

Here her voice trailed off. Wilber thought she was finished yet she spoke again

"These are the burning grounds. They're the last real obstacle before you reach the time gate. Solve this and you're in with a chance. But first ask yourself a question.

What was it that caused this place to burn?"

70

The Skies Fill With Crows

Smithy and Carruthers were deep in conversation when Crowhaven came out of the mansion, clad from head to foot in combat fatigues. They stopped talking when they saw him, stood to attention and saluted. It was obvious to the meanest observer who they were and what life they had led prior to this, despite their morning suits. The military left its mark for life and no man, however careful, could disguise it.

It had been quite a day already, what with the arrival of Young Muldoon and the instigation of Operation Ascension. Despite his outward civility and graceful manner, Crowhaven was not a kind man. Moreover he was a difficult man to work for. He'd awoken, just prior to dawn, in a foul temper and eaten alone in his den, surrounded by stuffed animals, whilst he awaited developments. Very much the Nineteenth Century Victorian collector was the Professor, happiest when he was taking things to pieces or predicting probabilities. In all things he engaged in, he insisted on absolute accuracy in the recording and reporting of events, not least in the outcomes of his many 'experiments'.

Looking up, he clicked his fingers and Smithy almost launched himself across the lawn.

"I'd appreciate more warning in future. You're beginning to look a little sloppy and we can't have that now, can we?"

"My apologies Sir".

The Professor did not respond. He heard and he didn't hear because his mind was elsewhere, racing simultaneously over a wide range of problems. Too often it went too fast for others to follow, filled as it was with spooling figures and ever flickering schemata. He saw numbers. Numbers in rivers. Numbers in space. Travelling numbers. Numbering changing, ticking down, or ticking up. In ordered sequence.

His world was a domain modelled with numbers. It was cool, vast and ordered and at any one moment he could be building or dismantling models of any number of structures, organisations or plans.

Temples, banks, airports, cities, worlds, galaxies, the Universe, the Multiverse. For him they were nothing more than numbers, all numbers, flowing, moving and shifting in sequences that he had often predicted. That was when he was happiest, when everything he surveyed moved in harmonious relation. No number was too big or too small for him to handle. In his world of numbers, he was God. The trouble occurred when other people entered his world. They knocked things off of shelves. He lost sight of where things were, where they should be. His world had been disordered by recent events. Somebody was messing with the plan. And they'd pay. By God they'd pay.

Without warning the Professor resurfaced from his sea of numbers and looked inquiringly at his aides.

"Why aren't you changed? It's 19.30 already."

Smithy cleared his throat, whilst Carruthers looked hard at the ground. It was a tried and tested routine, for both of them. In situations like these Carruthers had discovered it was always best to let Smithy do the talking.

"We've been monitoring events as they have been unfolding, Sir."

"And?" Crowhaven shot back.

"It's as you predicted Sir. The boy is a definite prospect. Four in the bag and the fifth winging its way towards him as we speak."

"And George?"

"Proceeding as instructed, Sir" Smithy replied, a smile plastered on his clean shaven face.

Crowhaven, with his hands grasped firmly behind his back,

began to pace back and forth. Plans were all well and good when they were in your head, or even on paper, it was their implementation that caused him sleepless nights. Oh he had a pretty good poker face but when the stakes were as high as this, well even he let things slip.

"I'm agitated, Smithy."

"I can see that Sir."

"I don't blame you Smithy. Events are not always controllable. I'd just appreciate it if you communicated change, rapidly, efficiently, effectively. I've never had cause to discipline you before; I've never expressed displeasure at your work have I? Never. But I am displeased now and trying to manage my mood. You know, you can see that, so hopefully you won't hold it against me or let it interfere with your work. I'm a very ordered man, you know."

"Indeed, you are Sir."

"I don't need confirmation from you Smithy."

"Right you are Sir."

Crowhaven paused and permitted himself a wry smile. He knew he nagged the lads but it wasn't personal, it was never personal.

"So what happened? Who do you suspect?"

Smithy was always thorough and he resented the implication that he was somehow at fault, but Crowhaven was the Number 1 and he must be respected. He had to handle his feelings of grievance, to bury them. Think, think. Only think. He instructed himself. With careful analysis, inductive and deductive logic, he would form a menu of possibilities. From these possibilities, strategies would evolve. Plans of action etc to be implemented with Crowhaven's approval. Now was not a time for self reproach nor precipitous action, but a time to be ultra cautious, quieter, slower, somehow more sensitive to his environment. So. How to proceed.

"Sir I could tell you what I think you want to hear or I could just tell you the truth. Which would you prefer?"

Crowhaven arched an eyebrow. Smithy's opening gambit was a bold one.

"Do you really have to ask that Smithy? Am I such an

unreasonable tyrant?"

Smithy's rejoinder was calculated to flatter in a minor key.

"You are a brilliant and a complex man Sir whom I respect more than any other. With that in mind I have to tell you we are still no nearer to discovering who or what has set this chain of events in motion. Everything could be as it appears or nothing could be as it appears."

Crowhaven took a moment to digest the contents of Smithy's speech.

"I don't like this, I don't like it at all. I prefer to act when in full possession of the facts, you know that, but here we're travelling blind, not light!"

His reverie was interrupted by a series of explosions up on top of the volcano and each of the men turned and looked towards them with something akin to astonishment. Flame and smoke billowed skywards indicating that events were taking a definitive turn.

It was Crowhaven who broke the silence.

"What am I seeing Carruthers? Can you enlighten me?"

Carruthers took out his radio and spoke into it for a full minute or so. Then he listened to the responses to his questions with marked care, in a state of rapt silence. Crowhaven, like Astapor, had eyes all over the place. He even had eyes up on top of the volcano, well hidden eyes that could not be tricked or panicked. After another thirty seconds or so, Carruthers called over and out and turned back to Crowhaven to report.

"You're not going to believe this Sir."

"Try me."

"The Alphabet Gang have gone rogue and blown three of the Russian's towers to kingdom come."

Crowhaven's eyes glazed over in delight.

"Go on..."

"But better than that the Russian has been forced out of his lair and is at large on the island. His forces, whilst heavily armed, are in disarray."

"There's more isn't there?" Crowhaven asked, staring hard into Carruthers' narrow eyes.

"Yes Sir, but not all of it good."

"Proceed."

"It would appear the Russian has emptied his silos and flooded the island with every kind of variant he has ever created. They are running amok, killing and eating everything in their path, even each other. If our reports are to be believed, the Russian is headed over to the west side of the island in a vain attempt to capture Young Muldoon and to prevent him joining up with his Uncle and obtaining the last of the crystals."

Crowhaven turned again at the sound of another brace of explosions. More smoke and more flame and another two of the Russian's towers up the swannie. It appeared too good to be true but was it? Crowhaven, responding to decades of sceptical appraisal seasoned by faultless logic, and not a little cunning, weighed his words and his options carefully.

"Might we postulate that the Russian, or another one of my colleagues, is running a scam, trying to overturn a long established order by forcing our hand, inducing us to act precipitously?"

"Hard to say, Sir," replied Carruthers. "It's a possibility, but as you can see by those burning towers not everything can be predicted. Not everyone acts as they are supposed to. We have to respond in real time. As of this moment the readiness is all. You know what they say about not looking a gift horse in the mouth."

"Indeed I do and as much as I loathe commonplace expressions I have to agree with the sentiments expressed in that last one."

Carruthers inclined his head in a short, economic bow.

Crowhaven took a moment to consider his options and rapidly came to a conclusion.

"Doubt aside, It's time to act."

"Yes Sir," Smithy and Carruthers chorused, glancing quickly at one another, fighting hard to keep the grins of their excited faces. This was what they had trained so long and assiduously for.

"Are the boys in place?"

"All three squadrons," Smithy reported. "Upwards of a hundred men in the field already. One on top of the volcano, one on the East End watching those damned cannibals and the third following the Russian's party. All dug in, all camouflaged, all awaiting instruction"

"Then give the order Smithy. Attack! Attack! Attack. Leave none alive."

"Yes Sir."

"None," Crowhaven reiterated, slicing the air downwards with his outstretched arm.

Carruthers changed the channel on his walky-talky and relayed Crowhaven's orders to each of the Squadron Commanders in turn. Within a matter of seconds the sound of machine gun fire began to break out sporadically all over the island.

Crowhaven beamed from ear to ear.

"It's done then."

"Indeed it is Sir," Smithy confirmed.

"Rest of the lad's ready?"

"All of them. Just coming down the eighteenth fairway now, all kitted out and ready for the Big Push."

Crowhaven wheeled and to his delight saw the men hoving into view. The second battalion was larger than the first and much better armed. Crowhaven felt his chest swell up with pride.

"Do you think the Russian suspects?"

Carruthers looked doubtful.

"Astapor is such an unknown quantity, Sir. You know as well as I do that the Russian can never be anticipated or controlled. Too damaged and too damn clever by half. Two minds in one body; one a mind of complete chaos and disorder; the second a mind of absolute and pristine order."

"And one never knows which one one is dealing with." Crowhaven said grimly.

"Precisely Sir," Smithy affirmed. "You have it in a nutshell, bounded in infinite space I might add."

Carruthers nodded thoughtfully.

"Whatever happens we are committed now Sir. There is no going back, as I'm sure you know. The Russian must be neutralised and permanently. After that we'll need to survey the lie of the land vis-à-vis the remaining Magi and their forces. Your elevation may not go unopposed."

Crowhaven turned and looked down the eighteenth fairway to where Battalion Two was marching, approaching him in six well ordered columns. By Jove, but they looked the business. Armed to the teeth and ready to do what must be done to secure the island. For progress, for science and exploration. Yes, he would move the island out of the dark ages and into the light. None would be allowed to stand in his way. No one! And if the Government Forces on the other side of the veil refused to play ball he would have to teach them a lesson or two as well. Time was a more deadly weapon than bombs had ever been. And anybody who did not understand that formulation was doomed.

The troops pulled up in front of the Manor House on the eighteenth green and rapidly fell into formation. Johnno called Ten-Hut and a hundred and fifty pairs of boots snapped to alert. Crowhaven ran a critical eye over his troops and gave an almost imperceptible nod.

"Stand at ease men."

The Battalion, as one, obeyed.

"So this is the moment we have all been waiting for. Down all the years, down all the days. All previous time was simply a preparation and it dissolves into this now, the moment of change. You know as well as I do that the Russian is a master of horror and surprise. So be prepared for anything and remember, shoot first. Ask questions later. Leave none alive, save the Muldoon boy and the Russian."

Carruthers' face clouded over, as though he didn't quite understand something.

"The Russian?"

Crowhaven laughed like a child given a new toy.

"Oh yes, I have plans for him too. Whether you like it or not, the

Russian is very much a part of all our futures. You don't throw a man like him away."

And with that he gave the signal for his men to form up and march out. Which they did without question. Within moments they had faded into the jungle en route to the Black Sands.

71

Final Dilemmas

Wilber staggered on alone, through the thickening fog, in a state of shock and desperation. The familiar rocks and trees that had constituted the island lay far behind him. The swaying palms and pines, the long grasses and mangroves, had ceased to exist along with his nearest and dearest. Uncle Patrick, Great Uncle Muldoon, his mother and father, the Alphabets, Caleb and even Lola were gone. Committed to the past like bodies buried in the ground. To rot and be forgotten.

Now the ground he covered was wholly other. The sand beneath his feet was pink and sugary, corrosive to the touch, and what few trees there were around him seemed made not of bark and branch but of flesh and bone, their leaves of skin. And they were full of eyes, those trees. Not just knots in ancient wood but functional organs, black and deep and knowing. Often in clusters, like spider's eyes, they watched. And mouths opened in the bloodied trunks and issued frequencies of sound and pitch almost impossible to endure.

Yet endure those hellish frequencies Wilber did as he half-ran, half-stumbled through the burning grounds where the air smelled of barbequed flesh and tasted of despair. Such a haunting place, where no one of sound body or mind would dare venture. Did that make him mad? He wondered. Then he let it go. There really wasn't time for conjectures of that nature...

And now finally, the storm began to break, that which had built steadily throughout Wilber's Running Time, began to pour down upon him. The swollen, black clouds that filled the overhanging sky emptied their fetid bags onto that which ran upon the earth below. The grey air was instantly awash and microscopic clouds of life teemed amidst the rain-slashed vapours. Breathing the air Wilber felt diseased, like he had a terminal illness. It tasted of iron filings and rotten oranges, that air, and it was enough to make you want to heave. But Wilber didn't have the time, not even to open his mouth and empty his guts. He had to complete the game!

Somewhere deep inside of him, a voice that sounded like his mother's begged him to stop to rest but he couldn't, he wouldn't, knowing that he would run until he dropped, until his heart stopped or he was blown to oblivion. As he plunged further and further into the burning grounds his sense of anxiety grew, knotting his stomach, leading him into an ever-weakening state of fear. It was one thing to be terrified of something immediate within one's environment, like a zombie or a croc, it was another thing entirely to be mauled by a horror one could not see, or even imagine. The deeper in he penetrated, the more vile the stench around him became, but also more strangely, the deeper in he got, the more charged and energised he felt.

Oh, the fear was still there all right, weighing him down, but it was not overwhelming him. He could function and do so well. And for the first time since being here, his feet knew where he was going. He did not need to consult a map or study a compass. The way was clear. To what he didn't know, but his sense of excitement grew and grew and that was the arrow that guided him now. The flaming torch in his hand guttered and threatened to go out, so Wilber stopped momentarily, removed his t-shirt and wrapped the sweat-saturated garment around the business end of his stick. The flame flared and revived, burning now with a green flame. He would have preferred to have wrapped the T-shirt around his mouth and nose, to alleviate the stench and lessen his suffering, but it was not a priority.

With naked upper half, he took off again. Beneath his feet he was fascinated to see the colour of the sand shift from pink to blue. And then looming suddenly on the left and to the right were huge, mist-veiled structures. Curiosity got the better of him and he stopped to examine one.

Then the realisation struck. The Burning Grounds were filled with ships and boats, of iron and wood from all ages. There were sailing ships, to be sure, from many a distant century but there were also modern trawlers and battleships too. It was like an elephant's graveyard with rusted spars for ivory and rotten hulls for spine and rib. Wilber so wanted to stop and explore, like any excited child in a new place of wonders, but he forced himself onwards. The lessons of the Cosmic Crystal had taught him the perils of distraction. To lose focus was to condemn oneself to failure, a watcher merely in someone else's game, confined to a labyrinth that was both prison and hell. But what of the final crystal? Where was it, could it be near?

On and on he plunged into the all enveloping fog. He should have been exhausted by now but for some reason, not yet clear, Wilber felt a great surge of excitement coursing through him, filling him with energy and hope. Delight even. He suddenly felt like a huge release was imminent and he raised his arms above his head so that his body was transformed into the letter 'Y'.

Why he did it, he couldn't say. All he knew was that he had pulled up, that he was running on automatic pilot and that something was coming. Wilber felt pretty nauseous. The air was minging, worse than Astapor's bog after a night on the borscht, but his fear was ebbing, his sense of possibilities and purpose growing. And there it was. He heard it and tensed; the sound of feet running towards him, over the blue sands. He could have legged it; in his present state he believed he could have easily outrun any pursuer, whatever their calibre. But something within said no. Stop. Face it.

Thus prevented, he waited, and the rain that had been falling steadily, intensified, lashing the sands with its stinging drops. And then from out of the fog a figure burst forth and Wilber gasped when he saw who it was. Dinosaur George Muldoon!!! And clutched in his arms, unbelievably was Lola. Wilber let out a howl of pain and joy such as the island had never heard and he ran and flung himself on his Uncle and soon they were both sobbing. The sense of relief was palpable. Crushed Lola, jammed between the reunited Uncle and Nephew was not quite so relieved, and let out a bat-like squeak. The Muldoons sprang apart and George set her down carefully, like she was a priceless statue, recently recovered from the sea. And there she stood, lank and wavering, a sinewy femme fatale with a killer look and a drenched barnet. Her long coat was soaked and but for the rain she would have broken out the cigars. Her black trousers and boots were filthy and her leather gloves were virtually ruined but she was on message and on song.

"Boys, save the hot love for later, we still have a job to do. You dig?"

Dinosaur George looked back at Wilber and cocked his head to one side.

"I found her crawling through the mud. She with us?"

"Err... yeah," Wilber replied. "She is." He shook his head in joyous disbelief. "George you're here! I can't believe it...but at the same time I always knew you'd make it. This voice inside said keep going, everything will be alright."

"Really?" George sounded dubious.

"So how did you get here?" Wilber asked.

"I ran."

As obvious as that was, Wilber couldn't help but be moved. Quickly they embraced and held each only with a force of love that would have powered a sun. It was only Lola's exasperated sighs that broke them apart.

"I hardly dare ask," Wilber gabbled, "but do you have it?"

A slow smile spread over George's rain-drenched face. Reaching into his pocket he pulled out a rag wrapped around an object and handed it to Wilber. Scarcely able to stand the tension, Wilber's whole body began to shake as he folded the sides of the rag away from the object. And there it was. The Fire Crystal, the Tetrahedron, The Eye of Astapor. They stood in silence and wonder and once more it was Lola who broke the spell.

"Boys, we're running out of time. It's 20:39. Just over twenty minutes left."

Wilber stared into the crystal's depths and then he scrunched up his brow and worry lines appeared.

"There's something wrong here George. It doesn't feel like the other crystals."

George nodded in agreement.

"That's because it isn't. Astapor deactivated it."

Wilber cursed and George arched an eyebrow.

"How'd he do that?"

"I dunno."

"Where'd you get it?"

"Too long of a story. It was beneath the labyrinth."

Wilber's eyes lit up.

"What about Uncle Patrick?"

George looked at the ground for long seconds and when he raised his eyes again they were red and bloodshot.

"He didn't make it. This is going to be hard for you to hear Wilber but he was in league with Astapor. They did some kind of deal. Patrick was always jealous of me and he was resentful of the fact I left the island without him. And he was tired and broken from living in a permanent state of anxiety and squalor. After Madeline died I couldn't face being here. I knew what I'd become so I ran and I left him and Uncle to their fate."

"It was Patrick's choice George. It wasn't your fault."

"I know that, but he came good at the end. He saved me and he suffered horribly for it. But through him I got out of the labyrinth. And from there I went into the Magma Chambers and found Astapor's guardians. There were nine of them and boy were they vicious and God were they strong."

"So where was the crystal?"

George suddenly looked a little embarrassed.

"Astapor had buried it in the brow of the Lead Guardian. He'd performed some kind of whacked out surgery on it, deranged Cossack that he is, and embedded it in the skull, but in a way that it was still visible. That's one of the rules that bind the Magicians I figured. The crystals have to be visible at all times to the Runners.

You can place any number of obstacles in their way but the crystals must always be in plain sight."

Wilber looked at his Uncle with admiration. It was obvious that they thought alike, that he, Wilber, was a chip off the old block. That was all well and good but there were still mysteries unsolved, still a line that lay untrodden between this moment and the End Zone.

"So what's next, George?"

George just looked at Wilber gone out.

"But I thought you'd know. I just had this overwhelming sense that you'd...."

"What? Have the answer?" Wilber spat, taking his cue from Lola for a change.

"Oh for the love of madness," Lola explained. "20:40!" she yelled at the top of her lungs.

"George I have collected, at no great risk to my person and my sanity, with your help admittedly, all five of the crystals. I have dispatched other children into oblivion in a cruel game of truth and lies. I have swum through alligator and crocodile infested waters, wrestled with harpies, endured psychological torments at the hands of Mr Hands and Mr Lapp and solved every riddle, puzzle and enigma placed before me to get here, into this moment, with all five crystals in my possession. It's a feat that has not been accomplished since the game began. When was that? What, 70 years ago? More? Now all you have to do is one thing, you just have to tell me how to activate the final crystal and get off this island, taking everybody who wants to come along with us. So, you know what I'm asking? So what's the answer?"

Dinosaur George Muldoon, a larger than life legend, polymath, professor and privateer just stood in the pouring rain, dripping, without a clue. Wilber felt in that moment like his soul would tear in two, like a sail caught in a hurricane. Time was ticking, time that they didn't have. What were they to do? At last a spark of recognition, or something, ignited in the Older Man's eyes.

"What is it George," Wilber asked, unable to mask his

desperation. "What do you know?"

"Down in the labyrinth, Patrick mentioned something about mirrors being not what they seemed. And they weren't. They were the doors out of the labyrinth. At first I just thought it was a cruel joke, but in the heat of the moment, the answer just dropped into my lap and I ran at the glass and smashed through it."

So the answer had been there all along. Wilber let his mind go slack. Didn't matter that the clock was ticking. Didn't matter that everything they had fought for would be lost. He cared and he didn't care. And in that instant, his mind took him back to Mr Lapp to when they had first met. To when Mr Lapp had infuriated him to such an extent that he had kicked him out of his hammock. Mr Lapp had been surrounded by Blue Light and Lightning had flashed in the air above him.

"What's that?" he had asked and Mr Lapp had replied, "It's a clue."

"Lightning," Wilber said.

George took hold of both of his hands as his nephew just stared off into the beyond.

"What is it Wilber, what do you know?"

"Lapp said that lightning was a clue and it is. Mr Hands said that all roads lead to the Burning Grounds. And they do. It's here the lightning will come."

"From the skies," George asked tilting his head backwards, "surveying the teeming heavens doubtfully.

"No, there's something hidden here. Something crashed and partially buried. The lightning will come from there."

Now it was George's turn to look off into the beyond. It was a while before he could speak.

"The burning grounds are different from the rest of the island. You must feel that Wilber. They have a heart, a centre, that sees and knows and there is a life in that centre. A life that Astapor drew here and trapped. He has found some way to harness the energy of that life but he has lied to it and misled it and now it feeds the island its rage and its pain. Look around you and you can see its agony etched onto the face of every tree."

"I can see it Uncle. It's plain as day. I understand now what I must do.

George shivered then and not just because of the cold.

"It isn't just boats and ships that have crashed here, is it? It's space ships. Beings from other realms and dimensions. Am I right?"

"You are. The tower complex sends out the signals and the volcano and the lightning opens the time gate. It's just one big, baited trap, the whole island. It was always set up that way. Although Astapor wages war against the human, that is not his real project. He plays a much bigger game, the games that Governments play. The real game is between the humans and the Star People. The Governments want them you see, along with their technology, and Astapor has learned how to trap them and to prevent them from communicating with their kin."

"How do you know all this George?"

"Because once upon a time I was part of the project. I was sent here to assist Astapor but I guess we both got a little sidetracked."

Wilber took a moment to digest this new information.

"So all that stuff about you being a dinosaur hunter..."

"Just a cover, a splendid story that gave me leave to roam the world, following my dream. It wasn't bones I was after though, but buried treasure, remnants of the lost technology of Atlantis. That's what lies behind the tech explosion that gripped the twentieth and now the twentieth first century. There's no way we could have grown at the rate we have without those finds, reverse engineered and dispatched to the world through dummy corporations. They appear independent but they are all under Government control. And despite the dog and pony show that plays on the daily news, the stage-managed wars and the threats issued from world leaders, seemingly opposed, there is just one Government, one power and it controls everything."

"George I just need to know one thing," Wilber said, feeling suddenly tired.

"What's that?"

"Is this game for real?"

Dinosaur George Muldoon took a deep breath.

"We can only hope so, Wilber."

It was not what he'd wanted to hear. It was an adult kind of an answer. Kids just wanted a 'yes' or a 'no' but adults talked in terms of maybe. Levels of maybe, of statistical probability. But he had to believe, he had to get back on the horse that had thrown him.

"So George, these beings are still alive?"

"Yes some of them but only the ones in the heart. All the other ships are derelict, their crews long dead and their cargo rotting. The one and only chance you have is to find a ship in the heart."

"Is there any guarantee they'll let me in?"

George pondered.

"We know they're intelligent. We just hope they are able to distinguish between good humans and bad humans. To date, they've only experienced the worst of us."

Wilber turned and walked away from George. If everything he had been told was wrong, how could he trust anybody or anything? It was an age where the lie dominated. The false pictures of fake news, fake opinion and fake ideas about what constituted success and reality. Humans, in this age, were unable to tell the difference between the lie and the truth between wrong and right. Everything had gotten twisted and bent out of shape. So how to proceed? He'd come up with just one answer. He had to close his eyes to what was going on outside, to other people's explanations and focus on his own perceptions, his own intuitions. In that way he could navigate, in that way he could find his true path.

"Thank you' for everything you've told me George, for everything you've done but I need you away from me now."

The hurt in George's eyes would have felled a charging rhino.

"I'm so sorry Wilber, for all the pain I've caused you."

"I'm not punishing you George. I love you and not just because you're my Uncle."

George nodded, tears flowing from his eyes.

"Now, I need you to go ahead to make sure that beach is clear for me."

"It won't be. They'll throw everything they have at you. They've too much vested in this experiment. All of them."

It was as Wilber had feared. Even those who appeared to be friends were part of a system that wanted to destroy him. He'd always known what he was and what he would become. Back in England, in Staffordshire, on the edge of Tamworth, the place where the two rivers met. It's just that the knowledge had been buried. Up until the age of 9 he'd been free of the knowledge but then like the Angel of Death, the knowledge had come for him. In the night. In his dreams it had come. That was when they had reached out for him, from their prison on this island. They had put their mark on him, branding him for life.

"The girls, get the girls together George. They are our last and only hope. If they stand with me we're in with a shout. If they don't, it's looking doubtful.

"Alright you got it," George agreed, the rain dripping off his bronzed face.

"Anything else you can tell me? Anything else I need to know?", Wilber asked.

"By now they will know you have all five of the crystals. They will feel the pull and they will launch. It's end Game now Wilber and the normal rules don't apply. During End Game they can attack and kill each, at least whilst you live. At the western gate and only at the end you'll see who stands with who."

George, realising time was short, grabbed Lola's hand and together they began to run, but they had only gone a handful of paces when Lola collapsed and George was once more compelled to pick her up and carry her. Wilber watched as they disappeared into the rain. Lola, though alive, haunted him. Feeling his way in the dark to the pulsing signal that reached out for him. That had always reached out for him. Only now he understood it and the message was both loud and clear.

72

Wriggle Room

Yabu took a long drag on his cigar, then exhaled the blue smoke wistfully into the darkening air. Seated on his throne of ivory and bone, on the torch-lit veranda, he was in a reflective mood.

For so long, life had been good on the island. The sun shone, and if it rained at all, it rained at night. There was always laughter, always so much to do. Lots of girls, lots of fun and best of all, lots of meat. To be eaten in any way you wanted to eat it. Raw, salted, cooked. And of course, he Yabu, was no slouch as a cook. Nothing he loved better than getting the gang together and tossing a few human limbs on the barby, popping corks and cracking beers, getting out the guitars for a sing-a-long or pounding the drums from dusk till dawn.

Yeah, life in the mangrove swamp might not be everybody's idea of fun but he had adored it there with the crocs and the gators and his people. Only that time was at an end now. But what a time. There was nowhere to run and soon they would come, expecting to be led. And what could he do but lead?

He thought back over the events of that day and Wilber's arrival. The kid was, it had to be confessed, a little wonder. Nothing less than a prodigy. There had been others down the years, as good, if not better, in certain aspects, but none had been the entire package. Of course he'd been helped by the Alphabets but he'd been hindered by other things and nobody or nothing could ever strip him of his achievement.

Not him, not Astapor, not no one.

Whatever happened next, and it was unlikely the kid would get out alive, it had been a privilege to meet him, to watch him work.

Yabu raised his glass of ice-cool champagne in sincere toast.

"Here's to you kid. You've been amazing."

He drained the glass in one long swig, then hurled it into the swamp and rose steadily to his feet. His suit had been replaced by black combat fatigues, boots, and a beret. His African Dictator look, he called it. Regardless of the seriousness of the situation he always needed to look sharp. That was the rule. How he wanted to stay but the call of the United Crystals could not be ignored. It tugged on him worse than any addiction he had ever known, and he had known and beaten many.

Closing his eyes, he saw the Western gate shrouded in cloud and darkness and the red sun disappearing behind it. No need to hoist aloft a crystal to see any more. The visions could no longer be escaped, not by sleep or drink, or any concerted act of forgetting. They had to be faced and addressed. No one could be a passive observer here; everyone was required to be an active participant in the unfolding drama.

The clanking of chains and the sound of marching feet told him his hour had come and he strode purposefully down the slatted walkway to where his servant Meruvel awaited him, chain in hand. He smiled and bowed low before his Master, then handed Yabu his pet. Yabu stooped and patted the twelve-foot croc on the head affectionately.

"Who's a pretty boy then?"

The croc seemed to smile benignly up at Yabu, who had raised him from an egg and fed him a hand every day. They were closer than lovers and Yabu trusted the croc more than he ever had or ever would trust any human. But in spite of these feelings of solidarity for the Reptile, it was the Russian who must be followed and obeyed.

"Everybody ready? Everybody here?" he asked, and Meruvel nodded.

"So be it. We'll approach the Western Gate via the Great White Smile, enjoy the sea and sand for the last time. Hope you packed your bucket and spade."

73

Screw Time

Lola and George were gone for now, perhaps for good. The night swallowed everything and if not the night, then the rain. Pounding down, streaky drops stretching, reaching out, becoming diamonds of light. In his eyes anyway. His upper half was unclothed, and whilst as naked as a horse, he felt nothing, not even the cold. Trousers drenched, trainers sodden, he felt solitary and alone.

Running, always running, towards the future, away from the past. Running to escape, running to catch a bus. Running out of time. Crucified by memories, by nostalgia and loss. The English way. And he was still English wasn't he? Crossing the line at sports day, breaking the tape, sprinting away from Mad Dog, leaping from the bridge into the swirling black river of chaos. Jogging down that long tree-lined drive at night, towards home, feeling the wind caressing his face and tousling his hair.

That was then and here was now. Or was it? Perhaps all time was now. Every moment occurring simultaneously, just at different points relative to the observer. What was motion if not his God? And what was his spirit if not breath?

And he was back in the moment, running again towards the heart of the Burning Grounds. Here was a desert of sorts where cloud met mist and mist met fog and the stinking wind crawled with disease. Every atom in the teeming air seemed to throb and pulse amplifying energies, relaying signals, signs, communications. He was not really alone. Separation was simply an illusion born of distance. Of a lack of light.

Left foot down, right foot lifting, arms pumping, lungs heaving, heart racing. Rain mingling with sweat, eyes wide open, pupils dilated. Pupils glowing. Coloured rings of light illuminating the iris. Tree rings. How those eyes had changed since the first moments of arrival. Waking up bathed by sun, partly submerged by the surf. Looking up at the trilithon. Hearing the pounding drums.

Seeing the colour of the waters for the first time. Green sea? Surely not, but 'yes.'

Glancing down at Crowhaven's watch, he felt its oppressive weight and silently cursed. 20:50. No time and all of time. Hating the pressure, reaching down, wrenching the watch free and hurling it into the rain, into forgetting.

Screw time.

And yet he couldn't escape it. What was he, if not a solitary hope for so many here. The first and final chance to escape, to find a bigger, better life, where one wasn't running away from something that wanted to eat you, every second of every day. He tried to keep his mind fixed on the task at hand but his heart betrayed him, diverting his attention back to Lola again and again. But she had looked ill. Thank God for George. She was the flame to his moth. He wanted to circle her for an age, then plunge into her luminous heart. An image arose unbidden, like a bubble from a wreck. He saw himself on a headland watching the blade of light from a lighthouse whirring round and round, round and round. Mesmerised he almost forgot himself for a moment but then he was back, scanning, searching, fearing. The fog had become denser, visibility poorer. Everything was intensifying. Mist, cloud, rain and vapours were interpenetrating, commingling, thickening until it was almost impossible to see.

Lost, with no sense of direction. Lost and yet feeling the magnetic pull of some energy, some centre. Crossing a threshold, the sand beneath his feet, changing from blue to yellow. Slowing to a walk. Walking not running, lights flickering on and off in the air around him. Like fireflies or Christmas trees. Demented patterns firing like neurons in the brain, over and over. Building pictures, signalling, perceiving. Something in the fog reaching out for him with the longest fingers, like razors or hooked claws. Flesh made metal, metal made flesh.

Shadows and looming forms, emerging from the fog. His breathing changing, his heart drumming irregular rhythms. The threat of a terror induced heart attack seized him and almost doubled him up, convulsed him, strangled him. Oh, how he wanted to scream but something had emptied his mouth of sound.

A buzzing like flies, a clanking like that of chains being piled, of trays full of keys being rattled. Sound but no sound. A mental sound. Machinery trying to start but failing to do so. Misery in that failure. An agonised howling coming out of a black, leafless, burnt tree. Wilber, shivering uncontrollably, but not with the cold. Eyes wide, wide enough to pop, alone in a white forest of nothing. And the boy, like bubble gum just wanting to pop. Just wanting to float up out of his body, out of the top of his head and be gone. Forever.

Slowing, slowing, feet slowing, finally stopping and eyes lifting to stare at the huge silver disc jammed in the sand. Thirty metres wide, at least, and ten metres high. Listing over to one side. Dented and cracked. Immobile and unbalanced. Endless bands of lights extinguished, windows smashed, metal not just rusting but rotting like gone-off meat. Smashed this, smashed that, smashed everything.

A sense of loss so acute, he let out a stifled sob. Stranded souls far from home. Alone in their agony, peering up into the darkness. Tortured by the drumming fingers of time. Unable to move, unable to reach for the sky, to hear the voices or see the eyes of their loved ones, lost. Not aliens but star brothers and sisters, feeling as he did, loving as he did, grieving as he did. Drawn here, dragged in and slammed down. Lied to and imprisoned, set adrift in broken time. Damn that Russian. Damn him for what he had done.

Wilber walked on, beneath the broken disc. He felt the emptiness within, the loss of life, albeit the pain remained to haunt this barren grove and poison the air. His own sense of loss grew as he walked further and further into the heart, past fallen ship, after fallen ship. And a line throbbing in his head.

I had not thought death had undone so many.

Empty derelict craft, once filled with teeming, joyous life. Explorers all, spacefarers all. Destroyed by the cruel whims of a tyrant. It all seemed so pointless that despair threatened to overwhelm him, utterly, but he forced himself onwards, like Sisyphus, out of a sense of defiance. Past ship after ship, all dark, all broken; crumbling hulks in the darkest corner of the darkest world. Abandoned, never rescued but drained, fed upon. How had they felt as the years had passed and hope had died? Had they consoled one another? Did they die in one another's arms or did they slink off into some dark place to die alone.

Despite the intensification of his despair, he kept on moving and in time there were no more ships, just fog and a wisp of breeze to keep him company. And then out of the darkness a light, as though from a lighthouse, picked him out and he remembered that long drive that led from the main road up to Muldoon Manor. For all of the misery of the world, he had always found sanctuary at home, at the end of that driveway. Regardless of who was there and who wasn't.

Walking down the blade of light he thought of home and smiled. He had lost, for all that he had won, he had run out of time. That much at least was obvious. But it didn't matter now, now that he understood what had brought him here, understood what had made him different, understood why he had suffered. It was all for this moment and for all that he, like these beings, was now trapped here, he would not despair. In his isolation he would reach out, he would find new hope and purpose and through communion, he would find the meaning that had once invested his life but had been lost.

He was what he had always dreamed of being, a knight in search of a grail, and here at last it was, the grail chapel, only it was a spaceship, not a church. Onwards he walked and in time the fog began to part and the light to soften. Now pink, now pearlescent, it soothed him. Then suddenly there it was, right in the heart of the Burning Grounds, the Final Craft, only this one wasn't derelict, it was still intact, still functional and still ablaze with light. And in a circular window, backlit by green light, a solitary figure looked down at him.

To him the ship looked like a silver eye, watching him. In truth it had always watched him. The only thing that was different was that he knew it now. The next thing he saw caused him to smile. Beneath the ship, spilling light, an invitation to enter. The metaphorical drawbridge had been dropped and he was free to enter, should he choose to.

Wilber paused and contemplated the figure in his turn as the black rain continued to fall. Then without a second thought he walked towards the lowered ramp and unbuttoning his satchel removed the Fire Crystal and held it aloft where the watcher could see. Then he walked on up the ramp with no muss and no fuss. It was just like getting on a a plane or entering a supermarket. There was absolutely nothing to worry about, he told himself. After all, he had nowhere else to go. Crossing the threshold, once more he paused and took a deep breath.

Inside the ship was cool and dry, yet he did not feel cold and upon entering he found his skin was immediately dry, along with his trousers, boots and socks. He stood and looked around. It was not as he had imagined it would be but then what had he imagined? A cockpit with flashing lights, a holodeck, bubbling tanks full of weird looking crustaceans?

There was none of that. If anything the interior looked more like a cosmetics counter from a 1970s High Street Store with atmospheric lighting and some dry ice. The walls though were strange and looked as though they had been made up of painted bricks. Nothing was smooth, everything was irregular, with some hidden purpose he found impossible to discern. What a place to spend eternity.

If he'd been out cruising the cosmos he'd have done it in a lot more style than this. He'd have wanted a spaceship three miles high with swimming pools on every level and robots to attend to his every whim. Lots of space and a lot of lifts. And screens. Everything voice activated and endless entertainments with rollercoasters and hi-fashion and sentient machines to design it for him, to his exacting specifications of course. And surgical labs to remodel his looks and extend his life indefinitely and...

Something was happening. The light was changing. A sulphurous, yellow haze began to fill the space around him, filtering down from some vent-like process up in the ceiling, and the air acquired a tang of oranges and metal. He screwed up his face at the taste and there drifting towards him through the sulphur haze was his watcher. It glided right up to him and stood close enough for Wilber to touch. In spite of himself Wilber resisted the temptation.

Over two metres tall, waif-like, clad in a robe of seeming black and white feathers the Watcher was a creature of singular grace and beauty. It was haloed in a trinity of colours; the layer closest to the body white, then yellow and finally blue. To Wilber it looked to be completely enveloped in a close-fitting, diaphanous 'skin' that glowed with an inner light revealing a conjoined heart and throat and two sets of eyes, one high up in the forehead, the other pair deep in a set of sculpted sockets. It was hard to tell whether it wore a crafted helmet or its face and head were biological in origin. A symmetrical being that could have been designed or simply evolved over aeons. Impossible to prove, on so short an acquaintance, but Wilber felt like he was in the presence of something ancient.

Without a second thought he held out the fire crystal and dropped it into the out-stretched arm of the attendant Watcher.

74

The Assembling of The Armies

The remaining Alphabets, following Antelope, loped through the fog and mist, away from the Burnt Grove, towards the Western Gate. They skirted the pink sands of the Burning Grounds in virtual silence. This was no drill. This was it! Apocalypse! The sky which had continued to darken throughout the course of the day, was now almost totally black, starless and black. Only the sea lent a little light and the trees, for some reason Crimson couldn't put her finger on, seemed to fluoresce. The red sun was almost spent.

Running with the pack, running through the twisted jungle, fit to burst, Frantic's anxiety had risen to an almost unbearable level. When there had been no hope it hadn't mattered but now that they were so close she could hardly bear to breathe. Could he do it? Could Wilber pull it off?

Def wondered about that too. Fang's dying screams still rang in her head but that was okay. To her it was soothing music, something to leave on repeat; gripping her bloodied axe she had never felt calmer or more certain of herself than she did right now. If this was the end then that was cool. They'd given it their best and gone down fighting. A death worthy of an ancient Viking was all she wanted. It was all she had ever wanted. Life was such a drag.

The sporadic sound of gun fire had given way to an almost constant stutter of machine gun and small arms fire. All over the island men killed other men and creatures that had once been men. In the East the Cannibals were being raked and shredded by Crowhaven's Third Battalion whilst up on top of the Volcano Astapor's guard had been reduced to a tattered, scattered remnant.

The variants from the 32 levels of volcanic hell, driven out of their siloes, suffered or thrived according to their various gifts. It was a bloodbath of epic proportions and soon the island became a killing field. This was it. The clocks had stopped and they had returned to the Year Zero. Here the gun ruled and the best trained and best equipped fought on the side of the English Professor. However, Crowhaven's soldiers did not have everything their own way. More than one fell prey to a zombie-mekon sandwich or a Scratcher's claws. Pell mell, they ran over every square foot of island they could find, chaos made flesh, blasting and shooting everything that crossed their paths, turning the Russian's creations into foaming strips of contorted meat, fit only for the knackers yard or a butcher's hook.

Rudi, close to breaking point, conjugated verbs in Russian or Serbo-Croat as a way of coping. She missed Semantic and couldn't stop herself from weeping like a willow, whenever she thought of her.

They ran in a wonky line through the last of the trees, feet pounding the ground, remembering their fallen friends. The fog and mist were so thick now, it was hard to see more than a few metres in front of where you ran. Towards End Game they moved, as those condemned to fight in a Roman Arena, against lions armed with rocket launchers and M16s. It wasn't a question of if one fell but when. There was no such thing as a fair fight here.

The dark, volcanic earth gave way suddenly to white sand and the beach they all called the Wave, a paradise of opportunities for those equipped with a surfboard and a powerful stroke. They walked the Wave, remembering happier days before this latest cull. Out to sea was clear of cloud, and white seabirds dived and fished in the black waters; no, if the fog came from anywhere it was from the Burning Grounds. Antelope, as ever led the way, brazen and fearless, listening for the sounds of approaching steps.

Or death swooping down on angel's wings.

And there it was, approaching from the northwest, in the stretching space between them and the Western Gate. The

Alphabets fanned out, limbering up and swinging their axes, getting ready for action. Under her breath Antelope raged and cursed. There should have been more of them. It couldn't end like this, could it?

From out of the fog, two figures emerged; behind them a small militia, of sinuous shadows emanating bellicose intent.

"Everybody ready?" Antelope called through gritted teeth.

"I was born ready," Def growled, counting the notches on her axe handle." Still room for a few more, she thought happily.

The tall dark lines bearing down on them gradually budded limbs and became recognisably human.

"Who is that?" Crimson asked. "They seem oddly familiar."

"You aren't wrong," Rudi interjected, her fluttering voice suffused with momentary joy. "Don't you recognise them? It's Lap Zhao and Albert Hand!"

The Two Magicians came closer and closer stopping just a few metres away from the stern-faced Antelope.

"Nice night for a stroll," Antelope deadpanned.

"Care to join us?" Mr Hands asked, returning the serve.

"Who's that with you?" Antelope said, indicating the bodies standing in the fog. It was as if the Alphabets were meeting their shadows for the first time and, in a way, they were.

Mr Lapp smiled.

"Antelope, these are your sisters. The Western Chapter of the Alphabet Gang. The other half of my army."

"Whose army?" Def chanted. "Whose army, whose army...?"

Mr Lapp looked at her oddly. He had never been able to fathom Def but she was a good fighter, so how much did it really matter?

"Girls, come and meet your sisters."

The shadows approached and stood like gunslingers looking at their opposite numbers. They were every bit as scarred as the East Island Girls. They had the same arrogance and the same ferocity; the same sense of loyalty and the same attitude of defiance. They would die for each other. That much was apparent. You didn't have to be a genius to see it. Self-empowered females who worked for the greater good of the group, not their own selfish need or glorification.

Antelope nodded and walked round the two magicians, approaching her opposite number. The shortest girl in the opposite pack, the so-called West Island Chapter peeled away from her clan and stood facing Antelope. Where the East Island Girls now ported double-headed axes, the West End Girls had what looked like medieval halberds, ranging from six to nine feet in length. Great for running people through with, at close quarters, not so great if your opponent had a sniper rifle or an AK-47.

Antelope sized up her opposite number.

"Seen any action today?" she asked, making pointed conversation.

"Plenty. You?"

"Plenty."

A pause you could have driven a herd of elephants through ensued, then Antelope eased back and extended her blood-stained hand. The other girl took it.

"Hi," she rasped, "I'm Zenith."

"Antelope. Not many of us left I'm afraid."

Call them out, Mr Lapp suggested.

Roll call? Oh well if that was what was needed.

"Antelope. Crimson. Def. Frantic. Rudi."

As each of the names was called the surviving East Island Girls raised their hands in salute.

The West Island Girls did likewise, Zenith doing as Antelope had done.

"Hen. Infra. Kaos. Ox. Queen. Tarantula. Ultra. Zenith"

The girls checked each other out. If they were to stand a chance, two must become one and now. There was no time to get better acquainted. No time to train or work out strategic objectives. They would just need to improvise and get stuck in.

"There used to be more of us too," Zenith said. "We had a full complement of letters when the sun rose this morning. Are there any more of us running around Mr Lapp?"

"Sadly no."

"And you kept us apart all this time? For what reason?" Antelope returned, her voice full of ice and razors.

"For just such a moment as this," Mr Lapp said simply.

"I don't see it. Do you?" This last question was addressed to Zenith.

"Me neither but I'm not sure it matters. We either fight beside them or we kill them now. Whatever you decide I'll support it".

Def grinned in appreciation. She liked this new girl. She had style!

Antelope considered.

"If it's a choice between them and Astapor, I'll take them. For now. Mr Lapp kept us separate but he also brought us together. He trained us and shaped us when we had nothing and no one."

"For his own ends," Zen added.

"You're right, I can't disagree but let's fight first and hold the inquiry later. We have a friend, a Running Man, who has acquired the five crystals we need to get us all off this damned island. He has twenty or so minutes to get to the Western Gate and open those locks. And we have to clear the way."

Zen nodded grimly.

"So we heard. We ain't gonna last long against automatic weapons."

"Then we'll have to use our cunning and that fog. You up for it?"

Zen scoffed.

"Like you need to ask. So who leads?"

"Wanna flip a coin?" Antelope asked. "Single combat would be my preferred option but the clock is where it is and we don't have time."

Zenith laughed and revealed filed teeth.

"Well if it means that much to you, you lead. Even if this is our hunting ground."

Antelope held out her hand again and Zenith took it.

"To the gate then, sister."

"To the gate."

It was a death or victory scenario. After today there would be no more running, for either faction.

Zenith turned to Lapp.

"So Mr Lapp, any more surprises we can expect?"

"One or two," Mr Lapp conceded. We may yet be able to swell our ranks a little. Mr Hand could possibly swing the odds in our favour.

"How?" Antelope asked.

"Heh! Mr Hands yelled, "that's my line!"

75

Deployment

Soon all of the wheels were in motion, spinning wildly, driven by ancient and hidden winds. Crowhaven moved down through the forest with his battalion, away from his mansion with its wraparound golf course and the comforts of home. The blue flags in each of the eighteen holes fluttered like medieval pennants high on a crenellated castle wall. It was going to be a glorious end to the day. Whatever resistance they met on the way, they crushed. Up on top of the volcano the first battalion had wreaked havoc and nothing there moved now. Down in the Cannibal village the second battalion was cutting a swathe through the ranks of the flesh eaters.

Everything was going according to plan, and Smithy and Carruthers beamed megawatt smiles. News from each theatre was relayed via radio link into concealed ear pieces that each fighting unit had been issued with. The Devil was in the details, was it not? The Professor's resolve had been rewarded. Soon, very soon the entire island would be his and he would be the Prime. First south, then west, the battalion ran, following the pathway that Wilber, Caleb and Lola had made just hours earlier. Ghosting through the jungle past the wrecked, partially eaten bodies of humans, Dinos and things that had crawled from the pages of Homer, all of them felt the forces of destiny stirring. The battalion moved quickly and whatever the island threw at them, they destroyed with flame or lead. It was all so beautiful and the air sang with bullets. In less than fifty minutes they had made it to the edge of the Burning Ground where Crowhaven called a halt.

"What is it Sir, Carruthers asked?"

"A moment's pause, that is all."

Crowhaven clicked his fingers and a soldier carrying what looked like a suit bag appeared. Without further ado Crowhaven began to undress and Smithy, Carruthers and the boys turned their backs and formed a protective ring around their glorious leader. Within minutes he was done and the transformation was wrought. The soldiers turned as one and looked with bemused amazement at the Professor, who having discarded his combat fatigues and most of the face paint, stood in an elegant black suit and a floor length electric blue cape.

Carruthers tried to stifle a snigger and Smithy bit down hard but couldn't stop himself.

"Going to a fancy dress ball Sir?" he quipped.

The look Crowhaven gave them wiped the smiles off both of their faces. There was something different about the Professor now. He was normally such an affable old cove, a chuckling crank but it was as if the blood in his veins had suddenly turned cold and blue. The light in his eyes had gone out and in its place a baleful reptilian stare remained.

"That's enough of that," he hissed and leant in close so that only Smithy and Caruthers could hear him. "Word of advice boys. When I'm on top of the volcano they'll only be room for one of you. Think on," he said, chuckling once more like that elderly uncle, the one who always gave you a fiver at Christmas and made inappropriate jokes about buxom young females.

Smithy and Carruthers regarded each other with dread, then turned their minds back to the task at hand. Crowhaven, meanwhile, stood on the edge of the pink sands looking towards the concealed heart of the Burning Grounds, but in the end he conceded defeat. He dare not venture in. Fog billowed out of the heart, obscuring all, but sending out a message. To enter would be to pay court to death. Looking first south and then north, he decided on the northern route and strode off, following the circular edge of the Burned Earth, in an anti-clockwise fashion. It was a path that would put him on a collision course with Yabu and his people.

Soon the rains came.

*　　　*　　　*　　　*　　　*　　　*　　　*

The Russian was not his normal self. Not that his self was now or ever had been normal. Drull and the other members of his bodyguard were growing increasingly nervous and that was a first for them. The Russian was unpredictable, but he was brilliant. They had seen countless examples of this over their many years of service, but he had never pushed them out this far. Everything that he had spent years building had been cast aside. The towers had gone, as had all those white coated scientists and red-robed surgeons, geniosos to a man. All his faithful servants, one by one, were being discarded. Would the same happen to them, and if this was the case when was a good moment to break away and make a run for it?

As of that moment they crouched on the edge of the Burning Ground, whilst up ahead the Alphabets jogged through the fog towards the white sands of the Wave. Abandoning Burnt Grove and its grisly remains, they had headed just south of west, with nothing more to guide them than the footsteps up ahead and the keen ears of the tracker's dogs.

Each man knelt in the sand, immobile, whilst Astapor assumed the lotus position, closed his eyes and straightened his back. A beatific smile radiated from his face. It was as though he didn't have a care in the world. Lurch, so far out of his comfort zone, had forgotten what comfort felt like, edged closer and closer to the Russian and when his master did not, stir gave a little whimper.

"Yes, what is it Lurch?"

"I was just wondering what you had planned for us?"

Fog drifting out of the heart of the Burning Ground obscured everything and so sound defined one's world. Rain was beginning to drizzle and from time to time the heaven's growled with thunder.

"In the land of the blind, the one-eyed man is king..." the

Russian said.

Lurch shook his head, in a most bewildered state.

"But the Cyclops is dead," he said in a hoarse whisper.

Astapor tapped the space above and between his eyes.

"You never really learned to see, did you Lurch?"

"I'm not a Magician, master."

"No but you could have been," the Russian opined and Lurch shuddered. Was the Russian losing the plot and what if anything could he see with his eyes closed. Away to the east the cannibals had begun to play their war drums and the night was full of death and unrest. Machine gun fire continued to shatter the silence. Whilst the pounding drums caused the night to hollow and sway. Lurch felt drunk and yet he never imbibed. Now why was that?

"Do you want to know what's happening, Lurch?'

"I'd love to," Lurch shot back.

For a long while the Russian said nothing and the rain that had only drizzled began to pore and then pound. Within minutes they were all of them drenched, yet Astapor was seemingly without care.

"He has all of them now"

"Who?"

"Who'd you think?"

"The boy?"

"Yes, Wilber has all five of the crystals and so we enter..."

Lurch grew suddenly excited. He knew the answer to this one.

"End Game."

Like a crocodile surfacing, Astapor opened his eyes and glared at the Scientist.

"Do you know what that means Lurch?"

"I do. The normal rules don't apply. You Magicians are no longer required to uphold your pact of non aggression. You can kill each other now."

Astapor nodded, seemingly impressed.

"That's right." he purred.

"But we're not doing so well, Master. Crowhaven has taken over most of the island. In terms of arms and strength he has the upper hand."

Astapor shrugged.

"The island isn't important, Lurch. Not really."

This, more than anything Astapor had ever said, terrified Lurch. Up ahead Drull had turned and was frantically signalling. The tracker's dogs were once more straining at the leash and it was game on.

A short way up ahead, the Alphabets were walking up the Wave towards a group of wavering shadows. At End Game all the toys came out to play.

*　　　*　　　*　　　*　　　*　　　*　　　*

The Watcher, for so Wilber thought of him, looked down at the crystal placed in its outstretched hand and then held it up to the light. The being's hands were quite extraordinary. There were five fingers and two thumbs, seven in total.

The number seven seemed suddenly very important.

Wilber, unsure of what to do in the company of so august a being, gave a little bow, whilst the Watcher rotated the crystal, examining it minutely. After a while the Watcher completed its inspection and returned its attention to Wilber.

Wilber watched and waited and was delighted when the Watcher returned his bow. Then he felt a tingling between his eyes and his head filled with the sound of a high-pitched whine, like a dentist's drill. Alarmed, he brought his hands up to his ears, sharply, in an attempt to alleviate the pain. In a second the sound dropped away and Wilber lowered his hands and gazed at the space on the Watcher's head between the two sets of eyes. There seemed to be another kind of eye there, a crystal, shaped like a fish bladder. Examining the face more closely he saw that there was no mouth and once again he found it difficult to distinguish between what was body and what was suit. How did it eat, he wondered.

"We don't."

Wilber almost jumped out of his skin. It was as though he had a

Hi-Tech speaker buried deep in his brain. His heart began to pound in his chest as he considered the implications of what had just happened. As his heart rate began to slow, he took stock and began to formulate a response. The Watcher waited in the arms of its vibrant silence.

"You're telepathic," he said simply.

"Most advanced species are, Justice."

It called him Justice and Wilber immediately saw his second name for what it was; a higher name, a star name.

"Are you the last?"

"The last here," the Watcher replied, "at one time we were many."

"Yes I can see that. The space outside is littered with broken craft, all of them empty. How come you survived whilst the others perished."

The Watcher regarded him for a moment.

"I had something the others didn't."

"And what was that?"

"You."

In spite of himself Wilber felt a smile breaking out all over his face.

"Really?"

"Yes. I've watched you for a long time, Justice. I'm afraid I've intruded on your life somewhat."

Images flashed into Wilber's mind then. Like high speed transmissions. Scenes from his life. Six years playing out in 6000 images in 6 seconds. Associating with the star people really sped you up.

"You made me strange," Wilber said, matter-of-factly. "You made me different. It was like I developed a really bad smell. People did not want to come anywhere near me after that. Even my friends abandoned me."

His voice trailed away. The hurt was still there but only in part. Like an afterburn.

"None of it matters though now," he added sympathetically.

"Oh?"

"I've run out of time. I'm no longer a Running Man. The sun has set on my ambitions I'm afraid."

The Watcher said nothing for a time but the quality of the light around it seemed to change. Three layers of colour became five. Magenta and yellow appeared, followed by orange, blue and white. Wilber remembered watching firework displays as a really young child and being so delighted he had clapped his hands together over and over. He felt like that again now.

Yes, in spite of all that had happened, he felt good. The Watcher was a very reassuring presence and Wilber trusted it. If this was it, if this was the end, he'd be happy just to lie down and let go. To die in the Watchers arms, in the hope that he could journey on, that there were other phases of existence. That was all he wanted now. Would his desire be enough though? Could dying be that easy? Forming the question in his mind was easy enough. The Watcher would respond and guide him.

Sure enough, the words began to flow again, crystal clear and so reassuring.

"You've had a lot to contend with Wilber. So many trials, so many different versions of events to measure and weigh. Truth, as you have found to your cost, is elusive. I understand why you want to set down your burden, but it isn't time yet. You must go on. You must continue"

"What's the point? The Russian has won. I'm out of time," Wilber said wearily.

"The Dark One, is not what he appears and neither is time."

Wilber let out a low groan.

"And I was just beginning to like you."

"Trust me," the Watcher replied, and reaching out, he placed a bulky object in Wilber's hand. The youth took it and then studied it. To his amazement he found he had been given Crowhaven's watch, the watch that, just minutes before, he had hurled into the darkness. Returning the watch to his wrist he glanced at the time and gasped. It was only 20.30. If the watch was accurate then time had slipped a hitch.

"Can this be believed?"

"Trust me," said the Watcher, and he held up the tetrahedral crystal, the four sided pyramid, for the youth to see. Once more Wilber gasped. Within the crystal's depths, flames seemed to rage. Without ceremony he handed it to Wilber who opened his satchel and placed the now activated crystal back within its allotted slot. The other crystals likewise now seemed to glow. Something had changed, something was different. The hardest part of the quest lay ahead but he had to continue. Yes, it was time to go.

76

Robed and Ready

Little by little, Mr Hand eased his way into the lead, as the party crept up the beach, in stealth mode, scanning the land around them for potential attackers. He looked a bizarre figure with his eagle feather head-dress, his tomahawks and suede moccasins, like something central casting would send for a joke version, of a re-enactment, of the Battle of Little BigHorn. Like the other Magicians he pretty much kept himself to himself and how he occupied his time and what his agenda was no one seemed to know. Yet whilst the other Magicians inspired awe, commingled with either hatred or respect, Mr Hand was something of a laughing stock. Whilst this was very much the case he seemed completely unphased by the looks of scorn and mockery that happened his way.

Mr Lapp, for his part, hung back with the West Island Girls who brought up the rear, whilst Antelope's clan dogged the steps of Mr Hands. It was clear they were approaching danger and the sense of tension ratcheted accordingly. They passed a broken down beach hut, made out of driftwood and thatched with palm leaves, and Mr Hand ducked inside without explanation. Mr Lapp, catching his fellow Magician up, ducked inside too, leaving the assembled Alphabets to wonder and wait.

Antelope soon grew apoplectic with rage.

"What in hell's name are they doing in there?" she hissed aloud. "They are going to get us all killed."

"Want me to go check?" Def asked.

However, there was no need. The Magicians were emerging

from the hut, but they were somewhat changed, sartorially speaking anyway. Black suits and billowing capes of magenta and orange replaced their indigenous costumes and they had a different air about them, like they meant business. The tomahawks were gone from Albert's belt and he now carried what looked like a harpoon. Lapp had also tooled up and had a Chinese Long Sword strapped to his back.

All of the alphabets regarded them with instant suspicion. Antelope folded her arms and stood gazing on with a face like fizz, whilst Frantic began biting her nails and tousling her hair simultaneously. Never a good sign.

Zenith stepped forward, halberd primed and ready for action.

"Are you here to help or hinder us?" she asked bluntly.

Mr Lapp regarded her coolly.

"We're here to stand with Wilber," came his easy reply. "To give him his shot and to clear the path."

"What's with the costumes?" Ultra asked.

"We don't have time for this," Def all but thundered, "Antelope what should we do?"

But Antelope was drifting off in some twilight zone of the mind where no one else could follow. Rudi saw it as did Crimson and they grew anxious. Since the Burnt Grove she'd been different. The Old Antelope, it seemed, had checked out of the building. Was it the trauma of all that they'd been through or was something else happening?

The island was still mysterious to them all. Just when they thought they had it figured out, new properties and effects emerged. No one was immune. Had Antelope succumbed to some bizarre psychological malady? If so, should she be relieved of command? But who would do it?

Precious seconds passed, whilst everyone assembled weighed their options.

Still the fog drifted out of the heart of the Burning Ground. Still the rain continued to pound, the black clouds to speed across the lowering sky and the sun to sink and bleed out the last minutes of its daily round.

Def leaning into Antelope squeezed her arm and whispered in her ear.

"Ant, you need to get a grip. You need to call this."

Zenith stalked over, her eyes blazing.

"What's with her? She doped or something?'

Def instantly enraged, wheeled and hoisted her axe to shoulder height.

"You leave her alone, or we'll be having words."

And there it was, in an instant, the seeds of their destruction. For all of them. Weapons raised with hostile intent, hate and fear crackling in the evening air. Girl against girl, east against west. A zero sum game played out in the black rain. The two factions of the Alphabet Gang were coming apart at the seams, their collective wound opening... the blood flowing freely, and so it would continue until their was none left to lose. Until the Gang, or what remained of it bled out.

It was then that Albert Hand spoke.

"I know what you're all thinking. This could so easily be a trap. We're Magicians, arch manipulators and liars, who think of nothing but our own needs. But that's the game he plays, with everyone. The Game of Divide and Conquer. The game of doubt. There's nothing he loves to see more, than the death of faith between people who have been friends, comrades, lovers. It feeds him. It amplifies his power. Don't succumb. You need to be smarter girls; need to be more mindful of your moods and perceptions. End Game messes with your head. Don't let complacency set in now and please, please don't let your paranoia get the better of you."

Rudi, her hand on Def's arm, watched what was happening in horror, tears pouring from her eyes.

"I just want to get off the island," was all she said.

That was perfectly reasonable.

"You've done well to get this far. Believe me," Lapp said.

"Oh we do," Antelope replied. "We do, but that's not the

issue..."

Here she paused.

"By my calculations we have fifteen more minutes of daylight and there is no sign of Wilber. The sun sets on every running man and woman. We've done well but have we done enough?"

Her voice sounded like she could crack at any moment. The tension was unbearable, and the thought of failing now was enough to drive anybody mad.

"Fifteen minutes. That should be ample," Ultra declaimed with more confidence than any one else in the group could have mustered. She lowered her halberd and the other West Island Girls followed suit. Not surprisingly perhaps Zenith was the last to comply. Eyeing Def, with bared teeth, she opened her mind and then her mouth.

"It would be so nice if everybody played by the same rules here Def but nobody ever does. Here the game is played with loaded dice. Here nobody is who you think they are. Isn't that right, Hand?"

Mr Hand, so used to being ignored or mocked, was surprised.

"Indeed it is, Zen. If you'll permit me an observation about time. I think it could help here"

Mr Lapp laughed.

"That's my arena, my friend, as you know, but please go ahead."

"With pleasure. End Game is the point where everything breaks down, where what lurks beneath the crust of the conscious mind breaks through and makes itself known. So much of who we are is hidden. We're strangers to ourselves, adrift in our own minds. But at End Game, we finally become who we are, for better or worse. All those carefully constructed masks crack, crumble and fall. Thousands of years of time pour their energy into a few minutes. Can't you feel time simultaneously stretching and contracting? All kinds of memories arising within you. It's enough to turn anyone a little weird."

It was Antelope's turn to frown.

"I'm seeing all kinds of weird stuff parading before my eyes. It's like having a thousand movies playing in your head. It's so confusing. I'm feeling rage now, like I never felt in my whole life. And I don't know who I am. One minute I feel like an old man, the next I'm a ravening tiger, then I'm my sister. Then I'm a bear, a snake, a flamingo. What is happening here?"

Mr Lapp was silent for a time. Then he spoke.

"It's time we all remembered who we are, Antelope, and what we stand for."

"What is End Game really?" Antelope asked. "Is it just a battle?"

"It is, but it's so much more than that. It's a rebirthing," said Mr Hand.

"I don't understand."

"Then follow me."

Mr Hand set off, long-striding up the beach, once more in the lead, with the Alphabets walking just a few paces behind him. He seemed to have a renewed sense of purpose about him, and a curious light of sorts illuminated his visage. From every side he was scrutinised, an object of sudden and obvious fascination. Each member of the separate gangs had in just a few minutes completely reversed what they felt and thought about him. There was that nagging feeling that he kept himself hidden behind that ridiculous head dress. So much could have been learned if they'd all just learned to see beneath that mask.

Was it too late though?

Watching the sea, Albert Hand appeared as he really was; a powerful Magus, fully in charge of himself and a Master of the Elements. They came to the end of the beach and the white sand turned to black, mostly powdered, rock. A remnant of a previous eruption no doubt, but when? A hundred years ago, ten thousand, ten million? So difficult to know unless you could read the signs. And the Magician in front so evidently could.

Mr Hand stopped and, as one, so did the remaining Alphabets and Mr Lapp. A new sense of expectation gripped them all. Fog continued to drift out of the Dark Heart of the Burning Grounds, as thick as smoke, but it no longer held the same sense of horror as it had before, and the sun, although almost down, continued to linger, splashing everything with a bloody red glow. The waves of the once green sea, now wine red, were splashed blue with little florets of phosphor as they exploded on the shore.

Standing immobile upon the shore, Mr Hand looked out to sea as though he was expecting something. Once more the tension built, but it was no longer a cause for existential doubt and terror. Now it brought excitement and hope. Listening, listening so acutely they heard a rhythmic sound, as bodies heaved and pulled together, dipping oars and hauling themselves over the darkened sea, towards the land where Mr Hand and Mr Lapp and those girls waited.

In a few short minutes, from out of the dark cave of the night, nine boats had appeared bearing numerous bodies all clad in bizarre apparel. As one they pulled, as nine they landed, as one they leapt into the surf and dragged the boats high up on the black shore. Reaching inside the boats they removed their weapons, an array of clubs, spears, swords and daggers, then they clustered around Mr Hand who turned to Antelope and smiled.

"This, my dear Antelope, is my army."

And what an army they were, clad from head to foot in bird-feather robes. A shaven headed, tattooed bunch of elegant thugs, more like dancers than warriors, feathered in black and feathered in white, infused with the spirits of crow and dove. Of peace and war. Lithe and athletic, androgynous and murderous, they acknowledged duality and yet transcended it. They were larger than life, because they suffused with life, though never coarse or commonplace, never unnecessary. They fired and inspired the Alphabets, helping them to believe that they had a chance, a fighting chance, where before there was only the certainty of death.

Rudi did a quick head count and found that Hand's Army was a little over eighty souls. She gave an excited whoop and would have performed a war dance but for the fact she felt a little self conscious.

The warriors turned, as one, when they heard her cry, and gazed at Rudi in mute fascination. Mr Lapp smiled, feeling the energetic shift in the group.

"We can lead you but we cannot fight for you," said Mr Hand. "If the Running Man succeeds today, we all of us can leave this island and proceed on our journey through time into new spaces. We can found new worlds and civilizations. We can give birth to new societies run along the lines of fairness, equality and balance for all, not just the favoured few. We will respect nature, taking only what we need, not what greed or hate dictates. We will live beyond fear and the rule of the Russian and others like him.

As you head into battle, remember these words. They will sustain and strengthen you in your moment of need. New rules and possibilities often demand sacrifices and we may be asking you to make the Ultimate Sacrifice. Mr Lapp and I know what we ask, that is why we will fight alongside of you. Our heads are on the block too. If we fall, we fall as one.

After today you will be compelled to obey no one save your own conscience. To step through the gate is to surrender one's power in order to gain one's freedom. After today, should we succeed, Lapp and I will no longer be Magicians. Our rods of power will be broken and not before time. Too long have we been marooned here, too long have we played this Game, his game. But after today that changes.

Not all of you will make it to the gate. Not all of you will cross the threshold, but all stand here in this moment to mark the possibility of real and lasting change. Turn now to the ocean from which we all crawled. Give it thanks and praise. As you prepare to fight one last time, look back briefly and meditate. See the best moments in your life. Remember them and those that helped to forge them. Remember your first kiss, your first victory, the times you've laughed and cried, the day you built something extraordinary, the day you buried a loved one.

Human life is but a moment. Seize that moment, savour that moment, make it count."

Turning to face the sea, Albert Hands raised both his arms and placed his feet together, to form the letter Y with his body. His army did likewise and the Alphabets and Lapp followed suit.

"Today we honour the Old Gods who came to earth from the heavens and created man in their image. We celebrate and we commiserate for the Gods, though wonderful, were often savage and cruel. And yet this island would not exist without them and neither would we.

We celebrate the Lost Continent and the Broken Civilization that men call Atlantis. Although broken, it can be reforged and it can rise again in each of us today. We acknowledge the darkness, yet we reach for the light, and that is why we wear the robes we do. Power without responsibility, knowledge without love can only bring destruction. Today we end that circle and return to the faith and humility of our forebears. Before the fall, before the time of pride and perversion, before the opening of the Box of Pandora."

"I have said enough. Fight with me sisters. Fight with me brothers. Reclaim what was lost."

77

A Disappearance

Lurch had never known terror like he felt in this particular moment.

It was like a pox that covered his body or a cancer that gnawed at his malnourished soul. It was so hard for him to imagine a future without the Russian in it, harder still to imagine a future that did not contain himself.

Death, to him, meant oblivion. The Long Goodbye, the Big Sleep. The horror of nothing. Better to suffer and be than not to exist, although at times he felt he didn't exist, that he was merely a product of someone else's nightmare.

Another round of machine gun fire filled the air and he ducked and flung his arms protectively over his head. He was shaking uncontrollably. It was not a pleasant feeling. Behind him Lurch heard one of Astapor's elite guards snigger contemptuously and he felt even more vulnerable.

Prior to setting out Astapor had called him aside and given him a gun, an antique Luger. He had watched with benign amusement as Lurch had tried to load and fire the gun. It had a full clip of ammunition. Lurch had half expected the gun to contain a single bullet, and that bullet for him.

"Master," he had said, with a note of pleading in his voice, "can't I have a machine gun. I think I'd feel far safer."

Astapor patted him as though he were a little dog.

"Leave the killing to the professionals, Lurch. It's what they are paid to do."

"But what should I do...out there?"

Here he had gestured to the world beyond the tower complex, a world he didn't know and because he didn't know it he couldn't control it. Life was only viable as a series of controlled experiments. The Russian had taught him that. It should be kept behind glass, in a sealed chamber and observed, as one piped chemicals into it.

But the tower complex was gone. The gates of hell had been opened and spilled out into his waking world. An insect bit him and he squished it dead with an instinctual swat. Then another insect bit him and another. He felt his eyes beginning to tear up and the edges of his mind beginning to fray.

This was not how his life ended? Surely.

The fog had yellowed and thickened and it was harder and harder to see where you were or who you stood next to. Drull and the Dog Man were up ahead but they were totally obscured. Beneath his feet the sparse vegetation had given way to white sand. So beautiful to look at but so difficult to walk on.

But walk he must, up the beach towards the gate. It was near now, he knew that, less than half a mile. What was that? Ten minutes of walking. And then what. He gripped the Luger and wondered if it would be safer to drift away into the fog and join the party once the shooting had finished.

Up ahead a faint burst of red light caught his attention. He paused in terror and then it clicked. Of course, it was the sun; its dying rays anyway. Nothing to fear. Carry on, carry on, he told himself, but his feet were glued to the spot.

Suddenly a spit of light swept through the fog and everything was illuminated. The guards and the Dog Man paused, fixed in light. Lurch had a sudden image of tissue mounted on microscope slides. Mounted and fixed. What was wrong with this picture? He span wildly around as light still clung to each man. He counted them off, included himself, the dog man and his dogs. What was wrong with this picture? And then the penny dropped. Of course.

The Russian was gone.

*　　　*　　　*　　　*　　　*　　　*　　　*

The sense of events speeding up dogged Yabu's footsteps as he led his ragged band of Cannibals, out of the swamp and down onto the sands of the Great White Smile. When the rains came Meruval handed him a stylish black umbrella which he rested on his left shoulder, whilst he handled Marvin the Man-eating Croc with his right hand. The others, lacking umbrellas, were soon soaked and cold. Marvin had been trained not to strain at the leash but it was some time since he had been fed and the normal proprieties were harder to observe.

Yabu didn't need the black cloud or the blood red sun or the sound of machine gun fire on the Eastern end of the island to tell his that things weren't going well. Crowhaven was firmly in the driving seat, having most of the men and the best of the weapons.

Worse still, according to reports, the Russian had gone AWOL. Having piloted the sinking ship into shark-infested waters, he'd bailed leaving others to pick up the pieces and face the heaving waves.

Would it be so very surprising if the Russian had abandoned them all? Yabu smiled as the thought passed through his mind, like a speeding night train, into darkness. No, nothing surprised him about the Russian. In so many ways now he didn't matter.

Yabu's mind turned to Lola. Perhaps she was the one he needed to fear. They had spent so much time together in the swamp, he felt of her as kin. She loved to watch the crocs feed, better still she loved to feed them herself, by hand. And she wasn't too picky about what she fed them. Certainly wasn't squeamish, that girl. She had observed him and learned from him, but did she actually like him?

Yabu, for all that he was a Magician, was haunted by a sense of uncertainty. He'd stopped trying to second guess the Russian. That was a shortcut to disaster. But Lola. He had told her so much, shared so much with her. But had she always coveted his throne, had she secretly sought to learn his ways so that she might replace him?

From the earliest days, the Russian had told him, she had always liked her meat on the rare side. As a sign it did not bode well.

"Lola," he murmured to himself, "I hope you've stayed true. I'd hate it if you were the one to destroy me."

A sudden blade of light swept through the ever-thickening, seemingly nicotine tinged-fog and Yabu froze. The beach was long, over half a mile, and they had travelled down most of it. They were on the section that abutted the Burning Grounds. It was a bottleneck. A very good place for an ambush as it happened and as he watched Yabu saw and understood that that was exactly what had happened.

Figures in the fog moved behind them. Figures in the fog moved in front of them and from what the light revealed, all of them held guns, machine guns. A quick head count, fore and aft, and he reckoned on at least seventy souls. Armed, trained and no doubt highly dangerous.

The figures in the slanting rain stopped moving and stood pointing their machine guns at Yabu and his Flesh Eaters who numbered in the high thirties. Oh they could wield an axe or a cleaver like the butchers they were, but they weren't soldiers and whilst there were one or two battered revolvers jammed into one or two belts it would not be an equal fight. Nor would it be a very long fight. Straining to see through the fog and rain, Yabu searched for any sign of Crowhaven. But the Professor was absent. Yabu couldn't really blame him. There might be glory reserved for the victorious dead but little else. Crowhaven would lay low and hang back until most of the work was done. Until most of the opposition were dead.

Sighing, he released his umbrella and let it fly off into the fog.

*   *   *   *   *   *   *

This was it. This was End Game. No going back, only forwards. Now that their numbers had swelled, now that Mr Hand had revealed his hand it was Game On. There would be much blood spilt and the outcome was uncertain, yet thank the Gods for

509

weaponry and battle.

So Def thought, so she felt as she jogged the final half mile surrounded by her surviving friends and the Bird people. Up ahead, silhouetted against the red sunset, she could just see the looming forms of the Western Gate. White sand lay behind them, now they ran on black volcanic rock, iridescent in places with intermittent shrubs, bushes and explosions of flowers. Here things teemed with violent life or there was nothing. In particular she admired the cacti that grew in such abundance. They reminded her of home and that made her scowl. Only way she was going home was in a box.

With Beth gone, Crimson felt more empowered than ever before. As much as she had loved Beth, she had felt as though she lived in her shadow. This was her time to shine though, however brief. This was her time.

Frantic's head, as usual, was scrambled. She had felt for so long as though she had been chained to a chair, unable to move, unable to be, unable to express herself. Her whole life had been a prison sentence. First her parents, then her teachers and then the Russian had all been her jailors, but amongst the Alphabets, she had at least known a taste of freedom. They gave her space and they soothed her when she felt violently mad.

But now was not the time to hang back, to restrain herself, now was the time for all that rage and grief to spill out over the side, to engulf the enemy.

And who was the enemy? Why anyone who got in her way!

Rudi felt as though she was only half in her body. Of all the gang she had been closest to Semantic and now her friend was gone. And all she could see was those sightless staring eyes, looking through a telescope of nothing at forever. Rudi wanted to cry and not to cry. She feared if she gave her vent grief, her heart would implode but if she didn't....she would die anyway. For now it was best to hold it, to hold on for the moment of explosion when her long buried grief could finally be released.

And Antelope, leading the charge, glanced across at her opposite number Zen and wondered if victory was even a possibility.

Clustered around the Western Gate were dozens of bodies, holding guns and they were all looking her way. What good could axes and bows and arrows do against assault rifles or M16s? It was a pointless, hopeless charge, like the Charge of the Bloody Light Brigade. The English Hussars had gone down having been foolishly launched against the Russian Guns and boy, did she know how that felt.

They weren't firing though, not yet. They were waiting, cynically waiting, for the girls to close the gap, narrowing their odds of survival. Not long to go, not long; just a quarter of a mile. And the rock was giving way to soft sand, black and clutching. So hard to run in, but run they must. The West End Alphabets were keeping up. Hen and the Ox looked handy and Tarantula looked well mad. Ultra and Infra were calculating the odds, points of attack and strategy, like there was a way out. Kaos crackled and the Queen sang. Around them the bird tribes, led by Mr Hand, had their arrows notched and ready.

And bringing up the rear, the celestial sweep, Mr Lapp, a smile kriss-crossing his radiance with hope. But now there was something wrong and the air was abuzz with the sound of angry metal. And as Antelope turned, she saw Rudi fall and realised that the fog, like everything and everybody else on this island had betrayed them. But her realisation came too late, for the German girl's bullet-raked and lifeless body was already crashing into the black sands. With guns in front and guns behind it could only be a massacre!

*   *   *   *   *   *   *

The five armies had arrived, seemingly as one, in the End Zone, all of them looking to score, each in their respective ways. Yabu and Crowhaven from the north, Lapp and Hands from the South, Astapor and his Russian 'Nazi's' from the forested interior to the East. They had skirted the spaceships and followed the Alphabets and the recently arrived Bird Tribe to the Black Sands. The Alphabets and their allies, suspended in fog, had been caught between a rock and a hard place, as had Yabu and his Flesh Eaters.

So now the board was set, the pieces that had been in motion were now in place. Death would be sudden and conclusive. The forces of Modernity would triumph over the merely primitive. You didn't have to be a military genius to see it either. Crowhaven's troops in every theatre had the upper ground. At the Western Gate they stood with their backs to the great, heaving, mass of sea that stretched into the darkness and beyond. The Professor himself was nowhere in sight but that was coincidental. Up at the Great White Bite Yabu, like the Alphabets, was outgunned and surrounded.

All it would take for Death to rear its skull head in every quarter would be for a gloved hand to fall. And once the armies had engaged, and the weaker had been cleared from the face of the island, then a new order would be established, one in which the Englishman, not the Russian ruled with a will of iron. The Five Armies would soon reduce to one. That fact was as natural as day. This was to be an absolute overturning of the established order. There was nothing partial about this particular takeover.

It was a certainty, or so it appeared.

But there were other forces in play, forces that others hadn't factored into their equations. In handing the Fire Crystal to the Watcher, Wilber had unleashed one of those forces and the Watcher rapidly went from being a passive observer to an active participant in the Game that came at the End. The Fire Crystal, placed back in Crowhaven's satchel, powered up and in doing so activated the other crystals in surprising and unseen ways and another series of forces was released.

Those crystals were not just well cut pieces of glass. They were sentient and primed, able to transmit signals that did things. Changed things. Like rules and laws and outcomes.

Death fluttered in the noxious air, full of its own importance, feeling it held the upper hand, but then the island tapped it on the shoulder and death, turning to snap, was surprised.

A second blade of light swept through the fog. For those standing on the Black Sands it was not difficult to pinpoint the point of origin of the light. It had come from the heart of the Burning Grounds. Four hundred heads turned and waited, watched and wondered, their minds temporarily drawn from thoughts of battle.

What did it mean?

And in an instant the fog rolled over and dissolved, the rain stopped falling and the clouds disappeared. It was a complete and utter transformation and yet more shocking still, was that time appeared to glitch, and the sun rose a little higher in the sky, almost as though someone had pressed rewind.

The bleeding sun ceased bleeding and emitted rays, first orange, then yellow, then white and then surprise, surprise, blue white. The temperature rose and light returned to sweep the island a third time. In the midst of a new born day, three peels of thunder rang out and three flashes of lightning issued forth causing all those assembled to shade their eyes. When they opened them again there stood Justice Wilberforce Muldoon, sword in hand with a determined look upon his face.

"Game on!" he cried and began to run towards the Western Gate.

78

Battle

Forming a cordon around the Western Gate Crowhaven's forces grinned and raised their weapons. On Wilber ran. On and on, into the Valley of Death.

"Aim...."

Wilber raised the decapitator as he sprinted forward and laughter spilled out of his mouth interspersed with shrieks, whistles and chirps in a torrent of incoherent babble. Carruthers smiled too but in an entirely different way. It was time to end this charade.

"Fire!"

And all around him a series of Dead Men's Clicks echoed in his ears.

Again he spoke, louder this time.

"Fire!"

The same mocking clicks.

"Fire! Fire! Fire!" He shouted, shrieked and screamed, desperation like a tidal wave overwhelming and finally engulfing him.

*　　　*　　　*　　　*　　　*　　　*　　　*

Smithy, momentarily blinded by the light, had shaded his eyes, when the third beam revolved and hit, as had his men both in front of and behind the black Magician's motley crew. When they came back to themselves they found everything had changed, that the tables had turned. Their weapons simply wouldn't fire. All that machinery and technological innovation counted for nothing.

Next to Smithy, his Second-In-Command, gripped his M16 by the barrel, wielding it like a club.

"You gotta be kidding," someone groaned.

"Fix bayonets," the Second yelled.

All down the line bayonets were fixed and the First World War sprang vividly into every soldier's mind. It had looked like it was in the bag. Not anymore.

Yabu, tasting the winds of change gripped his machete with an unholy glee. All around him the cannibals had come to life. Like him they scented blood, blood that wasn't theirs. Peeling off from the main body, the rearguard wheeled and charged back up the Southern Sands towards Crowhaven's gawping mob. In spite of their training, many of the soldiers broke ranks, span and ran. Skirting the Burning Ground they charged eastwards along the white sands, cutting up through the dunes back towards the volcano. Sand gave way to worm-riddled rocks then deep grass. Beyond the grass lay the cover of the trees but none of them made it.

For in the grasses Yabu had positioned a battalion of Reptiles. Man-flesh loving gators that would offer no quarter to any human. Haring through the grass, the once disciplined soldiers, dropped one by one, screaming as they were crunched and shaken into pieces.

Yabu counted them off as they fell, stepping through the Magic Door of death and vanishing without trace. All would die in agony, scared and alone, mauled and shredded. So many horrors were still to come. There was to be an eruption of horrors, so terrifying that even the winds would scream. End Game was to be heard as well as seen. Let the lava of wrath rain down on Crowhaven and all his little tin soldiers, Yabu thought exultantly.

Hope as a dimension of human experience could collapse and vanish so easily. The rearguard wheeled again, seeing the gators concluding their work. Time to charge again.

*   *   *   *   *   *   *

Lola and George emerged from the Burning Ground as the fog cleared and the wilting sun revived. Charging Wilber, off in the distance, Caleb's blade held high, formed a focal point for George. Desperation seized him and terror clawed at his heart, not for himself, but for his nephew. To get so far and to fall for lack of support would be the greatest cruelty imaginable. George still carried the girl and Lola reclined in his arms, like a dying black swan. He so wanted to cast her aside but found he couldn't. They were attached at the navel by some invisible umbilicus. Why or how he didn't know.

As Wilber did, so Lola babbled. The vapours or her guilt had clearly addled her wits.

"I crawled here along the shale, on my hands and knees, through the damp tresses of seaweed, out of the sea. They thought I was dead, those stupid men, but I wasn't dead, you cannot kill what is already dead.

Do you understand now?"

George plainly didn't so she continued.

"He hurled me down and I sank into the sea but he should have known not to do that. The sea is my element. Clinging to rocks smothered in limpets, I eluded them. Up on the cliff they watched, but they did not see. Then they turned on each other like rabid dogs. Yapping canines tearing each other to pieces but not quickly. Oh no they took their time. Did it real slow. In the end it was death by a thousand cuts. In and out of time they ran."

Here she paused and her eyes rolled into the back of her head, only to resurface again, violet in colour, ablaze with sudden rage.

"You're not listening to me George."

The voice was not Lola's and it brought George up short.

"What?"

George's eyes sought the horizon and with a sudden and excruciating jolt he saw and understood that once more the sun was descending. Like the poem said, nae man could tether time nor tide... not indefinitely anyway. Not even the thing in the dark heart of the Burning Ground could do that.

Time was back on the table, riding the air, over the ground, like a prize stallion towards the finish line. And unless Wilber crossed the finish line before it, all would be lost.

"George!" the voice hissed out of Lola like air from a punctured balloon.

"You're not listening to me George. You never listened to me!"

George pulled up short, his heart pounding as he remembered that fatal day up on the cliff. Running then, running now, as fast as his legs would carry him. Reaching out with his hand to stop him, to stop Astapor from pushing her over. But no...no...no... in every nightmare he had ever had since that fateful day, he was always too late. Madeline fell, she always fell into the swirling waters.

And she hit and broke and sank and never surfaced. The sea swallowed her like the whale swallowed Jonah. But it had never regurgitated her, never spat her back out onto the sands until now. And in spite of everything George stopped and looked down at the recumbent girl, still in his arms. Looked down only he couldn't see Lola's face any more, only Madeline's.

"Do you know how I felt George when I hit the waves? Liberated. Between the two of you, you were tearing me apart. I wanted to go then, I so wanted to go, but the sea has a mind of its own. I had no shoes and no socks on and I sank. And they watched me and soon I was enveloped in a bubble of air and I could breath, full fathom five and all that and I felt as if I was floating on air. They took me to him then, the Ancient One, in his Cave of Forgotten Forms. At first I was scared and then he showed me his mind. What he had in store for me, for all of us. He changed me in so many ways and then he launched me onto a shoreline I could call my own. Off of this island, out of this nest of dragons I could be myself. On the night of the new moon I emerged on the leeward side of a boat to find a new world and a new sky full of stars.

"Yes, believe it or not there are thousands of islands here, not just one, and most of them are populated with wonders, not horrors.

With beauty not terror. But the Russian has fogged your mind, so that you can see no other island but his. You are as addicted to this game as he is. You can't see past it but you must learn to, George. You must learn to, if you are to have any hope of survival and dare I say it resurrection."

George stood gaping, his mind twisted, his heart convulsing. The agony in his soul almost overwhelmed him because finally he understood something about himself he had always denied. As much as he had loved Madeline she had always gotten in the way. And on some level he had always wanted her out of the way. And Astapor had understood that. In dropping her over that cliff he had done them all a favour.

It was only George who had clung to his pathetic myth of lost love and betrayal. Both Madeline and Astapor had seen it. Why had he not?

The Russian was what mattered. The Russian was the only thing that had ever mattered or would ever matter. And finally he didn't need to deny that. Callously... honestly George opened his arms and Lola dropped like a stone onto the rocky floor with a thud and an ouch. Up ahead the Western Gate beckoned him. There the green sea heaved and hauled, spewing memories out onto the sands. And with them questions he had never dared ask.

Behind him, lay the past, rotten and broken like those sundered, derelict ships, lured by the Ultimate Wrecker with his false lights and cunning tricks, onto this island rock, to be chained and studied. And he, George, had assisted in this process. He had helped the Russian every step of the way. The question was, could he imagine a life beyond that, but more importantly, why was he really running at full tilt across the Black Sands, after Wilber?

Was it to help him or to kill him?

*   *   *   *   *   *   *

George wasn't the only one having problems. Antelope's mind was swarming with visions she found hard to comprehend. All around her, bullets whizzed and people fell, hitting the ground hard, only to roll and stop. It was all so abstract though, life and death, love and hate. Life was no longer simple, not something she could understand or interpret anymore. She no longer knew herself. Did that matter now? After all the running it was almost over. The gate loomed large. Two hundred metres had become one hundred metres, a hundred was soon to become eighty.

The Running Man was so close she could almost reach out and touch him.

Yes, in spite of all the speeding metal flying his way, Wilber was still running. Crowhaven's troops were still blocking his access to the stones. Astapor was still nowhere to be seen. And all around her, the Alphabets still ran. Well, most of them. Some of them.

Another round of hostile chatter from the machine guns and Tarantula and the Ox thudded into the black sand, punctured over and over, through lungs, face and heart. Demolished like old buildings by that wrecking ball, reality, they bled out and ceased breathing, their eyes staring sightlessly up into the now-clear night air.

It was then Antelope saw him. The handsome soldier with the blank expression, raising his gun and pointing it at her. She watched him as he watched her, one eye open and one eyed closed, staring down the barrel of his gun, fixing her in his sight. His finger began to squeeze the trigger, to add pressure incrementally, as he had been trained.

Such a pretty face, Antelope thought. She imagined them dancing together in a club, him holding her tight, pressing his hand into the arch of her back, the lights pulsing, the music pounding, him leaning in towards her, their lips meeting, tongues reaching and...

Click.

She flung wide her arms and tilted her head back, inviting death to take her, all of her, into his arms, forever.

But she felt nothing and her legs carried her automatically over the last thirty metres of sand towards the boy of her dreams.

Click, click, click.

Antelope accelerated but the world around her seemed to freeze. The cold, young soldier's face, so certain, was suddenly full of terror. His fear was almost touching and it would have melted Antelope's heart if she had been able to feel it at that moment.

But at that moment she couldn't. The pain of her dead was still too raw and anyway the axe was already in motion. Such a pretty face. Such a promising face. So masculine. And yet without the certainty of a loaded gun to back up his frail sense of self, the soldier was nothing. Just a frightened little boy waiting for her axe to fall.

And fall it did, diagonally, across that pretty face of his. The features were suddenly pulp. Eye, nose and mouth just a red slash. He didn't have time to scream but he didn't die immediately. In the sands he writhed for three long minutes in an agony he would have thought impossible before he finally found stillness.

By that time, Antelope was long gone and three other bodies had fallen prey to her axe. After all this time it was so easy for her. Like lopping the heads from daisies.

Where had she heard that expression before? She tried to find the answer but her mind was blank. The long lines of waiting soldiers waited no more. Their smug expressions had been expunged and their neat formations broken. Chaos held every frenzied body in its grip. Bodies whirled and swirled, ripped and slashed, clubbed and pierced until the world seemed composed of nothing but hacking arms. Screams and cries filled the air and blood spurted, sprayed and pumped out of the punctured and the hewn onto the black sands.

To Antelope it was an exhilarating nightmare, but one in which the net, once huge, had now closed and held every thrashing body in its mesh. Now the net was being lifted from the water, a dripping mass of blood and plasma, brain and vomit. In her mind's eye she saw it.

She hoisted the axe again and again, swinging downwards onto fallen bodies or cross ways from left to right, lopping heads like daisies. Where had she heard that expression?

It was all so abstract and yet in the last few minutes her world had become coherent again. She understood who she was finally and what her purpose was. Her world was smaller now that the bullets had stopped flying. The battlefield was a narrow strip of land perhaps fifty by thirty metres full of heaving bloodied forms. Neither guns nor bows were of use here. Swords worked, knives, axes worked. It was all so gloriously medieval.

Around her, the bodies fell thick and fast and before she knew it, Antelope found herself facing Crowhaven's commander Carruthers. He had lost his beret and his forehead bore a deep gash, as did his left leg. Bloodied but unbowed, the arrogant fool sneered contemptuously at Antelope.

"Mucky little unit aren't you. You're so dirty, you're unfit for service. Lie down like a good dog, won't you and receive chastisement. I'll make it quick I promise."

He gripped his machete in his bleeding right hand expecting Antelope to crumble but Antelope wasn't even there. In her mind's eye she was running up a long flight of stairs, from the dark basement up into the bright white light. The stairs were bright too, bright yellow and there were many people on them, like her, heading up endless flights into the light. Nothing and no one could be allowed to get in her way.

Antelope remembered games of tag she had played back in kindergarten.

Those games of chase me, chase me, led down memory lane, back to the nursery where old toys rotted, but as sweet as that time had been, she didn't have time for it now. Certain memories were like birds she held in her hands and let go. Some had white feathers, some black but they all flew upwards into the pulsing white light and in time they vanished.

But before the light, there was a great blue sky, which bathed the stairs on which she ran. Great forms floated in the sky, geometries of all shapes and sizes. She was aware of one that had her name on. An upended magenta tetrahedron with a square base, surmounted by a transparent dome. It hung in the air, awaiting her arrival.

Immanence was all, as was the music that filled her now.

Suddenly upon the stairway an obstruction appeared. A great, black crumpled box full of trash and broken parts. She needed to move it, to sweep it aside, so she dropped her axe, letting the weight of the double-bladed weapon do the work, and then rapidly hoisted it aloft again, in a dazzling upwards sweep. The box flew into the air, shattered and scattered and Antelope ran on, up and up, pounding the stairs like it was Christmas morning and she was in search of all her presents.

Behind her something fell but she was already gone. Nothing would come between her and her presents. Everything that wasn't gift-wrapped was to be ignored or destroyed. To her it was all the same.

79

Blood on The Dancefloor

Yabu's machete dripped with blood and gore and his face was similarly covered. Many of the Cannibals had fallen but that didn't matter now. All that mattered was that the board wasn't fixed, it was in motion again. Just up ahead, the Western Gate towered. The black sands glowed with blue electricity. Behind him lay the white sands and the many bodies of Crowhaven's army. Those that hadn't fled into the long grasses where his gators waited, had been carved into future meals and lay awaiting collection.

Without the aid of their machine guns they were nothing. The Professor's army was being decimated and there was nothing he could do about it but where was the man? It was time they had a chat about his retirement plans.

Glancing to his left he saw the Alphabets advancing as a body with Mr Hand and his Bird Tribe. Both groups had taken heavy losses, being attacked as had he, from in front and behind, but their fighting spirit was still intact. If anything, the loss of their friends had galvanised them. They fought with absolute and utter fury, impaling and chopping with total abandon.

The girls had exposed the boys for what they were. Second rate children with little or no taste for hand to hand combat. Yabu chuckled and his eyes, blazing with red fire, flicked this way and that.

Mr Lapp had peeled off with some of Mr Hand's fighters and were tackling The Russian's Bodyguard, who like Crowhaven's toy boys hadn't brought much to the party other than their Mausers. Drull was always the exception, having picked up the axe of a fallen Alphabet, was making mincemeat of the Bird People. However, his compadres weren't doing so well. Four of them had been dropped and now the Bird People were backing off and Mr Lapp was making his stand.

Lapp turned momentarily and caught Yabu's eye. They each of them nodded to one another and then Lapp turned his attention back to Drull who let out a low roar and charged at Mr Lapp. The Magician held his ground, smiling with grim amusement. Yabu didn't fancy the giant's chances.

Pausing momentarily to enjoy the spectacle, he wheeled and scanned, searching, ever searching. Aah there was Wilber, right in front of the Western gate wielding his blade like a trained professional, slashing and dropping the few remaining soldiers of Crowhaven's little band as though they were creatures without consequence.

Yabu eyed his watch. 20:53. Seven minutes left and it was very much 'on'. As thrilling as any world cup final in the history of the beautiful game, this was!

"Come on," he shouted, "come on!"

Eyes again in motion, ravenously searching and finding Antelope. Behind her in a spreading puddle of dark blood lay Crowhaven's commander Carruthers, an axe embedded in his chin, bisecting his face, up to the space between his eyes.

Antelope striding towards Wilber, picking up a bore spear from an impaled soldier. Striding out, a strange look in her once beautiful eyes.

Yabu's mind shrieking, shrieking, like a trapped woman in a burning building.

No, Antelope, no.

*　　　*　　　*　　　*　　　*　　　*　　　*

Lola hauled herself to her feet and, ever the cat, brushed herself down, sweeping the sand from her long coat and ripped T-shirt. She pulled up her leather gloves and surveyed the scene unfolding before her eyes, on the terminal point of the western shore. She felt a little light-headed but not unwell.

"And death came into the garden and kissed the children..." she murmured to herself.

Running westwards towards the gate was George. Damn him! Why had he dropped her? Why had he left her? They were supposed to go in together. Crowhaven's army had been all but destroyed and as she watched, Drull fell, headless and dead, victim of Mr Lapp's years of fastidious martial study and training. Lurch and the Dogman, now dogless, lay cowering in the sand and Mr Hand's Bird people surrounded them, spears pointing downwards.

It appeared to be almost over. All that remained was to mop up and then it would be time for Wilber to slot in the crystals and for everyone to go home. If there was such a place. In spite of everything, Lola felt uneasy. Where was he? Where was the Russian?

Then she stopped and heard a sound that caused her heart to beat faster and faster and her eyes to fill with tears. From behind her the sound of marching feet and howling humans. From out of the heart of the Burning Ground came the Professor, at the head of a host of two hundred or more soldiers.

And straining on reinforced leads, yellow-headed attack zombies foaming at the mouth. In a moment she saw and understood and then out to sea a new sound and new motion. Dozens of boats filled with hundreds of armed soldiers and a form in black, leaping out of the lead boat as it touched the shore, and striding up the sloping sands towards the Western Gate.

Standing immobile in the sea, the surf rolling over his feet, hands on hips, was the Russian.

*　　　*　　　*　　　*　　　*　　　*　　　*

The pitter-patter of boneless feet, rain clad, hammering holes into the mud was all Wilber could hear. His head was full of voices, gabbling and shrieking; voices not his. A low-pitched, sinister voice was whispering to him. It was as though he was possessed.

"Don't forget to tell them little willy," the voice chundered, "the bungled and the botched, the crotchless saints and vipers, the arse wipers, the spit lickers and whittlespits dragged up and out of their lime lined pits. Those disgusting little girls have opened the gates to hell and now all our nightmares will crawl out of the barred darkness to play."

Reeling, he pressed his hands into his ears. This was not what he wanted to hear, not now that the prize was so close. The line of soldiers in front of him were all staring at him, in mockery and splendour. Such a glorious display. Fighting hard to regain his centre, Wilber steadied himself and stood upright looking first forwards and westwards, then spinning through 180 degrees, to peer backwards and eastwards. The Game had flipped once more, as though someone had pounded on the board with a gloved fist and made all the pieces jump, causing them to land on different squares. It had been over. A conclusion had been reached. He'd seen it and his heart had leapt with joy and hope. But not now, not anymore.

The Russian's forces had lined up in front of the Western Gate and now Crowhaven's Second wave, led by the golf-mad professor were emerging from the Burning Ground, seemingly immune to the toxic effects that had rendered the zone No-Go since the year dot.

Then the voice was back filling Wilber's mind with unwanted words of advice.

"Wilber, dear Wilber, you must learn to rotate your hells. Wipe that dust from your dirty mirror, pig boy. You may reveal the true monster's face. Not that you'd ever want to see it. You couldn't punch clay that ugly. It would destroy you."

Here it paused to laugh. This was a new kind of torture, one that made hanging, drawing and quartering seem preferable.

"If the wind blows, the plague flies are elsewhere. If the rain drums, the plague flies are elsewhere. If you are high in the mountains, the plague flies are elsewhere. But if you're warm and no winds blow or no rains fall, if the sun shines, then the plague flies will surround you. If conditions are perfect for you, so will they be for the plague flies; they will feast upon you and plague is imminent. Oh yes, rotate your hells!"

Clutching his ears like his head might explode, Wilber emitted a high-pitched scream and mustering whatever strength remained, broke into a final charge. Up ahead the Russian grinned. There was still so much to enjoy in End Game.

*   *   *   *   *   *   *

But the Russian wasn't to have everything his own way. Once more the mood had changed along with the energy state of the island. A sudden intensification had gripped everyone moving on the Black Sands. It was as though lightning was crackling in every cortex, speeding everything and everybody up, robbing them of fear and restraint, making them more committed in their application of force and violence. It was as though everybody was running up endless flights of steps, making quantum leaps with every step, shifting energy state with every breath. Everybody, regardless of whatever their pasts contained had without warning become Running Men and Women. Now everyone was converging on a point of light, the hero or heroine of their own stories. Now everyone had meaning and a purpose. At the top of that seemingly endless flight of steps, a spaceship awaited to take each and everyone of them away. All they had to do was keep on running and stay alive.

*   *   *   *   *   *   *

End Game was not just for the few but for the many; even so it came at a price. That which had been hidden or lied about, forced its way up through the slime, the filth of the unconscious and erupted in storm, overwhelming the appearance of order. Fractures became splits, which became gaping wounds that gushed with the red rage of total madness. And not just a laughing or a desolate madness, but a violent madness, commanding all those who experienced it to kill without remorse and to go on killing. Not just the usual suspects either but people like George and Antelope, and most shockingly Wilber...

George's vision of Madeleine had unhinged him. He thought of Wilber and he saw that it was he, not Astapor who was the enemy. Kill him and the darkness would vanish from the island forever. Suddenly everything was so clear. Taking his machete from his belt he ran towards the boy with just one thought in his mind. With joy in his pounding heart, George saw that his quarry was near and that his head was set at a precarious angle.

The curious light that had for so long settled over the Burning Ground had gone out and the fog had dissipated, revealing the broken forms of the rotting, rusting space ships.

Crowhaven's troops, led by the Professor, moved slowly over the sands towards the Western Gate, away from the Watcher's nest. There they were awaited by the Russian Line. It was as though they were two great jaws, lined with serrated trinities of teeth, being brought slowly, inexorably together. All those caught in that gaping maw would be shredded and crushed, impaled and torn. The image brought a beaming smile to the Professor's thin lips.

A smile which set, like a dying sun when he was thrust suddenly aside and a dark, hugely bearded form, darted past him, galloping towards the similarly running Dinosaur George Muldoon. All lines of force were converging on the Candidate, who, like Hercules had completed all his labours, save the final one. The stones were unlit and as no crystal had been placed in its allotted slot the game was still in motion and moving towards a disastrous conclusion.

And why? Because like George, Antelope had been unhinged by exposure to her own unresolved conflicts. In the blink of a cobra's eye she had gone from Amazonian Queen to Mata Hari with more than a dash of the kamikaze in her make up. Like George, when she looked at Wilber, she saw not just an enemy, but a carcass on a meat hook, dripping blood. The image caused her to swing her bore spear in the direction of the red-eyed boy who only had eyes for the grinning Russian.

Unperturbed by any considerations of treachery, Antelope began marching towards the unsuspecting candidate. Her eyes became slitted and her rage swelled like the belly of a pregnant woman. But she would give birth to death, not life. Hoisting the spear to her shoulder she called out Wilber's name in a roar like a fighter jet. As Wilber turned in filmic slo-mo she swung the spear back but before she could throw it, Yabu's blade pierced her heart and she toppled as George moved in behind her to take her place.

Eyes blind with rage he readied his killer blow and Wilber, frozen to the spot, gazed up at him with uncomprehending eyes. Another cry, louder than Antelope's, tore the night in half, and both Wilber and George turned to see Great Uncle Muldoon screeching to a halt just yards from them. The old coot was sweating like an Eskimo in a sauna and his face was glowing the colour of Ribena. First he pointed at George in accusation, then clutching his heart, his mouth working like a fish out of water, he pitched forward and face-planted. After five astonishingly violent convulsions Great Uncle Muldoon twitched and was still.

The shock of his Uncle's death was enough to snap George out of his murderous reverie and bring him back down to earth with a bang. What had he been thinking?

80

Aftermath

Lola's run, slowed to an amble then a balletic walk. Finally, she halted and stared down at Antelope as she writhed, gasped and bled out. Yabu's blade had just about cleaved her heart in two, but it had been broken long before that. George knelt beside her as she drew her final breaths and held her blood stained hand. There was nothing else he could do. Antelope had made her choices, as had he.

After a while she was still and George let his head sink down, his long hair covering his face. He could not recall a time he had felt as low as he did now or quite so defeated. Wilber, for all the death that surrounded him, was still fixated on completing his task. Slowly, in a reverie he walked the final few metres towards the Western Gate and reached out to touch the stones. The black sands beneath his feet seemed to shimmer with blue electricity as he made contact and his hair stood on end, as though he had just touched a Van der Graaf Generator.

Def, standing beside Zenith, looked stunned. Watching Antelope fall had taken the wind out of her sails, driving her into a state of shock. Her usual response to grief was rage and endless violence but the savage fact of Antelope's betrayal was something she couldn't process. Gravity bore down on her and she couldn't move.

Yabu, walking past her, paused momentarily before stooping to retrieve his bloodied weapon. He cleaned the blade by gripping it in his gloved hand, then pulling the blade away from the hand in a smooth, sleek motion. His face was grim and it was obvious he had taken no joy in this particular kill. Something unique in his experience.

George raised his head, glancing from Yabu to Def and then Zenith. The other Alphabets were similarly in a state of shock but already the question hung in the air. Who would assume control? A new tension could be felt, explosive and unpredictable. Would fighting break out again and if so who would be killing who? Perhaps the Russian and the Englishman would simply stand back and let nature take its course.

Seconds stretched and still nobody did anything. Neither Def nor Zen felt inclined or able to act, nor could any of the other girls for reasons no one dared articulate. Finally, it fell to Lola to get things going again.

"Well don't just stand there, do something!"

It was a line worthy of a Carry On film but no one so much as tittered. Nobody moved and with a look of utter distaste on her face Lola rolled her eyes, strode over to Wilber and tapped him firmly on the shoulder.

"So... Get on with it! Get the crystals out of the bag and into the stones"

When he didn't react, she gripped his wrist, then wrenched and twisted it, to check out the watch strapped there.

"Five minutes. You've ample time."

Wilber looked completely bewildered.

"I'm not sure I can, Lola."

"Why ever not?"

George stood up, likewise perplexed.

"Yes Wilber, why not?"

Wilber tilted his head and looked up at the star filled heaven as if the answer was up 'there' written in star light.

"I dunno. It would just seem... well, err, disrespectful." Here he paused and stared at the fallen leader of the Alphabet Gang.

"Antelope's dead!" he mewled plaintively.

Def, brandishing her axe, went puce and gnashed her teeth so violently, blue sparks flew. For a moment it looked like Wilber might lose his head.

"Oh get a grip Wilber! Just about everyone's dead. Like one more matters."

For once, Lola found herself in agreement with Def.

"Listen to the surly metal freak Wilber. For once in her sad, depraved life, she's right. Antelope sold you out and would have gored you like a prize pig, if Old Croco hadn't pulled off his machete magic. Nice shot by the way…"

Yabu grunted, secretly pleased to be praised.

Here, Mr Lapp stepped forward.

"We've had our differences Yabu but that shot was one in a million."

George stepped into the ring looking less than comfortable, his hands raised to placate.

"As true as that statement is, I'm not sure it's entirely appropriate. I think a little sensitivity might be in order."

Lola's scoff was audible halfway across the island.

"This from the man who claimed he'd nurse me and who ended up dumping me on my head whilst he ran off to murder his nephew."

George had the good sense to look pained.

"I was conflicted, that was all. But I got over it."

"For now," Lola muttered under her breath.

Ultra looked at Infra and Infra looked at Ultra.

"This place really messes with your head," Infra dead-panned.

"No shit Sherlock!" Ultra shot back.

As true as this statement undoubtedly was, Mr Hand wasn't really following the patter. Instead his awareness was fixed on Wilber and what had emerged from the deep. The sun's descent had been momentarily arrested but it had resumed its arc and darkness once more stole across the face of the island. The time to act was now and quickly.

"Wilber, the Russian is coming. For all of us. He walks now, away from the sea and across the sand towards us. He has a couple of hundred men with him and he is less than a hundred metres from us. Do you not see him?"

"Yeah I see him alright," came Wilber's retort.

Mr Hands spun then and pointed back towards the Burning Ground from whence Crowhaven and his new force had emerged and were stalking towards them.

"And that way...over there. You see? That is the direction that Crowhaven approaches us from. And he too has a large force of armed men. And they, too, don't look friendly!"

A smile lit up Wilber's face. He looked like somebody had slipped something into his tea.

"I can see him. I'm not blind you know."

Mr Hands, now shaking, knelt in front of Wilber and took his hands gently. As though Wilber's hands were made of feathers.

"You need to act now, Wilber. Now is a time for doing, not thinking or talking. Place the crystals on top of the stones. Only you can do this. We cannot help you. We cannot even touch the stones. Tell me you understand."

The note of desperation was obvious in his voice but that didn't phase Wilber. He was calm, he was way too calm.

81

Odd Bedfellows

Quickly, all too quickly, the Russian and the Englishman closed the gap, marching their armies towards the survivors of the Charge of Black Sands. Each helmeted soldier bore a shield and a nine-foot-long Boar spear. The trappings of the modern had been forgotten and the ancient had returned. The scent of Atlantis clogged their nostrils but there were echoes of other cultures too, of the Greek and the Roman, of Sparta and Athens.

Coming to a halt, the two Generals surveyed the remnant of those who had stood against them.

"A valiant effort," cried the Russian, clapping his hands sportingly.

"Sadly to no avail," added the Professor, joining him, "but at least we know the lay of the land now, who is loyal and who is not."

George folded his arms and regarded each faction with disgust.

"I see you pair resolved your differences."

"Quite," said the Professor. "You should know by now George it is not wise to bet against the Russian."

At this point Wilber stepped forward beaming from ear to ear.

"Lovely to see you again Professor. You too Astapor. What a wonderful way to end the show. I'm guessing everybody is here. No more hidden reserves. No more caged bodies. No more surprises. Come on in lads, come and join us."

Detaching himself from his army, Astapor skirted the Western Gate and approached the gaggle of survivors. Mirroring his actions, step for step, the Professor likewise came forward at a rapid pace. The two Generals, although confident, were still cautious. First

Astapor and then Crowhaven motioned for the surviving Bird Tribes and Alphabets to drop their weapons, kneel and place their hands on their heads.

When the last of the ragged remnant had complied, they resumed their approach.

Soon all of the Magicians, Wilber, George and Lola stood round in a circle and to complete the round, having miraculously survived was Lurch. The Russian, seemingly heartily pleased with himself, took on the role of Master of Ceremonies.

"Good of you to be so magnanimous Wilber. You really are the best we've seen. I would be honoured if you could join me at my beautiful home."

Lurch, although delighted with the outcome of the Last Battle foolishly felt the need to enlighten Astapor as to his current domiciliary status.

"I'm afraid you have no home Master, it burnt down."

Astapor made a fish mouth, there was a thwock and before anyone knew what was happening Lurch had pitched over, an arrow in his back. No one so much as gasped when he hit the ground, dead.

"It's easy to be magnanimous when you are the Victor," Wilber observed.

Crowhaven burst out laughing.

"Indeed it is Wilber but that isn't you is it? Now hand over the crystals, my satchel and the watch. We need to reset the Game Board and get you chained up.... I mean bedded down for the night."

The Professor appeared delighted with how things had turned out and also with his turn of phrase. The Russian however was somewhat less exuberant; he wasn't smiling but regarded Wilber as though he were a block of marble he was going to chisel into a masterpiece.

"It seems Wilber I underestimated you."

"I'm afraid you did Count. This time it will cost you."

82

The Watcher's Eye

The quality of light was changing yet again, and once more darkness was denied admittance into the world. The old sun had almost bled out but it seemed a second sun was filling the sky now, but not with red light, rather with green. Rising from the seemingly dead heart of the burning ground was the Flying Eye, the eye in the sky.

The Watcher's Eye.

It was no longer as it had been when Wilber had first approached it. Now it appeared less like an eye and more like an egg, an egg that was cracking. Such a curious object, so bizarre and yet so compelling. All the assembled turned around to look at it but not all could hold its gaze. The Magicians could and did, as did Wilber and the Alphabets, Lola and the Bird Tribes but the armed lines of soldiers found they could not.

Their heads filled with static and the sound of screaming children. The revenging hordes of the fallen ran through their minds, plundering and pillaging what little sanity remained and the soldiers could do nothing but scream back, gripping their ears in the hope that those ghastly cries would go away. It was torture. They writhed, dropped to their knees, and cried out for their masters to save them, but all Astapor and Crowhaven could do was watch them dumbfounded. Some curled up in the foetal position and began sucking their thumbs. Some prayed to Gods they wanted to believe in, others impaled themselves on their own spears.

Wilber watched all this impassively, a curious light around him. He took no delight in the suffering of others but all of these men who knelt and screamed had been tortured, murdered and mocked. They had dispatched thousands of men, women and children with impunity justifying each and every horror to themselves with that age-old disclaimer…

"But we were only following orders."

That simply didn't wash anymore. Every soul carried a record of their past deeds in every atom of every cell in their bodies. Even in the light around their bodies. It was a brutal fact. Everyone was responsible for their own choices. That was the price of freedom. He knew on some level he had always believed that. Now they would too.

The sky was a green marvel, like Matisse had inked it in; a verdant, algal green pulsing with life and healing, growth and protection. It mirrored exactly the hue of the sea. Now, sea and sky were one. Wilber, George and the others watched in amazement. For the first time in a long time they saw the world through a child's eyes in all its glory and wonder. The jaded, jaundiced cynicism of life in the third millennium faded and ebbed away to be replaced by hope and the sense of renewed possibilities.

Even Lola felt it and her violet eyes shone, purged of all the twisted hate and cruelty that marred her soul. Wilber, seeing this, moved over to her and slipped his hand into hers. She took it without looking at him then squeezed the hand. Wilber's insides turned to goo. His life was complete.

The sea and the sky seemed to dance together. The male and the female principles conjoined in an act of ecstatic union. It had always been there, it was just that no one had seen it. Or rather only the few and they had been dubbed mad. The waters seemed to blaze with light, alive with phosphorescent forms that made the waters glow with rainbow cascades. It was the light of Christmas trees and neon signs, lightning and crystals, of phytoplankton or photocopiers. All centuries seemed to coalesce into this now and glow with the light of a million stars.

It was the best night of fireworks any of them had ever seen. All they needed now was a little Mozart or Drum 'n' Bass, perhaps a light ambient froth, seasoned by Stravinsky and then their lives would be complete.

Instead what they got was their ears filled with the screams of torturers and murderers. But not for long. The Eye had risen to a height about ninety metres above the heart of the Burning Ground and was moving westwards, towards them. As it moved, the once desiccated zone burst out into bloom and trees, flowers and shrubs sped out of the earth in an accelerated growth cycle. Soon the jungle was thick there and paradise once more touched the earth.

Flowers of pink, yellow and blue rioted in abundance filling the air with trilling sounds and harmonic peels. The island, like the people, was open to healing. Everyone watched in joy and amazement, everyone but the Russian and the Englishman.

Astapor had Crowhaven by the throat and was strangling him like an unwanted kitten.

"You were supposed to blow it up. You were supposed to destroy it!"

With bloodshot, pleading eyes the Professor rasped out a response.

"We did. We sprayed it with flame and blew it to high heaven. There's no way anything could have survived that."

This simply served to magnify Astapor's fury.

"Well something obviously did! Look!"

The Eyeship was now almost directly above them. All around it, waves of electricity and what appeared to be static, pulsed outwards filling the air with curious geometric shapes. To gaze into the shapes was to have one's mind vajazzled. Wilber thought once more of the images of Kalibi Yau manifolds he had gotten hooked on whilst surfing the web. He saw them for what they were now, points of dimensional overlap and collapse. Tunnels into multiple dimensions.

Now the ship was directly above them. It hovered, completely immobile and without sound. The eye was gone and now only the egg remained. Each form was part of the same force, only in different phases of a universal process. This was a transitional phase and the egg was cracking. From the centre point one could see a dark circular window and here the watcher stood. From the black window emerged a clockwise spiral which turned once, twice, three and a half times. Electricity crackled in the folds of this great spiral, energy of every hue and frequency. Before their eyes they saw matter becoming pure energy and energy becoming matter. All belonged to one substance on a spiralling quantum stairway that led from the earth up into the stars.

Suddenly, without warning, purple lightning issued from the egg, splitting the sky in every direction. On the earth the belligerent soldiers howled as one and their bodies shimmered, swirled and faded into nothing. It was as though they had never been there.

The Englishman and the Russian, well used to wonders, had never seen anything like this before. Never. Not in all their experience. Talk about signs and wonders. This was one. The Professor looked like he was about to burst into tears and the Russian was incandescent.

"That isn't fair," he was saying, "that is simply not cricket."

Then in the blink of an eye his self-pitying tears had turned to quivering rage. Reaching into the folds of his tunic he retrieved a cruelly curving knife and lunged at Wilber, but Yabu, ever cautious and ever sly had anticipated this. Pushing Wilber out of harm's way he gave a low whistle and Marvin who had been lying as still as a log amongst the heaps of corpses sprang into action, seizing the Professor by the ankle and dragging him off towards the pulsing green sea. His screams split the scene but only temporarily. Soon he too fell silent and peace returned to the island once more.

But not for long.

Out at sea, beyond the Great White Smile, the putt putt putt of a ship's engine caught the air and drew the attention of the assembled throng. Rubbernecking, like passing drivers at a Road Traffic Accident, the survivors turned to gawp only to observe Hogarth Macready run his vessel aground.

Deliberately, apparently.

A rope ladder dangling, from the bow of the ship, on the port side, supported the lumbering Captain's weight as he descended to the Black Sands and began running, or rather waddling towards them, as fast as his stout legs would carry him. He wore a long coat and had a distinctly piratical air. To his shoulder an African Gray parrot clung, that muttered and cursed like a Cornish Fish Wife. All he lacked was a wooden leg and an eyepatch. At one point he paused to draw breath and all feared it might well be his last and that his legs or heart might give out under him, but at the last moment he composed himself and resumed his course making a bee line straight for Wilber.

Everyone waited breathlessly to see what would happen, even the Russian.

En route he passed Crowhaven, still writhing in Marvin's jaws and without breaking his stride he reached down and whipped off the soon-to-be ex-Magicians cape, which he placed in a well used plastic bag and continued on his way.

When Hogarth arrived he stood directly in front of Wilber, and swinging his arm, slapped the youth's face as hard as he could.

"Jump to ship mate, look lively."

Stunned out of his torpor, Wilber hurtled towards the pentagonal five-gated structure, with the Captain following close behind him. It was as though the tortoise had become a hare and the hare a tortoise. Oh Aesop! One thing the Captain could lay claim to was strength, if not agility and in two shakes of a lamb's tail, he had positioned himself at the foot of the nearest trilithon and was ready to give the now animated Wilber a leg up.

Cupping his hands into a stirrup he urged Wilber on.

"Giddy up lad, or this rotting hulk of an island with its black sails will close its doors behind us!"

A little flowery but Wilber got the gist. Leaping into the fat captain's cupped hands and using his broad shoulders as leverage, Wilber half vaulted, half scrambled up the twelve-foot high stone megalith. Hauling himself into a standing position, he stood atop of the Western gate and surveyed all before him, his eye in particular drawn up the side of the volcano to the smoking ruins of

Astapor's tower complex. Those below him saw a purple silhouette set against a pulsing green backdrop, whilst above him, the suspended egg ripped through a series of rapid colour changes. It was as if the ship were burning off layer upon layer of accumulated memory. The dross of years spent in a state of incarceration perhaps.

Yabu flicked his gaze over to the Russian who stood as immobile as the rest of them, watching Wilber emptying the satchel, taking out each crystal and setting them down, oh so carefully.

Wilber glanced at Crowhaven's digital watch. The glowing red numbers revealed it was 20:58. Less than two minutes left on the clock. It was unbelievable when he considered what he had been through in the course of a single day. Incredible to discover that a single day could change one so totally and absolutely. Close to exhaustion, yet strangely energised he placed the first crystal, Crowhaven's cube into its slot atop of the lintel, on which he knelt. Then he moved around to the next. It was quite the high wire act and he had to be careful not to trip.

On one hand he could be quite dextrous, could Wilber, on the other a ridiculous clutz. Best not to screw it up now. Round to the next lintel, to slot Yabu's octahedron in place, with the sound of his raging blood pounding in his ears.

Round to the third lintel to slot the icosahedron in place, then the fourth. Here he paused as he held up Astapor's fire crystal to the light. Then in it went.

Round and round the roses... to end at the beginning. All of creation was a garden, after all.

Taking the final crystal, the dodecahedron, in hand, he placed it without a second thought into its slot as the clock ticked down through its hairline to zero point.

It was, as Jesus allegedly said at the end...finished.

The green light that had flooded everything dimmed and went out and the sun emitted its final red rays and disappeared beneath the horizon, leaving no afterglow trailing in its wake, only darkness.

All anyone could do was wait now. Wilber pressed the small

button on the side of Crowhaven's watch and the digital numbers illuminated, only now they were white, not red.

The time was precisely 21:00.

Precious seconds passed, everyone as nervous as Schrodinger's cat on a hot tin roof.

"George," Wilber cried plaintively, "shouldn't something have happened by now?"

Immersed in total darkness the survivors stood and waited and then a sound reached every ear, a sound that made the blood run cold.

The Russian's laughter!

83

Macready Takes Charge

A match flared in the darkness. Applied to a wick, well served by oil, swilling around in the base of a storm lantern, it further illuminated the scene casting shadows worthy of a Gothic Horror Movie. Hogarth Macready, having lit the lamp, hoisted it aloft and searched out poor cowering Wilber up on the stones.

"Well, did you slip 'em in shipmate?"

"Every last one Captain."

Macready shook his head dumbfounded.

"Are you sure? Check 'em again!"

Wilber tiptoed round to each slotted crystal to verify none were loose or not quite touching the sides, but they all were. Returning to his starting point on the leeward lintel, he knelt down and called softly down to the captain.

"All present and correct Sir."

Macready harrumphed and stamped his feet in irritation. He'd been following events closely, floating round the island on his barnacle-encrusted craft. Like others in the know, he'd been watching and waiting for an opportunity like this for years. The idea that he could get back to earth in a time zone he recognised appealed greatly. Too much time spent on or near the island was enough to drive anyone to drink. Or worse. It was time to change up and he was damned if he was going to let this opportunity slide.

"Get down from there boy!"

Wilber nodded, dropped into a sitting position, then swung and turned round, lowering his body till he was hanging off the leeward lintel. From there he let go and plopped easily into Macready's waiting arms. The Captain set him down, then clutching his plastic bag stalked over to the watching group and set up camp in their midst. Folding his arms and scowling he looked like he meant business. Wilber joined him. Everyone wanted answers.

"So, what happened?" Macready asked in a tone that suggested in his youth he had been used to demanding money with menaces. "This whole business has the whiff of fish about it and somebody needs to start talking. Now!"

Here he looked pointedly at Astapor, holding his lantern up at eye level so that the Slav's high cheekbones stood out in harsh relief. If he hadn't been a psychopathic scientist, Astapor could so easily have been a supermodel.

The Russian shrugged.

"Who died and made you God?"

Macready was not impressed.

"Oh is that the way you're going to play it, is it? Wilber!"

Wilber took the proffered plastic bag, removed the crumpled blue cape that had been thrust inside and draped it around the Captain's shoulders. Then he did up the clasp. Macready stepped back and preened. Lapp, Yabu and Hand clearly impressed, clapped politely.

"It takes more than a cape to make you a Magician," the Russian snarled. "Anyway the position is not even vacant. Professor Crowhaven..."

Here he was interrupted by the sound of violent splashes and terrified screams followed by a deafening silence.

"...Would appear to be permanently indisposed," Wilber concluded smugly. "You're just going to have to face it, Count. The Professor will not be returning to work, nor will any of your soldiers for that matter."

The surviving Alphabets and the people of the Bird Tribes, who had gathered around the periphery of the circle cheered and roared like it was the end of term and school was out.

Wilber, his dander well and truly up, jabbed his right index finger in Astapor's direction.

"Oh and by the way, you're finished and what's more your reign is over!"

The Russian looked quizzically at the agitated youth.

"Are you sure Wilber?"

The Magicians stood and stared at each other. The bodies of the fallen surrounded them but they remained alive and unbloodied. It was so typical. Wilber, more from habit than anything else glanced at his watch. 21:05. It was past the appointed hour and by this point in the proceedings he was more than a little irritated. Something should have happened by now. He hadn't come all this way to light the blue touch paper only to have the rocket fizz, sputter and not launch. That was not the way this movie ended.

But what to do?

The fog had cleared and night had become day and then night again. The darkness that enveloped them was totally impenetrable. No starlight, no moonlight, no flashes of phosphorescence. It was as though they had been dropped into a deep, dark black hole that had plunged them into a state of nothing. It was awful, like trying to imagine a world without computer games or electricity or pain killers. Now anything was possible and time hung suspended, like a blade poised to fall at any moment, but absolutely nothing was happening and the future they had dreamed was set to arrive at any moment, looked like it had been postponed. Indefinitely.

"Any ideas?" Wilber asked, turning in desperation from Magician to Magician but no one said anything.

"George?"

"Yeah."

"What do we do now?"

"I'm not sure we can do anything. It's like your friend... what did you call him?"

"The Watcher."

"Yeah well, as soon as he was released, he hit the road to the stars and left us all in the shi... manure. Chin deep, it appears. Not that I blame him. Anyone who spends any length of time here goes radio rental. You know, mental."

Here George stuck out his tongue and widened his eyes.

Wilber felt his irritation beginning to rise like mercury in a thermometer as the water bubbled and frothed. A titter, like a muffled fart, seemed to creep forth from the Russian's lips and Wilber dead-eyed him.

"But are we sure he's even left?"

Every head tilted backwards and surveyed the starless darkness. Up above the air was still and seemingly empty. But did it only seem? Did it only resemble the thing it was not? Perhaps the Watcher was still there, suspended in its web of knowing immobility. Appearances mangled and ruined you on the island. Nothing and no one was what they appeared to be. As much as Wilber had resisted that meme, it had him in its claws and was squeezing him, squeezing him and soon he'd vomit most of his major organs onto the black sands, polished and gleaming like glass and scream himself into a state of insanity.

But no, no. It could not be so.

Surely the Aliens were not so callous that they would leave the humans on the island to rot in their stead? Wilber considered this proposition wanting to believe in its impossibility. But he couldn't dismiss it. It had to stand.

Lola tapped him on the shoulder and he turned to survey her heavily shadowed face. Meanwhile, the rest of the restless throng kept their eyes on the sky in the hope that the firework show would soon begin.

"Lola, what are you thinking?"

"That I love you Wilber. Sort of."

"That's nice."

He squeezed her gloved hand affectionately. It was nice to look into her eyes and not have his view obstructed by her shades. Her violet eyes seemed to whirl and fizz simultaneously. Quite the show was Lola. Quite the circus but a circus of emptied cages where all the lions and tigers roamed free. Such a wonderful spectacle, even when she set you on fire. He'd never been in love before and now he was. What a bummer. Such exquisite torture. Then in spite of how messed up he was inside, Wilber kissed her and she kissed him back. He had expected her to taste bitter, like arsenic or vinegar. But she didn't, she was sweet, like sherbet or snakebite.

George, sensing movement, lowered his head to look at his nephew. It was as though they'd just lost the World Cup Final on penalties after a gallant shoot out. He'd rarely felt so desperate and he found his eyes seeking out the Russian's. Astapor, sensing George thinking about him, had his eyes fixed on his one-time best friend and collaborator. Together they had heard the chimes at midnight, together they had punched holes through time, together they had dragged countless aliens down out the tree of stars to study and fleece for tech. And advancement.

Such wonderfully evil days. But so addictive. Life without the Russian was an agony and a bore. No wonder he'd almost switched sides, working to destroy Wilber and not to aid him. But at the last moment he'd pulled up at Beecher's brook and refused to jump. He wouldn't plunge the dagger into his nephew's back, regardless of what was on offer.

Poor antelope had not been quite so loyal.

A sudden vision assailed his senses.

The sea beyond the stones was bubbling and submerged pools of light could be seen shining up from out of the depths. It felt as if the sea were about to surrender long hidden secrets. Could it be that alien craft would rise up out of the ocean, take them all on board and fly them to the Promised Land? That was a vision he could get with. Suitably exciting, cinematic even but would it, could it happen?

Tapping Wilber discreetly on the shoulder George leaned in and whispered in his ear.

"Is it just me or is there something happening out to sea?"

Wilber scanned the darkness for signs of happening but there was nothing doing.

'It's just you. What do you think you saw?"

"Lights down beneath the waves."

It would have been so lovely if something had been lurking in the depths, maybe the missing piece of the puzzle, and that compelled by some magical and benevolent force it had risen, unbidden to point the way, releasing them all from the dual agonies of ignorance and anxiety.

Wilber, conceding defeat turned, to the Russian.

"So Astapor, what's next? Where do we go from here?"

"Where indeed?"

The slimy Cossack was giving nothing away.

"Why don't we just chop him into pieces and feed him to the sharks. It's no less than he deserves," the Captain growled. With the tide coming in, it wouldn't be too long before his beached ship began to float again. They could dump his remains out in the bay and good riddance to bad rubbish.

"It looks like a stalemate situation, Wilber," Lola suggested, her voice sympathetically resonant.

"You didn't mean what you said earlier, did you?"

That quaver was back in Wilber's voice.

"You mean about the Game being a gigantic con, that there are no sunlit pools at rainbow's end. Truth is Wilber, we're kind of in uncharted waters. There's no map, no signposts for where we're going, just your gut."

There was wisdom in these words. The Russian seemed to think so too. But what were they missing? What was the new game that had been set in motion and how did you play it?

84

Reboot

"Face it Wilber, it's over," the Russian said. "There was no way of winning"

'I don't believe you," Wilber said softly.

"But you should. After all, you've won."

In the wake of this statement there was an absolute silence, broken only by Zen.

"Don't listen to him Wilber, he's just trying to tie knots in your head."

Wilber tried to let it go but found he couldn't.

"What do you mean?'

"What indeed?" Astapor said, sadly. "You are the best that has ever been, the most wonderful player of this sick game, a game that cannot be won."

"But why?" Wilber shrieked. "Tell me or kill me, but please, just don't leave me hanging."

"The gates are open, Wilber," the Russian said with a shrug. "You're free to go. So go."

George was frowning.

"Don't listen to him, Wilber. He's lying. It's what he does. This is just like him. He's a genius...but a total liar!"

The Russian bowed his head, as though defeated.

"If you step through that gate you'll destroy everything. It's not just the island that will be destroyed either but an entire Universe. We are all of us, contaminated. Shadow beings."

"And what does that mean?" Wilber mewled.

"It means we don't matter," Mr Hand replied.

"Because we're not matter." Lapp added.

"Then what are we?"

"Dark Matter," Lola said gaily. "Or is it anti-matter? Whichever's worse."

"It's called the Law of Destruction," Yabu said, by way of an explanation. "There's no escape, not really. Step through the gate and everything implodes."

"So why do you play the game?" screamed Wilber incandescent with rage.

"Everyone's got to have a hobby," Astapor said, sounding both pained and apologetic.

"Can you ever forgive us?"

Wilber wanted to pull out all his teeth and gauge out his eyes with spoons, formerly the property of mandrax addicts. He was on the brink of total and utter madness and suddenly he understood Astapor's laugh. What else could you do in a state of utter hopelessness but laugh like a loon, until death came with a studded collar to lead you away to oblivion.

"But why do you believe this?"

"Because it is written," Yabu replied sagely.

"Just because it's written doesn't mean it's true." Wilber said, his voice cracked and hoarse. "Come along with me. You just have to trust that everything's going to be ok. If what the Russian says is true I have activated the time gate. We can all go back home together."

Silence. Then giggles, then titters and then laughter, full blown gale force laughter. From everyone. Soon the entire throng was rolling on the black sands, paralytic with mirth. Wilber didn't know whether to scream or cry. In desperation he turned to the only one that really mattered. Lola. Even she was laughing, tears streaming down her face.

"So how did you learn about the island, Lola? About the rules and the Law of Destruction."

"From him," she said, pointing at Mr Lapp.

"And who told you?" Wilber asked, turning to Hand

"He told me," answered Mr Hand, pointing at Yabu

"And who told him?"

"Crowhaven told me," Yabu pitched in

"And who told Crowhaven?"

"I told him," the Russian replied. The only one not laughing.

"And who told you Astapor?"

The Russian shrugged.

"Ah, well that's a very long story and I'm not sure you have time."

Wilber crammed his fist in his mouth at this point and bit his fingers, then he removed his fist from his mouth and smiled. He was learning.

"On the contrary, it would appear I have all of time in the world, but please give me the short version. I'm ready for it now."

Astapor folded his arms and made a fish mouth. It made him look like a Mad Halibut not that you'd ever tell him that. Not unless you had a death wish.

"The Dark Father told me his story."

Everybody looked at the Russian and everyone was still; the Bird Tribes, the Magicians, the remaining Alphabets, the Muldoon's; not one of them moved a muscle. Why? Because this was significant information. Wilber, having nominated himself as head of the inquisition nodded slowly as if he understood something no one else did. Only he didn't.

"So who was this Dark Father?"

"He didn't have a name. To me he was just the Star Father. He was here when I arrived."

"And why did you come here?"

Astapor gave Wilber his hangman's grin.

"After Auschwitz I thought I deserved a holiday."

Wilber gulped. It was one thing to hate the Russian, another thing to deal with him directly. For a few moments Wilber fell silent, his mind churning and bubbling like a pot of Cannibal Soup. It was Ultra who stepped up and threw her hat in the ring.

"What did he look like?"

"I never saw."

"Why? Was he kind of Mummyish?"

The Russian considered.

"I suppose so. He was quite ill by the time I got to him. He lived on top of the volcano, presiding over the island from his Gothic Schloss. A most unfortunate piece of architecture. Like him it had to go. As I recall his entire body was clad in bandages, as though he'd been ravaged by leprosy but his eyes were exposed. I'll never forget his eyes. He didn't so much as stare at you, as through you."

It took a while for this to sink in.

"Describe them," Lola said, folding her arms.

"His eyes?"

Lola nodded.

"Yes."

"Well they were black; his eyes were very black, like dark caverns. That I remember. They were more like holes you fell into than eyes. They emitted no light and from them there could be no escape."

Ultra gulped.

"Sounds terrifying."

Astapor found this amusing.

"To you maybe. I found him quite stimulating. I sensed a great mind lurking behind those eyes. You know what they say about eyes being the windows to the soul. In his case it was true."

Muldoon was surprised by this statement and immediately sceptical.

"Not a word I'd expect you to use Astapor. Soul. A little bit last Millennium, don't you think."

The Russian regarded his old friend with something akin to pity.

"The soul is a terrifying reality George, as well you know; something humans have tried to condemn to the slag heap of dead ideas with little success. Yes, in spite of all, it has suffered at the hands of materialist philosophers and so-called scientists, the soul is persistent. It's biding its time, waiting for the right moment to make a comeback. Last millennium or a future century? Both possibly. Perhaps its good for all time."

George scowled and turned away as Lola stepped right up to the mark for another round of questions.

"About those eyes... what did you see there? How did exposure to them change you?"

"Hmmm." Astapor paused, clearly thinking. After a while an answer seemed to emerge from the depths.

"Yes the eyes were black but his soul was blacker and not entirely his own. There appeared to be other things in there with him. Sometimes he let you see images from his past. He let you loose in his mind."

Ultra found this idea both alarming and scintillating.

"Was that a nice place to be?"

The Russian chuckled, clearly amused by Ultra's ridiculous question.

"Depends on your taste I suppose. An amusement park it was not."

Wilber, having felt the ice-cold wind stream out of the Russian's mind, thought it better to treat the Magician with a little more respect.

"So he just sort of projected the images into you."

The Russian regarded Wilber with bemused affection.

"Yes, he showed you himself in flashes. As though by lightning. It was he who had impaled armies and feasted on their screams, it was he who created riots and revolutions down the centuries. He who profited from wars. He, who taught men to desire power over others, suppressing kindness and compassion and thoughts of love. He, who taught people to fear the truth about their own thoughts and feelings, to fear hell and judgement. He who taught the art of fear to the few so that they might rule over the many."

"Sounds like a right bundle of fun.

Zen was not impressed. Neither for that matter, was George.

"Perfect blueprint for you then."

"You might say that George. Now, as always, you lack the ability to see the bigger picture. The Star Father has always been here directing humanity's destiny from within and from without. From

553

near and afar. Whether you can see him or not. Whether you believe in him or not. He's there. He runs everything and he has predicted everything. It's what he does."

85

The Good Book

The Russian was clearly enjoying the direction events had taken. His army had been defeated, quite literally dissolving into the ethers, his allies had been destroyed, his life's work obliterated along with all his 'experiments.' He was surrounded by enemies, every one of whom wanted him dead and yet...and yet...he still controlled them; he still ran the show. George was flabbergasted, Wilber appalled. How did he do it? How had he achieved such mastery?

Kaos, who up to now, had been silent chipped in with a question that was curiously pertinent.

"Why would you wish to follow one such as he?"

The Russian smiled sadly.

"He taught me everything I needed to know about power and control. He taught me how to run the island, preparing me for a future that is racing towards us over the waves at full tilt."

Kaos looked pained.

"Not my kind of teacher."

"Perhaps and perhaps not. Say what you like about him but he was a liberator. And not just for me, but for all of you too."

"But he couldn't last," George sneered.

Anger flashed in the Russian's eyes.

"You want me to apologize George, to say I wish I'd behaved differently. I don't. I took the crown; it wasn't offered to me. And why? Because there's only room at the top for one. He had to go, but not before he told me everything about this island. And of course there was the Book. In the Book it was all written down. The rules and principles by which this island is governed were codified and sanctified hundreds of thousands of years ago. He simply inherited that wisdom and applied it. As did I."

Wilber, his eyes gleaming, was suddenly fascinated.

"And where is this Book?"

"It was destroyed when your friends saw fit to burn down my Tower Complex."

"How convenient. So we've no actual proof that what you say is true?" George asked, going on the offensive."

"I told you the Book was destroyed," the Russian replied coldly.

George was clearly not satisfied and turned to the Magicians.

"Any of you see it?"

Each one shook their head in turn.

"So everything you think you know about the island comes from that Book. And yet the Book has been destroyed," Wilber said in summary.

"That is correct. That is why you cannot leave. Any of you. The sun has set and darkness has come to the island. You, Wilber, like everybody else will become a permanent resident here as of tomorrow when the sun rises. You'll have to choose a side and an army, or like these crazed girls you can live on the outside and take your chances there."

"And what of the Game?" Zenith asked.

"You know the answer to that one Zen. We must continue to play the Game. The crystals must be removed and reset. We must prepare for those yet to come."

"But why, why must we continue to play?"

"Because if we don't then things will fall apart. The island has a purpose and a direction. It's called the Game. Stop the game and the island will fold in on itself. You think that what we have now is hell. It's not. It's heaven in comparison with the hell the island can create for us. We humans are weak and predictable. We need structure. We need organisation. We need to exist in a permanent state of war. I know it's hard. I know you hate me and want to kill me and maybe you should. But for all I've done, for all I've suffered at the hands of other people I want the island to continue and I want the human race to go on, with or without me."

There was a stunned silence. The Russian had always been hidden away, safe in his towers behind a barbed wire fence. Above or below ground he had always been protected. By concrete, reinforced glass and bullets. But not anymore. He stood amongst them and he controlled them, not with force but with a story, a narrative. A story with holes, a story that generated doubt and disbelief and yet was it a story that any one would dare refute?

It was apparent that the survivors had reached a crossroads, and that suddenly, against all odds, the past hell that they had all lived through was more appealing than the future heaven they had all been imagining. The Russian watched each and every face. Saw the thought penetrate. Saw doubt spread like a contagion. Saw hope die. Saw victory within his grasp. He had achieved checkmate with just a King and a Pawn. And yet he did not gloat, did not cheer or turn cartwheels, he simply waited and watched. It wasn't over till they all walked away. It wasn't over until... a voice that had been musing piped up again. Astapor believed that he had silenced that voice but he had not. The voice belonged to Wilber.

"But you never tested it?" the Voice said.

A nervous ripple of laughter passed amongst the survivors.

"What?" the Russian replied, trying hard to prevent his contempt from breaking through.

"You never tested the rules. You never tried to go through the Gate."

"Isn't that obvious? If I had there'd been no gate, no me and no you. No island. No world. No Universe. Nothing"

The wind had dropped to a mere whisper.

"Really?"

Wilber's voice was softer than the dying wind. The light from the storm lantern lit up his features in such a way that he appeared to be a creature of flames, a being of fire. The effect was unique and disquieting. The Russian sighed but nobody took their eyes off him. They all continued to stare.

In time, he felt compelled to speak.

"The Law of Destruction was quite clear on that point. If just one person was to go through the gate the island would collapse in on itself and we'd all experience not just mind shatter but bodily disintegration. So no it seemed prudent not to."

"Really?"

A longer pause, one the Russian felt disinclined to fill. He had spoken and his word was final. A smirk creased Wilber's features.

"So you took it all on faith. You never employed your reason."

A sharp intake of breath from several members of the assembled throng indicated that Wilber needed to watch his step, that he had perhaps gone too far.

"I employ and deploy my reason every day, boy, and soon you will be feeling the slicing edges of my reason."

Everyone froze. The Old Astapor was just like the New Astapor. He just wore a different expression...from time to time.

Wilber sensed the danger but after all he had been through, he was immune to it.

"But can't you see, this Star Father lied. That the house he built is a house of lies. And you believed it and you passed it on. Then they believed it and passed it on, so that it became a reality, an apparent fact. But its not."

The Russian stood as still as a statue. Silence was his only move now. Crimson watched him and as she did felt something shifting within her.

"So what is it then, an opinion?"

"A myth?" Queen queried, likewise doubtful, feeling the shift too.

"A legend?" Lola added playfully.

Wilber felt his smirk expanding into a full smile.

"No, he's the Legend," he said, nodding towards George.

Lola, playing her part well, had the intelligence to look perplexed.

"But why is he the Legend?"

George staring daggers at the Russian seemed torn by something, an event perhaps in his past that he was ashamed of but which he now needed to bring forward. But could he? Did he have the strength?

"He knows," George said, his eyes filling with tears.

"And what does he know George?" said Lola softly

"He knows I got off the island and that I came back."

The Russian's eyes clouded over and the whole aura around him seemed to darken.

"Not through that gate, you didn't," he hissed pointing at the Western Gate.

"You mean there are other gates?" Def roared.

"Yes, there are many others, hidden beneath the island, a whole network."

"And I knew..." George confessed, "that was why Astapor was so intent on catching me and silencing me. That's why he let you go, Wilber. He knew all along that you would run and that they would block you at the end. But with me in the picture..."

"As a kind of wildcard," Zen suggested.

"Yes, there was always the possibility I'd spill the beans and bring down his House of Cards."

The silent Russian was clearly incandescent with rage. "Traitor!"

"Who to? You and the glorious cause? I denounced both you and the cause years ago."

"Say what?" Def couldn't believe what she was hearing.

Wilber stepped forward.

"It's true Def. George and Astapor were partners once upon a time. They loved the same woman, only that woman loved George more. When Astapor found out, he went nuts and killed her."

"Liar!" the Russian screamed, turning puce.

Wilber rolled his eyes and continued.

"I'm sorry Def, about everything, but we've got to keep it together. George is not the enemy.

Def gripped her axe and sweat poured from her brow.

"Traitor," she whispered in a voice not her own.

"No!" Wilber said.

"Yes!" the Russian screamed. "He betrayed you all. He's the mole. He should be the one to die. Go ahead Def, swing the axe."

Wilber took another step forward and raised his arms.

"If you have to kill anyone Def, kill me."

"Did you know?' Def asked in a strangled voice.

"No. He told me on the way to the spaceship. I believe him."

"Why?"

"Because he's my Uncle and I love him."

And now it was the Russian stepping forward. The rage that had flashed across his face like a desert wildfire was gone and now he grinned a sickly grin of one demented. He knew something, that much was clear. He had cards up his sleeve and now was the time to play them.

"He lied to you, Justice."

"I know and I forgive him." Wilber folded his arms and stared at the earth.

"He didn't just lie about that," the Russian wheedled. "Want to know about what else?"

"Don't listen to him Wilber," George shouted in warning.

But it was too late.

"He's not really your Uncle, Justice, he's your father!"

George roared like an enraged lion and prepared to pounce but Mr Hand was quicker and had him pinned in a Half Nelson.

"That is low," Def said, in disbelief. "Say Wilber, do you think the Russian is too tall? Should I make him a head shorter?"

"There'll be no need for that Def. I'm Ok." Wilber half mumbled.

"Are you sure?" the Russian goaded, twisting the knife.

"For now I'm focused on sorting out this mess. I'll square anything else later. Ok George?"

George, with lowered head, spoke again in a near whisper.

"Ok Wilber. Not now, later."

Wilber took another deep breath and began considering his options. Everyone watched him to see which way he was going to go. But it seemed he was struggling. Perhaps there were too many options. Perhaps there just wasn't enough information. Perhaps he just wanted to throw caution to the winds or himself off a really high building. It was really hard to tell. But once again the tension had cranked itself up to a whole new level. Everyone was feeling it but it was Hogarth Macready who broke first.

"Wilber, you know he's a liar. An evil manipulator with not one saving grace. Why not just call it? Whatever you decide we'll honour."

George lifted his tear-stained face and looked at his son.

"Hogarth is right, Wilber. Do what you feel to be right? You can't always proceed according to logic and statistical probabilities. Sometimes you just have to trust your gut. Know what I mean?"

Wilber considered his father's words.

"Whilst I don't actually trust you any more George I think there is still some validity in what you're saying. Therefore, I have decided..."

Here the Russian cut across him

"You know you can't trust him so why listen to him? If you do, you'll destroy us all."

"This is mental," Kaos said with a resigned sigh, "really mental. We're already well into extra time, and we need a result, mate, so just do it. Decide! We either go through one of the gates or we walk back the way we came and pick up our lives. As to him," she said, "looking at the Russian, "I don't think this island needs him. And if you need somebody to hoist the axe, I'll do it and it'll be a pleasure."

Wilber nodded in acknowledgement. Crimson appeared to agree with Kaos.

"I'm willing to risk it if you are."

Everybody was looking at everyone else trying to figure out which way to turn. Was this democracy in process or mob rule? Did it matter any more? They'd all been through so much together, it would make a mockery of those they'd lost, if they just allowed the status quo to return to what it had been before Wilber's Run. The Russian was the only one who appeared not to agree.

"You can't do this!"

George shook his head.

"I say they can!"

Queen, like her sisters, was on the cusp of a paradigm shift.

"I'm sick of living in a state of fear. It's time to make a quantum leap and move on. I say we just do it."

Ultra let out a whoop.

"I'm sick of not having a change of underwear."

"Or any toilet paper," Infra said, agreeing with her friend. Often it was the major things that swayed you. Sometimes it was having an itchy bum!

'Yeah," Def growled; "it's time we put these Laws to the test. I don't want to stay here for what remains of my life. I've had enough of this place. I'm with Ultra. Let's do it!"

Mr Lapp stepped forward.

"Girls, ever since you got here I've tried to guide your footsteps. I didn't want to be a back-room General and I've never asked you to do anything I wouldn't do myself. I grieve for all the sisters lost and I regret not doing more to help you."

Here he paused to weigh his words and when he spoke again, he sounded pained.

"Blindly believing is not the way, but if you've decided to take that leap of faith, I'm with you."

"Let's do it!" Crimson yelled, punching the air.

The Bird tribes and the remaining Alphabets took up the chant.

"Do it! Do it! Do it! Do it! Do it!"

Wilber raised his arms and the mob fell silent. Zen, turning to Lola, put her hand on the girl's shoulder.

"You coming Lola?"

"What?"

"You can be one of the gang, if you like."

"You mean that?" Lola sounded stunned.

"We've been too hard on you. Too judgmental. You were right about a lot of things. Besides, we need to restock."

Lola, normally so cynical, was flattered.

"Sounds like a plan."

Astapor, increasingly marginalised, was not a happy bunny. Reaching round, behind his back, he pulled a concealed revolver from his belt and pointed it at Lola.

"If you take one further step I'll shoot you."

Wilber let out a gasp. Then Def laughed.

"Guns don't work anymore stupid."

"Sure you want to test that theory out Def? The guns didn't work because of the intervention of the creature in the craft. Now the creature has gone, it's likely they will. You might be right but are you sure you want to put it to the test? How sure are you, you're right?"

"You'd shoot your own daughter?" George asked, aghast.

More gasps. More shock. More revelations.

"I'd kill anybody who would be so stupid to put me at risk."

Fearlessly George strode up to Astapor and swung his fist, connecting with the Slav's jutting chin. The Russian was out before he hit the ground, the revolver dropping beside him.

"I'm not having that. Go for it girls."

86

Five Ways

With the fall of the Russian all hell seemed to break loose.

The magic circle that had contained all of them shattered and everyone scattered. This was it, now or never. Other torches were kindled and soon flaming faggots filled the air like buzzing fireflies. Every one ran around the pentagonal structure that composed the Western Gate like they were kids at playtime in a high wind.

It wasn't actually one gate at all, but five. Five gates but only one choice.

Everything now was up for grabs and huddled conversations were the norm. It was assumed that the first person through could detonate Apocalypse or simply disappear. That could mean annihilation or it might mean they were free, delivered to a sun-bleached road of parched whale bones or some futuristic city or maybe even the deck of a spaceship. Perhaps you got what you wished for, or maybe you got what you deserved.

Wilber talked to anybody and everybody and little by little the groups formed up, yet the vexed question remained. Who would go through first? Eventually the running too and fro and the dashing about abated and everyone was still. All eyes turned to Wilber in expectation but Wilber was having a hard time of it again. It was like he had a faulty TV in his head that for some reason kept changing channels.

George, out of the mass of waiting bodies, pushed his way through the crowd and laid his hand on Wilber's arms.

"You ok...son?"

"I'm not sure."

"You look weird again."

"I feel weird again."

Lola pushed her way forward and took hold of Wilber's hand.

Everybody is prepared to go through one of the five gates, Wilber. We have divided up into five groups. It may be that if the thing works we will all go off in different directions. Or we may all just crash and burn."

"Speculation is pointless," Wilber said blankly. "We've just gotta do it! Right?"

Hogarth Macready, somewhere near the back of the crowd piped up with a booming voice.

"Well said Ship Mate." And I guess I'm the best one to go first."

Wilber's eyes grew wide. The crowd parted and Macready stood unveiled. Some of the Bird Tribes, a handful of cannibals and the Captain's mate stood behind him, looking scared but excited.

"You ready Captain?"

"I was born ready lad."

"How many are you?"

"Fifteen, at the last count."

Wilber's eyes flicked over the assembled throng. After a while he was able to confirm the Captain's count. For all that he had only spent a short time in the Captain's company he felt a great affinity with him. He was a big man, in every way, but there was nothing morbid about his obesity. He was a happy fatty, a doer as well as a gabber. Rough as a badger's arse but more precious than porcelain. Wilber was going to miss him when he went through, but he hoped and prayed that wherever the Captain landed, it was somewhere he would be happy.

"Alright. Know which gate you're going to take?"

"I do. This one," Macready said, indicating the dark empty doorway that faced south. The crowd wheeled, reoriented and finally repositioned themselves for the start of the main event. Wilber, George and Lola stood to one side, whilst Hogarth and his stalwart band stood facing the gate and their soon-to-manifest destinies. They took a few moments of silence to steal themselves, preparing for the Great Leap Forwards...

There was no wind and only flickering torches lit the scene. All eyes were fixed on Macready whilst his eyes were fixed on the darkness that lay through the open doorway.

"Ready Hogarth?" George asked. "It's now or never."

The Captain didn't seem quite ready to make the jump to lightspeed.

"It's all such a mystery you know. This island, people, the sea. I hope that if we make it...I hope if we make it, that there will be answers. I want to know what came before us. I am an old man shipwrecked in flesh but I want to play the tapes back, rewind them to the beginning of time and see it all unfold. That would be heaven for me. After that I wouldn't mind sleeping for a while. Forever even."

"Stop it. Stop it. You're doing my head in. Just go," Lola shrieked like a banshee. A little extreme but everyone felt as she did. Too much.

The Captain gulped and took a step. Gripping the stone pillars on either side of the door with his massive ham-like hands, he felt for a moment like blind Samson chained between the pillars of the Great Temple. Should he not pull the temple down around their ears? No, he should step through and make like a man of dignity, not a broken prisoner.

He took another step and then another. The outer world seemed to fade, the world behind him seemed never to have existed. It was as though he had been here before, the moment before he was born perhaps.

In front of him, he saw water, a great blue ocean and his heart leaped into his throat, tears into his eyes. Could anyone else see this or was it just him? A lump came to his throat and up ahead he saw his Old Ma beckoning to him.

"Momma," whispered Old Macready, "I'm coming home."

Letting go of the pillars he stepped through and took a step towards the heaving seas. Would a new boat await him, he wondered.

On the outside it was all happening. As soon as Macready had stepped through the gate he had been enveloped in a kind of mist that made it impossible to see or track him. Then the torches had gone out and all had been plunged back into darkness. For a brief moment there were gasps of horror and shrieks of incipient madness and then quiet had returned. The air seemed aflutter with angel's wings as up out of the sea a tetragonal form, a pyramid of light, haloed in blue and orange and white light arose and flew towards them. Despatched from the Temple of Poseidon it illuminated the dark sands and the patiently waiting survivors of the charge.

Soundless it flew and settling over the five gates it hovered, silent and motionless. It was like the Star over the Stable in Biblical times; the best kind of fireworks display, the best kind of gift, after all was light. Then the three dark stones that formed the southern face of the pentagon began to glow, as though from a light within. Stone turned to crystal, darkness to blue light. The gate had activated to roars and cheers. Hats were flung into the air and crooked polkas were danced.

Suddenly Hogarth found himself standing on a beach and away to his right not a boat but a bridge, a bridge across the ocean. He walked towards the bridge and then onto it. There were multiple coloured streams of light. He chose one, stepped into it and disappeared without a sound. The others in his group followed him and soon all were gone. On to the next place. Wherever and whatever that was.

Yabu stepped up next and those who remained moved round with him to the next gate, which faced towards the South West. Without a second thought he stepped through the gate and promptly disappeared. As he did so the gate powered up, glowing with bright yellow light.

Mr Hands was greatly cheered by this and led his great flock around to the North Western gate. Wilber, George, Lola and the Alphabets followed him. The island was quickly emptying. Soon there would be no one left. Certainly no humans. And perhaps that would be for the best.

Standing before his gate Mr Hand was not lost for words.

"Always the echoes of former worlds and phrases return to haunt me. But a record can be played more than once. It can be played over and over. But can the same river ever be crossed twice?"

"Meaning?" Wilber asked, perplexed as ever by Mr Hand's odd pronouncements.

"You've gotta know where you're from to know where you're going."

And with that he stepped through the Great Gate which responded with a red orange glow. All of the western gate was lighting up like a beacon. It was a far cry from the Walsall Illuminations, although there had been similar levels of violence.

"This is it," he said, gesturing. "The future, now".

And promptly disappeared. It was just the Alphabets now, then the Muldoons and Astapor, who lay on his back, eyes shut. Mouth open. Such perfect teeth he had and not a filling in sight. Wilber tried to pay him no mind and to focus on what was important, but he had such complex and conflicting feelings about the Russian that he found it hard not to stare. Plus he was in a state of shock. Three groups had gone through three gates and everything appeared to be working.

When Hogarth had gone through the gate he'd closed his eyes, expecting the worst but it hadn't happened. The Russian had lied. Victory was theirs, so why did it feel so hollow? Wilber cast an eye back towards the island, where he has spent the last eighteen hours running. Looking into the darkness he shivered. The sky seemed to teem with menace and invisible forms were ever in motion behind the veil. This place wasn't just an island, he thought then, It's so much more than what it appears to be. It's a zoo and a library, a school and an exhibition of devices of torture, some medieval, many futuristic.

But was it a game?

And if so, who had designed it? The Russian had lied. The Russian always lied. He had sold them the idea that the gate was rigged to blow. That it was all a trap best avoided. And they had, as a body, defied him, that he could go boil his head for all they cared. They were going through and damn the consequences. And they had gone through and were still going through but was that the best course of action?. Were they not perhaps doing what the Russian wanted them to do?

What was that called? Reverse Psychology. The words came tumbling into his head then. To get people to do the thing you wanted them to do, you suggested the opposite. If they hated or mistrusted you, they would do just that; the opposite. A simple equation, a baited hook and they had taken the bait. Hook, line and sinker, as the cliché ran.

Wilber felt a light pressure on his shoulder. It was George... rather, it was his father again, looking down at him with concern in his eyes. The girls had moved round past the White Gate and stood facing the Magenta Gate with Mr Lapp. A curious sense of inertia seemed to grip them all. It was like that moment prior to going into an exam. Feeling sick and apathetic, wondering if you'd done enough work, made the right choices.

"What is it Wilber, you look weird again?" his father asked, trying but not quite managing to keep the note of irritation out of his voice.

Wilber shook his head.

"Something doesn't quite sit right here George."

Everyone turned to look at Wilber with tired eyes. It had been a very long day and lots of people had died. After they stepped through the gate the island would be all but empty, returned to its pristine and human-less state. All would be quiet again. All would be better. The island could sleep and rest and await the emergence of the next dominant species, no doubt hoping they would be less destructive than the humans had been.

George laughed uneasily.

"Bit late in the day for doubts old son."

For some reason that made Wilber mad.

"I'm just being true to myself is all. Like you always claimed you were."

"And I always was Wilber. But I'm human. My feet are made of clay, just like everybody else's. And without my youthful indiscretions you wouldn't be here and this wouldn't have happened. The future would be somewhere else entirely."

"You can't know that," Lola interjected. She had retraced her steps and stood at the transition point where the Magenta Gate became the White Gate.

"The Game has played out," George stated simply. "We've won."

"But have we?" Lola asked, suddenly in earnest.

"I'm not so sure. It just feels like a bad movie I can't quite buy into." Wilber's anxieties had increased exponentially, no doubt ramped up and affected by Lola's qualms.

"Exactly. Exposition. Action. Romance, then more Action. Twists, turns, betrayals and counter betrayals. And that final unexpected twist, that sting in the tail you didn't quite anticipate. Although you'll claim you did after the fact. All delivered at a cracking pace."

Lola, although infuriating, was on to something, but George was having none of it.

"What else could you ask for? What else do you want?"

"How about the truth?" Wilber shot.

"First casualty of war," George countered.

Wilber looked at his father, askance. What was really going on here? And why the sudden whiff of fish.

"Look, can we just get going? This place is giving me the creeps," Infra called, from the space before the Magenta Gate. It was a mood that was affecting them all.

87

What Could have Been

From behind the veil of the night there was a sudden growl of thunder and a flash of light. Wilber froze and closed his eyes. Flicker on, flicker off. It was there, the answer, staring back at him from the darkness within his own mind. The truth was not out there, but inside, he reasoned but it was hidden, or rather it was hiding in plain sight. Why could he not see it? Why the resistance. Staring into the darkness he began to shake. When the truth emerged, would its face shock him? Would the shock of it kill him?

Lola was at his elbow, pressing her cold hand to his wet face.

"What is it Wilber, what can you see?"

"The island from up on high. Like I'm floating above it, looking down. Not quite in my body, but in a body. Like I'm an eye or something. The island isn't what I thought it was. It was set up as a quest narrative, a board game, but it's a game played with loaded dice. Right?"

"Right," Lola echoed, unsure of where this was going but happy to follow.

"So what do you know?" Wilber asked.

Lola considered

"Well I know it's not a good idea to feed the cannibals."

George rolled his eyes.

"Consulting the femme fatale. Policy or idiocy, you decide."

"Shut it George," Lola hissed. Then in much softer tones. "Go on Wilber."

"So how would you explain all this?"

Not one to be silenced, George cut right across Lola's

injunction.

"Isn't it obvious? It's a Scooby Doo type mystery, with seemingly supernatural elements. Riddles, puzzles and frights galore. And it's over. You won. So let's go through the gate!"

"We're missing it," Wilber asserted blankly.

"Of course you have questions. We all do, but we need to follow through now, Wilber. Regardless."

It was Zen who had spoken and her words sounded like sense.

Wilber lowered his head and considered his options for the longest time. When next he raised his brain cage, he was decided.

"Aright. Go. And take my blessing with you."

Def shouldering Mr Lapp aside paused on the threshold and looked back.

"This one's for Antelope!" she said as she stepped through and promptly disappeared.

"Treacherous bitch!" Lola spat.

"Bit of respect for the dead, eh?" George said with obvious distaste.

With Def's departure the fourth gate had illuminated from within, sending a thrill through all who remained. It would have been nice to share a tinny and toss a few shrimp on the barbie but now was not the time. They would all, no doubt, meet again on the other side of forever. Wilber raised his right hand and waved somewhat tearfully. Lola rolled her eyes.

"Right, time to go," she called imperiously clapping her hands together briskly like a 1930s School Maam.

The other girls took the hint well, and promptly followed Def through the Magenta Gate, one by one, each waving at Wilber as they disappeared into the light. In a reversal of the other departures, here it was obvious that the Magician would go last. Mr Lapp, ever the philosopher, smiled benignly. After the last of the girls had disappeared, Lola walked up to him and tapped him on the shoulder.

Lapp turned, expecting trouble. Instead all he got was a proffered hand which he took and shook.

"I never had the chance to thank you for helping us. You kept the flame alive. You helped forge and then reforge the Alphabet Gang and for that I shall be eternally grateful."

"Thank you Lola. Your gratitude is appreciated."

He turned to go then, anxious to be on his way, but Lola gave a little cough as though she were clearing her throat, and he paused again. Lola took a step forward, a step closer to the Magenta Gate prompting Wilber to let out a sudden, shrill, unexpected cry.

"What do you think you're doing?"

"What does it look like?" Lola returned, sounding like her own eternally, exasperated self again.

"It looks like you're abandoning me!"

"Well 'abandoning' is a pretty harsh word to use..."

"But it's true!"

Lola sighed.

"In essence, yes."

Wilber looked like a caged animal about to be destroyed for a crime it had not committed.

"But don't you love me?"

Lola on the cusp of saying something Wilber didn't want to hear changed her mind, and her tone.

"Every inch of you."

"I sense a 'but' hanging in the air," Wilber said, his lower lip quivering.

"With you there's always a butt hanging in the air," Lola quipped.

But no one so much as smiled and Lola sighed, uncharacteristically wistful. The line had perhaps been a little lame. Parting was such a hassle, especially when people couldn't take a hint. Mr Lapp stood to one side and Wilber walked up to the girl he had assumed was now his girlfriend. Fate, it seemed, had other things in store though. George stared at the ground sensing something bad was coming, whilst Wilber, once more, took Lola's hands in his and waited for the girl of his dreams to speak.

She took her time.

"Caleb always thought he was so much smarter than everyone else in the room. But he wasn't. And now he's dead. What he was, was messed up, real messed up."

There was another pause. Wilber, trying to be understanding and sympathetic, found himself just staring at the pale-faced girl, with his reserves of patience fast running out.

"And?"

"And in a perfect world I'd have fallen in love with him and my love would have healed him and he would have been made whole. We'd have married and had children. Together we'd have overthrown Papa, but not killed him. We'd have caged him, humanely of course and we'd have led happy and fulfilled lives, serving the needs of the less fortunate and pursuing our environmental interests."

Wilber wasn't quite following the logic here.

"But I'm not Caleb. I'm not an orphan. I have a father, albeit he's the man I thought to be my Uncle and of course there needs to be conversations about that..." here he stopped and turned to frown at George, who smiled sweetly back at him, "but that's for another time, not today. What I am is together. More together than Caleb ever was and I won the Game... if indeed it can be won...anyway I completed it and it's still all to play for."

Here Lola looked perplexed.

"What's all to play for?"

"Us! You and me. Me and you. Lola I love you. Come with me."

Lola looked tempted, for about three seconds then she shook her head.

"Nah. It ain't me. Happily ever after doesn't exist Wilber. Just in fairytales and lame movies. I'm in it for the kicks. I don't want a husband or a boyfriend. I just want lovers and lots of them. The Buddha counselled non-attachment and I'm down with that. Capiche? So please little angel boy, suck it up and don't be needy. Remember the good times..."

"There weren't any good times," Wilber deadpanned, "just endless running and mass murder."

"That is the story of humanity I'm afraid," Lola replied, with a somewhat philosophical air, "and I don't believe it's going to change any time soon."

"You're so cynical," Wilber spat, his frustrations turning to venom.

"Yeah I am. But as of this moment I'm still alive and as you say it's still all to play for."

Wilber looking back over his shoulder, stared down at the recumbent Russian.

"But what about him? What about your papa? Don't you want to save him? Don't you feel the least bit of familial loyalty towards him?"

Lola looked monetarily pained.

"Why should I? He bred me, as an experiment and used me to do his bidding. He tolerated me, manipulated me and hell, he beat me when it amused him to do so. He wasn't exactly a model father. When I asked him about my mother he said she was an irrelevance. When I asked him about the meaning of life, he said that it was to dominate everything and everybody, to make the world in your own image. That all means were acceptable, that conscience was the first thing to be destroyed along with any thoughts about God or a Higher Power. He told me that no one was coming to the rescue, that you had to rely on your own resources. When I asked him about love, he said it was an illusion. When I asked him what he would do in my position, he said he'd try to kill his father and take over. So I ask you Wilber, in my position what would you do? Sling him over your shoulder, take him back to Muldoon manor and try and build some kind of relationship. Sorry kid, it ain't gonna happen."

"Lola, come with me!" Wilber pleaded.

"No. I'm getting off. I'm not getting stuck here. No way. And I'm not getting lumbered with you either. It's the Magenta door for me and you'll just have to deal with that."

"But the Alphabets hate you. They always have and they always will."

"And I hate them but I'm ok with that. It's hate that makes the world turn, not love. Hate that gets things done. Hate that makes the magic happen. And if you can't see that Wilber you're blind."

And with that Lola was done. Without a backward glance she strode through the Magenta gate, fizzed like lemon sherbet and disappeared. Mr Lapp shrugged and following the ninth and final Alphabet through the gate on a journey beyond sight and sound, stepped through. He looked for a moment like he was going to say something profound but then he stopped himself. Enough had been said already. Less was most definitely more and anyway there was no one left to listen. No one that mattered to him personally anyway.

Sayonara, the winds seemed to hiss in his wake. And good riddance.

Now four gates glowed in the darkness and just Wilber and George remained. The silence between them was deafening. Sound was not entirely absent but it didn't comfort or soothe. All they could hear, either of them was the repetitive, droning crash of the waves in the darkness. Like evolution, it went on and on until it stopped...forever.

"This is not the ending I had imagined," Wilber finally offered.

"Me neither. I had hoped for something a little more triumphant. And upbeat. But it ain't gonna happen, is it," George replied, lost and disconsolate. The adrenaline had gone and now the Game was over, what exactly would they replace it with?

"Do you think it's best that we just keep on moving?" Wilber asked.

"It's all we can do," George said, striding off into the dark. He returned after the passage of three quarters of a minute with Great Uncle Muldoon, dead in his arms. Wilber looked at the dead man in a curious way. It wasn't as if he was horrified. He had seen more than enough death in the past eighteen hours not to be phased by the horror of burned, slashed and mutilated bodies. It was more that he was bemused and bewildered by the lifeless body. The moment didn't feel entirely real. If anything, his memories seemed more real than the moment. How could that be?

Without speaking they both of them moved around to the White Gate that faced towards the North East of the Island. Everyone else had gone. For all that they knew, they were the last living souls on the island. Black Sands was a charnel house where the dead lay oozing blood and plasma. Nothing else. The island had entered a post-human state. What species would emerge next as the dominant force. If any?

Wilber's thoughts returned to the events of the recent past and how his family back home would respond to his story. It wasn't exactly believable. It wasn't exactly explicable, come to think of it. In an offhand way he asked a question that had been troubling him for some time but which he had buried.

"Why do you think Uncle Patrick did what he did?"

George thought about this for a moment.

"I don't know. He must have had his reasons. We just have to accept that he's gone, Wilber, and get on with our lives."

Wilber nodded.

"There's still a lot we need to sort out."

George gave a forced laugh.

"You're telling me, but not today, eh? Let's just get back home or wherever it is we're going next."

Again Wilber nodded in agreement, then they turned to look into the blackness beyond the pillars and lintel that formed the as yet unilluminated White Gate.

"It's what I imagine death will be like," Wilber said. "A gate into blackness and who knows what. Possibly nothing."

"Ever the optimist, Wilber."

They chuckled at this together before the laughter died on their lips.

"Best to travel hopefully, George, eh?"

"Yeah."

"You go first...dad."

"You sure?"

"Not really, but yes...it feels right. Like I should be the last to go through. Like I'm the cherry on the icing, the one to sign, seal and deliver all this."

Simultaneously they looked back at the Russian.

"What shall we do with him?" George asked.

"Leave him to me, dad."

The heaviness in the youth's voice turned George's blood to ice. But it wasn't his call. Not any more. Wilber was no longer a boy, not some wet-behind the ear's muppet who knew nothing about anything really in particular. He was a man. A free agent with his own thoughts and an ability to make his own decisions. And then to take responsibility for them.

"Right then."

George, carrying great Uncle Muldoon in his arms, was faced with the same dilemma as Mr Lapp. What to say. The answer was easy really.

Best to say nothing.

"See you on the other side then, Wilbs."

"Hope so," Wilber said simply.

And with that, George stepped through the gate and disappeared in a storm of swirling atoms. The fifth and final gate illuminated and an orb of white light rose up out of the previously dark centre, forming a dome over the pentagonal structure. Watching, with gaping jaw, a series of images began to circulate within Wilber's mind.

He saw the survivors of the Charge, forming groups, then choosing one of the five gates. He watched the last few seconds on the clock rolling over, as the sky changed colour. He observed himself climbing, then positioning the crystals on top of the lintels, each in a recess, into which they fit snuggly. He saw nothing happening and heard the gasps of shock and sudden despair. Then he heard the sound of Astapor's hapless laughter, echoing off the stones. Then he saw the subsequent activations of each gate, saw each gate as a unique lens, offering different pathways and different visions of life. He saw the remaining Alphabets with Lola stepping through and disappearing, heading off into a future full of possibilities. He saw that it had all been for something and that his hope was still alive. And looking up he saw for the first time the night sky full of stars, unfamiliar stars to be sure but stars nonetheless.

And he understood then, that this was the conclusion of something big.

88

Parting Is Such Sweet Sorrow

Wilber set off walking then, in a clockwise direction, around the stones. Passing each gate a new series of images filled his mind. This was not for now, he knew that without being told, but for later. Best just store it away and forget about it. Events would play out in their own way and in their own time. If the island had taught him nothing else it was that. Trust was rewarded, but trust backed up by a plan, by hard decisions and committed actions.

He completed first one circuit, then a second and finally a third.

On the threshold of the fifth gate, the White Gate, that faced in a North Easterly direction, Wilber paused and gazed back at the Russian who now stood on the black sands staring back at him, lost in his own moment of wonder. And scattered about the sands, the bodies of those who hadn't made it, the fallen, both friends and foes alike. Hundreds of them, poor souls. Possibly thousands. Some he knew, many he didn't and never would. Call them whatever's best: the unlucky, the lost, the victorious dead. Call them whatever epitaph seemed most fitting and appropriate. Or call them nothing. It wouldn't matter to them.

As the Hero of the Moment, as the New Legend, his right and his duty was to be the last to leave. And in stepping through the Fifth Gate he knew now, he would seal each and every gate behind him so that none might follow him.

What had he become in the course of eighteen hours, running from one end of Five Mile Isle to the other, Wilber asked himself. What had he become if not a Moses, one initiated into light. A boy from nowhere who had led a scattered mass of people across a desert, parted the waves of the Sea of Light and then led them to the promised land or rather promised worlds. It was not in his gift to see where each individual and group had gone, or even if they were safe but he sensed that they were. He believed that every individual, good or bad, who had stepped through one of the five gateways would have their own worlds of challenge and adventure to explore. But it was not for him to know. Not now. Not ever.

The black clouds had gone, along with the blood red sun, dragged down beneath the horizon and the sky seemed to purr with a velveteen darkness, studded for the first time, in a long time, with points of light. Wilber gazed up into the night sky, wondering where he would be transported when he stepped through the time gate, wondered which star up in the firmament he would end up orbiting? Yet for some reason he couldn't quite fathom, he wasn't ready to step through. Not everything had played out here, some deep inner knowing told him. The shaven-headed man in black, who floated on his own Sea of the Dead, watching him, told him that. Try as he might, he couldn't understand it. How was the Russian still alive? And why had all of the other Magicians survived? What magic did they and Astapor possess that their many acts of evil and cruelty should not be punished with death but rewarded with life.

Wilber looked down at the sword he had dropped onto the sand, when the armies of the Russian and the Englishman had been defeated. Walking toward it he picked it up and examined it, as though for the first time. It was Caleb's sword, his decapitator. The little emo's pride and joy. The edge was razor sharp and had put pay to many a savage zombie and stealthy creeper. It was an implement of death but it was also a work of art. How that was so he couldn't quite fathom. All Wilber knew was that it was true and that he was no longer the same boy who had stepped onto the island just hours before.

His mind began to race then and he imagined himself back in the spacecraft with the Watcher. Was the creature still watching him or had it, in finding its escape, forgotten about him? A sudden stabbing impulse brought him up short and caused him to look back at the Russian and in an instant everything was clear. This was the last scene of the last act, but before the final curtain could fall, one last action remained. And before he stepped through the White Gate, he knew what he must do, what he had done, ever since the moment when he had first set foot on the island; he must run. But not away from the Russian, as he had before, but towards him.

A breath of wind, feather light, brushed across his face and raising high his fallen comrade's sword, he began to run towards the Russian. The distance between them was halved, then halved again. Twenty metres from the Siberian tiger, Wilber let out a war cry such as he, nor any other had ever made, upon the island. Within his cry every echo of every moment of pain and fear and terror reverberated, every loss, every taunt, every slight flew forth but alongside of all that pain all he had gained in will and strength and self belief.

The Russian, black eyed and immobile, did nothing but stare.

And all Wilber could do was run towards him, counting down the metres, as he had counted down the hours, the minutes and seconds in his quest to free the island from the tyranny of the Game and the Dark Russian Master, who was its Architect and Marshall.

Ten metres became five, became two... And the sword fell in an arc... and the Russian smiled.

And though victory was his, Wilber stopped. Stopped the fall of the blade, prevented it from slicing through the Russian's neck, severing his carotid and the spinal cord, causing the scarlet blood to spurt and spurt in greater, then lesser arcs, stopping the head from falling through the night air and hitting the black sand with a dull thud. He had every reason to do it. The tears fell hot from his eyes, for Caleb and for Uncle Patrick, for Great Uncle Muldoon, for Beth, Semantic, Crimson and Edie. For Madeline and for Antelope. Yet he could not do it.

Slowly he lowered his sword and gazed into the dark eyes of the Russian who gazed back at him with an inscrutable air. Wilber had never felt so cold, so lost and defeated as he did in that moment.

There was no conversation to be had, nothing to be said and yet something remained between them. Some bond or relationship that had yet to be revealed and without that knowledge Wilber could not go on. He expected the Russian to draw a weapon and slay him. Some concealed blade or crossbow. Maybe a poisoned dart or a throwing star?

But nothing happened, nothing but an enormous roar behind them accompanied by the shaking of the earth and the heaving of the mountain. And way out to sea an answering roar and the rising of a wave, the greatest wave this version of the world had ever seen, over a hundred metres high, tearing across the nighttime ocean towards the the thundering volcano, spurting arcs of lava upwards, ever upwards into the night sky. Even standing upon the sands, Wilber could feel the heat from the Volcano searing across his forehead like a desert wind, a khamsin from out of the Sahara. And the Russian smiled and turned his head, as rising from the Burning Grounds, a hundred spinning silver ships took to the air, after decades of imprisonment.

And the night lit up like a Christmas tree and off in the distant sky a star expanded to a colossal size and began pulsing out coloured bands of light, now orange, now yellow, spinning and fizzing like a Catherine Wheel. Wilber oohed and aahed like a Firework Virgin, immune to the twin dangers that were racing towards him in the form of both burning rock and water wall. But the Russian knew and Wilber, roused from his reverie, understood too. Understood that he had passed the final test. The test of the fire crystal. That he was truly a Master of all of the Five Elements, as was the Russian, as still a sphinx before him.

And in that moment of understanding Wilber finally turned to go, as the sky filled with fire and that killer wave rose to tower and race, as he had raced. As the lava poured forth in molten rivers consuming all that had been. As the island began to sink. As the seething, snaking winds ceased their relentless war and grew still. As the last remnants of the eight burnt out towers were swept aside and the trees exploded. As all of these things happened, Wilber ran for the last time.

He ran as fast as his legs would carry him. Ran till his lungs burned and his body blistered with the great heat. Ran as though his life depended on it and of course it did. Ran to the stones and through the gate, the fifth in number and for the second time that day he had the sensation of falling on the brink of forever but this time not in an unblinking scream but in a moment of golden laughter where all creation was one vast and joyous joke, both riddle and game to be played as each player saw felt. Played for the joy and glory of all.

Played with a Spirit of Exhilaration, beyond Good and Evil.

89

The Last Laugh

Never under-estimate the Russian. Anyone who had ever played a game of chess with him would tell you that. Grandmasters the world over would caution you. He is one of the world's greatest strategists because he is able to convince anyone and everyone that he is moments from defeat. Seconds from disaster. That he cannot possibly recover from the wounds dealt him. That too many of his pieces have been taken from the board. That he has been overwhelmed by madness, by grief and rage. But always he will turn you and you will not believe it. You will not believe it because you will not want to believe it even when he invites you to destroy him. Of course he will offer every advantage. He will load the gun himself and as he hands it to you he will beg you to release him from the agony of his past mistakes.

And you will raise that gun, exulting in your own genius at bringing this monster to heel and you feel justified in pulling the trigger. Not once, but over and over. But you should know something, it will be your brains that crawl down the walls, not his. And do you know the last thing you will hear as your consciousness slips away into oblivion?

His laughter!!! His laughter for all eternity. And that is the hell he crafts for anyone who has the temerity to believe they can best the Russian at a game of Roulette. And so now he turns as the hundred metre wave rushes full tilt towards him and the molten rivers rush towards him.

And do you know what he does? Alone at last on an island he claimed decades ago and bent to his will. Do you know what he does? He drills a hole through time and escapes. He does what none would believe possible. Certainly none of the four, recently escaped Magicians who travel far beyond the sands would have believed it but eternity has swallowed them. So who cares? And Astapor walks away over the black sands, watching the last of the silver ships as they head down the coloured funnels of spinning orange and yellow light towards that distant star grown momentarily huge.

He walks and watches as the last ship disappears into eternity and the spinning lights are swallowed once more by that distant star, which having done what it came to do, recedes back into the vast fabric of the night's sky. A pebble placed on a beach, a splodge of colour on the grand painting of eternity. The Great Maya, the Never Ending Illusion.

Over the sands and into the forest. Not long until the lava pours forth. Not long till the wave strikes but long enough. No ship will bear him hence tonight. Fire and Water and Molten Earth will see to that. But perhaps the winds, who long ago he charmed, will.

And there it is. There it awaits. Not a life raft exactly but fulfilling the same purpose. A tethered balloon, filled like Crowhaven with hot air! Hopping into the basket, he fires up the burner and quickly dispenses with the dangling weights that loll like tongues over the side of the wicker nest.

And up she rises into the night sky. Up, up, up and away and, as if by magic, a wind arises, propelling the Russian away from the falling, burning rocks and the lava plumes into the Night Sky. Up, above the towering wave he climbs, the water wall which strikes the island and washes over it. Washes over the lava rivers causing steam to rise and the ocean to bubble and boil. Born away safely into the velvet night, safe from the revenging fires and rage-filled waters the Russians eyes search the horizon for the coming dawn and that which his vision has promised. Not just a new island but a new world. No death for him, but rebirth!

90

One Last Game

Stepping through the fifth gate, the white gate, Wilber couldn't believe what he was seeing; stacked bands of rainbow colours, shimmering and pulsing. And a final vision of golden coins raining down from on high, showering him with hope for the future.

He closed his eyes, took a step and his ears filled with the sound of laughter and when he opened them again he clapped his hands in astonished appreciation, as though applauding the Greatest Show On Earth. For after all the agonies they had shared, there stood the Legend that was Dinosaur George Muldoon, his father, waiting for him, lounging at the top of the drive, that led through the wood, and past the lake, to Muldoon Manor. Great Uncle Muldoon was laid out on a verge, looking quite presentable for once, due to his face being covered by George's blood-stained jacket. Smiling, as Wilber approached, George threw wide his arms and embraced his nephew

The time for tears was over and for all that Great Uncle Muldoon lay cooling in the sun, the object of attention for a great many hungry flies, both recognised the time for what it was, a moment of triumph. Yes, in spite of the suffering of so many, today was a day of celebration, for recklessness rewarded, for tyranny vanquished.

"Been here long?" Wilber enquired waggishly.

"Oh an age," George quipped.

Both of them fell about laughing

"So after everything we've been through we're right back where we started?"

George smiled.

"Yeah but we're different people now and it's all just beginning."

They walked on, down the drive, basking in the noon time sun, chatting away as if they had not a care in the world. Half way down the drive, they passed a boy in a Victorian Costume carrying a Union Jack. The boy was running and he almost collided with Dinosaur George.

"Where are you going in such a hurry?" George asked, unable to contain his amusement.

The boy eyed George with obvious distaste.

"And what's it to you?"

"Just interested is all," George replied, seemingly immune to the young boy's rudeness.

"Well I'm just off to the party."

"And what's the occasion?"

The boy shook his head, quite put out.

"The coronation as if you didn't know. Where have you pair been," the boy asked with obvious incredulity, "on the moon?" And he ran off laughing, as though he had cracked a funny joke.

"Dreadful hair cut," Wilber remarked. "Anybody would think he'd been shipwrecked on a desert island for a decade."

George tried to laugh, keen not to sully the mood, but he couldn't quite do it.

"He's on his way to the coronation in fancy dress. Wonder what that's all about."

Wilber, with his astonishing mastery of fact, put two and two together.

"The Queen must have died," he said glibly

"Oh well," George replied, "Had to happen sometime."

They carried on walking and rounding the bend in the drive saw, what for both of them, constituted home. Muldoon Manor. The ancestral seat, the family pile. And yet there was something not quite right about it. The gardens were in pristine condition with the lawns recently mowed and the roses in bloom, yet it all seemed just a little bit tatty, in a bit of state. And if anything the foliage and the flowers were more spartan than they remembered them, as though they had shrunk back and not grown in a very long time.

George stopped walking and stood and stared, and Wilber watching him, grew nervous.

"What is it dad? What's wrong?"

"Don't know," George said tersely, "can't quite put my finger on it."

Just then they heard a familiar sound and turned to look at one another with more than a modicum of concern plastered onto their faces. The clip clop of hooves on the driveway would once have been a familiar sound at Muldoon manor. But now, surely not. And then sure enough emerging from the courtyard a horse and carriage, driven at quite a lick; the coachmen, like the occupants and the boy they had passed earlier, clad from head to foot in period costume. The look the driver gave them as he passed was nothing short of murderous, but given their recent experiences they weren't easily phased.

The coach and its horses galloped on up the drive, disappearing as they went round the bend, leaving the two Muldoons with an even greater sense of consternation than before. What did it all mean?

"More fancy dress and no sign of a car," George muttered to himself.

Just then, from out of a side door, in an old wall, that George didn't remember being there, a man approached them with a horse whip in his hand. His mutton chops and whisky sodden eyes did not bode well and his manner was nothing short of appalling.

"What do you think you're doing here?"

"We live here," Wilber said, sizing the man up in case of possible violence.

The man screwed his face up into a violent sneer.

"Live here. Preposterous! Are you drunk?"

"No, but you obviously are," Wilber retorted, unconcerned as to whether he was heard or not.

"I beg your pardon!" the old duffer cried, his voice rising, his dander obviously well up.

A sudden look of horror crossed Dinosaur George Muldoon's face and he seized the man none too gently.

"What year is this? What year?

"Are you mad? Why it's 1837. What year did you think it was?"

George, obviously shocked, let go of the trembling fool who turned and staggered off in the direction of the house in a somewhat haphazard fashion. Mid way to the door he turned again.

"You're trespassing, you are! Breaking the law, so you are! Now, I'm orff to get my shotgun and if you're not gone by the time I'm back you'll be leaving this estate with your arses powdered with shot. The pair of you!"

And having delivered his threat the aged bore disappeared into the house in search of weaponry.

George and Wilber stood frozen to the spot, looking at each other in dread. Neither was capable of speaking as it dawned on them what exactly had happened.

Theirs, it would appear was a Victorian return, not an Elizabethan one. Wilber's history was hazy but he seemed to recall that 1837 marked the beginning of Victoria's long and illustrious reign. It was a reign that would last an age, or 64 years to be precise, and it would see in a new century. In the coming years they would observe the birth and maturation of an Age of Empire, in an age in a time that, for them, was already history. They would read the newspapers, knowing pretty much what would happen and when. They would watch untold buildings and columns rise and they would watch all of their hopes turn to ash, condemned to live in a century not their own. They would be forced to watch, knowing like Cassandra, what would come but powerless to stop it.

It was as though they had stepped out between two rolling columns of stained glass time and the columns had promptly stopped rolling.

Wilber had a sudden vision and he felt his once, buoyant heart begin to sink.

Away in London, Nelson's column span in the midst of a floating cloud and set images to dance through his processional mind. In his imagination, watched by lions, he was no longer Moses but a boy fallen, fallen like Icarus. And why? because he had flown too close to the sun. And through the open door, where the red-faced, mutton-chopped bully had disappeared in search of his shotgun they heard the sound of music. At first, the all too familiar anthem and the singing of drunken patriots filled the air but then came a change. A livelier air, perhaps a polka, something with a Slavic Spirit took its place.

Yes, something distinctly Russian. And that sound of laughter that had accompanied Wilber through the fifth gate, turned to a scream of horror and pain. He should have known, should have heeded the warning that hell awaits anyone and everyone who has the temerity to believe they can best the Russian at a game of Roulette. He should have known. After all, it was a game the Russian had invented!

And it was a game he always won.

Acknowledgements

For Edward and Shirley Goodwin, my parents, for their unstinting devotion and support. For Jan Goodwin for getting me started. The Rowe Family for their art and endurance: for my Godson Zephan for the early brainstorming and my Goodrow artner Al Rowe for being part of this journey, working through the ideas, the edit and production of this book.

Simon for the trees. Tim Boyle for taking me to Atlantis and Jayne Derbyshire for bringing me back. Gratitude to Plato for the myth and Blavatsky for the mysticism. Colin Wilson for inspiration along with Barbara Hand Clow and John Michell for the Dimensions of Paradise. Bev and Michael Lear for greening the man. Mr Stuart Sadley for musical direction and those mixtapes. For my Australian Family Li, Greg, Shirley and Ani for spiritual support and guidance. Phillip Preece for early discussions about things that mattered then and matter now. Reeves for the poetry and the passion. Jonathon Haber for trials and tribulations, Peter Myers for mountain adventures and Forbes for dragon chat. Jo Lesley for Godot and turning Telford into a stage. Barry Atchison for theatrical lighting. Emily Whitehead for introducing me to Rooster Byron. Billy Wa for links with Mother India and the world of British Waterways. For Brian Todd with whom I have heard the chimes at midnight. Chris Hewkin for introducing me to the sea and getting us safely back to shore. Brother Paul Leishman for the gift of mind and music. Rufus Ruffcut, Carl Barton for teaching me the gentle art of rally driving and the power of all things Stoke.